Jonathan Gash

LOVEJOY

Jonathan Gash

LOVEJOY

Paid and Loving Eyes

The Great California Game

The Lies of Fair Ladies

This edition first published by Cresset Editions
in 1993
an imprint of the Random House Group
20 Vauxhall Bridge Road
London SW1V 2SA

ISBN 0 09 182133 9

Jacket photograph of Ian McShane as Lovejoy © BBC

Typeset in Baskerville 10.5/11.5 by
Pure Tech Corporation, Pondicherry, India
Printed and bound in Great Britain by
Mackays of Chatham

CONTENTS

Paid and Loving Eyes

To
The ancient Chinese god Wei D'to, protector
of honest books from harm, this honest book
is humbly dedicated.

Lovejoy

For
Susan, and children everywhere.

CHAPTER ONE

The lovers were making the van sway. I had to get out, from seasickness. The night was perishing cold. Donk found me sheltering under trees in the drizzling dark. He's the antiques trade's only profit-making messenger, has a rotten old motorbike.

'Lovejoy? Your pot's tonight. Nine o'clock in the harbour barn.'

My heart fell and rose. Armageddon time, and me minding a pair of illicit fornicators in a furniture van.

'Sure, Donk?' I looked at the van as it reached orgasm. Just my luck. First paying job for a fortnight, and paradise – antiques – spoils the money. No, that's not right. It's gelt that does for antiques, not the other way round.

'Josh said hurry. That'll be a tenner, Lovejoy.'

Donk's messages are all ten quid, payable on delivery. I climbed up into my passionate van's cabin and fired the ignition.

'I'll owe you,' I called as he yelled after me. People don't understand. Antiques are urgent. Anyway, the lovers inside wouldn't notice that their trysting-place was barrelling through the rainy night at sixty. Passion is mostly oblivion. I'm an antique dealer, the only real one left. I know passion, and passion knows me.

There's a wharf in town. Not much of a harbour, but its access to the sea is well used these two thousand years. Four furlongs of paving overlooking an estuary, two cranes, a few warehouses. Ships come from the Continent – two thousand tons, max. They bring fertilizer, we send grain. The system, and the cargoes, are unchanged since before Caesar landed. I drove slowly into the barnyard, and parked by the railings. Five posh motors, I saw. The gang was all here.

The orange cabin light had buzzed on miles ago, querying the journey. My lovers must now be replete, ready for off to their separate homes. I sighed, reluctantly pressed the release. Just when you wanted ardour prolonged, lust lets you down. I'd wanted them to orgy on so I could referee the battle of the pots in the barn.

'Where are we?' the woman was asking as they stepped down, looking about.

The man said, 'I felt us moving.' I should hope so. They came at me together, under the shelter of the loading bay. I'd not seen either of them before. Secrecy's the hallmark of Gaunt's Tryste Service.

'Driver!' the bloke snapped, tapping my chest. I hate that. 'What's the meaning of this? We . . . boarded at a countryside lay-by. And you put us down . . . *in a harbour*? Where are our limousines?'

Door-to-door limo service is included in the price with Gazza Gaunt's luxury fornication pantechnicon. You get a well-stocked bar, an opulently furnished interior, and cosy privacy wherein to wreak your savage sexual desires on your lover's willing body. (Lover, like batteries, not included.) Then you primly return home to your husband/wife/children worn out saying you've had a hard day at work/college/committee. It costs a mint, though folk keep coming back for more. Well, a woman wants first a lover, then a husband, then a lover. It's love's roundabout. Guess who confessed that her nature was 'too passionate', her desires 'violent'? Queen Victoria, that's who. Gazza, the shrewd operator who runs the waggons, says four-fifths of his customers are regulars.

'Lovejoy?' somebody called from the barn doorway. 'Fight's on. Josh says come now.'

'Get me your head office?' The bloke was outraged. He was a stout glary sort, with the familiar non-face of a TV politico. 'I'm supposed to be at a sales conference in Nottingham.' Well, lies stay cheap.

'Look. I'll bell you taxis,' I offered desperately. Two bulky goons loomed in the light. Silhouettes threaten, don't they?

'Lovejoy,' one goon intoned, quiet with menace. 'Life or death, lad.'

'Coming,' I cried, shuffling anxiously on the spot. Threats make me do that. 'Look, mister. I promise –'

'Fight?' the woman asked. 'What fight?'

There was relish in her mellifluous, husky words. I recognized the response. Women love conflict more than men. In the oblique light of the loading yard she looked stark somehow, black and white yet languid with the serenity of the well used. Lovely. Money's easier to spot on a woman. They like it to show more. Smallish, slender, intense, voluptuous. I loved her.

'Diana.' Her bloke was furious because of my prolonged stare at the bird. 'You can't surely –'

'*What* is life or death?' She actually licked her lips.

'Counting, Lovejoy.' The goons were moving down the loading bay. Diana glanced at me, at them, her excitement growing and showing. God, but women interrupt your thoughts.

I swallowed, looking from him to her. You can't help wondering how they made love. I mean, her on her side, her back, hands and knees, with him . . . ? 'You can wait in the van. I have to go.'

'Can we watch, Lovejoy?' She was thrilled.

'They'll wait inside,' I told the heavies, passing them the van keys to prove I was obeying. The goons shrugged as brains failed to raise the game. I went up the wooden steps, the man behind me expostulating every pace.

'What's the contest?' Diana asked, eyes alight.

'Between two pots, love.' I added sardonically as she exclaimed in disappointment: 'The prize is everything.'

'You said life or death, Lovejoy. Whose?'

'Always mine, love,' I said, and went into the light where the contest was to be fought.

'Wait —' the woman was saying behind me. I heeled the door shut in her face.

CHAPTER TWO

God knows how gamblers do it, but they fill any place with smoke. It's beyond belief. I can't see the point of smoking, which only proves I too was once an addict of the stuff. Fear beats craving in the craven, hey?

The barn is ancient, oak beams and wattle and daub. Hereabouts such buildings can't be altered – unless bribes bend law. Josh Sparrow, the barn's owner, is a fierce upholder of preservation laws. They've given him a rich living. He competed with avaricious builders to buy this bit of the waterfront years ago – then announced it was to be East Anglia's Folk Epicentre. Conservationists rejoiced. They even gave him some award for Caring Commitment. Since then, the barn's been used solely for illegal activities, gambling, meetings between factions of villains, general mayhem. Josh gets really narked when Pennine pipers and Lithuanian dancers want to hire it. I keep telling him to change its name, but he likes the classy sound.

'About frigging time, Lovejoy!' said our paragon of epicentric culture.

He's always got a half-smoked fag dangling from one side of his mouth and goes about half blinded by his own smoke. Josh is forty, twitchy, always smells of fruit gums, plasters his hair down with some oily stuff. It must come free because he's a stingy sod.

'Been driving for Gazza. They're outside.'

He tutted through his smokescreen, this devout Episcopalian who deplores sin. He owns twenty-five per cent of Gaunt's Tryste Service. The holy quarter, I suppose.

Of the half-dozen people here, I saw I could ignore seventeen straight off. They were the brawn, the retinues, recruited duck-eggs with less than one neurone apiece. I hate them. Why do these ham-and-blam brigades line walls everywhere from the UN to the White Hart tavern nowadays? The world's getting like mediaeval frigging Florence, I've-more-assassins-than-you. Two birds, fifteen blokes, the usual ratio since equal rights dripped into the well water with the fluoride. They've all seen Ronald Colman films and dress early United Artists. I was cold, chilled, wet, hungry.

Three cheap chairs were arranged in a row in the middle of the barn floor under a cone of yellow light. The gelt sat there, idly contemplating the infinite, certainly not speaking.

Josh didn't count. The two protagonists standing to one side twitching nervously didn't count. I went forward into the light and stood before the prile. Grovelling's served me pretty well on the whole. I quelled my sense of degradation. Shame's no big spender, so doesn't count either.

'Evening, John. Sorry I'm late.'

Big John Sheehan's an Ulsterman. He actually should have counted several, but morphologically notches only *uno*. That is to say, he sits in a casual attitude of unsmiling threat. He clears his throat, you shut up until you're sure it's not the prelude to a sentence. His sentences, however you define the word, compel attention.

'?' his expression asked.

I explained about the Tryste job. He examined my face for perfidy, nodded okay after a heart-stopping moment.

'Josh gets docked half-crown in the pound,' he pronounced in that soft Belfast accent I like. Half-croyn in the poynd. 'Sloppy, Josh.'

Sweating slightly – well, muchly – from relief, I said hello to the other two gelties sitting alongside him. Strangers. During politenesses I worked out what forgetting to remind me about tonight's battle would cost Josh. Big John lives in pre-decimal money because he hates confidence tricks, unless they're his. Two shillings and sixpence out of every quid was an eighth. Of all Josh Sparrow's income for the month! Christ. For me, that would have been zilch. But for me it would have been a different punishment.

'Evening. I'm Lovejoy,' I said humbly.

'Good evening,' one said. 'Jan. To assess the antiques.'

Elegant, suave, twenty press-ups at dawn, cholesterol-watcher. Tanned and immaculate. Had a gold-headed walking stick. Fake Edwardian, so not all that good an antiques assessor. Cosmetics stained his fizzog. Well, takes all sorts.

'Get on with it,' the other growled.

Rotund, heavy breather, thick features veined with thin purple lines. His teeth would be mostly gold, if ever he laughed. His cigarette slummed beside John's cigar and Jan the Assessor's slim panatella. But I bet No-Name could do as many press-ups as anybody else. And weighed heavier. He wore an overcoat that could buy three weeks in Gazza Gaunt's sexy conveyances, bird included.

'Right, right,' I fawned swiftly. The two contestants came nervously forward. Their big moment.

'Who's first?' Big John asked. And when nobody spoke decided, 'Home team.'

'No,' the bulky geltster gravelled out. 'The Yank first.'

I didn't start to shake, but came close. Six suits leaned away from the wall. Big John's line did likewise. The two gangs looked at each other with that serenity hoods wear before war starts. We all froze, except for trembles.

Big John nodded. 'Right, Corse.'

The world relaxed, thankful it could orbit safely until next time.

Josh Sparrow dragged on a couple of floodlights, falling over wires and needing three goes to get the plugs right while his serfs carried a small japanned table in. I couldn't help staring at Corse. I was thunderstruck. I'd never seen Big John countermanded before. And he'd backed down. It was like learning that God picks his nose. Feet of clay, or something.

'Lovejoy.' Josh was telling me things, and I wasn't paying attention.

'Eh? Oh, aye. Ready.' I stepped out of the limelight.

The American advanced. She was dressed casually but clever, if you follow. Frocks can look almost exactly the same, cheap or rich. But some slight difference instantly tells you that one is a shop-bought end-of-sale good-riddancer, and the other classy and extortionate. This was the latter.

'Phoebe Colonna,' she announced, cool as you please.

She faced the three, standing for all the world like a girl about to recite. Small, hands folded. The pool of light made an arena of the flagged floor. No other lights, just the single shaded bulb above. The japanned table gleamed. I could make out the pale shirts and collars of the nerks around the arena. A mini-circus.

'Before I begin,' she preached, 'I particularly want to thank you gentlemen for the opportunity of presenting my work here in East Anglia. You will observe that I have paid particular attention to the composition of the glass incorporated –'

'Get on with it,' Corse growled. His catch-phrase.

Phoebe gamely kept up her prattle as she hurriedly beckoned a serf forward. He carried a covered object.

'– questions of design integral to the complexities of rationale, creativity-wise . . .' Et mind-bending cetera. I bet she'd slogged, postdoctoralwise, to be that slick in balderdash.

I watched her reach out, still lecturing away, and gently lift the cover as floodlights splashed on . . .

Only on the Portland Vase.

'Lovejoy?' Josh timidly interrupted her to warn me, stay where I was, but by then I was already across and staring down at the object. Lovely, truly bliss. I started smiling. Time hung about for a minute or several.

'Can I?' I asked.

Phoebe checked with the three by a quick glance. Josh tutted, coughed away a smoke spume. I lifted it from its stand. Flat disc base, not the knobbed amphora type. Beautiful work. She made to point, guessing I was some sort of referee.

'See where I effected the cameo relief carving – my own patented blowing process – of the white outer layer?' She was so proud of her work. I could have eaten her.

'Thank you, Phoebe,' I said. My eyes had filled for some reason. Eyes are stupid.

She was moved. 'You appreciate beauty, Lovejoy.'

Her vase was covered, I retreated, Phoebe smiled out of the way, and on came Steve Yelbard. He was a real artisan, decisive, no cackle, just put his piece down, lifted the cover and stood aside.

Thin, in overalls, scuffed boots, pencil behind his ear, he looked ready to make another ten soon as somebody got a furnace started. Another Portland Vase. Fake, of course. Which is the truth word for a copy, look-alike, reproduction, simulant.

I didn't need to go over to it. Excellent work. Interestingly, his was the full amphora type, base dropping to a rounded point in its stand.

Now the Portland Vase is famous. Everybody knows it, and its story. Any Roman cased glass – layers made separately then heat-fused – is beautiful. The most gorgeous of all is the Portland. Cobalt-blue translucency, it looks solid black unless you try to shine a light through. Opaque white glass figures adorn it – Peleus and Thetis, a tree, a cupid, some sort of sea dragon, you know the sort of thing; all those deities whose names you can never get the hang of. That's about it, really, *except that there's only one*. The British Museum has it. And here we were with two. Isn't life grand?

Corse the charm-school graduate grunted, 'Shift. Let's look.'

I stood aside. Steve Yelbard waited, talking technology with Phoebe. His eyes never left her Portland. She talked attractively and laughed merry laughs. The three rollers stalked round, looking at the two glass pieces. They hadn't a clue. A roller is a big investor in antiques. Any old, or even new, antique will do as long as it's worth a lot. They're nerks on the whole, but usually dangerous. I cleared my throat. Nobody stopped talking. Steve was the only one who looked at me.

'I saw your exhibition in St Edmundsbury, Steve. Not bad.'

He brightened. 'My prototype?' He grimaced. Real glass-makers always apologize, knowing nowt is perfect.

'Two prototypes,' I reminded him. 'One's base was disced, like Phoebe's. You decided against it?'

'I believe the original was in a true Greek amphora shape. The point removed and later replaced with a disc. Lovely, but twelve centimetres –'

'Twelve point one.' I nodded. 'And a different blue.'

He took instant offence. 'I wasn't shunning the challenge, Lovejoy. It's a question of what's artistically right.'

'No talking!' Corse snarled.

I leapt away and shut up. Jan was chattering, displaying his awesome vocabulary, making an impression on everyone listening, chiefly himself.

'There's a positive vibrancy of intellectualization, risk for risk's sake, atavistically speaking . . .'

And all that jazz. Phoebe was smiling, pointing out features of her superb vase. Lights were being trained while the gelt men peered and squinted at the two Portland Vases. Talk about a bloody pantomime. They got fed up after a few moments and strolled back to their chairs. Josh fetched me, plucking at my elbow as if trying to unravel my shabby jacket.

'Well? Which, Lovejoy?' Time for me to point the finger, and get either Steve or Phoebe a fortune or penury.

The floodlamps were extinguished. The shade cast its golden cone over me. I stood there like on trial. For an ugly second I thought how frigging unfair this all was. I mean, just because I'm me, they shovel this responsibility –

'Yelbard.' I ahemed to clear the squeak, tried again.

Jan swivelled, looked at Sheehan, Corse, then me.

'That's preposterous!' he exclaimed. 'The American piece is fabulous! It's perfection! Why, the Yelbard replica is . . .'

Silence is refuge when tyrants differ. I stayed silent.

'Lovejoy?' Big John interrupted.

Corse was darting suspicious glances. His goons came off the wall. So did Big John's. Jan pranced to the table desperate to prove me wrong.

'What's the point of asking Lovejoy?' He indicated Phoebe's piece. 'I've made a lifetime study of ancient glass. I tell you this divine piece could be the original Philip Pargeter replica! It's totality is perfection –'

'What's this pansy mean?' Corse grated. 'I came here for a 'ckin' definite. No maybes! You can't put money on a frigging maybe!'

'I think you'll find, gentlemen,' Phoebe interposed smoothly, 'that

Mr Fotheringay is correct. I based my work on the famous reproductions of the original Portland Vase made by Pargeter and John
Northwood, dated 1876. You will find –'

'Lovejoy,' Big John said quietly. 'The arts man says you're
wrong. Why?'

I'd rather have stayed in the rain to catch my death of cold
among the trees. I swallowed to get my voice going.

'Because he's right, John. Because the American girl's right, too.'
I nodded at her Portland. 'It's beautiful. But she didn't make it, did
you, Phoebe?'

'What's this beautiful shit?' Corse spat a stream of saliva in
disgust. I moved my foot in time. 'We're here to back the best *fake*.'

'There's only one fake here.' I glanced at Steve, who was starting
a slow smile. 'Steve's.'

'I don't know what you're trying to pull, Lovejoy –'

Phoebe's face suddenly went ugly with fear. Her voice pitched
higher. Odd that terror uglifies a bird, when passion beautifies them
so. But it was either her or me, with Corse signalling his suits into
their ominous lean. I cut in.

'There are several copies of the Portland in glass, Mr Corse. Not
counting Josiah Wedgwood's famous pottery jasperware efforts. It
started with Edward Thomason at Birmingham Heath, 1818 –
unfinished. Then Pargeter and Northwood had a few goes. Some
bloke called Locke in mid-Victorian times . . .'

I petered to silence, not because I'd run out of things to say, but
because Big John had frowned slightly. Slightly's enough, to cowards.

'How come the lassie knew his name?' he asked.

'Whose name?' Jan said, face draining. Big John meant him.

Nobody answered, far worse than uproar.

'Look,' Jan said, trying a laugh that convinced nobody. 'I'm well
known. I write for a dozen periodicals. I –'

'As Tiffy Tiffany,' Sheehan said. 'Your newspaper name.' His
voice goes softer, the more threat within. 'You're anonymous.' Hurt
showed in his brogue. 'I *paid* for that information.'

All the suits were edging closer now, glaring. I looked about but
there was nowhere to go.

'Please,' Jan was saying, tone ascending like a prayer. 'Please. I
had to make sure. Don't you see, Mr Sheehan? I *couldn't* leave an
investment this big to mere chance!'

He was squeaking in fright. The girl was trying to get out but
the circle of hoods closed. She struggled genteely a second, then tried
indignation.

'Well! If you can't listen to reason . . .' All that. Useless.

'We been done, John?' Corse scraped a cough, cast his fag end in rage. 'The Yank bitch and this poofter?'

'It isn't like what it seems!' Jan was shrilling, frantic, appealing desperately to Big John. 'This is serious money! A fortune –'

'Ronnie,' Big John said.

Three cube-shaped hoods came and hauled Jan away. When I looked, Phoebe was already being bundled out of the rear door. It slammed with echoing finality. I tried drying my clammy hands on my trousers. Steve seemed frightened. It's the safest way to be. I know.

'Lovejoy?' My cue from Big John.

'Phoebe was showing you a genuine old Pargeter copy. She'd not made it herself. That way, she'd win this contest and get the job.'

'And our money . . .' Corse choked, his face a vast sweaty plum.

'Josh,' Big John intoned.

Josh Sparrow came at a low creep, quivering and bleating. 'John, I swear to God. On my mother's life. My baby's head. I never had any notion there was a scam. I honestly don't know what's happened –'

'What did?' Corse grunted.

Happen? My turn. In a wobbly yodel I managed to start. 'Your competition was to fake the Portland Vase. Phoebe submitted a repro made in the 1870s, by famous old glass-makers. Steve here submitted his own work.'

'You sure?' Corse loomed over me like solid cumulus.

'Positive. Hers felt antique. Steve's doesn't.'

Corse's great puce visage cleared. He rotated, looked at Big John. 'Here, Sheehan. Is Lovejoy a divvy?' And got a nod, thank God.

'I am, yes, I am!' I said, desperate to show I was agreeing with everybody, especially BJS. I'm pathetic. I was still cold.

'That's okay, then,' Corse said, to my vast relief.

'Josh,' Big John said, as everybody relaxed and started shaking hands on unknowable deals. 'Six and eightpence in the pound. For four months.'

'Right, John!' Josh croaked brightly, grinning as if he'd just been awarded a knighthood instead of having to cough up thirty-three per cent of his income for the next twelve weeks for letting mistakes happen on his territory. Still cheaper than death, though.

They paid me a groat and let me go, into that slippery old rain. That was the start of it.

Sometimes a vehicle can seem a real pal. A goon gave me the keys as rain chilled my face and motor-car doors slammed and serfs lurked about the loading bay. I stood watching them go, weakly raising a hand – ignored – in salutation to Corse, then Big John. The vehicles splashed past. Other saloons started up, roared after. No sign of Phoebe Colonna, or Jan Fotheringay of great renown. Gulp.

Alone and safely out of it.

I got in the cabin and sat there in the darkness to let my sweat dry. Escape comes in many guises. Across the estuary, lights winked. The harbour's opalescent sheen toned the night sky. Peace. I started the engine, drove out, heading along the wharf towards our town's orange sky glow.

Then the customer's buzzer sounded loudly in my ear, frightening me to death.

'Lovejoy?' a woman's voice said on the intercom.

Diana? Still here? I thought the goons had run her and her tame shag back to the limousine-riddled lay-by whence they'd come.

'What the hell are you doing still in there, silly cow?' I swerved nastily, yelled into the squawk-box. 'You made me jump out of my frigging skin.'

'Thank goodness,' the intercom said with relief. 'For one moment I thought you were one of those hulks, Lovejoy. Find a quiet place where we can talk.'

'Get knotted, missus,' I said. I was blazing, really narked. 'You're going back to Gazza Gaunt's garage –'

'Or I'll complain that your incompetence exposed the Tryste Service to the police, my influential husband, the Vice Squad . . .' Women's voices go sweet when they threaten.

'The Drum and Fife's got quite a nice secluded lounge,' I said politely, swallowing a bolus of pride.

'Good, Lovejoy. You learn quickly.' It was a purr. She'd never swallowed pride in her life. I could tell. she'd defend her pride with blood. I wish now I'd remembered that, but once pathetic, always.

CHAPTER THREE

The Drum and Fife is a posh roadhouse, a cut above spit-and-saw-dust. To my dismay the place was heaving when I parked in its ancient flagged courtyard. I was too fed up to try anywhere else, and went to undo the passion waggon's rear door.

The lady stepped out, tutting because I'd no umbrella for her. I'd have used it for me, if I'd had one.

'Does it never stop raining?' She drew her collar round her.

'God left the taps running when he built East Anglia.'

'Well?' She gazed at the tavern. 'What are we waiting for?'

'Your, er, gentleman.' He hadn't emerged. 'Worn out, is he?'

She smiled in the exotic coloured lights that taverns string about themselves these days. 'Jervis left,' she said, and walked among the gleaming wet carapaces of the motors.

I scrambled to lock up and ran after her, hunched, through the worsening downpour. Why is it that hotels and suchlike spend a king's ransom on their fronts, yet their rear view is all drainpipes, steaming windows looking into horrible kitchens, rusty tubes?

Naturally, my 'nice secluded lounge' was thronged. Upstairs rollicked to the thump of some band. People dressed to the nines stood about chatting. You'd never seen so many carnations. A couple snogged in the coffee alcove with the abandoned passion reserved for strangers at a chance meeting. This wore hallmarks of a wedding.

'Sorry, missus,' I said, catching my streamliner up in the foyer as she stood looking about where to go. 'We picked a bad night.'

'No night's bad, Lovejoy,' she said, smiling. 'Days are hell.'

Her eyebrows demanded action, so I found us a place in an inglenook, a phoney iron grate with a cold fire. I looked my disgust. Spinning tin reflectors and a threepenny red bulb in plastic, pubs think they're Designer of the Year.

'Get me a martini, Lovejoy. No lemon.'

Bloody nerve. I nodded obediently, signalled with exotic mouth-ings to a puzzled wedding guest in the crowd. I'd complain about waiter service when it was time to go. She should get her own frigging drink. I was hired to drive the blinking love truck, not flunkey drinks for her.

I gauged her as a crowd of youngsters tore whooping through the foyer. Balloons ballooned, streamers streamed, dresses flounced.

Upstairs, cymbals crashed and an announcer bellowed something inane to prolonged applause. God, but weddings have a lot to answer for.

She looked different in the tavern's subdued lighting. Lovely, yes, but harder than her voice had suggested. I'd only seen her in rainy darkness before. Now, she was thirty, give or take a yard. Small but gorgeous. And so confident you could only admire her. Legs you could eat, figure you couldn't leave alone no matter how you tried. Skin alabaster perfection. Hair a delight –

'You approve, Lovejoy?' she asked.

Sarcasm makes me go red. I must have been staring.

'What d'you want, missus?' The description I'd been looking for: lush, but hard.

'Get me a cushion,' she said, extracting a cigarette from a handbag worth the whole Drum and Fife and expecting somebody to leap forward and light it. A bloke did, smiling eagerly.

She jerked a plume of smoke slowly, pursing her mouth in a way that almost stopped the show, and ignored him. He went his way, dazedly delighted to have been spurned by so gorgeous a creature. Aren't we daft?

'Get your own frigging cushion,' I heard myself say, and thought, oh, God. Now a bad report to Gazza.

She looked at me – actually at, as opposed to including me in the scenery. She did the woman's no-smile hilarity, the appraising gaze that makes you feel a prat.

'I meant, er, what do you want, lady?'

Driving Gazza's Tryste vehicles can be a real pain. He has three of the damned things. They're known among us by a crude double nickname – the first word rhymes with truck. You can land right in the mire. Reason: the course of true love does not run smooth. Whoever said that knew a thing or two. The last time I'd driven for Gazza was to a beach near Brancaster. The lovers inside had had a terrible fight – the woman a black eye, bleeding nose, the bloke scratched to blazes. Both had appealed to me in yells and screams to judge the rightness of their separate causes. The police wahwahs had come. A right shambles, me declining any knowledge of the battling lovers. Luckily, Gazza has an understanding with the chief constable, so all was smooth bribery and corruption. Gazza blamed me and didn't pay me, the swine. Tonight's success was my attempt to show new-found efficiency, and I needed the money.

'What happened in the barn, Lovejoy. I'm intrigued.' A direct order. Tell, or else.

'It's like this,' I began.

'Excuse me, sir. Madam.' A real professionoil suaved up, three trainee slickers in tow. 'Mr Prendergast, manager. Do I have the honour of addressing one Lovejoy?'

'One has.'

Jodie Danglass smilingly raised her glass to me from a stool in the long bar. I pulled an ugly thank-you-for-nothing grimace at her, for bubbling me to this yak. She's pretty, new to the antique trade, with thrilling legs. She talks crudities in her sleep. I mean, she looks as if she might sometimes possibly do that.

Prendergast smiled, tache, dark pinstripes, teeth a-dazzle. I smiled back, scenting fraud. It's the one thing I'm good at, being one myself.

'The Drum and Fife welcomes you! Could I offer your lady and your good self a complementary drink, sir?'

'No, ta. We're just going.'

Fraudsters have to do the driving. I was interested to see how he'd put screws on me.

He twisted with a smirk. 'Could you value the antique painting on display in the foyer? Naturally, the D and F would recompense you. Perhaps a complementary sojourn . . .'

'There is no antique painting in the foyer.'

He gyrated, darting his assistants a quirky tight-mouthed smile. I'd said something he hated. 'Did one pause to look?'

'One didn't need to.' If there'd been an antique painting in the foyer, it would have pulled me like a magnet. It's the way we divvies are. Folk only believe you if you put on an act. That's why police look menacing, bank managers dress sterile, judges pretend deep thoughts. Everybody goes by appearances. I should have remembered that, too.

I sighed, made my excuses to Diana. The foyer was only a step. The painting was beautiful, a Turner watercolour of Venice. Scratched, rubbed, the paper's surface scarified just right. The colours were exactly his, the dark-tinted paper brilliant.

'Lovely.' You can't help admiring class. I felt smiling.

Prendergast blossomed, beaming. 'There, sir! Thank you! I knew that you would authenticate –'

'No, Mr Prendergast. It's nice but naughty. Fake. But done clever. She used the right watercolours, see? She had the paper made specially –'

'Fake?' He reeled. Minions rushed to support him, but I was fed up and moved away. What do folk want, for Christ's sake? He'd thought the painting miraculous – all in a second it's ugly? Like everybody else these days, blinded by money. Disgusting. I felt sick.

'Come on, love.' I grabbed Diana's arm and hustled her through the departing bride and groom's mob. Confetti snowed from balconies. People screeched and hollered. Delight was everywhere. It can really get you down.

Somebody had glee-painted my van and tied balloons all over it. *Didn't Tarried – Just Got Married!!!* in pink clung to grammar and my van's sides. Joy abounding's pretty depressing stuff. Sometimes I wish it would bound off somewhere else. I rammed Diana into the cabin, climbed after.

'Budge up, love.' I fired the engine and we moved off to a clatter of tins tipsy nerks had tied to the rear bumper.

'Who's this she, Lovejoy?' And when I looked at her blankly in the dashboard glow, 'You said she.'

'The faker? Oh, aye. Looks like Fanny's work. Runs a children's society. Husband's a parson. She's a friend.'

Her lips went thin. 'Friend? And you betrayed her, for a night's free stay in a tavern?'

Women are born judges – of everyone else, never themselves. Ever noticed that?

'It was either her, or Turner.'

We drove in silence for a few miles, during which I got wetter still by pausing to remove the tins. I got us on to the trunk road. I was dying to get shut of Diana.

'You didn't look at the painting, Lovejoy.' Women never let things drop, do they? 'When we arrived, you just pushed into the lounge.'

'I never said I did look. In fact, I said the opposite.'

She was getting me narked. I should have returned her and the van hours ago. The evening was becoming supportive psychotherapy.

'You betray friends, yet you won't betray Turner, who's *dead*?'

'Dead?' That did it. Deliberately I slowed the van. I always start going faster in a temper and police radars skulk everywhere after nine o'clock. 'Ever seen a Turner painting, love?'

'Several. A friend of mine has at least two –'

'You've seen the greatest paintings in the history of the universe, and have the frigging nerve to say Turner's dead?' I should have chucked her out there and then, fifty miles an hour. If I'd any sense, I would have. 'You silly ignorant bitch.'

'*What* did you –?'

I closed my mind to her. I was too tired. 'Tell Gazza, love. And your influential friends. And your famous Jervis bloke. But let me be.'

Fame is shame. I suddenly realized I'd recognized her paramour, the mighty Jervis. He'd triggered off that sense of something shameful, so he must be famous. Fame really *is* shame. Aren't the most famous football teams simply the ones who've kicked everything over the grass, season after season? Aren't Olympic champions merely the ones on the biggest dose of corticosteroids? The most famous politicians the crookedest? Except in antiques, where fame measures beauty and true human love, fame is shame.

Now, here's the really odd thing about that night. She didn't mention the argument to Gazza Gaunt at all. Not a word. I reached the bypass, pulled in, transferred her to the waiting limo, and saw her off without a single cross look.

More amazing still, I reached Gazza's depot and signed off about ten-thirty with no trouble. He was pleased, because cleaning ladies come to repair love's ravages in his Tryste vehicles, eleven to midnight. And I got a bonus.

'Bonus?' They're usually what other folk extort from me. An incoming bonus was a novelty. '*For* me? You sure?'

Gazza laughed, slapped my back. He's a great back-slapper, is Gazza. He has a brother who clubs non-payers and uncooperative workers, so I didn't mind this sign of approval.

'Double bunce, Lovejoy. You really created an impression on that lady.'

Here was the odd thing. Gentleman Jervis had been very definitely miffed at my harbour detour. And the bird Diana had taken the hump when I was rude. So a *bonus*? Really weird. Gazza's never given a bonus in his life. Extracted a few, yes.

Doubtfully I inspected the notes. Strangerer and strangerer. I must have done something right, but what? Like a nerk, I forgot this vital question, pocketed the wodge and went on my way tiredly rejoicing.

This particular night, rejoicing meant Almira. She has a grand manor house in Birch near the church, and this quiet little cottage by the sea inlet. Mansion for august familial propriety, nook for nooky so to speak. Says her husband runs a chartered bank's investment company or some such.

Dinner was planned for seven-thirty, then passion till dawn. Arrangements don't have the accuracy they used to, I sometimes find. I think it's mainly because women don't get their act together. I was starving, could have eaten a horse. I got the bus down the estuary to Burnhanger, and walked into a flak storm. Luckily, Almira accepted my explanation that the taxi I'd got from town had run over a badger, and that I'd insisted on taking the poor injured animal to the vet's at Lexton. Naturally, I'd had to stay with the creature until I knew it was going to live. I was so moved by my tale I welled up. Finally she forgave me, and said I was just a lovely, sweet thing. Back on the right lines, thank God, I had the grub. In my honour she'd come off her perennial staples – whittled carrot and a lettuce-wrapped nut – and cooked food instead.

The passion began about one in the morning, and lasted to six-forty-five a.m. That's when she gets up to feed her bloody horses and bully the serfs.

She barely had time to make my breakfast before she had to streak off in her Jaguar. And even then she forgot my fried bread. Women really nark me. All night to work out the right breakfast, and still she gets it wrong. Can you believe it? Typical, that. It's time women learned to get organized. Probably comes from having nothing to do all day. I slept on, the sleep of the just.

CHAPTER FOUR

My cottage is a short distance from town, slumped beneath thatch in its overgrown garden wilderness. Our village isn't up to much. Historically a recorded failure over two millennia, it's shown no improvement since King Cymbeline, another local loser, lost all to Rome. I don't like countryside, but for once was glad to get back to my bare flagged floors even if I did have to pay the extortionate fare on the village bus. Almira would go berserk when she found me gone – I'd promised to wait until eleven, but once you're awake you can't just stare at the ceiling, can you? And I'd money in my pocket, my bonus from Gazza.

The phone was cut off, and electricity. Par for the penniless. This narks me. I mean, what if I'd been an old-age pensioner, shivering, wanting to call Doc Lancaster? Lucky for them I wasn't, or I'd have pegged out and made them feel really sorry. The post was on time, eleven o'clock delivery. I brewed up as the post lass shovelled bills into the porch. She came in.

I'd built a fire of beechwood, starting it with yesterday's un-opened letters, and got a kettle on.

'Burning evidence, Lovejoy?'

'Some old logs, Mich.' They were beechwood. Two pounds of beech soot to a gallon of water, boiled briefly, then decanted and evaporated to dryness, is the ancients' recipe for bistre, the pigment Old Masters drew with. A lot of forged antique drawings were due to appear in the next antiques auctions, after which my electricity and water supply might miraculously get switched on – if Fanny delivered the fake antique paper on time. Some local swine was testing my Old Master forgeries for the right antique watermark, using beta-radiography, so I'd had to pay Fanny's exorbitant prices and she'd never even seduced me, the cow. I ask you. Beta-radio-graphy's simple: you put a radioactive source under any paper, with a film on top. Leave it a while. Develop the film. And presto! A photo of the paper's watermark! It's a cheap and simple foolproof test of antique paper (which is why, of course, antique dealers avoid it like the plague).

She was telling me off. 'Michelle, not Mich. It's our anniversary, Lovejoy. Don't I get a card? Flowers?'

I stared. She laughed, a tiny sprite of a girl with a smile that makes you forget how hopeless the mail is these days. I like her, a red-haired pest.

'Two years I've been teaching you my name.' She disapproves of my habitat's coarser features. 'Never a word of thanks.'

'Who needs letters?'

'I'm valuable, Lovejoy.' She perched prettily on the divan, wrinkled her nose at its unmade condition. 'You didn't sleep here last night. Nor the one before.'

'So what? I was, er, busy,' I said lamely. Women make you feel guilty even when you've done nothing.

'You still with that rich tart, Lovejoy? You didn't ask me why I'm valuable.'

'Why're you valuable, Mich?'

'Because I'm a winged messenger. Tinker's at the Treble Tile, very urgent. And a posh lady in a monstermobile is asking Dulcie where is Lovejoy Antiques, Inc.'

That would have been almost worth another stare, but the kettle boiled just then and I had to dash to find my two mugs. Michelle lay in an *Olympia* by Manet posture. Dulcie's our village postmistress. Michelle has a phone thing on her pedal bicycle. I groaned inwardly, except Michelle heard me. It'd probably be Diana repenting of her bonus.

'Tell Dulcie to get rid.' I held up the mug as a bribe.

'No sugar.' She smiled and waggled provocatively out, doing the trailing-fox-fur mime. I felt worn out. Not even noon, and already hunted. Is it me? Everybody else has such control.

Tinker's my barker, a filthy shuffler who lives partly on ale and pickings, but mostly on me. He's my rumour-ferret for antiques. The best in the business, he assimilates news by osmosis. I mean, he can stand in a remote village pub all day long, gradually getting more and more kaylied, then tell you just before he falls down paralytic at midnight what's gone on at auctions in Ipswich, Norwich, even the Midlands. My part of the contract is to see his boozing slates are paid, every tavern in the Eastern hundreds. Magee's Brewery should send me a turkey at Christmas.

Michelle came back inside, closing the porch door, I noticed. She's almost a pal, as far as the Royal Mail services go. I gave her the cracked mug because it cuts my lip.

'Now, Lovejoy,' she said. 'Blackmail time.'

'Who're we doing over?'

'Me,' she corrected. 'I'm blackmailing someone.'

That sprawl out of Manet's famous painting was almost exact, except there was no Nubian slave, no black neck ribbon. And Michelle was clothed. I looked about for blackmailees. Me?

'Me?'

'You, Lovejoy. Pay up, pay up, and play my game. Two years' flirting is two years too many.'

'Or what?' Gawd, I'd not even had a swig. I tried to sound defiant.

'Or your parcel goes missing.' She smiled, laid her mug aside, beckoned with a crooked finger. 'It's registered, stamped, sealed, insured –'

'Parcel?' I licked my lips. I wasn't due any parcel. No antiques come through the legit post these days. I wondered about my past scams. Had that bloke in Ribblesdale finally decided to sell me his assortment of children's rattles? I'd been after them for a twelve-month. Mainly silver Regency, but with two North American Indian tribal baby rattles the most valuable of all. Sounds daft, but they'd buy a decent house, freehold, with furniture thrown in. Or had that Amsterdam dealer weakened, and sent me his Napoleonic prisoner-of-war bone sailing-ship model on approval? Worth a new car any day, especially with slivers of horn –

'Interfering with the Royal Mail's illegal.'

'I'm unscrupulous. Yes or no?'

I hesitated. It had to happen, of course. Women always have the final say. It's really only a question of when. It wasn't right. I knew that. I mean, Michelle had just got wed. Her new husband is a tough road-mender, all brawn and beef, this week labouring on the village bypass. And women always blab. I sometimes think that's why they do this. All these arguments totalled a resounding no. But antiques are antiques.

'Okay.' Being cheap costs, I find.

'The door.'

Obediently I went to wedge a stool behind it – the lock's wonky – and bumped into Jodie Danglass. She was entering briskly.

'Hello, Lovejoy. I knew you'd want to thank me for last night's . . .' She saw Michelle and beamed even brighter. 'Should I say sorry, or offer congratulations?'

Michelle swept out. Even a post lass can flounce if she's a mind to.

'Look, Mich,' I tried lamely after her, but got nothing back. She seized her bike and pedalled off in disdain.

Jodie was done up to the nines. I eyed her. 'You're not winning my heart, Jode. You're down on points.'

'Come, Lovejoy. Wear your very best. You've a customer. Sports centre in Ladyham.'

'This gear is it.' The new recreation place she mentioned was for the megamoneyed, not scruffs the likes of me. But a rich antiques customer must be obeyed.

She looked me up and down. 'Well, they said come whatever.' She smiled, brilliant with intimacy. 'At least *I* know you're spotless underneath.'

See what I mean? They can't help bragging they've nicked the lolly. It narks me. She had her motor at the gate. I got in, asking who the customer was.

'Not the foggiest, darling. Thought you'd tell me. She phoned me ten minutes since. Offered more than I make in a week to get you to Ladyham.' Jodie squeezed my leg, a cruelty with her shapely pins scissoring seductively as she drove. 'Didn't your persuasive tactics work last night, then?'

Last night? She'd seen me in the inglenook at the Drum and Fife with good old Diana, of bonus fame. Was Diana the customer? I settled back for the journey.

'Not my knee when I'm driving, Lovejoy.'

'Sorry.' She'd started it, then blames me. See what I mean?

The Nouvello Troude Sports and Recreation Centre dwarfs Ladyham, a village of insignificant size and zero fame. More of a hamlet, really. One pub, a stream, a church, a gaggle of houses old as the hills. And, new on the outskirts, a giant complex of tennis courts, buildings filled with desperates pumping iron, swimming pools and diving boards. They've even flattened fields into running tracks and steeplechase courses. It's obscene.

Jodie parked by the slummer's entrance – the smallest motor in the proper car park was a Bentley – and we entered the perfumed interior. Talk about plush. A log fire – no rotating tinsel glow lights at the Nouvello Troude, thank you. Wilton carpets, a glass display case of genuine Manton flintlock long arms on the wall, chandeliers. The reception hall was baronial, panelled and adorned. Very few of the loungers looked athletic. More of a club atmosphere, really, broken only by the sound of quiet chatter and somewhere the tap of a ball.

A couple of women gazed up, smiling, sipping interesting liquids, waiters hovering to bring more. Conversation resumed, with low laughter at my scruffiness.

'Mr Troude, please,' Jodie told some serf.

The kulak practically genuflected into the carpet's pile at the name and swayed ahead of us, giving backward glances like a keen collie.

'Who's Troude?' I asked in a whisper. We passed along corridors with original watercolours every few yards, Doulton decorative moon flasks, oviform vases and figures on small pedestals. This was class.

'Somebody who wouldn't bring your Diana into a place like this, Lovejoy.' Why *my* Diana? Why were we whispering like spies?

On to a glamorous balcony, plusher than any West End hotel. Beautiful people strolled, in or out of dressing-gowns. Some lounged, drank. Others basked under lovely complexion-gilding glims, and drank. Still others stayed in their designer dresses, and drank. All ogled, looked, drank. I felt uncomfortable. We sensitive plebs do, among the surreal and glorious.

'How d'you do. Lovejoy?' Troude was a slender, sun-crisped Latin, gold bracelets and chains against chestnut tan. His shirt alone could have bought my cottage, its two dud mortgages included. 'Welcome to Nouvello Troude.'

'Ta.' I felt I had to say that, though he'd only shaken my hand. Wiry was the word. A bullfighter's physique. He'd be a natural on a horse. Maybe, I thought hopefully, I should introduce him to Almira, get her off my back, so to speak.

'Miss Jodie. I thank you for conducting Lovejoy hither.'

A faint bow, no handshake. Get thee gone, Jodie, was his message. She made a smiling withdrawal. Conducting hither? Christ Almighty.

'Please sit, Lovejoy. Drink?'

'Tea, please.' I'd been done out of my home-brew, not to mention Michelle. The world owed me.

A sudden screech made my blood run cold. I thought, oh, no. Not here, the one time in my life I'd made posh. But it was. Sandy, as always larger than life.

We were on a balcony above a swimming pool. The plunge was not one of your echoing glass-domed halls filled with floundering Olympic hopefuls. Beautiful: palms, small courtyards with exotic plants, rimmed with natural walks, genuine grass (indoors? How the hell?). And a few dozen glitterati, the men shapely look-I'm-stupendous, the women mouth-wateringly luscious. No more exotic plant, however, than Sandy.

'Coooeee! It's me! Lovejoy!'

In a bikini, for God's sake, and a floral see-through dressing-gown, off the shoulder, with high-heel sampan shoes in magenta-studded gold. I went red. I honestly can't see the point of making yourself look a pillock, but it's how he is. Everybody was tittering.

'Hiyer, Sandy.'

He came over, doing a sexy slink. I moved back a bit. His eyelashes raked the air of his advance. God, he looked a mess. Mascara, rouge, lipstick. And . . . I stared.

'You *love* my earrings, Lovejoy!' he crooned. It was a threat. With Sandy, everything's a threat. 'Aquatic motif! I'm a prince – well, *princess* – between two frogs!'

A live frog sat dismally in the bowl that dangled from each ear loop.

'Er, great.' I hesitated. You daren't offend Sandy's dress sense. He and Mel – you always offend Mel anyway, no matter how hard you try – are antique household furniture and Georgian-Regency antiquers of mighty opulence. They inhabit a converted school-house and barn not far off, and despite appearances are shrewd, aggressive dealers. 'Do they hurt?'

'My earrings?' He tittered, gushed round to see everybody was paying close attention. 'I'd *love* it if they did!'

Folk chuckled. Sandy shrilled a laugh.

'The frogs, I meant.'

He rounded on me, spitting malice. 'More worried about reptiles than about *me* you hideous *ape*, Lovejoy! You spiteful, inane, inept *failure* you!'

To my dismay he burst into tears, teetered off at a lame sprint in his high heels. I called a sorry, Sandy, after him, but knew I was for it. He'd not forget that, or forgive. I sighed an apology to Troude.

'Sandy's an old friend, sir. Not', I added anxiously in case it got back to Sandy and landed me in still deeper trouble, 'old as in aged. Old as in good.' Good as in . . . ? I gave up. I'm hopeless explaining at the best of times. With all these sweet-lifers smiling at my discomfiture, I began to wish I'd stayed at home. At least there I'd have got ravished by Michelle, and earned my parcel.

'You really did mean the frogs, Lovejoy!' Troude was interested.

'Course. The poor buggers were . . .' I cleared my throat, rubbed the words from the air with a gesture. 'The poor things were trapped. It must be horrible.'

He paused to allow three uniformed varlets to serve tea. Sterling silver, I saw. Other balcony tables had silver plate. Troude must be a high-flyer. You can't count new silver, new gold, new anything. Only antiques matter. But society assays worth as wealth.

A peasant stayed to pour, grovelled in withdrawal. I eyed Troude. A man of multo wealth and much, much more. That explained Troude's aura. Confidence? Authority? In that instant,

Troude became my rival. Don't misunderstand me: I don't mean pistols-for-two-coffee-for-one, all that. But this man was the focus of the whole Nouvello Centre. Kicking order having been established, we sipped tea and admired the decor. My one advantage was that I could wait longer than he. Like Prendergast of the Drum and Fife, an antiques perpetrator has to put the screws in. Your screwee's job is to wait, and hope to get out in one piece.

'This leisure complex cost a fortune, Lovejoy. You like it?'

'Sumptuous.'

'You hate it.' He sighed, not put out in the slightest. 'It's a curious feature of civilization that administrators escape blame. Future archaeologists will clear the rubble, and reconstruct, what you see about you. They will be appalled at its sheer bad taste, find my name on the foundation stone, and blame me for crassness.'

'You own it, eh? I'd rather have had the fields.' Which is saying something because I hate countryside. It's superfluous. I can't honestly see what's wrong with concrete. The Nouvello was still a good argument for environmentalists, though, even to me.

He smiled, made that open-palmed gesture that isn't quite apology. Italian?

'To the *salotto buono*, appearances are everything.'

The business oligarchy, the ancient blood line of the gentry. No, not Italian. That hint of sarcasm revealed more than it hid. It sailed close to contempt, but what for?

'Look, er, Mr Troude. I'm sorry I spoiled that scene. I didn't mean to annoy Sandy. And I am sort of busy —'

He allowed a fawner to hurtle forward and light his cigarette. His glance swiftly backed the girl out of earshot. 'Lovejoy. The reason I invited you is that I hear you have a precious gift. I wish to use it. Would you be agreeable?'

'Use how?'

His expression was nearly amused. 'Your gift only works in one way. I know, you see. It is not a skill that can be passed or taught.' His cigarette hand paused, but only for an instant. Two waitresses clobbered furniture aside racing to supply the missing ashtray. I felt the waft of vitriol in the air. They left, to tremble somewhere else, guilty of omission. Jobs would roll.

'You know a divvy?' I was interested.

There's not many of us. You can always tell people who've see it before. Folk who don't believe are the majority, and simply don't want to believe.

'Yes, one. He suffered an unfortunate accident.' He shrugged without visible expenditure of energy. I wish I could do that. As soon as I got home I knew I'd be trying to do it in the mirror, quirky smile and meaningful eyebrows. I'd fail. Comes from living near the Mediterranean, I think. 'I miss him.'

'For what?'

'His divvying gift worked for most antiques, Lovejoy. Not all types, but enough.' He exhaled smoke. Studious, but it wasn't scholastic learning. Monetary reflections hung in that smoke, not classicism. He was a roller, not a caring antiquarian.

'Will he get better, your divvy?'

Troude hadn't called divvying a skill, or an aptitude. Gift. He'd said gift. A believer, all right. Suddenly I wanted him to be a cynic, and me far away from here.

'Alas and alack, regrettably no.' Hither, *and* alack? Maybe he liked Errol Flynn remakes. Play is life, for the rich. 'Our divvy was old, and his gift sadly fading. I immediately started looking for a, forgive me, Lovejoy, a substitute. A full year ago. Even before he . . . became unavailable.'

'I don't know if I'm up to doing a lot,' I told him frankly. My hands were sweating. I managed not to shake. That was pretty good, seeing I now wanted to know if he'd killed old Leon in Marseilles. 'And I've some deals on.'

'Cancel them, Lovejoy.' He was so pleasant, smiling with teeth off a dentist's advert. 'You will be splendidly recompensed. Unless, of course, your display with the Portland was a deception, and you yourself a fraud.'

How did he know about the Portland Vase fakery contest? I smiled. I quite like caution. 'I'd have to think about it.'

'I shall arrange to appraise your gift Lovejoy, if you don't mind. You will be given a generous retainer.'

'Doing what?'

'A small task. Judge a few antiques, maybe move a little antique silver.'

Sounded easy. I often did such jobs, vannies we call them. 'Get my old Ruby out of hock, I'll shift anything anywhere.'

He smiled at my quip and gave his non-shrug shrug. 'Ruby? An auto? Very well. There is one small question.'

There always is. I stilled. 'Yes?'

A crowd of elegants strolled on to the balcony. They chattered less noisily when they saw Troude, but just as happily.

'You are a northerner, yes?' He was French. Definitely. He'd nearly said *oui* like they do, the yes a reflex terminal. When I nodded,

'Your parents? Grandparents?' He was very intent about it. Still, whatever turns folk on.

'One granddad a wild Irishman from Kilfinnan. One grannie Scotch, from Kinghorn in Fife. A granddad and grannie darkest Lancashire back to the year dot. Mixture, really.'

He relaxed with disproportionate relief. Funny, because grampa talk bores people for miles around.

'That accounts for your gift. A Celtic element. But no French?'

'Sorry.' I did the only sort of shrug I know, a feeble imitation of the real thing. I was thinking what gunge. He declined my offer to write down my address, inferring he already knew it by heart or that his minions would.

Sandy carolled a farewell from the upper balcony as I took my leave. His shriek of laughter made all heads turn. He'd replaced his frog earrings with on-off neon fishes.

'Naughtily nautical, Lovejoy!' he trilled. 'You admire?'

I just hoped the electric fishes were not alive. I left, muttering an apology to Troude. He came with me to the entrance to see me off. I swear even the squash balls muted as he passed.

'Sandy is not our most serious Nouvello member,' he said. 'Everybody is fond of him though.'

We parted amicably enough. His giant limo took me to town, dropped me off at the Antiques Arcade by the war memorial.

Safe now among crowds of shoppers, I watched the motor recede. I felt vaguely tainted, as if my skin was about to erupt. Troude had come unnervingly close to saying something else instead of Nouvello member. I desperately needed Tinker and a phone. I'd kill Jodie for landing me in all this, silly cow. I saw Almira's car approaching, and ducked into the Arcade. It's safer among antique dealers. At least you know they're sharks and out to get you. Friends and lovers are infinitely worse.

CHAPTER FIVE

There's a main trouble with anything good. Like with women my question is, why can't they see how much we crave them, for heaven's sake? (The answer's that maybe they do . . .)

The trouble with antiques is fakes. The trouble with fakes is antiques. Just as in any war, greed is the instigator, and dithering uncertainty the determinant, of success. Thus antique dealers become a happy band of mourners at the funeral feast for casualties in an unending conflict.

Our local merry mob of antique dealers occupies a few crevices of dereliction. They've installed a small bar since the boozing law changed, to sell liver-corroding liquids at extortionate prices. The whole Arcade is nothing more than an alcove of many alcoves. You'd walk past it with hardly a glance. Wise folk do just that.

The usual chorus of jeers and imprecations rose to greet me. They were all in, bemoaning (a) the cheapskate public, (b) being broke, and (c) having this priceless Rembrandt/Wedgwood/Michaelangelo genuine antique that they're willing to let go for a few quid as a special personal favour to you/him/her/anybody . . . The siren song of the dealer.

Frederico grabbed me first, looking more like Valentino than Valentino. He's from Wigan, but cracks on he's never been to gaol. He wore a green suit by mistake, because he's only Irish on Fridays. Mondays he's from Tuscany.

'I've got a couple of things, Lovejoy!' He hisses this terse sentence, looking furtively round shoulders, trying for Fagin in the next amateur *Oliver*.

'Over here when you've a minute, Lovejoy,' Liz Sandwell called. I waved, brightening. Her tough boyfriend wasn't with her. 'Got what, Fred?'

Fool for asking. You need never ask, not with Frederico. His act's something to do with the ferries from the Hook of Holland. They dock at Harwich bringing loads of tourists. He gets caught out sometimes, finds he's claimed to speak a tourist's own lingo. Also, he only talks gibberish, a handicap for so determined a communicator. It's not my fault if I get confused. He dragged me to his alcove – a plank, a chair, a battery light, two boxes.

'Lovejoy,' Donk interposed, breathing fury. 'You owe me. That message –'

'Sod off, Donk. I'm busy –'

But he wouldn't be put off with IOUs, promises, tales of misery. Only when Frederico shelled out the dosh did Donk leave. I think civilization's got a lot to answer for, now trust's gone. Which raised the interesting question why Frederico paid up for me. He's never done that in his life.

'It's genuine old glass, Lovejoy. Honest. Every sign!'

'Oh, aye.'

One of his two boxes yielded a lovely little sweetmeat glass, its stem faceted and its foot scalloped. The dealers all around went quiet and started drifting over. Frederico made insulting gestures to repel them. It worked. They retreated muttering, narked and envious. Old glass is valuable beyond common sense these days. If you find one, order your blonde and two-litre Morgan and spit in your general manager's eye.

'See? Genuine 1780.' He sounded as if he was offering me surface-to-air missiles, peering about.

'Sorry, Frederico.' His paddy green kept getting me on the wrong track. 'It's duff.'

'No!' A cry from the heart. The other dealers chuckled, resumed chatter, pleased their friend would lose a fortune.

This is always the hard part. The glass simply didn't reverberate in me. Therefore it was dud. How to find explanations other people would understand . . . ?

'Look, Frederico.' I held it up against the bulb, though daylight facing north's best. 'Glass isn't a solid. It's a supercooled liquid. Think that, and you're halfway there.' Pointing, I showed him. 'Old glass – anything before 1800 – *must* have tiny air bubbles. Modern glass has virtually none.'

'But the iridescence, Lovejoy!' He was almost in tears.

You feel like knocking their heads together sometimes. Can't the blighters read? Being basically fluid, glass interacts with air and whatever crud's around. So over the years, wetness – in air, ground – causes its surface to iridesce, due to laminations. Think of microscopic scaling, and you've almost got it. Light gets bounced about wrongly in the glass, causing the effect. Sadly, dealers and the thieving old public jump to conclusions, the daftest but most constant folly.

'Somebody's dunked this in a cesspool.' It can take two cesspool years to get the right quality of iridescence. I've had three good fakes – Laurela at Dovercourt makes them for, er, friendship's sake – steeping in a marsh near here since last Kissing Friday. I sluch them out to check, every fortnight. It's grim, because one of those yellow-beaked black ducks has nested on the very spot, interfering little blighter.

28

'I've a certificate, Lovejoy! The industrial chemists –'

Now he was really agitated. I looked at him with real surprise. He's a con artist, so should know that every antique fake doing the rounds has more certificates than an Oxford don. The trick is to slice a piece of genuine ancient iridescent glass surface from some antique, and have it analysed – then sell the certificate to a dealer, who'll pass the testimonial off as belonging to some fake drinking goblet he happens to have.

The other box made me hesitate. He was so miserable. I waited. He waited. Liz Sandwell called. I looked expectantly at Frederico. He said nothing, forlorn with his dud glass.

'Look, mate,' I said, with sympathy. The poor bloke had pinned his faith – his greed, really – on scooping the pool. 'Get a few fakes from some old genuine piece, and cement them to your fake. The old trick. Then it'll sell at any provincial auction. And you can use your certificate to authenticate it.'

Hope filled his eyes. Avarice works wonders. 'Cement how?'

Narked, I walked off. Dealers are useless. I mean, Theophilus wrote how in his *De Diversis Artibus* in the eleventh century. The world hasn't read it yet.

Liz Sandwell was better value. I kept looking back at Frederico's other box. It pealed chimes in me, reverberating.

'Eh?'

'I said go halves, Lovejoy.' She smiled, a lovely offer. But you have to be sure what a woman's offer actually is. I keep making this mistake.

My throat cleared. 'Halves of what?'

'Not me, Lovejoy. This illuminated panel.'

'It's rubbish.' I turned on my heel.

She caught me. 'Why, Lovejoy?'

Because it didn't utter a single boing. Except Liz wanted a reason reason. So I looked at her neffie panel. A parchment egg tempera painting, St Sebastian dying heroically for something or other. Lovely, the right style and everything. If I'd been a buyer I'd have said Early English, worth a small house. Then I looked across at the dejected Frederico.

'I'll tell you why, Liz, if you persuade Vasco Da Gama there to show me the antique in his other box.'

She went and wheedled, returning in a trice with the box. The closer it came the more certain the chime. I swallowed to wet my throat for speech. Talk is problems.

'Can I look?'

Frederico, offhand, nodded. I reached inside the humble cardboard and felt a warm loving living thing slip smiling into my palm. I lifted it out, my soul singing.

It was beautiful. Besides glass, the one class of antiques that has stormed ahead of the world price spirals is that of scientific instruments. This was superb. For sheer price it could have bought the whole Arcade, and the street too I shouldn't wonder.

A travelling sundial. Octagonal base, incised with lines and numbers, with a recessed compass. Its gnomon – the little raised bit that casts the shadow – was shaped like a bird. Four hour scales, and latitude marks for 43 and 52 degrees North. You would adjust the bird gnomon for whatever latitude you were sailing in.

'Michael?' I heard my voice ask. 'Is it really you?' I rubbed the grime, licked a thumb, tried again. And it was.

Michael Butterfield – spelt right, thank God; contemporary fakers got his name wrong, like Smith the great porcelain faker did with Wedgwood – was an Englishman in Paris. For over fifty years he turned out superb works of genius. Naturally, from 1670 on his brilliant creations have been forged, stolen, faked, copied, like all things bright and beautiful. A true hero of talent. Can you imagine him, striving for perfection by candlelight when all around was filth and degradation, with –

'Sit down, Lovejoy.' Liz was holding me.

'No.' I pulled away from the silly cow. They treat you like a cripple, women. 'How much, Frederico?'

He looked amazed, me to the sundial. 'It's only brass, Lovejoy.'

'Butterfield made in silver and brass, nerk. How much?'

A distant cough sounded, coming nearer with a pronounced Doppler. The vibration shuddered through the Arcade. A flake of paint gave up clinging to the wall under the force. Tinker was approaching along the High Street.

'You sure, Lovejoy?'

He was asking *me*? Gawd above. 'How much?'

He licked his lips, tried to take his dial back. I kept it. Just because an instrument's made of brass doesn't mean lunatics can't damage it.

He glanced at his duff glass. 'I thought it was the other . . .'

The other way round? I might have known. A put-up job. Who'd given him the two boxes? No wonder he'd got the wrong suit on today. With tears in my eyes I replaced the Butterfield dial in its box and handed it over. Neither the fake glass nor genuine instrument was his to sell. Life is a pig.

'Sod off, Fred.' Where was I? 'Your parchment, Liz.'

''Ere, Lovejoy.' Tinker came in, shuffling behind his thundering cough like infantry following a creeping barrage. 'There's a tart wants you over at —'

'A sec, Tinker.' I gave the filthy old devil the bent eye, to restrict my trade secrets to a few square miles. His idea of tact is to pluck my sleeve in a theatrical mimicry of stealth, while booming out anything confidential as if yelling from a distant shore. I'd promised Liz a reason reason. I scanned her illuminated parchment.

'Blue, love. They should have used lapis lazuli instead of Prussian blue. Diesbach discovered Prussian blue in 1704, centuries too late for your mythical mediaeval monk.'

Actually, I'd have given modern French ultramarine a go, made up in egg yolk. Better still, I'd have re-re-remortgaged my cottage, and bought quarter of an ounce of genuine lapis lazuli. I hate fakers who're too flaming idle. So what that genuine lapis lazuli's the costliest pigment on earth? Ha'p'orth of tar and all that. Tip: get round the experts on this vital point by mixing a proportion of Guimet's synthetic ultramarine, available since 1824 for heaven's sake, with twenty per cent ground-up lapis. You finish up with an almost perfect faker's blue —

'That posh tart with the big knockers, Lovejoy,' Tinker interrupted. 'Her's a frigging pest. Wants you outside.'

'Thank you, Lovejoy,' Liz Sandwell said sweetly, retrieving her parchment. 'You may go, seeing duty calls.'

I leaned away from Tinker. His breath emerges very, very used. Must have been drinking solidly since dawn. His old army greatcoat was stained, his mittens filthy, rheumy eyes bloodshot, his stubble encrusted with food residues. I was pleased to see him in such good shape.

'Same one looking for me round the village early on?'

'Nar. That was just some whore, Lovejoy.'

'Can I listen?' Liz was enthralled. 'Or are you inaudible?'

Tinker got annoyed. ''Ere, miss. You keep yourself to yourself. We've work to do, if you haven't!' His attention returned to me. 'Young folk. They're all on tablets. I blames this free education.' He has theories like hedgehogs have fleas.

'Come on.' I got him out of the rear entrance, and we made the Three Tuns by diving among the alleys.

'That posh tart, with them frigging nags.' He inhaled half a pint at one go, settled back with a sigh. 'The one you've been shagging since Wittwoode's auctioned them funny frocks.'

Which being translated meant Almira. Tinker was reminding me that she and I met at a local auction of funny frocks – Tinker's phrase for the most beautiful collection of Continental eighteenth-century dresses ever seen in the Eastern Hundreds. Tip: embroidery's still the cheapest way to buy into the antiques game, but not for long, not for long. I thought deeply.

'Who was the woman asking at the post office?'

'Told you, Lovejoy. That whore.'

It wasn't right. Tinker's very strait-laced. He didn't call people whores, unless . . . What was it Jodie'd said? About Diana being not quite the sort of woman a gentleman like Troude would allow in the Nouvello? To me, Diana'd come over as a bonny bird simply having sly sex with some magnate who couldn't risk scandal. What more natural than to use Gazza's lovemobile, driven by that pillar of virtue Lovejoy? Surveys say seventy-two per cent of us are hard at illicit love affairs, surveys say. I wonder how they missed the remaining twenty-eight per cent. To work.

'Something's niggling, Tinker.' I fetched him another three pints, lined them up on the table. 'Sandy showed up yesterday in Ladyham –'

'He would, bleeding queer,' Tinker snorted. 'Never out of that frigging Frog centre since it opened. Put up a tithe of the gelt, he did. Like your tart.'

My headaches usually come on pretty gradually, unless they get help. I pressed my temple to slow things down. Tinker was rabbiting on.

'Wait, Tinker.' Tart and bint are simply females in his vocabulary, but a whore was a whore was a . . . 'You mean Almira?'

'Aye. Know how they got the land? Did the old dole shuffle from that poxy club, Mentle Marina.' He growled. I raised a finger just in time. He spat phlegm noisily into a drained glass, gave a pub-shaking cough, and recovered, wiping his eyes on his shredding sleeve. 'It only worked because that poofter's pal's some rich Continental git.'

Too much. Both temples were pulsing now. I was a nerk between two throbs . . . My mind finally clicked into gear. Sandy's earrings. Princess, between two frogs. I tried to recall Troude's comment. He was observing that I hadn't got Sandy's joke. One, Troude. Number Two . . . Who was Number Two?

'Almira? She financed the place?'

'Her and that frigging pansy. They got a kitty up for some Frog. Has his bleedin' nails done at the barber's, just like a poxy tart. Don't know what the frigging world's coming to, Lovejoy.' He spat expertly on to the carpet before I could restrain him. 'Her lawjaw's got four houses. Did you know?'

'Who?' Now quite lost.

'Always at frigging Ladyham, him. Says he once rode for England.' He snorted in derision, which from Tinker is a pubclearing operation that nearly blew me off my stool.

'Rowed, like boat?'

'No. *Rode*, Lovejoy. Frigging horse!' He cackled, wagging his head. A couple of brown pegs trying to pass as teeth littered his gummy grin. 'How can you ride a horse for England? That's not proper racing, like the Grand National. What a berk! Him in Parliament. He's never there. What we pay him for, eh?'

It would take more than a casual chat to disentangle Tinker's rumours. I gave up. Almira's husband an MP, and a banking company lawyer to boot?

'Antiques, Tinker.' I tried to get back on the rails.

'Oh, aye.' He grimaced. 'Sorry, Lovejoy. Baff's dead.'

Silence for the departed, mostly to absorb shock. It was like a blow on the temple. I honestly couldn't see for a second. My vision slowly cleared.

Baff's a talkative, friendly sort of bloke. No more than twenty-five. A refugee from the army – some regiment giving up its colours after half a millennium. Baff settled locally with a bird called Sherry down the estuaries. Nice bloke. I like, liked, him a lot. He hadn't a clue about the porcelain and jewellery he tried to sell, of course. An average antique dealer, mostly by theft. Tell you how he stole in a minute.

'What happened?'

'Got done over last evening. Some yobbos. He was working a seaside ice-cream stall. They did him for the takings.'

Dully, the facts clunked in. Baff died on the way to hospital. The spoilers vanished in the crowds. The Plod were questioning some youths, but nobody was charged yet. Fat chance, in a thirty-acre seashore all caravans and holiday-makers.

'Watch it. Your tart, Lovejoy.'

Almira was alighting from her motor. She's so splendid-looking that folk slow down to watch – blokes to lust, women to tot up the cost of her clothes.

Alacrity called. 'Tinker. Find Steve Yelbard. You know, the glassie. And Phoebe. Donk should know, if anybody.'

'Dunno, Lovejoy.' I slipped him a couple of notes, so he could keep supping ale, his only source of calories. 'The Portland Vase

final? That Phoebe's a snotty cow. That bugger Yelbard's worse –
he's honest.' He spoke with the gloom of the antiques barker, to
whom honesty's the ultimate cheat.

'Get on with it.' I made for the door, preparing a smile of
welcome for Almira.

''Ere, Lovejoy!' Tinker was rolling in the aisles. One of his jokes
loomed. Wearily I waited in the doorway for the hilarity. 'I'll bet
you give her a better ride than her nags!'

And he literally fell off his stool. I eyed him gravely as he
recovered, cackling helplessly, blotting his eyes as he climbed back
up. A couple of blokes down the bar looked at each other uncom-
prehendingly.

'Very droll, Tinker,' I said sombrely, and left to the tender mercy
of Almira.

She was there, glowering on the pavement. I started with surprise
and rushed to embrace her with thankful exclamations.

'Doowerlink!' I cried, giving her a buss. 'You're there! Where
did you get to? I left the note saying definitely ten-fifteen at the war
memorial! I was absolutely frantic –'

It's the one way to cast doubt into a woman's mind, hint that
she's mislaid some vital message.

'Ten-fifteen?' she asked, mistrustful.

'Yes, love!' I was so impatient. 'We've missed our chance,
doorlung! The holiday I was planning!' I sighed. 'The last places on
the flight went at twenty-to. Oh, hell!' I took her hands, gazed
sorrowfully at her. She looked about guiltily, tried to recover her
fingers from my vice-like grip.

'Not here, Lovejoy.' She was trying to look casual for appearance's sake.

'They couldn't hold the seats. It was a charter flight.'

She was looking hard, seeing pure truth shining nobly from my
eyes.

'You've been planning a holiday, Lovejoy? For us?'

I went all soulful. 'It's little enough, Almira. I mean, you take
me out to lovely meals. And that weekend on the coast.' I looked
away, biting my lip. 'This was all I could afford.'

'Oh, Lovejoy.' She started to look guilty. I was pleased, making
headway. 'I'm so sorry. Was it very dear? Only –'

'No, love.' I went proud. '*I* wanted to treat *you*.'

'A lovely idea!' she said mistily. 'Where did you leave it?'

'Eh?' People were pushing past on the pavement. I kept having
to move aside for prams and pushchairs.

'The note.'

'Oh, by the window. Propped up, where . . .' Where it could easily blow away, so ending the lies necessary on the subject.

She drove me to my cottage. Where my ancient Austin Ruby waited, glamorously restored and out of hock. I was overjoyed. Suddenly frightened, too, for who could afford to settle an expert car restorer's six-month bill? Overjoyed, yes, but aware of how deeply I now was in Troude's scam. And its enormity.

'Is this old car yours, Lovejoy? I didn't know you had one.'

'Neither did I, love.' I said weakly. We went inside and made smiles. I couldn't help thinking of Baff Bavington.

CHAPTER SIX

Women talk in the pluperfect vindictive, as the old crack has it. All the same, there's not much wrong with malice – as long as the arrow falls short if it's aimed at me. Why it's such a constant for birds, heaven alone knows. They relish the stuff.

'Who gave you that car, Lovejoy?' Women never let go, but I've already told you that.

'Eh? Oh, had it years, love.'

She padded about the room shivering, moaning about draughts. Finally zoomed back, freezing, complained I'd pinched her warm bit and trying to manoeuvre me out of it.

'Whose bed is it?' I demanded. Frigging nerve.

'I've never seen your motor before.' All suspicion.

'The Ruby? It got cindered. Thought I'd seen the last of it.'

'Restored by loving hands, I see.' Rich women see a lot. 'Who paid? Another woman? Seeing your electricity's off, and the phone.' She lifted her head from the pillow. 'And seeing you were going to take me on holiday, Lovejoy.'

See what I mean, about women never trusting people? She'd be on about this for months. Luckily we'd not last that long.

'Some bloke forked out. Part of an antiques deal.'

Shrewd Lovejoy's quicksilver brain was equal to the task. I took her delectable body in my loving embrace, and raised her head so our eyes locked. I said, most sincerely, 'There is no other woman, dwoorlink.'

'You're sure?'

'How could there be? To prove it, we're going to a superb new place for supper tonight. The Nouvello Troude at Ladyham!'

Her relaxed body went a fraction unrelaxed. 'Ladyham?'

'You know it?' I smiled, still most sincerely. 'I expect you wealthy landowners dine there all the time.'

'Nouvello? No, darling. I've never been. But Ladyham's rather a way, isn't it? When there are so many places nearer.' She burrowed beneath the sheet, ready for a new smile. I felt myself weaken. 'Let's go to Barlfen. It's on the waterside.'

'I'd like to try the Nouvello. I've heard it's really posh.'

'Can I persuade you, Lovejoy?'

I was determined to get her to Ladyham, the lying cow. She

co-owned the massive new leisure centre, whose boss, Troude, had just hired me. She and Sandy had partly financed it. Yet she's never been?

'Can I, darling?' Her mouth was everywhere, her hands crawling up my belly.

'Right,' I said weakly. Being ridiculous is my lifestyle. 'Barlfen. Sevenish okay?' Pathetic.

The Ruby was lively as a cricket. They'd done a good job at Sugden's garage. I called on Suggie. He came grinning to meet me. His two apprentices were overjoyed to see my Ruby, God knows why. They always say they're sick of it.

'Nice old crate, Lovejoy.' Suggie's always wiping his oily mitts on his overalls.

'Ta for doing it, Suggie.' I tapped its bonnet. 'What's the fastest I can do?'

The apprentices laughed out loud. They were itching to undo it again, start afresh on the damned thing. Barmy. Imagine mending engines all day long.

'Eject if you hit fifteen mph, Lovejoy. Downhill.'

'Ha, ha,' I said gravely. 'The bill get settled, Suggie?'

'All done.' He was over the moon. 'Thankful to get cash in hand these days, with that bloody tax.'

'Great, great.' No receipt, no trace of payment. 'Who collected it?' I asked casually. 'Only, the bloke left a letter on the driving seat.'

Suggie's grin faded into wariness. 'Best post it to him, Lovejoy.'

Kicking myself, I beamed, nodded. 'Why didn't I think of that? Cheers, lads.' I should have thought up a better story.

Just to show them, I notched a good twenty mph leaving their lane, but cut down to my usual sixteen when the Ruby started wheezing. The clatter still came from under the rear wheels, but elegance has to be paid for. I drove with pride into Sandy and Mel's gravelly forecourt. The Ruby trundled to a halt, silenced thankfully.

Mel was packing a big estate car. Cases on the roof, the interior stuffed with gear. Pot plants too, I saw with dismay. Oh dear.

'Wotcher, Mel. Going on a sweep?'

A sweep is a swift scouring of the countryside for antiques. Whether you use fifty technicians like the BBC in its *Antiques Road-show*, or a series of village halls like Sotheby's, or even if it's just yourself, it's basically foraging and returning loaded with antiques, the joy of mankind. But this was no quick trip. My heart sank. Had Sandy and Mel fought again?

He paused, strapping the cover over the heaped roof rack.

'No, Lovejoy. Leaving.'

Sandy and Mel are constants in the antiques game. I mean, they're forever quarrelling, parting in tears and temper. Then it's the big reconciliation and they resume dealing – shrewd, money-mad, but knowledgeable. They have a knack. Their latest success was finding a collection of wrought-iron German snuffboxes. Don't laugh. These were only half an inch tall, but were gold-inlaid, damascened, and genuine eighteenth century – if they're genuine eighteenth century. You know what I mean. Sandy and Mel's nine boxes were brilliant, original, and authentic. Their like in one handful will probably never be seen again. I nearly cried when some undeserving Yank bought them for a fortune. I eyed Mel. The less exotic of the pair, unsmiling, always cross. I was unhappy, seriously.

'Leaving leaving, Mel? Or just leaving?'

'Leaving squared, Lovejoy.' He tested the strap, stepped back. 'That's everything.'

He looked at me. Sorrow began to creep about. This looked truly grim. I'd seen the scene a hundred times, but never quite like this. The long silence made it worse.

'Mel?' I said, nervous.

He gazed about. 'Just look at it, Lovejoy. Converted school-house, a barn. Not bad, decoratively first rate. Three hundred years old, sound as a bell. Stock at valuation.'

A notice board announced it was for sale. My spirits hit my boots. This was real. Mel and Sandy, splitting? Like Tom and Jerry going separate ways. Unthinkable.

'Why, Mel?'

He knew I wasn't asking the price, and smiled deep woe. 'Sandy's gone in over his head, Lovejoy. You know how he is. Anything different.'

'I saw him at the Nouvello.'

'Mmmh.' The non-word spoke volumes of mistrust, almost fear. He tossed me a bunch of keys. 'He doesn't know I've gone, Lovejoy. Give him those.'

His anguish was all the worse for being quietly veiled. I mean, I don't understand how two blokes and all that. But love's a pretty rare plant. In this life there's nowt else – except antiques and they're the same thing anyway. I don't know what I'm trying to say, except I was upset. You can't really believe the Sandys and Mels of this world, not really. Like, they've parted every four or five days, tantrums and sulks, as long as I've known them. But when any partners finally separate, there's a terrible dearth. Almost as if two such transparent phoneys were really among the few genuines in the whole Eastern Hundreds.

'Mel, look,' I hated this. 'How about you phone Sandy and maybe meet him in the Marquis of Granby?' It always worked before.

He was already firing the engine. I felt cold. 'No, Lovejoy. It's over.'

He had sunglasses on. We'd not had any sun all week. For a minute he said nothing, while I tried to think of some magic phrase to cure all this. I get desperate when things suffer.

He said, 'You were kind, Lovejoy. So many aren't, you know. True kindness leaves no place for gratitude.' He glanced around the barnyard. 'It's only a small token. You'll do their gambado anyway. It's your nature. But advice from a friend, if I may?'

'What?'

'For once, just this once, don't help, Lovejoy. Not anyone. Friend or foe. Or you too'll finish up baffled.' He meant don't do what Troude wanted, now Sandy was his backer. 'I'm at my auntie's in Carlisle.' He hesitated, then smiled that terrible smile. 'Can you take another word of advice?'

'Yes?'

He indicated the steps up to the small office he and Sandy shared. 'Steal the Kirkpatrick. It's the best piece left.'

'Steal?' I yelled indignantly after him as he drove out. 'Steal? I've never stolen a single thing in my life! I'd not stoop so low . . .'

Gone. I heard the motor slow by the dairy, turn near the Congregational chapel. Its sound dwindled. Nothing. I looked at the forecourt. The jardinières were gone. The lovely Roman terracotta in the window was gone. I was furious about what Mel'd said. For Christ's *sake*! Cracking a malicious joke like that. Surely it was a joke? A sad attempt at humour as he'd driven out for the last time, to conceal his heartache? As long as he didn't really mean it. I mean, what sort of a rat would rob his friends?

The forecourt was empty, except for me. Nobody about. I looked at the bunch of keys he'd given me. At the steps. At the For Sale notice. And thought. Kirkpatrick?

Cornwall Kirkpatrick was a stoneware potter. American, Illinois. He decorated his jugs and whatnot with cutting satire – snakes as politicians, with biting inscriptions saying how horrible they were. His fantasy urns and geographical pigs (I kid you not) make you sleepless, give you bad dreams. Skilful, but alarming. And very, very pricey. So rare, they'd buy a good month's holiday any day of the week. I always sell them – give some other poor blighter the nightmares instead.

But to *steal?* From friends? That's the action of a real gargoyle, a despicable cad.

Only to test the door handle, I went up the steps. That meant I had to try the keys, open the door. And have a quick look round, see the Kirkpatrick was still there. Only for security and all that, because you can't be too careful. I found it in my hand, Mel's Kirkpatrick jug. Criminal to leave it. I mean, clearly it needed looking after, right? I decided I'd better take it home. Not stealing. No, honest. Not genuinely *stealing.* Only, somebody had to care for it, right? So I wrapped it up and hid it in the Ruby's boot, just so it wouldn't get stolen. There are thieves everywhere these days.

Baff's house was on the way, so I drove there, more by instinct than anything else, wondering how much I'd get for the Kirkpatrick jug. Only 1870s, but packed with potential. I felt truly heartbroken over Sandy and Mel, but notched an exhilarating twenty-two on the bypass, in a lucky wind. Omen?

Baff Bavington's a breakdown man. He's a lazy devil, is Baff. My brother used to say that lazy people aren't lazy – they're merely clever. Breakdowning is a way of nicking antiques from unsuspecting ladies who live alone. You can do it to elderly couples, too, but Baff never did – after one incident when some old geezer turned out to be a dead-shot colonel with a twelve-bore.

Sherry's his missus. She used to help him out, for authenticity's sake. Baff's standard trick was this: break down, engine boiling over or something, in the very gateway of some old dear's house. Baff knocks – can he please have some water for his radiator? (Sherry smiling anxiously from the motor.) Baff takes the pan of water, while Sherry nips round the back and susses out the house. She slips a window catch, or inserts a sliver of comb into a lock to make it easier to pick. There's even a spray you can get that makes a window impossible to close properly – I'd better not tell you its name, or you'll all be at it.

That night, back comes Baff, cleans out your antiques and other valuables while you kip. Easy.

The boyos – real hard-liner antique robbers – despise breakdown merchants because police always have their number. Within an hour of waking up, the robbed old lady's on the blower to the Plod. Who of course have a score of other reported breakdown-style thefts in the vicinity. Somebody always has the car's description. And Baff's. And Sherry's. Who suddenly need alibis . . . et relentless cetera. No, the boyos want scams you can do unscathed and often. Breakdowners are the lazy antique thief's theft. It's also risky. Which is why Baff's done time.

Sherry was grieving in her mother's cottage, which is where she and Baff live. Mum's their chief alibi, forever in court testifying to the innocence of her daughter and Baff. I knocked, went through the sordid courtesies folk use to ward off grief.

'You were a real friend to Baff, Lovejoy,' Sherry told me, sniffing. My friends were having a hell of a day. Was it just me?

'That's true, right enough,' her mum said, dabbing her eyes fetchingly at the mirror. 'You'll miss Baff's trade, Lovejoy.'

The ugly old bat showed all the grief of a road sign. A pro. And Sherry, a lovely plump woman with a penchant for old-fashioned hairstyles, scrolls on her forehead, was only going through a let's-pretend sorrow, half an eye on a telly quiz show. She knew I knew, only too well. She hostesses with excessive zeal on the town bypass, between helping Baff's breakdowner jobs. I discovered Sherry's exciting pastime accidentally, when doing a night valuation for Big John Sheehan. The Ulsterman had taken a liking to some display silver at The Postern, a crude hotel of creaking antiquity. He'd told me to drainpipe in and suss the silver, see if it was (a) genuine, and (b) worth stealing. Everybody knew it was in three cabinets, second floor. That night, I'd started out to obey – only to step on two heaving fleshly protuberances in the darkness. Both turned out to be Sherry, plying her hostessly trade in a manner unorthodox and a mite unexpected. Next morning she'd sought me out, frantic lest I divulge all to Baff. I'd gone along, because women have hidden persuaders. Anyway, silence spared Baff heartache, right? But why was an idle sod like Baff – sorry, *requiescat in pace* – why was he doing an extra night job?

'I'll see the lads have a whip-round, Sherry,' I said gently.

Her face lit up, instantly shedding sorrow at the sound of monetary music. 'You will? Oh, Lovejoy! That would be marvellous! I don't know how I'm going to manage, what with . . .'

She petered out, pinkly remembering our first nocturnal encounter and its mutually beneficial consequences.

'Never mind.' Embarrassed, I made my farewells, paused at the door. Mum absently borrowed her daughter's eye-liner. 'Here, Sherry. Baff actually working, was he?'

'Baff?' Her mind reluctantly left thoughts of how much money the more sentimental antique dealers would chip in for her newfound widowhood. 'Yes. He was doing a sea-front stall. They'd phoned him. Good money, Lovejoy. Of course,' she added hastily, in case word got back and diminished Baff's friends' generosity, 'I haven't had it yet.'

'Look,' I said. 'Let me collect it for you. Where'd you say it was?'

She got the point instantly. 'Selveggio Sea Caravans. On the Mentle Marina waterfront near the funfair.'

'Er, did Baff leave any antiques around, Sherry? Only, he owed me a couple of items . . .' He didn't, but it was worth a try.

'No, Lovejoy. We'd had a run of bad luck lately. So many people have dogs and burglar alarms these days.'

'Never mind, love,' I said nobly. 'Forget Baff owed me a thing.' I felt really generous, pardoning Baff's non-existent debts to me.

Sherry came to see me off. She closed the door and stood on the step in the darkness.

'Lovejoy. I'm quite free now.' She straightened my jacket lapel – no mean feat – and smiled beguilingly. 'It's hard for me to accept. But you've no regular woman, have you? Maybe you and I could get together. I could pop round, see if you needed anything.'

'I'll bring your money round later.' I bussed her, cranked the Ruby out of its moribundity, and chugged out of the tiny garden heading for reality.

This is half my trouble. I can cope with more or less anything, except with events that change in mid-stream. Like, here I was expressing my genuine sorrow over Baff's mugging/killing, only to find myself propositioned by his bird who was more interested in hitching up with a replacement bloke and getting a few quid. It felt weird. Sandy and Mel actually separating, Baff getting done.

When I'm bewildered, I head for antiques and sanity. The auction called. My best-ever fake was back in town. But first, a fake historical interlude, at a genuine knight's gathering.

Because I'd promised, I went to Sir Edward's Event. I didn't want to go. It's near Long Melford. Every year they select some historical date by chucking dice, then re-enact the trades and village life of that particular year. The whole village is at it. They wear period garb, serve period-style food and drink on trestle-tables. They dance to reproduction musical instruments. It's a bit too hearty for me, especially if they get things wrong. It's still quite pleasant to see the children done up in a make-believe old schoolhouse, farriers shoeing horses with a travelling forge, all that.

The grounds at Sir Edward's are given over to the Event, two whole days. There must have been three hundred people there,

counting us visitors. Admission costs the earth; this year it was to
raise gelt for Doc Lancaster's unspeakable electronics that he tortures
us with. A good cause, our luscious choirmistress Hepsibah told me,
laughing, as she took my money. I wandered in among the mob,
hoping nobody would see me slope off after a token grimace at the
jolly scene. Enthusiasm has a lot to answer for.

At Pal's joiner's bench, though, I really stopped to really look.
He had a table.

'Wotcher, Pal.' He's an old geezer, does the woodwork scene
every Event. 'Rain held off, then, eh?'

'Thank God, Lovejoy. Want a genuine antique table, Anno
Domini 1770?'

The table was lovely. I stared at it, worrisome bongs not
happening in my chest. It was labelled *Sideboard Table, Chippendale
Type, c. 1770*, with all manner of fanciful descriptive balderdash; *from
the home of a Titled Norfolk Gentleman* . . . The surface got me, though.

'Genuine is it, Lovejoy?' Jodie Danglass, no less. Sir Edward's
Event was a burden for me; it was extraordinary for Jodie.

'Course it's genuine,' Pal groused. He's pleasant, until you differ
with him on some opinion. 'Think I'd kill myself doing a surface
like that, do you?' He went on lathing a piece of wood, using a
rigged-up sapling drill. That's only a rope stretched from a stooping
sapling to your instep. Grudgingly I watched him. Better skilled than
me. 'Borrowed it from Sir Edward's Hall.'

Well, the local bigwig might have had a fake made by the
original methods. But nowadays? Except . . .

'Are you all right, Lovejoy?' Jodie asked.

'Stop nagging.'

We went to get served by a little girl. Dilute mead, quite good.
'That surface, love.' Perfect, with the sheen only the hand of man
can create. 'I'd heard somebody say last week they'd seen a mint
Sheraton side table in the Midlands, the surface unflawed, perfect,
original. I didn't believe him. But for some craftsman still to be
faking so good these days –'

'Looked genuine to me.'

She sounded quite indifferent. I nearly choked. Antique dealers
think nothing of the things they're supposed to know, understand,
admire. I saw red. 'Listen to me, you silly cow. See over there?' The
little girls serving the mead had a kitchen table, virtually a plank of
chipboard with four machine-made legs. 'That'd take any nerk less
than an hour to make, household drill and buffing pad. But that . . . ?'
I looked across to where Pal was pausing to light a fag. Somebody

shouted a criticism, were cigarettes in period? He waved back apologetically, took no notice, grinned with an addict's afront. I was to remember that grin, in far, far different circumstances.

'That?' she prompted. She looked as disturbed as I was, probably thinking how near she'd come to making an offer for it.

'You buy a log of mahogany, love.' I described its huge shape with my hands. 'Not the forced spongy wood they import nowadays, but the slow-growing natural unforced trees you have to pay the earth for – if you can still find one in the raped wild forests. Then you – top dog, as they used to say – straddle the log over a saw-pit. Some poor sod – bottom dog – climbs down into the saw-pit. You get an enormous woodman's curved two-handled log saw – itself a valuable antique, because nobody makes them now. Hour after hour, you saw the log lengthways to make a plank . . .'

It takes me like this, the shame, the ecstasy of antiques. I'm the only man living to have done the whole thing, start to finish. I couldn't move for a week afterwards. I paid a fortune for seven stalwart farm lads to partner me on the saw-pit I'd dug in my garden wilderness. They'd given up, one after the other, and left calling me barmy. I'd slogged on, hands like balloons, bleeding and blistered.

'Then you take your sawn plank of mahogany. You plane it flat. Takes three days.' Jodie was looking at me, mesmerized. I could have swiped her one. Antique dealers and fakers think of automatic electric planers, gouging drills you work with a button while having coffee and a fag. I heard somebody shouting for me from over where the horses were. I yelled back a sod off, pressed on. 'Then comes the hard part.'

They'd worked barefoot, mostly, those ancient cabinet-makers. All heroes to me. When the table's surface was smooth as any hand-plane could make it, they'd got children – often their own – to beg or buy fragments of broken brick. The children ground the brick pieces to dust in a pestle and mortar. They'd then winnowed it, casting the dust up into the air.

'Coarser brick-dust particles fell first – resisting the air, see? The children, toddlers to seven-year-olds, caught it on bits of fustian, in a bowl, anything. The finer particles were caught separately.'

The bloke was still shouting. Torry from Beccles, pockets full of phoney silvers as usual. I rose to move away, sickened by my tale anyway. Jodie caught me. Her eyes were huge. 'Wait, Lovejoy. The children?'

'No sandpaper in those days, Jodie. The maker smoothed it with brick-dust. I've done it. You rub the flat tabletop – coarse powder first. Your bare hands, to and fro along the wood's grain, hour after hour.'

'But don't your hands . . . ?'

'Aye, love. They swell, blister. The skin shreds. They weep on to the dusty wood. The dust becomes a paste, of skin fragments, brick-dust, blister water, sweat, blood. Think how it must have been. Virtually naked at the finish, dripping pure sweat. But you kept going. You had to, or you and your children starved, literally.' My voice went bitter. 'I had delusions at first. I would do it exactly as those ancients did. What a pillock! I lasted two hours. After a week's rest, another two hours.'

My skin had peeled first, then blistered from my raw palms. I'd used my elbows. Then I'd stripped naked, and stood on the tabletop with bare feet, shuffling the brick-dust up and down the wood.

'See why it's special, having a genuine Sheraton table? A modern Formica job's machined in a trice, virtually untouched by human hand. But the heartwood of an antique table's *still got the craftsman in it*. His blood, sweat, flesh, it's there in the living wood. Is it any wonder a genuine antique *feels* different? Modern furniture is chemical-covered chipboard. The real antique is a person. It's a friend living with you.'

'That's . . . lovely.' But she'd started out to say something very different. Well, truth takes you different ways.

'Know how long it took me, Jodie? Sixteen weeks, to repeat three days' work of a seventeenth-century man.' I tried to give her a grin, defuse the talk. Her face was all alarm. 'I had to keep resting to battle on. Pathetic. You women have it easy, love. The work of your sisters three centuries ago is still within your reach. Look around.' Across a patch of grass two milkmaids were hand-milking some Jersey cows, admired by a small crowd. Other girls were washing clothes in the fountain, beating garments on stones. People wandering among the stalls were laughing, joking. Oh, so very merry. 'You women can still give it a go any time, cook, wash, bake, skivvy for fifteen hours a day. You'd be tired, aye, but could still congratulate yourself on how marvellously you'd relived your grandma's routine.'

'And you?'

Answering took a long time. 'Ashamed, Jodie. I'd thought myself fit. I knew what to do, God knows. But the long-dead craftsmen defeated me.' I looked across at the village church. 'You graveyard's full of the old bastards. Any one sleeping there could wake today, step out, and produce brilliance like us modern clever clogs couldn't do in a month of Sundays. Admitting that is the shame of my life. It does something to a man. See, love. A woman can always claim she's prettier than the Queen of Sheba, that Lady Hamilton's hair was a mess and her own isn't. We blokes have more absolute comparisons. And we lose out every single time, to those that've gone before.'

'Can nobody do it nowadays?'

'That sideboard table Pal has on show there is a fake, Jodie. But it's been done using the old methods. Must have killed somebody.' I snorted a half-laugh. 'Until now I'd thought I was the only bloke alive who'd ever made a genuine fake. Get somebody able to repeat the old processes nowadays, you'd be a millionairess by teatime.'

'Then why don't they, Lovejoy?'

'Because the old methods use up people, not gadgets.' Well, I should complain. I'm the one who always argues people first, things second.

That is all I want to say, for now. We saw Sir Edward tottering towards us. He's a boring old devil, so I left Jodie and went to watch the morris dancers. That's something else I'm no good at, either.

CHAPTER SEVEN

Once upon a time, antiques were a rarefied pursuit for scholars. Oh, don't misunderstand. A few titled gentlemen really did pursue antiquities all over the ancient world. They spent fortunes, founded private museums in attics. Great, but kind of chintzy.

Until July, 1886.

In that month the great antiques hunt began, when an auctioneer intoned 'Lot One' – and the Duke of Marlborough's Blenheim Palace's magnificent art, furniture, statuary went under the hammer. That gavel was gunfire that reverberated round the world. The Great Antiques Rush was on. Think of a rocket soaring upward, that's never yet begun to fall. Okay, it's levelled off now and then, but always resumed rezooming prices into the stratosphere.

Now, we're all at it. Clever people draw graphs of antiques' values, starting back in that lovely summer of 1886. Don't be fooled. It's not a mathematical proposition. It's not philosophy. It's a scramble.

Umber Auctions took over from Wittwoode less than a month after he got nicked for 'discretion', that hoary old get-out by which auctioneers absolve themselves of blame for trickery. They behaved like a new Prime Minister. Wholesale sackings, Under New Management posters everywhere, advertising campaigns – then no change. The same whifflers drift aimlessly about hoping to make a few quid on the side, crooked auctioneers, crooked vannies, crooked antique dealers moaning that the antiques are pure unadulterated gunge. It still stank of armpits and stale smoke. I love it. An auction has paradise within. All you have to do is look.

'Lovejoy.' Practical was over like a shot, trying to pull me to see. 'What d'you reckon?'

Even before we pushed among the grumbling dealers I knew it would be the same old fake. You have to laugh at blokes like Practical because they're a waste of time, yet sensible in a weird kind of way. He fakes only the cheaper end of antiques. Not badly, but not well either. Fortyish, thin, stained with his famous watercolours. He uses his jacket for a rag, so half of him is always rainbow, the other half taupe tat.

'Good?'

I looked. The famous George Cruikshank, who died in 1878 or

so, illustrated Charles Dickens's works. He also sketched as he wandered, producing little watercolours that have never really caught on. You can get genuine Cruikshank for less than a week's wage. This is the sort of thing Practical fakes – hence his nickname. Old Masters 'aren't practical'. Cheaper, less risky forgeries are.

'Not bad, Prac. Not, definitely not, good.'

My tone disappointed him. 'Give me a tip, Lovejoy?'

'Get a couple of decent old frames from Farmer. New fake frames are a dead give-away. And stop using tea to mimic foxing. Everybody nowadays knows to look for a sharp rim. Leave the watercolour surface undamaged. Say it's just been cleaned. And for heaven's sake stamp its reverse, Prac – you can buy a fake Agnew's stamp for ten quid down the market.'

I turned away, exasperated. Folk drive you mad. Then I paused. Seeing Diana enter from the street, swivelling every head, made me think.

'Here, Prac.' Voice low – antique dealers have three-league ears. 'You still a neb man?'

Door-to-door con tricks come in many guises. The commonest among antique dealers is the 'neb man'. The old game where you pretend to be a council/social worker/health inspector – some kind of semi-authoritative official. You talk your way into somebody's home, filch a small antique, and scarper lightly on your way. It always works. In fact, it's so easy I sometimes wonder if people actually want to be tricked. 'Neb' comes from the old word for the peak of a cap – as once worn by officialdom's intruders. You still see market barrowboys and bus crews surreptitiously touch their foreheads, symbolizing touching a neb, to signify an inspector's on the way.

'A bit. Why?'

Practical hates doing it since he lost his teeth. No smile. A con man needs a smile. Too much booze had rotted his fangs, and pot teeth were looming from the dentist on Chitts Hill. For Practical, it had been the Year of the Tooth. I watched Diana out of the corner of my eye. She was urgently questing, not strolling. Drowning, not waving. I ducked. I'd my own problems.

'Done anything round Mentle? Ladyham?'

'Me and Baff did turn and turn about. I sold him Mentle a month since.'

'Ta, Prac.'

I promised to see Farmer, persuade a frame out of the stingy old nerk to help Prac out, and eeled towards the door. It was then that Donk saw me and yelled my name. A right pest he was turning out to be. I had to stand upright and pretend I'd been casually inspecting an Eastern mirror mounted in a brilliantly cut mother-of-pearl surround. Diana came over as soon as she could, all the oafs deliberately not getting out of her way.

'Hello, Lovejoy. I thought I'd find you here. Can we speak?'

'What do you think of this?' I seethed with disgust. 'Leave mother-of-pearl in sunshine, you never get its glisten back. A waste of all that lovely carving.' Actually, there are ways, but they're not good.

I went with her, but only so she wouldn't give me that can-we-talk? routine. I hate it. It's all they ever say on telly soaps: *Can we talk?* As if you have to set up a Security Council before telling a bird her dress is a mess and you love her. God, but the world needs me.

'My own fake's here, Di,' I said shyly. 'Want to see it?'

'Which is it, Lovejoy?' our greatest failed lover butted in to ask.

Dicko Chave. He's hopeless, which is to say an average dealer. A pompous, bluff bloke, he's proposed to every woman in the Eastern Hundreds, rejected every single time. Nobody knows why. He's begged me to tell him where he goes wrong. I'm stumped. I mean, an ex-officer, doesn't drink much, his own house, keeps accurate tax accounts would you believe, church-goer, shoes polished, reliable as a Lancashire clock. You'd think women'd find him a good prospect, if only for economic reasons, but no.

'Sorry, Dicko.' I now regretted boasting, even quietly, to Diana. Already dealers were sidling up to listen. The auction prices would fall now, from general suspicion. My Sheraton would have to wait for its deserved adulation until after it was auctioned. I took Diana's arm.

'Lovejoy. Won't you introduce me?' Dicko asked, wistful with his unmarried smile, drawing himself up for social niceties.

'I'm sorry,' Diana snapped. 'We're busy.'

'Oh. Perhaps some other . . .' We were out of the door, which wafted after us: '. . . time'.

See what I mean? Diana hadn't given him a glance. Yet Dicko's polite as well. Strange.

We went, brisk with purpose, to the Tudor Rest across the road. Not far enough, but their coffee's the only drinkable coffee in East Anglia. Hank the Yank runs it, needless to say. A triumph of caffeine-soaked heredity over environment. She chose a corner place after prolonged inspection.

'Expecting being stabbed, love?'

No levity. My heart sank. Deadly earnest time, and an auction about to start a hundred yards away. I have rotten luck.

'No time for wit, Lovejoy. What did he tell you?'

A pause while Hank TY himself served us. He has three wait-resses, but they do sweet nothing – as far as observers can see, that is. But Hank is a very happy proprietor. He admired Diana, tried to extend his delivery with chat, and failed at least as badly as Dicko Chave. He retired hurt to his kitchen, but not too hurt. Giggles arose from there within seconds.

'Troude?' I wondered about the wisdom of this meeting. I mean, why was she asking? 'Why're you asking?'

'I suggested you, Lovejoy.' She did that woman's head-shake that loosens their hair but makes you feel they're girding for war. 'I have to know if he hired you.'

'Is he your pal, Di?'

She lit a cigarette with aggressive intent, spouted smoke. She was mad all right. I began to regret that bonus. She was here to cash in on the obligation. No need to ask whose obligation, either. It's always on mine.

'If you call me Di once more, Lovejoy, I'll throw you under the next bus. Understand?' I nodded, to get the rest of the ballocking. 'Monsieur Troude and I are good acquaintances. We have difficulty keeping in touch, under the circumstances.'

'Mmmh.' She'd said about some husband. Maybe a club member? Investor? Or was that Member of Parliament's wife a regular iron-pumper there? I had to go careful. 'Mr Troude just said he'd be in touch.'

'That means he has hired you, Lovejoy,' she translated for her own, not my benefit. 'Have you a pen?'

She lent me a gold pencil from her handbag. I wrote the address on a menu. She held out her palm, but I honestly wasn't trying to pinch her pencil. For God's sake, everybody forgets to return pencils, don't they? Anyhow, I'd swap her rotten gold propelling pencil any day for a genuine Borrowdale graphite, the best writing tool ever made since the world began. It was back in the 1560s that gales uprooted an ash tree in Borrowdale, Cumberland. A man happened to see pieces of a strange solid in its up-ended roots. Curious, he felt it, and saw how easily it blackened his fingers. He used it to mark his sheep, and graphite – stone that draws – was born. Sensibly, folk began enclosing slivers of graphite – 'English antimony' – in a lathed wooden tube and hey presto! I hadn't realized I'd been telling her out loud. She clipped her handbag closed. I think I was beginning to like her. She smiled at something achieved, and I was sure.

'I'll make it worth your while, Lovejoy. Keep me informed. In more ways than you can imagine.'

Her hand touched mine, a promise on account. Promises have the half-life of snowflakes, which makes me wonder why I fall for them. You'd think I'd learn.

'Won't Troude be narked, if I blab to you?'

'He'll be glad, Lovejoy. No need to let on, though. Let's keep it just between ourselves.' She rose to go, leaving that red crescentic reminder of lust on her cup rim. 'Oh, Lovejoy. *Parlez-vous-Français?*'

'No, love.'

'School slanguage, though?'

'*Plume de ma tant*ie's all very well, love, but teaching doesn't get you very far. Here, love. You forgot the bill.'

'Oh.' She paid up with a kind of surprised amusement. 'You know, Lovejoy, I rather think we're going to get along. It's some considerable time since I've had a partner I could rely on.'

We said goodbye, me promising – I do it too – to let her know the instant Troude showed up. I found Hank beside me watching her walk up the brough into town.

'You're a lucky swine, Lovejoy,' he said. 'She looks a really great lay. How much a trick?'

First Jodie Danglass thinks Diana's socially unacceptable. And now Hank jumps to the same conclusion. Most be some allergen in the pollen.

'She's my client, Hank,' I said airily. 'Antiques buyer from, er, Michigan. Paid quarter of a million for a collection of Philadelphian teapot lamps last week.'

'An American?' he cried delightedly. 'And I thought she was Paris France! Nice trace of accent.'

'Educated there, Hank. Cheers.'

He went back in to resume his onerous labours making waitresses giggle in the kitchen. I went across the road more thoughtful than before. Suddenly there seemed a lot of France about, where France wasn't.

The world restored normality when Tinker caught me up and dragged me into the Ship Inn. He had Steve Yelbard waiting, victor of the Portland Vase competition.

'Hello, Steve.' I let my delight show. 'Congrats. Your glass-work's beautiful. Here, let me get these . . .' I ordered ale for the three of us, which was numerically equal to six – four for Tinker, one each for Steve and me.

We spoke for quite some time. He was a nice bloke, not able to tell me much. Genuine, as far as I could tell. More interested in glass than breathing. An enthusiast after my own heart. I asked if he'd visited anywhere locally besides Long Melford where he was staying, was told no.

Steve told me about Jan Fotheringay. 'I got a note saying he had a commission for me, copying some varied-knop bell-mouthed wine glasses, but he didn't show.'

'Newcastle, eh?' I sighed. Even a fake 1734 vintage glass, with its knops shaping the stem with lovely variation, yet in exquisite proportion, would send me delirious. Newcastle's glass has never been bettered – and I do include Venice. They are nearly priceless. 'You do your own wheel engraving, Steve?'

'No. Got a Dutch bloke.'

I laughed. 'Traditionalist, eh?' Even that long ago, our glasses were sent to Holland for engraving. The real difficulty is making sure the air-beaded ball knop isn't a fraction too large. Some glass-maker fakers run amok when they try for the most valuable – 'Eh? What, Steve?' He'd said something.

'Jan. Terrible luck.' Steve tutted. 'His motor home. Didn't know he was a drinker. You can't tell, can you?'

'Mmmh,' I went. I'd get it from Tinker later.

And that was that. Steve knew nothing about Phoebe Colonna, despite strong views on her morals, substituting a Victorian replica for one of her own. Unscrupulous, he called it.

'An American trait, Lovejoy. Spreading all over the world.'

So we parted, me and Tinker waving off this pure-minded forger who'd discovered America was to blame for all our wrongdoing. God knows what the Old World would do without the Yanks to blame for everything – blame our horrible old selves instead, I suppose.

'Tell, Tinker,' I ordered.

'Dry old day, Lovejoy.' He threatened a rumbling chestiness. I flung a couple of pints down his throttle in the nick of time. 'That poofter Jan lives in a motorized caravan. Its engine caught fire driving through Archway. He lost the lot.'

'What's this about drink?'

'Pissed as a newt, Lovejoy,' he said inelegantly. 'The Plod checked his blood. Insurance'll shell him like the bleedin' plague. Out of hospital, magistrate'll chuck the book at him.'

'That bad?'

The long hand of Fortune? Or the longer, more decisive hand of Big John Sheehan, Corse, both?

I remembered then I was going to Barlfen with the lovely Almira, and made a run for it. From my chat with Steve I was practically sure there was no connection between the Portland Vase competition and this Troude bloke. And sure too that Almira was only pretending she had no investments in the Nouvello venture in Ladyham. After all, she might have an old flame on the board, and simply be doing him a favour, right?

It came on to rain about then. I saw no new omens.

CHAPTER EIGHT

That evening was straight out of *Casbah*, me staring soulfully through candleglim at the beautiful Almira, who smiled mistily and whispered sweet everythings. The Barlfen Rest turned out to be the nook to end all nooks. No diner could see any other diner unless she was at his table. It was like a rabbit warren. You wended among ferns and carved ornate screens. Clever old Almira, to suggest – well, insist on – this place.

'Lovejoy, darling.' Almira was all for cottage work again. 'It's time to go.'

I'd had her pudding, disappointingly non-filling sorbet stuff. She'd seemed to expect me to eat it, the way women do. 'Wait, doowerlink. Please.' I pretended to temporize, slipped in an order for profiteroles. 'I have something to say.'

'Yes, darling?' Women love appetites in action. Almira was happy to see me nosh. I waited for the discreet serf to retire. It took longer than I wanted, because I'd had to wrestle the waitress to the best of three pinfalls for enough cream.

'Our holiday,' I said. I wanted to appear soulful, but you can't when scoffing your third pudding, so I let instinct guide me along. 'France. Next Friday. Can you get away?'

'France?'

She went faint. Her hand crept to her lovely throat. She was wearing genuine amber – orange-coloured, not Chinese red, no trace of that ugly sectoring that gives amberoid mock-ups away in oblique light. Lovely thick complete beads, matching near as amber ever can. Low-cut, her swan neck without a blemish. No wonder women rule.

'I checked. There's another flight next Thursday. I paid a deposit.' I looked proud.

'But Lovejoy . . .'

'I know exactly what you're thinking.'

'You *what?*' Now pale as well as faint, her voice going.

'Don't worry. I've made the arrangements through a travel agent near St Edmundsbury. You husband will never trace it.'

'Oh, darling,' she said, frantic. 'I couldn't possibly come, not to . . .'

Not to France? I thought, but did not say. I watched her scrabble out of the pit I'd dug.

'It's the . . . the competitions, Lovejoy,' she said with bright invention. 'I'm training three showjumpers for the point-to-point. I'm so sorry, darling. You're so sweet to think of it. I must recompense you for all the cost you have put into the idea, darling.'

'That's kind, love.' I eyed her. I was really narked. What if I really *had* paid a holiday deposit? 'Promise me you'll come some other time. How about Greece?'

She reached across the table and squeezed my hand, eyes glowing with unbridled love or something. She almost collapsed from relief. 'I promise, darling. Greece sounds lovely.' If I'd said Greece first we'd already be on the Great White Bird. 'Anything you want, Lovejoy,' she offered, gay now the threat of France was all done.

'Doowerlink,' I said mistily.

Anything, but keep off Troude's properties at Ladyham and Mentle where Baff got killed by louts, and book for anywhere but France? I was suddenly out of my depth. I told her to settle the bill because I was in a hurry. She obeyed with suppressed excitement, and we scurried from Barlfen with unseemly alacrity to make savage passionate smiles at my cottage.

She was sound asleep when I eventually rose and stole away with all the stealth of a fairground. I cranked the Ruby into life, and had it clattering resentfully through the drizzle towards London in minutes. I'd hidden the matches, so even if Almira heard me she'd have had a hell of a time lighting a candle to get dressed and catch me up.

Four o'clock in the morning, I was chugging down Highgate Hill when the Ruby croaked to a standstill next to the stone marking where young Dick Whittington had paused with his cat on his dispirited retreat from London and heard the bells chiming out promises of Lord Mayorality and fortune. I paused to listen. Only the tap of the rain on the wheezing Ruby's bonnet. It looked fit for Casualty. I went in to find the nearest unvandalized phone box. Enquiries gave me Jan's newspaper number. With a lot of shinannikins I got somebody on a night desk and explained I was Jan Fotheringay's doctor with urgent news for the next of kin. They had a conference of some sort, reluctantly gave me a number in Tooting Bec. I rang.

'Hello,' I said sternly to the sleepy but harassed bird who answered. 'This is the Whittington Hospital. I'm Dr, ah, Pasteur. Some confusion has arisen about Jan Fotheringay's, ah, designation status.'

'Yes, Doctor. This is Lysette, his next of kin,' she said breathlessly.

'I knew there would be trouble. It's this dual nationality, isn't it? He *was* born in Switzerland, but has lived here all his life. The tax returns are in such a mess from it.' A sudden switch as she realized the hour. 'He's still in a stable condition, isn't he?'

'Well, his condition is . . .' I crackled and hissed like a failing phone. We in East Anglia know the sounds only too well.

Armed now, I entered the Whittington Hospital and asked to see the night sister. I was Jan Fotheringay's long-lost estranged brother who'd just heard the bad news.

'Hello, Sister,' I said, going all desperation when they found her for me. 'I can't thank you enough for looking after my brother, Jan. Lysette in Tooting Bec says he's had a terrible accident. Can I see him, please? Our poor old mother does pine so . . .'

'It's just as well you came, Mr Fotheringay,' the night sister said sadly. 'A terrible accident. You can see him. But you must fill in this form. Name and address, please.'

I complied, narked. I mean, I'm basically honest, so why all this malarkey? Women ought to realize they have an obligation to trust me, but they never do.

The ward was long and thin with dismal green walls. Patients snored, rumbled, twitched, groaned. Gruesome machines did their blinks, wheezes, clanks. The hospital reverberated to clicks and clashes, the whole nocturnal symphony of dins combining to make healthy innocents shudder. If they don't use ether any more, why does its perfume linger?

Jan was unrecognizable. He lay on a bed that seemed a complex tangle of tubing in a plastic bubble. The bubble itself was tubed up like an astronaut. Jan was riddled. Even his tubes had tubes, fluid dripping in and fluids dripping out. Shiny metal cylinders squeezed and relaxed. Monitor screens bleeped and blooped. Dials showed numbers. Mad dots chased other mad dots across green glowing oscilloscopes. I felt ill.

The nurse caught my arm, helped me to a chair.

'I understand, Charles,' she said quietly. 'Seeing your brother like this is bound to be a shock. Put your head between your knees. I'll bring you a cup of tea.'

Silly bitch thought I was queasy. Ridiculous, because I'm not the sort to go giddy seeing somebody who's poorly. My vision returned slowly. My clammy hands eventually stopped shaking. Sweat dripped down my chin on to the floor. God, but hospitals have a lot to answer for. It took me half an hour to feel myself again, and even then the sight of Jan was enough to make me emigrate.

'Can I speak to him, Nurse?'

'Yes. But you won't go too near.'

She retired back to her illuminated desk, a pool of light in a sanctuary straight out of Goya, head bent beside the lamp, all else in darkness.

My head was bent too. 'Jan?' I said to the plastic sheeting. My breath condensed on it. 'It's me. Lovejoy.'

The figure didn't move. You could see bits of his features, mottled and scaly like a fish gone bad. Couldn't they cover his burnt bits up, for God's sake? He seemed to be lying uncomfortably, and not on proper bedclothes either. Didn't they give sick folk a proper mattress? Hell flaming fire.

'Anything you want me to do, Jan?'

'I haven't got a brother.'

Barely audible. I found myself looking about guiltily, but the night nurse wasn't in earshot. 'I lied. They wouldn't have let me in otherwise.'

An arm moved – well, some place the limb should have been shifted slowly. Tubes trailed with it.

I said, a bit apologetically, 'Stop frigging me about with this Jan the Critic gunge. You're from Tooting Bec.'

'How did you find out?' No laughter, but I felt he'd be amused if they lifted the hospital off him.

'I phoned the newspaper. Said I was your doctor. They told me your address. I phoned the girl there. Lysette, isn't it?'

Astonishingly, I saw an eye open to hold me in its gaze. Not such a nerk after all, lying here with that alert bright orb steady on me.

'Why're you digging, Lovejoy?'

This was the hard part. I hesitated. 'I have to know what happened after they took you out of the barn that night down in the harbour.'

Silence. No feeling of a would-be smile now. More like would-be fright.

'Listen, Jan. I'll guess. You just tell me if I go wrong.' I licked my lips, planning ahead. 'The hoods threatened you. You got scared, decided to make a run for it. You commissioned Steve Yelbard as a decoy, didn't show. You got your motorized carvan, and heading through Archway had an unexpected accident –'

'Accident.' The limb moved.

'Was it Corse's men?'

'Not even a crash.' He sounded so tired. 'They made me watch

57

while they burned it. They threw me in the door. I heard them laughing. I hit my head and couldn't move. It was all afire. Some passing football supporters pulled me out, the nurse told me.'

'I'm scareder than you, Jan. I'll say nowt, and do less.' But I'd had to know. I mean, I've worked for Big John Sheehan quite a few times. 'Was it Corse, or Sheehan's lot?'

'Neither. They set me running, Lovejoy, but they wouldn't care where I went.'

Odd. 'Where were you going?'

'Back to Geneva. I thought I'd be . . .'

'That's enough, Charles,' the night nurse said, quietly interposing. She looked ready to deal with a million tubes in a million horrid ways. I'd learned enough. I thought.

'So long, Jan. Keep going, eh?'

'Lovejoy.' I bent my head to hear the whisper in spite of the nurse's tutting. 'My address, my –'

'Safe with me, Jan. Cheers.'

On the way out, I almost bumped into a bonny dark-haired girl. She was hurrying towards the ward from the lift's cacophony of clashing doors. She didn't spare me a glance, just hurried on past. Lysette? I'd bet a quid.

Sometimes, I wonder if everybody doesn't go through life desperately trying to avoid being seen. It's as if we've all committed a murder, and have a nagging terror we might get spotted. Oh, I know we go about pretending the opposite, wearing fashionable clothes, sprucing ourselves up to catch the eye. But that's only surface ripples. Deep down, we strive for anonymity. At least, some do. Like me. I'm a chameleon in search of a colour against which to stand and vanish.

Especially to Cissie.

Lovejoy, her note said, as if I hadn't enough to do. *Come immediately. It's urgent. I shall be in until eleven.* No signature. I knew who.

Yonks since, I mentioned a wife I once had. Cissie'd become a half-remembered dream. I couldn't even recall her face, not that I'd tried. Like a pillock I drove obediently through Lavenham, wondering why the hell I was bothering. Marriage isn't what folk say it is. Bonding's pretty loose stuff, and marriage knots aren't. In the first place, it's hard to find any spouse who behaves as if morality's there in strength. Second, married couples never agree on what marriage actually is. For me, I simply hadn't understood that getting married to Cissie did not constitute a proper introduction. Mind you, who can fathom birds? Why, for instance, was the Marquis de Sade's missus Renée unswervingly faithful to him all the years he was in the Bastille, only to leave him the minute he got sprung? You tell me.

Their house is enormous. I'd only ever been there once before, to deliver her share of the belongings. She'd banished me, her belongings and all, threatened me with the police if I ever showed again. I'd been delighted to comply.

'My usual Tuesday visit, Katta,' I said to the maid.

She emitted a brief tubular screech, her signal of humour. A vast emporium of a maid, is Katta. She never stops spreading across your field of view. She's been with Paul – more about him in a sec – since he went to school on the Continent. Probably rescued her from Castle Perilous, and kept her on ever since.

'Oh, you!' she gave back, wittily. It's all she's ever said to me. It comes out, O keeyoo.

'Announce Lovejoy, Katta, if you will.'

She rolled ahead like a billowing cloud fast-forwarded in a nature film. You have to admire a bird who grapples anorexia to a frazzle.

'This way, Lovejoy,' said Cissie, walking sternly between us, not glancing at me. I was deflected into a drawing room where Paul stood, trying his distinguished best to seem in command. It was doomed to fail within five furlongs of Cissie.

She walked sternly to the fireplace and swivelled sternly. (If any spaces happen in the next few sentences, insert sternly; it'll save endless effort on my part. Cissie is stern personified.) Blondish, exactly the right height-to-weight Quartel Index from working at her figure in pools and leotards, exactly the right height, clothes, teeth, attitude. She's the most depressing example of perfection that ever crippled a bloke. Imagine a gorgeous death ray, you're close.

'Lovejoy,' she snapped, 'you have to help Paulie.'

'Why'd you not invite me to your wedding?'

Note the absence of greetings, won't-you-sit-down. What the hell was I doing here? I make me exasperated. I mean, I'd had two whole months of being wed to her Churchillian imperatives, enough to last several reincarnations, and here I was reflexly coming back for more. I'm beyond belief. I honestly get me wild.

Paul is a posh lawyer, investor. City gent. He looks the part. I say that with all the derogatory effect I can muster. It's all Paul ever does, look the part. I think he's just a suit. Occasionally, like now, he can seem really lifelike when despair shows through, but he's still only a Madame Tussaud replicate escaped from gene control.

'In trouble, Paulie?' I kept pretty meek at this stage, because I can fly off the handle.

'You must do as Philippe Troude says,' from Cissie.

'In trouble, Paulie?' Me, still meek.

'I said you must work for Philippe,' from between Cissie's perfect teeth.

'In trouble, Paulie?' Still meek, still on that old handle.

She swung on him in fury. 'I *told* you he'd be insufferable!' she honed out. There's no other word for her speech. It's a whine, a mosquito in your earhole at night that wakes you up flailing air, or a distant forester with a band-saw in the woods of an autumn. But the word doesn't work for Cissie. She never, never ever, whines. She shrills, screams, shrieks, thunders, but never whines. Honing, that scrape you get from metal on a honing stone, is the best words can manage.

'I. T. comma P.?' I said, so affable.

'Listen to me,' she honed. I stepped back. The band-saw had moved closer, and forests give absolutely no protection from the likes of her. 'Paulie has invested a great deal – a *very* great deal! – in Monsieur Troude's enterprise. He's not going to suffer on account of a worm like you, Lovejoy!'

Like at The Hague and the UN, her arguments always plead her own case in the guise of philanthropy. I listened with a sudden glim of interest. Why me?

'Why me, Paulie?' Still a meek handle-hanger.

'*Tell him!*'

Half the trouble was, I've only to see a couple and my treacherous mind starts asking absurd questions. Like, how *do* they make love? Does he ever ravish her over the breadboard? Or in the garage unloading shopping? What do they say during grunts of passion? Have they ever wept in prayer? What charities do they support? Does he squeeze his blackheads? Hers? If so, what does he do with the end-product? Is he a mattress-wiper, or a surreptitious flirter of the rolled-up . . . ?

'Lovejoy! Pay attention!' honed in my ear. I honestly swiped at an imaginary mosquito. Paulie had been droning for ages. What with Paulie droning and her honing, they were a concerto of sound Schönberg would have envied with his mere twelve tones. Tone, hone, drone. I stood there, an imbecile amid exhortations.

'. . . investment opportunities balanced against shortfall fiscal inputs retrograded leverage-wise . . .' he was saying. (I'm making this up; I haven't a clue what actual words he was using. Like I said, an investment lawyer. You get the idea.)

'. . . cullage from antiques reinvested across the board,' he said. And stopped.

'And?' I prompted. He'd got to the only word I could understand, antiques.

'And what?' he asked. He even managed to drone that.

'What do you want me to do?' This is so typical, rich people greedy to be richer. If you want to become rich, don't invest everything, and don't spend virtually nothing. Simply buy a good, rareish antique. That'll do the job. You want to know how? Right, a tip: Knocking around this old kingdom of ours are some thirty white-enamel-face long-case (so-called 'grandfather') clocks, with the most unusual dusty pinkish floral decoration on the dial. Birds, vines, leaves, the odd tendril, all painted so very slenderly. Simply go and buy one, average market price. What a rotten tip! you exclaim angrily, because the average long-caser is a whole month's wages – expensive, no? Answer, no. Because that delicate manganese decoration signifies a value ten times that of the average grampa clock. See? Instead, prats like this Paul–Cissie molecule want to be moguls overnight. Hence the contumely.

He looked pleadingly at Cissie. She glared. 'Lovejoy knows all the time, Paulie. He's just being aggravating.' She made me sound like a tooth abscess.

'Words of one syllable, please.'

'Help Philippe to identify certain genuine antiques overseas, Lovejoy. So he can reimport them here, for auction on the international market. Otherwise the profit vanishes.'

She paused, to my relief. I felt like I'd got clogged ears from swimming underwater. You know how your hearing goes thick after being in the plunge for an hour?

'The percentage return is –'

'*Paulie!*' from honer to droner. He fell silent. Very, very wise of him. Disobedience was not tolerated in her ranks.

'Why aren't the antiques being auctioned off on the Continent?' I should have asked Troude that.

'*Lovejoy!*'

Exasperation's not much of a response, is it, but it's sometimes all you can get from marriage. Escapers know that.

'Can't be done for the price,' I said blithely, but still with a dollop of that good old meekness.

'What kind of financial package are you –' droned Paulie.

'Shut *up!*' from not-tell-you-again Cissie. 'He means he doesn't want to, Paulie.' She rounded on me. 'You know Paulie's invested our life savings in the scheme, Lovejoy.'

Everything polarized. What some folk'd do without the first

person singular, God alone knows. Cissie's policy is, third person = abuse; first = the cause of righteousness. I thought, blimey. Then got intrigued, because I couldn't remember ever having thought that Cockney expletive before. Blimey, from the old English curse, blind me if I lie. Why blimey now? I'm no Cockney. Some trigger had set me off.

'Shake him, Paulie!' she was honing.

'Do if you dare, Paulie,' I said evenly. 'I didn't come up the Stour on a bicycle.'

He lowered his hands. I felt sorry for him. He should have got out while he was still alive.

'You have to, Lovejoy,' he said. 'Please.'

How desperate it had all suddenly become. I was intrigued. I mean, for Cissie even to summon me to her presence was a step of grimsome magnitude. What an interesting scheme Troude's was. Maybe the way to obtain more facts was to play hard to get?

'No, ta.' A little unmeekness had crept in after all, which only goes to show you can't depend on practically everything. 'See you. May you live for ever.'

It's the Chinese backhanded compliment. I chatted all the way to the front door with Katta. She did her soaring yell of a laugh and said, 'O keeyooo!' I liked her. She's the only one talks right in that house.

The Ruby for once sparked at the first crank, and was off the starting grid like a racer. It was glad to be out of it.

CHAPTER NINE

The lamp hours were ended when the Ruby shuddered to a stop. Almira's Jaguar had gone. Even so, I entered the cottage like a night-stealing Arab, in case. She'd vanished all right. Hadn't left any grub, thoughtless cow. Sulking, I bet.

I went to bed. The divan was cold, but I didn't mind. No tubes, no plastic bubble. Over and out.

The tube machine was coughing, regular as a metronome. I came to in a sweat, realized it was only Donk's motorbike in – repeat, actually inside – my porch. Motorbikers live on the damned things. Makes you wonder how they go to the loo.

'Lovejoy?' Donk yelled at me, peering round the door. 'Get your skates on, you idle sod. It's eleven o'clock. Sun burning your eyes out.'

The old squaddies' shout made me feel queasy, remembering what had nearly happened to Jan Fotheringay, chucked into his burning caravan by anonymous arsonists.

'Urgent message, Lovejoy. Pay up. And you still owe me.'

I lay and thought while Donk's wretched machine spluttered and fumes enveloped the world. Diana, Troude, or even Big John Sheehan? Or a normal thing like an antique, *Deo volente*? What choice does a bloke like me have?

'Right, Donk.' I roused and paid up.

'Ta. Message is, get to Mentle Marina. Noon. Jodie Danglass'll be there.' He backed his bike, stuffed the notes down his jacket front. 'You're a jammy sod with the birds, Lovejoy. I saw that MP's missus leaving.'

Diana? Probably still paranoid about Troude hiring me. I was halfway back to bed when I paused.

'Hang on, Donk. When?'

'Three hours since. I come up earlier.' He paused as an idea struck. 'Ought to charge double, two journeys.'

'Donk,' I yelled to stop him. 'What d'you think of her motor?' Donk's engine mad.

'Give anything for a maroon Jag, Lovejoy. Who wouldn't?'

And silence.

Five long minutes I stood there naked as a grape, staring unseeing at the garden where the robin flirted for its morning cheese and the bluetits mucked about and the hedgehog trundled.

My mind kept going: Donk saw Almira – she of the posh motor

– leave my cottage. He'd called her, what, that MP's missus. I'd
thought her husband an investment banker. She'd explained his
absences by fluctuating share prices and such. What had Tinker said,
in his confusing report that day? Now, I reckoned Diana's bloke was
an MP. Hadn't Diana said as much, Jervis somebody? Was *he* that
pompous Jervis, love in Diana's lap? It flickered in my memory.
Donk is only a messenger, admitted. Motorbikes think only of haring
down the bypass at ninety so they can go even faster coming back.
But they see an awful lot of people in a day, and know more than
most. Was Almira Jervis's tart on the side? If so, why did she haunt
my restful hours? *Or was she Mrs Jervis?*

Having deducted only bafflement, I drove to Mentle Marina in
time to meet Jodie Danglass at noon. I was worn out.

She came to meet me, handbag swinging and hair blowing in
the onshore breeze. I warmed to her, though I still hadn't quite
worked out why suddenly she was so prominent on my horizon, so
to speak. Children were watching a Punch and Judy. Those weird
nasal voices and everybody getting hanged or beaten put the fear of
God up me, so I refused to advance towards her and waited where
I could see the donkeys trotting across the sands.

'Have I got the wrong accessories, Lovejoy?'

'You look exquisite. This where Baff bought it, Jode?'

She looked about, didn't point. 'No. That caravan site on the
north shore. They have a funfair, disco dancing, open-air pub,
amusement centre for the yokels.'

We could see it, three furlongs on. First time I'd been at Mentle
for a couple of years, when I'd bought a fruitwood lowboy – as the
American dealers always call these 1720-ish small tables. I love
applewood furniture, and paid a fortune in IOUs for it to a seaside
landlady. (Don't be daunted by the rather lopsided appearance of
the little drawers, incidentally. It's bound to happen to gentle woods
like apple after about 150 years. In fact it's a good honest clue to
authenticity, in a trade which badly needs such.)

'The south shore being where we're heading?'

'Yes. Two distinct halves, Mentle these days. BT.' We started
walking. 'Before Troude.'

The sands gave out midway along the sea promenade. There a
few geological pimples, which pass for cliffs in flat East Anglia, rose
with obvious effort to form a headland. A walker's path climbed its
contours through flower arrangements and decorative bushes so you
could stroll with your ladylove while avoiding the ice-cream sellers
and balloon touts.

'He own this Mentle Marina too?'

'The lot. North-shore funfair, caravan site, pubs. He's the big shilling, Lovejoy.'

With Almira Galloway and Sandy among his backers. But backers for what? The thing that worried me most, though, was the knowledge that Baff wouldn't have got his part-time job unless the boss said so. Not only that – around here you obeyed this Troude prude. For some, or any, reason. Even if it meant taking a duff job that ended in a planned blagging by yobbos. How had Baff, your average minnow, mortally offended a marina mogul to earn that doom?

We walked the prom, short-cutting the headland, coming on the marina itself with unexpected suddenness.

The place had been all fields, until excavators dug out a series of shallow bays and opened seacocks to let the tides in. Then it became a mesh of inlets, jetties on a mathematical grid design. Seagulls love it. Posh folk sail yachts down the coast to throw parties for other nauticals who throw parties back. There's a lock gate, but only to charge boats entering and leaving. These seaside places are catchpenny.

'See the building? Only finished three weeks ago.'

A feast of modern architecture, the squat ugliness was breathtaking. Wrap-around windows gave a monster view of artificial bays. Its artificial lighthouse blinked red and green port and starboard lanterns from artificial masts. Artificial sails stuck up from the deck-hatch roof, across which artificial spray whisked every few seconds. Artificial rigging displayed signal flags depicting some non-message. Only the seagulls weren't artificial, and I wasn't sure about some of those.

'I love it,' I told Jodie. She looked at me with ? in her eyes. 'Only practising.'

We were expected. Jodie was given a polite thank you by Troude in a blazer-and-Henley rig. Neckerchief with gold anchors, and a flying pennant blazer badge. The lounge was extravagant with ships' wheels and marlinspikes and capstans and two of the most grotesque figureheads you could ever imagine. No place to get drunk. You'd wonder what you were looking at.

'See you, Jode,' I said, smiling to show I wasn't daunted by the lady sitting with Troude. He even had a captain's cap nonchalantly on the couch beside him.

'Thank you for coming so promptly, Lovejoy.' He smiled differently in daylight, but still the ruler of all he surveyed. Or, in present company, possibly not?

'How do you do, missus?' I said politely. 'Lovejoy.'

She gazed with utter indifference. Not at me, note, but vaguely in my direction. But there were a few boats gliding the briny behind me, so I couldn't be certain.

'This him?' she asked Troude. She didn't care one way or the other if I was me or not. I could tell.

'If it's me you want, missus.'

She looked at me, not quite hailstones but getting that way. 'I won't tolerate idiocy, Philippe,' she said.

'He's nervous, Monique.' He introduced her. 'M'selle Delebarre, Lovejoy.' I sat at Troude's gesture of invitation, thinking, she's the boss and he's only her nerk, captain's cap or no captain's cap.

Surprisingly, I didn't think I was. Nervous, I mean. In the lounge, staff were preparing for an influx, but keeping quiet and respectful. No customers, which was odd. I've never known a sailors' bar that wasn't heaving with maids and matelots.

'I won't wait all day,' Monique said. A cryptic lady, of very little patience.

Blankly I smiled at Troude. He looked at me. She drummed her fingers prettily. I yawned a bit, started watching the boats. One was fluttering its sails, having difficulty braking or something coming into its moorings. Monique was slim, but she'd had to work at it. A calorie job, no mistake. Her figure gave her away, in spite of the minions who'd slogged to make her appear less voluptuous than she was. She belonged among those fashionables who think a woman's got to look cachectic to be attractive. She'd not quite made it. Her hair was dark, lank but with sheen. Her face hadn't enough make-up on for me, but then I'm a magpie, want them to wear tons of it. They rarely do.

'Make him, Philippe.' She'd lost patience.

'Pick it out, Lovejoy,' Philippe Troude said.

They meant the miniature model lifeboats on the glass-fronted mahogany cabinet against the wall by the door. Two of them, each made by a man who hated the other in the frightening days before there were any such things as modern lifeboats. Historical models are all the rage these days.

'What silly sod spoiled the oars?' I asked. Troude gave a swift give-away glance of triumph at the woman, almost wagging for praise. He was crazy about her, and she didn't give a damn.

'The oars are exactly level,' La Monique said, coming to.

'They shouldn't be. Willie Wouldhave made that model. He cut them different lengths in 1789.'

It was a scandal that led to the most terrible row, back when those events could ruin a man for ever. As always, the wrong man got fame and fortune. The honest man starved to death.

That year, a fearsome gale ripped across the River Tyne driving the brig *Adventure* onto Herd Sands. Ashore, Tynesiders watched appalled as the crew drowned. A prominent local tycoon called Nicholas Fairles offered a money prize to anyone who could create a rescue boat able to withstand the ferocious local seas.

Enter the goodie, one William Wouldhave, honest genius of that parish. He was a dour, morose, barbary bloke who didn't make friends and influence people. In a dazzling fit of intuition, he abandoned design, and opted for buoyancy. Against all contemporary notions, he built a strange-looking boat with a cork layer actually sheathing the boat's sides. Greenland style, in shape. The ten oars were strangely of different lengths, but did the job. It seemed ingenious, clever, even brilliant. Willie cooled his famous temper, and basked in the glow of being, for once in his heated life, odds-on favourite in the great rescue-boat competition.

Enter the baddie, one Henry Greathead, who made a duff, mundane boat – sail, mast, no special buoyancy to speak of. A really average plain boat without much to commend it. Very long odds, Henry Greathead's nowt-new rescue boat.

Except his best friend was none other than Nicolas Fairles, head of the South Shields committee. Who naturally awarded Henry the award, prize money, the accolade that would guarantee him fame, fortune and honour.

And poor hot-tempered honest Willie Wouldhave? The committee invited him in, and gave him a guinea as consolation, 'second prize' they called it. Angrily he flung the guinea back in their faces and stormed out, to die in the poverty that bitterness always seems to bring.

And the rescue-boat committee? *They let Henry Greathead pinch Willie's superb design.* He received a fortune from Parliament. The first modern 'lifeboat' was made, and did its first famous rescue the following year. And Henry Greathead was given medals, prominence, did lauded lecture tours, got gold medals from Royal Societies . . . I won't go on, if you don't mind. It makes my blood boil. Lifeboat men still call the brilliant design 'Willie's Corkie'. The inevitable monument is to both men, the extolled gainer and the sore but honest loser.

'I don't know,' Troude was apologizing to the gorgeous lady.

'The other one, then.' She spoke dismissively. No tea and crumpet for poor old Philippe tonight.

'It's dud, lady.' I was narked. I wanted to go and see where Baff got topped, not play her silly game. 'Move your pins.'

'Pins?' For the first time she lost composure. Her accent intensified slightly.

'Legs. The chair you're on's supposed to be provincial Continental, with a French mortice-and-tenon joint. The pin's like a dowel, to hold the joint. The French', I added to nark her, 'say *goujon*. Sorry I can't say it proper. It stands proud from the wood, in time. Fakers construct it the same, but have to dye the protruding end to get the shade right. It's darker.'

She moved as if to inspect the chair beneath her, pinked slightly and didn't. 'We paid . . .'

'Aye, well you've been done.' I rose, said thanks and started to go. She'd thought I'd been lusting after her legs all the interview. I had, of course, but only after I'd seen the too-revealing darkened shiny *goujon* head on the joined chair she adorned.

'Wait, Lovejoy, if you please.' Troude came hurrying after, now more of a go-between. He'd been a god at the Nouvello. 'Please inspect the Sheraton table –'

'Fake, Mr Troude.' I'd given the small table a glance on the way in. No gongs sounded in my chest. It was a fake no older than last Easter. But the surface worried me. Beautiful, made with endless unrelenting slog. I didn't know any faker still did wood finishes that perfect, not since old Trinkaloo died last Candlemas. But still a fake, if an excellent one. How odd to see one this excellent at Sir Edward's Event, and now another so soon. Dunno why, but I felt sickened. Something I'd eaten? 'Inspect? No, I won't,' I told him, still going. I could see a couple of boats dipping into the wind as they tacked to make the harbour. 'You've mucked me about once too often. I'm sick of you planting stuff in the Arcade, switching stuff with Frederico in case he was more of a crook than you suspected. It was pathetic. I resign.'

'That is impossible, Lovejoy.' He tried to get ominous. 'You are an integral part of the grand design.'

Even I had to grin at that. Grand design? Was he about to march on Moscow, for God's sake? I sighed, and pushed through the doors shaking my head. The most depressing thing about people these days is that they all talk as if they're deciding on global nukes when instead they're merely wondering if they should go down the pub or watch the match instead.

Jodie Danglass fell in with me as I reached the north shore after twenty minutes' fast walking. I was at the ice-creamio.

'Can I have a lick, Lovejoy?' She wasn't smiling, but women laughing at you never are. I know.

'No,' I told her, narked. 'Get your own.'

She bought one, raising her lovely eyebrows as the ice-cream man laughed out loud. She put her arm through mine. We went to watch the sea, leaning on the railings. I like seaside, as long as it's like this, with boats and plenty of folk on the sands and all the dross of the fair. The trouble is there's too much of our coastline left undeveloped: secretive, dark, silent, tree-lined, remote, where hardly anybody goes and nothing happens except uncontrollables like Nature's cannibal act.

'How come you're their dogsbody, Jodie?'

'Happened by, Lovejoy.' She spoke too casually.

'Pay good, is it?' A little lad on a donkey was frightened. His dad pelted up, did a rescue. The little lad fell about with hilarity. It had been an act. The dad scolded, started laughing. The mum was furious. Even the donkeyman laughed, shaking his head. Lots of acting today at Mentle Sands.

'Not bad.'

I watched her tongue on the cornet. The white ice-cream seemed to like going in, sweep by sweep. I found my throat had gone dry. She was amused.

'When do we move on, Lovejoy? As soon as you are sure I'm getting less money than you? Or when you've decided you might stand a chance with Monique Delebarre?'

Move to where? She hadn't guessed yet that I'd resigned from Troude's brood. She detested Monique. I went along with her misunderstanding. Maybe she couldn't believe that somebody would actually refuse Troude and the lovely Monique. 'Dunno. I expect we'll know soon enough. That the stall?'

'As Baff was on? No. The police took it away as evidence. It was hard luck. Poor Baff. He just drew the wrong lot. Accidents happen, Lovejoy.'

Yes, well. Except a yobbo mob picking on a seaside vendor can sometimes be directed. Then it's no accident.

'Ta for the company, Jodie. And the intro. I appreciate it.'

'No time for solace, Lovejoy?'

She'd finished her ice-cream. I watched her lovely mouth assimilate the tip of the cornet, and listened to the faint crunch as it achieved total bliss on entry. My ice-cream was running in a hot melt down my wrist. I had to chuck it in a waste-bin. Seagulls swooped, shrieking deprivation.

'If you like. La Delebarre's antique chair was a fake, Jodie. And somebody'd "improved" the oars on Willie Wouldhave's model. Thought that was still in South Shields. How did they get it? Must have money to throw away.'

We walked to the Ruby, me dawdling to see her legs.

'They wanted some you couldn't have seen, of course, Lovejoy. Taking no chances. One thing.'

'Mmmh? Get in.' I got the crank handle.

'Since we left the marina all of a sudden I'm Jodie. Until then you drove me mad calling me Jode. Why?'

She didn't like it. I could have kicked myself. I give me away to women all the bloody time. I'm pathetic.

'Shut your teeth.' I swung the handle. The Ruby groaned awake, started a reluctant muttering, rocking side to side. 'You women are obsessed with your own image.'

Lovely teeth, beautiful shape, and a complicitor in Baff's murder. I watched her laugh at me. I had to explore further, with whatever means I had.

'That's more like the Lovejoy we all know and love.' She actually said that.

One of Galileo's girlfriends was a corker. A real stunner, Artemisia Gentileschi was. The reason we know so much about her is that she strolled about her dad Orazio's studio naked, driving his apprentices crazy with lust. One apprentice, Tassi, couldn't stand it. He raped the gorgeous Artemisia, and history – with the vicious impartiality history sometimes achieves – recorded the horrendous consequences.

Poor Artemisia's dad Orazio (pal of Caravaggio, his only other claim to fame) sued Tassi. The court scene was enough to scar you for life. It certainly scarred Orazio's lovely daughter. The law saw to that. In a variation of today's courtroom tortures, the Roman court insisted on thumbscrewing poor Artemisia – presumably on the logic that truth needs forcible encouragement from females. A doctor's examination of her pudenda was conducted in front of the goggling courtroom rabble. The apprentice was found guilty. Artemisia was justified, her honour restored.

Not enough. She went ape. Can you blame her?

An artist's daughter to her very soul, she revenged herself with exquisite talent. Before, her paintings depicted nudes and more or less holy scenes, all grottoes and haloes. Now, they showed stark vengeance in the bluntest and most aggressive way possible. Her *Jael and Sisara* – that event which the Bible tries to persuade us was

God-approved, where a bird drives a nail through the skull of her
kipping cousin – isn't quite as gruesome as her *Judith Decapitating
Holofernes*, but neither's a laugh a minute. The rest of her post-court-
room period's the same. Message: some nerk ruined Artemisia's
self-image, so look out, world. The two dozen or so of her paintings
on show in Florence were the only exhibition I've ever seen where
the crowds stayed totally silent as they shuffled from one macabre
painting to the next. Superb artistry, yes. One thing got to me. It
was the serenity on the face of the decapitating, hacking, sawing,
nail-toting, hammering, skull-piercing birds. And all of them were
Artemisia. Revenge is sweeter for outlasting the revengee, eh?

See what I mean? Muck about with a bird's self-esteem at your
peril, or wear a parachute. As I drove from Mentle Marina I realized
I'd been careless. My galling diminutive for Jodie had vanished as
soon as I'd realized she was one of Troude's people, hook, line and
sinker. Quick as women always are, she'd spotted something in my
manner. Lucky she'd guessed wrong about my staying hired, or she'd
have guessed I'd rumbled her.

Nothing for it but to accept Jodie's company. We drove to my
cottage. I thought of ice-creamio stalls, and composed firm decisions
about not going to France. I didn't want to go. But why were so
many people determined I should? Jodie made such life-or-death
problems vanish into ecstasy.

CHAPTER TEN

There *is* no battle of the sexes. No such thing.

Never mind that everybody talks about it, says it rages all the time. It doesn't exist. Reason? Everybody's on sex's side. And it wins hands down.

Of course, we pretend like mad that there is. What utter hypocrisy. What a hoot. Women, like sex, won any conflict long before the starting whistle blew. They knew so. And why? Because they're the only supply.

Mind you, sometimes sex can resemble all-out ground war. It did that afternoon with me and Jodie. I actually found myself staring at the bruises on her, in horror that I must have done those. She laughed, called me stupid, asked if I offered the same service to all birds or was it just her, light chit-chat the way they do when they've proved you're an animal in infant's clothing. Nothing we can do about that, either. I wondered why a woman like her would put up with an oaf like me.

'You know something, Lovejoy?' She was almost purring, while I cursed and tried to find the kettle and swore blind somebody'd nicked my tea bags. 'I could go for you.'

'Like we've been holding a novena?'

'Who's the latest bitch?' She tutted when I glared round at her. 'I don't mean your popsies. Or that whore you drove for Gazza the other night. I mean *the* latest.'

'What've you done with my sodding milk?'

It was curdled in its bottle. Astonishing. The weather must have been thundery. Or was it simply old? I could remember buying it . . . whoops, a *week* ago? God, time flies. I looked hopefully at her, lying in that recumbent dreamy posture that brings back the ache.

'Fancy nipping up to the bungalow shop for some milk, er, love?' I'd tried for Jode a few times during, but passion had interfered with reason and Jode hadn't quite made it. I vaguely wondered if Jodie had.

Well, that really set her laughing, shaking so her breasts came to be the only thing in the world. She was still laughing when I chucked in all thoughts of brewing up and waves on the seashore went dot dot dot. It was only afterwards, on the way to see Gobbie, who'd know about Leon the French divvy if anybody would, that I

72

started wondering if she was so badly hooked on Troude that she would willingly go with a scruff like me on his orders. To keep me on the chain?

I've no illusions about love. I believe, honestly do believe, that women do what they can get away with. I mean, take any staid reliable lady. Supposing she meets Handsome Jack; he says, Come, dwoorlink to some resort – safe from prying eyes, cast-iron excuses for her family and loved ones. He's rich, romantically unattached, excellent company, amusing. What does she do? Spurn this upstart with a Victorian avast-ye-Satan? No. I honestly think ninety-nine point nine recurring per cent of respectable matrons would say yes, and go for that hidden lust, only they'd call it secret romance.

I'm not being cynical. I'm being sad, realistic. Nothing against it. It's just that we're somehow compelled to act as if we all believe that morality wins hands down. It doesn't. We know so.

Gobbie, know-all and undeceived. That is to say, he's old as the hills and seen it all. He even knows – knew – Leon.

I found him at a boot sale. For those unacquainted with East Anglia's pastoral pastimes, this isn't selling footwear. You fill your car boot (trunk in Americese) with any old dross, take it to the appointed place – playing-field between matches, schoolyard, village green – and pay to park your gunge-stuffed vehicle among other GSVs. Then you sell your rubbish to anyone who'll take it, and buy everybody else's rubbish to take home in your poor groaning old motor. It's recycling at its best. If it wasn't for boot sales, the world'd be nipple-deep in tat. Gobbie was there, staring morosely at the teeming field.

'Wotch, Gobbie.'

'Hello, Lovejoy.'

This sale was in aid of scouts and guides and brownies. Novelty yodellers did their stuff on a mock-up bandstand. Tambourine singers competed. A youthful morris team wore itself out ruining the village cricket pitch. Brownies served tea and crumpets heavy as lead. Fathers shifted crud from one car to another. A gaggle of antique dealers scavenged and prowled. I recognized a few, Liz Sandwell, Merry Halliday, Rhea who gives sexual favours for genuine Georgian furniture, Capability Forster who designs your garden then sends his lads to nick valuable antiques from your home. Harry Bateman too, I saw with surprise. His wife Jenny's hooked on some non-starter, but doesn't care. Big Frank from Suffolk, silver-mad and on his umpteenth wife.

'Gaiety gone mad, eh, Gobbie?'

Gobbie's so named from his long-range spitting prowess. A true cockney old-time dealer, Gobbie. And a veteran of the Continental night runs for the antique trade. Retired.

'Riot, son, innit?' he said drily. 'Got a prile of ointment pots, though.' He tapped his bulging coat pocket. He only deals in secret now he lives with his daughter. She thinks antiques degrading.

'Goo' lad you, Gobbie.' I eyed him speculatively. 'Any Singleton's?'

Singleton's Eye Ointment has been on sale within living memory. It was originally Dr Johnson's (not *that* one) of 1596. Singleton took over three centuries back, selling the stuff in parchment. These pots had a few name changes over the years, but after about 1858 became Singleton again. Look for early unglazed examples, the rarest. You still find ointment pots pretty cheaply – a day's wage on average. Boot sales rarely charge more than a few pence for anything, so Gobbie'd done well.

'Here!' Some bloke rushed up, pointing, furious. 'You in charge? Those little bastards are dancing on the cricket pitch, for Christ's sake!'

I knew there'd be trouble. A leaf blowing across the hallowed turf can cause heart failure in village cricketers. I saw a dog shot once for wandering on our village's.

'Leave it with me, sir,' Gobbie intoned, to my astonishment. 'I'll move them directly.'

'I should flaming well think so!' The bloke tore off to be furious elsewhere.

Gobbie resumed as if nothing had happened. 'No Singleton's, but still not bad.' We watched the parades, the turmoil of milling folk. Then, 'You in with that Frog, son?'

'Resigned, unpaid. Glad to be out of it.' I was relieved he'd spoken first. An astute old bird is Gobbie. He'd probably guessed why I'd come the instant he saw me wander in.

'Best is not to be noticed at all.' Gobbie looked about the field. 'Know what, Lovejoy? The old antique game's coming apart. Looks safe, ordinary. Feels corrupt, horrible.'

'Shouldn't you be doing something about them dancers?' I was worried the kiddies'd catch it from that cricket goon.

'Eh? Nowt to do with me, son.'

Blokes like Gobbie make me smile. I can't help it. He'd sounded like our bishop, telling the cricketer he'd handle it. Now there was a disturbance out there, three adults arguing, the furious gent pointing angrily towards us, the morris dancers faltering, hand-kerchiefs fluttering slowly to a stop.

'Leon was something to do with Troude. Right, Gobbie?' There are so few divvies around, each of us had heard countless stories of the others. It's pub gossip in the trade. Troude the high-flyer wouldn't know that.

'Leon snuffed it.' Gobbie's old eyes took me in. 'You sub?'

'Aye, substitute. Silver imports, Troude said.'

Gobbie snorted. Folk came hurrying our way, all furious. I was sick of their bloody cricket pitch.

'Much he'd know, silver or owt else.'

'Is he not an antiques roller?' I was astonished. Why did Troude need me, then? 'Or a dealer?'

Gobbie's laugh of derision set him coughing, a gentle ack-ack-ack. 'Him? There's no such thing, Lovejoy. Not no more.' His bleary stare raked the approaching mob, but he spoke only of the antique dealers, now arguing over some fake. 'Just look at those buggers. Nobody knows naffink no more. Twenty antique dealers, not one has a clue. All they want is a few quid. Wouldn't know an antique if one bit them in the arse. Troude neither.'

People talk truth, you listen.

'You distinctly said –' the cricketer started heatedly, while organizers and brownies surrounded us, all yammering.

'You didn't rope them a different square,' Gobbie said, pontifical in reprimand. Lies didn't alter his tone one jot. I marvelled. 'I wrote to your secretary last week telling him to rope them off a separate square. Avoid misunderstanding. Not the kiddies' fault. They were told, dance in the roped-off square.'

'I got no letter!' the cricketer cried.

'See?' the brownie mob cried righteously. 'See? *Inside* the roped-off *square!*'

Gobbie announced, 'Rope off a different square. They got permission. You didn't do your bit.'

They all left, still arguing, the cricketer scurrying for some rope. I looked curiously at Gobbie. Some blokes simply exude status. You have to admire fraud, wherever it walks with style.

'Know when antiques wus, Lovejoy?' The old visage cracked into a dozen little smiles. 'Fifty year since. I played the violin, dance bands in the Smoke. Then the talkies came, fiddlers out of work everywhere. Became an antiques runner. You should've been there. Running down Aldgate, three o'clock of a rainy morning. Hauling trestles up Cutler Street silver market – not that frigging shed they got now, the real one. The barrers in Petticoat Lane, iron wheels sounding like tumbling coal on the street stones. Old Tubby Isaacs singing on his whelk stall – real live eels – top end, where you could look at Gardner's Corner or Aldgate Pump. Nobody about in the shiny black morning 'cept real folk.'

'What happened, Gobbie?'

He came to, bemused, astonished I was still there. 'Gawd knows, son. Everybody became a great greedy herd, just feeding and fucking, never lifting their heads to look. See Maisie?'

'Mmmmh?' I knew Maisie, fair, fat, forty, fly-by-night with the reliability of a weather forecast.

'Says she's been antique dealing six year. I told her, "No you not, ducks." She got narked. You're the only one who knows what I mean, Lovejoy.' He paused. The antique dealers drifted. Their argument would linger through several nights' drink-up times at the pubs. 'Nice here in the country, though. Daughter, grandkids, her bloke good-hearted. No telling anybody what I seen.'

He has bad feet, did a practice shift of weight, wanting me to ask.

'What've you seen, Gobbie?'

His smiles coalesced. It was strangely beautiful. 'I seen a Thomas Tompion clock on a street barrer, Lovejoy. Seen a Hester Bateman inkstandish pledged for a half-a-crown Derby roll-up bet.'

He made to go, with that I'm-hurrying gait of the arthritic.

'Ain't no antique trade no more, Lovejoy. Nor no dealers.'

'Leon the last, eh?'

He halted, staring at the dancers being triumphantly roped off by the cricket-club man.

'Last but for you, Lovejoy. Watch out, son. They did for him in a loading accident. Some roadside in France. Heard from a box shipper. Me mate, 'fore the London docks went posh.'

Well, old matelots tell each other things.

'But why did they top Leon, Gobbie?'

'Dunno that, Lovejoy. Word is, he wouldn't play along.'

'With what?'

'Gawd alone knows.'

'Here, Gobbie. You really running this lot?' I couldn't help asking.

His face parted in a great grin round one tooth. 'Nar, son. Dunno what they're all on about.'

And off he shuffled. Box shipper, one who exports container loads by sea. Mate, a Cockney's drinking partner, trustworthy to the hilt. To do for, to kill seemingly by accident so there's no fallout.

'What can I do, Gobbie?' I called after him. I meant to repay the favour.

He didn't stop, laughed ack-ack-ack. 'Bring times back, Lovejoy. I'd give everything for just one last scam.'

The old soldier's laugh. You used to hear a lot of it, old sweats who'd been in the trenches. Inaudible beyond eight yards.

'Look.' The cricket secretary came, sweating heavily, pointing in an aggrieved manner. He'd seized on me, authority by association with the old magic man. 'Look. I can't have those children dancing on the bowler's approach run.'

'Sod off,' I said sourly, and left through the hedge. People get my goat. Everybody wants solutions for their problems. Who helps me with mine. Bloody nerve.

Falsehood may be the bride of truth, but in murder and antiques it's legend is her lover. Old Gobbie meant that Leon had been topped. Like Baff, though the means of killing was different. Two deaths, Troude the common factor.

Stopping off before I reached town, I went to sit in a tavern yard. They rig up pot plants, swings, a children's zoo – rabbits, a guinea-pig, hamsters, smug chickens – with trestle-tables for you to swig ale on. It encourages families to come.

Troude hadn't mentioned Leon the French divvy, not by name, so I was guessing. I knew little of the bloke, except he was famed in subterranean antique lore. He's supposed to have helped the Louvre, in its multitude of nefarious dealings among Continental antique dealers. Just as a roving football scout spots schoolboy talent in a Sunday park then clandestinely phones a First Division club, so Leon – no surname ever whispered – would spot that staggering convent altarpiece, let's say a Lorenzo Lotto painting, and for a consideration contact some Louvre stringer. The convent delightedly accepts a pittance (less than a hundred dollars) for their old daub, whereupon the Louvre then announces the discovery of a priceless old Lorenzo Lotto painting, got for a song! (Well, a song plus Leon's cut.) Imagine how sweetly ye heavenly choirs do singen over such a triumph! Lawyers join in, soon as the courtroom opens. Incidentally, if you think I'm making up this Lorenzo Lotto story, don't ever go into the antiques business.

Leon was a power, made a good living. Except suddenly I was uneasy. How much of all this was fact, and how much lies or legend? Troude, posh in his richdom, lived remote from my level. I mean, I'd never heard of him a little ago. This is the trouble: penthouse princes see us from a height, as eagles see ants. And I'll bet one thing for absolute sure – those eagles don't know one single ant, whereas we ants can identify every individual eagle down to the feathers on the tail.

The pub was quiet, hardly a soul in. Almira's motor arrived, it came like a military band. Two old soaks on the bench lusted at her stridey figure as she advanced on me to stand akimbo, glaring.

'Are you avoiding me, Lovejoy? And who's that mare in your cottage?'

Who indeed? Two children stopped admiring the little zoo to stare at this aggressive newcomer.

Better look downcast, I decided. I hung my head in sorrow. 'Still there, is she, dwooerlink? She's haunting me. I had to escape.' I shrugged, all pent-up emotion. 'It's not her fault, Almira. She's going through some crisis.'

She blazed on. 'That doesn't explain –'

'Why the hell does she come to me, though?' I paraphrased her forthcoming sentence. 'I can't solve her frigging love life.' I gestured her to sit down. She did so, reluctantly. I eyed her. Yes, time to give her a gentle reprimand. 'Your phone, love. Is your husband having it tapped? Makes some funny noises.'

'My phone?' New thoughts for old, I saw in her face. 'There were no messages, Lovejoy.'

'That proves it. Somebody wiped them both off. Is he back?'

'Who?' She looked at the two children, now standing listening beside us. 'Go away!'

They didn't move. 'Why's your mummy cross, Lovejoy?' Peggy, the taller girl, asked me gravely.

'Because I won't do as I'm told,' I said. They were shocked. So also, I saw, was Almira. She tried to smile, to show she detected no double meaning.

'Run along, children,' she said tightly. She wasn't used to brats. She'd say that, soon as they were out of earshot.

'You have to do as you're told,' the titch Justine said sadly. 'I've to wipe my own button. I can't wee on the tortoise.'

Lucky old tortoise. 'That's not fair, chuckie,' I said. Somebody called them and they went disconsolately towards the tavern's side door.

'No, Lovejoy. Jay isn't home for several more days yet.' She'd had time to think. Now, Jervis isn't all that common a name. But it definitely does start with a jay. She tried to be seductive. 'I'd like us to take a run out tonight, Lovejoy. Stay over somewhere. London, perhaps? I've a friend who says her cottage will be free for us to have a week or so on the Continent. Will you come?' Lips wet and luscious, seduction at its most powerful.

Drawing breath, I prepared to say no, resist her. She was offering unrestrained passion, but it was me who'd be walking into danger now the moment had come. 'Course, love,' I said. My mind complained she'd baulked at France a short while ago. Now it was the Continent at all costs. Why?

As I went towards my Ruby she actually came out with it. 'I'm not used to brats, Lovejoy. You have such odd patience.'

See what I mean? Sometimes you can guess what women'll say, or even do, but you're no nearer. I'd have to do an exploratory stint on Gazza Gaunt's Tryste waggons.

'Good heavens!' I patted my pockets. 'Forgot to pay! My cottage, half-five. You will come, dwoorlink?' I looked anxious.

Almira hesitated, but didn't want a row on a pub forecourt. 'Half-past five, Lovejoy. Shall I tell Claudine?' She tutted at my uncomprehending stare. 'About her cottage in France, Lovejoy.'

'The sooner the better, dwoorlink!' Like hell, I thought.

I hurried inside, paused long enough in the taproom to hear Almira's great motor start and pull out, relaxed and went to the off-licence bit, tapped on the hatch. There was hardly anybody in the bar, all unfamiliar faces.

'Wotch, Tone.'

Tony grinned through his window. 'Mummy ballocked you, Lovejoy?' So Peggy'd blabbed. He gave me a glass like an undine, his cruddy special welcome. To me most drinks are unfathomable.

'Who's making Justine wipe her own bum? And why can't she pee on the tortoise?' I'm her godfather. Much good it does either of us. I've to drink Tony Crookham's poisonous liqueurs and Justine gets oppressed.

He fell about, sobered. 'Good to see you, Lovejoy. Hear about Baff?' Tone was always quick on the uptake. It was the real reason I'd stopped by.

'Whatever was Baff thinking of, taking a part-time job? He wasn't so badly off as all that. I saw his missus.'

'Hasn't everyone?' Which gave me food for thought.

'Who especially, Tone?' I'd asked the question outright like an idiot before the penny dropped. Tony was uncomfortable, leaning back to check along the bars for ears.

'Word is Baff did the breakdowner on some foreigner's place.' I almost said it with him. 'On the outskirts of Mentle Marina.'

'How did you hear, Tone?' The one question no publican ever wants to answer, or have friends ask.

'Sherry mentioned something about it,' he said, all on edge, speaking quieter still, looking round. 'Only in passing.'

Well, well. Still, we godfathers are responsible only for the morals of our goddaughters, not of their parents. 'Course, Tone,' I said, and took my leave.

Nothing to do with me, I told myself as I cranked my Ruby and leapt in while the engine still cared. Tony's wife Georgina's a lovely Irish redhead, tall and slender with the air and breeding of the aristocrat. And she's sexually superb. I meant to say I think she looks as if she probably is.

So somebody in Troude's syndicate had had Baff murdered. A rum world.

Chugging out and on the town road, I wondered about people. Look at Tony and Georgina. Nice people, known them for years. I'd stayed in their tavern during a spell of homelessness, and we'd stayed friends. Yet Tony slopes off from Georgina, who'd make any bloke's breathing go funny, to Sherry, a bird of great sexpertise but minimal other attributes. A frosty old lady I know once told me her mother preached, 'It's for the man to try/ And the woman to deny.' Well, more marriages founder on that reef than any other. Maybe Georgina was busy denying, so Tony sailed elsewhere? You never know what goes on between a bird and her bonny, do you. I clattered the Ruby to Gazza's garage. I'd never thought of his shag waggons as a form of marital breakdown service before.

CHAPTER ELEVEN

Everything's luck. Who you end up loving, finding that priceless Old Master painting, getting away with murder. And you get no help. I mean, set up infallible rules to guide you in life, and you're still as baffled. There's a group of nations called G7 – they do things with international money. They met in England a bit since. Would you believe, a Japanese collector paid a fortune for the blinking crappy modern chairs they sat on? I understand less and less as time goes by. They could have bought some antique chairs for half the price.

It's my own fault. I'm a mine of pointless fact. Like, Queen Victoria and Prince Albert's wedding cake was 9 feet 41/2 inches tall (can't help you into centimetres if you're a decimal nut). Also, Equatorial Guinea hasn't a single cinema, tough on local film buffs. Furthermore, Engels, Marx friend-of-all-mankind's sidekick, wanted 'ethnic trash' exterminated – he included Basques, Scots Highlanders, South Slavs, anybody he called 'backward'. Aristotle was first translated into English in 1620 . . . See? Mind like a ragbag, all contents useless – except, when some bit's oddly not.

There's one old dear in our village says we all know what's coming, that we prepare for it the whole of our lives. I tell her she's a daft old coot. She says I'm unwilling to believe the obvious, which is ridiculous because my mind's always crystal clear. It's just that occasional flukes sometimes make you think, good gracious, how lucky I knew that odd scrap about Mrs Hannah Glasse's cookery book being worth well over a hundred times more than its look-alike contemporary pirated edition! Or when you've just looked up the measurements of a loo table – nothing to do with lavatories; for the Georgian game of lanterloo – only to land on one the very next day. The trouble is, sometimes you discover which bit's the important one in the most unpleasant way, or when it's too late.

Sandy was all over the front page, I saw from the evening edition. I was in Gazza Gaunt's yard, having some grotty machine coffee, when I caught sight of the headline in Mercy Mallock's paper. I asked for a look.

'Sandy's invented a new political party, Lovejoy,' she said. I read, gave it back. 'Europe Time, it's called.'

'What's up?' she wasn't smiling.

'My bloke's left me, Lovejoy.'

'Barmy sod.'

Mercy Mallock's the only woman driver Gazza employs, presumably on the grounds that blokes are macho tough and can defend his clients should the need arise. It's a laugh. I'm off like a hare at the first hint of trouble – to call on somebody like Mercy, truth to tell. She used to be some notable's bodyguard, believe it or not. Her hobbies are kendo, karate, all those martial arts that sound like food additives and consist of kicking people in white pyjamas. She is of surprising daintiness for all that, graceful and always groomed, looks a stunner dolled up. Now, she was in some sort of boiler suit.

'He was never satisfied, Lovejoy.' She was sitting on the running board of her van. 'Not that,' she added quickly at my look. 'I was area champion two years running, trained with him every night. He left me for a woman shot-putter from Stourbridge, built like a sumo. How can I compete?'

Impossible. 'He's a nerk, love. Any bloke'd give his eye-teeth.' I didn't run him down too much, because women are odd. I didn't want her rounding on me in his defence. 'Want the night off?' Mercy's passion waggon was the last in the yard, waiting to go. I was the only driver without a van.

'No, Lovejoy. I'd better keep going.' She gave a wan smile in the yard's lights, fluorescents of ghastly pallor. 'Is it this hard for a man who gets rejected?'

'Dunno yet,' I said, to give her a smile. Didn't work.

Ten months since, I hired her – nothing illicit; Mercy's honest – to eavesdrop on some antiquarians at the London Antiques Fair. It was really disappointing. They were meeting to decide what antique books they'd bid a million dollars for (surprisingly only six: Shakespeare's First Folio, 1623; the American Declaration of Independence, 1776; Audubon's *Birds of America*, 1827-38; *Don Quixote*'s First, 1605; the Gutenberg Bible, 1455 or so; the *Bay Psalm Book*, 1640). They commissioned a counterfeiter, Litho from Saxmundham, to forge the twenty-pound notes to buy the books with. Litho forges by lithography, a printing process using stone developed two centuries ago by Aloys Senefelder, a mediocre playwright wanting to facsimile his plays on the cheap. I made nothing of it, but it drew me and an excited Mercy together for the one time we ever made smiles.

Gazza came over, the big business. 'Nothing for you, Lovejoy. Mercy, here's your ticket. Pick up at the moorings by the Black Boy, code word Heaven. Forty minutes.'

'Thanks, Gazza.' She gave me an apologetic look. Her van was the newest and most luxuriously appointed of the lot.

I sulked, to get Gazza's mood right, then left dejectedly, but not as dejectedly as all that because it was all working out just as I wanted. I flagged Mercy down at the intersection to cadge a lift. It's not allowed – Gazza sacks you for less – but I'd once been especially kind to Mercy and it worked.

'Did Gazza say the Black Boy, love?'

'Yes, Fremmersham.'

'Give us a lift, love?' I climbed in quickly, not giving her a chance to refuse. 'Console each other.'

'You too?' She gave me a glance, pulled away. A cracking driver, million times better than me. I find almost all women are. London bus drivers rattle you round like peas in a drum, unless they're women. Birds drive smoother, and just as fast.

'Getting over it, Mercy,' I said, all brave. 'Her family's titled, rich, Oxford. You can imagine the reception I got.'

She squeezed my arm. 'Poor Lovejoy. That the blonde, Jocasta, who has the racing-driver brother?'

I was startled. I'd been making up my heartfelt sadness, or so I'd thought. I couldn't even remember a Jocasta. 'Don't, love,' I said, almost in tears. 'It hurts too much. Let's talk about something different. I might go on a Continental holiday soon. Play my cards right.'

'Where?' She glided through the gears. I wish I could do that. 'I love the Continent, Lovejoy. Beautiful weather, lovely scenery. They take an interest in their food, real life, art.'

Honest surprise lit my countenance, I hoped. 'Didn't know you felt like that, love. France, I think.'

'Lucky you, Lovejoy.' She sighed, patiently allowed a cyclist to pedal over the level crossing before the barrier descended. Most drivers I know would have shot the amber and terrified the cyclist out of his pants. 'I lived there so long.'

'You did?' More raised eyebrows. I should have gone on the stage. 'Oh, aye. Weren't you a courier or something . . .?'

'Bodyguard, actually. Didn't you know, Lovejoy?' She smiled, gave a rather shy titter. 'I know I don't look like one. That was the trouble with Gay.' The cloud settled again. Gay's her karate feller, but nobody jokes about *his* name.

'Fancy!' I said, yanking the subject back where I wanted. 'I've never met a bodyguard before. What did you actually do?'

'They hired me after I became pentathlon champion.'

'Didn't it feel . . . odd?'

'Because I'm a woman, Lovejoy?' she demanded, stung.

'Eh? No. I hardly noticed that. I mean, being responsible for some politicians you'd never heard of.'

'Bankers, actually.' We reached the town bypass and pulled out coastwards. Fremmersham's on an estuary some five miles out. I looked at her face in the dashboard glow. Pretty, composed. Barmy old Gay, that's all. Swapping shapely Mercy, for a weightlifter. There's nowt as daft as folk. 'I spent my life at airports, shepherding stout men with briefcases.'

'Can't imagine you doing that, Mercy.'

'They asked me to stay on. Mostly they're Dutch girls, on account of their languages and because they look the part. I was lucky, on account of Dad.'

'Got you the job, eh? Influence counts in banking.'

She glared at me, touchy. 'I got the job entirely on my own merits, Lovejoy! My languages. Just because my hobby's sport doesn't mean I have to be thick.'

'Right, right.' I lapse into a modern vernacular when I want to placate folk, trying to sound like I'm just from a disco and full of fast junk food. The rest of the journey was uneventful, because I made it so. We chatted about her loss of confidence now her Gay had given her the sailor's elbow, her hopes, her sports, her having to give up the flat. Routine incidentals, you might say, that make up life's plenteous pageant.

At the pick-up, I stayed well out of sight, just watched her lights dwindle from the taproom bar, then merrily tried to get a lift back to civilization, away from the lonely estuary and its one tavern and boats swinging in the night breeze. Mercy Mallock was in my mind. I felt more cheery than I'd done since hearing about Baff getting topped.

Lucky enough to get a lift from Spange, a dealer without portfolio – meaning not an idea in his head – I made it to my Ruby and thence the White Hart, and organized a whip-round for Baff's missus. A paltry sum, but plenty of IOUs made it seem more. Enough excuse to see Sherry, anyway. So I left smiling. Quite a good evening, really. I'd covered some ground. Oh, and I'd made arrangements to see Mercy again, the point of it all. If France loomed as ominously as it seemed, I wanted allies.

But just how far things had gone was brought home to me as I was leaving for home. Donk came hurtling in just as I made the outer door. He had an envelope. Reluctantly I paid him his message money out of Sherry's whip-round. Only borrowing. I'd owe.

'Urgent, Lovejoy. Meeting's in an hour.'

'Eh? It's bedtime, for God's sake.'

'You heard.' And off he thundered. I glanced guiltily about, in case any of the antique-dealer mob had seen me misuse their donations, brightened at the good omen when I saw they hadn't, and opened the envelope. In the solitary light of the forecourt I read Jodie's rounded scrawl. The meeting with Troude and one other would be tonight, quarter before midnight, outside the George.

Some hopes. I wasn't their hireling. They could take a running jump. So I lammed it down the dark country road to my cottage, brewed up, sat and read a couple of antique auction catalogues that had come, generally faffed about doing nothing, and settled down by about one o'clock.

Which was how I came to be heading for France. Not quite instantly, but in circumstances definitely beyond my control.

CHAPTER TWELVE

A book was published in 1869 entitled, *Autograph of William Shakespeare
. . . together with 4,000 ways of spelling his name.* Which may sound loony,
but represents some bloke's unstinted endeavours. You have to
respect it. Some other bloke wrote the longest poem in the language,
five ponderous volumes on Alfred the Great – as unreadable as it
sounds, as neglected as it ought to be. Pure endeavour. The Eastern
Hundreds has more than a fair share of endeavouring eccentrics –
this in a nation of eccentrics – so we're belly-deep in weirdos. It was
therefore no problem to find the world's greatest sexponent, at
one-thirty on a sleepless frosty morning. I wasn't surprised to find
Forna Lux wide awake and lusting. Everybody knows Forna Lux,
but is especially wary of her because she knows everybody back,
which isn't good news if you pretend holiness.

'Lovejoy, babbikins!' she screamed into the phone. I held it a
mile from my ear, but was still deafened. 'What've you got?'

Forna is her own invention – I mean her name. She denies ever
having received any cognomen. I don't believe her. Obscure of
background, indeterminate of accent, no known family, Forna has a
serene individuality that defies pinning down. She lives alone, on
information culled from anywhere. She says she's written seventy-
nine books under that name, all on sex and ways of doing it. I like
her. She's a slender yet blowsy middle-ager with glittering teeth,
peroxide hair, and wears more gold than a jaunting gypsy.

'I need your help, Forn,' I said into her screech. 'Sorry about
the late hour.'

'It's early, babbikins!' Her voice is that shrill noise chalk makes
on a school blackboard, if you remember that far back. Sets your
molars tingling. 'You know me, always at it!'

The laughter almost melted the receiver. I waited it out. Forna
works harder at her records – perversions, lists of clients seeking
ecstasies of a hitherto unpublished kind – than most antique dealers
do theirs. I like a professional. No, honest. Standards mustn't be
allowed to fall.

'A certain bloke, Forna.'

'Can't be done on the telephone, babbikins,' she cried. Come
round if you're desperate. Same position, same old place!'

She has a knack of making the most mundane phrase suggestive.

I sighed, got dressed, found matches for the Ruby's headlights. Twenty-past two I was chuntering into Forna's Furnace.

Lest I give the impression that all the Eastern Hundreds are mad on surreptitious goings-on, what with Gazza's outfit and all, I ought to explain that Forna runs her own publishing house. It's respectable, as such places go, with a logo, two secretaries and a small printing works near Aldeborough. She's the dynamo and prime mover, though, and runs it from her cottage in Sumring, a hamlet trying hard to be noticed for something else besides Forna. She has automatic locks on the doors, successive stages of entry under banks of hidden cameras.

'Enter my inner sanctum, babbikins,' she screamed.

Several locks later, I passed through the last of the reinforced doors. A sitting room, with one Turner seascape, watercolour, testifying to her taste among a load of Art Deco nymphets and erotica statuettes you can't keep your eyes off. Forna wore pink satins, impossible pink lace flounces, synthetic pink furs. She always wears a ton of make-up, which I admire. I chose a chair at a distance, got nowhere. She cuddled me on the sofa, poured me a drink I didn't want.

'Wants, babbikins?' she shrilled in my ear. 'Every man's got those. I want yours, that's all!'

'Ha ha, Forn,' I said gravely, hoping for fewer decibels so I could at least hear the answer. 'Any news about a bloke called Jervis, or Jay, related to Mrs Almira Galloway?'

'Cost you, Lovejoy.' A trace harder now, but still octaves above top C.

'What?'

She contemplated that for a full five minutes. When I first knew her she was quite soft-hearted and had a dog called Frobisher, but it got killed when somebody ran over it. She abandoned business for a six-month, then resumed with a heart of flint and a disguise to match.

'There's a young artist I know, Lovejoy,' she shrilled. I leaned away, hoping my auditory acuity would survive. 'Has an old bike. My cousin, actually. He needs money for art school. Is there much of an antiques market in old bikes, Lovejoy?'

This was the squeeze. Forna always wants to help her cousin's lad who's always manfully striving to better himself. Her bloody cousin must breed like a frog, the number of times I've helped him with antiques. Were there other clients, bankers helping this same unfortunate striver with fiscal problems, clerics helping him over theological humps, engineers giving useful tips about his gas turbines?

'Bike? Tell me, and I'll tell you, Forn.'

'No, dear,' she screamed. 'You run down the different sorts. I'll stop you when you get to the one he wants to sell.'

'A German baron produced the first bicycle, a walking machine with a steerable front wheel, back in 1817. Your, er, cousin can't have one of those, just on probability,' I began. Give her her due, Forna listens intently, takes it all in.

'Wood, were they?'

'Mostly, but very popular. A Dumfrieshire bloke invented workable levers to drive these walking machines about 1840,' I said, watching for a glimmer of recognition in her eyes. Nothing. 'You'll know the velocipede, Forn. Pierre Michot made about two hundred a day in the 1860s, but sold out for filthy lucre. They're not too rare, but cost.'

Her eyes sparked. 'Maybe it was one of those, babbikins?'

'The penny-farthings are the best known,' I went on, heart sinking at the price I'd have to pay, but I desperately needed to know more, and I'd scraped the barrel for information. 'James Stanley was the genius, a little Coventry chap who made fixed pedals for the front wheel.' I got carried away. 'Posh bicycle clubs became all the rage, with bright uniforms and personalized bugle calls. Labourers were barred – muscular strength was unfair, you see, to effete aristocrats in the team.'

'I think maybe it was one of those,' Forna said, eyes now brilliant with pleasure. For pleasure read financial relish.

'His brother's son, John Stanley, made the one you'd recognize today, Forna. Equal wheels, chain drive, brake and bells. These Safety Bicycles were a terrific advance, highly sought among modern collectors. The Rover design was the pattern . . .'

'That's it!' Forna cried. I heard no more until I'd watched the midnight cops-and-robbers film while she searched her records in some secret cupboard with a whirring door. I kept wondering where I'd get the price of one of John Stanley's original Rover bikes from. Of course, the bike itself wouldn't show up. I'd pay for it, then she'd promise it, promise it, promise . . . Then, by mutual agreement, the antique bicycle and her artistic protégé would turn into slush and vanish down the gutters of time. For a bird who lived on hard news, Forna's income fed on fiction.

'Here, babbikins!' She emerged and sat, pouring a new drink.

'Jay for Jervis Galloway, Lovejoy,' she shrilled. 'A Parliamentarian, not going to stand at the next election – an expected large windfall from some unspecified new business. Politician of mediocrity. Turncoat. Conservative to Social Democrat to Labour. Wealthy by his missus, a dick-struck cow who fox-hunts.'

'That it?' Almira would love her description.

'No.' Her voice sank a little. 'Heavy money into coastal development, Lovejoy. A syndicate of antique dealers funnels money through him into Mentle Marina. Philippe Troude I know.' She smiled. 'He buys more love potions than a wizard. Struck on some French woman with high connections.'

It matched, but added a little. 'He your client, Forna?'

'Did I say one bike, Lovejoy?' she cried. 'I meant one of those velocipede things as well!'

'Good heavens,' I said evenly. 'What a lucky lad your cousin is! Troude your client?'

'Has been since he opened his marina complex, Lovejoy. No harm in the man, not really. Pays on the nail, pleasant with it.'

She told me his foibles, bedtime idiosyncrasies, tame stuff really. I hardly listened. Four in the morning she was still wide awake, answering some incoming call. I left knackered, wanting to kip.

Yet back at my cottage I couldn't rest. The parcel delivered by a relenting Michelle was inside the door. I'd passed it a couple of times, reeling from the bonging but too worried to've taken up its challenge. Now, I opened it with care. Very small, an ovalish velvet box that barely covered my palm. And a note saying sell it on commission in London, not anywhere local. It was from Baff, RIP. *Anywhere else but the eastern hundreds, Lovejoy, you have the connections, I have not any more you see how about a 3/7 is that okay with you good luck no questions asked mate, never seen playin cards like these, they seem complete set as far as I can tell, regards, Baff,* he wrote with Elizabethan disregard for scriptural refinement.

The velvet case contained fifty mica (thus transparent) oval slivers. At first, I couldn't work out what the parts of faces and bits of apparel and hats and wigs were painted on them for. Then I saw on the bottom one, painted on solid heavy copper, a Cavalier-like gentleman looking at me, dated 1641. It bonged me stupid. A spy-master's set of disguises! I'd never seen a complete set before. I picked one mica slice at random, superimposed it on the oval miniature portrait, and the Cavalier had changed into a swarthy turbanned Turk. Replace it with another mica oval, the miniature became an exotic bewigged blonde lady with exquisitely huge breasts

89

tumbling from her bodice. No playing cards these. My hands trembled so badly I had to set them down.

In troubled yore, disguise mattered. A spy-master – like Mrs Aphra Benn, the heroine I keep on about – wants to send, say, a message to a secret ally. But letters could be opened, like Mary Queen of Scots', and you'd be for it. Carrier pigeons could be hawked on arrival, then all was lost. Messengers were intercepted, bribed, waylaid. A problem, no? So your spy-master has an innocent parlour game distributed to secret sympathizers. They look like partially painted mica slices sort of, with roman numerals on each transparency. The secret sympathizers – Royalist, Parliamentarian, whatever – going about their daily business would receive an innocent letter for birthday greetings, some such, bearing a date or some numeral. The sympathizer hastens to the children's nursery for a merry game of Appearances, and casually notes the matching numbered slice. He superimposes it on the miniature portrait, and finds himself now staring at . . . at a middle-aged woman pedlar! Get it? He now knows that the next secret messenger *must* be of that description. They were Flemishmade, usually, and are unbelievably rare. I'd only ever seen one complete set before, and that was on a BBC *Antiques Roadshow*, where the expert didn't know what they were for and thought them a simple entertainment. Some entertainment!

But.

This pack I'd actually heard of before. They'd been sold at a local auction a year since. I'd missed them by a whisker, arrived too late to bid. Tinker told me they'd gone to some French bloke who lived near Ladyham. For a fortune.

Had Baff pulled the breakdowner on Troude? And been exterminated for his pains? From then till six o'clock in the morning I sat and thought. And thought.

Then I cast caution to the winds, walked up the lane to the phone by the chapel and phoned Almira.

'It's me, love,' I told her. 'Let's go.'

'Oh!' she said, brightly gathering her wits. Somebody was with her. 'Very well, ah, Claudine. I'll come right over.'

Two hours later, I was shivering in the minutest aerodrome you ever did see, at Earls Colne. We flew in a thing called a Piper Saratogo, which looked like a sparrow that had swallowed a watch. I closed my eyes, and dozed through a flight, a landing, an interminable drive, and finally came to a rest where oblivion awaited between clean white sheets. It was broad daylight everywhere except in my head.

CHAPTER THIRTEEN

Opposites aren't. I always find this. Murder, when you go into it, tries to be something else, like unwonted killing, not quite murder as such. Motive's the same; it isn't anything like an explanation. The only two things that stay what they start out are love and hate. They're white-hot hundred-per-centers, complete of themselves. Idyll therefore is not idyllic. I could have told Almira that, if she wasn't a woman and therefore likely to laugh at whatever I said. It's the way they are.

So, in lovely France, in a pleasant house miles from anywhere, with two lovely ponds in the lovely garden, not another building to be seen from the lovely stone terrace, lovely herbaceous borders to gladden the eye, lovely exciting Almira for the one lovely exciting essential, and lovely food baked or whatever by unseen hands below stairs, I was utterly bored sick. If heaven's like this, I thought, screaming inside.

That fourth day in France was the real landmark. I woke up, came to. Almira was lying beside me on the bed. The house was an odd shape. The main bedroom had the disconcerting feature of being open to the rest of the house, so when you turned on your side you could see down into the hallway and part of the living room. If a door to the left was ajar you could also see the feet of an elderly lady called Madame Raybaud who cooked and gave instructions about where things had to be left. She went berserk when I moved a bag of groceries half an inch. Centimetre.

The place was silent, except for Almira's gentle breaths whoofing on my shoulder. It was early afternoon. You've to go to sleep after noon grub for about an hour. You get used to it, but it's a terrible waste of effort. I lay on my back, sweating from the heat, and gazed at the ceiling. Shadows on the plaster walls, a portrait of the Madonna, a crucifix, not much furniture, though some quite old, of local rusticity that I liked.

Almira turned over. The thick fluffy mattress clung to you for dear life whatever you did, but me and Almira had conquered that by compelling passion. She was good, vibrant, desirous, didn't simply lie there waiting for you to get active. She joined in with an eagerness I'd come to relish. Mind you, I relish inert birds too, so there's no means of telling which is best. I looked at her sleeping form, and felt a warmth that shouldn't be there. Birds get into you, and then you're helpless. I'm not afraid of commitment, no. How could a bloke like me be scared of loving one bird for life, to the exclusion? I'm decisive, sure, definite. It's my character.

The window shutters looked simple but had a folklore all their own. Simple hooks got you mad by staying hooked just as you thought, here comes daylight and a vision of the valley. I wrestled silently with the damned things, finally got them open enough to see out. Windows are for looking from, not blocking up.

Our house was a size, on the shoulder of a vale with a river coursing below. No anglers that I could see. Back home they'd be out in droves with coloured umbrellas and odd hats and flasks, murdering minnows. No other farmhouses. Small fields, I noticed, no cattle in them to speak of. Where the hell did Madame Raybaud hail from? She came on a bike. It made me smile, thinking of Forna's cousin. She'd have to wait for her fee now.

There's nothing to see in countryside, is there, so I leaned on the sill, thinking of Baff. East Anglia was as depressingly rural as this, so possibly not far away out there an assortment of strange characters lurked possibly as exotic as ours. Was there a Dicko Chave, perfect gentleman, proposing to any bird who stood still long enough? A Sherry, giving exciting welcomes to hotel guests for a consideration? Glass faker-makers like Phoebe Colonna and Steve Yelbard? Did Gallic versions of Gazza's Tryste Service trundle these dusty lanes, bearing Dianas to some costly nocturnal lust? I found myself shivering, don't know why, chucked trousers on and padded downstairs.

The terrace was a longish paved area under vines and clematis, between foliage that fell away down the hillside. No definite edge to the garden that I could see. It blended with scrub. Lazy smoke rose from the greenery. Did we have beavering gardeners as well as a cook? We were complete, a nuclear family or something. I looked at my feet. Very odd, but the strangely new slippers fit me. I'd tugged them on without thought. These trousers weren't mine. They were new. I'd brought nothing except what I'd worn when, practically walking in my sleep, I'd stepped out of Almira's motor. She'd brought none of my things, silly cow. That's the trouble with women, never . . . never . . .

Some fault in the logic halted me. I sat on the wall at the end of the terrace. Nobody'd know I was here. No phone, no nearby village. I'd walked along the lane for a couple of miles, finding only a couple of cottages set back from the verge, orchards, a field or two, woods. It was picturesque rural tranquillity at its most poisonously repellent.

Almira's motor vanished some time during the first night. I'd heard it go, but not been in a condition to look. I mentioned it to Almira but she said it was going for a service, so that was all right. I find preconceptions go wrong on me, especially about countries. That's what I meant about opposites. Maybe some old snippet from history was making me uneasy about being in France? Like, Richard the Lionheart got shot while besieging some local town here. With gentle nobility, he died lingeringly, forgiving the enemy archer – who was then literally skinned alive for daring to kill a king. See what I mean? France is gentle, noble. Or France is lies and cruelty. Preconceptions. I'm the same about women, always wrong. Men are easier.

My logic started to niggle. I've had one or two birds – well, all right, maybe more than that. Experience has got me nowhere but, all the same, women do stick to certain patterns. Like, this holiday was never on Almira's impulse. It was planned, down to the last detail. And – the vital bit – women are obsessional packers. Go away for two days with a bird, she brings the kitchen sink and eleven suitcases of superfluous tat. Not only that, I thought, watching a bee rummage in some flower, but a woman packs like a maniac. It's her nature. Agree a weekend away next Easter, she'll strew luggage all over the bed that very day with seven months still to go. And if you're slack about your own packing, they'll furiously start on it for you. I don't know why. Probably they've not got enough to do. You just have to ignore it, like Wimbledon Fortnight. I haven't got much in the way of clothes, never have. Almira'd brought in a selection of clothes the first day – or had they already been here, waiting? I'd been too knackered to observe. She'd had a thrilling time, kitting me out in new trousers, shirts, a selection of shoes. She said it was a French door-to-door service. I hadn't found my old crud. Almira had chucked it. 'You look smart, Lovejoy,' she said, delighted. Four days . . . *I was now anonymous.*

There was a path down the hillside garden. I'd been down it before. It went past one of the pools and finally an old well. That seemed to be it but for a copse further down where the path petered out. I found myself walking down it, for nothing. I was suffering badly from withdrawal symptoms – not an antique shop for a million miles. See what I meant, what's wrong with Paradise?

Wood smoke drew me among the trees. It was surprisingly near. A smouldering garden fire, a brick cottage, two oddly silent dogs chained to a stake, both looking at me with mistrust, and music trying to suggest Spain concealed beyond the doorway.

'Monsieur?'

I jumped a mile, but it was only a grave-looking, stocky man, clearly some gardener. He held a hoe, was quite pleasant. School French always lets you down, but you're sometimes forced to give it a go. I tried. His face took on a surly what's-this-gunge expression. I came to recognize it as a hallmark admix of French scorn and impatience, reserved mainly for me.

'Hello. *Je suis* Lovejoy,' I said. '*Je visite avec Madame, dans le maison.*'

We talked similar stuff for a few breaths. He invited me in, gave me some drink that produced an instant headache. He was Monsieur Marc. He was a gardener, I understood. I was not a gardener. What is it that you make like *métier*, Monsieur Lovejoy? I buy of chairs and of tables, Monsieur Marc, especially *plus vieux*. French wears you out. I could ask him if he liked apples or *poires* and how old was his Mum, but replying to counterquestions, ever my bane, was hopeless. I thanked him a million times, because thanks is easy. He saw me off after I'd told him the flowers were much more better *comme* the *fleurs dans* England, not is this not? I tottered past his dogs – weird; I thought dogs did nowt else but bark. Maybe stunned at my syntax.

His hoe hadn't been a hoe at all, I saw as I left. It was a sickle, slotted bayonet-fashion underneath a longarm. But that was all right, wasn't it? I mean, out here in this rural peace a gardener'd need a weapon, *il* practically *faut*, right? Foxes, heaven knows what. Did France still have boars, wildcats, worse? I felt protected, snug even. Good thinking, Monsieur Marc. I returned to the terrace, where Madame Raybaud was setting out tea. She had her own idea of what English afternoon tea was – heavy scones, butter and jam, Earl Grey and a kind of clotted cream in small ramekin pot things. Lovely, but so far we'd not had a single pasty. Almira came down looking a picture in a summery saffron linen and matching shoes, good enough to eat. No problems with her declensions, I noticed. She and Madame Raybaud prattled on about Monsieur and talked laughingly of groceries. Clearly old pals. I had the notion that Monsieur was not me, but how would I know?

Often I wonder if there's all that much to do in heaven except look out. Oh, Almira and I were really enjoying ourselves, I thought over mouthfuls of Madame's thick scone. How could it be otherwise? Gorgeous bird, no worries, fine weather – though I'm the rare sort who actually likes rain – pretty garden, passion on demand with a lovely compliant woman, watching her sunbathe and occasionally swimming in the larger of the two ponds. People'd pay fortunes. It was just my festering discontent. Most of it, I decided, smiling across the terrace table at Almira's lovely face, was simply withdrawal from antiques. I get symptoms worse than any addict. I just can't help it. Women tend to get narked if you own up, tell them you're dreaming of some sordid antiques auction. They think you're criticizing them for making you bored. It's because women love holidays. I don't. Holidays, like a number of other things I mentioned a bit ago, aren't. To me, they're hard work.

Sorry to go on about holidays being truly boring gaps in life, but I'd noticed a few features of Almira's behaviour. I knew this place was owned by her schoolfriend – I'd forgotten her name – and guessed that probably Almira had visited before. But a woman walking about her own garden behaves very differently from one who's merely coming through, so to speak. Even if she's shacked up with her very own lover with hubby safely slogging elsewhere, she looks totally different. She touches this bougainvillea, that oleander, with possession somehow. Women do it to men as well, so you can tell what's going on before it hits the newspapers if you keep your eyes skinned. Even if you don't want to spot unpleasant truths, sometimes you can't help but see the obvious.

This house was hers.

Certain conclusions are inescapable, once a fact hits home. The Almiras of this world can't live without a phone. No wires proved nothing nowadays, in the cellular-phone aeon, so there was communication about. Yet I'd been told otherwise. If this was Almira's secret love-nest, she'd still have electronic wizardry. If it was her husband's family nook, he'd be even more likely to have wires humming between here and political headquarters.

Once a lie creeps on to a tea table, you're done for. The scale of the deception scarcely matters. Like contamination defiles a feast, or a stain ruins a dress, it's spoilage city. Okay, Almira might want to keep me away from contacts, the way a holidaying bird excludes all those clamouring duties she's left behind. But one fib compounds another. The keys to Almira's motor had been hanging on the wall of Monsieur Marc's cottage. She'd only one set. The keyring's fancy, with one of those dotted inbuilt lights they give you at Sandor Motors. I knew its logo. I'd asked them for one when they mended my Ruby once. They'd told me to sod off. I'd not said anything. So Monsieur Marc was more than a full-time gardener. So what?

'Look, love,' I said brightly as we finished nosh. 'How about we have supper out tonight? Maybe see a nearby town?'

She smiled, fond with possession. 'As soon as the car's back, darling, we shall. I want to walk through to the river down below. Madame's just been telling me there's a lovely lake somewhere near. I'll get directions from her, shall I?'

'Lovely, dwoorlink,' I replied, most sincerely.

One more lovely and I'd go mental. But I smiled, and wondered when they'd come. Our holiday was only supposed to be ten days. If they delayed much longer there'd be hardly any time to shift their antiques. If any. I felt pretty sure I knew who we were waiting for. I wasn't quite correct, as it happened, in fact not even near.

Incidentally, don't hide from fraud. Hiding from it's the easiest thing to do, and always brings disaster. Yet we do it, every single day. The fact is, fraud is always – for always read but *always* – clearly recognizable. You sense that your husband is deceiving you with another woman? You tell yourself, heavens, no! Can't be! He's merely edgy because of things at work ... The checkout girl is doubling up your grocery prices? No! She's a pleasant lass, always smiles ... We trick ourselves. Complacency's so cheery. Facing reality is hell.

Once, I went to a night lift in Cambridgeshire. I'd been in a Cheesefoot Head pub when this maniac wandered in and surreptitiously showed a fragment of shredded silver. My chest bonged like Great Tom's clapper and I was across the taproom like a ferret. The bloke let me touch it. Honest Early Christian silver, seventh century. I almost wept.

'Look, mate,' I told him. 'You a moonspender? Give me three days. Name's Lovejoy. I'll have a syndicate together, honest to God. Money up front.'

A massive aggressive hulk shoved me aside and showed me his craggy yellow teeth. The pub went quiet.

'You're off your patch. I've heard of you, Lovejoy. This be local business, boy.' He had two enormous goons for help he didn't need. It's always like this, because field finds of Dark Age silver can bring in nearly enough to settle the National Debt. East Anglia's taverns have this illicit trade sewn up. (You're supposed to tell the Coroner, who on a good day promises you maybe perhaps some reward money, possibly, with any luck. Whereas illegal syndicates pay cash on the nail, the night your little electronic detector goes bleep. Guess who wins?)

'Okay,' I said. I didn't want to get left in a dark ditch. 'You called Poncho? You'll know I'm a divvy. Want me along?'

Which did it. Poncho hired me for a few quid and a free look at the treasure as it was dug up. We drove out in tractors – tractors, for God's sake, on an illicit night steal of pre-mediaeval buried silver. All the stealth of a romp. Cambridgeshire wallies – antique dealers working the bent side – are like this, half business acumen and half gormless oblivion.

We were dropped in some remote place. I'm clumsy at the best of times and kept falling over in the pitch. Countryfolk go quiet after dusk, except when they're cursing me for being a noisy sod. Just the five of us, including the moonspender with his detector and earphones. No moon. I wanted to go straight to the spot and get digging, but away from civilization rural people suddenly acquire a terrible patience, think nothing of standing still for an hour so's not to disturb an owl or a stray yak. I can't see the problem. They made me sit down on the ground so's not to make a din, bloody nerve. All I'd done was stay still. I was excited at what we'd dig up.

The field was standing grain. I'd asked a few times why didn't we get going. Nobody was about. Poncho growled that he'd thump me silent if I didn't shut up. After a whole hour, I drew breath to ask if there were rival moonspenders bleeping their discs at our treasure out there but Poncho's hand clamped over my mouth. His two goons were suddenly gone. They returned twenty minutes later, suddenly four instead of two. We all ducked out then, and finished up in a barn two miles away interrogating two sheepish oldish chaps. Poncho was furious, but our moonspender laughed all over his face when the goons lit their cigarette lighters as the barn door clamped to.

'It's only Chas and Dougie!' he exclaimed.

'Hello, Lol.'

They stood there crestfallen, blinking. We should have had Joseph Wright of Derby to paint the scene for posterity, intriguing faces illuminated by the stubby glims. Two more innocuous gents you never did see. Thinnish, grey of hair, meek of mien. No trouble here. I walked round them, curious. I'd never seen gear like it. They carried a short plank, a huge ball of string. The one called Dougie wore a flat cap with wire hanging from the neb, like a threadbare visor.

'You were in my field,' Poncho growled.

'No, we were just making a pattern. Honest.' They were scared. They'd realized we weren't police.

'It's all right,' the moonspender said, still grinning. 'It's what they do.'

'They'm grain-burners,' a goon mumbled. The barn chilled at

least twenty degrees. The two blokes went grey with fear and started vigorous denials. Countryfolk are vicious if they think you'd dare damage crops, haystacks, farm gates. Really barmy, when there's so much rurality to spare.

'No,' Lol scoffed, laughing. 'They're artists, loike.'

And suddenly I twigged. 'You two from Outer Space?'

They looked even more embarrassed. 'We do no harm.'

Poncho wasn't satisfied. His illegal night lift had been spoiled. He wanted blood. Lol explained that Doug and Chas were the crop circlers.

'They make rings in the grain. Bend the wheat down –'

More growls from the goons. Farm people, they hated this.

'What for?' Poncho had to know.

I joined in, to spare a couple of lives from Planet Mongo. 'It's in *Nature*,' I told him. 'There's whole books now on crop markings. There's even an institute – right, Chas?' And got eager but terrified nods. 'They're flying saucers. Some say.' I had to smile, using the old expression. Some say – *and others tell the truth.*

'It's only you two bleeders?' Poncho said, amazed.

Chas said yes. 'I like wheat fields, but Doug here likes making patterns in barley because the grain heads hang –'

'We don't spoil any crop, honest!' Doug put in, nervy at the countrymen's hatred.

'It's just a fraud,' I told Poncho. 'They're famous, but unknown. Studying the crop markings is a new science, cereology.'

Poncho took some convincing. 'You', he finally sentenced the shaking pair, 'are banned the Hundreds. You hear?'

They agreed, and were let go – but only after the night lift was accomplished: a silver platter and a chalice, sold on to a Continental dealer two years later, I heard down the vine, and miraculously 'discovered' in a Belgian attic when an old house was being demolished. Thus authenticated, the precious silvers joined the 'legitimated' mass of ancient treasures given wrong attributions in the museum collections of the world.

Fraud. When speaking straight off to the moonie in that Cambridgeshire pub, I'd forgotten one of my own laws of antiques: Fraud is everywhere, *so never ignore it.* See? One fraud compounds another, spawns off a third, a fourth, for greed feeds off the whole evolving mass of deception. Meanwhile, the brave new science of cereology goes on, as more and more mysterious crop markings show up everywhere . . .

And I durstn't hide from Almira's fraud any longer.

CHAPTER FOURTEEN

The lake was quite a size, as jumped-up ponds go. We walked along a little shore among trees that tried to get their feet wet but couldn't make it. Pretty. There are quite a lot of flowers in the woods in France. That's all I wish to say on the subject of their countryside. Rural lovers can keep it. They can have ours too, as far as I'm concerned.

'It hasn't rained for days, Lovejoy!' Almira was like a young girl, running ahead, pointing. 'The ground's lovely!'

Ground? Lovely too? Jesus. Mind you, a woman's alluring shape makes you think of possible ways to counter yawnsome nature rambles, so I smiled, but she skipped away, enticing.

'Not here, Lovejoy. Wait till the summerhouse . . .' She caught herself quickly. 'Madame Raybaud said there's one along here.'

Well, deception is as does. I cooled, looked across the lake. Nobody was about. We weren't being seen and it all seemed private, so why suddenly the reserve?

'Lovejoy!' she exclaimed, flushed. 'I said no! Wait. It's just along here . . .'

We managed to get her breast off my hand and make it round a small promontory to where a logwood cabin stood. It seemed mostly windows. A boathouse, a rough track leading into the trees. Nice – sorry, *lovely* – if you like being remote. It was locked, but – surprise! – Almira guessed exactly where the key would be on the lintel. More clues to ownership: she didn't have to look for door-handles. I felt that same sense of a woman *in situ*.

It was getting on for four o'clock when we came to and donned enough clothes to show respectability if a passing racoon or whatever happened by. She decided to brew up when I moaned neglect, and laughingly went to clatter in the kitchen. Big kitchens in France, but no ovens to speak of. Stoves by the score, though. I stood on the verandah to look over the lake.

Sunshine's not all that bad, when it's the golden ambery kind you get in late autumn. It's the straight up-down stuff of broiling summer I hate. I stand in shade wherever it lurks. So, to one side of the sheltered projection over the boathouse slipway, I watched the lake and the weather and what a load of crap countryside is. Then I heard Almira lal-lalling to a tune, and smiled as the light came on. I had an Auntie Alice once who lal-lalled to any tune on earth. She could turn Vaughan William's Sea Sympathy into lallal. I edged nearer the corner to listen, smiling. Which was how I came to see him.

It was Marc, leaning on a tree. That sickle thing hung in his belt. He carried a shotgun the way countryfolk do, broken over the crook of an arm, barrel down, stock under his elbow. Hands in pockets. Plus-fours, thick jacket, small hat with feathers around the band. Slowly I drew back. It's movement gives spies away. That and, I thought sardonically, being too sloppy when you think the opponent's a duckegg. Like Marc did me.

Quickly I made the kitchen, demonstrating affection to see what happened. She pouted, glanced at the window, shoved me aside, did that playtime mockery women engage in to promise passion when they've got a minute. Which meant she knew Marc was trailing us. Hence the absence of sex on the sunshine shore.

'Dwoorlink,' I said, all misty, when we were sipping in the bay window. 'I've an idea! Let's sleep here tonight!'

'Oh, Lovejoy.' She smiled, but close to tears. 'You're such a romantic. But it's impossible.'

'Why?' I was bright as a button. 'Can't you see? Nobody near us, to see us or hear us . . .' I halted, uneasy at the words' familiarity. I'm no wooer. Women see through me.

'Because,' she said. It was meant to sound light-hearted, but came out unutterably sad.

'Because what?' I took her hand. 'I've never said this to any other woman, love. But I honestly wish you were the very first woman I'd ever met. I want us to —'

'No, Lovejoy. Don't say it.'

She turned away, real tears flowing. I was uncomfortable, more upset than she was, because I'd almost nearly virtually honestly been about to say something unspeakably dangerous. I felt myself go white inside, if that's possible. Why had she stopped me? Usually women go crazy to hear such daftness from a bloke. Was she acting, then? Or even more chained than me?

We spent the rest of the time proving merriment to each other, that this was a holiday affair of the very best kind. We made it home at the very edge of light.

And saw a Jaguar making its throbbing approach towards our very own front door. Like I said, I almost got everything nearly right — another way of saying everything wrong.

'Good heavens!' Almira exclaimed in a way that told me she

was furious we'd not returned earlier. Probably planned how we'd be sipping aperitifs or something clearly innocent when he arrived. 'Look who's here! How ever did you manage to find us, Paul?'

With a man of vigour, you'd say uncoiled from the car. Paulie unravelled.

'Good evening, Almira.' He'd been ordered to sound portentous. 'Lovejoy.'

'Wotcher, Paulie. Alone, I see.'

'Afraid so. It's Cissie.'

'Oh, aye.' When was it ever not? I didn't say it.

'She's ill, Lovejoy. She wants you to come. I phoned home to find you, Lovejoy. And heard you were here, at your friend Claudine's chateau, Almira.'

Suspicious, but maybe true.

'What are you doing in France, Paulie?' I asked, eyes narrowing, ready to disbelieve.

'We were on our way to Marseilles, a clinic there. Cissie's been ill, took a turn for the worse on the journey. I got her seen at the local hospital. She's there now, Lovejoy.'

It might just be true. I looked at Almira, who was being all concerned. 'Oh, poor thing,' and all that. I wondered how genuine we three were all being. He honestly did look distressed. But was Cissie truly honestly ill, or had Paulie merely been ordered to do King Lear?

'Come where?' I gave back, wary. Coming on Cissie's orders was no simple matter.

'The general hospital, Lovejoy. It's about forty miles. I'll drive as soon as I've got myself together.'

Madame Raybaud hove into view, sombre of mien. Old women everywhere have this knack of sensing morbidity. They're drawn to it like motorists to an accident.

'Poor thing!' et sympathetic cetera from Almira. 'I hope it's nothing serious . . .?'

His eyes wavered. 'I . . . I'd better let them tell you there,' he said. 'She wants to see Lovejoy. For his help.'

If he was acting, it wasn't bad. If it was genuine, it was, well, a totally different game. Maybe not even a game at all.

'How come you know Almira?' I asked, still wary.

'Know each other?' She gave me her huge eyes, a half-incredulous laugh. 'This is no time for silly jealousy, Lovejoy!' She coloured slightly. 'Paul has been my investment counsellor for over six years!'

So the party line was that she knew about Cissie and, formerly, me. And about Cissie and, now, good old Paulie. Therefore Cissie knew about Almira and me, and wouldn't blab to Jay. One thing rankled, though. I'd never known Cissie pass up a chance to stab an orphan kitten, let alone make a cutting remark about my indiscretions. Cissie would have slashed me with some remark about consorting with rich married women. Apart from that little flaw, their combined story could just be true.

'Why does she want me?' I asked. She never had before.

'She wants to tell you herself, Lovejoy.' He looked at me, then away. 'We've not got all that long.'

'Oh, my *God!*' from Almira, starting indoors to find some packing to burden us with. 'Come *on*, Lovejoy! Get *ready!*'

An hour later, we hit the road in Paulie's Jag. I looked back several times, but we weren't followed, far as I could tell. I perked up. Maybe the hospital had some antique medical instruments for sale. I know a collector in the Midlands gives good prices for mint surgical stuff. I'd ask Cissie, if we were on speaking terms. I wondered if she knew the word for charades in French.

CHAPTER FIFTEEN

Maybe it's the ambience – or one of those other words that sound full of the ineffable – but foreign hospitals seem more scary. Our own always smell of overboiled cabbage, resound to the clash of instruments and lifts whirring down to green-painted underground corridors with lagged pipes chugging overhead. Hideous but knowable. Hideous and unknowable is worse.

The day slid into dusk as we drove. What little I could see of the countryside was sculptured. Quite classic, really. From a prominence in a small lane you could see the line of sea with a small ship, though I'm bad on direction. Almira sat in the back, talking Poor Cissie's Ordeal and occasionally sobbing, though women's tears are often not. I dithered between doubt and doom. I mean, I didn't even want to be here. I wanted home.

'How come you're here really, Paulie?' I asked in a straightish bit. Don't distract the driver.

'Ah,' he said. He hadn't been told what to say when cross-questioned. But it still didn't mean fraud. Like I said, he's thick.

'In France,' I said. 'If we are in France,' I added to rub it in. Then I thought, hey, hang on. What had I just said? *If we were in France and not in some other country!* But once you're out of your home, you're roaming, right? What did it matter? I wish I could remember details of the flight in with Almira.

'Well, ah, you see, Lovejoy,' Paulie was saying, lost, when Almira put her oar in.

'Didn't you mention you were coming over for Cissie's health, Paul? That clinic, Marseilles?'

'Indeed I did!' with a shade too much relief for my liking.

'What sort of clinic? What *is* wrong with her, anyway?'

'She'll tell you, Lovejoy,' Almira reprimanded. 'It's lucky we were so near! Don't pry.'

The motor-car numberplates had that cramped French look. Or Belgian? Dutch? German? Why was I worrying where exactly we were? Nothing I could do about it. I couldn't read the road signs. We hit no motorways. We must have been somewhere pretty rural because I didn't see a major road. The villages we passed were memorable for postcard-style fetchingness and unmemorable names.

'Anyway, nothing wrong with a holiday,' Almira added.

No money, clothes only what I stood up in. I could hardly make a run for it.

'Very little,' I said, to show how good I felt except for my deep nagging concern over poor old Cissie.

As we drove into this small town, I glanced at Paul, under cover of turning round to say inconsequentials to Almira. I'd never really seen him this close, never to take a real shufti. He was a worried man. I could tell. His posh sort never really sweats, just becomes behaviourally focused. Were he a man of action, he'd be taut, lantern-jawed, keen of eye. But he wasn't, kept looking at his watch, other cars. And even once let his speed slacken a few miles. Making time a shade too good? He'd been ordered to arrive dead on. I wondered who by.

The hospital was small but genuine. Nurses, people waiting, an ambulance or two, some poor soul in blankets being trundled between the devil and the deep blue sea. Pain in any amount's really authentic, isn't it? I waited with Almira while he did the *bonsoir* bit with a starched clerical lady at the longest desk I'd ever seen in my life.

'We can go up,' he said. An audience with the Pope. I felt quite cheered up because his drone had come back. Until now his voice had taken on a near-human quality, really strange.

It's hard to walk along hospital corridors. Not because they're uneven but because your feet feel guilty all of a sudden, as if they'd no right to defile the shining surface. I hung back, letting Paul and Almira go first. Genuine all right.

The wing we reached – two floors up and a nurse with a mortician's look – was quiet to the point of stealth. No din. No rattles of equipment. Doors closed, frosted glass, charts looking pessimistic as charts always do. Along three corridor doors, no less, and me finally really apprehensive. With this degree of care, Cissie was for it. No bonny Lysette, like you get in the Whittington at Archway, I felt with a pang.

'Please wait,' we were told. Paul was admitted. Then I was beckoned, and in I went.

It chilled me. Why every grim hospital interior has to be aquarium-lit I don't know, but it scares the hell out of me. The room held one bed, Cissie inside it, pale, her legs under a blanket. Nearby, but mercifully unconnected, were those bleep screens, gasp machines with paired cylindrical concertinas poised to squeeze, tubular glass valves, silvery switches. It looked like a rocket launch. The one honest light barely made a single candlepower. She seemed asleep.

Paul wakened her, after asking the nurse if it was all right. Cissie opened her eyes.

'Hello, er, love,' I said. Nowhere to sit. Doc Lancaster once told me that hospital telly soaps always go wrong in making their actor doctors sit on the edge of the bed, and approach the wrong side of the bed. I crouched to peer at her, trying to work out what I was for.

The nurse warned, 'One minute.'

Cissie's eyes opened, surprisingly clear. 'Lovejoy,' she whispered. I was shaken. I didn't know she could whisper. I must have recoiled, expecting her honing voice. 'Paulie,' she whispered. 'I want to speak to Lovejoy alone.'

'Right, right, dear.'

'The nurse too,' Cissie ordered, with a trace of her old asperity. She groaned, shifted slightly with the nurse's help.

The nurse left too, glaring as if this was all my fault.

Five minus three left me and Cissie. Her eyes closed for a little while, some sort of pain.

We'd lived marital a fortnight, then six weeks for intermittent skirmishing before the separation. It was the fastest divorce on record. She'd married Paul on the first permitted legal morn.

'Lovejoy,' she whispered. 'I wanted to say I'm sorry.'

'Eh?' I straightened, honestly found myself edging away. Abuse, yes. Hatred, aye, sure. But an apology? I felt I'd walked onstage in the middle of *The Quaker Girl*. That unreal.

'I know you must hate me, Lovejoy,' this whispering stranger said. She seemed to sleep a few seconds, blearily came to with appalling effort.

'No, er, Cissie,' I whispered along.

'Yes.' She fixed me with unnaturally bright eyes. 'I was cruel. I was wrong.'

Wrong? Cruel? Sorry? It was beyond my experience. 'No, er, don't worry. It's all . . .' In the past? Did one say things like that, times like this? 'It's okay.' When of course it wasn't. Okay for Lovejoy, not quite okay for somebody dying.

'I want you to do something, Lovejoy. If it's too much, then please say no. I won't bear any grudge.'

Please too? 'What?'

She wanted to move on to her side a little, and signed for me to move her round a little.

'I'll get the nurse,' I said, worried sick.

'No, Lovejoy. I don't want her to hear this.'

I held her, found myself cradling her body in an embrace that would have seemed like old times, except we'd never done this before, not with each other anyhow. Her face was close to mine, her eyes huge.

'What is it, love?'

'Paulie's a fool. Not a patch on you, Lovejoy.'

Not exactly the time to say I'd always known he was a pillock. 'Oh, well,' I managed.

'Please. I want you to help him, Lovejoy. Is it too much to ask, Lovejoy?' She coughed a bit. I tried to cough for her like a fool, holding myself stiff at an awkward angle.

'I don't know what it is I'm to do. Nobody's told me anything. Is it this Troude thing, something about silver shipments?'

'Paulie's in too deep with Troude. He's so desperate for it to succeed. All it is, they are storing some antiques, for export somewhere. It needs a divvy. Say you will.'

'Maybe,' I said, instinct keeping it so I could escape moral bonds should I want to off out. Gentleman to the last.

'I can't blame you, Lovejoy. It was all my fault.' She slipped away then a while, came to after an inward struggle. 'I'm frightened, Lovejoy. And leaving things in such a mess for Paul makes it worse.'

'I'll do it, Cissie,' I said. Instinct yelled to steer clear of the phrase at the last second, failed.

She drove it home. 'You promise, Lovejoy?'

'Promise, love.'

She sank back with a profound sigh. I was just taking my arms away when the nurse came in to say I had to leave, it was time for Mrs Anstruther to rest.

'Blood transfusion due in ten minutes.'

'Right, right.' I looked at the still figure breathing so shallowly, thinking of her in a plastic tent, the mask going over her face, drips being adjusted. 'Bye, Cissie love.'

Her eyelids fluttered. She said nothing. Paul came. And Almira, who said she wanted to say goodbye to Cissie. She was in tears. Paul was silent. I went along the corridor and watched the night outside with its strings of lights along distant roads through the darkness. It had come on to rain.

The way out was hard to find. I managed it third go. Only once did I discover something strange, and that was more by misjudgement than anything. It gave me pause. I stayed among a crowd of visitors getting something to eat down a corridor off a sort of outpatients' place. I heard an odd laugh, odd because it was familiar and shouldn't have been there. I sidled out and stood under the canopy thing looking at the rain.

An ambulance bloke came past, smoking to advertise the benefits of sickness.

'*Pardonez-moi, Monsieur,*' I got out. 'What is this that is this country, silver plate?' My French just made it.

'France.' His voice mocked my sanity. He strolled on, adding a critical suffix about foreigners, especially me.

As if it mattered, like I said. Except that Cissie was going to die in France. I'd seen the terrible diagnosis written plain as day on her chart. Diseases strike terror into me. Pathetically, I wondered guiltily if it was catching. How long ago had it been? I tried to work out. Could a disease lurk, only to spring out...? Gulp. I'd been pretty tired lately. But coping with the rapacious Almira would have weakened a randy regiment, so there was no telling. Three silhouette nurses talked inside the porch across the forecourt. A tubby girl gave an odd whoopy laugh, cut it for professional reasons. Matron would scold.

'All right, Lovejoy?' Almira, at her most sympathetic.

'Aye, love.'

'Lovejoy,' from Paul. 'I'm sorry. I...'

He looked so lost I even felt sorry for him. 'It's all right,' I said, wondering what the hell I was saying. I was reassuring him that I was fine. 'I mean I'm sorry.' Even that didn't sound right.

'We should get back, Lovejoy,' from Almira. Paul said he'd drive us.

We finished the journey in almost total silence, except for Almira saying if there was anything we could do, Paulie, just get in touch, not to bother giving any notice. How, without a phone? I didn't ask. He nodded, kept glancing at me as if I was somehow more injured than him. I tried to force myself, but couldn't reach out and shake his hand. He didn't offer, either, so that was all right.

'Cheers, Paul,' I said as we did that silly look-at-the-floor shuffle folk do at such times. 'Be seeing you.' Would I?

'Yes,' he said, brightening. He went downcast, probably realizing that it was Cissie's dying wish that was possibly going to get him out of some scrape.

'Not coming in for a nightcap, Paulie?' Almira asked.

He seemed to lighten in hope for a second, then something in her expression clicked and he shook his head with the nearest he could manage to resolve, and dutifully got back in the Jag. Once a serf, nowt but. A night bird did its barmy whoop noise. It sounded so like a girl with a funny laugh.

'Better get back,' he said. 'Thanks.'

Almira bussed him farewell. 'Give our fondest love to Cissie.'

'Lovejoy.' He was trying to say something as he fired the engine. 'Thanks, old chap. I really do mean it, you know.'

'That's okay,' I said.

Me and Almira waved him off. He had the radio on as he turned up among the trees, headlights a cone of light dragging him swiftly away. It was that clarinet tune that hit the charts practically in the Dark Ages, something about a carnival.

'Poor Paul.' Almira said. 'Poor Cissie.'

'Yes.' Something felt very odd. That night bird whooped.

'Lovejoy.' She stood close, under a night sky fast clearing of scudding cloud. Stars were showing, and a moon they call a night moon where I come from, thin as a rind and reddish-tinged.

'Yes?'

'Cissie . . . It's no reason for us to be any different, is it? She'd want us to live exactly as we are.'

'Would she?' Odd, strange, queer, weird.

'Yes.' Very vehement. 'There's very little holiday time left. Just let's remember that, darling.'

There is something in this relief theory, that the misfortune of others shoots us so full of relieved thank-God-it's-not-me sensations that we instantly go ape. That night Almira and me really did go over the top, cruelty melding passion and desire in a frenzy so near to madness there was no telling where lust began and delirium ended.

The night seemed to last a week. Which was just as well, because holiday time was over, and fighting time was come.

CHAPTER SIXTEEN

'Good heavens! At last!' Almira cried from the terrace after breakfast.

I too expressed pleased surprise, the sort you see in those terrible old 1950s B films where rep-theatre acting glossed all emotions into mannerism. Being a genuine phoney's easy.

Marc drove Almira's motor up to the house and alighted with a flourish. He prattled something about having fought the garage to a standstill, demanding Madame's *voiture* back *immédiatement.* She was thrilled. I pretended I genuinely thought it had been driven from a nearby town instead of from Marc's cottage two hundred yards off. Marc retired, proud with achievement.

We beamed assurance across the coffee cups. I played along. I mean we said practically everything. Almira had already wondered sadly how dear Cissie was this morning, and how Paulie was bearing up. What a pity there was no telephone! This odd nagging feeling returned, that I was being led towards a distant but quite safe destination. Everything above board, nothing hidden. Great, eh? Lucrative, with Troude's assurances that money would flow in.

'Cissie told me about Paulie's investments in an antiques project, darling,' she finally said, doing her bit. 'You promised to help.'

'Mmmmh,' I concurred, doing mine.

She was ravishing, today in lemon yellow. 'It's Philippe Troude's project, isn't it?' She gave a half-laugh. 'Well, with Monsieur Troude arranging everything, nothing can possibly go wrong. He's a billionaire, Lovejoy!'

Over those curly bread things Madame Raybaud seemed to think were breakfast Almira seemed excited, under her thin disguise of transitory grief for Cissie. It'd be today. No woman can hide the delight of anticipation. It was there in her eyes, her moist lips, her showy manner. I've already told you about fraud. Remember the crop markings? And how *that* little fraud had become legitimate, even founded a whole new science? The only hassle came when it intruded into Poncho's fraud, which had itself spawned other new frauds . . .

And guess what! A message came! A messenger on a Donk-type bike rode up, solemnly handed Almira an envelope, got his chit signed and offed.

'Not bad news I hope, dwoorlink?' I said anxiously as I could on half a grotty bun and a swig.

Almira read the note. 'It's from Paulie, darling. Philippe Troude is here. Can we meet them today, talk over the arrangements. Thank goodness it's not bad news about Cissie!'

'Thank goodness!' I agreed. How lucky Almira's motor was back in time, I thought but did not say. But as long as antiques loomed I'd be happy. You can trust antiques, the crossroads of loving, murder, deceit, forgery and corruption.

'Now that we have the motor, dwoorlink,' I suggested, knowing the answer, 'have we time to look for an antique shop?'

'What a good idea!' she said brightly, telling herself she thought I'd never ask.

We hit the road. The keys were in the ignition. No concealment of direction, no angst over questions. Lovely chatter, pleasant talk about how she really admired the views, how much land France seemed to have, how much prettier France was than the Low Countries, don't you think, darling? Which told me I wasn't ever coming back to Madame Raybaud's domain, or the shack by the waterside with the hunter in the woods.

Through quite mountainous countryside – though goose-pimples look hilly if you live in East Anglia – Almira drove with ease and accomplishment. Driving on the Continent you have to think hard every inch because they drive there on the wrong side of the road. Nothing wrong in that; it's just their way. But Almira's expertise showed she wasn't new to these cack-handed roads. Nor did she need to inspect the signs, just casually notched them off.

Almira was quite at home here, thank you.

We avoided the big national highways. It seemed to me there'd only to come some sign promising a D, A or N road for Almira to cruise off down some rural snaker. I didn't mind. Nice to see open air, towns and that. I felt the odd familiarity of a newcomer to France. Maybe it's the names. Villiers I remember, because there was once a Villiers engine, now highly collectible on old motorbikes. And a river called Anglin, very appropriate unless I've got it wrong. We drove forty miles, then stopped for coffee at a tavern. Hills rose in the distance. No, Almira couldn't tell me which they were, but there was a map somewhere in the glove compartment, darling . . .

See? No secrecy, no possible subterfuge. Mrs Almira Galloway was clearly nothing to do with the Troude scheme financed by Paulie et al. She was just along for the ride, so to speak.

As we talked and saw people roll up, stop for a chat, smoke and coffee, then trundle off, I prepared my sentence. And asked the serving lass if there was a *ville* nearby *avec un* antiques *magasin*. I'd have been quarter of an hour disentangling her swift joyous reply but for Almira, who cooed why didn't I ask, for heaven's sake? And drove me six more miles. To heaven.

'There's always one antique shop, Lovejoy,' Almira was pacifying me for the eleventh time, getting narked like they do when you ask quite a reasonable question. 'Don't keep on.'

'We should drive to the next town,' I grumbled. 'Happen the bird got her wires crossed.'

'We've hardly looked!' she was saying, when I stopped and felt a bit odd.

The town was hardly that. Set among small fields, it was on a little plain, a river not far off. It seemed amateur, somehow, but didn't care. Houses of that peculiar Frenchness, dry ground, trees indolent, unlike our busy East Anglian trees that are always hard at it – God knows what 'it' is, but they always seem to be giving it a go, stirring the air to a brisk breeze. Maybe it's our skies, never still. A few cars, a horse and trap, a lone flag proclaiming nationality. The windows of houses always look strangest to me in a new country. Flowers competing on opposite sides of the main street.

'This way, love.'

We crossed the main street. Three or four shops, a small restaurant, some men drinking outside at tables under an awning. A lane led up from the thoroughfare. I felt the oddness from that direction, towards the church. Less than a score yards along stood a yard, with a bow-fronted shop boasting antiques.

Remember this, for money's sake.

French furniture either goes ape in fashions so distinct from ours that your mind boggles – rococo chairs so ornate you sometimes have to work out where your bum goes. Like the fashion to implant floral decorative Sèvres porcelain plaques in the surfaces of cabinets about 1774 on, glorious but overwhelming unless you care for those horrendously smiling masks of women and lions that ornament the corners and frieze. Or it does the other thing, goes individual with a strange elegance that I love more. Oddly, the great furniture-makers were often not French at all, though they sometimes learned their craft there. Like David Roentgen, who sold in Paris but worked in Neuwied.

I stared. In the yard was a small converted Citroën truck. I reached to uncover the bureau more, but the odd feeling died. I let go, and turned in disappointment to find a diminutive bloke standing next to me. Gave me a jolt.

'Er, *bonjour, Monsieur*,' I said. '*Je désire pour regarder votre* antiques.'

He sighed a long French sigh and shot a mouthful of exasperation at Almira, who explained while I wandered to where my sensation grew stronger. It's exactly like that hot-cold game of children's parties. You *know* when you're standing next to the real thing, even if it's only a mildewed crate.

'. . . need, Lovejoy,' Almira was saying.

'How much? *Combien pour acheter*?' I told him.

He gauged me. He was the slyest man I'd ever seen. Even his direct appraisal was an oblique squint-eyed effort that never quite made your face. Then, when you'd finally given up and turned aside, you'd find his quizzical shifty eyes trawling after you, taking you in. He'd have made a cracking spy.

'This is not for sale,' Almira said after a voluble interrogation. 'The bureau on the car is.'

'*Je désire acheter le* contents *à l'interieur*.'

'?' he asked Almira.

'*Non*,' I said. I knew that *flic* and *agent* were police-laden words, and he'd gone even shiftier. '*Mais je . . . aime beaucoup* what is inside, Monsieur.' I remembered I hadn't a bean.

Almira told him I was an antiques collector. He brightened shiftily, and tried to pull me back to the piece on the truck.

'*Pas* the *tromperie* fake,' I said. '*Mais le vrai un*.' Just in case he managed to sly his way round this syntax, I added, '*Le vrai un. Dans votre* box.'

He tried telling me all sorts about the priceless magnificent late eighteenth-century bureau, just arrived on his truck, but I wouldn't have it. At last, slyly he undid his crate – already the screws were out – and slyly exposed a fire screen laid in the bottom. I went weak with delight.

Sometimes, mixing styles can be so dazzling that even the simplest object becomes glorious. I mean, can anything be simpler than a fire screen? Anything rectangular that stands up will more or less do the job, right? But Georges Jacob in the last quarter of the eighteenth century made a meal of rectangles. He married the new classical style with the older natural period. Another foreigner – Burgundian – he was a riot with the Parisians, and even did a brisk export trade to posh gentry in England. It was good enough to eat. The screen itself was slightly arched gilded wood, carved with sphinxes, arrows, twists on the support columns, cornucopias on the feet. Little garlands and ribboned top, all carved with unbelievable skill, showed just what they could do in those hellish workshops.

'*Est-ce-que à vous, Monsieur?*' I asked as best I could when breath let me.

He was ruminating slyly at my response, said something shifty to Almira.

'He owns it, Lovejoy,' she said, staring. 'But it's not for sale.'

'Everything else on the planet is,' I countered. 'Ask him.'

The piece smiled up at me from its bed of polystyrene grot in the crate. The screen's panel was a wonder, embroidery pristine as the day it was finished, florets in plum on a beige ground. Lovely. Some people say antiques are just inert materials. They're not. Antiques know what we think of them. Forgeries don't have feelings, but sure as God the real things do.

'. . . Lovejoy.'

Almira interrupting. 'Eh?'

'He says no deal. Buy the bureau on the truck, or nothing.'

'Tell him to stuff it.'

And I went outside to the car. She stayed behind to say no ta to Sly. We left, me burned up at having to part from that wonder. I could hardly speak until we'd driven out of the place.

'That fire screen was magic,' I told her, courageously not weeping. 'The bureau on the truck was a copy, modern, of Roentgen's work. He was famous for his stupendous gliding parts – drawers, doors, rests – and marquetry. He's become more faked than most Old Masters, especially here on the Continent.'

'What *is* the attraction, Lovejoy?' She was driving, perplexed. I sighed. You can't tell some folk, even if you're crazy about them.

'Roentgen's skill was so terrific that even the makers of automata – you know those little working models? – got him to make their models.'

'So? Couldn't you buy that fake bureau, and make more money on it than the genuine fire screen?'

'Of course.' You have to be patient. 'But the antique is alive and beautiful. The other's a load of dead planks.'

She was exasperated. 'But *profit*, Lovejoy!' Like I'd never heard of that old thing.

'Bugger profit,' I said crudely.

It was several miles before she spoke. We were pulling in to a town car park, quite a sizeable place with Paulie and Philippe Troude just arriving at a café and the lovely Monique preceding them in.

113

Almira said, 'Lovejoy. Are antiques, well, real people?'

Women can surprise you, even when you think they've run out of ideas. 'That's right, dwoorlink. I only wish that real people were real people.'

I made it sound a joke. But I was only thinking how curious it was that a rare genuine antique like that Georges Jacob screen had turned up in a dump like that village shop, with a superb valuable fake like the Roentgen bureau in the same yard. So I smiled and said I loved her. She smiled back and said she loved me. We were sickeningly sweet.

'Paulie and Cissie will be so grateful, Lovejoy,' she told me. 'I'll go across with you.'

Carefully not holding hands, we crossed briskly. No antique shops in sight, so I didn't care. I wish I'd been more discriminating. It's foolish to obey women, because they're usually wrong, but what can you do?

Paul emerged as we went in. He tried to reach for my hand to say so long. I passed him with an out-of-my-way look. A wimp's a wimp because he's determined to stay one. I'd no patience.

'Where to?' I asked Almira. Except that she was no longer with me. I looked round. She'd gone. And Paul.

'Monsieur.' A waiter ushered me through a scatter of diners, and from then on it was no game. Couldn't expect it to be, because antiques never are. But I felt utterly at peace, so serene. Antiques, even if they aren't mine, are the breath of life. I had to be near them at any price, and felt close.

CHAPTER SEVENTEEN

There was a lunatic survey not long since. I read it in Doc Lancaster's waiting room midst ponging infants and wheezing geriatrics. Two things Make the Heart Sink, the magazine shrieked, 'Parting After Sex' and 'Meeting Somebody You Want to Avoid'. Well I'm sure the first is wrong; parting after sex is a pretty good idea. But the second is dead on. Bingo-time.

I entered this little nooky room above the café. The Heart Sank as I recognized the bloke seated at a polished table. That is to say, I'd never clapped eyes on him before in my life, but I recognized him all right. He was Superior Officer, fresh from military command of the most exacting kind. I hated him instantly, his ideals, his purity of vision. Nothing wrong with being a soldier, but there's one sort that chills the blood. They have the light of eagles in their eyes, and smell cannonfire sipping yoghurt with the bishop. They are patriotic, loyal, unyielding. They cost lives – hundreds, thousands of lives. And I'd only one – none to spare for the likes of him.

'This is Lovejoy, Monsieur.'

Troude was pleasant as ever – in fact, I instantly saw Troude in a kindlier light. Beside Monique's lacquered delectable hardness and the colonel's crew-cut ramrod stiffness, Troude was almost pally.

'Monsieur Marimee will control the process,' Monique said, *ex cathedra*.

Marimee fixed me with a gimlet eye. Clean-shaven, steel-grey hair, slightly sallow, lean as a whippet, he looked ready to jump from the plane at a cool eight thousand feet. Odd, but the table – a humdrum modern folding job straight from the nosh bar below – instantly took on a desperate polishy appearance, like it was on parade. It's the effect these blokes have. Of course he had a file. He opened it, threatening me with his eyeballs.

'You are a criminal.' The English was a bit slidey, but clear with meaning.

'Not much of one.'

'You are an *ineffectual* criminal.' He flipped a page, gave it no glance. I was getting the treatment. Authority ruled; his, nobody else's. My silence riled him. He rapped, 'Answer!'

'The question . . . ?' I wanted to obey in the meekest manner possible, do his job and exit smiling. Not much to ask.

Stupid to needle him but I couldn't help it. He appraised me from under eyebrows borrowed off an albino beetle. Troude fidgeted. He wanted us all to go forward in harmony. Monique was impatient with the entire world. Some women give the impression that an execution is the only way out.

'Insubordination will not be permitted, Lovejoy.' He got the name right, so his English was wellnigh perfect. 'This project requires absolute compliance. No discretion is permitted.'

He'd nearly said or else. I slipped it in to complete his meaning. Or else he'd shoot me? Then they'd lack a divvy, and they needed one.

'Very well.' And I added, 'Sir.' I saw he said it inwardly with me, satisfaction easing his stalwart frame for a second. His military mind wanted only to talk to chalk, like a superannuated teacher. 'What project?'

'Recovery of items from a location to be specified.'

'Very well.' The scent of fraud trickled in about here, ponging the nostrils. For recovery read robbery. 'Sir.'

'You are not curious about the items? The location?'

'I know you will inform me when the time comes, sir.'

His eye glinted. 'You have served?'

'In an army? Once. I was a famous coward. And ineffectual.'

No curled lip, but he hated the levity. 'Ineffectual criminal *and* soldier!'

Troude's sudden agitation warned me not to reply that maybe the two occupations shared lifestyles. I swallowed it.

'Is it the Commandant's wish for me to leave the project?'

Monique started. Troude almost fainted. Marimee found himself in a quandary. Gratified at the title, narked by having to admit I was valuable, he found refuge in an order.

'You will continue until the mission is completed.'

His project had become a mission in half a breath. I sighed. My famous instinct was yowling for me to get the hell out, run like a hare, swim back across the Channel. Cissie was dying in the hospital, believing in my promise.

'Very well, Commandant.'

'There will be two phases. The first will be in Paris and possibly London. The second will take place in a certain location to be notified. Time-scale: immediate, and within three weeks respectively.' He leaned back. The room relaxed slightly. He looked at me hard, hands behind his head. Immediate did not mean instant, it seemed. 'Questions are permitted.'

'I work alone?'

'No. You will have two assistants in Phase One. Phase Two is not for your ears until One is accomplished.'

'I will receive enough, ah, tools to carry it out?'

'Planning has been exemplary for both phases.' He shot to his feet, abruptly showing a non-punitive emotion for the first time. Troude looked wary, Monique irritated at some coming digression. I shrugged mentally. Okay, so I was not to query the perfection of his military mind. I'd not argue.

'Your nation, Lovejoy, is *despicable!*' he shouted.

Eh? Another mental shrug got me through that, but he was boss and implacable threats lay thick all about. I know when to bend with the gale. Marimee marched to the window, clear eyes seeking snipers out there on some distant hill. My whole *nation?* Maybe France'd just lost to us at cricket, whatever.

'Your tabloids speak of *losing* your empire, as if it was mislaid on your London buses! The truth?' He swivelled, fixed me, swivelled back, an animaloid gun turret. 'The truth is you *gave it away!* You proved spineless in the crunch!'

This sort of stuff bores me to tears. Who the hell cares? So obsessional historians score points off one another. It's no big deal.

'Your immigrants retain their national identities, *n'est-ce-pas?* Each group as distinctive as they were in Hong Kong, Kenya, India. Like', he sneered without showing whether his lip was really curled or not, 'the so-wonderful Americans.'

'I think it's what they want to do,' I said lamely. He'd seemed to be waiting for an answer.

'It is behaviour without *soul*, Lovejoy! In France, we *blend* immigrants! They become French. We fight for principle! As we fight for our language. English is barbaric, a degraded hybrid! India alone claims six thousand of your "English" words. Your music is bastardized, assimilating Trinidadian . . .' I won't give the rest, if that's all right. It's a real yawn. For God's sake, I thought as my mind switched off his claptrap, if a tune's nice, sing. If it's not, don't. It's not exactly a proposition by Wittgenstein, for Christ's sake.

His assault when it came frightened me off my chair. He leaned at me, yelling, '*And you don't care!*'

'Er,' I said, returning. I'd almost shot out of the door. 'Well, I know some folk do. There's a lot of interest in ethnic dances and whatnot . . .'

'You surrender your national heritage!'

What the hell was he on about? I was here to shift some antique silver, and the nutter earaches me over reggae and steel bands? Troude caught my despair, shot Monique an appealing glance. She intervened. Her luscious mouth moved.

'Lovejoy. You will receive daily orders from the assistants of whom Monsieur Marimee spoke. Depart for Paris immediately.'

'Very well.' Assistants who rule? If her mouth said so. I'd do anything for it.

Marimee controlled himself. His outburst done, he sat with fixed calm. I didn't like this. Serenity's not that sudden. It comes like a slow glow from a candle. His tranquillity burned up like an epidemic. Wrong, wrong. The bugger was barmy. 'Immediately now or eventually now?'

She almost smiled, but didn't. '*Maintenant*, Lovejoy.'

'Very well. Good day, Commandant.'

As I reached the door Marimee spoke with clipped precision. 'I regret to inform you that Madame Anstruther died at twenty-three hours precisely.'

'Eh?' I halted. I didn't know any Anstruthers. Except I did. Paul Anstruther. And of course Mrs Cissie Anstruther. I looked back at them, hand on the knob. Waiting stupidly for some sort of qualification, perhaps. Like, well, Lovejoy, not quite as in *dead* dead.

Troude was looking at the threadbare carpet. Marimee's eyes were opaque, done this a thousand times before along established lines, no need for any kind of display. Monique was looking at me curiously. Every time she stared it was as if I was seeing her for the very first time, a kaleidoscopic woman. This time's look was quizzical: how will you react?

'Very well, *mon commandant*,' I said, and left. Useful old phrase, very well. Stands for a million different things. I've often found that.

When I got to the car park, Almira's motor had gone, of course. And Troude, Marimee, Monique Delebarre, were already motoring away from the café into the thin traffic. I'd lost an ex-wife, my wealthy mistress, any means of transport, finance, and I was alone in a strange land. I felt a desperate need of two assistants, with orders. They were to be here *immédiatement*, for Phase One had begun, according to Colonel Marimee.

They arrived about ten minutes later. Life went downhill, with variations.

CHAPTER EIGHTEEN

You never know with new people. You meet them, and form instantaneous judgements. Mine are always wrong. I'm truly gormless. If I met Rasputin I'd think him St Cuthbert and only clue in when the body count increased. Like my assistants, when finally they arrived. Nobody can be as wrong as me. They proved it.

Standing idly by the traffic lights, I wondered if Colonel Marimee was as militarily superefficient as all that. I mean, I was here, poised like a greyhound in the slips, ready for this phoney antiques scam, and where were my two assistants? Luckily, French drivers don't let you cross, so I didn't feel out of place waiting. I reasoned that ice-cold Marimee had planned this little interlude as a kind of initiative test. These military minds think straight lines. The last time I'd done one of these what-nexters they'd put me down in the Yorkshire moors in the deep midwinter so I'd die. I'd saved myself by kipping with some cows in a byre until daylight. The sergeant put me on jankers a fortnight for cheating. See what I mean? But here, lacking cows and initiative, I loitered, hoping my assistants would finally get fed up and come for me.

Their motor was a mundane thing. It passed, dithered, pulled in. Two roaring forties, him balding and specky; she smiley and talkative. They had a dozen maps out. I barely gave them a look, then a faint chime bonged deep in me. I bent down to peer inside their car. On the back seat was a very, very interesting chair, tall, thin, with six cross-struts for back support. Genuine Astley Cooper! I knocked on the window. I must say, they put on a good act.

'Yes?' the driver asked. His wife nudged him. '*Oui?*'

Scotch, thank God. Out of the declension jungle! 'Hello,' I said. 'Lovejoy.'

He glanced at his wife, probably checking that I was the right bloke. They probably had photographs of me in the glove compartment. Sensible to make sure, really. I could be anybody. 'Could you please guide me to the Paris road?'

'We never get the maps right,' his missus said, smiling.

Good cover! Shrewd. I beamed. 'I could show you,' I said loudly, to show the world this wasn't prearranged. A really accidental encounter, *tout le monde*! 'If you'd give me a lift.'

'I'm not sure . . .' he said, doubtful. I thought that was overdoing it, but the bird shoved him affectionately.

'Och, away, Gerald! Simplest thing to do!' He undid the rear door and I climbed in. 'Mind that crofter's chair, Lovejoy. It's very valuable.'

'Lilian,' Gerald reproved as we pulled away. Why did he want her to be so circumspect? The antique was his signal, after all. Well, we all were treble secret I supposed.

'Och, he's all right!' Lilian said of me, warm.

'Astley Cooper,' I said, smiling my thanks. She was bonny, as well as a superb judge of character. 'Not a crofter's chair. Not a farthingale chair.'

'It's a Regency spinning chair,' Lilian said. She adjusted her vanity mirror to see my face.

'Nor that, love. Sir Astley Cooper was a surgeon, knighted for operating on the Prince Regent. He designed this chair to teach little children to sit upright.' They went silent. An odd pair, these, seeing we were on the same side. Had I missed some code word? 'The other names are daft. Nice to see one of Astley Cooper's chairs left plain. Goons nowadays decorate them with everything but Christmas lights.' I chuckled, but on my own.

The motor swerved violently. An open tourer shot close to us, horn blaring. A girl shook a fist at us, furious, blonde hair streaming. The young bloke with her was straight off some telly advert for South Seas surfing.

'Bloody idiot,' I muttered. The tourer's lights were flashing. Both youngsters seemed angry, though Gerald was driving with a Briton's usual guarded suspicion. 'That was their fault.' Criticize other motorists, you're in.

'I'm obeying the rule of the road,' Gerald said anxiously.

'Course you are,' Lilian said, her pride stung. 'Always impatient. Same as at home.'

The tourer dwindled ahead. In newfound comradeship we relaxed into those where're-you-from and heavens-my-auntie's-from-there conversations that substitute for instant friendship.

'We're looking at places,' Lilian said, too smooth by far as Gerald reasserted his motor's rights. 'For time-share holidays.' Aha. Their cover story.

'Good idea, time-share,' I said, thinking pretence the party line. Maybe the car was bugged? 'I'm hitchhiking.'

The journey was pleasant, they eventually relaxed. Banter-time as we rolled – Gerald never raced – towards Paris. Luckily, I saw a

Paris sign before they did, pointed it out as if I'd known all the time. They'd started up a small travel business. 'Everything will be leisure, hen, in ten years.' Lilian was emphatic, but in a practised kind of way I couldn't quite accept somehow. Still arguing about prices, the cost of renting a shop front in Glasgow . . .

'Dearer in East Anglia,' I challenged, to get her going. Women hate admitting that other people suffer more expense.

'You live there? And you think that's dear? You come up to Clydebank, you wouldn't know what'd hit you for prices! Gerald bought a . . .' The motor straightened after a small swerve, with this time no flashy youngsters cutting us up while overtaking. '. . . a share in a tour operator's. It cost the *earth* . . .'

Gerald and Lilian Sweet, of Glasgow. Travel concessionaires. I listened, prattled, watched the scenery drift by. Marimee would have been proud of the three of us. Not a word passed our lips about the mission we were all on.

We stopped for nosh twenty kilometres short of the capital. I grinned, said I'd stretch my legs. As Gerald locked the motor with meticulous precision, Lilian took me in properly for the first time.

'Are you short, hen?'

'Had my stuff nicked, love. Pickpockets.' Stick to the pattern. Plenty of traffic about now, people have directional microphones these days. I could hear Marimee bark orders.

'We'll stand you a bite, won't we, Gerald?'

'Oh, aye.' He didn't seem keen, though. Maybe Marimee checked their expenses. Lilian got her dander up and he surrendered. We went in this Disney-Gothic self-service for the loos. I was first out, and got collared by a flaxen-haired aggropath. He slammed me against the wall. My breath went shoosh! It was the sports-car maniac who'd bawled Gerald out on the road.

'What's the game?' he said, through gritted teeth as they used to say in boys' comics.

'Game?' I gasped, going puce. 'Let me breathe for Christ's sake! I wasn't even driving!' Bog-eyed, I tried to point into the self-service. Let him throttle Gerald or Lilian. But not me.

'Drop your two friends. Wait by my Alfa. Thirty minutes!'

'Right! Right!' Quite mad.

'An' if you don't . . .' His eyes were so near, so pale, watery yet clear. The opposition hired madmen. You humour madmen, then scarper. I tried to nod, managed a weak smile.

'Kee!' The delectable blonde bird slipped up, nudged him.

And they were gone, into a murky-lit grotto place with slot

machines and winking screens. I went jauntily towards my own couple, smiling at the prospect of grub looming. Henceforth, I would stick to the Sweets like glue. That Marimee should have told me there'd be dastardly foes on route. Typical. Always half a story. No wonder Gerald Sweet was ultra-cautious.

'Let's see what sort of food they have, hen!' Lilian led the way in. 'I hope they have a nice hot pasty!'

Love flooded my heart for the dear beautiful woman. A pasty! She knew my desperate need. I caught her eye in the mirrors. She coloured slightly, but it may only have been the steam from the cooking. Gerald was anxiously checking his pockets, craning to see his motor wasn't stolen. Lilian laughed self-consciously.

'Gerald's a real worrier, Lovejoy!' she told me. 'Up all night phoning home to see the . . . the business hasn't folded while we're away!' Good. She was careful too.

I cleared my throat. 'Really,' I said. Then as Gerald turned at my tone, 'Nothing wrong with being careful, is there?'

'No, Lovejoy,' he agreed, and for half an hour gave me a lecture on how easy it was to get caught out in business. I noshed like a trooper, listening with half an ear. He was becoming more like Marimee every second. I promised to owe them the cost of the meal, got their phone number and address. They had it ready, to my surprise. Real pros, excellent cover.

As soon as we hit the road, I showed true military-style initiative. I deflected us down a road soon after leaving the service station. We shook off the two gorgeous loons in their Alfa Romeo. I was so thrilled.

The hotel was quite small, on the southern outskirts of Paris. I liked it, but maybe it was the relief of being back in a town, free of that terrible pretty countryside everywhere. There was a garden, a fountain thing, lights and tables outside. I've a theory that it's the Continent's weather that permits folk to be so laid back. In East Anglia you could never put awning umbrellas out, scatter romantic candlelit tables round an ornamental grove unless the weather gods freak out into a spell of sun. You've only to step outside for it to teem down.

They said I should stay for the evening meal. Then, as Gerald was about to start on his phone marathon, Lilian suggested they lend me some money. They were only sticking to the pattern laid down by Marimee but I felt really touched. I accepted, with great anxiety and swapping of bank-account guarantors, and got a small room in the garret. A lot cheaper than our own hotels, I was astonished to learn.

Supper, Gerald finally wedded himself to the phone, and I was left with Lilian. It was getting on for ten o'clock. It crossed my mind to tell her how I'd cunningly outwitted the opposition back at the pit stop but thought better of it. Was I expected to chat about everything that happened? Probably not.

'He'll be telephoning now until midnight,' Lilian said.

She looked bonny. No specs now, earrings, a lace shawl that should have been Edwardian but was disappointingly repro. We were in the garden, looking down into the rock pool. Only three other couples remained, talking softly.

'He works hard,' I said. I meant it as praise.

'Och, nobody more than Gerald!'

Well, I suppose Marimee was giving orders for tomorrow. Was the silver lift to be done in Paris, then? Or was that tale now to be discarded, as the cover story it undoubtedly was? I felt things were imminent, brewing up to action. Maybe Gerald had better be warned about the two aggressive enemy.

'Look, love.' I glanced about. Any of these diners could be the opposition. 'This is a bit public.'

'Public?' She seemed to colour slightly, but I couldn't really tell in the low glim. 'What . . . ?'

'They'll hear.' Through the lounge window Gerald was visible, nodding, reporting in, taking notes. 'Even from inside the bar.'

She looked towards the hotel, seemed a little breathless. 'It's risky, Lovejoy. I'm not sure if I know what –'

'My room,' I suggested quietly. It was quite logical after all, the one place that had not been prearranged. They'd had difficulty finding me a nook.

'Oh, Lovejoy.' She was worried, glancing at the building, the other diners, two waiters. 'I've never . . . I mean, what if Gerald – ?'

Typical woman. A bloke's got to take charge some time, hasn't he? I had my arm through hers.

'We've got time before Gerald's done, love. It'll be safe.'

Which was how we entered my small single-bedded room together, in an ostentatiously non-clandestine way that probably announced skulduggery louder than a tannoy. Inside as I closed the door, she paused.

'Lovejoy.' She was all quiet. I bent my head to hear. Very sensible in the circumstances. In those spy pictures a transmitting bug's small as a farthing. The hotel could be riddled.

'Yes, love?'

'I . . . I don't do this sort of thing.'

What sort of thing? 'I don't either,' I whispered encouragingly. 'We're in this together, love. I'm discretion itself.' I decided to prove it. 'I had a tussle with that blond motorist at the service station. I saw him off.' Well, it was nearly the way it happened.

'You did, hen?' Her eyes grew even larger. 'Oh, that's wonderful! Gerald isn't really very . . . ' More colour. 'Well, physical, Lovejoy.'

'Doesn't matter.' I glowed in her admiration. Not much comes my way, so I have to glow where I can. 'I can cope, love.'

'Lovejoy.' Quieter still. I was stooped over her now, both of us standing there. We hadn't yet put on the light. 'I'm not quite as young as I was. I'd hate to disappoint you.'

It's one of my observations that women are more practical than us. But that only holds true for ninety-nine per cent of the time. Once in a hundred, their minds go aslant. They talk tangents. Here we were, spies doing our surreptitious best, and she starts on about age. Women's tangents mostly concern numbers, I find. Years, hours, fractions of a penny for mandarin oranges, when little Aurora was actually born to the split second. Daft.

'It's the way I want it, love,' I whispered, all reassuring. 'You're exactly right.'

'Oh, darling.' Her shawl fell as she put her arms round me. It's not often my mouth gets taken by surprise, but this time it was startled. Her breast was beautiful, though I stabbed myself on a brooch that made me yelp. Just shows how thoughtless modern women are. Edwardian ladies had amber beads to cap the points of their brooch pins, so that marauding mitts of amorous gentlemen didn't get transfixed in a ration of passion – cunning, this, because a dot of blood on a white-gloved finger when reentering the ballroom meant suicides in the regiment.

'Shhh!' she said, breathless still. I joined in the breathlessness as we made the bed and still I hadn't managed to reveal my doubts about Colonel Marimee's mission.

'Dwoorlink,' I managed, as nature started to decide the sequence of events.

'No, Lovejoy. Please. Say nothing . . . '

I did as I was told. It's my usual way. Sometimes it works out for the best, as now. She was lovely. And it's any port in a storm, isn't it.

Love never comes without problems, but sometimes they come in a way that shows you've had no right to stay thinking. I mean,

I ought to have said how attractive she was, this lovely woman. Maybe, it seemed to me in the instant before ecstasy engulfed the universe, I should have admitted I wasn't much, just a bum wondering what the hell everything was all about, give her the option to pull her dress on and light out leaving me, as it were, standing. But I obeyed, said nothing, learned nil, and managed only bliss. If anybody from the opposition was actually listening, we fooled them. She was superb.

An hour later I took her to her door, two floors down. She unlocked it. Gerald wasn't in yet. She pulled me in, just far enough for a parting snog before shoving me gently away.

'Will I see you again, Lovejoy?'

'Eh?' Blank for a second, but she was right to stay in character. We were travellers with the hotel hots. 'I couldn't go on without that, love.' It was easier to say than usual. Her eyes filled. 'It's true, Lilian. You were magic.'

We whispered a few more phrases, enough to convince any eavesdropper, then I stepped reluctantly into the corridor as somebody came upstairs.

And I glimpsed something round Lilian's neck that made my blood run cold. But I managed to keep smiling, nodding goodnight, as she put the door to and I went for a well-earned kip.

God knows how I'd failed to notice it. Heat of the moment, I suppose. Only a small gold medallion, with a monogram. Its initials, SAPAR, round the periphery, struck into my brain and set my two lonely nerve cells clanging like clappers in a bell. Stolen Art and Purloined Antiques Rescue.

But quite the most frightening was a single gold letter stencilled in the centre, larger than the others Letter H. Lying on my crumpled bed, I found myself shivering like in a malarial rigor, except this was much, much worse. I wondered for the first time who Lilian and Gerald really were. And the gorgeous golden maniacs in the posh racer. The world had unglued, to clatter all about me. Marimee would have me shot twice a day for a week. Paul, Almira, Troude, Monique, were on a dead loser. And me? I was in the worst-ever trouble of all.

H stands for Hunter.

Time to run.

CHAPTER NINETEEN

About sexual emblems.

They have a fascinating history. The antiques that have filtered down to us oftener than not go unnoticed. In fact, I'd go so far as to say that sexual antiques get shunned. Women, as with everything else on earth, hold the key.

In every age, every fashion, sexual artefacts flourished. They do now, except we won't admit it. My favourites are nipple jewels. Not merely studs in the nipple's eye, but lovely pendants with question-mark supports for pierced nipples. All the rage late in Victoria's reign, the ancient world's fashion came round again. Breast tassles, some with erotic tails of hair, tiny whips, even fine blades, offered all kinds of fetishes for the women who preferred to mount her own performance, so to speak. Merkins were natural, in an age of wigs, though very few survive. These flattish wigs made for the pubis – smallpox tended to denude your genital hair – mostly human hair in kid leather, were desirable enhancers. They came adorned with every kind of jewellery, including gold stitchery. Belly jewels, implanted precious stones actually surfacing through the skin, spectacular ornaments for the genitalia, they've all had their day.

Because more boy babes died than girls in those past days, women outnumbered us. Superstitions ran rife about conception, a must for a woman to hold up her head. The more she produced, the better. With ineffable logic, they decided that the greater the arousal, the more certain the chance of fruition. They invented with ingenuity and skill. They called in seductive lady helpers of great beauty, who'd excite to passion – using any devices they could think up – then escape from between as husband and wife came together, to coin a phrase, with an almost audible clang. Hence the toy phalluses, images, statuettes, paintings, erotic prints from the Far East, precious gems (of course of the right birthstone significance, because you wouldn't want your rival to benefit simply because you'd used emerald instead of ruby, right?). I've even seen one locket, made for some Victorian lady, which contained the beautifully carved miniature male genitalia of sapphire on one leaf, and the female sculpted of amethyst on the other. Conjures up the charming image of a demure lady praying in church, fingering her locket, which, being firmly closed, made the male and female jewels inside the locket unite in the most intimate manner. Presumably she was born in February, her lover in September – and note that astrological stones aren't quite those of the calendar months. Semiprecious stones became a means of communication. Diamond, emerald, amethyst and ruby look rather rum in a linear gold mount, but they spell DEAR to the observant swain. I've seen a fairly modern platinum-mounted one of feldspar, a gap, then chrysoberyl, then kunzite – the gap standing for 'unknown'. Incidentally, if you see kunzite – violet pink of different colour depths as you rotate it – in a brooch for its name, then the gem's really not a genuine antique, for G.F. Kunz was an American at the end of Victoria's reign . . .

Where was I? The gold-lettered pendant on Lilian's gold chain. Husbands give their ladies depictive jewellery showing occupations. Gerald was a SAPAR man. There's only two grades in SAPAR's organization: A for the admin, legal, research lot; H for the self-effacing, but ruthless, hunters.

Escaping, that's where I was. On the run from H for Hunter Gerald, the clever swine.

First, nick a motor. Fifth car I tried, I got in, started up with ease. Reasonably modern, so it wouldn't conk out and embarrass me. Hot-wiring a motor at a somnolent night town's traffic lights attracts attention.

Knowing what theft is exactly, is Man's dilemma. I thought this abstruse quandary as I guided my new possession from the hotel car park and zoomed back the way we'd come.

Stealing a car, possibly to save my life, was not theological or moral theft. The Church teaches that stealing bread to save your starving children isn't. As the lights on the south-east road lit my reflection in the windscreen, I worried in case the Church didn't teach any such thing. If it doesn't, it ought. Naturally I felt sorry for the lady whose dawn would be clouded by her missing Peugeot, but I didn't choose to be here, driving wrong-handed into gathering night rain. Everything simply wasn't my fault. She looked quite smart, did Madame Jeanne Deheque in her photo snap, with her deliberate hair and long eyelashes. No credit cards, maps, nothing to help a stray escaper, the thoughtless cow. Typical woman.

The memory of the service station on the main road was fresh in my mind. No passport, no knowing where I could find refuge. But I was pretty sure I could find the town, the car park, the café where Marimee had grilled me. From there, it would be easy to trek back to Almira's house and the chalet by the lake. Thence filch my passport, and home. No speeding – French cops are death to dashers. I was the sedate motorist. Enough petrol to last a lifetime. I settled down to a steady night drive.

Gerald had been pretty cool, all right. His cover, a travel agent looking for time-share accommodation, bonny homely wife along picking up the odd antique for the business premises. No wonder he spent hours on the phone. No wonder they exchanged glances when their casual hitchhiker knew an Astley Cooper chair and all of its off-key names. But a SAPAR hunter? Gulp.

The Mounties get their man. Sherlock Holmes wins out. In antiques scammery, the SAPAR hunter's the one to avoid. Whispers tell how two or three of them – there's only ten, would you believe – have actually killed thieves who proved reluctant to disgorge the booty, before politely restoring the stolen antique to its grateful legitimate owners.

Nowadays, antiques are the big – read mega-galactic – new currency. Drugs and arms sales are still joint leaders, but only just. Antique fraud is closing fast on the rails. Greed is powered by everybody – terrorists, politicians, Customs and Excise, Inland Revenue taxmen, governments, international auction houses, you, me. Most of all, though, it's the absence of honesty. We all have eyes to love the delectable antiques they see, but they're paid eyes. Paid but loving. And that means hired, because money cancels love. We pretend it can't, but it does.

Since every antique worth the name's on the hit list, the world clearly needs seekers after stolen antiques. Scotland Yard's Fine Art and Antiques Squad is largely impotent. Oh, statistics emerge now and then, to claim that three per cent of stolen antiques get recovered, but who knows? Answer: nobody. Even I get blamed for the world's pandemic of antiques theft, for God's sake. That's *really* scraping the barrel for the lees of logic. You want the truth? Great Britain alone has 16,000 lovely Anglican churches – and lets one get battered, robbed, pillaged, *every four hours*! It can't be me alone, right? You see, crime pays. Less than twenty per cent of our police forces have art and antiques fraud squads, so what chance has holiness? (Incidentally, that 'squads' is a laugh – they're mostly one bloke each in a dusty nook; Scotland Yard's entire mob is two.)

People place some reliance (note how carefully I worded that?) on the Art Loss Register. Others swear by LaserNet. I swear *at* both. You pay a fee to see if anybody's reported as stolen that antique you want to buy. They collect records of antique thefts. Auction houses joke along with their Thesaurus system. Why joke? Well, you just try matching any ten catalogue descriptions with the objects they purport to describe, and you'll finish up in tears of laughter, or worse. It's hit or miss. Like the Council for the Prevention of Art Theft, they're new and blundersome losers against impossible odds.

But SAPAR is different. For a start, it's not listed in any antiques glossy. No list of subscribers, in no phone book. Its employees are practically ghosts. I know antique dealers who've been in the business quarter of a century who believe there's no such incognito mob. If it hadn't been for an utter fluke – making love to a SAPAR hunter's missus on the hoof – I'd never have spotted Gerald. Having his wife along with him for cover, and giving me a lucky lift, was possibly the one mistake he'd made in his life as a hunter. I just hoped I'd shaken him off.

Three-forty in the morning, I made the lane past Almira's country house. I drove on, collected my wits, had a prophylactic pee against a tree, put the car off the verge in the wood, and walked silently to the gate and down towards the house.

You can never return. Nobody ever can. It's one of my infallible rules. Call in at your old school, see the playing fields where you scored that super goal . . . Mistake: the place is a housing estate. Visit your old church? Hopeless: it's derelict, tramps lighting fires in the vestry. Detour through your old neighbourhood, all heartaching nostalgia? Don't: it's a biscuit factory. Slink, like now, through a French grove towards the holiday home of a lady you awoke night after day for yet more unbridled lust? Error cubed. Even if it's to nick your own passport, get the hell out. Returning is wrong.

My other infallible mistake is to disregard my own rules.

The house seemed still. A high-powered motor stood on the moonlit forecourt. So good old Paulie was here, doubtless boring somebody stiff as usual. No other cars. Was Almira's at Marc the Nark's cottage, watched over by his pair of hounds? I stared at the place for a few minutes, dithering.

The way in, which I'd planned during my drive, was through the rear. The ground sloped up towards the road above at quite a steep angle. It was as if the house was sunk into the earth that side, leaving the front standing free. Split levels always help burglars. They're easier to climb, which means less of a drop if you have to escape fast.

No balconies, though, except one looking south towards the lake, so it wasn't all beer and skittles. Drainpipes, rough stone with crevices. I used the old drainpiper's trick of filling my pockets with a variety of stones from the ground. Find a space where the mortar's missing, you can slot a stone in to serve as a mini-foothold. I smiled as I started up. 'Swarmers', as the antiques trade calls cat burglars, are mostly slick. Some I know would have already done the job and been at the Dover crossing by now. The roof over the main bedroom was only ten feet up. But being cowardly does no harm.

Quiet, careful, I climbed. My belt I'd removed and tied round my neck for a good handhold if I came across any hooks. I must say, when I'm scared I'm quite good. I honestly think I could have made quite a decent living at burgling.

The roof astonished me by being more of a problem than the wall. Can you credit it? Up there, spread-eagled on a slope of tiles formed like a rough earthenware sea, I found myself baffled, thinking, what the hell do I do now?

Then I remembered the fanlight. It had figured largely in my daring plan. Never closed, it showed the night sky to anyone gazing obliquely up from the bed. I'd learned that. I began edging across towards the moon's reflection that defined the window. Odd, I could smell cigarette smoke. I halted.

Was somebody kipping, or not kipping at all, in Almira's bedroom? Having a smoke? I heard, definitely heard, a man clear his throat. A resounding *yes*! I was stymied.

Choice reared its aggravating head. If the bloke inside was Paul the wimp, it would hardly matter. I could simply walk in, scavenge my passport and off out of it. He was a drink of water, and I'm not. But what if I walked confidently in to find some mauler waiting for me on, say, Marimee's orders? Did Paul smoke? Oh, Christ. I'd forgotten.

Within arm's reach of the louvre window, and nowhere to go. Daft to slither across to silhouette my head against the moonlit sky. Bedrooms? Three others, I knew. What the hell was the bloke doing sleeping in Almira's bed when the other guest bedrooms were all free? Surely they were?

And the light came on, blinding me. I almost yelped with fright and cringed, terrified reflexes trying to shrink me into invisibility on the roof. I could be seen by anyone in the woods above the house.

'Katta.'

Paul's voice. Katta? Who the . . . ? *Katta*? Cissie's Continental maid. No good staying baffled. I had to risk something, or stay treed for good on Almira's damned tiles. Two silent shifts, and I slo-o-o-owly peered over the edge. Obliquely, safer now the bedroom was brighter lit than my heavenly space, I looked down. Onto Paul and Katta.

He was in paradise. I've been there, and knew instantly a million things I'd only ever guessed at. Until now. Katta's vast naked form was kneeling beside him. Him supine, she hugely tumescent, working away, her head raising and lowering like a feeding animal's. His hand was on her nape, his other cupping her pendulously swinging breast. His neck muscles were straining taut as he arched, striving towards the bliss that is oblivion. She was laughing. How she managed to, God knows. Her hands were on his hips, pinning him to the bed. It was a rape, a gift, Katta's enormous fatness rocking flabbily over the recumbent man. I've made it sound repellent, I suppose, but it was beautiful. Poets should have been there. Was it the contrast, her spreading flesh and his lean length? Or the fascinating incongruity of Katta's unbelievable mass seeming to chew him into docility? Or her shaking with laughter while he soared towards detumescence —?

A car door slammed nearby, and another. Footsteps scrunged gravel, and voices spoke casually down on the forecourt.

And I hadn't heard a thing, so engrossed by the lovely scene on the bed. I froze, couldn't for the life of me look away.

'. . . have six or seven of them staking it out,' a bloke's voice pontificated.

'If that's enough. You know what he's like, Jervis,' Almira countered. 'I have the key.'

'Not really,' Jervis said. A good try at wry humour. 'You two *should* be able to advise!'

'Don't be offensive.' Jingle of keys, sound of a lock. 'Always the politician, Jay.'

'It has its advantages, my dear.'

Katta heard the door, quickly lifted her head, mechanically wiped her mouth using the back of her hand. She rose with the strange nimbleness of the gross, evaded Paul's agonized, stretching hand, and trotted from my sight. Paul groaned, covered himself, put the bedside light off. I ducked away. God, I felt his deprivation, poor sod. Robbed, a second from ecstasy.

And that was everything. I thought for quite a few moments, up there on the moonlit tiles.

You see, I'd glimpsed Katta's face as she'd lifted her mouth, spitting away joy unbounded, and it was wrong. Her face wasn't right. Oh, it was Katta, sure. But her expression should have been anxiety, worry at being discovered, what the neighbours would think, et familiar cetera.

It hadn't been any of those. It had been utter shock, almost fear.

The sort of revelation that tells all, especially about whom she's suddenly so scared of walking in through the door.

When she'd heard the last of Almira's sentence and Jervis's rejoinder as they'd opened the front door, she'd been halfway across the carpet. *And her swift fright had instantly evaporated.* She'd even turned, given Paul a charming rueful smile, blowing his tormented features a kiss from a mouth suddenly formed into an exaggerated tantalizing pout. Katta had slipped out of the room much calmer than she'd shot away from their love-bed. So she'd been frightened to death of someone finding her and Paul – then suddenly not given a damn when the intruders were merely Almira and Jervis. How come?

It took me quite a while to escape from there, passportless. I didn't care. I was almost pleased with life, as I made it back to the car and drove back to the trunk-road service station, to wait for the golden pair to come.

They captured me while I was having some grub in the self-service. The swine didn't let me finish it, either.

CHAPTER TWENTY

'Lovejoy.'

Here he came, Narval the Throttler, plonking himself down opposite, extermination in mind. God, but he had the most electric eyes you ever did see. Killer's eyes, staring, seeing only their own madness. She stood hands on hips, looking for a surfboard and a beach. Why did she have marks on her arms?

'Kee.' I had a mouthful. 'What sort of a name's that?'

'G.U.Y.' The girl was cool, languid in a warning kind of way. Bored witless. She'd be at least as much trouble as Kee. I spelled the name to myself. Guy. He was Guy, say Kee. 'Guy Solon. S.O.L.O.N.'

'Up and come, Lovejoy. Now.'

'Right.' I seized a fragment of grub, and upped and went.

'You're in trouble,' Guy said conversationally. 'Veronique'll explain.' This made him laugh, a whine interrupted by giggles that never made it. I felt in sore need of allies. Mercy Mallock?

'Trouble,' she said, laughing too. We were so cheery.

'Who from?'

'A high-ranking officer.' Veronique looked at me. I was shocked. Her eyes were a vigorous blue, so bright they seemed illumined from within. Standing beside this pair of clones as Guy unlocked his motor I felt like the coalman. I'm never well turned out at the best of times. After my climbing efforts, no wonder Veronique's gorgeous radiant orbs scored me as a tramp.

'Someone with standards, eh?' I prompted. They only laughed. Their brittle merriment was getting me down. I hoped it wouldn't last. I longed for Lilian's seductibility, even Gerald's anxious friendliness. (No, cancel that. No hunters, please.)

We took off in a Grand Prix start. Whiplash Willie hit the road like he had seconds to live. Veronique yabbered into some phone while I tried to find the seat belt, seemingly a triumphant account of their recapture of some wayward nerk. I tore my eyes off her. She sat in the rear seat. I was lodged perilously beside Guy. No wonder he was on a permanent high, with a bird like her. But how to keep such a creature? You'd have to be the world's greatest powerhouse of excitement, handsome, constant dynamite, rich. I glanced at Guy and sighed. He seemed all of those things. We ripped through France, two deities and a scruff.

And made Troude, and the place we were going to collect the antique silver from. Sometimes, absolutely nothing is true. Ever noticed? This was one of those times.

It was a garden party. I was astonished, then embarrassed, then mortified. Talk about wealth.

'Welcome, Lovejoy!' Troude greeted me with such calm pleasure I could have sworn it was nearly genuine. He advanced across the grass beckoning waitresses and acolytes. 'So glad you could make it!' He did his merry twinkle. 'Your wanderlust is cancelled, Lovejoy. Henceforth, adhere to the schedule.'

'Henceforth I shall, thither,' I promised. He said schedule the English way, 'sh', not the American 'sk'.

The enormous mansion wore lawns like skirts extending in all directions. Groves, garden statues, pools, small summerhouses, it looked a playground. Primary colours everywhere. The house itself was regal, symmetrical, balustrades, wide stone steps up to a magnificent walk. I'd thought Versailles was somewhere else. Or maybe France has a lot of them knocking about.

The guests were even more ornate. They looked as if they'd brought summer with them. No rain on their parade, thank you. Cocktail dresses the norm. From there, every lady zoomed upward in extravagance, Royal Ascot without the horses. I looked at a statue of a discus-thrower. I could have sworn he was breathing, put it down to imagination. I was nervous in case I was going to cop it for going missing.

'Now, Lovejoy! None of your famous bashfulness!' he chirruped. A glass appeared in my hand, cold as charity, moisture on the bowl. Ancient Bohemian glass, too. Beyond belief. (Watch out for modern Bohemian fakes – they are our current epidemic. The best are vases, costing half a year's average wage if genuine, the price of a railway snack if fake. Sixteen inches tall, ornate damson-coloured vases engraved with forests and deer, they're basically a tall lidded cylinder on a stem, such a deep colour it'll look almost black. Sinners buy these fake Bohemians, then sell them at country auctions as genuine.)

'Come and meet some of our visitors!' Troude was saying. 'You've already met Veronique and Guy, I see!' He chuckled, introduced me to a charming couple from Madagascar who had a yacht. 'Lovejoy hates sailing,' Troude told them. 'Though his next movie's about a shipping disaster.' He glanced at me in warning. 'That wasn't confidential information, Lovejoy, was it?'

'No, it wasn't.' It also wasn't information.

'Lovejoy's company has four wholly-owneds in LA,' Troude said, smiling. 'He changes their names on a weekly basis!'

The couple from Madagascar laughed. Troude laughed. God, but I wished we'd jack it in and stop laughing. Even Monique, among a crowd of admirers, was laughing. I looked again. That discus-thrower really had actually breathed. Laughing too? Here came Paulie and Almira. How close were they, really?

'Lovejoy.'

'Wotcher.' God, I hated Paulie's name, the swine. I couldn't help scanning the garden party for Katta. Difficult to hide anybody that fat. 'Almira.'

'Hello, darling,' from Almira, on edge but laughingly. 'Sorry I had to dash. But you got here!' She was exquisite in a stunning flared dress of magnolia, usual among this slender clique. And she was getting away with high heels, when the other women had gone for less rakish footwear. I'd have been proud of her, if I hadn't noticed her husband Jervis Galloway, MP, deep in conversation among a gathering of colourfuls. Nobody introduced me. It was Diana's paramour Jay, all right. When I drifted his way I got deflected. The statue breathed again.

'Come, Lovejoy!' Troude was affability itself, steering me round, introducing me, saying I was here to finance movie deals with Italian money. I kept my wits about me, saying the deal was for five movies and all that. I clammed up when people asked who'd star in them, said that was still being negotiated.

'He's cagey!' Troude laughed. The people laughed. Even I laughed. And now a statue of The Three Graces, naked women embracing, breathed. And a zephyr gently moved their hair.

'The movie industry's crazy,' I laughed, to laughter.

Talk, chatter in the golden sun, Veronique and Guy being delight-edly admired strolling in their magnificent world, everybody loving or lusting after Monique – more sedately dressed than the others, dark green with silver jewellery. And Marimee there, looking not quite at attention. An orchestra played soft airs in a wrought-iron pagoda. Lully? Something that way on. Everything was superficial, no digging deep for motive or disgorging woes. It was so beautiful it troubled me.

I sought out my Madagascar couple. They looked ready for the Olympics. Everybody was gold and gorgeous. I felt sick. They wanted to talk about yachting, sails and motor engines, races I'd never heard of. He was a friend of the Algerian couple, the man explained, brought into this syndicate by the Mexican couple. I wondered, was it one per nation? If no, I was superfluous, seeing Almira'd fetched hubby J for Jervis. They liked the idea, they told me, surreptitiously lowering their voices. I said I did, too. They asked me how long it would take. I asked from what to what. From start to finish, they asked. I liked their intensity – first time anybody had stopped laughing – but said it depended on how soon we got started.

'Can I take him away?' Troude begged, just as I'd noticed that the shadows cast by the sun hadn't moved, though the trees in the distance had glided quite a foot or two along the background of the orchestra's summerhouse. How come?

'See you later,' I smiled, going with him. I looked at the grass. It was non-grass. Pretty good fake, but definitely bud.

We headed for the house. Was this whole dump some sort of film studio? A set? I looked forward to getting inside to see if it was real or just a giant doll's house that turned continually to face the sun just like its garden. A mansion house that stays put while its gardens swivels is in deep trouble.

The house felt real, lovely and genuine. I keep saying how a house responds when you step in through the door. It susses you out and thinks, who's this newcomer? If it likes you, it welcomes you. If not, then you'll never be happy there. It's a person, is a house. Be polite to it. I silently commiserated with it for losing its real garden, in exchange for a look-alike turntable phoney lawn plonked on top. Maybe their antique silver was here.

Marimee was there before us. 'Lovejoy did well with the cover story,' he said. 'Lovejoy will receive sanction for the default.'

Default? Sanction? He meant mistaking my – no, his – assistants. I nodded, received a grateful glance from Troude. Monique came with Guy and Veronique. We reached a conservatory facing a walled yard with roses and trellised arches.

'Nice.' I broke the ice. 'If only it'd stay still.'

Troude smiled. No laughs now, tension in the air. Maybe they too were to be sanctioned for letting me escape?

'Why did you return, Lovejoy?'

'Ah.' Why? I'd got clean away, then come back to find my pursuers. I should have thought this one out, quick. 'I'd no passport. I owed it to the memory . . .' I caught myself, cleared my throat. Start again. 'I promised somebody I'd help.'

Marimee nodded, one curt sharp depression of the chin to signify approval. For him that was a flag day.

'It is safe to speak here,' he said. He stood facing, legs apart, back to the window. 'Here we plan the robbery. Here we decide the fate of the valuables. Here we allocate duties.'

'Here we will say what you're up to?' I put in. Troude did an appealing look, the sort he was now starting to nark me with.

'Silence!' Monique said. It cracked like a whip, shutting me up. What fascinated me was it also clammed Marimee.

She walked to face us. I noticed Marimee made way for her, and it wasn't politeness. She boss, him corporal.

'The brigandage is already decided,' she said. Bland's the nearest I can come to, for her attitude. Nobody could possibly dispute the number of the Number 7 bus, her tone informed us. 'The *projet* is fixed. There will be two rehearsals only.'

'Here?' I asked again, thinking of those statues and the rotating gardens. 'Only, isn't it a simple export job?'

'That silver story was a lie to get you here, Lovejoy.'

Cool. It had worked. I was undeniably here.

'You have objections?' Like asking if I had a coat somewhere.

'Yes. Ignorance, mainly. What do we nick, and where from?' Note that I didn't ask why. 'And who's in the way?'

'Details,' Monique said, with a smile like an ice floe. 'Others see to details, Lovejoy.'

And she walked off. Veronique stepped aside, proving to be in the way, taut, her hatred glinting like distant spears. Not all friends, then, amid this much laughter.

Leaving us. 'There will be three stages,' Marimee clipped out. 'Stage Three the robbery. Stage Two rehearsal. That is all.'

'Eh?' I was blank. 'Two from three leaves one. You missed out Stage One.'

Marimee's moustache lifted in what might have been incipient mirth. 'That is you, Lovejoy. You buy.'

'Buy what?'

'Antiques.' He made me sound thick.

The others were looking. Troude was trying to elbow me gently from the conservatory.

'What with? From where? What sort?' I got mad, yelled, 'I've no frigging money!'

Marimee paused, eyed me with utter disgust. 'Imbecilic peasant,' he said scathingly, and strutted grandly on his way.

'Come, Lovejoy,' Troude said gently. 'Let's go.'

'Where to, for Christ's sake?' I was so dispirited. I wanted to go home.

He patted my shoulder. 'You're the antiques divvy, Lovejoy. Wherever you say, but mostly Paris. Guy, Veronique.'

On the way out I saw Katta, demurely waiting on in black

waitress garb beneath an awning. I looked her way, waved once. She smiled, I swallowed, thinking of her luscious wet mouth in action, managed to smile back. Paulie and Almira were talking near the orchestra. Pity Cissie wasn't here too, I thought without a single pang. This was the sort of do she always enjoyed, as long as she had somebody to ballock for doing the wrong thing In Company, a terrible crime in her book. Maybe she was here? In spirit, some people might say. Not me.

Jervis looked away when I passed quite near him. As we left the eating-drinking-laughing cheeriness, I glanced back to see if Katta was just watching Paul or actually doing something. And saw the house from a new angle. It stayed in my mind. I've a good memory for pictures. I'd seen it before, or some place very like it. And it wasn't any country mansion, not then. It was heap big business, the sort a low-grader like me would never even get within a mile of. In some advert? Yes, sort of definitely.

Until then, I'd not known what to believe. I mean, soon I've got to tell you about international antiques robbers, and I will. But so far I'd been thinking along the lines of, well, those dozens of St Augustine's sermons, AD 400 or thereabouts, discovered in the Mainz public library. Priceless, easy to nick, pass them off at any customs border post as boring old committee minutes, and make a mint. Especially apt, since that French historian uncovered them on that dusty German shelving in 1991. Something like that. Now, though? Now I knew it was no bundle of ancient 'crackle', as parchments are known in the trade.

'Shall I drive, Guy?' I said. 'Race you to the scam, eh?'

'*Merde!*' he said rudely. 'I cross the border in one hour! You'd take a week!'

'Only joking.' Which meant Switzerland, of course. I'd been too dim to work it out. We were going to do the Freeport International Repository.

Inside I laughed, and laughed, and laughed. Some jokes are too good to ignore.

CHAPTER TWENTY-ONE

Paris is beautiful. I mean it. Oh, the traffic's noisy – everybody's water-cooled motor horns on max for no reason – and a city's but a city. Yet it surprised me. Small. I'd expected something massive like, say, New York or London. Paris gets to you by cleverly putting all its bits within reach. Unbelievably, it's a walker's city. And its charm isn't synthetic polyurethane gloss; it's natural. Sweet yet protein, so to speak.

They, my golden pair, booked us in at a small hotel by the simple process of screeching to a heart-in-the-gob stop at the front door and strolling in, ready to remonstrate with whoever came forward to remonstrate. The booking-in process wore me out. Guy remonstrated, Veronique remonstrated in a crosstalk act straight from music hall. I got an upstairs room. There were only about fifteen rooms in the whole place.

Nothing to unpack, I opened the window and was captivated. The famed Paris skyline really truly exists! Jumbled roofs, chimneys, windows with tiny balconies. Church spires here and there, television aerials, wires, a splash of washing, pots flowering on sills, now and again a flat roof, an old man having a sly kip, children skipping to some chant. Beautiful. I turned, smiling, and jumped. Veronique was standing silently behind me. I hoped she wasn't one of those steal-thies.

'What do you see, Lovejoy?'

'Eh?' She looked sullen, brittler than usual, narked as hell. 'Never been before, love. Didn't know what to expect –'

'Decadent enough for you, Paris?'

A glance out showed me the same charm. A woman across the way was seeing to her pretty window box. 'Looks fine. I'd thought skyscrapers, black glass boxes filled with bankers –'

'Decadence!' She glared past me. 'It needs thorough cleansing, Lovejoy! Of parasites that drag her down.'

Well, there's not a lot you can say to this gunge. I'd been wondering how far it was to Monet's garden, but didn't risk asking while she was in this black mood. I couldn't see many parasites, but no good arguing with a bird.

'You don't see, do you?' Baffled, I started to edge past her into the room. 'The tourist's vision.' She spoke hate-filled.

'Look, Veronique. We're tired. That hell of a drive –'

She grabbed me and with ominous strength dragged me to stand looking across the street. 'Calm? Tranquil, Lovejoy? Pretty? Can you see Notre Dame from here?'

'Dunno.' I was only trying to be helpful, please the silly cow, but she started to shake.

'You know what I see, Lovejoy? I see unemployment – French jobs stolen by foreigners! They pour in to bleed our money, give nothing back! To France: The Last Land Before the Sea!'

'Really?' Polite, I managed not to yawn. These days it's politically upright to grouse about this kind of thing.

'Unemployment! Misery, resentment! You think you have strikes across the Channel? Not like we have strikes! We have more grievances! Recently, every French port was closed. Nurses on strike this week, all public transport in France next. Farmers riot. Our . . .' She struggled over the word, spat as she said it: ' . . . autobahns are blocked by fighting lorry drivers. The airports are in uproar, barricades everywhere. Pretty, the view?'

'Yes,' I said simply, because it was.

'You are determined to be stupid.' She let go, stepped away. I'd been close enough to be intrigued by the faint division across her hairline, but looked away.

'I can't understand,' I suggested lamely, but thinking, what does a girl this lovely want to wear a wig for? 'I think France is bonny. Political things blow over. They always do.'

'We French sink under a morass of foreigners! Frenchness is losing its identity. You know Romanian roulette, Lovejoy?'

'Russian?'

'Fool! Romanian immigrants here market imported Romanian women! Thousands are shipped in each year! It's *obscene!*'

She sounded likely to kill anybody who disagreed. I hesitated. Change the nationality, you can collect a million such moans in any bar anywhere in the world. Every nation's at it, same old grumbles against governments, changes, taxes. It signifies nothing. I can't honestly see the point of shoving the clock back to some Good Old Days. We all know they never existed. What *was* wrong with France? I thought it superb, fetching, full of interest. They even have a Mushroom Museum in the Loire Valley. Ever since Louis the Fourteenth the Sun King ordered mushrooms, France has –

'It's a pity,' I tried soothing. She was still trembling. Was it rage? 'But there's nothing you can do.'

She smiled a crooked smile, oblique with vile meaning. Her hand stroked my face. I didn't like it – unusual, this – and drew away. 'Oh, yes there is, babee,' she said.

Just then Guy called from the next room, and she left. I shivered as the door closed. I never have a watch, so I had to estimate a lapse of five minutes. I went and knocked.

'It's only me,' I said to the handle.

Veronique opened, let the door swing while she returned to the bed. Guy was sprawled out of his skull, warbling incomprehensibly. She was already naked, reeling. On the bedside table, a couple of tinfoils, spilled white powder, a tiny mirror, a syringe. A smarting pong filled the air. She was giggling as she tumbled spread-eagle over Guy, whose hands moved over her. I swallowed, backed out.

'Sorry,' I stammered. *'Excusez-moi, s'il vous plaît.'*

'Come back, Lovejoy!' Veronique carolled. They erupted in laughter as I meekly crept away. 'I can handle two!'

Aye, I thought, shaken. I'd only gone to see if they'd mind if I went for a stroll. Druggies. I had two crazed junkies on my hands. The charming skyline of roofs, all colours and textures, was still there. It was coming dusk. I stood at my window to watch it. The distant roar of traffic reassured me that this aerial stillness was founded on the brisk bustling life of a stunning city below. Just my frigging luck, I thought bitterly. My exquisite assistants were zooming deranged through some stratosphere powered by illegal chemical toxins. The gentle 'antique silver' job had become a major scam, with loony political overtones, and I was no longer a mere courier. I was the main player. Which told me what Colonel Marimee's logic would be if the enterprise plunged to failure – I'd cop it. Guy and Veronique would blame me, of course. The pattern was already established by the Sweet episode. Marimee had promised me sanctions and penalties, all because that golden pair had been late. Hindsight, blindsight.

This scam had a bad odour. I needed a friendly face, the sort I was used to. The kind, in fact, I could depend on for absolute unreliability. I went for a walk on my own authority, to clear the cobwebs and mentally pick my way through a selection of friends back in East Anglia.

Paris has it. Really, honestly has it. Oh, I'd slowly become aware that France looks with a vague – sometimes not so vague – mistrust at its capital, same as Italians regard Rome. But she has a quality to life, and quality's rare. And never cheap.

Bravely risking all, I had a coffee in a small nosh bar. The people chatted, smoked. The traffic snarled away outside. Lights were showing. Rain was coming on. You get a kind of osmosis in such places. Even before you know the layout, nostalgia seeps in and you start remembering things you never even knew, about streets, names of squares, statues and buildings. That you've never seen them before hardly matters. They stroll alive out of your subconscious. God knows how they got there in the first place, but that's unimportant. It's the way civilization is. It pervades, doesn't need highlighting.

With some surprise, I noticed how mixed a folk the Parisians were. And the accents! Becoming attuned to cadence, I was now able to pick out some differences. And the garb! There seemed a number of North Africans about – or was I wrong, and they were older inhabitants than most? I definitely heard a snatch of Arabic. The serving lad sounded Greek, and two artisans covered in a fine dust were Italians. A cosmopolitan city.

Grinning like an ape – smiles are never wasted, when you're a stranger in a strange land – I left, walked down to the corner. Greatly daring, I returned and walked to the other corner. Quite a large square, two trees barely managing, some seats, a couple of cafés. Starry Starry Night, with some minuscule motors occasionally racing through and vehicles parked in improbable spots. I stood a minute, rehearsing school words, then went for it and triumphantly bought some notepaper and envelopes. I was really narked that the serving lady served me without noticing my huge cultural achievement. I sat and scribbled a letter home. A wave of homesickness swamped me, but I stayed firm and finished it.

Then I went out, found a pay phone, painstakingly followed the directory-enquiries saga. The phones are quite good in France, unlike everywhere else except Big Am. I got through the trunk dialling in one, to my utter astonishment. Even phoning the next village is enough to dine out on in East Anglia, and here I was –

'Hello? Can I speak to Jan Fotheringay, please?'

'Who is it?' The same bird, Lysette.

'Lovejoy. It's very urgent. Hurry, please.'

'He's resting.' God, she was on the defensive. I might have been . . . well, whoever.

'Listen, Lysette. I'm on Jan's side. He knows that.'

By the time he came on I was frantic, seconds ticking away. 'Jan? Lovejoy. Jan, if I ask for you to come to France, as translator, adviser, whatever, will you?'

'I'm still not mobile, Lovejoy.' He sounded worn out. Just when I needed the lazy self-pitying malingering sod. Aren't folk selfish?

'Jan. It's serious. You know it is, and getting worse by the hour. You won't be allowed to survive. I won't either. Mania stalks out here, mate.' I gave him a second, and yelled for a decision. The pillock, buggering about when I was . . . 'Eh?'

'You're right, Lovejoy. Where?'

The hotel, I told him, but he'd have to come immediately because I'd probably be there for only a day or two more. I'd leave some message if he didn't quite make it in time. Like a fool, I babbled profuse thanks as the line cut. For God's sake, I was trying to save him too, wasn't I? I seethed indignation thinking about it.

My second call took longer, but fewer words. I said there was a letter in the post, containing my best guesses. 'Positively no obligation,' I finished lamely, the salesman's lying assurance. 'Help me, pal.' I tried to limit the pause, but it went on and on until my voice got it together. 'Please,' it managed. What a lousy rotten word that is.

Hoteltime. Maybe by now my golden pair would be unstoned. Did people say destoned, or is that what you do to plums? How long did junkies take to come down? I really needed Mercy Mallock, sort these sods out with her karate.

There are occasional non-French motors around in Paris. So I wasn't at all concerned when a car bearing a striking resemblance to Gerald Sweet's motor trundled out of the square as I moved away from the phone by the two trees. I mean, a car is a car, right? I was so definitely unconcerned that I made a long detour, just proving how casual I was.

Back in the hotel, I showed me and the world that Lovejoy was cool by peering down from the window at the passing cars for at least three hours before turning in. I didn't switch the light off, because I'd not switched it on. Good heavens, can't tourists tour? I'd known the Sweets were heading for Paris, hadn't I? So they were here, exactly as expected. So what? God, but my mind's ridiculous. Sometimes it gets on my nerves, bothering me hour after hour with inessentials. I didn't sleep that night.

Seven o'clock, I was downstairs in a panic having that nonbreakfast breakfast they give you, one measly crescentic pastry and a cup of coffee. It was urgent to do something in antiques that looked really legitimate, even if it never is.

Which means auctions. It's practically the definition.

CHAPTER TWENTY-TWO

Roused, bathed, and having conquered the breakfast charade, I strolled the morning streets until Veronique and Guy came at a run and we embarked on our impending spree.

'Did the Colonel say how much money we had to blue?' I asked, but only got shrieks of laughter.

'We must avoid the Parisian winds,' Veronique said at my look. Her coat was heavy, its high collar surprising. 'Paris has only wind tunnels. London's chaotic streets give protection.'

If she said so. I thought it mild if fresh. Guy thought of nothing but his next tumbleweed and roaring his motor through impossible thoroughfares. I'd never met a bloke like him for getting off the starting grid. We'd no sooner walked round the corner than he was in his motor, revving like the maniac he was.

'Antique shops were sprinkled about the arrondissements, Lovejoy,' Veronique explained, her head wobbling and jerking as she tried to talk against the lunatic's darting accelerations between delivery vans. 'An arrondissement's a Paris district, with a mayor, a town hall as you call it, everything. They're numbered in a spiral on maps, from centre outwards.'

'Which one has the antiques?' There should be a special nook in heaven for the bloke who invented roofs for motor cars. And one in hell for the bloke who took them off.

'Sixth. I think', she added, managing to sound dry, 'near the Luxembourg Gardens.' Women nark me. It was clearly my fault, I'm not French.

'There are true antique shops, Lovejoy, and *brocanteurs*.' Guy screeched a mad screech at the word.

'*Brocanteurs* are what you call junk shops, second-handers.'

'Have you a big flea market, love?' I tried to explain Petticoat Lane, Portobello Road, but she was there ahead of me.

'That's where we're going, not your posh shops. *The Marché aux puces*. On Saturdays to Mondays, bargains galore.' Her dryness reached sarcasm.

'Turn back,' I said after a momentary think, which at Guy's speed meant a least a million miles out of our way. 'The sixth arrondissement, please. No dross today.'

'No, Lovejoy,' Veronique said. 'We've got a planned sequence.'

'Do as you're frigging well told,' I said, all quiet and quite calm. 'And tell your frigging loon to do the same.'

You can't muck about when it's antiques-time, and I'd had enough of her dryth and his mania. I wasn't here by choice. I wanted out of their daft unknowable scam. The only exit was by doing my job, then lam off leaving them to it.

She stared at me over her shoulder. '*What?*' Guy actually shouted in astonishment, so loud that pedestrians turned to look.

'You heard.' We screeched to a stop at some traffic lights. Guy revved his engine, Fangio on song.

'Lovejoy,' Veronique said, tight-lipped in the erotic way women show fury in public. 'You will obey orders.'

'Ta-ra, love.' That's the advantage of a bucket seat. You can spring lightly – or even clumsily – into the churning snarling honking Paris traffic, at risk of life and limb, if you're feeling specially suicidal, or even fed up.

Guy swore incomprehensibly, Veronique shrieked warnings, threats too I daresay. The traffic crescendoed to deafen the city. But I was free, and off down a side street like a ferret. It seemed to have no motors in it, by some extraordinary Parisian oversight. I walked a bit, looked back. No sign of Veronique, nor Guy. Nor his motor, thank God. A bloke passed me trundling a handbarrow, which cheered me. Reality was about.

Without any idea of where exactly I was, I found a nosh bar and tried to negotiate something to eat. The stout man seemed surprised to be asked for a lash-up so early in the morning, but responded well. It's really being served with eagerness. Back home you get a surly uncooperative grunt like in Woody's cafe, but this man seemed really pleased. He did me some scrambled eggs – he'd no real notion about kippers on account of my language barrier – and some hot sliced meat I didn't recognize, some eccentric jam, an astonishing variant of tea, toast by the ton, and some hot cylindrical bread things. After, I asked for some vegetable soup with more of his scalding bread sticks, then some cake (cold; I insisted on *froid*, non *chaud*). He turned out to be good on cakes. I had four small ones, then slices of a big dark monster with embedded fruit. He brought his missus out to see. She tried giving me some red wine, really weird this hour in the morning. She understood with regret that wine, to me, came *après* tea o'clock. She pondered – which you do gesticulating volubly in Paris – then brightened, and brought out some liqueur. I had to accept it, but slung it into my tea to dilute the stuff. I took a few cakes for the road, and paid. We all rejoiced.

We even shook hands, more oddity. In East Anglia you shake hands with your new brother-in-law and that's it for life. Still, when in Rome. I felt fit at last. No sign of my helpers, all to the good.

Taxi at the main road, and I was on my way to Antiquaires, wherever that was.

'Louvre des Antiquaires, Monsieur,' the driver explained.

'*C'est* it,' I agreed. '*Merci, Monsieur.*'

He told me more, but I wasn't exactly sure what. If I'd had enough words, I'd have asked him to hang about, take me to the sixth arrondissement later on, but decided to quit while I was winning. I'd escaped from my assistants and had breakfast. No good pushing my luck. It was about eleven o'clock when he dropped me off on the Rue St-Honoré, with warnings about the prices antique dealers charge. I said ta, unworried. I knew all about those.

The building wasn't old as such, and looked restored. Quite a crowd was streaming in. I joined them, milling with increasing optimism. It seemed nothing less than a huge antiques emporium, with some two hundred-plus antique dealers stacked three levels high. I was astonished to see notices advertising afternoon lectures on antiques, illustrated no less. There was an exhibition of French end-of-century dress and jewellery. I'd never seen the like in my life. Did French antique dealers actually *want* their customers to learn, appreciate, the antiques that they had to pay through the nose for? They'd go berserk at this sacrilegious idea back home. What a place!

A beautiful feeling enveloped me. I stood against a wall, eyes closed, savouring the loveliness of antiques to come. How much did Colonel Marimee say I could spend? The thrilling answer: *he hadn't!* So I could go on until Guy and Veronique caught up and stopped me. *That meant as much as I liked!* I went giddy. If it wasn't for antiques, God would have a hard time, same as me. Luckily, faith scrapes it together and forms a quorum, but only just.

'Monsieur?' Some gallant moustachioed custodian touched my arm, asked if I was well.

'*Très bon, Monsieur, merci,*' I said. I was too overcome to explain about Paradise. A doorway instruction sheet promised that all the antique dealers were professionals keen to settle the hash of Customs, give certificates where appropriate, and could arrange shipment to anywhere against a fee.

Hang the cost, I thought, somebody else is paying! And sailed into bliss.

Money has a lot to answer for, but is never really to blame. We're the villain of the piece. Money's merit is its divine right to seduce. Never is it more seductive than when you've got plenty, plus a command to spend, spend, spend. Like being in a harem, with permission to have any bird as takes your fancy. But there's one hitch. All antiques are beautiful, alluring, but only some are honest. The rest are forgeries. See the problem? With a spend-and-be-damned bottomless purse, the urge is to simply buy everything, on the grounds that you're bound to net the genuine pieces. Yet to a purist like me that's the ultimate treachery. Why? Because you're encouraging dross.

Not only that, I thought as I stood inhaling the beeswax and varnish nectar of the first furniture dealer's showroom. Money seduces by its power, fine, but its power is almost irresistible.

Look at Italy, for instance. More funding scandals than the parson preached about, and more famous art than any nation on earth. No scandal so great as the Signorelli shambles, which is a warning about money power. Luca Signorelli was an artist who in 1499 was commissioned for 180 ducats to finish the paintings begun fifty years previously by the immortal Angelico, in the wondrous cathedral at Orvieto. Signorelli was ecstatic – he wanted to stun the authorities into awarding him their next contract, which was fresco-ing the lower part of the chapel. With exalted vision he stormed on, executing brilliant, dazzling work. He even invented new techniques – like his gold-covered wax-point underlaying to cause the reflected candle glow to shimmer when the congregation looked upwards. In other words, a masterpiece, to be preserved at all costs.

Enter weather, permeating rain, humidity, working over the centuries to despoil and erode. (Also, in 1845, a touring load of Russian nobles, who unbelievably *washed away Signorelli's dry overdrawing* on the frescos, cheerfully convinced they were improving matters.) Then – as if time, decay, and predators were not enough – enter politics.

It's not for me to complain. I'm no better than I ought to be. But honestly, when the Italian Parliament votes a special law, the '545', enabling some 300,000,000,000 lire for the care of Orvieto and Todi, arts lovers everywhere have a right to ask where it all went to, right? Not for me to ring Signora Parrino, Minister of Arts, and ask what the hell possessed her. Why *did* she lend 100 billion to a certain corporation the day *after* she'd left the post? 'Where is it now?' a baffled enthusiast asked the innocent, honest Assessore. We all know the poor bloke's reply: 'Disappeared.' How? Dunno, nobody knows anything . . . And even the sterling, upright, efficient and honest, Soprintendenza is meshed and helpless. A fraction of gelt creeps back from That Company when a fuss is raised, but the rest stays salted.

Politics always bulges the sinister corridor curtains where big money flows. The Soprintendente who raised Cain about the vanishing moneys allotted to Pompei's restoration was replaced with Byzantine alacrity. The lovely and outspoken lady who tried to ginger Venice into honesty has gone. Okay, it's politics. What I want to know is, are the priceless masterpieces stashed away in the Galleria Borghese's (permanently closed!) *quadreria* still there? Reasonable question, because the restoration money isn't, not any more. It's been disappeared, it's politics.

'Buy it, Monsieur,' I said, coming out of the trance.

'The plate, Monsieur?' The dealer was suave, polished. 'Yes. It is genuine Palissy. You observe the carefully worked snakes, and leaves of plants —'

'Not the fake, Monsieur.' His partner, a smart middle-aged lady, wore a genuine Breguet watch on her fitted jacket — you can tell them from their plainness, the matt background and narrow chapter ring showing up the plain hands superbly. 'Breguet et fils, Madame?'

'Yes,' she said, pausing uncertainly. That meant not pre-1816, but still a valuable watch.

Palissy was a Huguenot glass-painter, one of the unlucky ones. Even though the royal family patronized him, he still died in clink. When he turned to pottery, he got good whites without tin oxides. No mean feat, because you have to put on a translucent lead glaze and let the white clay underneath show through. Everybody fakes Palissy, though, except his small plates. And this was a big exotic one, but without a single chime. Fake.

'The Majorelle, Monsieur.' I smiled hello at it.

A water-lily table, little over two feet tall. Called so because it was carved literally to look like a water lily. Not truly an antique, except to avaricious Customs and Excise, who want everything older than fifty years down in their little ledgers. About 1900, Art Nouveau ran riot, basing everything on Mother Nature. It's bonny stuff, if you've the stomach, but I can't honestly take such blunt copying, however polished the tamarind and mahogany, the gilt-bronze lily buds, creepers crawling up furniture legs on to the top of the damned thing. Majorelle was a lone cabinet-maker, who knew wood. Pity he didn't go straight and make proper stuff (apologies if you're an Art Nouveau nut. Wish you better).

'To be shipped, Monsieur?' The lady was sizing me up: non-

French, a new buyer, non-haggler and pretty much unconcerned with a few percentage points here and there . . .

'My assistants will tell you, Madame, later today.' I scribbled a note for the price as marked, thanked her profusely, and withdrew. She tried catching my attention but I was off into blissland. I find it really quite easy keeping tabs on the antiques I buy. The difficulty is remembering where. I suppose women have this trouble when they're on a spending spree, except they like to scoop everything up as they go, which saves bother. But I had assistants. What did I pay them for, for heaven's sake, if not to help? I always finish up doing the donkey work. Not today.

A little over an hour, I'd bought forty-seven antiques, almost all furniture and genuine, for a fortune in IOUs. 'My assistants will be along *immédiatement*,' I carolled every time. 'Name of Solon . . .' I'd not seen a single piece of furniture that had made me queasy, in the way that Troude forgery in the Mentle clubhouse had. I felt the serenity that comes when rewakening after love. Love is moreish, same as antiques. I hurtled out from the place, collared a taxi and told him anywhere in the sixth arrondissement, starting with the very best antique shops. He was pleased, warned me darkly against the dealers. I said ta, I'd watch out, and tipped him well. He called out his warning after me. I waved, keeping an eye out for Guy and Veronique.

And plunged into the separate antique shops, not sparing the grottier *brocanteurs*. I must say, the stuff was pretty good. Oh, forgeries abounded, as always, and nothing wrong with that. Fakes provide mirth, where very often there is only weeping and gnashing of teeth. I was happy to see the usual dross of Dutch fake silver – and I *don't* mean fake Dutch silver – with its phoney marks, its duff baroque 'strapwork' so gross and unlike the real thing. You've only to see one genuine piece in any museum to be warned off it for life. Why the Dutch love faking Louis XIV silver, heaven alone knows, because they're no good at it. Electrotyping's more of a difficulty, because you do this by making a mould from an original, say a valuable bronze. You coat the copy with plumbago, as we forgers (sorry, we honest copyists) still call black lead, then sink it in a bath of electrolyte. Wire it to a chunk of copper, give it a little current, and sit back. Copper covers the copy's surface. Clue: it will be beautifully fine, deposited atom by atom, unlike the real bronze, which is rough.

The piece I came across didn't need the test, but I gave it a knuckle tap for old times' sake, and heard the tell-tale clunk instead of the lovely faint singing note of genuine bronzes. I smiled an apology to the dealer, then bought a fake painting. It was a mediaeval Madonna and Child, so say, on solid wood panel, done in the true old style. It would have fooled me but for my chest's stony silence when I touched it.

Still keeping a watch for my two nerks, I asked, 'Can I see the reverse, Monsieur?' (Please – *always* look at the back. Here's why.) It was American hickory of the sort we call pignut: very straight, coarse but lovely smooth grain. It's a beautiful elastic wood, can resist any amount of thumps. In spite of these qualities, it doesn't last, so is highly favoured by forgers for painted panels. This faker had really done his stuff – glued several small panels together to make one large one. And he'd stuck them like Theophilus did in the eleventh century, mixing quicklime and soft cheese (I really do mean cheese). Theophilus thought highly of this method, and so do I.

'I'll buy it as a fake, Monsieur,' I suggested. He was outraged, scandalized, overwhelmed, underwhelmed, and finally whelmed. I gave an IOU. My two assistants would be along . . .

There were plenty of antique shops, a few with two or three proprietors. And still no sign of my golden pair. The rest of the time I concentrated on furniture, with a few other antiques here and there. I bought an especially fine piece of fake Strasbourg faïence, but pretty old. I liked it because Strasbourg faïence was copied right from the off. (You often get the number 39 underneath, because fakers misunderstood the significance of numbering. Once you've seen the original brilliant carmine you'll never get taken in; even modern fakers can't match it.)

An hour I worked, darting quickly in and out of shops, eyes open for Guy and Veronique. Eventually I went down an alley, feeling worn out, and settled to a nosh in a busy restaurant. I sat where I could see the street.

Less than forty minutes later I was back in the shops, buying, testing, looking, sounding pieces out, rejoicing fit to burst in a way I hadn't for days. I could hardly keep myself from choking while examining furniture, on account of the robbery that was going to hit the street come nightfall. I could even pinpoint the exact shops. In fact, I returned to one and bought a Davenport drawing-room desk. I'd passed on it first time round, but saw it would be right in the robbers' firing line and probably get marmalized when the ramraiders struck. It was too bonny to die.

'Can I have it taken out of the window's sunlight, Mademoiselle?' I begged the dealer. 'Only it might fade.'

'In three hours, Monsieur?' I'd promised her my assistants would be along. But she complied.

Captain Davenport's original desk-and-chests had desktops that slid backwards to cover the chest, for use in a narrow ship's cabin. Adapted for a lady's withdrawing room, the desk surface could stay projecting, supported by pillars on a horseshoe platform. Yellow walnut, and lovely even if it was Victorian.

Which gave me time to inspect more closely the bloke pacing the pavement. A fly lad, tough, fit, earring. I hid a smile. He'd been in the Louvre des Antiquaires, then here, consulting a card list and catalogues. A dealer never misses somebody putting ticks on a catalogue. Sign of an innocent, or somebody not innocent at all. One thing about ramraiders, they're the least subtle thieves in creation.

The ramraider's one of Great Britain's exports. Just as we invented most of the world's sports, in order to lose at them in the Olympics, so we're indefatigable inventors of scams. The bluntest, not to say most aggressive, robbery in antiques is the ramraider. It's so simple it's almost beautiful. At least, it would be if it wasn't destructive.

Method: take any van – and I mean steal, nick, thieve. Weld scaffolding poles to the rear bumpers to form a battering ram. Early in the owl hours, you reverse at speed through the window of any convenient antique shop, shattering whatever protection it's got. Spill out, go straight to the antiques your sussers have previously marked on a rough sketch-plan you've learnt by heart. Load up, and be off and out of it in less than ninety seconds. Again, I do mean that quick. The London and Provincial Antiques Dealers' Association has been moaning for years about the eruption of ramraiders in the Thames Valley. The best (for best read worst) thing is that it's thieving to plan. Exactly like the art works – Van Gogh, Old Masters – in France, Holland, Germany, during the 1980s and early 1990s, it's theft by prescription. One place in Leeds got hit three times in as many weeks. I'm against ramraiders, actually, because they're pro hooligans. That is, they go straight for whatever they're told, never mind what's in the way. They'll shred any painting, mash any furniture, to reach the priceless pieces they've been sent to steal.

How did I know the lank lad with the soiled jeans and golden earring was a susser? Well, who else would pace a street of antique shops like a drum major, his lips moving as he did his phoney 'stroll'? Then, unbelievably, pause to mark the distances down! Where I come from these daredevil youths'd starve. The pillock thought himself among a load of dupes. I hadn't known the ramraiders had reached Paris, but here they undoubtedly were.

'Monsieur?'

God. I found myself shaking my head, tut-tutting audibly. I smiled apologetically at the girl. She was smart, really well turned out. I apologized. 'The traffic, Mademoiselle! I admire your Parisian drivers' skill. So fast!'

We prattled a bit. I said what splendid stock she had. She was pleased I liked it, tried to persuade me to buy some more. I told her my name, Lovejoy. Claire Fabien offered me coffee for a *merci beaucoup* and a smile. We talked of the antiques locally. I kept an edgy eye on the window, twice almost starting up as I imagined a couple of blond heads, subsiding to chat some more, false alarm. I was drawn, through no fault of my own. I realized after an hour that I should get on, hoover up more antiques, and rose to go. I hesitated.

'Look, Miss Fabien. Might I give some advice?'

'Indeed. I should be grateful from one so knowledgeable.'

'Please. Tonight, remove your antiques. To a storeroom, any borrowed pantechnicon.'

She looked at me, at the street. 'But why?'

'I have a hunch, that's all.' I said my goodbyes, telling her to be sure to give my tardy assistants a receipt.

And that was that.

I did thirty-one more shops, not counting the *brocanteurs* which had mostly duff stuff except for an orrery I picked up for a song. 'Orrery' after John Rowley made a model of the solar system for the Earl of Orrery in 1713. They look like those mobile hangings that were so popular ten years ago, except stuck on to a small stand. It was cheap, the *brocanteur* told me, because the ivory base was all bent and split to blazes. I pretended hesitation, though I was almost sure it was pre-1781 because that was the year Herschell discovered the planet Uranus and there was no sign of it on this orrery's whirlies. With an actor's reluctance, I paid him four-fifths of his asking price with a scribble. Straightening old ivory's the easiest thing in the world: steep the ivory in dilute nitric acid for some days, judging it as you go. It slowly becomes astonishingly bendable, and translucent. Gently force it into shape, then let it dry. That's all there is to it. An old orrery's worth a fortune.

Congratulating myself, I mentally thanked Paris for a marvellous day. I went and stood at the corner of the oblique X intersection of the Rue de Rennes and the Rue d'Assas. As obvious as a spare tool, it was still a full hour before Guy the Prat leapt on me, snarling. He was shaking badly, teeth a-chatter. He'd missed a dose.

'About frigging time,' I said. 'Here.' I shoved the shoal of promissories at him. 'You've an hour before they close. Better split them with Veronique or you'll miss some. See you at the hotel.'

'Lovejoy!' It was a howl. I've never seen anybody so enraged, so desperate. Across the road Veronique was shrieking abuse at a taxi and some motors trying to cut from the Luxembourg Gardens. Jesus, what a durbar. 'Come back!'

'*Bon chance*, Guy.' I strolled off with a wave, pointed to an imaginary wristwatch.

With the sun setting, shops closing, motors getting madder, the driving crazier, I sought out a restaurant and had a whale of a time noshing everything in sight. The waiters finished up laughing at me for my misunderstandings of the menu, but were thrilled at my hunger. Well, I was starving, hardly eaten a thing all day. I felt restored, made whole again from contact with lovely antiques. I drifted about the darkening city, then retired for the night. Guy and Veronique weren't back yet. Still chasing up my antiques? Or, my smile dying, catching up on their vital dosage somewhere? But the antiques had made up for everything. And not a single one had made me feel ill, though I'd seen hundreds of polished surfaces, fake, genuine, phoney, simulants, look-alikes, copies, filiations, shams, authentics twindled into double, marriages of scores, hundreds of pieces. Which makes you think that something was more than radically wrong with Colonel Marimee's scam, whatever that might be. And with Guy and Veronique's assistance, whatever that might be.

And even with Cissie's death, WTMB?

CHAPTER TWENTY-THREE

'Not *that?*' I heard myself exclaim, swiftly returning to ingratiate, 'Quite, er, splendid!'

The famous Paris auction centre is a mess. Imagine Sotheby's, Christie's, Bonhams, the rest, together in one new building like a corny copy of a provincial bank. It tried to emulate the nearby bourgeois façades. I beamed falsely at Veronique and Guy.

'It's marvellous,' Guy bragged as we approached. 'Space for four hundred cars, every-hour parking.' He would think of motor cars.

'We need antique auctions,' I reminded. I didn't want Colonel Marimee getting on at me. 'I did my bit yesterday.'

'You bastard, Lovejoy. *We* did all the work!'

'Oh, aye.' I went all laconic. 'So why'd you need me?'

He growled, his sign of wanting to land me one.

'I'll show Lovejoy round,' Veronique swiftly told Guy. 'You see Dreyfus. Fifteen minutes.'

I watched Guy shoot into the building. I didn't like him to be so zingy, behaving like he had stars round his head, and asked, 'He okay, love?'

'He's fine.' She halted so I bumped into her. 'No more questions like that, Lovejoy. Today we begin.'

Like what? I asked myself, narked. All right, maybe I'd sounded full of mistrust about his crazy stare and dynamite style. I'd only been trying to help, in a caring sort of way.

'Thank God. Where are they?'

We entered the place. She spoke offhand to three blokes who accosted us, beckoned me with a tilt of her head. I felt a sneaky pride in being with somebody so lovely.

'For a start, Lovejoy, this is the Hôtel Drouot.' I nodded I'd heard of the great focus for Paris's auctioneers. Not a hotel at all. 'Rebuilt in 1980. Sixteen salerooms, each with storage space, three selling floors from central foyers. Temperature – controlled storage, bond areas . . .'

'Great.' Only sixteen? Did that explain the grumbles of international dealers? Mind you, I'm prejudiced. There's nothing wrong with auctioneers that retirement wouldn't cure.

'This way.'

Just think of the wasted corridor-miles humanity's logged over the centuries! If it wasn't for flaming corridors we'd have colonized the universe yonks ago. As it is, we're all still plodding down boring corridors, trying to reach our respective launch pads.

Dreyfus was a small pleasant bloke, so respectably dressed he had me notching my own markers of suavity – curling lapel, slanted tie, shirt without a top button, grubby shoes. We greeted each other warmly. He had a partitioned office. No antiques in the inner sanctum. The sofa table by the wall was a dud. Or maybe not so dud? Its luscious surface patina felt right, but the table seriously wrong. It was brilliantly done, looked exactly right. The four feet with their castors gave an authentic bong. But the resonance of it mixed with that terrible fraudulent surface made me nauseous. I looked away.

'Jacques Dreyfus,' he said, twinkling, 'and no relation! Beautiful, isn't it?' He'd be quite at home in any language. 'It will be catalogued soon.'

As a fake, I hoped. The old trick. Its base, castors and all, were nicked from a genuine cheval mirror – 'swing dressers', dealers call them. In Regency days they'd had to make them strong, to take heavy glass. Cheval mirrors are not so valuable, even now, so forgers marry the support to the best flat heartwood. Presto! Your 'genuine 1825 sofa table' – and we challenge anybody to do any tests they like. Your usual patter is, 'No, take your sample for chemical analysis from the feet, please – the tabletop is irreparable, you see ...' The tests prove exactly right for 1820, and you have your certificate of authenticity. Then you buy some old wood, fake up some feet with castors for the cheval mirror, and sell *that* as completely genuine. Only now your patter goes, 'No, take your sample for chemical analysis from the ebony-inlaid top, please. The base is irreparable ...'

'The system,' Veronique said. Impatient women aren't new, but there was a new edge to her voice. Social-philosophy time? I'd hated the bit I'd already received.

'Our auction system in France endures,' Jacques said cheerily, 'despite all attempts. We operate a monopoly, though the Common Market lawyers wring their hands in Brussels.'

'I'm ashamed of my ignorance,' I put in. I moved from the chair to sit on a low couch, trying to get away from the distress of that ghastly hybrid.

'The Compagnie de Commissaires-Priseurs de Paris has control- led auctions since the eighteenth century, Lovejoy.' He rippled his fingers like a pianist gathering pace. 'The auction firms – *études* –

can have offices wherever they like, but must rent a saleroom in the Hôtel Drouot for a sale.'

'Must?' That would account for the gripes of the non-French antiques traders. '*Il faut?*'

Jacques chuckled at my pronunciation. I began to like him. I was doing my best in a mad mix of French and English.

'*Il*, as you perceive, *faut*, Lovejoy. We are also forbidden to prepare our own sale catalogues. Those are formed up, descriptions of the antiques and all, by a corps of experts certified by our Government.'

'Is there a guarantee?' I asked without thinking. Then I had to struggle so as not to see Veronique tense at my question. I'd have to be even more circumspect. I've the brains of an egg.

'Thirty years.'

'The expert cataloguer is more important than the *étude*, then?'

'That is often the case.' Jacques Dreyfus smiled with guarded apology at Veronique, who was busy pretending she was bored. 'The money is the other, Lovejoy. The Compagnie holds half the sale money until the year's end.'

'And dishes it out when it wants?' I was aghast. 'Don't the big boyos mind? They're subsidizing the small fry, right?'

He shrugged that Gallic shrug. 'The smaller *études* don't have to catalogue each sale.' He looked at Veronique in exasperation, smiley still. 'It's the way things are.'

'No more, Jacques,' Veronique said. Guy came zooming in. 'We must show Lovejoy your collection.'

I brightened. 'Antiques? All as good as your sofa table, Jacques?'

His smile was quite brave, in the circumstances. I had a vague idea he'd sussed me out, but wasn't sure. 'I believe exactly!' He wanted to show me a saleroom. I asked for a loo first, please, and received directions.

There, I was violently sick, retching and leaning gasping against the tiled wall until I could retch no more. I put my forehead against the cold surface a few minutes. Afterwards I rinsed my face in cold water and emerged pretending a kind of I'm-casually-interested-looking-about. Veronique and Jacques Dreyfus were waiting in the foyer. Guy had streaked off somewhere.

'Are you all right, Lovejoy?' Jacques asked. 'You're white.'

'Fine, thanks.' My head was splitting. I grinned like a goon, having remembered where it was I'd been sick like this before, and why. 'Have we far to go?'

'With you along, Lovejoy,' Veronique said through thinned lips, 'the answer's yes.'

Me and Jacques chuckled merrily. In my case – and maybe his? – it wasn't much of a chuckle. But I thought hard of having got my letter off, overloaded with stamps from a tobacconist, and managed something near a jovial croak.

We drove in Dreyfus's motor, a more trundlesome job than Guy's zoomster. I kept sane, and more importantly in a non-puke state, by exclaiming at the Parisian landmarks – the Seine, the Arc de Triomphe, the bigger-than-expected Sacré Coeur – then a double through tangled streets to finish up in an unprepossessing district within sound of trains. It looked the sort of district Paris shouldn't have, grotty, down at heel, soiled.

'This it, Veronique?' I let my surprise show. I was getting fed up with being careful all the bloody time. It's always me gets the headaches.

'Yes, Lovejoy. This is it.' She spoke French with vituperation. I looked about as Jacques parked the motor.

Some darkish children played, stood about. The filthy street wore debris like medals for indignity. The house fronts were frayed, no real paint. The doors looked battered. A couple of windows were patched with cardboard. The aroma of exotic cooking filled the air. It made me hungry as hell, but I had a sour feeling that more sickness lay just around the corner.

'This way, Lovejoy.'

It might have been a church hall, some sort of meeting place, that we found after a few hundred yards. Down steps, with a reinforced door to shut the world of staring children out. Two bulky blokes stood in bulky-bloke attitudes, suited for funerals. They knew Veronique, accepted me without a glance, but listened to Jacques. Paymaster?

We went through an arched doorway. Guy was jangling away, talking non-stop to Colonel Marimee, gesticulating, joking, a riot. The place was crammed with furniture, much covered in sheets. Note that small point: hardly any paintings, ceramics, and no display cases filled with antique jewellery.

The Colonel gave a terse instruction to Guy and stood watching us approach. We signalled our arrival with various degrees of sub-servience, all except Veronique, who perched provocatively on a polished surface. I swallowed. Montaigne said that however high the throne, we all still sit on our tails.

'Inspect these items and report, Lovejoy,' Marimee commanded. 'You have thirty minutes.'

'*Oui, mon commandant.*'

He meant me. I avoided spewing on his brilliant shoes, and walked down the first line of furniture. The pieces were of a muchness. The larger of the two hulks preceded me unasked, flicking away the dust covers as I went. Jacques Dreyfus followed.

French furniture caught fashions from its neighbours. People say that, yet it's a bit unfair, because France started a number of styles of her own. It's always said that France filched Italian joinery in the Renaissance, Flemish marquetry in the seventeenth century, English mahogany styles in the eighteenth and so on. True, but don't forget France's flair. You have to see the originals – not this load of gunge I was being shown. In skill, France's antique furniture is a front runner.

A tulipwood cabinet stopped me. Supposed to be 1775, it sported four plaques of Sèvres porcelain set into the panels. Small, but a fortune at any auction, if you believed it. I bent down to the plaques. Plants, spring flowers. Carnations, three tulips, lilac, with that lovely apple-green border Méreaud loved. He was the highest paid of Sèvres porcelain decorators, though of course he'd died two hundred or more years before these fake plaques were done. I knelt to look closer. The carnations were exactly right botanically. The tulips, being easier, also were. The lilac was wrong. I've a tree growing in my own unkempt garden, and have tried to imitate Méreaud and his equally skilled pal Léve often enough to know. Somebody had copied as best they could from an imperfect picture of the real thing.

That sickness made me giddy as I rose. I stumbled, fell on a nearby table. I withdrew my hand with an involuntary cry. I'd checked my fall mechanically, touched its surface. It burned me like a chimney from hell.

'Pardon, Lovejoy,' Dreyfus said, helping to steady me. I apologized profusely, saying it was too long since breakfast. Colonel Marimee curled his lip at my offshore weakness. I went with pretence of care, pausing now and then as if thoughtful, but the nausea was almost shaking me.

'Very good, *mon commandant*,' I said to Marimee. Almost all of it was sickening. I still wasn't sure how much of the antiques game he understood. Nor did I know how much he was supposed to know. I could hardly see.

'Adequate? Yes or no?' he demanded.

'Adequate, *mon commandant*.'

'*Bien.*' And left, terse nods all round. There was no relaxation of the atmosphere.

'What about transport?' I asked Veronique. 'I mean, do we have to arrange it, or will they call for it?'

'Who?' she asked back.

'Well.' I was thinking while I was still on my feet, holding the sickness at bay. 'You said we can't auction it here. Hasn't it got to go to the Hôtel Drouot to be sold?'

'Stupid,' she snapped, as I'd hoped she would. 'We aren't selling. We've gone to a great deal of trouble to . . . afford it. And it's a fraction only.'

She was going to say buy, then didn't. My throat cleared itself as I tried to stop it saying, 'Is it all furniture? What else we got?' *Don't say tapestry, upholstery.*

'Wall tapestries, mainly,' Veronique said, starting us off out of the storehouse. 'And of course upholsteries. People say they're more expensive than the furniture itself. True?'

'Always has been, love. Got papper mash stuff?' *Don't say yes.*

'Sure,' she said. 'Thirty papier mâché pieces. Right, Jacques?'

'Good,' I said, meaning bad, bad, bad. They'd have paper filigree too, the bastards. I nodded a nod as good as the Commandant's, then got driven back to the hotel, where I bade them a smiling so long, and with the relief of the afflicted was spectacularly and constantly sick in the minuscule bathroom. The image of those dark staring children watching us in that shabby street, with their blistered hands and old-young faces and blunted expressions was in my mind. Dr Johnson's crack came at me: 'Remember that all tricks are either knavish or childish.' I thought, please help me. Come soon, pals. You can't leave me to do this alone. My insides were empty, except for this feeling of murder. I saw only the lavatory bowl for half an hour.

The day was waning – all Paris seemed on the wane just then – when I left the hotel. I wandered brimming with nausea into the little square, sat on the seat beneath the tree, looked at the cobbles, put my head back hoping for cool. Clammy head, wet hands. The air felt heavy, muggy, too close to breathe. Somebody sat on the seat. I felt it nudge.

'Where the hell've you been?' I said, not bothering to open my eyes. 'I said come straight away. East Anglia's only forty minutes, for Christ's sake.' But I'd not heard a wheelchair.

'I had to see to Jan first,' she said, which would spring anybody's lids. Lysette, no less. 'He needs special care.'

'You're no use,' I said. This is typical. First time in my life I've ever asked anybody for help, and they send me an ignorant tart. 'Jan give any message?' The least he could do.

'Yes. He said to rely on me, Lovejoy.'

'Get lost, love.' I'd a splitting headache. I made to leave. What she said stopped me.

'I would have waited at your hotel, except for your company.'

What did she know? 'How much do you know, love?'

She was smaller than I thought, pale, composed. I felt a strong urge to tell her to clear off, but bonny women make you lose your gommon.

'Jan was hired to advise on antiques. There's heavy buying in East Anglia, France, all over.' She hesitated. 'He made mistakes. You can't be right all the time, can you?'

Well, yes. 'A divvy can. Antiques are easy, love. It's people queer the pitch every time.' She was trying not to tell me Jan started defrauding the rollers, Big John included.

'You're hateful! I can see what you're thinking, Lovejoy! My brother could no more cheat –'

'*Who*?' My headache belted me across the eyes.

'My brother. Jan's the gentlest, kindest, most honest . . .' Et sisterly cetera.

Wrong again. How was I to know? I'd honestly seen Lysette as Jan Fotheringay's bird. My shimmering vision tried to focus on her anew, without listening to her defensive dross. Jan had pulled the old Nelson, as the trade says. You are supposed to approve a multitude of fakes and genuine antiques – that is, decide if they're good enough to pass most scrutineers, like I'd just done – but he'd then condemned a few beautiful pieces as dross. Secretly, of course, he'd snaffled them, and made a fortune. The problem? It was the rollers' fortune, not his.

'Where's it heading, Lysette? Am I right, Switzerland?'

'Yes. I don't know when.'

That didn't matter. The square seemed clear of familiars still, but for one. I almost got better with relief.

'Look, Lysette. Good of you to come and all, but you're no use. I wanted Jan. He could tell me the backers, whose scam it is. You can't.'

'I can, Lovejoy. Some, anyway.' She named the ones I expected: Jervis, Almira Galloway, Monique Delebarre, Corse, Big John (she didn't call him that) Sheehan, and Paulie of course. And took my breath away by adding, 'Jan told me Mr Anstruther was frightened, but his wife drove him. She's Monsieur Troude's woman, you see, and got her husband's firm to invest everything.'

Cissie and Troude? My headache had only been teasing until now. Across the square, Gobbie spat with laconic skill.

'Got a car, love?'

'I can easily hire one. You want me to help, Lovejoy?'

'Please,' I said, nearly broken. 'Get one, and follow. We leave tomorrow, if I've guessed right. You'll have a travelling companion. An old bloke I know.'

Lysette smiled, suddenly bright and beautiful. 'I'll be there ahead of you, Lovejoy. If *I've* guessed right.'

We made a detailed plan. She left, me watching her edible form move across the cobbles out of the square. I gave her a few minutes, then went to where my real helper sat, thank God.

'Wotcher, Gobbie.'

'Hello, son.' He hawked up phlegm, rheumy old eyes watering. 'Who's the bint?'

'On our side. You'll be travelling with her.' I launched into money, surreptitiously gave him what I had to cover expenses. He'd told his daughter he was going to a regimental reunion, a laugh. I had to ask him, though. 'You sure you want in, Gobbie? It's okay if you duck out. I'll manage.'

'Like hell you will, son,' Gobbie said, grinning. 'You'll squirrel off and hide. I know you. You're a cowardly sod.' I had to laugh. A gappy geriatric grin and a brilliantly beautiful smile, both within a few minutes. Plus a home truth. And allies! Things were looking up.

'It'll be rough, Gobbie.' I paused. What had he said at the boot sale? 'Bring old times back – they were dangerous, remember.'

His smile was as beautiful in its way as Lysette's. 'Them's the times I wants, Lovejoy. One more, worth anything.'

'Remember you said that,' I warned him. I'm glad now I said that, too. 'Here, Gobbie,' I said on impulse. 'Want to brighten your day? Well, night? See a giggle?'

'A robbery? Here?' He was surprised.

'It'll be about two in the morning,' I warned. He fell about at that, guessing what it would be. And he was right.

Well, he would be right, with his million years of experience. He got a motor car, as I'd asked, and we sat there in the darkness looking out at the street. Gone two o'clock, and so far nothing. Odd how some people, especially older ones like Gobbie, seem at home wherever they are. I would have sworn the motor was his own, so familiar did he seem with –

'Watch, son.'

His quiet voice woke me faster than a yell. I'd seen nothing, but then my instinct's for survival. Gobbie's seemed entirely outside himself. Maybe it's because I've so much guilt, that unsleeping guardian of morality.

'Where?'

'Nothing yet.'

Nothing wrong with dropping off, but then I was tired. Old folks seem to nap like babies, in and out of sleep any old time.

'Glad I don't own a Range Rover, or a big Nissan.' They get nicked for robberies like the one we'd come to see.

'There goes one.' A Citroën, innocuous and plain, drove sedately down the night road, clearly somebody late back from the theatre. 'The scout,' Gobbie explained, sussing my wonder at his certainty, 'otherwise he'd have slowed a bit just before the traffic lights. Everybody does, unless he's trying to look casual.'

See what I mean? Only a veteran would think of that.

Mall-mashers, ramraiders, are a particularly English variant of the smash-and-grab. It's a dark-hour job, though of course you can change the batting order, like the most famous one, the 1990 Asprey ramraid that proved the landmark of its type. (They backed a truck through Asprey's window with wonderful precision – just off Piccadilly, would you believe – to snatch diamonds from the stove-in window.) It's a Newcastle-upon-Tyne speciality, averaging one major ramraid a day now, many of them hitting the same retail shops and malls time after time. They're exciting to watch.

'Here it comes, son. Wake up.'

'Which way?' I was asking blearily when it happened.

Two vehicles drove up, glided to a stop in the centre of the road. One reversed gently into position, then accelerated with a roar and simply drove into the antique-shop front. Glass sprayed everywhere, clattering and tinkling around. One or two shards even rattled musically on our roof. While I was watching, astonished and thrilled, the other was already hurtling into the next window. Neither had lights on. They reversed out, tyres crunching glass. Four hooded blokes dived from the motors and leapt through the openings. Each carried a baseball bat. It was a hell of a mess. I moaned at the thought of the antiques within, but what could I do? I'd warned the one girl I'd fallen for, Claire Whatnot.

The motors pulled to wait against the kerb, engines running.

'They got walkie-talkies, son,' Gobbie said quietly. 'See?'

Well, no I didn't. A couple of small vans came round the corner, dousing their headlights as they settled nearby. Two men to a van, I saw. Admirable organization. They ran the scroll gates up. No lights inside save a red direction node borrowed from some theatre stage.

'Christ!' I almost shrieked. Somebody opened our car door. A mask peered in, our courtesy bulb lighting to show his red eyes.

'Just watching, mate,' Gobbie said quickly. 'Good luck.'

'Fuck luck,' the hooded bruiser said. He held a club the size of a tree in his hands. 'Who're you?'

'I'm Gobbie. Lovejoy. Your tyres okay? Don't pull a spud.'

I thought. I don't believe Gobbie. Why didn't the stupid old sod simply gun our engine and scarper? Instead he makes introductions, pulls the ramraider's leg. Spud's the latest slang for a ballsup, after the catastrophe (or success, whichever way you look at it) of Continental raiders who'd tried to emulate our Geordie rammers in Amsterdam. Hoods nicked twenty Dutch Impressionists worth untold zillions from the Van Gogh – including Vincent's own *The Potato Eaters*, hence 'spud'. The loot sat meekly in the getaway motor which had a flat tyre. I could hear the blokes shouting, things smashing in the antique shops. God knows what heirlooms they were destroying.

'I heard of you bastards,' the bruiser said. 'Clear off when we do, right?'

'Different direction,' Gobbie said amiably.

The bloke disappeared, putting our car door to quite gently. The pandemonium along the parade of antique shops was increasing. The lads were rushing out small antiques. The first wave would snatch tom – jewellery, precious items such as miniatures, handies that could be scooped up. Then furniture, paintings. But only the ones that had been earmarked.

'Why'd he cuss us, Gobbie?' I asked, narked.

'He knows our scam, son. He doesn't like it.'

'He *what*?' A visiting ramraider team *knows our scam*?

'There they go.'

The first van slammed itself shut. The blokes piled in. It roared away, the Range Rover tearing after. The second slammed, the Nissan barelling round to leave the way it had come. The main van raced off, and that was that.

We drove away, taking the first left. I wondered if they'd battered through into the next-door place, which was Claire's, or whether they'd had orders not to.

'Gobbie,' I said, thinking hard as he dropped me off in the night near the square. 'He knew? Really *knew*?'

'Mmmh. You can always tell.' He paused, I paused, everybody

paused. 'Son? Is your scam going to finish up with them antiques they just nicked?'

'Eh?' I'd not thought of that. 'You mean, they were pinching them for *us*?' I'd nearly said Troude and Marimee.

'A thought, son. They were older blokes than usual, see? Them touring Geordies are all of seventeen, eighteen as a rule.'

The hooded raider had seemed thickset, maybe forty or so. Gobbie was right. Ramraiding's a youth's game. So why was an older bloke pulling a stroke like that?

'Like', Gobbie continued, gently nursing me into thinking, 'that lot of gorms last month as raided the Metro Centre. Did the wrong stuff, remember? Too young to know the difference between tom and tat. Did a beautiful rammer, got clean away, and found they'd nicked a display of imitation jewellery.'

Yes, I'd heard. It was desperately worrying. Too many variables all of a sudden.

'Any ideas, Gobbie?' I asked. How pathetic. Me supposed to be the leader of this private little side scam, and here I was asking a wrinkly for advice. I disgust me sometimes. I'd have dozed through the whole thing if it hadn't been for him, too. 'Forget it,' I said, and walked away.

'Night, son. See you there.' I swear the old sod was grinning. I was narked. One day I'll get the upper hand, then people'd better watch out, that's all.

CHAPTER TWENTY-FOUR

'Didn't the Commandant say something about London?' I asked hopefully in next morning's flying start.

Guy tore us through the countryside. I wanted some aspirin, but Veronique fell about when I asked. I was really narked. Just my luck to draw the one bird in the world without a ton of paracetamol in her handbag. 'Is this north?'

'He's quick on the uptake!' Guy cried, swerving, sounding his horn. I shrank in my seat as the wind ripped through me. Everything he said sounded copied from American films. Mind you, what's wrong with that? Same as me, really. Birds often tell me so.

Veronique was smiling. I was exposed in the bucket seat, my regular place now. 'He's a servant,' she said, turning to speak directly at me. 'Aren't you, Lovejoy?'

'Aren't we all?' I was worried about my helpers. I meant me.

'No!' she cried. 'You are *dull*! Like all the servile! Show you a sham clubhouse, a seaside toy, call it a marina, and you grovel like a dog.' *Et* withering *cetera*. I'd made a hit.

'I'm no serf,' I fired back. Staying a buffoon never did me any harm.

Not a bad description of Mentle, marina and all. So she – meaning Guy too – had been there? I thought about poor Baff.

From then on, I decided, I'd really try. I shone, talked instead of sulked. I began trying to draw them out, embarked on some funny not-so-funny tales, Actions I Have Known, scams, robberies (no names, no pack drill as people say), and within a few miles had her smiling. No mean feat, with Guy yippeeing, attacking every vehicle on the road. I slyly timed him, supposing he'd shot his lot before we started out. He'd have to pull in somewhere when his jangles got too much.

'I mean, I really like Alma-Tadema's paintings,' I was giving out when finally Guy started to become quieter, his driving less flamboyant. What, an hour and a half of belting along the motorway? We'd come out of Paris on the A6. 'What's wrong with detail, if it's lovely? He painted all the faces in his enormous crowds. But so what? Easier to fake.' I'd been on about the old 1980s forgeries, still around in some galleries.

'You're a secret luster, Lovejoy,' Veronique gave back in that encouraging reprimand women use. 'We heard.'

165

'Not a word to anyone, or I'll stand no chance.' I grinned apologetically, innocent Lovejoy, hoping but never really expecting. 'Where do you find anybody to do detail like Alma-Tad nowadays?' I hummed, trying to remember the melody of that old music-hall song. 'Alma-Tad, oh what a cad . . .' My Gran used to sing it in her naughty moods, dreadfully risky. It worked.

'Look in the right place, Lovejoy, you'll find anything.' Veronique's implacability phase returned for a second.

'Not nowadays, love. Forgers don't have the application. And if fakers can't be bothered, who can? You need time, money, love.' I chanced it as Guy, all a-twitch, began looking for exit roads. Veronique darted him a glance, nodded permission. 'Don't annoy me. I've lived like a monk since I arrived. Gelt's all very well, but I'm short on vital necessities.'

She burst out laughing, a beautiful sight, the wind, blonde hair flying, all shape and pattern. 'I *see*, Lovejoy! You're desperate!'

Even though they'd killed Baff, I was narked at her amusement at my expense. 'Look, love. Birds can go years without a bloke. We can't last more than a couple of days without a bird.' I was still fishing, laying groundwork. 'Everybody's . . . well, fixed up, except me.'

She was still rolling in the aisles at my lovelorn state when we halted at a service station. On the way in, I took a gander at the wall map, and realized we were heading east. Reims led to Metz, to Strasbourg. The E35 darted south along the Rhine then, to Zurich. A guess right, for once? No sign of the Sweets, which surprisingly gave me a pang. Lilian had been brilliant, for all that she was the wife of a SAPAR hunter. And none of Gobbie and Lysette.

'How long's this going on, Veronique?' I asked while we waited for Guy. 'I need to know the plan, when, some detail.'

'Why?' We'd collared some superb French coffee. She gazed levelly back, chin resting on her linked fingers.

'Good old Suliman-Aga.' I made a show of relishing my first swig though it burnt my mouth. Women can drink scalding, with their asbestos throttles.

'Who?' Very, very guarded.

'Your Turkish ambassador, brought coffeetime to France. About 1666, give or take a yard.'

She didn't say anything. She'd already been to the loo, as I. I realized I couldn't quite see the edges of her pupils, however hard I looked. Funny, that. I'd done my most soulful gaze a number of times, hoping. Though what I'd learn from seeing if the pupils were dilated or pinpoint, God knows. It's supposed to be a clue to drugs, but which size meant what?

Her eyes rose, held me hard with an intensity I didn't like. Lucky that Guy was the mad one, or I'd have suspected the worst.

'We were warned about you, Lovejoy.' She drew a spoony trail in a spillage spot on the table. I was starting to hate surfaces. 'I paid no heed. Now I'm wondering if I underestimated you.'

This is the kind of woman-talk I don't like. Had I been too obvious? I went into a huff. It's quite a good tactic, played with enough misunderstanding.

'Look, love.' I showed how heated I was. 'I'd rather finish this job and get home. If you're narked because I mentioned I'm a bit short of, ah, close company, then tell Marimee and get me sacked —'

'Sacked, shacked, packed?' Guy raced to the table, literally grabbing Veronique's coffee. 'Hacked?' He laughed so loud people looked round. He hovered about four feet above the floor, zingy, fully restored. 'Hacked, then *lacked*? Wracked?' Happy days were here again. I didn't need to look into his pupils.

'Guy,' Veronique reprimanded quietly as we rose to depart. Guy shrilled merriment, streaked off to the motor. We followed. 'You will be told everything, Lovejoy.' She wore a watch that could have afforded me a thousand times over. 'In three hours.'

'Three hours more at Guy's lunatic speeds'll have us in Vladivostok. Will we make it back to Paris? Only, I started fancying that hundred-year-old concierge. She's just my type — breathing.'

That gave her a crinkly half-smile. I felt we were more allies after that short break than before. I tried telling Guy to take his time. He bawled that we were to make Zurich before midnight, and whiplashed us into the traffic with barely a look. Correct, at last. Mind you, the million pointers had helped. Gobbie and Lysette would now meet me as planned.

'Daddy wouldn't buy me a bow-wow,' I sang, explaining to Veronique: 'Alma-Tadema used to play that to visitors on his early phonograph. Real class, eh? Was it the *onzième*?'

'Eleventh?'

'Arrondissement. Your warehouse, the cran. God, I've never seen so much reconstruction. Don't Parisians get fed up? Between the Place de la Bastille and the Boulevard Voltaire, wasn't it? Lovely, once. I'll bet, when it was famous for cabinet-makers.'

Silence. Guy nearly bisected our motor on an oil transporter.

'Mind you, what can you expect?' I said, blathering on. 'The City of Paris's planning department has no conservation section, has it? Cretins. That lets anybody do anything.'

More, but certain, silence. Funny, but now I was sure of their terrible scam my nausea had all gone.

Veronique didn't chat much more during that pacy journey, and I shut up. But I caught her looking at me in a mirror when she did her lipstick. I cheered up. An ally? Or did her languid look mean she was simply on different shotpot than before?

Three more pit stops for Guy to toot his flute and we were across the Swiss border. I felt bright, optimistic. After all, here was lovely Switzerland. Never having seen it, still I knew it was clean, pristine, beautiful, orderly, utterly correct and safe and lawabiding. Veronique seemed to last out on only one kite flight. Except a vein in her left arm was now swollen and bruised. At the border, Guy produced three passports, one mine. They weren't inspected, and we drove on through. I was so excited I nodded off.

'Lovejoy? Wake up.'

We'd arrived, quite dark. I stumbled out, bleary. The hotel seemed plain, almost oppressively compact. Stern warnings abounded in umpteen languages on every wall about baths, water, payment, lights, payment, doors, keys, payment. I didn't read any, but climbed the stairs – stairs were free – thinking that whatever Monique Delebarre's syndicate was spending, little of it went on lodging. Or was this doss-house strategically placed?

The microscopic room was dingier even than my cottage. One bulb flogged itself, leaking a paltry candlepower that barely made the walls. The place was freezing. I sprawled on the bed and thought of money.

Now I'm not against the stuff, though I know I do go on. It's really crazy how prices dominate. The UK tries to keep track by teams which examine 130,000 shop-shelf items in 200 towns, compiling the Retail Price Index, but it's all codswallop. Just as comparing antique prices. It's a hard fact that a lovely epergne, a decorative table centrepiece, weighing a colossal 478 ounces 10 pennyweights, was auctioned in 1928 for 12/6d an ounce, which equals 63 pence as this ink dries. Date 1755, by that brilliant master silversmith Edward Wakelin, no less. *And in its original case,* that collectors today would kill for. So where's the sense in comparison? Answer: no sense at all.

The only honest matching is by time. And I knew no forgers,

no artisans, who could or would devote time to making furniture exactly as they used to back in the eighteenth century. Except me. Yet Monique Delebarre and Troude and all seemed to have tapped an endless vein of superbs, by the load, by the ware-house.

Even though I'd no pyjamas I decided it was bedtime. Guy and Veronique were rioting and whooping in the next room.

For a while I lay looking at neon on-offs making shadowed patterns on the walls and ceiling. Antiques crept about my mind. Antiques that were laborious, time-consuming the way all creativity is. Like upholstery, tapestry, polishing furniture in a cruel endless method that only the seventeenth and eighteenth centuries ever managed. And, I'd bet, paper filigree, and papier mâché, that took many, many poorly paid hands. I think I dozed, and came to with somebody knocking surreptitiously on the door. I was there in a flash, opening it slowly, lifting as I turned the handle so it couldn't squeak.

Veronique.

My face couldn't have given me away, not in the semi-darkness of the street glow. She came in and stood leaning against the wall by the doorjamb. I was broken, thinking it would be my home team, Lysette and Gobbie.

'We off somewhere?' For all I knew we might have to steal into the night. It seemed the sort of military thing Colonel Marimee would get up to.

'In a manner of speaking, Lovejoy.' She closed the door.

Then I noticed she had a swish jewel-blue silk nightdress on, to the floor. She shelled the cardigan she'd tied round her shoulders, letting it fall. 'Guy's asleep, sort of,' she said quietly. 'Will an hour do? For somebody so deprived?'

My throat swallowed. My question was answered. Guy's bright episodes were sixty minutes, between doses.

'For what?'

She sighed, pulled me to the bed, pushed me gently down. 'You're hardly the Don Juan they threatened us about, Lovejoy.' She propped herself up on one elbow, and smiled down at me. She was hard put not to laugh her head off. 'I come into your bed in the night stripped, shall we say, for action. Does my presence give you any kind of clue as to why?'

... *they threatened us about, Lovejoy, when we crossed to East Anglia to murder Baff. And silk is the rarest, most labour-intensive textile. Get enough supply, and you could make enough fake antiques to retire on, if you'd a zillion obedient hands* ...

'Get that off,' I said thickly, clawing her nightdress while she hushed me and tried to do it tidily faster than I could rip.

Pride creeps into mind-spaces it shouldn't, I always find. Shame does too, but lasts longer. The trouble is, there's no way to resist, delay. Women have everything, which is why they get the rest. You can't stop them. Veronique got me, and I'm ashamed to say now that she was scintillating, wondrous. What's worse, I had a perverse relish, almost a sadistic glee, knowing that her bloke next door, stoned out of his skull, was the one who'd murdered a mate of mine. And maybe helped to do over Jan Fortheringay? I'd have to work that one out. I behaved even worse than usual.

At the last second I felt her hand fumble and cap my mouth in hope of silence. Women, practical as ever. It wasn't the end, and, shame to say, I was glad. I harvest shame while I've got the chance. Pathetic.

She left after the full hour. When she'd gone I think I hardly slept, wondering about bedbugs in this dive, but finding that antiques marched back in.

There would be others Veronique hadn't mentioned and I hadn't asked about. Like paper filigree, which the Yanks call 'quilling', the most painstaking antique of all. Ten years ago, you could get a tiny paper-filigree doll's house for a month's wage. Now? Oh, say enough to buy a real-life family house, garden, throw in a new standard model Ford, and you're about right for price. Inflation, the Slump of Black Monday, recession – the antiques made of tiny scraps of paper trounced them all. And their prices soar yet, to this very day. Go to see it done, if there's ever a demonstration in your village hall.

In the 1790s, Georgian ladies invented this pastime. They'd take slivers of paper so small that your breath blows them away if you're not careful. Me being all clumsy thumbs, I've tried faking these objects and they drive you mad. You roll the paper tightly, then colour it (before or after) and stick a minute slice down to a hardwood surface. Make patterns. Surprisingly durable, you can then fashion tea caddies, boxes, even toys, tiny pieces of furniture, whatever.

There are quilling guilds everywhere now, who preach it as one of the most ancient of arts in ancient Crete. Then it was a religious craft, purely decorative, for shrines and churches, only they used vellum. I've seen some on alabaster, to hang in a window so the quilling picture showed in silhouette – translucent alabaster was once used in place of glass, like in some Italian churches. The best quilling examples I've seen are nursery toys like minuscule kitchens, with every small utensil made of these small rolls, twists, cones, cylinders. And entire dolls' houses, rooms fully furnished. 'Quilling', I suppose, because North American ladies used quills of birds and porcupines, though there's a row about the word as always. Inventive ladies used miniature rolls of wax, hair, leather even, and decorated their purses, pouches, even their husband's tobacciana.

Maybe you don't think it's a very manly pursuit, hunting filigree quilling antiques? Let me cure you: take a look in your local museum – they'll have one or two pieces if they're any good – just to get the idea. Then try it. Make a square inch of paper filigree. Go on, I dare you. Know what? You'll give up in ten minutes. If you're like me, you'll get so mad you'll slam the whole load of paper shreds against the wall and storm out sulking to the tavern until you've cooled down.

No. Filigree takes application, skill, endlessly detailed work. Or loads of money, boredom, leisuretime. Or something much, much worse. I sweated, with fear.

As I lay there, hands behind my head and staring at the ceiling, I couldn't help listening to any sounds that might come from the next room. A few mutters, a single shrill scream of dementia from Guy, silence. No chance of sleeping any more tonight. I knew it.

When I next opened my eyes it was breakfast o'clock, the traffic was howling and daylight was pouring in. Shame hadn't really done with me yet. It pointed out that I'd awakened refreshed, you cad Lovejoy. I decided I was now willing to give my newly planned role a go. My jack-the-lad manner seemed to be working with Veronique, and anything that works with women is a must. What's a lifetime's liberal humanism between friends? I'd become the hard-liner, under Veronique's tender loving care.

So to Zurich, in clean, pristine, sterile, hand-rinsed, orderly Switzerland. To rob the biggest repository of saleable untraceable antiques in the world. The easy bit.

CHAPTER TWENTY-FIVE

The meeting was billed, quaintly, as 'Promotion of Exemplary New Arts'. I wanted to walk there, but Guy, sniffling and having to blow his nose every minute, objected and we did a murderous dash-stop-dash roar through the traffic. Zurich was lovely, fresh and splendid after the sickness of worrisome lovely Paris. It actually felt seaside, with the Limmit River running down to the broad sunshiny lake, the Zurichsee. We went down the Bahnhofstrasse – I was thrilled to notice the main railway station, because that's where me and Lysette and Gobbie were to meet. Guy dumped us off near the Rennweg. A sign up and left indicated the tree-dotted mound.

'Have we time to climb up?' I asked Veronique. God, but she dazzled this morning. You can understand the ancient Celts giving up the ghost when tribes of great golden people like her hove in. 'Only, it's the ancient settlement of Zurich. We could see the whole place!'

'No.' She paused, as near as she'd ever come to a hesitation. 'Lovejoy. What do you think of Guy?'

'For a psychotic murderous junkie he's okay.' I gauged her. The traffic passed down to the Quaibrücke, that lovely waterside. 'Why?'

'When this is over, Guy and I will finish.' She looked away. 'You are not spoken for, Lovejoy.'

More evidence that she'd accompanied her killer druggie to Mentle Marina, otherwise how did she know I wasn't heavily involved back in merry East Anglia?

'You mean . . . ?' She couldn't mean pair up. Not with me. I'm a shoddy scruff. She was glorious, rich, attractive.

'You are an animal,' she admitted candidly. 'With an animal's innocence. It is what I need.'

Why, the silly cow? I'd not even got a motor, nor money, unless this job paid. Odd, but I noticed that the motors reaching the traffic lights switched their engines off and sat in tidy silence until the lights changed. Fantastic, something I'd never seen before. What did they do it for? Save petrol? If I did that to my old Ruby it'd block the traffic for miles, never get anywhere, needing cranking up at every amber-red.

'And do what?'

'Live, Lovejoy.' She nodded at the city. 'Grand, no? Wealthy, no? I want everything, every experience. Guy must go.'

Women have the finality of their convictions, know goodbye when they see it. In fact, that little skill of theirs has caused me a lot of trouble. But the way she spoke sent a shiver down me. It was almost as if –

'Let's go, folkses!' from Guy, practically dancing between us. The district was mostly banking, exclusive and affluent. That Exemplary New Arts notice was a laugh. I avoided Veronique's meaningful side glance, but in the end couldn't resist giving her one. Contact lenses show an oblique rim, only just, round the edge of the iris, don't they? You catch it, if the angle's just so. And coloured contact lenses show it most. I was the only one not in disguise.

The place was a plush room within a hall, a kind of enclosed box inside a larger assembly space. Exhibition? It reminded me of those set-ups railway modelling societies use to create atmosphere for their titchy displays. I'd also seen one used for war games, nearer the mark.

'You come with us, Lovejoy,' Veronique said. Guy was chatting, waving, slapping backs, reaching for swift handshakes. Around the hall, two beefy blokes at each exit, hands folded. Three were in uniform, talking intently into gadgets. Once you got in, there'd be no way out. Nor could anybody outside get close enough to listen. The box occupied the precise centre of the vast hall. Mausoleum? You get the idea, that degree of welcome.

'Morning, Lovejoy.' Troude, a handshake. Lovely Monique, aloof. No sign of Almira, no Paulie, no Jervis Galloway, MP. 'I want to thank you for the work you've done for us. Selecting the antiques we needed to buy at the Paris auctions, your Paris sweep, checking the suitability of the, ah, reproductions. You have earned a bonus.'

'Good morning, Monsieur Troude. Thank you.'

We did that no-after-you-please in the one doorway and entered the darkened box. The door closed behind us with a thud. Colonel Marimee was on a dais, hands behind his back, facing the dozen or so folk already in. All were standing. Monique was beside him. It was lit with a single strip light. Battery operated, I saw with surprise. Couldn't they afford one from the mains? But a wandering flex breaches a wall, and this was –

'Soundproof, Lovejoy.' Philippe Troude was next to me, smiling. I'd been ogling. 'Swiss security, that they do so well. Banks, you see.'

'Good morning, ladies and gentlemen,' the Commandant rasped in French. This was his scene, everybody listening while he delivered battle plans. Monique translated *sotto voce* into English for the un-educated, mainly me I suppose.

The pair I'd met at that weird mansion-house garden party were standing nearby. I smiled a hello. They nodded back, tense. I felt my belly gripe. If they were worried sick, I ought to have at least a panic or two. Sweat sprang all over me.

The Colonel spoke. 'The event will be perfect. All has gone well.'

At Marimee's barks people looked at each other in relief. Satisfaction ruled. The audience was affluent, smooth, the women elegant. Dressing had cost a fortune. I expected a series of tactical maps to drop from the ceiling, red arrows sweeping around blue ones, but it was only the Colonel, in his element.

'There are two additional steps.' Marimee stared us all down. Drums should have begun, music pounding to a martial crescendo. 'First is financial. Another fourteen per cent is required from each syndicate member. Cash. Investment return will be commensurate. Immediate effect.'

A faint groan rose. I found myself groaning along, like a nerk. I hate that military phrase, as does anyone who's seen a reluctant soldier. This must be my doing, buying up Paris.

'*Mein Herr,*' some stout bespectacled put in. I noticed calculators were surreptitiously in action.

'No questions!' Marimee barked. 'The second step is accomplishment of the objective. Execution will be total effectivity.'

A cluster of three men, almost Marimee look-alikes except less showy, nearly smiled. The executors, if that was the word?

'That is all.'

'*Entschuldigen Sie bitte, Herr Colonel,*' the unhappy stout banker type said. I recognized a money man trying to wriggle out of spending.

'*Non*, Monsieur Tremp,' Marimee said in a muted voice. It shut us all up, groans and all. Except me.

To my alarm, I heard me say, '*Mon commandant.* I take it the items were all correctly bonded in Liechtenstein?'

'*Oui*, Lovejoy,' Monique Delebarre said evenly. But not before Marimee had hesitated. Him, whose first and last dither had been which breast when working up to his first suck. 'Thank you. That will be all,' Monique intoned.

We filed out of the stuffy little room, me asking Veronique if that was it. I'd felt claustrophobic in there.

The Cayman Islands, and little Liechtenstein, let you lob into bond any antique for seven measly days – then you can legally bring it out and legally sell it to anyone. (That's *legally*, got it?) In fact, you may even have sold it while it palely loitered. Our East Anglian antiques robbers love Liechtenstein because that one brief week gives us – sorry again; I meant *them* – time to forge a new provenance history, no more than a brief receipt, however sketchy, for the stolen antiques. Though nowadays everybody likes point-of-sale transfer, like in some Dutch or Belgian places that pay on the nail for any nicked Old Master, so making the sale legit. Zurich's bond currently is five years.

'What else is required, Lovejoy?' Veronique was smiling. 'How do you say, cold feet?'

'Cold feet, warm heart.' The best reply I could give. 'I thought we were going to get our orders, details and all that.'

'We have them, Lovejoy. The meeting confirms that all is on course.'

'For when?'

'For the time of execution. You heard the Commandant.' She smiled. Guy the burk was still chatting, prancing. Folk all around him were amused, in spite of the bad news about the kitty being upped. My belly warned me with an incapacitating gripe that execution has more than one meaning.

The hoods at the exits detained us until Marimee and his three clones left the security room. I was sick of all this cloak-and-dagger malarkey. I mean, why didn't Marimee just whisper his damned orders to us in the street? But pillocks like him feed on this sort of gunge.

They let us go in dribs and drabs, me and my couple last. Guy tried prattling to Marimee, but he ignored him except for one terse command I couldn't hear. It didn't quite bring Guy down through the Heaviside, but forced him into fawning agreement.

'Can I see the exhibition?' I asked Veronique. My plan was to bore Guy, literally, to vanishing point. 'Is it true the Kunsthaus has a Rembrandt? There are four galleries I want to go to. The Swiss National, the Landesmuseum, is a must, eh? It has workshops three centuries old from the Zurich arsenal! And I'm dying to see the Rietberg Museum.' Poisonously cheery, I knew my tactic would work, at least on Guy. Once I got rid of him, losing Veronique would be that much easier. 'Is it true its collection of Chinese art was got from East Berlin in a swap for Lenin's tea strainer? Then there's that other place called the Bührle Foundation. And St Oswald's . . .' I smiled an apology. Their eyes were already glazing. 'After all, one of ours, in a strange land, eh? I'll light a candle for him – if Swiss Lutherans are into ritual!' I chuckled into their shocked faces in the great foyer. 'Which first?'

It took an hour to shake Guy, then another to get rid of

Veronique. We'd reached two of Hobbema's landscapes when he finally cracked. He'd been twitching some time when he took Veronique to one side and muttered through his sniffles. She let him go, came back to me with questions in her eyes. I took her arm and kept up my dreadful heartiness, yapping non-stop. She'd wondered if my enthusiasm had been a pretence, a ploy to get her alone. I was repellently obsessional, dragging her round the adjacent gardens to see the Henry Moores and Bourdelles.

'I'm not into Magritte and Ernst, that lot,' I told her, pulling her along. 'We'll leave the new extension, eh? Let's go up to the first floor. There's a Hans Fries, *Adoration of the Magi*. Have you seen it? Only, you just guess how many times the bloody thing's been varnished, and with what sort. Try! I'll give you three goes, but here's a clue: it *isn't* copal varnish. Know why? Because if you stand about four feet away, then look away and quickly look back, you'll see a kind of shimmer –'

She broke, to my relief. 'I'd better go and see how Guy is, Lovejoy,' she said. 'Meet us at the hotel, supper tonight. Okay?'

'Okay,' I cried, giving her a ton of disappointment, riskily saying what if we get sudden orders, where on earth should I find them?

'Today's free, Lovejoy,' she said. 'There's one job for you tomorrow, then you're done.'

Done? my mind screamed as I grinned so long. Done *for*?

Cunningly, and I thought with skilled casualness, I mooched about to see her actually leave. Then I did a series of pretended quick looks in case she doubled back, or one of Marimee's goons was lurking somewhere in the art gallery. No sign. An hour later I walked openly to the main station, where Gobbie would be waiting, and Lysette Fotheringay. Return to normality.

Me and Gobbie were in the station when Lysette arrived. We were so cunning – in Information looking at these tiresome diagrams of railway networks – and simply walked away giving no sign. We went to a nosh bar – expensive, in Zurich – and apologized to each other for having to share a table. That legitimized our speaking together, my daft idea a kid could have seen through. Pathetic.

'Keep your voices down,' I warned them. Foreign languages carry; indigenous speech doesn't. It's always true. 'Say as little as possible. Good coffee.'

'Made proper Swiss style,' Lysette said with pride. 'Through filter papers, none of your French stewing process.'

I sighed. Two minutes, and already we were into national rivalry.

'Look, love. Cut that out, okay? I know we're in the most perfect, orderly, tidy, stable country in the world —'

Her face changed. 'You think so?'

'That's what they say, love.' Her sudden ferocity made me uneasy, and I'd had enough of being that. 'It's going to be our main ally. Steady police force, trustworthy citizens. The slightest anomaly must stand out like a torch in a tomb —'

'Mr Veriker, would you excuse us, please?' Lysette said to Gobbie. I stared at him. His name was Gobbie, for heaven's sake. Everybody knew that. Well, well. Who'd think Gobbie'd go and grow a surname? Him, of all people. 'It seems that Lovejoy's even stupider than we both could possibly imagine.'

'Watch your frigging gob, Lysette.' I was getting narked. Nowt but birds with hobnailed tongues since I'd left home.

'Come, Lovejoy. Perhaps, Mr Veriker, you'd like to meet us here in an hour?'

We left. I trailed after, sheepish but madder. It would be obvious now to anybody that we knew each other. She went down into a shopping precinct underneath the railway station. It was posh, with splendid boutiques, auto-bank windows, luscious grub, imported knitwear, a veritable Bond Street of superb design. Really Swiss, I thought.

'Your arm, Lovejoy.'

'You sure?' I was still furious. Fair's fair, right? I hadn't asked to come just to help her and her frigging pansified brother . . .

'Change?' An apparition said it in three languages, holding out his hand. Maybe four, five. I wouldn't know.

'Er, aye.' I gave him some. He looked derelict, almost in rags, and filthy.

'Change?' Two more drifted at me from nowhere, hands out. Lysette yanked me aside and we moved on among the people.

They seemed mostly youngsters, huddled in mounds. One or two sprawled. Most sat at a crouch.

'You encourage them to mug you, Lovejoy,' Lysette said, keeping us walking. 'It's a real danger. They sleep here or in doorways up above. I know it happens in all cities — and in lovely neat Zurich.' She sounded bitter.

'Only here, though?' I asked. I knew that in India the railway stations are great social concourses.

She did not laugh, gave me a look of scorn. 'You think you have drug problems, Lovejoy? Nothing like ours. The diseases that accompany it offer the proof.'

'In Switzerland?' I didn't realize I'd spoken aloud.

'Yes, here. The capital.' She drew me to the escalator and we made the open air.

'A few homeless in a whole nation . . .' I faltered.

'How much evidence do you want, Lovejoy? The report from the parliamentary commission which investigated our Ministry of Justice? It found that secret police gangs had records of thirteen per cent of the entire Swiss population on file.' She gave a wintry smile. 'So many Swiss subversives!'

'Your Swiss police?' My plans took another tumble.

'Of course,' she said sweetly, 'the files vanished when the commission report became, shall we say, famous!' She guided me along the pavement. 'Possibly because the secret army we call P26 might have to be unmasked further.'

Either she was off her nut or my plans were even wronger. She hailed a taxi, still talking.

'Economy? All Europe's ills we Swiss have in abundance. Rising unemployment, inflation, poverty, falling home ownership . . .'

I won't tell you the rest, if that's all right. I'm not scared of such talk, but there's too much going wrong everywhere, and it shouldn't. A bird I once knew used to say mine was the typical ostrich mentality, but it's not. I just don't want to hear bad things, that's all. What's wrong with that? I didn't look at what she pointed out on that taxi ride, struggled to deafen myself, shut her horrible words out. Lysette went for reprimand.

'It's no good trying not to listen, Lovejoy,' she was telling me as we finally came back. 'Those people in the Platzspitz were mainliners, druggies, pushers, narcos. Needle Park, that place I showed you. It's an open drugs mart, free needles on the State in hopes of lowering the AIDS rate. The suppliers make a billion francs a year . . .'

'Alma-Tad,' my mind sang, 'oh, what a cad . . .'

'We have *Zahfräulein*, tooth ladies,' she was waxing. I tried putting my hands over my ears. She leaned closer, spoke more directly. The taxi driver must have thought us insane. 'Spot checks on children's teeth – so they can start out really healthy derelicts . . .'

Do women never shut up? 'Oh, I wandered today to the hill, Maggie,' my cortex warbled. Thank God, we were back near the Limmatplatz and its massive Migros supermarket with the orange M.

'The Migros?' She'd glimpsed my relieved recognition, rotten cow. 'Our famous store, all things to all men!' She scathed on. 'We

Swiss are *so* docile! It is *1984*. Twenty-five per cent of us shop there daily . . .' We stopped at a traffic light, and I got out for air and freedom, leaving her to it.

She caught me up, no getting rid of her. I'd dithered, lost for direction. She took my arm. 'Switzerland has more drug OD deaths in six months than –'

'Love.' I stopped, broken. 'Please. I can't . . . I just, well *can't*. Don't you see? For Christ's sake.'

'You have social and political responsibility, Lovejoy –' She sounded like Colonel Marimee, in her own mad way.

'Lysette. Let's part, eh? You your way, me mine. Bugger everybody.'

'Community obligations –'

'Aren't, love. They drive me insane. I can't take it. I can only escape. It's all I ever do.'

'He's right, miss,' Gobbie intruded, thank God. How the hell had he got here? 'Lovejoy's a scrounger, has to travel light or not at all. He's a weak reed, wet lettuce, broken straw.'

'Here, Gobbie.' Narked, I straightened from my supplication posture. There's a limit. I'm not that bad. A lady pedestrian spoke sharply to us. We'd been blocking the pavement.

'Lovejoy must be educated, Mr Veriker,' from good old sterling standard Lysette. I could have welted her one. Sociologically minded people once took over ancient Babylon, and we all know what happened then.

'No, Lysette. Educators everywhere ploughed that one.' I reached out and wrung her hand. 'This is it. Fare thee well, lass. Cheers, Gobbie.'

He came with me. I was only half surprised. They'd seemed like a going concern, somehow, and him four times her age.

'You were right, son,' he said consolingly. 'She's too wrapped up in do-goodery. Time for a jar?'

'Well, as long as I'd one ally I'd give it a go. I've been alone in scams often enough. We settled on the nearest thing we could find to a pub. It was the glossiest dearest pub I'd ever seen. We found a quiet corner, away from some blokes with feathers in their hats talking of some shooting club. The thinnest glass of ale I've ever had served. Gobbie tutted, grinned.

'They'd get scragged serving this in my local,' he said. I chuckled obediently, working out how to tell him. 'Pity you and her didn't get on, Lovejoy,' he said. 'Now, son. Where do I come in? She won't give up on you, mark my words.'

'I know, Gobbie. Let's try survival, eh?'

'If you say, Lovejoy.' He grinned, loving every minute of it when things were going wrong, like now. He must have been the greatest antiques runner on earth when younger. I hoped he was still. He was all I'd got. Maybe I should have gone for Mercy Mallock after all.

CHAPTER TWENTY-SIX

That evening I had supper with Guy and Veronique. I'd been dreading it. We had incomprehensible but superb grub, a wine that didn't give you heartburn, and talk that did. Guy was at his most manic, once having to be fetched down from standing on his chair to give the restaurant a song. Veronique was practised in handling him. Twice during the meal he had to dash out to stoke up on some gunja or other. In the latter of his absences Veronique unbent, spoke freer than she ever had.

'You can see how Guy has outlived his usefulness, Lovejoy. Do you blame me?'

My throat cleared for action. I wish I could think fast near women. 'Well, no.' He was getting on my nerves too, though you never know what goes on between a bird and her bloke.

'You and I will make a killing, Lovejoy,' she urged softly. 'Me: languages, knowing the dealers, the art thefts, the Continent's customs everywhere. You, a divvy.'

'I've not a bean, love.' The waiters fetched some pudding thing that started to dissolve before my eyes. I started on it frantically before its calories vanished altogether. She offered me hers, but only after she'd had the icing surround, selfish bitch. That's no way to start a love partnership.

'I have beans,' she said, smiling. 'Plus, we'll have a small fortune after the share-out.'

That old thing, I thought sardonically, but tried to look gullible. 'To do what?'

'Your job tomorrow's to go with Monique Delebarre, Lovejoy. To the Repository. It'll be simple for you. You'll be told to separately consign the antiques and fakes.'

Now that she'd actually said the word, my heart swelled. Only temporary, but my most reliable symptom of impending terror. It's not uncommon with me, I find. And it always seems to happen when some woman starts projecting her expectations. I wish I wasn't a prat, and had resolve, will-power, determination, things to help life on its merry way.

'Maybe in the next reincarnation,' I said, of her offer.

'No, Lovejoy. This.' She held my gaze quite levelly even though I could hear Guy on his way back, working the tables like a demented politician. 'You have no choice. I've already arranged it with the principal backers.'

A slave? Well, I'd had my careers. 'If I say no?'

'You can't, Lovejoy. And won't want to.' She made some signal to Guy, quite openly. He saw it, promptly seated himself at a small party and instantly had them in fits, ordering wines and clapping his hands at the waiters. 'It's antiques that I'm offering.' She smiled at her plate, up at me. 'And the bliss you need. I'm the one for you, Lovejoy.'

'Antiques?' More grub, this time small dainty sweetmeats laid out round the rim of an oval dish thing.

'Why do you think the syndicate chose furniture, Lovejoy?' I listened with a carefully arranged expression of unenlightenment. 'Think what's happened to paintings, art, and you'll be able to work it out for yourself.'

Bloody cheek, I thought. I drew breath to tell her so. 'Can I have yours?'

She pushed her grub across without breaking step. 'Art theft is done to order. Thieves pierce any gallery, museum – and simply select items like catalogue shopping. Think of the Isabella Stewart Gardner museum in Boston – Rembrandt's *Storm on the Sea of Galilee*, how many millions of dollars? And Vermeer's *The Concert*. They didn't steal cheapos.'

True, what she was saying. Even when museums are supposed to be burglar-proof they still get done. And it's all preselection nowadays, like the ramraiders me and Gobbie'd seen. The robbers know what they've come for.

'We'd be the best pair on the circuit, Lovejoy. You to browse, pinpoint the genuine masterpieces in the galleries, me to organize the thefts. It's my special gift.' Her eyes went dreamy, a lovely sight. Repletion was in the air between us, and so far today we'd not touched each other.

'Did you design this scam?' The words were out before I could think.

'This?' She almost laughed, but derision was dominant. '*This*, Lovejoy? Do you know how long it has taken? Two *years*! Setting up factories in Marseilles, Birmingham and Bradford, Berlin, Amsterdam, Istanbul, Naples. Ptah!' She almost spat. 'That's your precious *this*, Lovejoy!'

Anywhere with a load of cheap immigrant labour. They'd be terrified out of their wits they'd be hoofed back to their home countries. People galore to work their lives away finishing off fakes with the same terrible effort our craftsmen had used two and three hundred years ago.

'But if it works, love . . .' I needled, for more. I could have killed her. I wish I'd not thought that now. Honest.

'An ox works, Lovejoy,' she said with that quiet intensity. 'A new Jaguar works swifter. I was against this scam from the start. I told them we must rob, instead of creating fakes.'

'Robbery's good,' I conceded, to goad her angry reminiscences further still. 'In East Anglia we finish a deal within forty-eight hours of doing a lift. I did one once – I mean, I knew somebody who did it – where we shipped the Constable painting in two hours flat, money in hand.' Money for Big John Sheehan, not for me, I was too aggrieved to say.

'Of course it's good! It's beautiful!' She almost climbed over the table in her vehemence. She poured me more wine. I drank it for the sake of appearances. 'And churches, galleries, museums – how often do they take stock, do inventories of what they have? Once every thirty years! That's survey-proved! Have you ever seen a private gallery with security worth a damn?'

More truths ripped from her tongue. I know because I was watching it closely. Banks go berserk if a penny is missing. Officers are cashiered for losing a regimental penny. The Exchequer burns the midnight oil over farthings. The Stock Exchange works dividends out to nine decimal places. But she was right. Paris's Notre Dame cathedral once learnt of a priceless sketch missing from its archives only when somebody overheard an American tourist saying he'd seen it in Washington.

'And thieves everywhere are incompetent!' She coursed on while I asked her for some more of that vanishing pudding. Well, you can cook too light, I find. 'Look at your London mob, over that Brueghel. Can you imagine?'

Well, yes. The lads had tried selling their stolen *Christ and the Woman taken in Adultery* to the Courtauld. The trouble was, it actually belonged to the Courtauld Institute in the first place. But the cracks they came out with in court gave everybody a laugh, some less bitter than others. The ramraider had abused me and Gobbie: *I heard of you bastards.* Nobody's softer-hearted than a crook, and that's a fact. A scam that depended on working immigrants till they drop endears itself to nobody. Except possibly the Moniques and Colonel Marimees of this world. And, dare I say, to the Cissies. And Guys? Veroniques? Almiras? Subject peoples have always been used thus, time immemorial.

It explained why Jan Fotheringay got done. And maybe Baff. And, possibly, the great Leon too. Unwilling to go along with the business once they learned of the cruelty involved? Jan, in on it until he sickened of the whole thing – probably never having known enough of the horrendous manufacturing processes. Baff coming across it by accident when doing one of his breakdowners on Philippe Troude's country residence. His mica Appearances spy-master's kit was proof of that. It all fitted. And Leon because he'd sickened of it, seeing the holocaust by attrition first hand . . .

'. . . fuck, Lovejoy.'

Brought me back. 'Eh?'

'I was saying', she repeated calmly, signalling to Guy, who started a deliriously jokesy farewell from his newfound life-longers, 'that we must celebrate our partnership in the oldest way. In fact I insist, Lovejoy.' Her mouth shaped itself on her lipstick. I stared transfixed as she screwed the red lipstick from its sheath, my throat sphinctering on a spoonful. I hate symbolism. It's never the real thing.

'What about Guy?' I croaked eventually.

'Yesterday's news, Lovejoy.' She continued sweetly as Guy arrived breathlessly, 'Guy. I was just telling Lovejoy . . .' She smiled knowingly into me while I frantically tried to shut her up. '. . . how here in Zurich our newspapers help antiques robbers. No sooner does a theft hit the headlines than adverts appear saying things like *Desperately Seeking Gainsborough*, or *Come Home Spitweg All is Forgiven*. It's the Swiss way of making a blunt offer for the stolen masterwork. In Munich too, of course.'

Looking sideways at Guy, I tried to laugh convincingly for his sake. But it's still pathetic to visit an ancient church expecting to see the *Virgin of the Snows*, and instead see a blank frame. The saddest photograph ever published is *Time's*, of an Italian pastor with his candle next to a framed photo of that missing masterpiece. She was right. We'd make a formidable partnership, a killing as they say.

We cemented our relationship that night. I allowed a decent interval, four seconds, before deciding to admit her when she tried the door. This is where I should report that I resisted her advances, stood firm against her seductive wiles, but can't. Shame and guilt were trumped in a trice. I relished every moment, and she seemed delighted at my willingness. Passion's nothing going for it except its total ecstasy, paradisical joy unbounded. I have a hundred logics that end up with me forgiven for each sexual transgression; they all depend on it being the woman's fault. Next morning, Veronique was purring, her wig on the pillow beside her. She was a redhead, I saw with shock. Her eyes were dark brown.

'Hello, stranger,' were her first words. 'Going to give me breakfast?'

Guy and Veronique, blond and blue-eyed as ever, delivered me – I almost said delivered me up – to Monique's huge saloon motor at nine-thirty precisely. Veronique seemed chilled, though it was quite mild. She huddled in a swagger jacket, breathing through her teeth the way women do when telling the weather off. Skilled with cosmetics, she'd disguised her neck bruises, thank God. She had kitted me out at an expensive outfitters along Pelikanstrasse. I felt done up like a tuppeny rabbit.

'You know the drill, Lovejoy,' Veronique told me as the limo drew in. 'Say nothing. Agree with Monique whatever she says. Pick out the genuine antiques. A list will be given you at the Repository. Allocate our fakes to storage, and our genuine antiques for forward shipment. That's all you do. Any questions?'

'Then what?'

Veronique smiled. She was worn out, quite on edge. I felt my spirits lifting by the minute now it was starting.

'Then you report to me.' Guy looked worse than the pair of us put together, and he'd had a good night's sleep. I wondered what he looked like without his wig, his coloured contacts, his meticulous make-up. He was beyond hearing, all senses stultified. 'I've planned for us, Lovejoy.'

'Right. How long'll I be?'

'Until Monique says, Lovejoy. We'll be here. Guy.' His name was like an order. Obediently he tried to pay attention, but it was a sorry show. *You see, Lovejoy?* Veronique's eyes asked me.

The driver was one of the hulks who'd guarded Marimee's briefing. He said nothing, flattened me against the upholstery by the force of his acceleration. I felt lonely, odd to relate, legitimately free of my watchdogs for the first time.

'Far to go, have we?' I tried, but got nothing from Suit. His neck was roll upon roll of fat. Underneath would be solid gristle. I'd never tangle with such as he. I sighed, settled back for the ride. Another giver of orders, for immediate compliance.

It was not all that long. Countryside abounds in Switzerland. Mind you, after Lysette's tour of Zurich's grotty grottoes I found that I wasn't as animose to the boring hills as usual. The Alps can be seen from the city, and I was pleased to get glimpses as we drove. Sherlock Holmes, though, said there's more sin in pretty countryside than in any sordid town.

A small village or two out, the motor pulled in and I was transferred to an even huger motor. It contained Monique.

'Morning,' I said. The Suit shoved me. I almost fell in. No reply. I sat as far away from her as possible. Never disturb a wasps' nest. A glamorous nest, though. Bonny hair, with a small hat bordering on insolence. You know that sort of encased, sheathed look some women achieve in a smart suit? Well, Monique achieved exactly that. The despond I'd felt when seeing her the first time, at Mentle Marina, returned in waves. Seeing a brilliant woman you know you'll never have always gets me down.

'Lovejoy,' she said, speaking slowly as if to an idiot. I was surprised. My name had never sounded nice before. Now I quite liked it. 'You have one task this morning.'

'To agree.'

'To obey.' A pause for it to sink in. We were driving along a narrow road. I could glimpse a lake, very beautiful. 'The Repository. You know it?'

'Of it, yes.' Taking the silence as invitation to continue, I went diffidently on. 'The world's great auction houses need a place where antiques can be safely stored. It charges buyers, vendors, antique dealers, so much a month.'

'Yes.'

More silence, so okay. 'It's security city, really. Vast. You buy an antique anywhere in the world, ship it to the Repository, and simply leave it there. Then sell it, raise loans on it, barter it, all without it moving it an inch. The bills of sale are currency among legits and crooks alike, like dollars.' I began to wax eloquent. 'They say that the world's drug money is laundered via antiques in the Repository while the antiques simply remain there under lock and key. Great scheme. And legal! I've seen a possession note change hands for almost half a million pounds, for a George III bureau owned by a SARL – that's a *société à responsibilité limitée . . .*'

Her eyes held me. I managed silence at last. I'm like this, stupidly unable to stop gabbing, a puppy trying to impress its luscious mistress. Pathetic. Plus I was scared.

She looked out of the window. 'Who is the woman. Lovejoy?'

'Woman?' She knew Veronique, because Veronique was her employee. Therefore . . . 'She's a bird – er, a girl I met.' I didn't say where. Lysette, she meant Lysette. And Gobbie?

'Where?' She was indifferent. The motor slowed on a steep incline, turned at the top. Lake, trees, distant snow.

'Actually in Paris. She's moving to Switzerland, with, er, her grandad. She's here in Zurich now.' I felt stripped, started a cringe of evasion. 'Look, Monique. You don't know what it's like. I'm living like a monk. She's the only chance −'

'Veronique.' Flat, bored. 'You've had Veronique.'

'Yes, well.' I tried hard for moral rectitude. 'I don't want to say things about her when she's not here, but I think sometimes . . . I think her bloke Guy's on drugs. It puts me off. Maybe she shares the habit. You understand?'

'Brother.'

'Eh?' That made me draw breath. Then exhale. Then inhale. Then exhale. 'Eh?'

'Her duty was to maintain you.' Was it still mere flat indifference, or was malevolence creeping in?

'Oh, she did! She did!' I chuckled, only it came out octaves wrong. 'Honestly, we've had a whale of a time . . .'

'Stop it, Lovejoy.' I stopped it, listened soberly. 'Today, we are dealers sending in a mass of antiques. They are of course the fakes, reproductions, simulants of the type you approved in Paris. The best of our manufacture. You will mark them for storage. Any that are authentic, genuine antiques, you will mark as requiring shipment. Understand?'

'Forgeries into store, trues for shipment. A bar?' Her eyebrows rose a fraction. I explained, 'Do I cut off the process at a certain number?'

'Gambling term.' Her mind, classifying away. She must find scruffs like me fascinating specimens. No wonder she was bored by everything. I was narked. I'm no arthropod. Time to tell her.

'Because', I found myself giving out nastily, 'we don't want them stealing the wrong lot, do we?'

'Stealing?'

'Your loony colonel's going to pinch the lot, Monique − the forgeries, that is. Plain as the nose − er, as a pikestaff. A kid could see that. Dollop a cran full of fakes. Make sure the Repository catalogues them as genuines. then get a mad mob to storm the building, pinch the fakes, and claim on the insurance.' It's called a spang in our talk, but telling her so would only set her etymology off again. 'The insurers'll naturally investigate the ones left untouched. Which will of course be the authentic genuine lot I earmark, right?'

187

She was smiling! Summer radiance covered the motor's interior. I swear she actually emitted light from her eyes like mediaeval saints did. It was really quite dazzling, for somebody evil.

'I'd hoped for something really original,' I went on, though now less shakily. 'The only original thing is the way you've manufactured the fakes. Immigrants, virtual slaves.'

'I did wonder,' she said. It was all so academic. 'You are sympathetic, Lovejoy. You see nothing of what is at stake.'

'I do not care for what is at stake.' I spoke it from an elocution class I'd never attended. I'd got calmer the more amused she'd become. 'Your syndicate are mad. You *imagine* the issue. It is simply not there.'

'We are here, Lovejoy.' The car was pulling in. 'Your name is Henry Getty. No relation.'

Getty? 'And yours?'

She nearly smiled. 'Mrs Monique Getty. We are married six years, are American, and own the collection we are now depositing.'

Three people advanced to meet us, stylish but sober. The Repository serfs, bright with beams of monetary affection.

'Wait for the chauffeur, Lovejoy.'

Mistake. I'd started to get out unassisted. 'Henry, dwoorlink,' I shot back, stung. 'My name's for my friends.'

Best I could manage, as the door opened and we went forward into the great unknown.

CHAPTER TWENTY-SEVEN

'Lorela Chevalier,' the woman said, smart as a pin, steady eyes. Not much change out of her, I thought, giving her my innocent millionaire smile and shaking hands. The other two proved mere serfs, oiling ahead to open doors, snapping into squawk-boxes. 'Repository Director.'

A woman of few words? I wasn't too sure I liked such novelties, but showed willing.

'Getty No Relation,' I said, typecast buffoon. 'Trade you Henry for Lorela. Deal?'

'How charming!' she exclaimed, but it was very practised and she kept her eyes on Monique. Women spot where power lies. I was instantly relegated, second-division status.

'Madame Getty,' I said lamely, out of it.

'How do you do,' from Monique, no sudden friendships on offer from Monique, thank you.

'Madame. You received our charges, conditions, prerequisites . . .?'

'Certainly.' We moved gently towards the house, me depressed because they'd slipped into French. Lorela broke off to spout a command in sideways German before continuing handling us. A lovely scoop of a face, the sort you'd trust instantly if she wasn't in antiques. I was among polyglots, handicapped by being an idiot in my own language let alone everybody else's.

The house was the carousel one we'd had that garden party in. Except it wasn't. I bet myself that this one would stay still. A disturbingly similar mansion house, in unsettlingly similar grounds. Copses, statues, lawns, everything within four hundred yards was uncannily similar. Only the sun was angled differently. I inspected the great pile as we strolled chatting along the terrace. Yes, virtually identical. The Commandant had done his groundwork well, down to the shape of the windows, doors, type of brick, even a stone buttress reinforcing the west wing. Typical military: prepare a model, then a precise life-size mock-up of the objective. Then go to war.

'Lovely house, Lorela,' I interrupted. Monique smiled with woman's complicity at the director. 'Been here long?'

'Twenty years,' from Lorela. 'The building's history, cited you'll recollect on the information we dispatched to you, is rather briefer than first-time visitors usually assume from the exterior.'

'Like many!' I chuckled. 'We've two or three phoneys too. Right, honey?' I gave Monique a squeeze. She didn't have me gunned down, but her stare lasered a hole in my skull. 'In Santa Monica Mountains.' I nudged Monique. 'Neeky here complains it's too near J. Paul Getty – you've heard of that architectural shambles down those foothills? Everybody's laughing at it.'

'They are?' Cool, cool Ms Chevalier. 'Isn't it a breathtaking concept? What did they describe it as, a secular monastery?'

I laughed, putting a sneer in. 'I'm not being critical, 'Rela, when I say that J. Paul G.'s a cardboard cut-out of the real thing – which real thing is *me*! But d'you see any de-light in having to go to Malibu to see the statues, then crawl up a Los Angeles hilltop for one of Cousin P.'s daubs?'

'Henry,' Monique said sweetly. 'Remember what we decided!'

'Right, Moneekee, right!' Buffoon, grinning, winking. I was repellent. 'No relation!'

'Fully understood,' Lorela said in her slightly American accent. Thank God they'd lapsed into English. (Hang on – why did I register that they'd *slipped* into French, but then *lapsed* into English?) 'You have brilliantly covered your origins, if I may say.' To Monique's raised eyebrows she smoothly added, 'Madame Getty will recall the security cover, detailed in the blue appendix to our advice brochures –'

'You excavate all possible approaches.' Monique nodded. 'I'm relieved to hear that our incognito status held up.'

'It's the reason we chose the Repository,' I cut in. 'In spite of your charges. They'm punishment, 'Rela, hon!'

We moved into the grand hall. Balcony, sweeping staircase, hall windows. Identical. Good old Colonel Marimee. His team only needed to stay a week at his country mansion to be able to creep in here at night and move around blindfold. Brilliant. Lorela, her Repository Director's horns out, instantly launched into a spirited defence of her fees.

'There are so many expenses!' she battled. 'You must be aware of the vast intelligence network the Repository must operate? All staff are security cleared. We have sixteen electronic, seven non-electronic auto systems –'

'You come strongly recommended, Ms Chevalier,' Monique said, which got me narked. Here was I getting the whole dump's security details, and she shuts her up. That's women all over. They can't plan. And nothing needs planning like a robbery. Hers or mine.

'Thank you, Madame,' from Lorela, leading us with the career woman's defined walk into a drawing room. She hadn't finished with me. 'You could go to cheaper . . . firms.' She hated having to mention competitors. 'Christie's, Bonhams, or –'

'Sotheby's Freeport Geneva, right? Lucky Number 13, Quai du Mont-Blanc?' I gave a sharp bark, digging Monique in the ribs. 'She hates the enemy, notice that? Trying to sound they's all *colleagues*! I like it! Commitment! Hustle, hustle, make a buck!'

Lorela gave a glacial nod. Serfs ushered coffee, chocolates, those small sweet things that get your stomach all excited but turn out to be teasing promises. The silver was modern, I noticed, and therefore gunge. Why not go the whole hog, serve plastic from Burger Boss? I scrounged some edibles from habit. The women pretended to taste one. I often wonder if birds think noshing vulgar. 'The difference is that the Repository is *the* Repository, not merely one more imitation.' I whooped in glee at her cool claim to superiority. Lorela Chevalier appraised me levelly. 'We have never, never ever, been burgled, Mr Getty. Other firms have. Which is not to say', she added, critically inspecting a maid's skill pouring coffee, 'that attempts haven't been made.'

'Henry adores the ins and outs of commerce,' Monique said distantly, to effect repair.

'Not me, Mow-Neekee.' I wouldn't leave the subject. 'Hate any kind of work.' I leered grossly at Lorela. 'Except one – know what I mean?'

'Your requirements, Madame,' La Chevalier said, struggling on under my barrage of vulgarity. 'Your possessions are to be in two lots, I understand. One group for shipment to a destination to be notified. One, much larger, group for storage until further notice.'

'Correct.' Monique held a cigarette for villeins to hurl platinum lighters at. 'My husband has decided he will select which antiques will go into which group.' She let her withering scorn for me show, peekaboo.

Lorela smiled, offered me more of the vaporous grub fragments. I took the dish from her, irritated, and had the lot, getting hungrier with each mouthful. What narked me was the cleverness of Monique's ploy. Spring my new identity on me at the last minute, as we enter the Repository, and I'd have no time to devise any alternative ploys. She'd say the play. Me dolt, her the brain – and that's how Lorela was registering us. I'd done exactly as Monique planned. For the first time I really began to wonder how far they were willing to go in all this, and felt truly disturbed. I was on a raft in the rapids.

'Your shipments are already in the motor park, Madame,' Lorela said. 'My apologies for the delay. The Repository insists on a thorough security scan of each vehicle before it can proceed to our unloading bays.'

'Had trouble?' I asked, an oaf trying to be shrewd.

'Over seventy robbery attempts in the past two years, Henry.' No harm in first names now the two women had tacitly agreed on my being a transparent idiot. 'Robbers hiding in bureaux, silence-activated robots sealed in a Sheraton commode.'

I brightened. I'd not heard of a silence-activated robot before. First chance I got, I'd ask Torsion back home if he could knock me one up, have a go at the Ipswich depot. Or had they already tried it in Newcastle? They're very innovative up there. Torsion's a Manchester brain, thinks only electronics.

'How long was its trigger mode?' I tried to work it out. 'They used a robot cable-cutter for that Commercial Street spang. It went wrong. Remote control's overrated, I reckon –'

'Henry.' Monique viciously stabbed a phoney Lalique-style ash-tray with the burning point of her cigarette, and rose. 'You don't want to tire Miss Chevalier with your famous stories. We'll get on. Come, Henry.' Like come, Paulie.

And they were off, speaking in German, French, anything but my lingo. I crammed the few remaining petits fours in my pocket to eke out life, and followed. I was right – anybody could do this, any time, anywhere. They didn't need me. Maybe, the intriguing thought came as we descended in a lift, they were making sure I wasn't employed by rival thieves? Now there's a thought . . .

Except, I saw as we went through doors on to a long wide loading platform, there was room for no fewer than six furniture pantechnicons backed up the ramp. Simulated daylight – never quite right to look at antiques by, but next best if rigged by experts. And clerks on old-fashioned high stools at tall Dickensian teller desks, snooping on all they surveyed. A humorous touch: their pens had prominent feathers. I smiled, not fooled. Every pen and pinna would be wired for sight, sound, gunfire.

'Simultaneous, then, Lorela?'

I laughed. A team of blokes in tan overalls were unloading the vans as they went. One queue of whifflers, antiques shifters, nurtured the antiques on to auto-trolleys, forming up at the end of the loading bay. There was no sound except the grunts and murmurs of the men. No fatties, no beer guts. They looked a fit lot. Thirty? With the clerks, about that.

'Queue theory, Henry,' Lorela replied without blanching. 'One line moves more expeditiously than several.' She ushered me and Monique to the head of the column. Two wall vents were already running conveyor walkways, each as wide as the lane leading to my cottage. One exit was painted yellow, one black. 'Here you will select the destinations, and check that your antiques have all arrived undamaged.'

'Well planned, Lorela!' I was starting to dislike this bird. There's such a thing as being too efficient.

'Your antiques for shipment along the yellow conveyor, storage into the black.'

'Excellent,' I said. 'Where do they lead?'

'That information is classified, Henry.' She smiled, indicated the workers. Not in front of the hired help. 'Personnel are not entitled to details that are inessential for their work sector. When you have finished, you shall be shown.'

'And the security?' I asked. 'Can't be too careful!'

Monique could have throttled me, which told me what I wanted to know. 'That I'm sure is also classified, Henry. Hadn't we better get on?'

When a woman says 'we' like that, she means you, not her.

'Sure thang.' I called for bourbon, though I can't stand the stuff, shouting let's get the hell on with it, and shelled my jacket, shoving a clerk off his stool. 'Hey!' I called as the vannies wheeled the first antique on to a disc-shaped area down below and stood waiting in the pool of light. 'Hey, Monique! All I need here's a green eyeshade to be calling the shots in the pool championship! Remember that time in Reno, Nevada?'

'Would Madame like to inspect our display of Japanese art upstairs?' Lorela suggested gracefully, signalling for the work to begin. 'I hope Madame will not be disappointed . . .'

'Thank you.'

There'd be trouble after this. I could tell from the way Monique walked, slightly faster than usual, straight as a die. Women don't walk straight as a rule, unless they're blind with rage. Check it. Watch a woman on any pavement, she proceeds anywhere but directly forward. Women waver, men walk ahead. It drives me mad when I'm in a hurry, always get stuck behind a bird and have to duck into the roadway at peril of losing my life simply to get past. Monique walked straight. Ergo, furious. And who at? I was doing my best, for God's sake. I mean, all this trouble just to case a storage dump was barmy. Mad military overkill.

'Okay, men,' I told the waiting crews of vannies. 'Zoom on.'

'One, Monsieur.' The first pair wheeled their trolley forward into the cone of light, halted.

'Turn it round, please.'

The men stepped aside. The floor revolved slowly, the piece revolving at viewing pace. An inbuilt turntable. Screens on the ceiling announced the piece's weight, the relative humidity, temperature, reflectances, dimensions scanned from a million angles. Equinoctial phases of the moon in Burundi too, I shouldn't wonder. Never seen so much data, and more searchlights than the Edinburgh Tattoo. Even the floor was illuminated, like in coffee dances. Monique and Lorela had gone. I relaxed.

'Look, lads,' I announced. 'I don't want a frigging circus. Just enough light to see the items. Switch off, and for Christ's sake stop everything spinning round.'

In silence, checking that I meant what I said, the clerks made the screens vanish to where good screens go. The lights dimmed to partially blinding.

'No frigging ears in your heads?' I yelled, really getting narked at their hesitancy. I slid off my perch and walked about, pointing. Turn that off, leave that on. Honest, you'd think this lot had never seen an antique in their lives, let alone handled daily intakes of the world's most precious antiques. I wouldn't have got so wild, except the first was a genuine card table, William IV, of the rare kingwood so dark it was almost purple. And not stained with a single dye! Lovely fold-over pattern, plain as King Billy himself always loved furniture to be. Dealers call these 'Adelaide tables', but the Queen had nowt to do with progress except import the Christmas tree to our fair land.

'Right.' I swarmed back up, looked along the clerks similarly perched, down at the whifflers in their tan overalls. Like a Le Mans starting grid, except this was interesting and important, and motor racing never can be. 'Light down to daylight candlepower. Floor still. No information.' And antiques somewhere around. Ready, steady.

Genuine. For a second I let myself bask in its warm glow, then came to. Into the yellow conveyor, right? Wasn't that the way round? Genuine antiques for shipment, fakes into the black for storage? I had to think to make sure.

'Down the yellow chute, lads.'

The pair wheeled the card table up the ramp, and unloaded it through the yellow entrance. A man accompanied it on the conveyor, standing like a moving duck on a fairground shoot, out of sight. You couldn't moan that lovely Lorela Chevalier was disorganized. Her – sorry, *the* – Repository ran like clockwork. No chinks, no loose cogs. I felt myself becoming intrigued. How was Colonel Marimee going to raid this place, get this lot out? Nearly four dozen vanloads, plus what was already here. Beyond belief for size. I felt proud to be in on a scam this big. It'd set them by the ears at the White Hart.

'Two, Monsieur.'

Marble-topped table, Dresden manufacture about 1729, give or take. Hoof feet, 'Indian' masks high on the table's knees to show trendy obsession with the cult of the Americas. Gilt gesso, very flash, beautifully preserved. Dealers would advertise it as mint. Except it was fake. Phoney, false, dud, it was still exquisitely made, by all the same old processes that the ancient craftsmen had used, in their hellish conditions . . .

'Eh? Oh.' Somebody had asked me what I'd muttered. I gave my glittering grin, but mirthless. 'Black. Storage, please. Next.'

And the next. Next. And next. Genuine down the yellow conveyor, false down the black.

An hour or so, I called a halt for a stretch. Clearly, I was here as a double-check, that the vannies hadn't pulled a switch somewhere along the way, right? Otherwise, anybody could have done it. Just sit there, sending our genuine antiques, the ones I'd bought in Paris or ordered Guy and Veronique to arrange bids for through the Hôtel Drouot auctions, down the yellow path, and the zillion fakes – which merely meant any others – down the black. I didn't feel proud, perched there saying 'Yellow', and 'Black' with the blokes sweating and lifting, trolleying the pieces in the viewing area.

Except it got easier when we resumed. The small items started coming sooner than I expected. But there was a mistake. It happened after I ordered a restart. The whifflers placed a plant stand, quite well made but modern and therefore dross, in the circle, and stepped away while the disc rose like an ancient cinema organ from the floor until it reached my eye-level, four feet away. Steps raked alongside so they could reach up. Then they brought in a small box I didn't recognize. By which I mean I really truly did.

It sat there, smiling, mystic, wondrous.

Dilemma-time. I'd not picked this little box out in Paris, at Monsieur Jacques Dreyfus's auction place, at the antique shops when I'd gone ape and bought everything genuine I could see. Therefore it should be fake, right? That was Monique's and Marimee's infallible plan. Me to buy the genuines, the syndicate to manufacture fakes. By separating the genuine antiques from the mass of fakes, I'd earn my percentage of this superb, flawless scam pay-out time. I'd got it right, hadn't I?

Now this box.

Onward shipment, the antiques I'd earmarked in Paris, right? All of which I'd seen, right? Therefore, I should recognize each and every single genuine antique, right? No problem.

The box looked at me. I looked at the box.

And, the Troude-Marimee-Monique scam scenario went, Lovejoy would funnel the fakes one way, and the genuine antiques, all familiar friends, the other. Okay?

The box sat there, waiting.

Now, I had my orders so firm I'd no doubts about what would happen if I disobeyed. Look at poor Baff. Look at poor old Leon. Look at Jan. I didn't want it to be look at poor Lovejoy. The rule was, make no changes. Monique said so. Guy and Veronique had been terrified out of their drug-sozzled wits when I'd bent them ever so slightly. The rule? Genuine antiques, ship; the fakes, storage.

The box smiled.

Genuine, pristine, beautiful, antique – *and I'd never seen it before.* It ought to be fake, so chuted down the black conveyor. Except it was genuine. So down the yellow. Except I'd never clapped eyes on it. So down the black. Except I recognised it. So yellow.

The box beamed. I smiled back. *Wotcher, Jamie* my mind went. 'Monsieur?' a puzzled vannie said.

'Sorry, mate. *Un moment*, please.'

A snuffbox, the colour of old tea, decorated with a simple engraved leaf. Not much to look at, maybe, but the genius that made it was one of the most lovely souls who ever lived. Yonks ago, it was the fashion to go and visit this crippled lad – legs paralysed as a child – in Laurencekirk. He had a great circular bed, and thereon he was stuck, for life. It had shelves, lathes, tool racks, a workbench, all within reach. There, this game youth made these boxes, plus others for tobacco, tea, needles, wools. He even made furniture, and unbelievably cased some clocks, worked in metal and engraved glass. His dander up, he stormed on making violins, flutes, even nautical instruments. A veritable ball of fire, was little crippled lame game James Sandy of Laurencekirk on his circular bed.

Even better, children used to bring him birds' eggs from the surrounding countryside – it's between Montrose and Stonehaven in what I, and others who also haven't yet lost their wits, still call Kincardine. Spectacularly, James Sandy used to hatch these eggs with the warmth of his body, then feed the fledglings and release them to the wild. Can you think of a more beautiful life? Especially considering how oppressed his dauntless spirit must have been?

'Monsieur?'

'Sorry, pardon, *entshooldigan*, er, I've a cold coming. *Un malade.*' I coughed, came to.

Jamie Sandy invented an invisible wooden hinge held by a small transfixing brass pin. Practically airtight, it was highly prized, since your pricey spice or costly snuff never lost its flavour. Eventually, their manufacture centred on Mauchline in Ayr under the Smith brothers during the Napoleonic Wars. Whole societies of collectors now fight over napkin rings, pipes, ring trees, walking sticks, all Mauchline ware in sycamore. But the real gems are these originals, made plain by little James Sandy in Laurencekirk. Okay, so they were only copies of touristy trinkets filched from Spa in Belgium. And okay, so it was a deliberate act of head-hunting when Lord Gardenston enticed a Spa souvenir-carver from the Low Countries to show the Laurencekirk locals how. But what's wrong with that? It produced one of the loveliest geniuses in that age of geniuses. It'd even be worth going to boring old Heaven one day, just to meet James Sandy.

This wasn't one of your machine-mades. Nor one of the Mauchline-ware sycamores with their nicotine-coloured varnished transfer-prints of Skegness. This was exquisite, by the original hand of an immortal. I looked away, uncomfortable. My duty was to stick to Monique's rule: fail to recognize an item, label it a fake and chute it down the black conveyor to storage.

And call James Sandy's work fake? Bloody cheek.

'Yellow,' I heard myself say calmly. Yellow for genuine, authentic, superb. Hang the cost. I could argue the genius's case any day of the week, even with Monique Delebarre and Colonel Marimee, Philippe Troude. And sighed as the bloke nodded and made for the ramp carrying Sandy's wondrous skill. Once a fool, as they say.

'Next, Monsieurs,' my voice went through a great calm. And so signalled the death of somebody I knew, somebody I shouldn't have killed at all, among the rest.

CHAPTER TWENTY-EIGHT

We were given a splendid tour. That is, we were finally shown our own stuff *in situ*.

'Vibration-proof,' Lorela Chevalier said, spinning in a doorway. 'Double reinforced glass, triple-access doors, tacky mats against quartz dust.'

'Thermal control a particular reliability?' I asked.

She darted me a hesitant smile, tried to make it genuine. 'Of course, Henry. Barometric pressure . . .' She started a routine prattle, from the Repository catalogue. I could have said most of it with her. Tonto MacIlvenny, our specialist blammer – destructive break-in artist who does over antique dealers' shops throughout East Anglia, but who charges travel expenses from our village – always carries a copy. It's a joke in the Arcade for the dealers to chorus bits from it when Tonto's done over some rival the night previous.

'Walls specially constructed to provide an –'

– effective barrier against any attempted intrusion, whether direct or by undermining, my memory trolled along. God, I could even remember where the catalogue's punctuation went wrong.

'– thus proving the most reliable storage system available.' Lorela got desperately brighter, sensing something amiss. 'These are coupled with a special security staff selected after –'

What would con artists do without the word 'special'? Not quite so well, that's what.

We endured the tour. We saw our genuine antiques being marked *Shipment! To be Notified!* through milky glass panelling, in a split-level storage compartment, the grimmest half-acre of protection I'd ever seen. I tried to look impressed. We peered through the thickest wobble glass on earth at where our superb fakes were being shrouded, ticketed, arranged, coded.

'Why's the storage separate from the others?' I asked, innocent. We'd come down a mile of corridors.

'The vehicles, Henry,' Lorela answered, having recovered from that twinge of doubt. 'It saves on moving shipment articles twice. Though,' she quickly added, 'the Repository is fully insured at Lloyd's against any kind of . . .'

And so to bed. We were offered nosh, which Monique declined,

maddening me. It's all right for them, but no sympathy for a hungry
bloke who needs regular stoking.

'No, thank you, Miss Chevalier,' Monique said. 'Henry has other
duties today.'

A cat can look at a king, they say. Ballocks, I thought morosely,
following Monique meekly out to our Rolls. Monique'd vaporize me
if I so much as mentioned lust, love, sex, desire, passion . . . Passion?
I watched her, more than the entourage who assembled to wave us
off. Passion? Monique must be moved by something akin to it, to
go to all this trouble. I made my *merci-beaucoups* and waved absent
goodbyes to Lorela.

'How long'd it take you, Monique, setting it up?'

'Two long years, Lovejoy.' She settled back into the plush
upholstery, practically purring. Replete? 'Your infantile behaviour in
there almost wrecked it.' She turned lazy eyes on me. 'For a moment
I wondered what you were up to.'

'Eh?' I gaped. 'I was helping, for Christ's sake! You women. I
got all sorts of stuff out of her. You'd never have noticed the
infra-reds, heat-activateds, periodic blips –'

She smiled, eclipsing the sun's reflected dazzle from the lake. I
swallowed, had to look away. 'You did quite well, I suppose.'

But it wouldn't have mattered if you hadn't done a damned
thing, Lovejoy. That's what she was saying. Once I'd divided the
wheat from the chaff, my usefulness had ended. For good. The
security of the entire Repository was somehow irrelevant. But why?
Colonel Marimee and his merry men were going to raid it, steal
everything I'd just sorted through. As if divining my worry, she asked,
'Can you remember the security detail, Lovejoy?'

I erupted. 'What the hell d'you think I was winkling them out
of her for, silly cow?'

She laughed, and the sun followed its reflection into shade. No
wonder poor Philippe Troude was hooked on her for life. But what's
the use of living in an orchard if you can only admire the apples,
never taste? Except blokes are funny. They'll starve in a prison of
their own making rather than walk away to freedom. We have a
bloke in our village plays a euphonium, the same musical phrase
over and over, hour after hour. People say he's loony, but he's not.
I asked him why didn't he learn something else, whereon he instantly
played me the loveliest solo I'd ever heard. The phrase he keeps
playing – still does – is one he wronged in a band concert ten, twelve
years ago. Came in half a bar late. His silver band lost the championship. Ever since, he's played alone in his cottage, sadly getting

it perfect, year after punishing year. He explained it all, anxiously bringing out the tattered music, showing me why his calamitous mistake wasn't really his fault. I said why not forget it, and simply join a new band. He looked at me like I was an idiot. See what I mean? Like Troude, languishing in Monique's disinterest instead of reaching out for Jodie Danglass who was crazy for him, or Diana, who was crazy for him. Or Almira WWCFH. Or Cissie, W. *et* eponymous *cetera.*

'Here, Monique. Why don't you let Troude off the hook?'

She stared at me. The Rolls drifted round a bend. 'I beg your pardon?' (No, not like that, more I *beg* your . . .) Meaning I was insolent. Women manage talk better than us. Maybe that's why we don't say as much as they do. Meaning talk as often. The thought lost itself in my labyrinthine mind.

'Jodie'd snap him up any day of the week. I can't honestly see the point.'

'Who?' She was astonished at what I was asking.

'The antique dealer, Jodie. Brought me to Mentle Marina that time. You tried hoodwinking me over that ancient model boat, the chair.'

'The woman?'

'Didn't you ever notice her, you selfish bi – ?' I cut off, humming and hawing my way out to safety. 'She's a friend. Was. Almost was.' And added lamely, 'Once.'

She said nothing, looked. Then clicked an intercom and gave Suit's pendulous nape directions in, what, sort of French.

We drove to a place overlooking a massive lake. Took us an hour to get there, which I could ill afford. I was desperate to meet Gobbie, see how many pantechnicons he'd counted. If Lysette had done her job, she'd have followed them, and I'd know all.

'Where are we?' We alighted at a beautiful vantage point. The restaurant overlooked a promontory, some sort of turrets visible below, a few pretty houses, trees. A tiny steamer drew a dark mathematical wake in the shimmer.

No answer, just a stroll into this expensive place. They swept aside the need for reservation, awarded us the table Monique went to as a matter of course. I followed, wondering if any second I was going to get the elbow. Suit reduced daylight near the doorway, standing motionless. She ordered, offering me the choice but deciding everything, the way they do.

'Lovejoy.' Here it comes, I thought. A duchess doesn't splurge on a serf for nothing. 'Tell me. Why are you not afraid?'

'Why?' Was I asking did I have reason to be scared, or why ask such a barmy question?

She was inspecting me. From nothing I'd been promoted to vaguely interesting specimen, a blundering troglodyte.

'You are a scruff, poor as . . .' Her education came good. 'An habitual criminal.'

Which raised the question of why she was bothering. 'Am I discharged the service, like your Foreign Legionnaires?'

Her expression clouded. 'You disturb me, Lovejoy. Most of what you say is imbecilic, except for certain phrases.'

'Look, Monique.' She was narking me more and more, and the bloody soup was frozen. It even had ice in the damned stuff. I gave it back to the waiter and said to warm it up, please. Even I can work a microwave, for God's sake. He started a distressed harangue with Monique in explosive lingo. She shut him up. He crawled off with my soup. She'd started hers. Too polite to complain, I suppose. I went on, 'I'm having enough trouble with the lingo. If it's declensions you're worried about you should have hired a certified linguist.'

'As you please.' I don't like it when women give in that quick, because they never do unless they're working something out. 'But I find it strange that you often move so surely in areas of which you are supposedly ignorant.'

'Eh?'

'It happened a number of times at the Repository. You detect human fondnesses which others might miss.' That took some saying, but she did it, with pauses. 'I'm unsure of you. Is it a quirk of speech? Or some intuition in your nature?'

My soup came back. The waiter managed not to chuck it at me, and retired rolling his eyes. 'Well,' I told her defiantly, 'he should have got it right in the first place.' Hot, at last.

'You mention the Foreign Legion. Our Red-and-Greens.' She looked at me as I quaffed away, but her eyes were somewhere else. 'Founded in 1831, mainly to sweep up drunken German students bothering our towns. But French in culture, as we are. You can never understand, Lovejoy. Your multiculture society is hopeless. We meld all comers into one entity called France.'

'Or else what?' I'd have had the rest of her soup except the waiter would disintegrate when I told him to hot it up.

'Or else they are superfluous to requirements, Lovejoy.' The main course came steaming, thank God. The waiter was learning. 'Our Legion's desertion rate was never half that of the American forces, though envious nations make much of our discipline.'

Our? I tried to find a resemblance to Marimee in her features. Well, thinking of Veronique and her brother Guy. And Lysette, more platonically related to Jan.

'We French face an onslaught, Lovejoy. On spelling – you'll not have heard of the criminals on Rocard's High Council on the French Language, who want to change the spelling of nearly a tenth of our words. Or the idiot bureaucrats of Brussels who want to change them all! To compel us, by economic force. What is Brussels, but a suburb of a suburb? France is under attack. Washington's population evaluers score Paris – *Paris!* – a mere seventy-two per cent. Our brilliant war record is decried as sham. Our superb wines are ignored – bribery among international judges! So we French now lead the world – in swallowing tranquillizers, twice the German rate! And in counterfeiting, of course. Along the Rue de la Grande Truanderie – the Street of Crooks, in your appalling language, Lovejoy – we excel in laserprinted fifty-franc notes.'

Nice does the best 200-franc notes, though, I'd heard, but wisely did not say. She almost hit two poor approaching waiters, who almost recoiled. She managed to stay silent until they'd poured the wine and retreated. 'Our President learns from the American Secretary of State that France depends on Ami nuclear technology, and has to admit ignorance of this at a public dinner table. Our airports score –'

'Can I start, love?' I was famished.

'– highly. But for what? *Perfume!* Nothing else!' Well I started anyway. 'Our empire is gone, our currency surrenders to the Common Market. We must eat foreign food, as ordered by foreign minnows in Brussels! And our great Marseillaise is to be bowdlerized. No longer *Aux armes, mes citoyens!* It's to be *All one, friends, dance hand in hand. Marchons* becomes *Skip on.*' She was pale, her lips bloodless. 'Rouget de Lisle will turn in his grave.'

'Politics is shifting sand.' I get uncomfortable.

'Once it was only the Americans – with their crass ambassadors. Camelot Country, whose President got the Pulitzer Prize for *Profiles in Courage* written by somebody else.' She became bitter, really vicious, the way all people speak of an envied friend. 'Still, it shows there are advantages to having a President with a father capable of making a fortune from buying up cheap liquor licences during Prohibition.'

'Your art –' I was sick of her and her bloody whining. So folk have faults. What else is new?

'Is thieved, stolen. You see the headlines, Lovejoy: *Paris: The*

Empty Frames! Our honour is shattered everywhere now that any hairy student actor can walk in and steal —'

'He wore a wig to look like a Rasta.' I had a mouthful. 'Pretty clever. Sixteenth arrondissement, wasn't it? Your Banditry Repression Brigade moved pretty sharpish.'

She fell silent. I looked up, waiting.

'You see, Lovejoy?' She'd cooled her ardour. 'You are informed. It happens too often.'

'Don't be daft, love. Everybody goes through a bad patch, even France. You've one of the loveliest countries on earth. Lovely lingo. Look at us. We drop clangers all over the place.'

'Clangers?'

'Faults, make mistakes. Christ, love, the Vatican's own postage stamps got their Latin wrong last year! And C-14 carbon dating's off by 3,500 years – when we thought it infallible!' I grinned. 'Sometimes errors help. Like that statue of Hercules. Second century, right? Its top half's in the Met – didn't they pay to have it smuggled out of, where, Ankara? No wonder the Turks went mental. Where're you from, love?'

'Marseilles.' It was out without thought. She shrugged, a pretty sight. A shoulder lifted, head a little aslant. Beautiful enough to paint, eat, love. Well, maybe not love. You'd never survive. 'Now my city is broke, unemployment rife. Shops close daily. The French population declines, replaced by a tide of immigrants who know nothing of France. The great docks have moved to Barcelona – *Barcelona!* – and Anvers. The influx of Africans is said to number only 56,000, clearly false.'

'So?' I said cheerfully. 'Incomers blend in two generations —'

'The main street was exquisite, Lovejoy.' She was toying wistfully with her food. It was a lovely pie thing, fish and mushrooms with some sauce stuff, vegetables undercooked, best meal on earth. I borrowed a bit from her plate while she talked, to help her. Her eyes were dreamy. 'La Canebière outshone the Champs Élysées for glamour and luxury. Now it's a series of cheap pizza stalls, an Arab souk where no self-respecting Frenchman walks at night unless with guard dogs. And even then you have to climb over filth, piled rubbish.' She focused on me. I was having her spuds. 'You don't think this reasonable, Lovejoy?'

'No, love. Not for self-indulgence. Londoners once petitioned against French immigrants for pinching jobs. Charles the Second had the sense to say no, let the Huguenots come.'

'Liberalism is weakness, Lovejoy.' She said it by rote.

'If you say so, love. Any chance of some more greens?' She signalled, the waiters sprang. 'I don't blame your dockies for demonstrating now the Spanish have abolished their Customs and Excise posts. Wherever there's a border barrier, there's a fortune in fiddles. That's what they're mad at.'

She watched me nosh. 'My lovely Marseilles' major product is now crime, Lovejoy. Gang wars, killings. France has left.'

'Anything I can do, love?' I honestly meant it. But what? Nostalgia's the only untreatable disease.

'You've done it, Lovejoy. Divvying.' She asked a bit more about Jodie Danglass, who she was, what she did, but in malicious tones that gave me goose-pimples. Ten minutes later, me still trying to scoff some profiteroles, she upped and offed without so much as a word of warning. And that was that.

'How many, Gobbie?'

'Fifty-two, Lovejoy.'

'Where to?' Fifty-two pantechnicons? Christ.

'South at first. Hell of a convoy.' He grinned. 'At first.'

'What do you mean at first?'

He was falling about, silly old fool. 'They didn't ever form up. They left in dribs and drabs. Know what, Lovejoy?'

'No?' *Every van looked slightly different.*

'They wus every shape and size you ever did see.' I'd counted on it. 'Lysette's chasing after three. She didn't know what she oughter do. They're labelled something about electricity.'

'The vans had different insignia?'

'Far as we could tell, son. We only guessed at fifty-two.' He went apologetic. 'Three entrances, see? Only two of us counting, from hiding . . .'

Pity. If I'd been there, I could have told whether they had been crammed with antiques or not. Instead, I'd been delayed hearing out Monique's Good Old Days saga.

'Right, Gobbie. That's it, then.' We were in a nosh bar near the St Peterskirche. I'd paid a king's ransom for two coffees and a cake. 'They'll hit the Repository in two days.'

'How'll they get the stuff out, Lovejoy? It's a hell of a lot to get in by legitimate means, let alone rob.'

'Wish I knew. Where's Lysette going to meet us?'

We left, me thinking I'd solved nearly everything, talking over old scams. The cafés of Zurich aren't a patch on the Paris ones, which have atmosphere. I know Switzerland pretends to be over seven centuries old, but that's a fib. But Paris really truly has it. I said as much to Gobbie, laughing. He looked at me doubtfully as we walked down a narrow street to the Fraumunster. I was saying what a high old time I'd had in Paris, racing Guy and Veronique round the antique shops, how I'd seen the main fakes' storage area there for the Troude-Monique scam.

Talking to myself. Gobbie had stopped. He was in the gloaming behind me, standing quite still. It was coming dusk.

'Gobbie?' I called back. 'You all right?'

He came on slowly. 'Lovejoy?' he asked. 'You do understand?'

'Eh?' I could have clouted the silly old git. 'Course I do! I'm the one called you in, you burk.' Maybe it was senility.

'Then tell me.' There was hardly anyone about. The Fraumunster was lit. We would have seen eavesdroppers.

'Tell you?' Of all the frigging cheek. Here was this old loon that I'd called out of retirement, accusing me of not sussing an antiques heist? I suppressed my anger, took a breath. I liked the old soldier. He and Lysette got on well. I didn't want her raging at me because of my temper.

So, strolling to the Fraumunster – clever architecture, I'm sure, but somehow threatening – I summarized the entire scam for his thick idiot brain. I mean, I'd only unmothballed him because he knew the Continent, for God's sake.

'Look, Gobbie,' I told him, words of half a syllable for his cretinoidal nut. 'These French raise a syndicate, see? Anglo-French money. They use it to create a zillion superb fakes, mostly furniture.' Christ, I'd given it to the old dolt clear as day. He'd seen the bloody vans filled with the stuff.

'And?' He'd gone all quiet. You can really go off people, even friends. I hated the bastard.

'And, moron,' I sailed on, 'they lodge them into the biggest antiques repository on earth. Got it so far?'

'And?'

One more 'And' and I'd do him. 'Then they nick them, and claim on the insurance – as if they were all genuine!' I chuckled, such gaiety. 'See? Now, the Repository's no innocent about security, so the Commandant will have egg on his face when his robbery team goes in!'

My laughter died away. He'd stopped. We were out into the Fraumunster's famous square, except it's got more side's than even Swiss squares should have. 'And?'

'Well,' I said, trying to recapture the moment. His old whiskery face was staring at me in disbelief. 'I thought me and thee'd hang about for the last act. See Marimee's face when . . .'

'I thought even you'd have spotted the obvious, Lovejoy.' His voice was so quiet I had to strain to hear the old loon.

'*Even* me?' I tapped his chest, choking on rage. 'Listen to me, you silly old sod. I brought you over because you wanted one last go at an all time grandy. What was it you said, at that boot sale? Bring the old times back. And I have! This is the . . . Gobbie?' I almost stepped back in horror. He was crying.

Tears were streaming down his face. I gaped. Men don't weep. We're not allowed. Old soldiers like Gobbie especially don't. They've seen it all. And why don't these silly old soaks shave proper, for God's sake?

'Gobbie?' I said dully. 'What's up, pal? I'm not really narked. Honest.'

'Lovejoy,' he managed, in a terrible silent voice I'd never heard him use before. I can hear it yet. Close my eyes, and I see him in that floodlit square under the towering Zurich church. 'What about the children?'

CHAPTER TWENTY-NINE

Needle Park, as they call it, is as unappetizing as, well, the same in any big city these days. The local gesture at liberalism, of a sort. Gobbie dropped me off. I'd told him I'd be an hour or so.

A few of the huddles looked derelicts, but some were astonishingly affluent. Several decent overcoats, a trilby or two, and one bird smartly dressed in a skirt suit of classic career-woman line. It makes you wonder. One group was actually auctioning drugs, the business ethic at play. I finally found Guy and Veronique round a sort of big candle among so-o-o-o happy friends. Guy shouted, some joke. Everybody laughed at me. If it centred on my stupidity, he'd be right.

'Evening, Guy.'

'Kiye!' several chorused my pronunciation. One added in a shrill roar, 'Khow kquaint!'

The laughter died. Somebody coughed, racked and shivering. One drank, offered me a sip. I declined, thanks.

'Chance of a word, please?' I asked. Guy, rolling his eyes, came, Veronique too. She looked in slightly the better shape. I turned after a pace or two and sized them up.

Here stood my two guardians, relaxed, cool. The same custodians, note, who had crumbled in near-terror when I'd gone missing for a few hours among the antique shops of Paris. A decided change, now I'd done my bit. Or now that I was expendable?

'You're not keeping track of me, Veronique.' I hoped for a reasonable reply. Guy seemed beyond it. 'Instead you're shooting the toot, or whatever you people say.'

She swayed, staring through me. Distant traffic stuttered sedately, the Swiss still methodically switching their engines off at a hint of a red. I wondered, is it to save petrol for the fatherland?

'Time off, Lovejoy.'

'Look. I've a problem.' I hesitated, hoping my bad acting wasn't over the top. 'I've the chance', I admitted nobly, 'of, er, seeing a girl. But I've some money coming in from East Anglia. To the hotel, next couple of hours, I think. I need it signed for.'

'Money?' Guy was on Planet Earth after all.

'As a draft. In my name.' I smiled apologetically at Veronique, who'd also momentarily tethered her mind to reality at the mention of gelt. 'I can't be in two places at once.'

'What girl?' Veronique asked.

'Nobody important, love,' I said. 'Not anyone *you* need worry about. But I can see you're busy . . .' That partly mollified her.

'I know!' cried Guy, almost leaping as the notion struck him. '*We'll* accept the money for you, Lovejoy!' I thought the penny'd never drop. 'Sign an authorization with the concierge, and we'll do it!'

'Thanks, pals.' I waved farewell. 'Oh, one thing. How long can I be away? Only, Colonel Marimee said I'd be needed.'

'You should be able to get in enough pokes before tomorrow night, Lovejoy.' Guy leered, fell over. Veronique started to haul him upright. Somebody nearby relieved himself into a small bush. Another vomited. God. Ecstasy, at these prices?

'See you back at the hotel, troops. Sevenish do?'

They called seven'd be ample. So the Repository would be a midnight job. I had twenty-four hours. They could buy a hundred comas with my money, as long as I was free of them for a bit. As it was, I got free of them for much, much longer.

Gobbie drove us out of Zurich. I tried telling him the way we'd come, me and my golden pair. I vaguely remember road numbers, but things never look the same returning. The old Italian proverb came dimly from some old Western film, look behind, not before. Fine time to remember good advice when it's pointless. He told me to stop telling him the way. Okay, so he knew the Continent and I didn't. No need to get irascible.

Lysette was along. Never known such a quiet lass. She only spoke at the first Strasbourg sign. I'd dozed off.

'Why is that money necessary, Lovejoy? I have credit cards.'

She smelled nice. She'd been there when I'd phoned the upright, honest Dicko Chave. He'd promised to wire me a load of zlotniks against some antiques I'd found. That story wouldn't have been enough to make him trust me. I'd had to invent a lovely unmarried lass I'd also discovered, as his new possible partner. He'd urged me to propose on his behalf. Poor old Dicko.

'The one commodity my addict custodians need is money. The scent of it winkled the time of the robbery from them.'

'They'll steal it, Lovejoy,' from old Gobbie at the wheel, his face lit by the road lights. 'You should have only pretended there was money coming.'

'No. They'd have guessed, then I'd have been in the soup.' I'd not said how much, but to addicts all money promises bliss.

We drove on. I'd not said anything to Lysette about the terrible truth that Gobbie'd made me face. I couldn't. But I suspected she'd known the true story long since. As I had. And maybe poor Baff Bavington had. And poor Leon, the French divvy. And Jan Fotheringay her brother. Jesus, but I'm thick. That's half my trouble. I'll work something out, then ignore the obvious if it's too horrible to contemplate. Birds are always picking at me for never facing up. Hateful, that they might be right. It's as if I know the words, the tune, but don't understand the song.

'Where did they go, love? Your three vans.'

'Lausanne.'

'Lausanne? Is that still in Switzerl –?'

'I've made a map with detailed directions, Lovejoy.' She spoke curtly. She meant I wasn't worth talking to. Next breath she told me why. 'I believe you already know the address.'

I hate it. A bloke ought to be allowed one or two tricks, even though they're transparent. I mean, we're not allowed to say when a woman's deceit is obvious, are we? But they can say whatever they like. It galls me. Women have too many blinking privileges for my liking. 'Did other vans turn up?'

'I counted eighteen, in Lausanne.'

So they probably all went there, By one route or another. I'd think of a cutting rejoinder to Lysette any second.

'Lovejoy?' Gobbie said gruffly. 'We're here. Paris. Where was it?'

The nausea rose within me. I'd been sick at my non-thought thoughts for a fortnight, longer even. Now I was back.

'Look,' I tried, surly. 'We'll stop for coffee. It's almost ten o'clock. We've not stopped or anything –'

'*Lovejoy*,' from Lysette. Gobbie said nothing, waited while traffic honked and motorists yelled imprecations.

'Right, Gobbie.' Where had we driven, that night in Dreyfus's trundlesome motor? Seine, Arc de Triomphe, Sacré Coeur, then doubled back to that sordid Paris-shouldn't-have-such-districts near the sound of trains. I managed to direct us through the knitted thoroughfares. We parked, by a fluke, and walked.

Lysette walked with her arm through Gobbie's, I noticed, narked. Gobbie occasionally made as if to glance at me, then avoided my eyes. It took us nearly an hour. We'd actually passed the doorway before I recognized the church-hall-type entrance down a few steps, cardboarded windows opposite, the same smell of cooking. It was wise to walk on by, in case one of those immobile beefy blokes had been left on watch.

'It's here, Gobbie. That's the way in.' Children were playing nearby, calling in foreign dialects. I didn't look at them. It was dark, the street lighting furtive. 'What now?'

'You two off out of it, Lovejoy. I'll look round the district. Be at the corner in an hour, eh?'

Gobbie shuffled away on his quest. Lysette came with me, to a small caff near the Deux Magots. When she did speak it was so unexpected I almost spilled my coffee.

'I should have taken you to the Procope, Rue de l'Ancienne Comédie,' she said quietly. We were at a pavement table. 'Benjamin Franklin went there. But your favourite would have been Voltaire. He also. And Napoleon.'

I would have liked Voltaire? How did she know? I knew I'd look him up sooner or later, be no wiser.

'There are whole books written on Parisian cafés, Lovejoy.' I quite liked my name, first time I could remember since Monique said it. 'Hemingway objected when the proprietors of the Closerie des Lilas – from its lilacs, you know? – made their waiters lose their moustaches. No longer chic, you see?'

'Oh, right.' There isn't a lot you can say to this quiet reflective stuff, especially from a bird like Lysette. You never know whether it's leading up.

'The Coupole has been supplanted by a monstrosity. Beckett, Henry Miller . . .'

My attention wandered. Nobody I recognized around the small square. Students burst into laughter at a nearby table. Two nurses slumped tiredly on window chairs, smoking. Nurses made me remember that gross but fantastically exuberant Katta. Wouldn't have minded her giving me something she gave Paulie. Isn't it odd how –

'Eh?' An important question had come up.

'. . . kill you, Lovejoy.' Her last words.

'Who?' People looked across with sudden interest. I must have yelped. I quickly smiled for the sake of appearances. I don't know what it looked like, but it felt pretty ghastly from within.

'The syndicate.'

Sweat beaded my forehead, started to trickle down my back. Jodie Danglass was their helper. Surely she wouldn't be party to anything so . . .? And Paulie? Or his slavish fatty Katta? The suave Troude? The chilling Monique Delebarre might, any day of the week. Guy and Veronique would slay their grannies for a bob, par for their mainline course. Colonel Marimee was deranged; I couldn't count him among the faint-hearts, and who knew how many goons he had to pull the rip? But Sandy, for God's sake? No wonder Mel had cut and run. Had Mel known how terrible the scam was? Worse, did Sandy?

'Why'd you visit Jan, Lovejoy?' Still flat of voice. 'I recognize you from the hospital, coming out of the lift.'

'Dunno. Worried about me getting drawn into something I didn't understand, I suppose.'

'Jan and Sandy have been . . . friends for months.' She shrugged. 'It's difficult. To be sister to a brother with . . .'

'Must be.' Jan and Sandy now? So Mel had good personal reason to scarper, not just money.

'You could leave, Lovejoy.' I wished she'd not fiddle with her spoon. I sometimes wonder if women nark me deliberately.

'Leave?' I said blankly. 'Leave? As in . . .?'

'Leave. With me. Now, when Gobbie comes, simply drive home.'

That quiet voice, her luscious hair, casual manner, the serene intensity of her Pre-Raphaelite features. All the time cerebrating away like a think-tank.

'*With* you?' She'd made me gape.

'Gobbie will make his own way. He knows the routes.' She raised her eyes to mine. I'd never seen such deep eyes, though they were at the front, if you follow. Not sunken, I mean. 'You must ask yourself why stay, Lovejoy.'

I really hate that. Asking me why's my business, not hers. 'Why?' I asked her.

'You must learn your own reasons, if you haven't already discovered them for yourself.'

'Look, love,' I said, peeved, frightened. 'This whole thing's made me spew up, drift around foreign lands with —'

'You're ignorant, Lovejoy,' she said softly. 'Ignorance of the simple kind, not malice. But it draws you out of your depth.' She coloured slightly. 'I would care for you, you see.'

Care for how? I nearly said, like you did your brother Jan? Mercifully, Gobbie wheezed into a chair, his eyes rheumy.

'Found one of their factories, Lovejoy. Within a stone's throw of the depot. Next street but three.' He cleared his gruff old throttle. 'I could tell you about it. Save you seeing?'

Lam out? That's what Lysette wanted me to do. 'No, Gobbie. I'll see.' It was me'd been sickened, suffered by avoiding the truth. This served me right. 'Stay here, Lysette.' I rose. She came anyway. I sighed. One word from me, birds do whatever they want. It's their version of loyal co-operation.

Distances in Paris never seem very far, not like London where sequential postal numbers signify districts miles apart. Paris is yards rather than furlongs. We were there in a trice, Gobbie flagging somewhat as we made the last street. I must have been hurrying. Lysette told me to take my time, that Gobbie had already done too much. She didn't mention her prodigious driving, staying on the ball, Lausanne and back, Zurich to Paris. And making mad proposals to a nerk like me.

'See that covered way, son?' There was a kind of projection from a long wall. It resembled one of those ironwork half-cloisters you get over the side entrances of London theatres, for early-evening queues that no longer come.

'Aye?' Several stacked street barrows. Steps, a few sacking-covered windows, some lantern lights, one or two bare bulbs. Rubbish littered the pavements. That scented cooking, metal clanking somewhere, a few shouts in non-French, a background hum. 'Is there a way in?'

'The steps go up, but have ones leading to the cellars beside.'

'So I go down?' Nobody along these pavements, not at this hour. I felt my nape prickle.

'No, son. You go up.' With resigned patience, 'Then you can look down into the cellar area, see?'

Now he was deliberately narking me. 'How the hell did I know they'd made it all into one?'

''Cos it's a workshop.' He was disgusted by my slowness. Lysette said nothing.

'Wait here.' I left them, eeled down the narrow street. The hum and clanking grew louder. Something thudded, shouts rose, then settled down to a hum. I went softly, looked back. Gobbie and Lysette had vanished. The air felt smoky. The light was only clear at the top of the street now. Here was gloom, foreboding, trouble. I almost started to whistle, like walking past the churchyard coming back from the White Hart.

Some sort of torch would have done me, but I'd not the sense. How had Gobbie managed it? Go up, he's said, then you can look down. The steps were of the old-fashioned sort you see in North London, iron railings both sides. Some gone, jagged pegs waiting to stab you as you fell.

The door was blowing faintly, sacking, outwards. No lights except some feeble glow – oil lantern? – from within. I shoved. To my surprise it scraped ajar. I stepped in. Somebody calling, others yelling, childish voices answering. A bloke threatening.

Glass, pieces of broken glass, on bare linoleum. Flaking everything, by the light of the oil lamp hung beside the stairs. Oil lamps meant no traceable electricity bill. Up or down? I went where the light glowed most, which was directly ahead beside the staircase. The place stank.

One unbelievable creaking woodwork step down, then a sheen from below. Round a corner, me shuffling inchwise and the hum growing and the shouts louder. If only I could have understood what they were saying. Lots of little voices, the gruff deeper voice yelling abuse. Near silence, then the hum resuming.

And I saw them, suddenly there, children down in the cellars. The floor of what had been the living room had been knocked out, almost ripped, the floorboards scagged at their insertions into the walls near my feet. They had been unceremoniously hacked away. I was near the margin. Another foot or two, I'd have tumbled over and been down among them.

Them? Three or four dozen children, bare-arse naked, working on furniture, planed mahogany, even some walnut. Lovely aroma of fresh heartwood. But it was looking down into hell. Straight out of the seventeenth century, the children were smoothing with their hands, feet. Some were standing on the wooden surfaces, holding on to rods stretched from cellar wall to cellar wall. Oil lanterns shone light.

The children's bodies glistened with sweat. Their hands bled. One little mite was weeping, trying to lick his palms. Another had actually fallen asleep. Even as I looked he got whipped awake with a riding crop.

They were polishing. One boy nudged his pal, keep going, keep going. Some chanted, working in time. One tiny mite went along the rows, casting up handfuls of dust on the worked surfaces.

The man walking down the aisles of furniture – five rows, three or four pieces a row – switched the air. I swear that he lashed a little lass from sheer habit. A couple of men were seated at a deal table beneath two lamps across from where I stood looking down, playing cards. Playing *cards*. Smoking cigarettes. The whipmaster looked at his watch, was downcast at the time and lashed here and there in annoyance.

Two smaller children burst in from the rear cellar door, trying to haul a plastic bowl. I recognized the technique. Brick-dust, doubtless.

The average age? It looked about six, at a guess. The oldest child was about nine, the youngest threeish. They were bloodied, blistered, hands and soles dropping sweat and blister water. They were all scarred, too experienced in life to be scared very much. One's shoulder was a carbuncled, pus-pouring red mass. It took me a while to move away.

Odd, but I walked from there without a single creak of the floorboards. I swear I glided. Odd because when you're desperately trying to avoid making a noise, everything you touch peals like thunder. When you don't give a damn, you don't make a sound. I actually *wanted* that whip-toting flogger to catch me. I'd have . . . I'd have run like a gazelle. I know I would.

'Gobbie?' I called at the corner. 'Where the hell?'

They were watching me come. Lysette said nothing. Gobbie said, 'Awright, son?'

'Stop asking that, stupid old bugger.'

Twice they had to call to me, correct my direction when I'd marched ahead, as if I knew the way and they didn't instead of the other way round. The motor'd had nothing thieved.

'I expected no wheels,' I joked. 'This sort of district.'

'Don't, Lovejoy,' from Lysette as we boarded.

I swung round in the seat, finger raised. 'Not another word from you, love,' I said. My voice was a hoarse whisper, astonishing, because I'd said nowt much. 'Not one.'

'It's not your fault, Lovejoy,' she was saying, when I lashed my hand across her face and she fell back with a cry.

'Now then, son,' Gobbie gave me.

'You too,' that funny whisper said. 'Get us to Zurich.'

'Via where?' Gobbie asked. 'Lausanne —'

I looked at him. It was enough. He fired the engine, and we flew from Paris like angels.

CHAPTER THIRTY

'Thanks,' I told them just before they dropped me off. 'You've been pals. See you at home, eh?'

'What're you going to do, Lovejoy?'

'Join the scam.' I gave Lysette a really sound smile. 'Get my chop, live in idle richness.' They didn't roll in the aisles. My jokes always fall flat. I can't even remember ones I'm told.

'You go careful, son.'

'Trust me.' Gobbie was looking at me oddly. Lysette stared at her knees. 'You know my address.' I hate that phrase, keep in touch. It always means farewell.

Darkness had fallen, or what passes for darkness in Zurich. That means lights everywhere, skies filled with sheen, lake reflecting every glim. Our village has an astronomer who keeps suing everybody for light pollution. He'd have a ball here.

'So long. And ta.' I waved from the pavement.

To the hotel. Guy and Veronique weren't in their room. I lay on my bed. Odd, but I no longer felt sick. I felt calm but hot, sort of flu round-the-corner.

Lysette had begun to speak when we were on the trunk road heading east. Steadily, without inflection almost, stating facts rather than wanting to tell anybody anything.

'There's still an anti-slavery society,' she said quietly, of nothing in particular. Nobody had said anything until then. I looked round and asked, 'Eh?' but she ignored me.

'It only scratches the surface. There are more child slaves now than in the whole of history. In leading industrial nations – us Western peoples – just as elsewhere. Nations sign the UN Articles against it, and take no notice –'

'Shut up.' My analytical thought for the day.

'Jan was approached by an illegal immigrant,' Lysette said in that grave non-voice of hers. She might have been reading football results. 'Her children were debt-bonded in Whitechapel. She asked his help, because she'd seen him photographed with one of the financiers. Jan was horrified.'

'Debt-bonded?' Gobbie asked it, knowing I'm stubborn.

'There are two forms of child slavery. Chattel slavery – old-fashioned slavery, bought and sold. It exists in North Africa, elsewhere.

There are cases reported every year in Western countries, even among diplomats' family servants. In debt bondage children work to pay off parents' debts – India, Pakistan, South America, Africa, the Philippines. I would tell you stories, but you would not bear them, Lovejoy.'

The stupid bitch had gone on and on. I stared at the ceiling, hearing Guy and Veronique arrive next door. They sounded three sheets to the wind, or similar. '. . . Ten thousand little boys were imported from Bihar to make carpets in Mirzapur-Varanasi. They were bought, bonded, simply stolen children. They work from four every morning until two o'clock in the afternoon. Then they are fed one bread *roti* with lentils, and work on to midnight when they're allowed to sleep after another similar meal. I learned this after Jan spoke with the woman.'

'What work?'

'Making nice carpets. Making nice bricks. Making nice polished gems for the elegant West End shops, to please elegant Western ladies. Quarrying stones, making matches, rag-picking, doing *zari* embroidery. And faking –'

'Ta, love.' I meant shut up. Some hopes.

'Plantations, domestics, factories.' Christ, had the stupid bitch never heard of inflexion? She sounded on automatic. 'Thailand's supposed to lead the world, Lovejoy. For exploitation of over three million child slaves, I mean: drug-packers, child prostitutes, leading exporter of bonded or chattelled slaves to the Gulf, Europe. Rong-mung Road, near Bangkok's railway station, the children are sold, to be chained workforces, or to baby brothels. Jan was horrified, not knowing, you see. He isn't commercially minded. They told him at the Anti-Slavery place. I think they said ten pounds sterling to buy one child slave, though you can get wholesale deals . . .'

'Excuse me, please. Can you stop half a sec, Gobbie?'

I stared at the ceiling some more. I'd actually uttered the words, remembering, in the privacy of my own hotel doss-house room. Gobbie'd not stopped, of course. How could he, million miles an hour on some fast roads? I'd grumbled, finally told Gobbie to shut her up. She'd only obeyed when Gobbie gravelled out, 'That'll do, Lysette.' Why did she never do as I said, only that gerontic old sod? It gets my goat.

'Lovejoy?' Veronique opening my door made me leap a mile. She laughed, eyes shining with that unholy thrill that came from within. 'What were you doing? I startle you?'

'Er, no, love, ta.' I was bathed in sweat. 'Time, is it?' *Every one*

*of Great Britain's old manufacturing towns, Glasgow to London, through
the industrial North and Midlands, immigrant children are beaten, flogged to
labour . . .*

'We've just had word.' She spoke coyly. 'It's tomorrow afternoon.
You can get on with your merrymaking.' She paused, hand on the
door, provocative. At least, she would have been provocative, except
drugs meant she was no longer Veronique. She was a trillion different
other folk, people I'd never met and didn't know. Like talking to a
chemistry set.

'Off?' I said stupidly, mind cogging slowly into action.

'Postponed.' She smiled over her lie, really more of a leer.
Hideous. To think that I'd – 'Worth it, was she?'

Lost. 'Worth it?'

'You look, how d'you say in English, shagged out, Lovejoy.'

Whoops. Forgotten I was supposed to have been wassailing with
a local bird. 'Superb, love,' I said weakly. Well, Swiss national
honour and all that. 'Beautiful.'

'Good as I?'

'Not quite, no.'

'Tomorrow, Lovejoy, you and I will make sweet music, no?'

'No. I mean yes.'

She smiled. I'd never seen eyes so brilliant. 'It will be such lovely
music, Lovejoy. Like never before!' Her sentences were fraying in
their chemical heaven.

'Great. See you tomorrow, then. Ah, the money, love?'

She pouted. 'You do not trust little Veronique?'

'Well, I need to, er, take the lady for supper.'

'Guy is sleeping, Lovejoy. He has your money. I shall wake him
eventually and bring it to you.'

She left then, me calling a ta, see her later, all that. I let their
bedroom whoopee start, heard them sink to silence, then departed
that place, taking neither scrip nor purse nor staff to aid me on my
way. Well, not exactly. I actually went into their room, stole Guy's
car keys from his jacket while they slept their sleep of the dust, and
nicked their Porsche. My lies were as good as her lies any day.

The Repository, I worked out as I drove, was model for Colonel
Marimee's mock-up. At the garden party, it had slowly swivelled,
the way military models do when top brass play tactical planning.
That way, the sun, moon, prevailing winds can be controlled, varied
to whatever time their plodding minds plan the action. It's called
actual simulation, as if there can be such a thing.

217

No daytime action, so night, with a moon as now, fitful yet businesslike. While admiring Lorela Chevalier's territory, I'd particularly admired the surrounding hillsides. Quite nice mountains, really. Two positions overlooked the Repository mansion house. One was severely wooded, the other somewhat more sparsely. I paused to look at Guy's map. The bloody thing didn't give me phases of the moon. Just typical, I raged. The one time I needed it, they leave it out. Cartographers don't deserve the money we spend on them, that's for sure. I'd been under fire once or twice, and knew that you want to look down on a target. You leave it in light, while staying in shadow. I watched for the moon as I drove. The wretched thing never seemed to stay in one position. Was it always like that? Ours back in East Anglia wasn't. Ours is tranquil, restfully there until it sinks behind some clouds to kip the day out. This Swiss moon rolled about like a puzzle pill, sodding thing. Dishonest.

Odd that I wasn't at all tired. Must be an adrenalin thing. Of the two sharp hills dominating the Repository, I'd already decided the one from which to watch the action. The wooded one, further along the twisting contoured road but more concealment for your actual coward. I felt excited, like going to a film I'd been awaiting. The Repository would be in darkness, leaving me blindly guessing which method Colonel Marimee had chosen to pull the robbery. Or the Repository would be lit like a football field, in which case I'd be the lone spectator at the grandest slickest action ever devised. I had no doubts about Marimee's military genius. He'd scam the stuff out somehow, no problem. I was quivering to see how, though. Tonight I'd have all the excitement, and none of the risks. Like a holiday. I had to stop myself from singing that Vivaldi bit about a hundred sexy maidens.

And after this, home. Please.

Off the road, on the summit among trees. Pity about Swiss trees, really, all pines or pine-lookers. No variation, planted by some maths teacher with a theodolite, growing to order. Snow, surprised me, mainly because some of it was starting to fall thick, unwieldy. A sky glow showed me direction, though I'd already worked that out. Left? I thought about the motor, backed it on a more pronounced part of the slope so I could hop in and release the handbrake to course downhill. If I needed, I could either race off uphill in the direction I'd been heading, or swing back the way I'd come. I'd decide later. If Marimee's men were slick and got the hell out in millisecs, I could simply drive off anywhere I liked, a simple innocent passing motorist. I parked safely.

Up into the trees, a slow climb. From the car clock I worked out I had plenty of time. Two whole hours before the rip happened. It was perishing cold, no wind but those big flakes falling. I was surprised. They seemed to ignore the trees and fall down anyway. Perished, I went back for the car rug. I was in a forest, for Christ's sake. Snow's supposed to hit the trees, lodge in the blinking branches, make pretty for wandering artists, not slip through and land on me. Stupid snow, Switzerland's. No hat, either. I hate getting my head wet. Under the blanket like a squaw, I plodded back up among the monotonous evergreens. Footprints now, I saw uneasily. Well, as long as nobody came by and glimpsed the Porsche, okay.

Fifteen minutes, me blundering into those straight tree trunks every few yards. I was sure the bloody thing moved. And I hated the big snowflakes that came on my eyelashes. I had to keep pulling my hands out and wiping my vision free, damned stuff. Why didn't Swiss snow give warning, like sending different sea winds so you could get ready? I call it basic lack of organization.

Then, of a sudden, the best seat in the house. The Repository was laid out like a toy below, lit by floodlights. Lovely old mansion, with extensions that weren't too bad as modern architecture goes. I could see the smaller separate place where our genuine antiques had gone for shipment. Mustard-coloured sills and doors, I noticed. Nice touch, Lorela. It was a cardboard cutout copy of Marimee's garden-party mansion. No, the other way round. The Repository was the genuine place, his the one with the copycat garden to practise on.

No real nooks in a Swiss forest, either. Once you stand still, a wind springs up, sends snowflakes swirling round your ankles. I finished up crouched down, close to a bole as I could get, hooded under my blanket. It stank, I noticed. What the hell had they been doing on the thing, for heaven's sake?

Looking down at the great house, I started thinking defensive. I mean, when I was a little lad, bits of those interminable Latin lessons stuck in my mind. Not very well. But it seemed that every time Caesar came across an *oppidum*, a fortified camp, he had to storm it for no other reason than it was there. Like, that's what they're for. The Repository'd had, what, seventy attempted robberies in two years?

All unsuccessful, too, Lorela implied. She exuded confidence: nobody was going to besmirch her reputation. Confidence is daunting. I thought back. I'd never heard of anybody doing the Repository over. Plenty of failures, yes, but that's life. Which was odd, very strange, almost so wrong it must be a fake story in itself. I mean, even the Tower of London's Crown Jewels have been filched in their time. Down below, a small vehicle moved in silence across the snow-covered grounds. Nobody alighted. Another vehicle moved to meet it, disgorging dogs. Six, four huge and two short waddlers puffing along, pausing to stare at the perimeter fence and wall. No men stepped down.

Except the more I looked at the place, the less I believed in it. Surely somebody could get in? Or were the guards in the blacked-out vehicles down there actually Marimee's hoods? Or in his pay? I was sure the Ali Baba must have been tried – hiding a team inside the antiques as they went into storage. Lorela had said as much. And all the rest of the thieves' dodges, the Oliver, the donk, the lep, trackle, bammo, the over-and-over, the shagnast, the burnout, the Sunday joint, the spang, not forgetting all the electronic scams the lads are at these loony-tune days. Yet there the famous Repository was, being gently snowed upon. Inviolate, pristine, virgin.

The floodlights went out. Plunge, all black. I almost exclaimed aloud.

God, but Swiss hillside forests are dark when you take electricity away. It was suddenly colder. The chill non-wind came that bit faster. I creaked upright to make sure I could still move. Was it the syndicate's first move, a fuse ploy? I peered, saw nothing. Just when I was getting really disgruntled, the floodlights slammed back on, frightening me half to death. Then, within a few seconds, off again. On after a count of forty-nine. After that they settled down to a steady hum. I don't like that abrupt bland crash they make, not even at football matches. It makes me think they're going to take off.

They stayed on, and I thought. A warning device? The Repository computer had programmed erratic switch-offs, and notified the various cop shops and guard depots accordingly. Any variation from the plan meant somebody intruding. You wouldn't need men watching. Police or other security teams' computers would detect any unwonted variance within a split millisec. Clever. Not new, but on this big scale a definite deterrent. I smiled, wondering if the Commandant knew. I'll bet he did. Was he watching even now, ready to go?

But fortified places aren't. Not really. They *all* get done sooner or later, because mankind's ingenuity is tempted to the task. Take that terribly secret Code Black place the Yanks have. You know the one, where the President and his High Command will go the instant nuclear war starts. It's so secret that the Federal Emergency Management Agency – it runs the place – doesn't even mention it in its budget, for heaven's sake. It's even left out of the Classified Secret FEMA's own phone book, except under 'Special Facility'. And nobody knows its name. Between our secret selves, it's called Mount Weather, secret code name SF, and is seven hundred secret acres of prime Virginia wooded land on County Road 601 some eight secret miles from Berryville near Washington. But if it's so secret, how come I know? It can't just be me and the United States President, can it?

Off. Plunge into darkness. I waited, counting. The floods crashed-walloped on after more than two minutes. Erratic, planned to be. Good thinking, Lorela. A game girl –

Engines, faint in the distance. I strained to hear. No vehicle lights that I could see, but then I was looking along the hillside ridge, so naturally wouldn't. Waspish, snarly sorts, two or three, churning and whirring. Jeeps? Something like them, anyhow. No pretence at stealth.

Nearer, savage gear changes, a swathe of headlights now, quickly extinguished, then on from another direction.

The floodlights plunged out with a crash. On in an instant. The vehicles' band-saw engines nearing, no lights now. What the hell? The two security motors in the illuminated grounds below had crawled away, leaving the arena empty. Curious how like a stage set it was, a studio's rig for some shoot-out, brilliant panto lights for the purpose.

The engines slumped. Silence. Me, the snow, the distant mansion elegantly occupying the illuminated terrain in that high perimeter wall –

Something went thump, a couple of miles to my left. I was still looking that way like a fool, so missed the Repository roof falling in with a cloud and shatter. I gaped. Two more thumps, so horribly familiar. The windows imploded, the whole front Repository wall falling in, bricks and dust and snow everywhere. I saw rooms, furniture inside, tumbling upwards into the sky. Flames whooshed out. The explosion felt like a charring oven wind.

Thump, thump. Silence. Thump. And new explosions from the Repository. The main building was being incendiaried. No, that's wrong. Past tense. The engines were already started, churning and snarling away. I stared.

The Repository erupted, crackling, burning, what was left of it. Only the storage place stood untouched.

'You silly buggers!' I yelled at the night sky, at the fires, at the beautiful buildings smashed to blazes in a few seconds. 'You stupid sods! Couldn't you have . . .?'

Couldn't they have what? They'd destroyed the syndicate's fakes, by the hundred. All of them, torched to oblivion. The result of all those child-bondeds. They'd created slave-labour factories, gone to absurd lengths to have the fakes accepted in the Repository, then blown them to oblivion? Not to mention hiring a mob of ex-Legionnaires, with the Legion's famed 'battery flash' of six one-twenty mortars. Why?

I'd seen it happen. Start to finish. The enslaved immigrant children, now the flaming rubble. Only the genuine antiques remained. Their building stood unharmed.

How long I stood there I don't know. It was only the sight of those two security motors crawling back to halt in bafflement at the appalling sight that made me move again. I started down the hillside, blundering so fast I missed my footing and several times went tumbling, but got myself up and ran on. Lost my blanket, of course, but who can trace a blanket?

The metalled road's surface jarred under my heel, practically knocking the teeth from my head. No sign of my red motor. I looked left, right. Which way had I come among the trees? The sky glow behind was brighter now, far more than the floodlight's glim, and orange. No clues. Had I angled right, left? I was sure I'd climbed directly up. At least, I was almost nearly certain I was sure.

Right. Only a guess, but that was the way Marimee's vehicles had come. The speed of the thing had been devastating. Famous Foreign Legion stuff, that, the flying column, the swift fourminute unlimbering, shell the enemy with one-twenties, and off. But mortaring the damned place to smithereens?

Something coming up behind me. I ducked into the trees, up a slope, ran and hid. The motor seemed familiar, if one ever can. I gaped as it came at a fast lick, slithering on the snow at the bend. I almost shouted, but something was closing on it fast. They arrived almost opposite me, the motor hitting a pine tree and sliding sideways, lodging there. In for the night, it seemed to say, after that run. The pursuing motor was a jeep. It stopped by simply sticking to the ground, the way four-wheel-drive militaries do.

A man got out, familiar, walking slow. He came at the saloon car. Its engine was still going, lights on.

And Gobbie looked out. Left-hand drive, of course, so he was my side. Marc walked at him, without speaking. He was armed, a long single-barrelled high-velocity job. I drew breath to bawl out, 'Leave him alone, you bastard.' But shouted nothing.

Gobbie must have known what was coming, because he raised

his fist to strike at least one blow before Marc clubbed him. Quite ineffectual, naturally. The Swiss simply swung his stock in through the car window, on Gobbie's temple. It splatted on the side of Gobbie's head, an abrupt, horrid thick sound that made Gobbie dead that instant. He fell away inside the car.

Marc opened the door, casually shoved Gobbie across with his foot, got in, moved the car a few feet to point downhill, and released the brake. He stepped out, watched the motor trundle down the slope. I thought, almost delirious, Hey, hang on, that's Gobbie. And did nowt. Marc drove his own vehicle in watchful pursuit. I saw his red tail-lights go on. And Gobbie's car slid, even where the road curved, straight into the trees. It crumped, burst into a guttering flame for a minute, then erupted with a whoosh.

Marc's motor drove sedately off, its light fading among the trees. My mind went. He murdered a pathetic old man, my pal. And I did nothing. I was afraid, scared, too terrified even to try to distract the killer. Who had stood a second beside Gobbie's car, pounding my old mate with the stock of his hunting rifle, a murderous washerwoman action.

That meant my motor was concealed upslope, my nonfunctioning brain went, or they'd have seen it, come hunting me.

In silence I waited, snowed on, quiet, still. The sounds of vehicles died. No lights as yet. Why not? Too far from the fire station? No police stations, this far from anywhere? Watchers don't get medals. They get life. Like all cowards. Like me.

A crunch from below sounded. I swear I felt a waft of heat on my face. Something more had exploded near some bend downhill.

My face was unbelievably cold, partly because it was wet. The snowflakes, I suppose, melting on me. You can't keep them off your eyes. Why not, if you can keep rain away? I found my – Guy's – motor untouched, no footmarks round it. They'd see mine when they came, unless the snow got on with it and obscured everything. Except people who carry out a reconnaissance like Marimee'd done, and who could obliterate a mansion as swiftly as I'd just seen, don't tend to leave loose ends. Marc the henchman hadn't. Police would surely have minions combing the hillside for traces of visitors. Snow may be good at footprints, but it's not so good at tartan blankets hanging from a branch. I didn't go back for it.

No lighter of heart, but with a vestige of something growing in me, I drove away from their direction, so avoiding passing the slope where a motor burned, in great haste.

CHAPTER THIRTY-ONE

The snow was tumbling like surpliced leaves, white and deadening, when I made the hotel. You couldn't see my window from the road, just a sort of lounge with curtains parted above the main doorway. I drove past slowly to check, then got scared. I didn't want Marimee's men, especially Marc, catching me in Guy's car and putting two and two together. I wanted them to continue acting by instinct, now that they'd, well, done their worst.

Making sure the street was clear, I raced up, slammed the brakes on, screeched to a stop a hundred yards short of the hotel entrance, and emerged from the motor whooping and screeching. I left the engine running, and slipped in silence down the alley a few paces off. Then I ran like a loon, coming up winded and sweating cobs, shaking like an aspen. Not as far away as I'd like, but the best I could manage. In my state I darestn't risk a café just yet, certainly not this close.

The streets were clear of pedestrians, more or less. Traffic had dwindled to almost nothing. I leant against the wall to wheeze some breath back, imagining how the sleepy bad-tempered desk clerk would emerge on hearing the racket, see the motor, and go indoors to complain – or not?

It was a good hour of walking before I returned to the area. I actually took a taxi, flagging one down with a tired boredom and telling him the end of the street, paying him off with much interrogation about what notes were which. We had a good laugh before he drove away. By then, of course, I'd told him my name, tried to translate it for him into German – he did an instant and better job, another laugh. And I'd asked him if he'd any antiques because I was an antique dealer. He entered into the spirit of things, saying no, only his cab. I laughed back, saying I'd been lucky in love tonight, tipped him hellishly, complained about his dry old Zurich snow. We parted blood brothers. He'd remember me if no one else.

Nothing. The street was almost deserted. I stood waiting, uneasy. A car passed the other end, its wheels mutedly crunching snow. Three inches, maybe more. The place was not white, not like our East Anglian snow. Something made it curiously slatey-grey. Was it the buildings, something in the air? Or did you need a mountain for contrast?

Waiting's no good. I walked slowly down the pavement to the hotel. Door closed against the chill wind. Swirls had left small piles by the steps. Guy's motor car was gone. Either Guy and Veronique had recovered from their oblivion and hurried to Needle Park for a shot of Yuletide bliss. Or something else had happened.

Nobody at the desk. That spoiled things, made my return less noticeable than it ought to be. I dinged the bell.

'Hello!' I called, smiles in my voice thrilling all available listeners. A difficult act, trying to look post-coital after what I'd seen. As difficult, indeed, as trying to pretend that one hasn't made love the night before when coming down to breakfast. Blokes manage it, leaving slight doubt in cruel observers' minds. But women can't. They look loved-in. Or not, as the case may be. Where was I? Pretending. 'Anyone there?'

'Please, Monsieur!' somebody called from upstairs.

'Oh, sorry, sorry!' I stepped across to peer up the stairwell at an annoyed bloke with a moustache and specs. 'My apologies, Monsieur. Shhhh!' Finger to my lips, I turned to see a thin angry desk man.

He remonstrated with me. He complained that this night was more trouble than any in all his experience. I wanted to know what was wrong, but stayed jauntily unsympathetic.

'Any messages for me?' I asked. On being given a surly no, I was astonished and not a little narked. 'But surely, Monsieur Solon my friend left the money that arrived for me? He promised to do so. Could you please check?'

He did. No gelt. I resumed. 'But Miss Veronique, my friend's sister. Surely she left my money? It is very important, for tomorrow I must buy a present for my friend back home . . .'

All in all it was pretty good. His lip curled at the mention of my companions. To my relief he told me they'd returned over an hour ago, leaving their car running outside. Accidents are caused by such irresponsibility. No, they had not deposited their keys. No, no messages. No, no envelope for me. No, he had not seen them. I got my room key.

The stairs creaked, telling the world Lovejoy was in action. For once I was legit. I grumbled loudly, authentically everywhere for when the police would come calling if I'd guessed right. I went into my room. My heart was banging. Have you ever had it thumping so you simply can't understand how other people can avoid being defened by it? Like that. I was shaking. I looked at myself in the mirror, washed my face, went to the loo, tidied myself up. I was worn out. Had my heart pounded this way, my hands shaken this badly, when Marc the killer had used the butt of his rifle on that snowy road?

Half an hour, I moved. Not like lightning, but trembling. I went out, closing but not locking my door – wasn't I simply visiting my friends in the next room? I knocked. No response. I knocked a second time. Nobody. I knocked loud, louder, loudest.

A bloke spoke to me in German from the end of the corridor. He wore a dressing-gown. Different bloke, no tache, no specs. I was relieved at another witness, explained in poor French I was trying to wake my friends who'd forgotten to leave my money at the desk. I tried the door as I was talking, exclaimed aloud as if pleased, and staggered in a sweat of fear into Guy's room. And gagged. No pretending any more, not for anyone.

They lay on the bed. The light was on. A syringe was in Veronique's arm, dangling, partly filled with blood. Guy lay beside her. The stench was sour, acrid. Vomit soiled the counterpane. Both were partly clothed. Bloodstains on their faces and bare arms, as if they'd pawed each other in some terminal dementia. White, white skin, whiter than the Zurich snow. The pallor seemed an aura. Guy's face was buried in the pillow, a pool of vomit forming an ugly meniscus along one cheek. It was Veronique that got me. She seemed faintly worried, as if trying to be serene but knowing something was going awry. This isn't part of the game, her attitude seemed to be telling me, so what's up, Lovejoy? Can't you explain to these men who've come stealthing into our room and who're giving us a dose we don't actually want this time? Yet there was no expression. There never is, in death. It's a vacancy, a marked absence. It was only me again, supposing.

I have no illusions. In that terrible split second when I was reading expressions into her posture to obfuscate, explain away the ugliness of the two bodies' cesspool state, the scatter of needles, the bloodstained syringes, the marks –

For Christ's sake, I'd forgotten to howl. I'd silently practised one before coming to knock. It didn't matter, because I found myself doing it anyway, creating enough noise to wake the – well, being sick as a dog on the landing, going argh-argh-argh like they do in the pulp comics when fighting. Only I was vomiting on the thread-bare carpet, reeling like a drunk, panting and trying to do my howl and failing. Always, always failing. My scene, I sometimes think. What I'd not shown for friends, I showed in grief for enemies. Typical me.

Gasping, sicking, pointing as doors opened and the no-tache man went past me and started hollering. I made my way downstairs, hardly knowing any longer if I was sticking to any plan. Pointing back upstairs, I reeled wherever my feet took me. I managed a brief word as the irritable desk clerk climbed slowly upstairs past me. 'My friends . . . !' I got out. He merely expressed outrage at the mess I'd made, and avoided stepping into anything Zurich might not be proud of.

Swiss trains run on time. I don't mean this as a political jibe. They simply do. Not as many of them as I'd like, and jiggery-pokery at borders, but nothing worth writing home about. Into France, into Paris, me kipping all the way, sleep of the just and innocent I shouldn't wonder. Sleep needs six hours a man, seven a woman, eight a fool. The old saying doesn't say who gets none.

Your feet do the choosing, I often notice. I got into a dozy little doss-house within a mile of that glass pyramid somebody conned Paris into buying. Worryingly, I was low on money. And I needed a motor now that, well, now circumstances had changed. First thing I did was get on the blower to Dicko Chave. God, but heartiness is a killer. I staggered from there like a beaten boxer. What with his indefatigable good cheer, his merriment, his stiff upper lip. I'm sure he'd be great in battle, but just to say hello to him was a burden. He'd bring more money over, he told me. Midday flight.

'Looking forward to meeting her. Lovejoy,' he'd said crisply.

'Her?' I'd bleated, in a panic remembering my super new mythical partner. He'd already financed her once at my Zurich hotel. 'Ah, well, you see old chap –'

'Toodle-oo, Lovejoy. See you in Gay Paree!'

That's all I needed. He was still blabbing cheer when I rang off, depressed. Things were getting too complicated. I wondered if I could reasonably nick a car, decided against it. There was Lysette, of course. Where? Sheer spite must have taken her off in high dudgeon. Being a bird, she'd naturally blame me so she was, frankly, out. My one chance of help, and I had to chuck her. Typical, but I felt utterly panned out, forswunked. It wasn't my fault things had turned out like this.

They'd repaired the ramraiders' efforts. I was pleased at that. The pretty girl – Claire, was it? – had done her stuff. I hoped I'd given her enough heavy hints to get her antiques out of the way. I stood opposite, watching the dealers in and out. It was along here that the ramraider had hated me and someone else, when he'd

peered in and called us bastards. Given such a clue, I should have
made myself face facts back then. Someone else, with more sense,
had. Nobody's more sentimental towards children than a crook. It's
a wonder the ramraider hadn't clubbed me there and then. In fact
he would have, but for leaving clues, collecting bloodstains. I'd
escaped such a fate, of course; lucky old me. Somebody else hadn't,
o.c. Lucky old me.

'Monsieur Lovejoy?'

Somebody touched my arm. I fumbled in my pocket for a coin
to give to this importuning beggar. You can't be all worked up about
child exploitation while ignoring the plights of others. I thought.
Here, hang on. How the hell did this policeman know my name?
Him and two police cars – so low on the ground, Paris bobbies'
motors are – and what was going on?

'You will accompany . . .' Long pause, then he made it: '. . . us.'

'Thank you,' I said miserably, and got into their motor. Best not
to say a single word of a foreign lingo straight away, or you get
spoken to at such speed you're lost in a trice. To show grovelling
subservience I added, '*Merci, Monsieur.* Ta.'

And got driven away to the police station. I wasn't quite ready,
but when is ready for the likes of them?

The place wasn't some grand Victorian dump, nor some black glass
rectanguloid. It seemed no more than a dullish office that looked
like a building-society branch office. I'd never seen people smoking
like their jobs depended on fags, but this lot were. All except the
lead bloke. He was an oddly motionless bloke with an ornate
waistcoat, the sort you saw years ago on telly announcers. The rest
of him was very, very serious.

'Lovejoy?' he said. Not to me, to everybody else. The police
who'd fetched me promised yes, this man was Lovejoy, and got sent
on their way. He had a good smile, events such a drag and couldn't
we get on with things, please, but I wasn't taken in. Police only have
three sorts of smiles, all phoney. They constitute threat. 'You're
Lovejoy,' he told me sadly.

'Lovejoy, Monsieur,' I agreed. '*Merci.*'

'Bring the lady in.' English his language, so no cheating.

And in came the beautiful Claire Fabien. She stood carefully
away from me. I smiled my very best, innocence radiating from me.
I rose, made to shake hands. She recoiled. I faltered.

'Miss Fabien!' I tried. 'The antique dealer! You remember me?
I bought several pieces from you. The Davenport!'

'Yes, Monsieur,' to the cop. Except now I looked at him he began to look less and less like a bobby. 'This is the man.'

'Of course I am *le même homme*, Mademoiselle!' I outdid Dicko in heartiness, beaming like him. 'Are you all right? In trouble?'

Waistcoat had not risen when La Fabien entered. I don't like blokes this motionless. Blokes normally shuffle about, hitch, shift feet. We don't stay frozen to spots, unless we've malice in mind.

'Lovejoy. You warned Miss Fabien against ramraiders.'

'Against who?' I asked, a puzzled innocent.

'You advised Miss Fabien to move her antiques, even into a pantechnicon.' The word came out stilted. 'Why?'

'Ramraiders?' I wrinkled my brow, theatrically. Clear the brow and into, 'You have them in France? Good heavens!'

'Very well.' This man didn't waste time on prattlers or phoney excuses. He let me off his hook too easily. 'To the English, crime is an amusing commodity. To the Germans a philosophical proposition. To the Americans a job.' I didn't know whether I was to laugh or not, so did. 'Monsieur. You ordered a large number of antiques for shipment from many antique dealers. Most spoke of your excellent choice. Payment was in cash, by two assistants. Could you please identify them for us?'

'Guy and Veronique Solon,' I said pleasantly enough and quickly. 'I was hired by them. Met them in a motorway restaurant when hitchhiking through your lovely country.'

'How did that happen?'

'Oh,' I said, smiling apology at Claire Fabien, taking so long, soon clear up this misunderstanding, 'we got talking antiques. Don't exactly recall how. They were international buyers. I stopped off with them at one or two places, window-shopping. They admired what little skill I have. I agreed to do a bit of purchasing on their behalf.'

'Why France, Monsieur?' A pause to avoid smiling. 'I believe like your poet, that it's curiosity, not devotion, makes pilgrims.'

'Eh? You mean me? Just trying to find new sources of supply. I'd run into a shortage of stock. You know how it is.' His shrug made an elbow-room of silence. I said to Claire, 'Did you get ramraided then?'

She glanced at Waistcoat. 'It was very terrible. They drove cars in the shop and stole. They ruined many antiques.'

'Kell do madge,' I tried politely, shaking my head. If she'd windowed the ones I'd ignored, the world had only lost a few poor-quality fakes. I looked at her with interest. 'You claimed on the insurance, Miss Fabien?'

Suddenly a little pinker than before. 'Of course,' she said stiffly. So she was pulling the insurance scam. Had to, of course – or admit that her display was muchly fakes.

Was it that give-away that decided Waistcoat? He rose, thanked me profusely, and shook my hand. Deadest mitt I'd ever touched among the living. I began to wonder if I'd landed in the French equivalent of our Fraud mob. I had the sense not to ask.

'Your intentions, Monsieur?'

'Oh, I was just about to look round the Louvre des Antiquaires, Monsieur. I've heard of the *Marchés aux puces*, and your Village Suisse, where many superb bargains –'

'Please do not believe all you read in the guidebooks, Monsieur. Though I am sure you require no assistance.'

'Thank you for your advice, Monsieur . . . ?' I'd see this sod again, I felt uncomfortably.

'Pascal, Monsieur.' He didn't smile. 'Easy to remember, eh?'

'May I walk you to your emporium, Miss Fabien?' I asked, gallantry itself.

She recoiled, no, no. Well, win some, lose some. And that was how I came to be sitting alone in the cold wind of the little square where me and Lysette and one other had met up and talked over what we were going to do. And where I'd made the decision, shutting out the truth and causing a friend to be . . . well, made unable to continue living.

The coffee didn't seem as good. I realized I'd ordered breakfast, this hour. I had it, then wanted soup and some other grub. The waitress was encouraged, brought a menu. I asked for more. She was pleased, said I could dine inside if I wanted. I realized I was the only one sitting in the square, everybody inside looking out. It must be perishing. A light dusting of snow was on the table. How long had I been there?

'It is too cold out here for your lady,' she said. A bonny lass, wanting humanity's loose ends tidying up.

'No, ta,' I said. 'I like fresh air.' I couldn't take Lysette, not at this stage. Not even if she would give me a lift to the rotating mansion of Marimee's syndicate where the great share-out would occur and I'd have something positive to do.

The waitress relaid the table and went in, disgruntled. She would have to brave the cool gale that fanned this glade with my next course. Cool gale? Some fragment of school poetry? What poet, Monsieur Pascal? She came across the square towards me. Overcoat now, I noticed, and different from a few minutes ago. I was shivering, but managed to stop it as she pulled the chair opposite me and arranged herself as they do.

'You will catch your death of cold, Lovejoy,' she said sternly.

'You'll have had your tea.' The old Scotch joke I told you once: Edinburgh folk say hello like that, too mingy to offer any. Friendly Glaswegians give you tea without asking.

'Wrong city, Lovejoy.'

'Where's the boyo?' I gave her, Welsh accent. 'Sure to be near, eh, alannah?' Irish for darling. Anything to strike back before I got arrested good and proper.

'Stop it, Lovejoy. I won't have this daftness. I want to know what happened. Not', she gave me in her best Clydebank reproof, 'what's in the papers, either.'

'Is it already in?' I was surprised, but then I never read them. Avoiding newspapers ensures a better quality of ignorance.

'What is it, Lovejoy?'

'Shouldn't it be Gerald asking these questions, Lil?' I nearly joked about talking to the organ-grinder, not the monkey. 'No good saying it all twice.'

She almost smiled. 'Cheek! Gerald's taking photographs, doing the recordings as usual. *I'm* the SAPAR field agent, Lovejoy, not him.'

I drew breath at that. 'You?' Cunning, to wear the SAPAR gold pendant as if it was a fond husband's gift, when all the time she was the baddy. 'I've never heard of a bird hunter before. Does that mean that when you and me –?'

'Lovejoy.' She looked askance. 'This is being recorded.' She meant Gerald was nearby with directional microphones on the go. 'Who is the girl Lysette?'

'Mind your own business, you rotten cow.'

Not a quibble, more of a learner's smile. 'Start from the beginning, please.'

'Sod off.'

'It's either me, Lovejoy, or Didier Pascal's unit. He's closing.' She paused. The waitress was emerging with my grub. 'Me, you might get some reparation. Pascal is already on to it. When he moves, the fur will really fly. And he does read newspapers.'

If I delayed the full explanation, disguised as a show of willingness to co-operate, I might yet give Marimee time to do the necessary damage. He was only the instrument, after all. The syndicate was the real enemy.

'Inside, then,' I said. 'Let's go somewhere warm.'

We passed the waitress. I made profuse apologies. She followed us, hating Lilian all the way back in, knowing this change of plan was all the woman's fault. It quite cheered me up.

CHAPTER THIRTY-TWO

The pity is you don't get many chances. Things should be different, but never are. Some folk make their mark. Like Jules Tavernier, a French painter of the 1880s. One of his paintings hung in Claire Fabien's shop; with any luck I'd call eventually and buy. He was no great shakes, Tavernier. But he made his mark by simply catching the boat to Hawaii. Unremarkable? Not quite – he did for Hawaii what Gaugin did for another exotic place. Now, he's immortalized, the epic painter of Hawaii's sublime and awe-inspiring terrain. See? One decision, glory for ever. Wish I was like that.

I got the taxi to drop me off at the factory I'd been taken to by Lysette and somebody else, the night I'd been made to realize. Shaking like a leaf yet bold as brass I went down the steps and banged on the door. I hollered, yelled, kept thumping, and finally somebody came. He looked North African, though how would I know?

'I wish to speak with the Commandant,' I told him. My ponderous French seemed acceptable, but in the darkness his cataract gave him a wall-eyed appearance. It put the fear of God in me. '*L'homme,*' I added for good measure.

He tried fobbing me off, shook his head. I thought of trying to bribe him. In despair I said the magic word. '*Je désire parler avec* Colonel Marimee.' His expression cleared, apprehension stalking his mind. He was the bloke who'd whopped the children. I could hear the noise going on, that faint bustle, chants, shouts. '*Il faut,*' I encouraged him, and had a go at telling him I'd been summoned by Marimee himself.

Ten minutes later I was in a long saloon motor between two gross toughs. That is, they looked and smelled like pimps, but were lean as laths, wiry and ready for anything.

'*Mon commandant,*' I said to Marimee, who oddly was doing the driving. 'I wish to warn the Colonel, with respect.'

'Speak.'

'I . . . I hate to say this, *mon commandant*, but today I saw sold, at the Louvre des Antiquaires, a piece of furniture that I deposited in the Repository.'

Silence. I cleared my throat, ready to embellish. His goons compressed me, simply leaning sideways. I said nothing.

'You are certain?'

'*Mon colonel*!' I said it as if proud with obedience, trying to be the good soldier I'd once failed to be.

'From whom?'

'It was loaded on a van, Monsieur. I tried asking, then became worried in case . . . in case . . .' His nod was almost imperceptible. 'I failed to get the vehicle number. I didn't know if I should ask Monsieur Marc or not, but –'

'Marc.' Flat, impersonal. 'He was there?'

'*Oui, mon colonel*. He received money. I was anxious not to be seen, you see. I blame myself, sir. I passed the emporium a little earlier, and thought then that some pieces being loaded up looked familiar. But I made absolutely sure of the last item. Should I have made a drawing of it for the Colonel?'

The motor didn't move. We'd simply driven round the corner and parked. The night streets were deserted.

'You asked for me, not Mademoiselle Delebarre. Or others who hired you.'

'*Oui, mon colonel*. My duty. I was assigned to you, sir. Only', I went on in spite of a distinct lack of encouragement, hammering it home, 'it seems to me that if one item was stolen, then *all* may have been sold the instant they were deposited. I cannot understand how or why this could be. It seemed to me my clear duty to the Colonel –' I'd looked up some words in a pocket dictionary for the purpose of fawning exactly right.

Compressed to silence by my tough book-ends. We stayed there an age. I tried hard not to sweat, tremble, babble, promise not to reveal a thing if only he'd let me go. I kept persuading myself I was a baffled bystander, trying to earn a bob or two, wanting home. Instead, my mind kept wondering how they'd kill me, what it felt like, if they'd use knives, dear God not *knives* –

'You have done well. You are discharged. Cross the Manche.'

Cross where? What's a Manche? The Channel! He meant clear off! I almost shrieked in a relieved faint, remembered to say yes, *mon colonel* and thank you, *mon colonel*, goodbye and it was an honour to serve under –

My foot hardly touched the floor before the car was off. I tumbled, lay there, letting the blissful sweat come as I stared up at the black sky. I'd done it, done it, done it . . .

Done what?

'If you think I'm flying in that frigging thing, love, you're mistook.'

'Lovejoy.' Lilian had an auntie's exasperation in her voice, though she was no auntie. It's the woman's inflexion, a kind of exasperation when a bloke doesn't obey instantly. It's the *I know what's good for you so swallow when I tell you* cadence of the nurse with the grueful spoonful, the *We're going to Bognor for our holidays* voice. 'You've flown in one before.'

'I'd been shot then.' I stood rooted on the airfield.

'You're not shot now.' She was half laughing, half screaming. 'We've ten minutes. For heaven's sake!'

'Helicopters fall down.' Two ground crew waited.

'It's the safest means of travel, Lovejoy,' Gerald's brogue put in. Why did he always sound doleful?

'You're not going,' I spat, narked. He looked offended.

'It's only an hour, Lovejoy. Lausanne.'

'Might as well be a million miles,' I argued. I'd gone clammy in spite of the wind – *wind*! Taking off in a frigging egg whisk in a frigging *gale*! Was the world mad?

'Less than two hundred and forty miles,' Gerald intoned.

'Shut up, you pillock.'

'Don't talk to Gerald like that, Lovejoy!' from Lilian, real anger this time to show me where I stood. Just because we'd made smiles, she was warning me. 'Didier Pascal's people found Lysette Fotheringay at your hotel. She's already on her way.'

To Lausanne? To where? I didn't say. 'You did ask for her to be found, Lovejoy,' from Gerald, fidgeting. I keep wondering how folk become what they become. Like, I'd have hired the meticulous, accurate, single-minded Gerald Sweet any day as a dedicated antiques-recovery sleuth, Lilian his travelling companion. Instead, it was the other way round. Why? I'd not had the courage to ask them if they'd picked me up by accident. I desperately wanted the answer to be yes, so chickened out.

'She'll be there?'

'Yes. They've already been gone an hour.'

'Driving, I'll bet! Why not with us?' So that Pascal could extract news from her in his black Citroën, that's why. 'I get airsick,' I protested feebly.

'She's gone through a lot for you, Lovejoy,' mourned Gerald.

I gripped his tie. 'Listen, you prat. I'm the one who's gone through a lot. Nobody else. D'you hear?' His bald head glistened. He nodded, puce, his eyes goggling. Even in that position he took orders from Lilian, glancing behind me to see what she gestured.

'Aye, Lovejoy. Sorry, man.'

'Aye, well.' It was a private helicopter. That alone chilled my spine. I mean, air crashes are always chartered, never scheduled flights, ever noticed? Or is it the other way about? 'It isn't Air France, then.'

'Lovejoy.' Lilian, the spoon, the Bognor holiday. The last words of the Old King came to mind: *Bugger Bognor!*

Nobody had asked me about a crashed motor on the mountain road above the Repository. In fact, there had been very little news given out about the whole thing, except *Explosion Partly Demolishes Furniture Storage Facility* sort of thing. Lilian had seemed quite proud of the media's inattention, silly cow. I'd told her my version, some even accurate. I had the feeling she'd believed most. It goes to show how poorly women co-operate.

'It's okay for you,' I groused, stung. 'Why doesn't a helicopter have a giant parachute . . . ?'

We fly south-east, the pilot started to tell us as his blades screwed the heavens and the engines deafened the world out. Gerald of course corrected him, giving points of the compass in millibars, whatever. Lilian held my hand unseen in the back seat, her cheek colour heightened at her dreadful temerity. I didn't squeeze her fingers back, having probably fainted with fright. We landed in a trice.

Lorela Chevalier was smart as ever, really beautiful. She greeted me in the foyer of the theme-park hotel as if we were old friends. I'd made it a condition that everybody else stayed away.

'Welcome,' she said, a beautiful slim volume between two attendants. They weren't the same blokes, but wore unresponsiveness like every armed squaddie. Why do weapons confer laziness on eyes, droops on hands, sloth on shoes? Somebody ought to research that. 'How do I call you?'

'Wotcher, Lorela. Lovejoy.'

Her eyes widened a little, settled into understanding. 'I've heard the name. That explains . . . Won't you come in?'

'No, ta.' Somebody was hang-gliding in the distance beyond the picture windows. You could see a couple of horses trotting, a small whiskey with coloured fringes being driven on a hand rein by a beginner, a liveried groom trotting longside. A lake shone through trees. A moneyed holiday location; this was no Bognor, 'Just show me.'

'Lovejoy,' she said ruminatively, leading the way to a lift. The two vigilantes came too. We descended without a starting judder. 'East Anglia? Poor. Unattached. No premises.' She turned her lovely eyes to add, 'Divvy? Like Leon Cabannes?'

'Like Leon Cabbanes *was*.'

She looked at me still. The lift door opened. A small train thing on a kind of rail set in the floor. She didn't move.

'Yes. Very unfortunate, Lovejoy. The old gentleman was coming on to our staff the same week he passed away.' No wonder Troude and Monique ordered old Leon topped.

The train thing had no driver. I stared at it, queasy. I'd already been brave once today. Twice was snapping your fingers at Fate. 'We get in that? How far is it?'

'It's programmed,' she said smoothly. 'It can't go wrong.'

'Like your hiring schemes?'

She stepped in, arranged herself, nodded to three blokes standing about in gold jackets. I sat beside her warily. We started off, just me and her. Smoothest ride ever, down a cement tunnel. She had no controls.

'Tell me, Lovejoy. Was that dead man anyone to do with you? There was a crashed car down a ravine with a body –'

I clouted her, really belted her, grabbed the handrail in front of me to stop my hands throttling. She sat still. The little train was three coaches long, enough room for two bums a coach, six in all. No goons with us. A few moments, then she found some tools and started blotting her face to the accompaniment of that faint rattle their handbags always make.

We glided through two intersections, same speed, slowed, then through a vaulted arch. Steel doors rolled away for us. We alighted in a huge arched place. Hangar? On pallets, furniture in covered and even transparent seals. A fork-lifter whirred across an aisle about eight yards away. Music played softly, Vivaldi's *Four Seasons*. No external exit that I could see. Colour codes, and a stand plan like you get to explain tourist vantage points, but here to show where antiques dollops were stored.

'No, nothing, Jim,' she assured somebody who'd stepped forward with a grunt to start extermination of the visiting maniac. 'It's fine, really.' She swivelled brightly. 'This way, Lovejoy! We arrange things here simply –'

I held up a finger. It was blooded. 'Shtum, love.' My knuckle was unfortunately bloodstained, her cheekbone bruised to hell, though luckily I'd missed her eye. I walked away among the stored furniture.

It took three-quarters of an hour to check a good enough sample. Her blokes unwrapped the pieces I chose in the coded area. They hated me every second. Without her restraint they'd have

237

marmalized me. Marimee's stuff seemed all there, every single fake. *Fake*, observe.

'The genuines?' I asked finally. Odd that the beautiful fakes didn't make me feel sick any more.

'I'm unsure,' she said, determinedly bright. 'I think they're here somewhere . . .'

'Don't frig me about, love. They're not.'

She nodded slowly, appraising me, lips pursed. 'I knew you were a divvy, Lovejoy, when, ah, when you —'

When I what? Painfully I thought back, an all-time first. The penny eventually dropped. 'When I directed the Jamie Sandy antique with the other genuines?'

'We always place one of our own, to mark a large deposit. Banks do the same, I'm told, using gold-bullion markers. Radio-isotope labelling has become routine, even for political documents. The other group are . . . at another of our storage facilities.'

I stood hunched, hands in pockets. It felt cold down here. No snow, no cold winds, no mountainside, no pines plopping snowfalls in earthbound gulps, nothing to melt on your eyes and set your eyes running.

'Get rid,' I muttered to the floor.

Some deep bickering, then her men drifted. You could feel their anger. I waited until I'd heard doors whirr and thump. I looked at her. Her cheekbone was prominent, blueish. I almost exclaimed aloud, asked who'd done that. Me.

'They'll be at you, love. Unless.'

'Unless?' She was composed, thinking away, lovely eyes on me. She had sense, this one. Ready for an agreement.

'Unless you say nothing at all to the authorities. And you can go on as before.'

'Which is how, Lovejoy?' She smiled because she was making me speak frankly when I didn't want to. Women have a nerve.

'You accept antiques at the Repository, show customers how secure your Swiss fortress is. Then secretly van them elsewhere, simply transfer the antiques to secret locations. Like this, under a holiday theme park. Good cover, disguised vans, the lot. There really *is* no Repository, is there?'

'Promise not to tell, Lovejoy?' Ah, good old question time. 'Ouch!'

Smiling had hurt her face. Served her right.

Pascal was filled with mistrust. I've been mistrusted by supercynics, and can tell. It says a lot for the Gallic character, I whispered to Lysette. She said to shhh, it was impolite to whisper in company. So why was she whispering?

He wanted to make a speech. I'd already said it wasn't necessary. We were crowded into a caravan trailer. Air conditioning whirred. Too many of us. Pascal had three goons along. There was me, Lysette, the Sweets, and some uniformed bobbies.

'It'll tip them off if you go in force,' I'd said when Pascal wanted to call his regiments out. 'They'll not come. You must wait until they're all inside, then bottle them. See?'

They settled for road blocks. On permanent stand-by, to be put in place when I'd given the signal.

'Lovejoy,' Pascal ordered, umpteenth time. God, but I wished the bloke couldn't speak English. They were all bloody linguists, except me. I mean, some Oxford goon's worked out that there's 403 septillion ways of combining letters in English – yet everybody else knows my language better. How come? I was especially narked that Lysette got on really well with Didier Pascal. What sort of a name was Didier, anyway? Sounded like a rocking horse, the bum. He'd already got Lysette to sit next to him, the eyes of a rapist. 'You will signal only when all – repeat *all* – the syndicate has arrived. You do understand?'

'I've said yes three times. How many more?'

The seven uniformed officers sat stolidly listening, though I think they'd already got organized. One asked, 'Where?'

'I'll show you,' I promised. 'Lend me a motor?'

'No,' Pascal said, exchanging glances with Lilian Sweet. I just caught her minimally shaking her head. 'We go together.'

Which was how I finished up sitting in a twitcher's hide watching the mansion house in the gladey garden below. It wasn't going round this time. Its garden was absolutely still.

Two days later, they came.

CHAPTER THIRTY-THREE

Living in close proximity with somebody you don't know is painful. I'm not one for chat; neither was Pascal.

The bird-watcher's hide was made of logging. No lights, no door for the opening in the wall, no glass for the long slit window. That was it. I'd got a blanket-thick overcoat, and Lysette gave me gloves. Gloves, the old Elizabethan lovers' gift. Binoculars with dulled lenses, and that really was it.

We had a loo outside in a rectangle of sacking, blowing in the wind. Basically sawdust in a large tin. Grub was already prepared for us, cold. Tea in a vacuum flask for me, coffee for Pascal. We had to make do. No talking was allowed, pleasing me.

The mansion house below seemed reduced, now the real deed had been done elsewhere. The garden I noticed was smaller than the Repository's, but the two prominences topping the hillside to our right were about the correct elevation relative to the building, and were wooded to about the same degree. Nicely chosen. I'd explained to Lilian Sweet and Pascal before I'd got stuck in this hole that the scammers' meeting was to be within the week. It only took me an hour to start wishing I'd kept my mouth shut and simply eeled away.

There from ten o'clock onwards, night. Midnight came and went. Twice I'd whispered had Pascal anything to read, got looked at. Faint starlight was all we had to see by. I tried looking down at the mansion house, the gardens, the little stream, through binoculars, but couldn't see a damned thing. Never could. I always used to pretend anyway, when it mattered.

If we wanted to say anything desperate, we were to write it down on a small notepad, pencil provided. No talking.

Within three hours I was starting to wonder what if they didn't come at all. I'd be found in this log hut in God-forsaken countryside starved to death years later, waiting for the syndicate to come. I imagined the scene, with great bitterness thinking of the grub there'd be, the lovely luscious women delirious with joy, flushed with excitement at the vast fortunes they thought they'd made from the scam, Monique queening it over everybody, having justified her barmy political beliefs.

And let's hear it for Colonel Marimee, ladies and gentlemen! With fanfares and party time and delectable birds so edible you'd almost forget to reach out for the grub and sink your teeth –

'Sssss!'

'Sorry, sorry,' in the lowest whisper. I must have groaned. I'd not had a pasty for as long as I could remember. I was famished as soon as we got inside this place.

They'd be readying for the ultimate celebration down there. Servants, I supposed in my entranced mind, by the score. Maybe Katta, with her luscious delectable mouth surmounting that gross pendulous shape. Lovely. And Almira, with hubby Jervis. And those Madagascar folk, so wealthy with their digits sheathed in gold. And the smoothies, Philippe Troude, Monique Delebarre and all. There'd be frolicking and wassailing in nooks and crannies everywhere, even before the announcement.

That would be the peak. They'd get called in to a separate room, maybe some baronial panelled hall with a log fire. Brandy, being in France, would be served, with canapés or whatever those little noshes were, on silver trays. Then they'd announce the sum they were going to claim from Lloyd's insurance. But only after they'd made the celebratory call to the Repository . . . I smiled, got admonished by a nudge. No chuckling.

The night passed. No cars arrived, except one that seemed to be Monique's. No passengers, no visitors.

Odd to think that Paul Anstruther had been Katta's sex focus (sorry, no pun intended) all these years. How on earth had Cissie put up with her? Except I'd learned that Cissie adored Philippe Troude. I began to think about seeing Katta's huge form writhing on the ecstatic Paul. God, but that would be bliss, some bird so vast you could hardly see over her. Would you want to?

But hadn't her reaction been strange, that night I'd unexpectedly eavesdropped on them? When the car doors slammed, Katta'd been really terrified. She'd leapt off Paul, not pausing to wipe her mouth until she'd been reassured – *by hearing Almira*. Then, and only then, Katta had relaxed, paused to tease Paul by giving him that erotic moue. Question: *Who'd she thought was coming?* Answer: Somebody she was *truly* scared of.

If I had a permanent bird, I'd know the answer straight off. I knew I would. It's as if a woman is your missing half. Happen I should get one, some day. Except it never works. I suppose in a way I'm like Dicko Chave, perennial failure. Except I nearly get enough, and Dicko simply lacks any. And settling down for good is impossible. I mean, what if you draw a Cissie? I knew the answer to that for sure.

Which raised the question why my mind kept coming back to her. Ambition unlimited, ferocity unleashed, anything for wealth, status. She'd married us – there seemed to've been no negotiations, just Cissie's determination – because she aimed to harness my divvying skills and gross a trillion. She said as much. She stormed off because I was uncontrollable, and her scheme didn't work.

My head jerked upright. I was stiff from leaning on the log sill. Mostly blackness out there. I occasionally tried standing up, stretching, swivelling like Olympic atheletes do after gulping their anabolic steroids before track events, but you get fed up with fitness so I sat down again. I sometimes looked at Pascal. He was a good watcher. I'd never met anybody quite like him before. Gallic equivalent of Lilian Sweet? If so, I'd seriously underestimated Lilian's talent.

Once, in early daylight of next morning, I woke to find him passing me photographs. Two children, both girls, one smiling doubtfully in a small garden pool, the other standing on the bank throwing a scoop of water, laughing. What, eight and fourteen? Yours? I asked with a pointing finger. He nodded, smiling, asked did I carry any photos? I shook my head, pretending rue. He shrugged, stood again at the slit window staring through his binoculars. And that was that, entertainment for the day.

We had stewed tea and coffee from our row of thermos flasks. One every five hours, our ration. Cold sandwiches of cardboard material. Sausages, well congealed in thickening grease, sliced ham. Couldn't Paris have raised its frigging culinary game? I wanted to demand, but caught Pascal's shrug and made do, trying to prove that I too could be a stoic.

No snow, but pretty cold weather, especially at night. I guessed Pascal's police'd not set up a rota. Rotas work well when sussing a possible place for a rip, until you actually need to replace the old watchers with fresh invigorated new. Then there's trouble. If it isn't a give-away from banging car doors, it's obvious that something changes in the street's pattern. I wasn't too sure about things in the countryside, even though that's where I live, but I knew the French had gamekeepers too. And those miserable sods can spot reeds misbehaving miles off.

Doing nothing's really weird. How do Trappist monks manage? Though I suppose they're allowed to read. Once, this bird actually hired me to do utter nothing. Honest, true. She was really flash, very chic. Wed, of course, she had a lad at boarding school, husband in mortgages. She truly hired me to just be there. And 'there' was simply nearby wherever she was. She even introduced me to her husband, who okayed the whole thing. For quite three days I thought I was a bodyguard, and went in fear of my life, scared stiff, until it dawned on me that I was mere decoration. I even asked Doc Lancaster if it might be one of those afraid-of-loneliness things. He sent me packing, the swine. Really odd. Can you imagine, a woman just wanting a bloke dancing attendance? They're strange. I overheard her being teased by her posh friends, chinless wonders, about her 'bit of rough', meaning me. I was deeply narked. On the way home we made smiles, me like a gorilla, she thunderstruck that her figment had suddenly become bestially real. I resigned that night. You won't believe this, but she thought a lifelong loveship had been sealed, whereas I'd thought I'd been punishing her. See how women insist on misunderstanding? Like Cissie, like Almira, like Jodie Danglass, like Lysette, like Lilian Sweet. They have the advantage of being underhanded. It's not fair. We've got to be honest and upright. Women can do what they want. It should be the other way round.

'Sssss!'

'Ssss!' I went irritably back. Okay, so I might have muttered aloud. No need to go berserk. Pascal settled. He'd only given me one small set of binoculars, but collared four pairs for himself. He was forever stealthily changing lenses, looking for some bloody attachment or other, getting right on my nerves.

Lately, I'd been trying to get my teeth right. Toothpicks always seem one of civilization's good ideas that never quite comes off, though the Romans used them. It doesn't bother me that Juliet only had (honest) four teeth in her head when, aged fourteen, she romped with Romeo. So I'd acquired toothpicks. For something to do I started digging. The best teeth gadgets are those electric rotary brushes you charge up on the mains, but I always lose the little things that go round and round on the end . . . Pascal nudged me. I mouthed an irritable *I'm awake, I'm awake!* and roused blearily to more misery.

The day seemed to have turned itself inside out far more than twice when finally Pascal tapped my shoulder. Something happening. I hope I hadn't snored. It was early afternoon. I looked out, fumbled for the binoculars. He pointed to my pair hanging round my neck. I peered, focused, got it blurred, tried again.

A big Merc. Whatever colour they paint them, a Merc always looks black. Ever noticed? Grandeur, I suppose. Even Hannover taxis look black, and most aren't. A bonny girl, slender as an arrow, arriving down there with a bloke. Servant out to say hello, show them inside. The motor retired, pomp in every line. I ticked the air to Pascal. He nodded. I'd seen them at that party, or in the hotel meeting at that security room. He nodded okay, keep looking. Irritably I nodded back that I was, for God's sake, don't keep on.

They arrived faster, increasing numbers. I started a pattern of gestures. Thumbs up, yes I recognized the couple from Madagascar, the bloke who looked something artistic, the slightly plump woman with too-young dress sense, her besuited banker husband. The German moneybags who'd asked the wrong question of the Colonel in Zurich. Then Almira, her husband. Philippe Troude with – heart in my mouth – a popsie having difficulties in stilt-like high heels on the drive surface. Definitely not Jodie Danglass, multo definitely. But yes, she'd been at the party.

Then, astonishment showing me how astonishment should be really felt, Sandy, in splendiferous garb, gold cloak, what looked like electric Christmas-tree lights flickering along the rim, ostrich feathers in an absurd halo. He looked ridiculous. Still no Jodie Danglass. But Corse the roller, last seen abusing me and the rest of the known world at Josh Sparrow's barn. I grunted with satisfaction.

Pascal was looking at me oddly. I smiled, indicated that all was going quite well. The numbers began to dwindle. Then ceased.

Nudge. He showed me the time. Two hours, the daylight not yet fading but definitely less encouraging than it was. Motors revved, cars lined up to one side of the mansion house. No marquees today, no tents or awnings, no sherry on the lawns. Some uniformed drivers smoked, one reading a paper. All cars were left-hand drive, Continental design. Pascal stirred, hands asking if that was it.

No, I gestured back. I opened my palms, fingers asplay as if holding a large ball. Many more to come, I indicated, though, waggle waggle, I still wasn't sure of the number.

How many, then? He was becoming edgy, scanning the sky. What for, helicopters? Dusk? Some additional help he'd requested should things start to go wrong and the whole syndicate looked likely to escape? Or something much much worse?

He indicated, drawing an imaginary net tight, that he'd got them in the sack, all the evil swine in one. Why delay? I shook my head. More would come, hold on, wait.

No sign of anything flying overhead. No signals from the trees. Nothing that I could think of or see. Only Pascal, finally watching me more than he watched the mansion house in the clearing below. I smiled a bit at him now and then, showing willing, offered him some of my tea, tried his coffee with a grimace. Not a single smile now, nothing but wary glances. It began to nark me. What the hell could I do, with the daylight now definitely losing interest and the mansion-house lights starting to come on, and me stuck up on a hillside in a plank shed with a cop? For Christ's sake, I thought, narked. You're a frigging copper, not Tracker Joe Wilderness. Get a grip, Pascal.

The motor came at last. Paulie's, the same one I'd driven in to visit hospital that day. No need to be prompted now. I was all attention. Without having even to focus, I saw Paulie halt his motor, leap out and scurry round to the opposite door, open it.

She looked smart, trendy even. And stern. She simply gave no acknowledgement of his politeness, and sternly swept by without a look into the mansion house.

Cissie always did run true to form. Katta heaved her enormously beauteous bulk from the low motor, and walked round the back of the building with one of the chauffeurs who'd been having a smoke leaning on the bonnet of his Bentley. I felt glad Katta'd be out of it, when whatever it was happened.

My finger gave Pascal pause. By now he was hopping from foot to foot, less taciturn than he'd ever been in his entire life, I shouldn't wonder. One more yet to come, I mimed, stabbing the air. Keep looking. Wait, wait. Hold them off, whoever they were.

And even as I recovered my binoculars, his motor arrived. Marc got out of the car, chucked the keys indolently to one of the other drivers, and walked into the building. I'm sure it was him. He carried a large suitcase-size thing, not so large he had to trundle it on wheels. I said nothing, just started a slow counting on my fingers, clearly trying to work out if I'd forgotten anybody. No, that was about it.

Still I waited. Why? Nudge from Pascal. He even scribbled me a line on his barmy notepaper, his pencil shaky, all over the place. I went ssssssh very softly, read his scribble, frowned at *Maintenant?????*, waved a downward palm slowly, take your time, mate.

I wanted his watch. He had an unbelievable three, honest to God, three, ripped one off savagely, thrust it at me. I stared at the hands, counting, my lips moving to show him I was on the job.

Marc would go into the assembly room. Only the syndicate would be allowed in, nobody else. That was their pattern. I saw the whole glitterati lot – can we take our drinks in? How much will the pay-out be? What claim we shall put in to the insurers? Isn't Colonel Marimee coming, then? Shame! Monique gorgeous, lovely, taking the place of honour on the dais. Would there be a rostrum? Lights?

Marc'd be going in now, smiling, handshakes, proud.

They would be chattering, talking of their expected riches. Claim for tons of priceless furniture in the Repository, share out. What were their expectations, really, when all was said and done? They'd have the perfect money machine, for slavery is eternal, pure, elementary, a model of perfection. Everybody's fatal siren call.

One minute fifteen seconds. Tick tick, silent second hand but shuddering me with its mute force. One eighteen, twenty.

What orders had Colonel Marimee given Marc the killer? To activate some switch on the case in the meeting? Probably. Or would the case be on auto? Or externally controlled perhaps? Had he told Marc it was an aiming beam for his famous flash mortar? Marc would believe he'd have a few minutes to get clear . . .

'Your watch, ta,' I said, returning it.

One minute forty seconds, plenty. 'Go now. No more, I'm sure.'

Pascal flipped a switch on a small box thing strapped to his shoulder and yelled into it, over and over again. It sounded like 'Lay-lay-lay-lay . . .!' He hurtled from the place leaving me alone, looking out at the building through the foliage. A motorcycle engine sawed the air, Pascal running like a rabbit through the trees towards the road.

A *crump* sounded. I felt the earth press up slightly against my soles. No waft of heat on my face this time, no blizzard, no residual crackle audible, no sky glow from a fading blaze, none of that, no snow on my face, no whine of Marc's car.

The drivers were bewildered down there. Two had run towards the mansion, then withdrawn. Maids and waiters emerged, scattering, shrieking, pointing. Katta came, smoothing down her skirt, perhaps from some motor parked behind the house.

A man came staggering round the side of the house, blood on his head, trying to wipe it. The drivers took him, shouting, beckoning. Some went to the edge of the drive, peering at the back of the building's west wing. Two thought, dived into their motors, stood free with car phones in action. A few windows had billowed out, sharding on the lawn. No smoke, no sign of fire, no bright flames. One thing, Marimee did a precision job, every single time.

An explosion, I guessed, in the syndicate's meeting. There'd be grave injuries, I shouldn't wonder, even deaths.

Helicopters headed over the trees, shining headlights. Four. Another, distantly, higher. Searchlights of amazing power. Motors shrieked and wahwahed along roads. Police were everywhere. It was very efficient, motorcycles roaring and those sharpedged police vehicles short on windows arriving by the column. I thought, why am

I so cold inside? Why am I not weeping? For Paulie, Marc, Sandy, all the others so recently living?

For Cissie?

I'd probably got time for a walk. Stretch my legs after all this standing about. So I left, walked down among the trees.

Goodnight, Gobbie.

CHAPTER THIRTY-FOUR

'Lovejoy!' The last person on earth I wanted to see, Dicko Chave. He was impeccably dressed, tweeds to his eyeballs, handmade leather shoes.

My heart sank. 'Dicko! Just in time, mate!'

He stood in the corridor, beaming. 'Had difficulty finding you, old chap. Some young lady guided me. Seems like everybody's talking about you there. Made a killing, what?'

'Er, aye. Look.' I was trying to explain my nakedness, towel wrapped round my middle. I lowered my voice. 'The lady – remember my temporary partner, that I want to introduce you to? She'll arrive in half an hour. I'm trying to get ready. Mind if we meet up in the residents' lounge?'

He almost fell over with enthusiasm. 'Certainly, Lovejoy!' He wrung my hand. 'Never forget this, old sport. You're a brick!'

I went in and shut the door in relief. Katta looked up from the bed. Credit where credit is due, a plump woman is real value. I realized I'd never seen her under the bedclothes. A natural counterpaner.

'Khoo theyet?'

'Eh? Oh, friend.' She flicked the towel from me. She stared. She had a smiley kind of stare, the most erotic I'd ever seen. She reached. She had an erotic kind of reach, the most erotic reach I'd ever felt.

'He naye-iss?'

'Aye. Yes.'

As we started to make smiles, and I groaned in bliss at the ceiling and she grunted with divine relish, a strange possibility came into what was left of my mind. I tried hard to register it for afters, so to speak, but failed.

'Lovejoy, *mon ami.*'

I'd been summoned before Pascal, the day after the deaths. He had two assistants with him. Lilian Sweet had Gerald and an official of some ministry. Two uniformed police worked transcribers. I'd never heard so much racket before, not even in a cop shop.

'*Oui*, Monsieur Pascal?'

'Did you know?'

Ponder for a sec. A minefield of a question. If I said no, he'd

248

say, What didn't you know? And thence et dangerous cetera into some Parisian clink. I could joke: Know? That France intended to demolish the Eiffel Tower in 1909, when it was a mere twenty years old, and build on the site . . .? but that'd nark him. You counter word tricks with a definition.

'Know? That the explosion was going to happen? No, Monsieur. How could I?'

'Indeed. How could you, Lovejoy?'

More mines. I nodded, grave and sad. 'Even delaying so long, I worried lest I missed a couple. That's why I took your watch, allowed myself only two more minutes. Less, even.'

'Marc was gardener-chauffeur at Mrs Galloway's lodge. The place you stayed as her lover when you first came to France, Lovejoy. Had you met him previously?'

Shrug, my own personal ineptly non-Gallic version. 'Vaguely saw him about the place.' I straightened, honour bound. 'But, I do not make any admission about the relationship between Mrs Galloway and myself. The lady's honour forbids me speak – '

'*Oui, oui*, Lovejoy.' He had a knack of making agreement sound disbelief. 'Your firmness does you credit. About the events surrounding the explosions at the Swiss Repository.'

'I was in Zurich when that happened, I believe. But I had nothing to do with it.'

'You observed no similarities between the mansion house of yesterday and the Repository?'

A shrug to dispel surprise. 'Similarities? I knew neither place. When I was taken to the garden party, for reasons that even now are unclear, I wasn't even sure where it was.'

'Lovejoy. There will be criminal charges brought. Their precise nature is yet to be determined. For this week you will remain in Paris. Thank you.'

And I left. They'd booked me into a small hotel near the Panthéon, which pleased me. I was to report three times daily to the bobbies. Each time, Pascal had to be notified in case he wanted me. I realized with a shock that Lilian and Gerald Sweet had an office, a real genuine office, in Pascal's division. Can you believe it? Their underhandedness took my breath away. What's happened to fair play?'

Katta was waiting outside Pascal's office on a bench, a picture of misery. She brightened when she saw me, leapt up and embraced me, cooing. I realized instantly that here was a woman filled with love's natural warmth. She'd lost Paulie, *requiescat in pace*, her precious plaything, and wanted another. Just to tide her over, I said I was free and did she have time for a chat. I'm always ready to do friends a good turn. Anybody'll tell you.

'Listen, Katta, love.' I stopped us just short of the lounge. 'One thing. I'm really happy.' Nothing settles a man's soul like a woman, but how do you tell her? 'What I mean is, ta.'

'Oh, kyoo, Lovejoy!' She simpered, in her thick mascara, plastered lipstick, hair greenish, cheeks really rouged. You have to hand it to birds. They have real style.

'There's one thing.' I hesitated. How to describe Dicko? The truth, when all else fails. Here goes. 'Katta, love. Dicko is, er, new to women. You understand? He simply doesn't know how to, well cope with a genuine female.'

'Chee is . . .?' Her purpled eyes widened. She actually licked her lips. 'Chee feerjeenal? Layke chyoo?'

Virginal like *me* for God's sake? I swear that sometimes I think she's putting it all on. 'Dunno. He's certainly a beginner. Okay? But he's a friend. So, well, go easy, okay?'

She seized me, grabbed me in an envelope hug and forced her lips on to mine. Her tongue rummaged my uvula. Passing hotel staff made approving murmurs. 'Senk kyoo, Lovejoy! Setch er geeft!'

Dicko was waiting in the lounge, bouquet of carnations at the slope-arms position. He shot upright. The poor chap was desperate, expecting another failure.

'Katta, may I introduce my friend Dicko Chave.' I was on my best behaviour.

'Chow doo yoh doow?' Katta got out, coy and shy.

Dicko shook her hand. 'Flowers for a flower,' he clipped out. The daffodils stood to attention.

'Heavens!' I exclaimed. 'That the time?' I left them beaming at each other. A hit!

Exit Lovejoy. I'd keep his loan, my fee for effecting a lonely-hearts intro. Fair's fair.

The street was abuzz with police. I watched from the corner among a small crowd. The factory was being boarded up. Cloaked folk stood gazing.

'It's no victory,' somebody said close to my elbow.

'I know,' I said.

'It will simply move on, Lovejoy. More legions of slave children, different guises.'

'I know that, too.'

'Mrs Sweet tells me there were five in Great Britain.'

'And the rest.' I always sound bitter, wish I knew why. I do try to sound light-hearted and chirpy. I've never yet seen me smile in a photo. I wonder what it is.

'They are introducing legislation . . .'

'Shut it, love.' When law steps in, truth flies out of the window.

I watched as the police loaded up the furniture, much partly completed, some hardly started.

'What will you do, Lovejoy? Now Katta and Mr Chave have got engaged?'

That made me turn and look. She tried to give me a hankie, silly cow. You can always trust a woman to be stupid. 'I've already got one, ta. Engaged?' I thought she meant hired.

'To be married, Lovejoy.' She was near to a smile. 'Katta asked me to give you this.'

Hotel notepaper.

> *Dear Lovejoy,*
>
> *Timeo Danaos et dona ferentes! My betrothed and I shall expect you at our wedding. Do bring a guest, darling.*
>
> *Love from your new neighbour,*
>
> *Katta*

What had happened to the accent? That's women for you. Me and Lysette strolled off. No good checking on the police now they'd finally got weaving.

'Mrs Sweet wishes to see you, Lovejoy, tonight. She'll call at your hotel.'

'She does?'

'It will take several sessions, I think, from the way she spoke. She has a massive inventory of antiques she wants you to check, before Miss Chevalier arrives tomorrow.'

'Miss Who?'

'Miss Chevalier. Monsieur Pascal told me there's a way to reduce the criminal charges against you, if you co-operate with the authorities here, Switzerland, Great Britain.'

'Meaning co-operate with Lorela Chevalier?' I'd saved her firm, her reputation, her antiques, her job . . . She'd tried to phone me at the hotel a thousand times. I'd finally left the receiver off the hook while Katta, er, swallowed my pride.

'I think so, Lovejoy. And Mercy Mallock will be with you soon. She faxed the hotel.'

'Mercy?' I brightened. 'What'd she say?'

'Her letter is too long, too personal, and impertinently presump-
tuous. You must have nothing more to do with her.'

We turned into the street gales, par for Paris. This was starting
to look sour. I mean, Katta'd served, as it were, her purpose in
detoxifying my soul with her unique brand of adventurous love. But
Lilian Sweet was a different proposition. Back in East Anglia I'd not
last an hour if word got about that a SAPAR hunter had decided
to cottage up with me. And Lilian had proved her determination
more than somewhat. I'd not shake her off in a trice.

Lorela Chevalier on the other hand had definite possibilities.
Lovely, attractive, feminine as a flower. But with the giant responsibility of her great Repository? And willing to offer heaven-knows-
what for me to replace old Leon? To live with the glorious Lorela,
in utter affluence, comfort, warmth, wealth, surrounded by the
densest collection of perfect antiques the world could assemble? I'd
die of ecstasy in a week.

No Paradise for the likes of me.

'Are you going to the hotel, Lovejoy?' I'd stopped at the square
where me and Gobbie'd met. And Lysette.

'Well, aye.' I felt uncomfortable. I'd nearly said I'd nowhere else
to go.

'Miss Danglass is waiting there, Lovejoy.' Lysette was standing
close. The wind whipped our coats about us.

'Jodie Danglass?'

'Yes. She's been waiting a while. She said she has urgent offers
from a Big John Sheehan, about some glass replicas he wants you
to market for him. He's asking after some Carolean mica playing
cards he bought from a young widow. It's rather complex, Lovejoy.'
Sherry Bavington, the bitch. She must have come calling, nicked the
micas from my ever-open cottage. I'd strangle the thieving cow, after
I got a lock for the door.

'Aye, it would be complex all right.' With Big John Sheehan it
was never easy, cheap, or straightforward. Sending Jodie to France
was his way of saying to the trade that he had nothing to do with
the child labour – not that anybody'd ever believe he had. 'She
mention which? The Portland Vases?'

Lysette's eyes were pure, that ultra-blue you get in Greek
paintings.

'Lovejoy. I don't think you should become involved in something
new, not just yet. Not with Monsieur Pascal's team still investigating.'
Pause. 'Do you?'

'No,' I tried, cleared my throat. 'No,' I said, firmer.

'Darling, I have an idea.' She smoothed my lapel. I hardly felt her hand. 'Paris can become rather crowded. Would you like to stay somewhere else? Only for a short while, not too long.'

'Stay?'

'Yes. Rest, read, have time to visit interesting museums.' She smiled, quite casual. The wind swooshed her hair across her face. She scraped it aside with a reproving tut. 'Some antique shops aren't quite played out. That sort of thing.'

'What about Pascal and Lilian, the rest?'

'Need we tell them where we are going, darling? I think not.'

'We'd never make it.'

She smiled. 'Oh, yes we would, Lovejoy.'

'You're not an antiques hunter too?' It was a joke, but came out despairing. What had I thought, those epochs ago: that too many people were paid but loving eyes.

'Not yet.' Her reply started out serious, emerged as a joke. I felt her smile.

'Let me think.' I stood there. She slipped her arm into mine, and we sat on the curved bench beneath the tree. 'Hang on,' I said. She'd put her arm round my shoulders, pulled my head gently down on to her shoulder. It was the wrong way round. I'm the masterful all-caring protective provider. She was the weaker vessel. 'If Jodie Danglass is here from home, and Lorela Chevalier is offering . . .'

'Shhh,' she went. Her fingertips pressed my cheek, turning me to her. She touched her mouth on mine, very soft.

Applause sounded. The café windows were crowded, grinning faces and salutations everywhere. She broke away, scarlet.

'Look,' I said. 'How about we try that, then? Might as well, eh?'

Took me less than ten minutes to talk her into it. One thing, I'd not lost the knack of persuasion.

The Great
California Game

For
Joan Kahn, with love
This book is respectfully dedicated to
the Chinese god Kuan Ti, patron saint of
wandering antique dealers far from home

Lovejoy

CHAPTER ONE

In antiques, everything is women.

Everything else is America.

I'm a convert to America. Like a nerk, I'd always assumed the Olde Worlde was a cut above the Yanks. Now? Now, I can't honestly see why they bother with the rest of us. They've got everything. Like beauty. Antiques. Wealth. And, strangely, innocence. So if you're a confirmed Ami-hater, better swap this quick for some improving literature, because this story's how I fell in love with the place through the genteel world of antiques – meaning the hard way, via murder, robbery, fraud, larceny.

Antiques make you live that way. I'm an antique dealer, every breath I breathe.

I'd been in New York three days, and seen nothing but hurrying crowds. I worked in a bar eatery. From nothing, I'd already worked myself up to the lowest of the low.

The Benidormo Hotel was as cheap as dinge could make it. The dozy bloke at the reception desk – a couple of planks flaking paint – made me pay a night's advance. His job was watching quiz shows. I tried to sound American, wrote my name as R. E. Lee, didn't tell him I'd just arrived from Hong Kong with nearly nowt, and found the right floor by trudging because I mistrust lifts.

A bird saw me in the gloomy corridor, a place for assassins. She was pleasantly laconic, overpainted. A little lad trailed her. I'm hopeless about kids' ages. Seven, eight?

'Can I help?'

'No, thank you.' The key tag said this was it.

She followed, stood looking from the doorway. 'I mean can I . . . *help*. Twenty dollars' worth.'

I gauged her. This young, they should be at home worrying about term exams. 'Unless you know where a job's going.'

She appraised me more frankly than I had her. I felt weighed. 'What can you do?'

'Anything.'

'That means you can do shit,' she said elegantly. I was trying to appear cool and streetwise, but women can always suss me. 'How long're you here?'

'Until I get enough to travel. I'm from California, studying in England.'

'Don't give me shit.' She made up her mind. 'I'm Magda, next door. No banging the walls when I'm working, okay?'

'Wouldn't dream of it.' That didn't sound slick New Yorkese. 'Sure,' I amended quickly. 'Lovejoy.'

She nodded. 'Whatever you say, Mr Lee. You're weird, y'know that? Try Fredo. Manfredi's. He kicked a counterman.'

'Fo' crackin' n' smackin'.' The little lad rolled his eyes to show drug dementia.

How had a kid this young learned about ecstasy? Magda saw my shock and said, 'Zole, meet Lovejoy. Short for Zola.'

'He's soft sheet,' Zole said with scorn. 'So's Zola.'

Maybe her brother? 'Howdy, Zole. What time does Mr Fredo open?'

Her eyes widened. 'Where you say you're from?' She gave me one of those number sequences which are pinpoint addresses in this extraordinary country. 'Get over there, Lovejoy. People'll be standing in line.'

I thanked her, locked my door and left. She too was leaving, would have held back but I dithered so we left together, Zole trailing and bouncing a worn tennis ball. I warmed to her. Considerate. I just didn't like the way she had me down as a prude. We walked a little way then she stepped into a doorway and wished me luck with the job. It might have hurt her feelings had I wished her luck with hers, so I merely said so-long.

'So-long, Rube,' Zole called with derision. What did Zole do while Magda took her clients upstairs? A New York problem. Unsolvable.

'Lovejoy? Take the bar.'

'Right, Fredo.'

'And that jerk's a chiseller. Watch the bucks.'

'Right, guv.' He meant a man at the end might try to evade paying. I didn't know quite what a jerk meant, but it isn't praise.

Manfredi's was as crowded as I'd yet seen it. I'd been lucky: Magda's name had counted; Fredo gave me a chance because some employee had Monday bottle sickness. That first night I'd worked until closing time, frightened by the sense of this big city. I'd got myself hired, and threatened about behaviour.

The drinks were a difficulty, contents I'd never encountered before, but at least I could clear tables and wash the bar counter.

Fredo watched all dozen of us workers like a hawk. The first day I'd seen him fire two of the blokes for fiddling money and general slowness. It taught me New York's message: earn your pay, or else. By the evening of the second day I'd memorized every drink, their prices, was hired on a daily basis.

'Guv? What's with this guv?' Fredo asked.

Fredo often looked at me, amused by my strange speech.

'Ah, it means boss, Fredo. Picked it up from the, er, Limeys.'

He chuckled, an amiable man. 'Sir yesterday, guv this. We'll talk English, yet!'

I chuckled along, grovelling being my strong suit when poverty's trumps. I'd stuck to the story I'd told Magda: I was heading back to California after years of studies in London. Lies come naturally to an antique dealer. I hinted I had a girl in New York, which was why I wanted this job.

The other bar hand was late this third evening and the rush about to begin, so I tidied things and got started. I couldn't help looking for the girl with the antique amber brooch.

Tonight she was in early, eightish. Theatregoer? Meeting her bloke from work? She always – in NY three consecutive nights count always – placed herself away from the door. I gave her a smile. That amber Agnus Dei brooch again. I tore my eyes away and started my job, saying 'Coming ride up!' and 'Awl ridee' like I thought everybody else was doing. Mr Manfredi had this complex system of double invoicing, which caused me a deal of trouble. But I'd mastered it, because I'd seen what happened to waiters who didn't. The idea in these American bars is there's a counter where customers perch on stools, while elsewhere floor space has tables for a waitress service. It sounds a rum arrangement, but it works. A dozen tables, swing doors onto Eighth Avenue so you could glimpse those fantastically long motors everybody drives, a score of customers, and that was Manfredi's Manhattan Style Eatery. Oh, I forgot to mention the talk – God, but Americans chat. And they do it to anyone, even though they've not been properly introduced, or have any reason. I'd never heard so many opinions – weather, politics, sport, traffic, the Middle East. That you might disagree counts nil. Strangely, I was starting to like it. You could say anything to anyone about anything any time. Surprising.

The chiseller proved no problem this particular evening. He was three parts sloshed and gradually slumped to a foetal posture less than three drinks and an hour after the boss had left. Josephus, our giant waiter who sang the livelong day, threw him out towards nine.

'Hey, Josephus,' I said soon after that interlude. 'What time's Mr Manfredi back?' At this social level, you start everything with Hey or Say-my-man. I was blending in.

'Doo any second, Lovejoy ma man.'

A bit odd. I remembered Fredo's words: thirty minutes. He never missed checking the till money. I clocked the time. Two whole hours, and no sign.

But it was a normal evening otherwise. The punters came and went. I served the vodkas, learned two more drinks recipes for my armoury. People from work, offices, the shops disgorging folk into Manfredi's. I can't help looking at people, wondering why they're in a nosh bar instead of home. The trouble was, three days and I'd seen nothing of America except that taxi ride from the airport, my grotty little pad with Magda plying her trade in the next room. And here.

'New Yorkers live on the hoof,' a woman's voice explained.

'I was just wondering.' My words were out before I saw who'd spoken.

She'd finished her meal, an enormous salady thing of avocado and chicken in deep crisp-heart lettuce foliage. That's another American thing, the meals. I'd never seen so much on a plate.

'Nobody home cooks.'

Her Agnus Dei wasn't as ancient as some, but brooches like hers are unusual. Once, new Popes issued wax Lambs for wearing in silver discs. This wasn't one, but could easily have been except for the amber. My chest bonged faintly the nearer I moved. Genuine antique. Norwegian? Swedish? She saw me looking. I went quickly to serve a lady's martini in that fearsome high-gin New York formula.

'You like my brooch?' Persistent.

'The Scandinavians' Agnus Dei pendants were usually silver. Amber's such a Baltic thing.'

She was mid-twenties, shrouded against the autumn cool, and pale featured. Long hair, nothing spectacularly fashionable. Slight, quiet, always reading.

'You know about such things?' Her grey-blue gaze took in my lapel badge. 'Lovejoy's some kinda name.'

'It's all I have, miss.'

She rocked with silent laughter and mouthed: Miss? I went a bit red, stepped down the counter to punish a suited gent with a treble bourbon. I'd quickly learned that Americans drink booze through shovelfuls of ice, God knows why. Even their beer has to be freezing. No, honest. It's quite true. Go and see for yourself.

'Sorry, Lovejoy,' she said when I drifted past her end. 'I'm a New Yorker. Rose Hawkins. Can you price it?'

See what I mean? Straight to essentials. In sleepy old East Anglia getting down to a valuation would take a fortnight.

'I'd need a good light. But it'll keep you a month. Around 1800 AD.'

'That fits.'

She looked at me curiously. For a few minutes I had to hear about baseball from three geezers, regulars in for the bar telly. Baseball – an unknowable ritual resembling our women's rounders – is as baffling as American rugby, which is all I ever hope to say about them for ever and ever. These fans kept explaining the ins and outs of the damned thing since they'd spotted my ignorance. Every religion craves converts.

'It was my great-grandmother's,' she told me next pass.

'Don't give me provenance, love, not without documentation. I've . . .' I caught myself.

'You've . . .?'

'I've heard it's safer. Never mind what dealers and auctioneers tell you.'

'Been to the exhibition, Lovejoy?'

'Exhibition?' I was casual, doing the mystique with ice and gin for a newspaper vendor. He called every second hour.

'Antiques. It's only two blocks, if you're interested.'

Interested? I'd give almost anything. 'I haven't time off. I'm new here . . . I mean, I'm new back.'

For a second I was proud of my vernacular, shortening my adverb; or whatever it is, American fashion. She began to ask me where I was from, all that. I gave her the Californian back from England, desultory patter between hurtling orders for drinks.

Then I noticed the kitchen was being closed. Last orders for grub. Lil the elderly boss waitress was collecting the invoice chits. Ten o'clock? Only nearby Apple Jack's stayed open later than us. No Mr Manfredi.

'Hey, Josephus,' I asked the big bloke. 'Fredo back?'

'Dunno, man. I'm zoomin', Lovejoy.'

'Doan look at me, honey,' Lil called.

A couple of customers gave amused advice. A lass left the kitchen, calling goodnights. The mousey-haired brooch girl stayed, said she was from some place called Greenwich Village. Like a nerk I asked politely how often she went home to visit. She seemed puzzled. I hoped it wasn't anywhere near California. Being merely one more illegal immigrant working for the Almighty Dollar makes you edgy. Fredo had twice asked for my social security number. Not having any idea what that was, I'd told him I'd bring it in tomorrow and tomorrow and tomorrow.

Outside the traffic was still hard at it, zooming to and fro. Police sirens were a standard feature, I knew by now. The first night I'd twice got up from my pit to see what was happening, but by my second night I was impervious, by today oblivious. New York's siren song, always there.

Josephus had called closing several times. Finally the brooch made to leave, smiling.

'Goodnight, Lovejoy.'

I was wiping the counter, washing glasses, keeping an anxious eye on the door for Fredo, not knowing what to do. Della, our cash-cheque lady, was locking up her pedestal and handing me the keys and donning her coat. I told Rose goodnight.

She left in the same door-swing as Della. Everybody was yelling goodnights to me, people giving me keys. Josephus was singing his folksy way out. I was desperate. He declined Della's keys.

'Dowan tra me, Lovejoy. I'm singin' in ma club tonight.'

'Oh, aye.' I'd forgotten. His big chance, some melody he'd written.

Which left worried me, the customers all departed, the greasy keys from the kitchen's street entrance on the counter. And Manfredi's Manhattan Style Eatery empty. Except for two cash registers loaded with money. Waiting. Gulp. Hurry back, Fredo.

Outside, sirens whooped. I stood there by my clean bar, wondering what to do. I went and turned off the lights in the kitchen. Only one storey, thank God, so no upstairs to worry about. I called a feeble inquiry into the Ladies' loos, checked the Gents' for lurking figures. I was alone.

With all that money.

Fredo's home number? I hunted high and low. I tried the New York telephone book, my first experience. Its size took my breath away. There was a Greenwich Village actually here in New York. And a Bronx! No wonder Rose stared when I'd asked her what state she hailed from . . . Well, might as well look for an Italian name in a haystack. I gave up, took off my apron, stood there like a spare tool, thinking worried thoughts.

My doss house hotel was a couple of miles southwest, so no chance of popping round to ask guidance from the dozy old bloke. Magda I'd hardly glimpsed since my arrival. Lock up? Last night

Fredo'd winkled out some tipsy customer with vigorous expletives and mucho muscle. Bums had to be slung out no matter what, and everybody was a threatening bum until proved otherwise. This morning I'd heard Della telling Josephus how she'd been mugged in broad daylight, her purse stolen with its credit cards. Danger land.

I bolted the door, but its lock was electronic – tap its buttons in the right sequence or it doesn't obey – so I achieved nothing more. Money, though.

All American money looks alike – hundred-dollar notes look like ones, fifties look like the rest. Weird. All decimal, of course, so my trick of translating into the simpler old pre-decimal guineas, pounds, crowns, florins, shillings, tanners, threepenny joeys, pence and farthings, which everybody could understand, wouldn't work here.

Homesick and forlorn, I made myself some coffee, putting a coin on the till for it, and sat wondering about the USA, with its enormous meals and streets all numbered in order so you couldn't get lost and everybody so cheery and . . . Like Rose, for instance. So direct, so willing to smile and talk. Most odd. So unlike us. I mean, as recently as 1989 Lord Dacre threatened to resign because his Savile Club decided to allow members to talk during breakfast, the bounders.

Somebody shoved the door. I leapt a mile, bawled a terrified 'Hey, go home, ya bum!' and switched lights on round the place. Silence, or what passes for silence in New York. That is, traffic, sounds of people speed-walking, talk, sirens, motor horns, occasional yells.

The bar now seemed cold and uninviting, even stark. There's something unnerving about tidiness, isn't there? I'm always lost when some woman comes to stay, tidies me into her pattern, washes sheets and gets grub by the clock. I like a little disorder. Manfredi's, all prepped for the morning, was an uncomfortable oasis.

Nothing to read, so I switched the telly on for company just as a policeman pounded on the outer glass panel, frightening me to death. His silhouette seemed convincing. I went to let him in.

'What's going on here?' he said, eyes everywhere.

'Evening, constable. I'm still waiting for Mr Manfredi.'

He gazed around. He was all dark leather pouches. The gun made me swallow a couple of times.

'New, huh?'

'Yes, constable. Barman.'

He walked about for a few moments, eyed me in what can only be called a threatening manner, strolled out without another word. I was relieved to see him go.

An hour on, I surrendered all hope and got some cold grub from the kitchen fridges. I made more coffee, though by now I was sick of the bloody stuff. The great survival trick is to avoid cinnamon. America must float on a sea of the wretched spice. They put it in rolls, things called muffins which aren't, in tea bags, in anything edible. Midnight came and went and the telly game shows went on and on. I barricaded the front entrance with chairs and a trough filled with giant greenery, tested the windows, listened horrified to somebody fighting outside, pulled out plugs, generally lessened the electricity bill for the dark hours . . . except there are no dark hours in New York, that insomniac's paradise.

A bench seat would do me. Towards two o'clock I unfastened a window, peering out. Motors still about, pedestrians, somebody falling over, neons blinking multicolour into faces, somebody running down a side street. And the grids steaming as if Hell was somewhere immediately below. I couldn't get used to the great funnels they stick into the roadway to pipe the gases high into the air. I latched the window, baffled. Grub finished, I washed the crockery in case the kitchen people went mental in the morning, and put the lights out.

The telly I left on, sound lowered. I dozed fitfully on the bench. Three or four times during the night I roused thinking I heard people trying windows, doors, but there was no one and I slept on.

CHAPTER TWO

Seven o'clock, and I was dismantling my barricade when Fredo came. He was there breathing hard, with the same bobby from the previous night. Fredo looked distraught, a piece of sticking plaster on his forehead and his wrists bandaged.

'Morning, guv. You okay?'

'That's him, Fredo,' the policeman said.

They pushed in. The law stood by while Fredo attacked the cash registers. I got fed up just standing about while they exchanged meaningful glances so I went and brewed more of that terrible liquid. I'd have made myself an egg but I once cracked one at home and there inside was an almost fully formed live chick. Now I wait for birds to do the cooking, or go without. After all, what are women for? They can't go about doing nothing all blinking day, not even in America.

The kitchen people were obsessional about their ovens, so I switched the electric ones on and lit the gas under the ones that looked as if they needed it. I heated some water, which I thought a really sensible move. We usually had quite a few people in for breakfast, who sat along the bar. I put the telly on, more unbelievable game shows with everybody clapping all the time.

'Yes, guv?'

Fredo was breathing hard, but sitting down now. The bobby was glaring. My heart sank. Morning of my fourth day in America, and it looked like I was for it.

'The money's right,' Fredo accused. His words hurt him.

I gazed blankly back. 'I know. Della tilled up last night.'

'Why's he talk like that?' the cop said.

'Who minded the store, Lovejoy?'

I thought that one out. Some idiom? Guarded the restaurant, probably. 'Stayed here? Me. I couldn't work the alarm.'

The cop looked troubled, but shrugged and left when Fredo gave him a series of long slow nods. That left us two, except Josephus trundled in like a sleepy troll and Lil, Della and the rest arriving, hallooing that 'Hi, there . . .'

'In here, Lovejoy.' Fredo walked with a limp as we made his office. He yelled for coffee through his hatch and got a chorus of cheery rejoinders. God, but morning heartiness is depressing stuff. I wasn't sure how much more I could take.

'Lovejoy. You stayed?'

Patiently I recounted my feat of having dozed on the bench during the night. He listened, staring.

'O'Leary was waiting for you to make a break for it.'

'Break?' Run away? As from a robbery . . .? My mind cleared. 'You mean the constable expected me to steal our money?'

Fredo corrected, '*My* money, Lovejoy. You barricaded yourself in. O'Leary heard. He covered the rear exit.'

I shrugged. So the police waste their time here as well. 'Big deal.' I brought out my Americanism proudly.

'Lovejoy. You stay downtown, right?' I still don't know what Americans mean by downtown. Ask what they mean, they'll define it a zillion different ways. They know where *theirs* is, though, which I suppose is what matters. 'And you're new off the boat, right? The money's right.' He pondered me.

'I know.' This was mystifying. And the outer doors were clicking as New York poured in for nosh. 'Look, guv. We've already said this twice round. Customers. If you want me to say it a third time, just call, eh?'

Apron, wash hands, and leap into a whirlpool of noisy greetings over the biggest breakfasts you ever could imagine.

Jonie, a lanky lad who shared Josephus's rotten taste in rotten music, told me Fredo had suffered an accident on Grand Central Parkway, been unconscious all night. Jonie was a merry soul who dressed like a jogger itching to go, laughed at his own joke: 'Business worries got him hospitalized, Lovejoy – and business worries woke him right up!' Everybody thought that hilarious. I grinned, quipped that dough worried everybody, got a chorus of 'Right, right!' and pressed on serving coffees, shouting orders and making sure the right sauces, pickles, condiments, were on hand for whatever customers lurked behind those mounds of steaming food we served and served. And served.

'Lovejoy?'

'Evening, Rose.' I was tired by eight. She was in, same stool, had her tunnyfish salad and sliced eggs and coffee and a glass of white wine.

'Want me to buy you a drink?'

I thought I'd misheard at first. 'Er, thanks, love. But I don't drink on duty.' Then I contemplated the alternative, the terrible cinnamon tea of America, and relaxed my rule but insisted on paying for it myself. She frowned slightly, heaven knows why. I got some American white wine.

'Why d'you lot import so much European stuff when yours is better?' I mused between customers, on the principle that compliments stop women frowning. 'Like your American cut glass.'

'Cut glass?'

'Late Victorian. It's miles better than . . . er, foreign antiques of that vintage.' I'd caught myself in the nick of time, reminded myself that I was a Yank, not an illegal immigrant hopefully passing through.

'You and antiques. We take in that exhibition?'

'Give me half a chance, love.'

'It's a date. Tomorrow afternoon?' She saw my hesitation, reminded me tomorrow was Sunday. I agreed with ecstasy. Antiques *and* time to think? 'Then you can concentrate on legit antiques, Lovejoy.'

She smiled, tilting her head towards the lovely woman in the corner who'd captured my attention an hour previously by her accessories. Her purse was a genuine Victorian Belgian gold-mesh chained handbag – I was practically certain it had a garnet clasp and a gold dance pencil on its chain. It may sound silly, but purses and handbags are still among the easier antiques to find. And they're still relatively cheap (though by the time this goes to press . . .) I must have stared rather. The woman, aloof from us rabble, actually used a cigarette case with the old Czarist tricolour enamelled between gold mounts. Surely not Fabergé, here in New York?

'Lovejoy ma man, Fredo wants you.'

I served one customer a gallon of bourbon (mounds of freezing ice, poor bloke) and left them to it. Josephus took over. He hated this. It stopped him singing because people along the bar talked and he had to answer. Fredo was in his office, ashen now.

'Lovejoy. You gotta do a job for me tonight, y'hear?'

'Tonight?' I was knackered. I'd never thought the prospect of snoring my head off in that grotty little hotel would seem like paradise. But Fredo looked worse than I felt. His eyes were bloodshot and he was slanted in his chair. He was on whisky. 'Shouldn't you be in hospital?'

'I been in hospital, goddammit.' He groaned at the effort, sweat pouring down his face. 'A thousand dollars for nuthin', send you home worse 'n before, for chrissakes.'

He was worrying me. 'Look, Fredo. Close Manfredi's just for tonight, eh? Call your doctor –'

'Lovejoy.' He spoke with drained patience. 'You do my outside job tonight, right? Juss *do* it, ya hear?'

So I got this job, dead on nine. Wasn't there some old play once by that title, where somebody finishes up shot? It didn't turn out like that. Not immediately anyhow.

When you're in some new country, city, anywhere, it's only natural to want to look, get the feel, be amazed at whatever's there to be amazed at. Tired as I was, I was impatient to see New York, walk and gawp. So far I hadn't had a chance. I'd been in two shops – I'd bought essentials, razor, street map and that – plus Manfredi's Eatery, plus my microscopic drossy pit. So Fredo's command to get in a taxi and go to a written address pleased me: chance to see New York at last! I waved to Rose and explained to Josephus and Jonie and Della and Lil, left them arguing the toss about who was to do what, and left.

The taxi man was local. 'I'm the only remaining New Yorker behind a wheel,' he told me. 'You're lucky you got me. Now, they're all African, Hispanos, Europe, you name it. Next month I quit, run my own service on Long Island with my dumb brother-in-law. He's a schmuck . . .'

I listened in bafflement as his family hatreds came out. I'd never heard anyone speak like this before. Was it the custom? To tell a stranger your native city stank from garbage? That you'd kill the mayor if you could? That your President shoulda done law' cos he's stoopid? That your son was a bum? By the end of the journey I was stunned. I hadn't even looked out of the window.

'How much?' I asked, alighting in this enormous driveway. A large house loomed above up narrow stone steps, an ominous place in spite of the lights and music on the terrace.

He spoke with disgust, explained, 'It's down to Fredo, my brother-in-law. You believe my luck?' And drove away into the glittering night leaving me standing there being watched by two silent goons.

One beckoned, examined my bag. I felt my nape hairs rise. Being looked at like that brings out the coward in me every single time. Life's always on the wobble, and men this tranquil exist solely to tip life out of control.

'My waiter's things,' I said, nervous.

Silence, broken after a couple of centuries by a woman's irritated voice calling was he here at last and get him in here. I received my bag and was shoved to the rear entrance, where another bulky goon was standing, knowing I was coming and saying nothing. His hands hung down. He made no reply to my nervous 'Hi there!'

'Where the hell have you been?' The same woman, by her voice, light hair and smart in dark blue and ruffles, comely but modern.

'I only knew a little while ago, ma'am. Mr Manfredi sent me. He's had a road accident.'

'In there. You're *on*. They're just going in.'

The place was beautiful in a modern way, by which I mean clean and spacious and wretchedly dull. As I changed into the jacket – slightly too big, but it had to do – I could hear music and a faint kitchen clatter. The aromas were mouthwatering. I managed to get the shoes on, too tight but no time to argue, and tried combing my hair. It never works. Ready.

'For chrissakes! What've you been *doing*? This way?'

Shapely walk, white gleaming corridors of below-stairs, following into a lift – incredible. A lift! In somebody's house! – then a pit-stop at some unnumbered floor.

'Manners above all. Y'hear? You done this before?' Her voice was a whispering bandsaw. This was a lady with whom I would never argue.

'Yes, ma'am.'

The place was plush. Other flunkeys were standing about the edges of the concourse. Pale lavender carpet, a grand staircase asking for gowned starlets to make riveting descents, chandeliers and antiques. Paintings on the walls that bonged into my chest and shut my mind off from common sense. A superb Chippendale library table which some lunatic had placed against the wall where its loveliness would be concealed. Sacrilege. Why not in the library, for God's sake? I found myself tutting in annoyance. The woman furiously told me to pay attention.

'The butler's Mr Granger. I'm Jennie, catering. The captain's Orly, okay?'

'Mr Granger, Jennie, Orly.' The white-gloved old bloke was straight out of rep theatre.

'Follow Orly's instructions. Don't speak if you can help it. Got it?'

'Thank you, ma'am.'

She wasn't a catering manageress. She was a very very frightened catering manageress. Like I was a scared waiter. I wondered if we were all terrified. On the way into the lavishly appointed corridor – too much rococo wallwork for my liking – I realized some flunkeys were more flunkeys than others. Two waiters were nervous as I was; three others similarly attired were not nervous at all. These were stiller than the rest. They didn't look at the guests. They looked at me, the other waiters, the spaces between.

'Just in time. That's Orly. Take position by him.'

Orly was an agitated smoothie positioned across the spacious entrance hall. Dark slicked hair, very mannered, slim, colourlessly delighted to be in charge. Only twenty guests, I counted, so nothing major.

Jennie glided away into the servants' regions. I took stock.

This was class. The ladies were glamorous, stylish from the certainty that all this richness would still be here in the morning. Looking young was their game. A couple were middle aged but doing brave battle – we'd have trouble selling spuds tonight. The men were monosyllabic, except for a garrulous laughter with silvered waved hair. Politician? The remainder were too economical for my liking. Economy always chills me. They were economical with smiles, words, gestures, though they'd have passed for a first-night crowd anywhere on earth. Dinner jackets tailored, rings a little too flashily genuine. There was tension in the air, with everybody eager to pretend otherwise.

We got down to it at a gesture from Mr Granger. The grub looked superb, but I was more interested in the antiques around the room. Twenty's no great number, is it, and I had time to fall in love with a vase on a pedestal – daft, really, sticking a Greek krater where us blundering servants might knock it off. These are worth a fortune. Think early Wedgwood if you've never seen one. It almost made me moan with lust. It stood glowing, its twenty-four centuries emitting radiance you can't buy. (Well, you can, but you know what I mean.) I kept trying to get near its inverted-bell shape to see if its two handles had ever been injured and re-stuck. The red-figure styles, like this, are the sort to go for. It was worth this whole house . . .

Orly gestured so I leapt to it, serving vegetables. Italian seemed to be the grub theme, but well done. Somebody expert in the kitchens tonight, thank heavens. Veal done in some posh way, broccoli, some sweet-aroma pale things I'd never seen before, and boats of other veg, it looked good enough to eat (joke). They left almost everything, ungrateful swine. It broke my heart. I could have wolfed the lot.

'Certainly, ma'am.'

The hostess was an elegant youngish blonde wearing an enormously long diamond neck chain from the shoulders. She'd indicated that a Spanish bloke wanted some grub, so I hurtled decorously, trying to look, as waiters do, that I'd just been about to get round to him any second. As I served – Royal Doulton, no less – I caught a momentary flash of complicity between two glances. Well, my business was to see this guest got his fair share of mange-tout peas, never mind if he had something going with the hostess.

'Lovejoy.' Orly's quiet murmur took me out of the dining room in a lull.

'Yes?'

He rounded on me. 'Pay *attention* in there! Can't you concentrate a single moment?'

'Eh? I am, I am!' I'd thought I was doing brilliantly.

'You're not!' He gave instructions. 'No more staring at the walls. What *is* the matter? You'll have us cemented in the East River. Don't you know who these people *are*?'

Well, no. 'Okay, okay.' I returned to the trenches as Orly clapped his hands imperiously for the waitresses to clear the main course away. I'd met blokes of Orly's temperament before, of course. His sort gets worked up over nothing.

The pudding was some impossible concoction – hot outside pastry with a cold fruit middle – which I served smiling to prove I was all attention. I almost dribbled into their dishes, I was so hungry. I even earned a smile from a dark lady in deep blue velvet who wanted some more wine. Her neighbour was a showy bloke who was all teeth. I was sure I'd seen his teeth somewhere on television.

And that was it, really. The reason I'm going on about this dinner is that it nearly got me killed. As in death.

It was afterwards that my problems began. The guests drifted out to a loose chat, drinks and coffee in the larger of the two salons. My first real glimpse into American affluence. It convinced me that America was and is the mightiest nation that ever was. It had quirks, I knew, for wasn't that a Thomas Cole landscape painting placed beside a genuine Persian seventeenth-century tile wall panel – over a hideous modern lounge suite? Well, no explaining what money will get up to.

One small incident: the host, a neat compact man who could shut people up by simply drawing breath to speak, made an announcement when everybody was sprung from the nosh. Orly signalled me to freeze. Mr Granger stood self-effacingly among the foliage. We serfs were not to be noticed.

'Ladies and gentlemen. A toast. I give you the Game.'

'The Game! Win, Nicko!'

Nobody stood, though everybody seemed happily enthusiastic. Oddly, the blue velvet lady, Sophie Somebody, had to strain her grimace to its limit. Didn't like games? I caught her careful evasion of the Spanish gent's gaze, and his of hers, because I was standing nearby her at the time with a tray – silver, a genuine antique Boulton and lovely to clutch. I was dying to look for the hallmark. She wanted some more wine. I naturally stooped to pour, and found something worrying.

She was wearing some lovely jewellery – except it was modern crap. Diamonds really are precious, but phony diamonds aren't. Maybe wearing non-diamonds in the super circuit was the reason for her concealed anxiety? There's nothing really wrong with a bit of fakery. I mean, look at me.

Mr Granger inclined his head. I zoomed for glasses, refills, after-supper chocolates. The glass wasn't quite Jacob Sang, but it was rich Edwardian so I was pleased. And Mrs Sophie Velvet caused me another pang a second or two later because I saw she'd put her glass on the Sheraton Pembroke table and the glass foot *was wet*, silly cow. She was moving across to speak with Spanish, whose wife was laughing merrily with the politician, so there was no telling how long it had been there. I crossed quickly, blotted it dry, whispered to Orly that I'd attend to it later, and the party chattered on with nobody noticing we were into danger time.

The guests left about one in the morning. I'd been helping to clear away. Then Jennie caught me examining the Sheraton piece, on my own. Its surface was marvellous, took my breath away.

'Lovejoy? What are you doing?'

'Eh?' I straightened up, worried by the stain. Satinwood can be a pig. 'Oh, there's a mark on this wood, ma'am. I caught it in time, but –'

'Sure that's all?' She was looking about suspiciously. I was narked at her tone.

All right, so there was nobody else about and Orly and the rest were packing up to go, but a mark is death even on the best furniture.

'Knock it off, love. These library steps are worth a mint.'

'Jennie?'

Light flooded down the lounge from a tall doorway. Nicko stood there, his wife Gina and the politician visible inside the room behind. It seemed to be a large study, loads of books lining the walls. Lovely.

'It's this waiter, Nicko. I caught him going through the drawers.'

I licked my lips in a panic. Jennie was looking at me in a mixture of apology and anger. 'There *are* no drawers, guv.'

We did the what's-this-guv-bit for a second or two. Nicko moved closer. I noticed two of the silent flunkeys had silently reappeared.

The host positioned himself directly in front of me, but his eyes stared obliquely off at an angle. It gave me the creeps.

'What were you doing?'

'It's a set of library steps made to look like a table. Sheraton often did that. And Ince and Mayhew –'

'Jennie?'

For a bloke with a quiet voice his words could penetrate. Jennie drew breath.

'Sheraton's the antique maker, Nicko. A couple of centuries back.'

Wrong dates, but I shut up in case Nicko disagreed. Might is right in these situations.

'What steps?'

Jennie hesitated. She didn't know. I carefully opened the Pembroke table to show them it was phony clever, as made by the immortal Sheraton. 'See? This table's really steps. Sheraton often did that trick. Made them like leather-covered stools as well.' Hadn't they ever looked, for heaven's sake?

Nicko glanced down. It might have been a plank, instead of the most beautiful furniture ever made by the hand of man. A cret, though a scary one.

'Has he excuse to be here?' he asked the air beside Jennie.

'Something about a mark on the surface, Nicko.'

'You crept in here? To check a scratch?'

I showed him that too, him staring off into the middle distance. Jennie examined it.

'Shouldn't we rub it off?' she asked.

'No. Leave it. Rub it well when it's hard, never straight away. It might not need repolishing, with luck.'

Nicko turned away, but like a fool I opened my mouth.

'Er, excuse me, sir. It was the lady with the zircons did it, not me.'

Jennie's sharp intake of breath should have warned me, but I'm basically thick. So I went on to describe how she'd put the glass down and moved away to talk to the Spanish gentleman . . .

Nicko inclined his head and Jennie went with him as they talked. Me standing beside the Sheraton, worrying what I'd said wrong. I was barely ten feet from them and couldn't hear a word. She returned as Nicko went to the study, the door closing behind him. The two Suits evaporated.

She looked at me. 'You're from Fredo, Lovejoy?'

'Yes, ma'am.' I paused, not quite knowing what was going on. 'You can check.'

She paced a step or two, not quite wringing her hands. For a happy supper party there was a lot of anguish here. I was tired enough to fall down. And us serfs hadn't been offered a bite, not even with tons left over.

Then she said, 'Zircons? Mrs Brandau wore zircons?'

'Yes. The lady in the blue velvet dress, ma'am.'

They paid me, got me a taxi back into Manhattan, making sure I had all my things.

Simple as that, and I'd earned a few dollars on the side. I was so pleased with myself. Like a milliard others, me and Americans were an instant success.

When I'm stupid I go all the way.

CHAPTER THREE

'New York's a collection of islands, then?'

Rose laughed, vivacious. The breeze along the boat kept blowing her hair. I'd have told her she was bonny, but she believed she was ordinary. They're full of daft ideas. We were just docking after a circular trip round Manhattan.

'The song, Lovejoy! To the New York Islands . . .' She pointed across the Hudson River, singing about this land being her land or something.

'Oh, aye,' I exclaimed quickly so she'd know I'd only forgotten for a sec. 'That barge?'

'Every day, Lovejoy. Garbage goes out on barges, dropped into the ocean. The city's almost blocked with the stuff we New Yorkers throw out. Unbelievable.'

'I'm struck by the buildings.' And I was.

Everything in a new country's astonishing, I know, but New York is beyond belief. Until then I'd only seen New York in rain. My images had been formed from cinemas, that skyline they always show you – skyscrapers, tugboats, traffic on those bridges, the same old longshot of people crossing that long street between blocks.

I now saw New York was beautiful, kaleidoscopically and mesmerizingly lovely.

Most of Manhattan's buildings are no more than three or four storeys, all different. And the ferryboat had steamed between forested hillsides and cliffs studded with lovely houses, chalets, countryside so colourful it could have been Tuscany. I was so taken aback I'd asked Rose, 'Are we still in New York?' when I'd run out of landmarks. Several people standing along the boat's railings had turned and laughed, made jokey remarks.

'Not often New York gets such a good press, Lovejoy,' Rose said as we watched the docking. 'Especially from a Californian.'

'Why not?'

She gazed at me. 'East Coast and West Coast. Sibling rivalry.'

'Oh, *that* old thing.' I laughed, I thought convincingly.

The city seemed really . . . well, bright. Remade yet sound, not at all like the brash New World I'd expected. And such friendly people. Preconceptions are always wrong.

We got a taxi.

'Hey!' I'd spotted something. 'There's a pattern. Avenues north to south? Streets east to west?'

Rose laughed at my exitement. 'Sure. The rule here.'

'And numbered!' I was more thrilled than Columbus. 'In *sequence*!' How simple it all was.

'Except for Broadway,' the taxi driver cut in. 'And lower n' 14th Street's real bad. Old-fashioned, y'know?'

He and Rose engaged in an incomprehensible dialogue about whether all even-numbered streets should all have eastbound traffic. I looked out. The place was heaving, for all that it was Sunday. Rose had told him to go round the southern tip of Manhattan to show me SoHo and Greenich Village. I thought it all wonderful. And I was safe here, which was more than could be said for the place I'd left.

More parks and open spaces and different architectures than the parson preached about. I was exhilarated when we stopped in West 56th Street to disembark. I had an ugly moment of terror about the tip. Rose explained.

'A tenth, fifteen per cent if you're pleased.'

We were standing in a quiet street outside an antiquarian bookshop of the name Hawkins. Hardly any traffic, and Rose looking distinctly flushed as she fumbled for a key. Why was she nervous? I'd not made any serious mistakes, not said the wrong thing.

'I work here, Lovejoy. I'd like you to see it.'

If she said so. I followed her up the steps into a pleasant but confined shop. She seemed a little breathless, talking too much.

'My sister's business, really. She's the one with the knowledge. I'm just a hanger-on.'

'Mmmh, mmmh,' I went, saying the books were really quite good, the usual lies. There's a feel you get from reading old pages that you don't from new. I thought Blake a swine until I read his own printing.

'That glass case holds Moira's special sale stock.'

I paused. Nothing special, save a tatty copy of *Martin Chuzzlewit*. It bonged me like the first edition, which is fine but common. 'Great,' I said heartily, trying to please.

'Of course, Moira dreams of the one really big find,' Rose said, switching lights on so I could be impressed all the more.

'Don't we all, love,' I said with feeling. 'Same back home. Er, in California.'

There was a desk at an angle between the cabinet and the door, with unanswered letters spread about.

'We have associates in England, France, Germany. Coffee?'

She had a silvery pot all ready, fresh milk in a carton, cups. Modern gunge.

'Please.' I didn't like Rose's let's-pretend conversation. But that alone wasn't what was worrying me.

One of the addresses I could see on the letters was not far from where I live. Lived.

'Moira's on the trail of something now.' Rose already had the pot making a noise. I watched her.

'Special?'

'Something drastic, fantastic.'

Oh, dear. I almost switched off. Antiques are an open invitation for every extraterrestrial to orbit in from Planet Greed. We're all avaricious, wanting Tutankhamen's gold bracelet for a song, dreaming of finding a Turner watercolour behind the wainscoting so we can ballock the boss and eagle off to Monte Carlo. And legends don't help, teaching us about King Arthur's lost crown, Shakespeare's autobiography, the fabled gold ship lost in the North Sea. Newspapers make us worse, always full of little lads digging up early Christian silver chalices, old aunties discovering that their plain gilt earrings are the ones Cleopatra lost in the Nile, all that. You think I'm against romance? Work a week in antiques. You'll get weary with reports of miraculous finds that turn out to be utter dross. It's always somebody else's exultant face under the banner headline, never mine.

Still, friends justify the means. And Rose was a sort of pal. So I smiled and went, 'Mmmh.'

'Moira was the same when she found that Book of Hours. Cream?'

'No, ta.' What's wrong with milk? 'Where, love?'

'Sixteenth-century, French.' She pointed.

'Eh? Oh, aye.'

Pull the other one, I thought. It stood there among the parchment bindings. Phony now, phony always. I think it knew it, too. But next to it was a tattered relic volume that beamed out enough radiance to warm any dealer's vitals. It was labelled Burnet, probably that Thesaurus which the crabby old doctor had published in Venice about 1700. (Tip: Nothing – repeat, zilch – has soared in price quite so much as the devotional Books of Hours did a few years ago. But be careful. Fakes are flooding onto the market, the better-class ones priced about the same as your average Rolls.)

'I play a game, Lovejoy . . .'

I on the other hand was wondering about the elegant woman sitting in the back room. She'd been there when we arrived. Rose knew it. She'd manoeuvred me round the wrong side of the desk so I wouldn't see her. Sister Moira? Only a glimpse, but I was sure she was the aloof lassie who sat and read in Fredo's. I'd caught her in the reflection of the glass door.

'What game?' Nicko had toasted some game.

'What I'd buy if I had the money.'

'The Burnet,' I said, in for a penny in for a pound.

'Not the Book of Hours?' I mumbled something in reply. She heard me out. Then, 'Lovejoy. How long will you stay?'

'I'm for California, as soon as I can. See the, er, folks.'

'What d'you get at Manfredi's?'

A slow inhale. American confidences have three-league boots. But I was being my up-front Californian self, so I told her and she shook her head.

'That's peanuts, Lovejoy.'

'I made some extra last night, waiting on at a private party.' I cursed myself for sounding defensive. Why should I defend stingy old Fredo? 'Fredo's okay.'

We talked of money in the book trade. Actually, book dealers are my least favourite antiquarians. They're demon elbowers at book fairs, chisellers with each other and worse with customers. Go to any provincial book fair in England. Booksellers' commonest moan is 'There's no books to *buy*!' Meaning there's a shortage of cheap rarities they – booksellers – can salt away for themselves. The elegant woman didn't emerge.

We finished the coffee, both pretending, and went to the antiques show she'd promised me. On the way I heard a girl yell abuse at a taxi. I heard a man tell another, 'Get outa here, ya bum.' We saw buskers playing wonderful street music. I nearly had my toes whisked off by every passing car. Noticed that the street corners are kerbed in iron! Asked why the manhole covers steamed so, got no answer. Learned the murder rate in New York topped anybody else's, though Washington was a contender.

But beautiful it is. Despite what happened it'll stay that way in my memory for ever and ever.

We walked alongside Central Park to the New-York Historical Society's place.

'Note that hyphen, Lovejoy,' Rose warned. 'They're compulsives!'

'Show me a museum curator who isn't.'

The elegant woman was there ahead of us, standing on the corner of West 77th, ostensibly admiring the Natural History place next road along. I didn't wave, but wondered uneasily about Rose's pale indentation on her ring finger. I knew from ancient Doris Day films that marriage holds a special place in American lawyers' hearts. Was I a prospect, Moira along to suss me? She followed us in.

The exhibition gobsmacked me. I'm not ashamed to admit it. Here was quite a small building, not many people about, getting little attention. And inside they'd pulled together a staggering display of Regency furniture. I've seen most of the stuff that matters. I simply stood there, gaping.

Remember preconceptions? Even though I'd landed hoping simply to somehow scrape the transatlantic fare home, I'd been an arrogant swine, imbued with that Old World toffee-nosed attitude: the United States of America's got no culture, not deep down.

The first glory I saw was a Hepplewhite piece, then a blinding Ince cabinet, two – that's *two* – Sheratons, then a Chippendale . . . I filled up, had to pretend I had a sudden cough. It was like suddenly meeting a houseful of friends and lovers.

There's only one way to greet people you love, including antiques. And that's to drift. I kept losing Rose in the process. Finally I chucked in the sponge of pretence as the hours flew away. Until then I'd been trying my best to be the returned expatriate. Now I thought, what the hell, I'll probably never even see Rose again. I started answering naturally when she asked about things.

'No, Rose.' I remember grinning like a fool. 'They loved brass. See that brass inlay, all round the sofa table? They couldn't resist it. Good old George the Fourth. He has more influence on everyday life through furniture and household decoration than we care to remember. Of course, he was a bit of a ram, women all over the kingdom . . .' I saw people looking. 'Er, he was a libertine . . .'

'Why did you pull a face at that one?'

'It's a fraud, love. See the woods? Coromandel's a devil to use, hard as iron, difficult to place just like the Regency makers did. In fact, it's as if they filed rather than planed. We use fierce electric sanders and routing planes. If you were to look with a McArthur microscope at the surface, you'd see microscopic . . .'

More folk listening, one gentleman stern, two others casual. And the elegant beauty. In an odd moment she'd crossed glances with Rose, though neither had shown recognition. I moved Rose on underneath a silver chandelier.

'There's only a dozen known, replicas excepted. Find one and you've pulled off the biggie.' That was a thought, because in the USA possession of a silversmith's die – with which each made his hallmark – isn't illegal, whereas back in dozy old East Anglia . . . So anybody could make a *new* silver chandelier, get an original Regency silversmith's die, and in a trice be the proud owner of a 'genuine' Regency silver chandelier, one of the world's greatest rarities . . . I wasn't really serious. Only daydreaming, as I told Rose when she called me to earth.

The clocks were disappointing. Some goon nearby started expounding about the 1820s being the peak of London's longcase clockmakers – the nerk called them 'grandfather' clocks. He would. This sort of thing's often quoted from the slithery catalogue spiel of auctioneers. You have to arm yourself with truth to counteract it. London clockmakers let longcase clocks alone after about 1804 or so, when the provinces took over. There was a bonny archtop bracket clock in mahogany I would have found room for under my jacket if I'd been the only visitor (only kidding) and a pearl ware Wedgwood jug with that priceless yellowish tinge they couldn't get rid of until they discovered that a little touch of cobalt made all the difference.

'For myself,' I was saying as we left – it shut at teatime – 'I'd rather have the lemonish tint.'

I ignored the glimpse of the elegant woman to one side of the entrance, because what did it matter? Her sister was overprotective. So what?

We shared a gentle meal in a self-service place and said so-long. Rose suggested we meet some time. I agreed because it's my only response with women. I waved her off near Columbus Circle, started walking.

I'd gone a hundred yards when I was taken in custody by a couple of plainclothesmen who flashed badges at me just like on the pictures and bundled me inside a motor the length of a cathedral. I was made to believe that any attempt at discussion would be ill received.

CHAPTER FOUR

It wasn't a police car, not like I'd seen. Some special division, arresting me for being an illegal alien? From gaol I'd write to Rose, c/o Fredo's nosh bar, or her bookshop . . . We'd driven into an enormous tunnel.

'Excuse me, please. Where are we going?'

Neither answered. My mouth was already dry, but it dehydrated some more. My anxiety gelled into fright. This was no arrest. At times like this I'm even more pathetic than usual, lost, helpless, every neurone on hold.

Emerging, daylight showed me signposts. New Jersey? Wasn't that vaguely in Los Angeles? Or not? TV late-nighters, hitherto my sources on America, are never precise on geography. Here was New Jersey, stuck right onto New York, as pretty as the rest of the place. Why I should be so astonished by trees, colourful gardens, chalets and imposing dwellings, handsome architecture, I don't know. I mean, I've never been to France or Tibet, yet I've read quite a bit about them. But here I was in the United States and ignorant as sin. Maybe it's that we *suppose* we know, when really we don't. Guilty, of wilful ignorance.

The grand house we stopped at was familiar even in daylight. And the frantic girl who came to wring her hands on the steps. She was pale as death, though bonny in her tope sheath dress. I had the feeling that somehow Jennie wasn't quite the same status by daylight. She'd been the catering manageress; now she was no more than a gofer. Terror still showed. I hoped mine didn't.

Mr Granger conducted me and Jennie across acres of carpet, modern crud attractive as an oil slick. For the same price they could have had a lovely Edwardian or Mesopotamian. It's the same with people who buy new dinner services or with household lace, late decorative glassware. Folk never listen.

Nicko was seated between two people. One was his wife. The other was Orly, erstwhile my off-table boss only now much less camp and very solemn. Daylight altered status all round. I prayed it didn't change mine too much. Mrs Nicko sat in an apple-green afternoon dress, emeralds picking light from everywhere. Lovely. Nice to see a woman choosing the right colours for once. I honestly do believe they make more mistakes in colours than in hair styles, dress, fashion, textures of materials, food menus . . .

'What's with him?' somebody was asking.

'Lovejoy. Tell Mr Aquilina what you said last night.'

I dragged my eyes from Mrs Nicko, licked my dry lips. My voice came out a croak. 'Er, well, Sheraton –'

Nicko gazed obliquely past me, still as a stoat.

'No. The lady, Lovejoy. Mrs Sophie Brandau.'

'Blue velvet? Yes. I saw her do it.' Suddenly I really honestly didn't want to be guilty of marking their frigging table. I wanted to prove my innocence to the hilt. 'Orly saw her. You served her the glass, Orly.'

I swear my knees were quivering. Sometimes I disgust me.

'He said zircons, Gina,' Nicko told the wall.

Mrs Nicko did a woman's meticulous non-smile that speaks volumes. I didn't want to get on the wrong side of her, either. She said, 'Truly, Lovejoy?'

Odd that bosses have first names in America. Was it the custom? Chat and fright are immiscible, the way chat and love are not.

'Well, the setting was a bit too much for the style,' I began helpfully. 'The ring stone was about J/K colour, Edwardian cut, put into platinum.' Faces blank in my pause for breath. Was Nicko going to go spare if I said I didn't like the setting? 'Er, I thought the mount crap – sorry, not well designed. There's a limit to what a slender Edwardian mount can get away with . . .'

Nicko's attitude had changed. Jennie jumped in. Fright makes a woman ugly, as if it scars her soul. Odd, because excitement makes them more attractive. I wonder why.

'Zircons, Lovejoy? Not diamonds?'

I eased. Was that all? Had I been brought all this way and scared witless just for society· gossip?

'You mean am I sure? Zircon shows a double edge. Diamond doesn't. You need a handlens to make certain, so I . . .' I glanced worriedly at Orly '. . . filled her water glass, handed it to her.' Into their silence I explained that parts of a filled glass can magnify.

'This zircon,' Nicko asked infinity.

'They're old-fashioned now, really,' I said, cheering by the second. Home ground. 'They were the favourite diamond lookalike once. Now there are superb cheaper manmakes.'

'How cheap?'

'Peanuts.' I spoke my Americanism proudly. 'Some cubic zirconias and whatnot you can buy for virtually the cost of cutting them. Even amateur jewellers turn them out.'

'So?'

I wished he'd raise his voice, give it some inflection now and then. Maybe it wouldn't put the mockers on me quite so badly. I shrugged.

'She should have had a synthetic.' This was none of my business. 'Some manmakes are red hot. I mean, cubic zirconias usually won't chip, which natural zircon sometimes does – not as hard, you see, though nothing's quite up to diamond. And finding a big natural zircon can be a pig because they're usually pretty small.'

More silence, everybody looking. I cleared my throat, running out of facts.

'Ceylon exports them. People used to call colourless zircons Matara diamonds, after a town there.' Pause. That was my lot, unless they got me a good library. 'I like natural zircon. Mrs Brandau's were terrific, though not worth much. Zircon,' I bleated on desperately, 'gets a bad press. Like colourless sapphires. You can't give them away nowadays, yet they're beautiful stones.'

No response. I began to sweat, casting about in my mind for more bits gleaned from my sordid past. Mrs Aquilina crossed her legs, driving me mad just when I wanted to concentrate. Jennie and Orly were intent, Nicko gazing off somewhere. His wife was nearly smiling, hard eyes on me.

'The woman,' she said softly. I swallowed.

'The only reason women wear natural zircons nowadays is if it's their Zodiac thing. Or if the setting's complicated and old and it'd take too long to have replicas made.' I gave a stiff grin. End with a joke. 'There's a lot of thieves about. So I'd use the antique phonys because the setting'd convince even if the gemstones wouldn't . . .'

And I wished I hadn't, because suddenly it was no joke. I learned that when Nicko moved. His head swivelled, but so slowly it was like waiting for a salvo. His eyes stilled me. Black as coal. I felt my feeble smile fade.

'Try him out,' he said.

They took me to a small room a mile down some corridor. God, but white corridors daunt your spirits, don't they. What's wrong with a bit of colour, for God's sake?

For an hour Orly and Jennie showed me stones of varying sorts, including zircons in various cuts, spinels and colourless stones, mounted and unmounted. I was worn out, but becoming less scared as I worked through the gems in their plastic envelopes. Mrs Aquilina came in to watch from time to time, smoking her head off but graceful with her cigarette and giving submerged looks. An elderly man called Sokolowsky had brought the gems. He sat by, saying nothing. Presumably the jeweller. He'd brought the instruments every antique dealer knows and hates – they tell whether a dealer's speaking the truth. You can put the fear of God in a jeweller by simply asking for a handlens, a microscope, a refraction gadget. (Don't let him tell you he hasn't got these essentials handy – notice that all jewellers have a little dark alcove behind the counter?) I was nearly thrown by a synthetic turquoise; the sod had treated it with paraffin, as if it were a natural stone, so I had a bad minute with the microscope. The most valuable instrument is an old pair of polaroid sunglasses, but I shelved that dealer's trick and did it all properly, for show.

All the while I was thinking, a brilliant-cut diamond of six carats isn't much less than half an inch across, if the proportions are about right. Sophie Brandau's zircons had been way above that diameter, from what I could remember. So her real ones must have been worth a king's ransom. Yet what did it matter if she'd decided to wear el cheapo copies? Women often do that for security, leaving their priceless tom in the bank. Sweating less, I handed Jennie the list of the forty gems they'd given me, and waited while the old bloke ticked them off, nodded, packed his stuff and departed with a wheeze.

Orly sat with me, talked animatedly and with open friendliness about last night's party, being witty about the guests, making me relax.

Then I was sent for by Nicko, who told the middle distance, 'He's hired.'

'Hired?' I glanced from Nicko to Jennie, to Orly, to Gina who by now had worked up into a genuinely frank actual smile, and very lovely it was.

'Well, thanks, er Nicko, I've already got a job. I honestly think I'd better stick with it.'

The world iced.

'Is he real?' Nicko asked, passing a hand in front of his forehead.

Jennie wasn't so pale now. She gave a hand flap. Two suited blokes lifted me off my feet and flung me out, along, down into a limo. All the way I was thinking: Hired? Hired for what? I mean, what good was I to a man like Nicko? To Jennie, Orly? To New Jersey, even, now I'd got it pinpointed on the world map?

I had a headache, my freedom, two jobs, and a growing terrible notion that I suddenly knew far too many people in America.

Thank goodness I hadn't told Nicko's lot quite everything about the blue velvet lady. Like an idiot, I actually thought I'd got away with something.

CHAPTER FIVE

That Monday started so odd that I began to wonder what I was doing wrong. Or right. I had a visitor, discovered a familiar face, and got yet another job.

The minute I arrived at Manfredi's I got an envelope. The place was hardly open when in came a Suit. It was the huge truncated man who'd sat beside the limo driver the previous night. He gave me a thick manila, asked for coffee.

'I'm Tye Dee, Lovejoy,' he said without blinking. He sat on a stool like a cartoon elephant, overflowing all round. 'I bring the word. Capeesh?'

'Sure, sure.' The word?

He watched me pour coffee, then left without touching it. Lil was close by and gave a phew.

'Ya got him for a friend, Lovejoy, ya gotta friend.'

Well, hardly a friend. I opened the envelope, found it stocked with money. Hastily I hid it and hoped nobody had seen. Josephus and Jonie were busy, and Della was in Fredo's office signing on a new waitress. Maybe this was my pay for my extra unknowable job. The speed of America was bewildering. Should I tell Fredo? Was there a message in with the gelt? I was scared to look, with Manfredi's starting to fill with breakfast customers. I gave Fredo the envelope to stick in his office safe.

That day, I started taking an interest in the bar's television. We always kept it on. As the hours slid by in a cacophony of talk I kept watch, throwing in the occasional comment about politicians, bankers, showbiz personalities as they showed on screen. I wasn't being nosy, you understand. Just human. Fredo had been blunt: I should say nothing about the special job he'd sent me on. I understood that. Us illegal immigrant workers love anonymity. But there's nothing wrong with learning about a city, is there?

By evening I started activating the customers. I'd got nowhere with the telly.

'Hey, man,' I responded to one enthusiast who'd challenged my supreme ignorance about New York. 'I'm from the West Coast. What do I know?'

He was a regular, a cheery early-nighter from Brooklyn. I got

him onto local politicians, easy with so many news bulletins on the
million TV channels they have.

'See, N'York's a kinda special case,' he told me, well into his
third manhattan. 'This city's the world's business leader. The Federal Government should help, 'stead of trying to tax us out of
existence.'

A lively debate struck up. Everybody seemed to be from somewhere else, but with know-all opinions about running New York.

The elegant lady – she of the Belgian gold handbag – was in
the far corner soon after six, silently reading, but listening.

'Look at the way Washington treats N'York . . .'

'Mmmh,' I went, polishing glasses, serving. 'Sure does.'

Background was my role in life. Get enough money for the fare
homeward. Until then, be silent as wallpaper, your friendly barman.

'Hi, Lovejoy. Remember me?'

'Hi, Rose.' It was a careful greeting. She'd cautioned me yesterday about saying 'Howdy'. I was narked, but she'd said it's cowboy.
'What can I get you?'

'You have to ask, Lovejoy?'

Tunafish salad, sliced eggs, coffee, glass of white wine. And her
usual end stool. I served as Brooklyn's argument heated up. Lil
chipped in. It was all so friendly. Lovely, innocent, and so American.

Still no recognizable faces on the news. Good newscasters, a
hundred times better than ours back home. One up for USA.

Maybe it was preying on my mind, but by now I was almost
certain I'd seen *two* of the faces before. I could only have seen them
on the news. I'm hopeless with names, but I love faces. The trouble
is we disguise ourselves with posh speech, fine clothes. We go about
hoping everybody thinks we went to a better school than we actually
did. Or that we're richer. Anything but truth. Faces are often the
only way in to the real person beneath. I wish I'd remembered that.
It might have saved a life.

Rose spun out her meal for well over two hours. By then
Manfredi's was quiet, the cheerful arguers reduced to sports grum-
blers. She put it to me as I passed her the chit.

'Lovejoy. Moira wants to know if you'll call. Maybe come round
for coffee after work?' She smiled at my hesitation. 'She'll pay the
taxi to your hotel.'

'I'm not good with relatives, love.'

'A paying job, Lovejoy. Antique stuff.'

She was speaking confidentially. Nobody else within earshot.
'Fine.'

She slid off the stool. 'You remember the address?'

'It's the only one I know in New York.' She left a tip, to my embarrassment, but Della barked at me when I demurred.

'We're taxed eight per cent of our salary, Lovejoy. Refuse a tip, you're subsidizing Uncle Sam.'

'Thank you, miss,' I called after Rose. A minute later, the elegant woman in the corner also left. No coincidence, not any more. She was Moira all right. But why the secrecy?

What harm could a third job do? I'd already got two. I joked my way towards closing time. Fredo quietly told me he was pleased I'd done well at Mr Aquilina's, and to leave an hour earlier that night. He looked rough and tired, so I said I'd stay. He insisted. I obeyed.

Nineish on a wet New York evening isn't beautiful. I walked carefully, keeping to the well-lit areas as Rose had told me. I saw some old geezer preaching God is Love and was coming to exterminate us. Two blokes were brawling on the pavement with drunken sluggishness. People in doorways start soliciting an hour after dark, demanding change and offering packets of God-knows-what. Taxis always seem to be heading the opposite way.

Odd, but the dozy old man on the hotel counter gave me a greeting, his first ever. Really unnerved, I climbed up to my grotty pad, and found Jennie there. Now, I always keep the room key whenever I'm in a hotel, so she was a surprise.

She didn't move, just pointed to the chair opposite. No smile. I exhaled, having had some ludicrous notion of asking what the hell but deciding the better of it. Where Nicko's catering manageress was, various goons wouldn't be far behind.

'Zircons, Lovejoy.'

I was beginning to wish I'd never mentioned the bloody things. 'Did I get some wrong, then?' I meant the jewel tests they'd made me do.

'No.' She was eyeing me like I was a curiosity. For women this is nothing new, but I'd thought America would be different. 'Hundred per cent. Even the mounted gems.'

Oh oh. I knew what was coming. There'd been a piece of beautiful amber in a Balkan wooden carved mount. I'd loved it. These votive pieces are religious objects, nothing truly valuable in themselves but exquisite antiques. (Take care. There's a zillion forgeries about, usually copal resin with carved walnut wood, mostly made in Italy.) It had chimed warmly at me. It was authentic all right. At the time, I'd vaguely wondered about the coincidence. Rose's amber, now this.

'One of which you didn't even touch, Lovejoy.'

'Miss one, did I?' I said brightly. 'Well, get the old soak to drop it by and I'll —'

'Sokolowsky says you didn't. A wooden-cased amber pendant. Yet you scored it genuine.'

'He'd nodded off, Jennie,' I lied quickly.

'We video everything at Brookmount.' She stood, walked the one pace and twitched the curtain. It shed dust over her. 'You're some sort of divvy, Sokolowsky tells us.'

Good old Mr Sokolowsky, not as sleepy as he'd seemed. And who was this *us*?

'Guesswork.'

'Could you repeat the test, Lovejoy? On other items of our choosing?'

She spoke with authority greater than that of the usual serf. Jennie was big medicine. In fact, I bet that she and Nicko . . . I tried a disingenuous smile, little boy found out.

I said offhand, 'Sometimes guesses work.'

'Life or death on it, Lovejoy?'

I swallowed. 'Er, look Jennie. I, er . . .'

'Just tell me the truth.' She was simply asking, perhaps even a little sad. 'If you aren't a divvy, that's fine. Nicko wouldn't blame you, for a skill you haven't got. If you are, that's fine too. Just don't lie.'

Her voice had gone hard. I nodded a yes.

'Only for antiques, Jennie.'

That made her think. She started to speak, cut out, reached inner agreement.

'Very well. Be here two o'clock tomorrow. Nicko has an idea.'

'I'm sorry, but I . . .' Her expression changed to a light sleet. I smiled my most ingratiating smile. 'Right, right.'

She paused on her way to the door. 'Good luck, Lovejoy. Mrs Aquilina is very . . . strict with all employees.'

'Meaning what?' I asked, but the door wafted her away into New York, leaving me alone.

Lovely lass, worried sick and living on her nerves. Nicko her lover, yet she warns me about Nicko's wife's fearsome nature. I could do without all those implied threats. But that tip about Mrs Aquilina unsettled me.

I put the telly news on to get the time, and coming back from the washroom with my one towel I caught sight of a face I recognized. It was Brandau, his wife Sophie beside him. That was why I couldn't decide why it was one face or two. I switched off and went out to get a taxi, smiling at the irony. Maybe they'd be in some newspaper tomorrow – if newspapers in America did what newspapers do all the time back home, simply filch their scoops off the nine o'clock news and pretend.

'Sorry I'm late.'

Rose let me in, more flustery than usual. I'd have said edgily excited, had I known her better.

'I'm pleased you came, Lovejoy.' She smiled me into a chair, sat with an intent frown.

'Do you know anything about Sherlock Holmes, Lovejoy? Conan Doyle?'

'Nothing. I remember the Basil Rathbone films, though.'

She winced. I sighed inwardly. Was she one of those truly boring fans who dress up?

'Not quite the same thing as Dr Watson's accounts, Lovejoy.'

She made it a reprimand. I mmmhed to show I thought the same, though quite honestly these nerks who forever delve into fictional characters as if they were real people annoy me. She spoke as if Dr Watson was real, which tipped me the wink that she was one of those loons who'd come to believe the writer's fantasy. It's a danger we all skate near.

'Dr Watson didn't write the stories, love,' I said clearly, to nip delusions in the bud. 'He was fictitious. The real-life physician was Conan Doyle.'

'Lovejoy. My sister has made a lifelong study of the Holmes literature.'

'Good.' I waited. Rose was acting on Moira's instructions.

'I've a proposition, Lovejoy. Your antiques expertise convinces me you are the right person.'

My newest new job loomed. I donned a pleasant you-can't-mean-me smile. 'I doubt it, Rose. You need an antiquarian if you're making a collection of Sherlockiana.'

'Let me tell you a story, Lovejoy.' Rose was hovering, tidying piles of papers, quietly placing books. 'It's the most valuable of all modern manuscripts.'

'Not that old joke about some beautiful?'

It was honestly meant as a quip, but I saw her face set in anger, suddenly suppressed. She knew instantly what I meant. A 'beautiful' in the antiques trade is a long-lost treasure. Captain Kidd's chests of gold, King Solomon's Mines, Chippendale's secret warehouse in Wapping, that ton of priceless pearls hidden under Birmingham, the whole dustbin of burdensome fable which troubles us antique dealers night, day and dawn. I'm not being unromantic. It's just that the public ought to grow up. George Washington's secret treaties with the Emperor of China, King George or Napoleon are so secret they never existed at all. See what I mean? Getting close to myths is dangerous. You start believing.

She calmed, with effort. 'Lovejoy. I expected better from you. It's a matter of simple record that Dr Conan Doyle wrote *The Narrative of John Smith* about the time he married Louise Hawkins. His first novel! The manuscript was lost in the post.'

Well, what's in a name? Though I should talk, with a name like Lovejoy. I tried to remember. Conan Doyle? It's one of those names which slip in and out of consciousness like sparrows through your headlights, gone unremarked. I'd better own up.

'I know nowt about him, love.'

'My father's people came from Southsea. Where Dr Conan Doyle practised. Where, in fact, he wrote it.'

'This being the Sherlock beautiful? The *John Smith* novel?'

'Of course.'

Pity. I decided that the USA was now a terrible disappointment. America should have done better. What about all those ancient land deals with the Red Indians? The lost deeds to whole silver mountains? Columbus's long-lost maps, Captain Henry Morgan's treasure from sacking Panama? If I started starving here I'd have to fake a few Eric the Red mementoes . . .

'Thanks for the offer, Rose. I'd best be getting back. Big working day tomorrow.'

Rose watched me rise. I hesitated, but what claim did she have on me? I mean, okay, Rose had befriended me. And I'd welcomed it. But that didn't mean I had to listen to her barmy ramblings.

'See you,' I said cheerfully.

I was making my way to the door when Rose spoke. 'Moira?'

The elegant woman stepped into the room. I'd assumed the little door led to a closet, toilet, some nook. Careless old Lovejoy.

'My sister, Lovejoy,' she explained apologetically.

'You'll help us, Lovejoy.' Her voice was as melodious as she looked, but with added threat.

'Not me, love.'

'Lovejoy,' Moira said, perching on the desk with such style that like a fool I stopped to gape. 'Late of Hong Kong. Before that, East Anglia.' She even gave the address of my cottage. 'Divvy, wanted by your own police. By antique dealer syndicates. In debt to seventeen antique dealers, two finance houses, three mortgage companies. All that plus six lawsuits, Lovejoy – as soon as I have you deported as an illegal alien.'

Rose was pale as her sister spoke. I dithered, returned, cleared my throat, looked at the time. Nigh midnight, and me being blackmailed into balderdash.

'You've got the wrong bloke, Moira,' I tried for the record.

'Rose?'

'Yes, Moira.' Rose passed me a sheaf of typewritten notes. Taking them, my mind went: My career was documented pretty well, but with that bizarre slant with which libel uses truth. 'We are associated with antiquarians in England, Lovejoy. It took only an evening's phoning. People didn't even have to look you up. They already knew you.'

See how falsehoods spread? I was indignant with the sly bitch, but swallowed my ire. Why was deportation such a threat? Maybe America deports illegals to wherever they want to go! I could try for Australia, if they'd let me. Yes. That was clearly the way. Resist this attempt to blackmail me into helping the loony women. Bluff and double bluff. Be strong, show defiance. The American Way!

'All right,' I said weakly. 'What do I have to do?'

Being in the greatest of all lands is all very well, but antiques are antiques. And money rules. I was fast learning that America knew money. It is very, very dear to the US of A's big beating heart.

In my time as a dealer I've seen all sorts of legend about priceless antiques. Every dealer has. Crazy, daft, loony – but they've generated fortunes, liaisons and affaires that have led to multiple murders, robberies galore. I've seen a million ancient charts to Lost Cities, King Solomon's Mines, Merlin's magic wands, Beethoven's missing symphonies, and extinct species of plants living on under the Cotswold Hills. All pure imagination, maybe nothing more than wishes formed of faded sorrows. But – remember this – *all* confidence tricks have a basis in greed. And cons make money, right?

So I did a little diligent spadework using New York's phones. And after a fortune in coins so minute I kept dropping the damned things, I got through to Thurlough in Buxton, Derbyshire. It felt really strange talking with somebody on the other side of the Atlantic but who sounded within reach. I had to shout over the night traffic.

'Thurly? Lovejoy. I haven't got long.'

'Lovejoy? Do you know what frigging time it is?'

'Sod the time, Thurly. Look. A Sherlock Holmes bookseller . . .?'

'The best?' He took time off to complain to his missus that Lovejoy was ringing at this hour. They sounded in bed. 'That'll be Brian Cheeryble.'

Cheeryble, opposite the British Museum, up those rickety stairs. I got Thurly to find me the number, and when he tried to suss me out told him I had a chance of an earthenware bust of Conan Doyle, probably a modern fake. He rang off still grumbling, old misery. Brian Cheeryble. He'd know about any Conan Doyle grailer, if anyone would. I'd not contact him until I'd learned what I was really contacting him about.

CHAPTER SIX

The commonest question is, how can you stay poor yet recognize antiques a mile off, by vibe? The answer's pretty grim: imagine having responsibilities to every antique you ever met. A divvy has exactly that. It comes with the gift. Like being Dad to all the children on earth, you never know where you are, what to do. Even the Old Woman who Lived in a Shoe only had forty kids. She had it made. She should have been a divvy, and learned the hard way.

Plus this thing called crime. Tell anyone that you're a divvy, and you can see evil thoughts flit through their minds. And they aren't innocent good-heavens-how-interesting thoughts. They're greedy how-can-we-use-this-nerk-for-sordid-gain thoughts. I've seen it a hundred times. And don't pretend you'd be any different. You wouldn't be. Why am I so certain? Because avarice rules, that's why.

Antiques = treasure, yes indeed. But some are more equal than others.

Look at your average newspaper. In one week the Greeks re-excavate a temple to the God Poseidon in Corinth, and Boston University architects date it a sensational 665 BC; the Chinese find their earliest known celestial map – painted on a tomb's vaulted roofing over twenty-one centuries ago; and two new living species of fly are discovered in Wales. I'm thrilled by the first two, because they're antiques. But the flies are a yawn. Don't misunderstand me – I'm all for conservation. Flies have to manage as best they can, and have wings and whatnot to do it with. But antiques can't. They have nothing except soul. And they can only become fewer and shoddier, as we batter and revarnish and 'mend' them whenever we think we'll have a hamfisted go . . . See? Somebody has to be on their side. So far, I've only found me.

Two o'clock I went to my crummy hotel, and found Zole in the lobby trying to lever open something under the desk.

'Hi, ma man. Watch yo back, Lovejoy. Tye's waitin' n' baitin'.'

The greetings alone are enough to wear you out. 'Hello, Zole.' I warned him in the passing that the desk dozer was coming back down the corridor, and saw him ease silently out into the street. A minigangster, that one. What had he said? Watch my back?

Tye Dee was waiting in my room, talking with Magda. He turned from her the instant he saw me, cutting her dead. It seemed odd at the time, but not later. I gave her a wave, got one in return.

Quarter past, we were in a skyscraper's lift rising in grand style. We shared the lift with a suave bloke wearing an antique stock pin in his tie, the cret. Can you imagine? It had the true zigzag stem – I could actually see its shape – projecting slightly from his idiot modern tie. Well, I'm used to these Flash Harrys back home so I just glared a bit when he got out on the eighteenth floor in a waft of expensive aftershave.

On the nineteenth floor Mrs Aquilina was waiting. Not Nicko, not Jennie.

Sumptuous was the only word. I stood in the doorway being searched for concealed ironmongery by Tye while she strolled and blew cigarette smoke towards the vast expanse of windows. She wore a confining black dress, scallop neck, and looked half as young as before.

'Clean,' Tye announced in his gravelly bark, and closed the doors as he left.

'I don't doubt it.' Mrs Aquilina avoided smiling, gestured me to sit opposite, a callous trick to play on someone undergoing enforced celibacy. A log fire seemed genuine. The air hummed coolth. The vast flat was dull as ditchwater, everything modern and expensive and thoroughly objectionable. Tastefully decorated, but who cared?

'Today I'm going shopping, Lovejoy.' She had aloofness, but not her husband's terrifying knack of speaking to distant planets.

'Yes?'

A pause. She didn't drum her fingers, but was impatient. She returned my gaze, squared. 'You're going to buy me some jewellery.'

'Sorry, missus,' I said apologetically. 'I'm not well up in modern stuff. You've got some good tom shops in New York –'

'You proved your worth with gems, Lovejoy.'

'Spotting Mrs Brandau's jewellery was accidental, Mrs Aquilina.'

'Sokolowsky gave you full marks. Yes, Blanche. Martini.' A bonny maid appeared and vanished. I wasn't offered any revelry. 'One hour, Lovejoy. Go and dress. Be in the foyer. Dee will show you.'

Dress? I was already clothed. I rose and like an idiot thanked her. For what?

'One thing, Lovejoy.' She ground out her cigarette. 'I will not tolerate any more insolence. Last warning.'

'Right. Thank you, Mrs Aquilina.' I almost nutted the carpet making an exit bow. Blanche's glance avoided me as I left, but it felt sympathetic.

Exactly an hour later I was in the foyer, standing like a lemon with Tye Dee. I kept wondering how I'd been insolent. I'd done my maximum grovel, agreed with everything she said, not complained when she'd not offered me any victuals. I'd been for a shower, shaved again in case I'd missed a chin patch. I was hungry as hell, not having had time to snatch a bite while hurrying down the New York canyons.

Tye Dee had inspected me doubtfully when I arrived. 'You okay like that?'

'Fine, thank you.'

Kind of him, I thought in my innocence. He looked monolithic, even bigger in daylight. I felt as if I were standing beside a gasworks. I watched people come and go through the foyer.

'Lookin' at people?' he said after a while, suspicious rather than interested.

'Eh? Oh. I try to guess what they do.'

The foyer was marble and brass. A modern desk was set out for the receptionist, flowers and notepads and console, a couple of couches for waiting serfs. Except Tye had told me to stand beside him at the windows. A doorman in comic opera regimentals strode about marshalling taxis and leaping to serve. Mostly ladies, one or two with the tiniest dogs you ever did see. Fantastic. One was no bigger than a mouse, and wore a collar worth me twice.

'Rum world, eh?' I said conversationally.

'Uh?'

'Rum world, Tye.' I nodded to indicate the diminutive hound being passed to a liveried chauffeur. 'Bet that dog's got more servants than —'

He did an odd thing. He spun me round to face him. It took hardly any effort on his part, but I was held in a vice, completely immobile. I'd never seen anybody move so fast. His face lowered and he spoke softly.

'You say nuthin', Lovejoy, less'n you're spoke to. Got that?'

'If you say so, Tye,' I got out, throttled.

'No names. We're not here, see? Gina's our total responsibility.'

He lowered me to the ground and let go. I straightened and recovered my breath. Don't speak. Don't mention names. Protect Mrs Aquilina. Do as you're expected to do, which meant be invisible and anonymous. Take the money and do the job, in whatever order either comes. I sighed inwardly as the lift went and sundry serfs leapt to fawn on Mrs Aquilina as she emerged. Okay America, I thought, you're the boss. I too advanced, smiling the anxious smile of the abject ingrate.

She swept by me without a word, doors parting and kulaks bowing and scraping. I trotted after, a humble ninth in the entourage. Except there was something wrong. And it wasn't that Mrs Aquilina also seemed mad at me. It was that a bloke stepping forward in the morning coat of a hotel manager had a luscious eighteenth-century stock pin, ruby head and zigzag stem, in his lapel. Lovely stone, glamorous design, gold mount all just the same as earlier. I've only seen about six in my life. Now two on the same day, in one building? Were there scores in New York? And he'd grown a moustache – in an hour?

'Excuse me,' I said, plucking Tye's sleeve as our lady stopped and we all collided up against each other.

'Shtum.' It was more than a hiss, not proper speech. I only wanted to explain about the bloke with the tiepin, ask why a stylish gent in sunglasses and suave gear would want to change into serf's uniform. Was he too one of us hirelings, on perpetual guard against New York's unknowable mayhem? If so, it was overdoing things a bit. This Nicko lot seemed to live on its nerves . . . Then I saw Tiepin look at a dark blue motor down the street, surreptitiously raise his hand. Two men. Tye was facing the other way, though he scanned the traffic closely as we left the foyer for the pavement.

Mrs Aquilina got into her limo. I recognized the driver. Tye said, 'Hi, Tony,' so that was all right. I made to follow her into the motor. She rounded on me from the interior.

'Out!' she snapped. I'd never seen anybody so furious. 'You look like a hobo! *Out!*'

Tye hauled me back onto the pavement, saying desperately, 'Wait, Gina –'

'*Andiamo!*'

Tiepin disappeared into the building, moving faster than a major domo should. They stroll, august and serene. This one was . . . escaping? Definitely at a fast trot. Wrong. Our limo containing Mrs Aquilina moved off, I thought a little slower than normal. And Tony's gloved hand reached out of his window and slickly tapped the limo's roof. Why?

The big blue motor down the street started up, rolled after her no more than sixty feet.

Tye was signalling to a taxi – so the strange motor with the two men couldn't be ours. Therefore they were . . .

I barged the commissionaire aside, grabbed his posh metal stand and heaved the damned thing into the road, catching the blue motor. Two other cars swerved. The blue limo tried hard, but dived into a skidding yellow taxi. Tyres squealed, glass fractured and horns parped.

A passing scruff delightedly went, 'Wow-eeee, man!' Drivers began bawling with that immediacy New Yorkers manage so easily. I'd never seen so many gestures. Even pedestrians joined in, exclaiming and gesticulating and thronging about. Tye had vanished. Some friend, I thought bitterly. Just when I wanted him.

The commissionaire had me in some deathlock. It had taken ten seconds. I was alone, the centre of attention. In one minute flat I was arrested. The druggie bent to peer in at me as I was clouted into the police car. 'Wow-eeee!' he cried after us. I wore handcuffs, heavier and more serviceable than ours. The policemen were about two stone overweight, and brutal masters of invective. Genuine police, at last. I'd made it back to normal.

CHAPTER SEVEN

Well, all right America, I still love you. I just have my doubts about your constabulary.

New York's joke is 'You can't beat our cops'. True, true. (They do the beating, get it?) I was black and blue when I came to rest among other miscreants, but nowhere did it show. Clever. My face and hands were untouched, yet I could hardly stand. They slung me into some pit amid sounds like a clanging echo chamber. Nine of us, mostly wearing jeans, tattered denim and truculent sneers. I avoided eye contact, slid down the wall bone tired. I realized that irritating groaning was me. I stopped, hoping to avoid attention.

'What yo fo, bo?' somebody asked me, a treble bass voice.

'Attempted murder,' I said to the single bulb a mile out of reach through a grid that covered our domain. It was hardly a glim, but hurt. I closed my eyes.

'Who'd ya trah?'

'International art dealer.' I'd worked it out. By the time this lot learned the truth, I'd be deported, shipped home for my long-awaited trial elsewhere.

This time I got 'Whafo?' and 'How?' I was among sociologists. A doze was called for, out of all this. If they'd let me. Gaols and violence are synergistic, not mutual exclusives.

Somebody was picking my pocket. Talk about inexpert. Where I come from he'd starve. I roused to answer when somebody shook me, asking.

'Eh? Oh. I'd done him a load of antiques. He didn't ...' Americanisms might save me from being butchered as an Olde Worlde guest on these shores. '... he didn't make wit de bread, man. I threw a hotel stand at his motor, uh, automobile.'

As improvision it wasn't bad.

'Shoulda trahd yo gun, man,' the resonant voice said. I'd never heard such a bass, quiet as that.

'Boss says no guns. He'll be ...' What was Americese for infuriated? '... real sore at me for this.'

A desultory talk began while I tried to rest. They discussed ways of inflicting death and/or destruction without guns. They thought my effort with the stand feeble.

The clamour from the clink intensified. Like living in a foundry. A couple of people came and went, subjected to the same interrogation I'd undergone. My few dollars went from my back pocket. I dozed fitfully, was hauled out for interrogation twice – reason for blamming a vehicle, causing mayhem in Manhattan – was thumped back to the cell. We'd shrunk to eight, one clearly stoned out of his mind on spiritual substances. He was clobbered to the floor by the treble bass voice. I did my weary slide, now blacker and bluer.

'Hey, man. Bettune?'

'Eh?'

The bloke who'd slammed the druggie was crouching by me. He was a giant, even bigger than Josephus.

'Yo dealer man. Bettune? East 74th?'

What the hell was he on about? I squinted up at him. 'Boss says no names, man.'

'Rahd own.' Right on. The great head nodded slowly, big as a bison's and biblical with it. He waited a moment, staring at me with vast bloodshot eyes, then snapped his fingers and without having to look caught a clutch of dollars somebody instantly passed him. 'Yo cash, man.'

'Thank you.'

I remember very little else for seven or eight hours after that. Somebody playing a mouth organ, everybody having awkward pees with everybody else grumbling, the druggie waking to the shakes in a screaming fit, that persistent clanging, occasional shouts, vehicles wahwahing outside.

They called me about six in the morning. Except it was the brightest-suited lawyer I'd ever seen, all smiles and brilliant teeth. A holiday camp of a lawyer if ever I'd seen one. He knew everybody, slapped backs, had a million jokes, a cheroot, expensive tan, and a briefcase chained to his wrist. It held one sheet of paper which he produced with a magician's flourish. I never did learn what was on it, but it sprang me.

'See yaz, Lovejowa,' boomed the bass after me.

'Oh, yes. Bye. And thanks, er . . .' How did he know me?

'Busman. West 42nd station, yo in town.' The bass varoomed a laugh octaves down.

'Cheers, Busman.'

'Name of Gordino,' the lawyer told me, shaking my hand. I blinked at the light while he signed at a desk. I'd never seen so many police in such a hurry. Like a commuter rush, barging past and yelling things like 'Yo!' They had more hardware on their belts than most tinkers' carts. 'This way, Lovejoy.'

'Er, thank you, Mr Gordino. It's most kind of you to –'

'That's all, Lovejoy.' He muttered the instruction from the side of his mouth, impressing me. I knew I'd be trying to do it in front of the mirror as soon as I made it back to the hotel.

As we left the cop shop he made a regal progress, acknowledging everybody, any rank and role. 'Hey, Al! How ya goin'?' and 'Tom? Okay Thursday, get beaten by a slicker handicap?' Our departure was a crazy crosstalk act, him the cheerleader, pally police an amiable gauntlet.

We made the car park and he changed into a bitter unsmiling man.

'You bastard,' he said, lips tight, sinking into a saloon. Tye Dee was sitting beside the driver. It was Tony the roof-tapper. He said nothing, so neither did I. Gordino cursed me. 'You double mother of a bastard. Never try that on me again, ya hear?'

'Right, sir,' I said anxiously.

'Why the frigging fuck you not lay out the wire?' he said through his slit. If he loved the police, he hated me for not laying out his wire. I nodded blankly. 'It took me nine – repeat nine – long hours to find you.'

'I'm sorry. I promise.' But promise what? So far, nobody in America had understood me. And I was lagging in the comprehension stakes by a mile.

Gordino mopped his face with a crimson handkerchief. He was trembling, here in broad daylight. I looked out, trying to see where we were going, but Tye's eyes caught me in the rear mirror and I sank down so as not to see.

'Double bastard,' the lawyer muttered a couple of times.

We drove out of Manhattan, some tunnel to somewhere. Wherever it was was sure to be beautiful, leafy, affluent, and baffling as the rest of America. I started scratching, having caught lice from the gaol. I wondered about Busman, Bettune, 74th Street, having my money returned by robbers for nothing. And, of course, why I was a swine to Gordino on account of some wire. And why Tye Dee looked scared for his skin. I was scared for mine, of course, but that was normal.

It was about eight o'clock, the morning rush hour. I drew breath to suggest that I'd best be making tracks for Fredo's bar, but stayed silent.

It was more than a yacht. It was a cruiser, white as a goose. Twin masts and striped awnings. They didn't have vessels like this in the Blackwater at home. This was a cocktails-and-caviare boat, not a coastal slogger ready for gales such as I was used to. It was the only vessel at the small pier.

The crew weren't uniformed so much as standardized, which was much less reassuring. Only half a dozen of them, but fit and wary. One just stood there in the stern, scanning the distant wooded riverbank and talking quietly into his chest whenever another boat glided by.

I went up the gangplank after Gordino. He was into his windmill mode, the big hello and cheroot, pretending to throw up over the side when the boat rocked slightly in a wash.

'Follow on,' Tye Dee said. He was uncomfortably close behind me.

It was a lovely morning, the sun already up and a few boats plying the water. Cars winked windscreens on tiny roads parallel to shore. A few gulls planed over. Several other yachts were moored further downriver. It felt good to be alive. God, but yes it did. I warmed again to America, not solely because there was Gina Aquilina in a white towelling dressing gown observing our arrival from under an awning on the top deck.

Nicko cooled my pleasure at this nautical scene. His stare was somewhere to the northwest, his voice sibilant. Jennie wasn't there. Orly was, seething at me as usual.

'Lovejoy's done well,' Nicko said. 'He gets bonused.'

Bonus a verb too? I grinned, but my face wouldn't play, stood there like a lemon.

'Tye, man.' Nicko heaved a moderate sigh. 'About you.'

'Let Lovejoy tell it, Nicko,' Mrs Aquilina begged. Funny sort of begging, though. Quiet, yet the words piercing everybody's reluctance. I spoke up, worried about the outcome but avoiding scratching at the lice. Fleas get poems written in their honour. Lice are just misery.

'Why didn't you warn Tye, Lovejoy?' she asked.

'About the men in the motor? I . . . I didn't know if I was wrong.' I'd explained about the tiepin man, his sudden moustache and quick change, his running exit, the signal to the two men. Except I'd tried, and Tye had almost flattened me. I left that bit out.

'Why didn't you warn Gina?' Nicko asked.

This one was more difficult. A simple lie to save Tye's bacon was fair, but dare I try the same for Mrs Aquilina? The space between husbands and wives is a minefield.

'I . . . I was too slow getting into the motor car, Nicko.'

'He looked like a hobo, Nicko,' his wife said.

'I'd no other clothes, you stupid cow!' I yelled, narked. Then swallowed myself into docility again. 'Sorry, missus.'

'Good.' Nicko nodded to the distant shore. 'I like that. He lies good.' He thought, glanced at the shore where Tony waited by the limo having a smoke. He wasn't relaxed, kept looking up at the yacht. 'Berto?'

Gordino said, 'Lovejoy told nothing down the precinct. But he shoulda got on the wire, saved me a ton a trouble.'

'That's okay,' Nicko forgave. 'I like that. He told nothing.' He stared at Orly. 'He's filthy. Clean him up, bring him for *prima collazione.*'

Breakfast! Grub on the way! And bonused! I was in some sort of favour, an experience so rare I'd been slow to realize it.

'Who's the broad?' he asked the river.

'Rose Hawkins, Nicko,' Tye replied for me. 'Bookseller. She's hot for Lovejoy. Has some book job for him is all.'

'Excuse me, er, Nicko.' I ducked slightly as his head rotated. It turned like a gun's swivel mount in a turret, stopped short of my face, thank God.

Silence, except for seagull sounds by the galley portholes.

'Er, can I ask Mr Gordino to do something? I'd pay – well, owe him, if it's okay by you.' Mrs Aquilina had a sudden alert interest, a stoat about to start its rabbit-transfixing dance. 'There's a bloke – guy – in the police station. Can you try to help him? Busman. He was kindly.'

Nicko thought, said okay. Gordino asked, 'Chico? Spic? Nigruh? Wasp?'

'I don't know his surname. He's just called Busman.'

Mrs Aquilina stifled a giggle. Nicko's gaze reached me this time, like a puzzled Last Judgement. He decided I was thick. 'Orly. See about Tony.'

Orly nodded, left us for a moment. We all waited. The rest seemed content. I kept clearing my throat, shuffling, whistled a bit until I realized it made me feel more ridiculous.

Two crewmen went down to Tony. He stood on his fag end, almost came to attention as they approached.

'Nicko,' he called, in his voice an ugly quavering. 'Can I speak wit you?'

Nobody moved or answered.

'Er, I think Tony's calling, Nicko . . .' I petered out.

The crewmen shoved Tony inside the motor. One sat behind him as the other drove the car up the slope and away. Sacked? Perhaps for lacking vigilance? On the boat life instantly resumed.

'Right,' Nicko said. 'Let's go.'

'To help Busman? There's no need for us all,' I thanked him. 'Just Mr Gordino, if he could . . .'

Nicko departed, shaking his head. The lawyer sprinted ashore after darting me a malevolent glance. The crew sprang into action. Orly left at a peremptory signal from Gina. There are some people who, whatever they do, look as if they're always sweeping up after the boss. Orly was one. Mind you, Gina would be lovely to associate with in any circumstances – or so I thought, then.

'Don't go, Lovejoy.'

'Yes, Mrs Aquilina?'

Tye Dee beckoned a crewman, who eyed my measures doubtfully. They had gone below through heavily varnished doors.

Gina was so desirable my throat had practically closed. I stood, mesmerized and in difficulties.

'I'm grateful. You saved my life. You know you could have gotten yourself shot?'

'Well.' I struggled with my airway.

She gazed out at the river. Sunlight consorts with a woman, doesn't it? I looked. She turned to gaze at me.

'There's only one thing makes a man take a stupid risk like that, Lovejoy. I just want you to know I understand. But it's out of the question. However, you deserve some sort of reward. You can have your pick of the staff. As long as you are discreet about it, and the girl goes along.'

I pondered. What the hell was she saying? That I was lovelorn? That I'd acted from adoration, or what? I got breath and was about to explain that she'd got it wrong. I mean, don't misunderstand me. She was blindingly beautiful, and knew it. And I'd have given anything just to, well. But when a living creature's in mortal danger, I mean any bloke in his right mind would do the same thing without weighing the pros and cons, right? I've rushed across motorway traffic to save a bewildered hedgehog before now. It's what people do. Instinct or something.

'Well, Gina . . .' Then I thought. My one brain cell shrieked to beware.

It's this business of women and love. It lies at the root of all of life. Everybody loves a lover, true. But does every woman love a lover equally? Not on your life she doesn't. Oh, they adore Abelard,

crazy for Héloïse. They revere Romeo's lust for Juliet, John What-
sisname for Lorna Doone. And here was the lady who had everything
– power, wealth, beauty, youth – saying openly that she approved
of me, your one-off destitute scruff, solely because she believed that
I'd fallen for her. Of course, she was right. But it was true for her
maid Blanche, for Rose Hawkins, her imperious sister Moira. For
Della, Lil at Fredo's bar, for . . . No. The great mistake loomed. Hell
hath no fury as a woman substituted.

'No, thank you.'

'What?' She leant on the ship's rail, taking stock.

'No, thank you.' I tried to look abashed, embarrassed, brave but
melancholic. A bidden blush never comes, does it? It's only when I
try to seem supercool that I go red. 'I know you're out of my reach,
Gina. I'll not settle for less.'

'Of all the . . .' Her anger faded. She turned away. 'Get below
and clean up. You look like a derelict.'

I went inside to find Tye, more cheerful than I'd been. I'd risen
in Gina's esteem. And my determination to stay pure needn't last
more than a few minutes. There were several maids laying for a
party on the upper deck arena. As long as Gina didn't find out.
She'd not want me to lower my standards.

The engines started and nautical sequences began. We were
going on voyage.

'Chico, Spic, Nigruh, mean colour, Lovejoy.' Tye Dee was swilling
a whisky while I showered. (Dear USA: need your showers be so
forceful they slam you against the tiles?)

Colour? How could Busman's colour help? There couldn't be
more than one with that nickname. I soaped industriously with a
loofah. Lice are simple to shed. Damage the fragile little things and
they've had it.

'Another thing, Lovejoy. Orly and Mrs Aquilina are . . . friends.
So's Jennie and Nicko. Okay?'

That halted my scrubbing for a second. I resumed, slower.
'Thanks, Tye.'

'And ya get took, ya phone Gordino. Okay?'

God, but whisky stinks foul in the early morning. Its aroma
almost made me gag. I'd bagged my clothes in plastic, and tied the
neck. A crewman's gear was laid out on the bunk. My second job,
at last? Dressed, I went and lost my way a dozen times.

Breakfast was gigantic even by American standards. Gina finally
came, had an ounce of orange juice and three grapes. Orly had a

couple of pancakes. Nicko had a croissant and coffee. I had hash browns – thick fried mash – and everything within reach. Three times I narrowly escaped having syrup poured over it all.

During the gargantuan nosh I tried asking where we were going. The Hudson? No, for we were amid several islands. The Statue of Liberty, and us turning away northwards, bridges ahead and a crowded mass of habitations to the right.

Gina was being amused. 'How marvellous to see you eat, Lovejoy! The galley will be delighted.'

Well, there was no telling where my next meal would come from. And you can't muck hunger about, or any other appetite for that matter.

'I'm worried about Mr Manfredi, er, Gina. He'll be in the middle of his morning rush.'

'That's taken care of, Lovejoy.' Then, just as I was settling down to the new batch of grub, 'You seemed to take a particular interest in Sophie, Lovejoy. Why?' I rescued myself from a choke. 'Sophie Brandau, Lovejoy. The lady in blue velvet.'

'I saw her bloke on television. I looked their name up.'

There's not a problem in human affairs that crime can't solve. So crime had to be my explanation.

'He's a politician, Gina. I was scared, because I'm in political trouble.'

She was enjoying my discomfiture, chin on her linked hands, very fetching 1920s while Orly glowered. Nicko and Tye were listening.

'I'm not American,' I confessed. 'I'm from East Anglia. Illegal immigrant, trying to work my way home. I'm wanted by the police there.'

'We know, Lovejoy. You're not exactly our streetwise New York spoiler.'

Sandpaper grated nearby. We all looked. It was Nicko, laughing, shaking up and down in his deck chair.

'Lovejoy. You think you'll put the bite on Denzie Brandau?'

Nicko fell about. It really narked me. I'd been so American I'd convinced myself completely. Gina was nodding.

'Through Sophie, perhaps,' she murmured. 'Except generosity's never been her strong point.'

She and Nicko exchanged glances. Tye Dee was with me still, noshing but keeping out of it. Orly put his oar in.

'Lovejoy'll be able to try his hand at exploitation – when the Brandaus come aboard this afternoon.'

We were turning towards the east, leaving Manhattan behind. I felt entitled to ask, myself again.

'Is this still New York?'

'Both sides. We're headed for Long Island Sound.' Gina extended a hand. Orly leapt to take it, haul her up.

Nicko showed no emotion as Gina and Orly paired away. He was reading from a folder. I avoided asking the obvious. Their business.

'Excuse me, Nicko. What am I here for, exactly?'

He didn't look up. 'To help decide fraud, Lovejoy. And play a game.'

It didn't sound my thing. I lowered my knife and fork.

'I'm sorry, Nicko, but I want out . . .'

Tye suddenly shoved a plate of scrambled eggs and waffles across the table, warning. Nicko hadn't interrupted his reading.

'Great, great,' I said quickly. 'Look forward to it, Nicko. Fraud's my thing.' Thereby being responsible for the deaths of two people. One was a foe, one a sort of friend. And one was nearly me.

For an hour I stood on the after deck watching New York glide by. Tye described where we were. The names were oddly familiar, the places resonant of some primeval dream time: Queens, the Bronx, Yonkers, New Rochelle, Brooklyn. The old jeweller Mr Sokolowsky astonished by coming out to stand and reminisce. He was amusing, got me laughing about local quirks in buying silver, pricing jewels, a goldsmith's slender finances ha ha ha. A witty old bloke with shrugged-off humour. Orly passed by once, to say I was to 'get something decent on by the time we hit the Sound'.

'Long Island Sound,' Tye translated. 'That's where it happens.'

'Oy vey,' Mr Sokolowsky lamented, shrugging. 'Happenings should wait a liddle now and then.'

Gina sent her Blanche with a message that she wanted me. It was to do with clothes. She'd had the vessel combed for clobber. It was highly fashionable, which I am not. I settled for some loose grey trousers and a white shirt. She pulled a face when finally I showed myself. I grimaced back, grinning to set her laughing. It was the last laugh for some time.

I wanted to know what happened to Tony, if Berto Gordino had managed to spring Busman, what Della and Lil were telling Rose when she came by Fredo's and asked where I'd got to. But by then the boat was thrusting through some narrows into Long Island Sound, breath-taking in its expanse and shores, and my duties began.

CHAPTER EIGHT

They started coming aboard about mid-afternoon. I watched them from the rail, a mere bystander like the crew.

Glamour isn't simply something in the eye of the beholder. It's a kind of heat, emanating from the glamorous. But it's cold, heat that doesn't warm. Which I suppose is one way of saying it's radiation, the stuff that eventually kills. This thought struck me when I recognized a familiar elegant lady ascending our gangway from a small power boat. Good old Moira Hawkins was accompanied by Sophie Brandau and her politician husband. My head didn't quite spin off, but my breathing went funny. Was I the link? I hated this notion, because chains have a tough time. A score or more arrived, laughing and full of that strange chilled charm only the rich exude.

Long Island is, well, sort of a long island, if you follow. Everything tends to astonish me, so America had it made. But why should I be dumbfounded by the Atlantic's proximity? And by Long Island's enormity, its beauty? Glamour is America's par, wealth an incidental. Everything's so vast that your eyes run out of vision. Tye Dee was supervising the welcomes – which probably meant seeing they all arrived unarmed – so I'd nobody to ask. Old Sokolowsky had vanished. How strange that he was along, on a fantastic cruise like this. Mind you, the same went for me. Except the old jeweller and me were two of a kind; different bookends, same purpose. Sokolowsky was the experienced gelt merchant, techniques to his fingertips. I was the . . . the what? Neither Gina nor Nicko had mentioned antiques, which is basically what I'm for. Sole purpose in life. Tye Dee was simply a trusted bouncer, with his thick holster bulging his chest lopsidedly. Orly was Mrs Aquilina's 'friend' again today.

It was a pleasantly open day, light breeze, rich thick American sunshine. Innocent, fresh.

The little boats shuttled between the shore and us. A small township, its streets open and the traffic casually undeterred by the growing aggregate of Rolls-Royces and lengthy American cars I couldn't name. How pleasant to live in such a place, I was thinking, when I saw Jennie alighting from a limo with a fat man. They made quite a pair, him flashy and corpulent and Nicko's lassie slender and pert. Wasn't I thinking a lot about gelt? Something in the climate.

Fatty and Jennie were the last, the occasion for much jibing from the party on the after deck.

'Hey, Jim!' one voice yelled through the growing music. 'Antiques doin' okay, keeping you late.'

'Don't hold your breath, Denzie!' the fat man bawled as his boat slowed. 'You politicians ride on my back, man!'

Desperate needling, it seemed to me, but it earned a roar of laughter. You can say anything in America, as long as you grin. Orly's shoulder tap made me turn. I wished he'd stop doing that. Worse, he prodded my chest.

'Lovejoy, go help Bill in the bar. You know how?'

'Yes.'

'Tell Tye to close the rail. Mr Bethune's always last.'

Antiques, Jim Bethune. Busman had asked about some art dealer, Bettune . . . Orly shoved me so I almost stumbled.

'Move ass, Lovejoy.'

'I'm hurrying, I'm hurrying.'

Correction: *almost* everybody in USA is charming. If Orly prodded me once more I'd break his digit, in a charming sort of way of course. I sprinted to obey, fuming but silent.

The pace of the Aquilinas' party was sedate, compared to Fredo's in full spate. It was noisier, and the grub went almost untouched. I was astonished at the transformations the guests had undergone. They'd changed, instant butterflies, even Jennie emerging gorgeous from the cabins.

Bill the barman was twice as fast as I'd ever be. He was tall, lean, tanned, wavy-haired, the sort I always think must be every woman's heart-throb, straight off a surfboard. Blokes like him evoke archaic slang.

'Handle the ladies when two come together, Lovejoy,' he ordered. He didn't tap or prod. I warmed to him.

The women? I went red. Barmen the world over hate women customers. Men are more decided, can be served fast. Women take their time, change minds, negotiate. That's why sluggardly barkeeps get the slowest jobs. And me a veteran of Fredo's famed happy hour! I swallowed the insult.

In spite of being narked I slotted in, doing my stuff, trying to remember to maintain that wide American smile. The crowd swelled to thirty, as guests already on board before the influx made their colourful entrances amid hullabaloo. Quite frankly, I admire people who put on a show of style. I mean, it's something I could never do in a million years. The women were bonny, slim, slick. I'd never seen what I call evening dresses worn during the afternoon before. Jewellery gleamed genuine gleams and antique settings bonged into my chest, but I kept my mind on my job, trying to please. It was a pretty scene. I avoided Mrs Brandau's eye, didn't look at Jennie, tried my damnedest not to lust too obviously after Gina when she queened into the deck arena amid a storm of applause. The men were not my concern.

Denzie Brandau was smooth, suave, your friendly politician. He was perfectly attired, cuffs mathematical and suit impeccable, his manner subtly saying that he was slumming but was too polite to say so. Power anywhere is a threat, very like glamour.

'Hey, Bill,' I said in sudden thought as the bar slackened. Other serfs started circulating with trays of food to encourage the starving. 'Am I replacing Tony?'

'Sure are, Lovejoy.' He was shaking a cocktail. I watched enviously.

'I can't drive.' A lie at home, but true in America.

'Drivers we got. Only here in the bar.'

'That Tony owes me ten dollars,' I invented.

Bill dazzled the ocean with a brilliant grin. 'Then you are strictly minus ten, Lovejoy. Like for evuh.'

We chuckled, me shaking my head at the vagaries of fortune. I tapped my foot along with the music, smiling with the peasant's pride as Fatty Bethune staved off his anorexia by wolfing all the grub within reach. Oh, I was so merry. And my soul cold as charity. Tony was extinct. My fault? I leapt to serve as Sophie Brandau and Gina drifted to the bar asking for bloody marys. But a lone neurone shrieked outrage. What the frigging hell did it matter whose fault it was? I get narked with myself. I don't run the frigging universe. I only live here.

'Lovejoy tends to ignore the ice,' Gina said mischievously. 'Something in his background, I suspect.'

'Is he new?' Mrs Brandau was distantly bored by serfs.

'Practically.' The hostess took her drink. 'On probation, you might say.'

'I aim to please, madam.' Grovelling's pathetic, but my job.

The ladies drifted. I turned. Bill was watching me. He wore his professional smile, and spoke softly.

'Lovejoy. Don't look murder. It shows.'

'Ta, Bill. It's er, all that grub.'

'Hungry? We get ours during the Game.'

•

'Will it be long?' I noticed Blanche undulating past, mingling merrily with a tray of edibles. I love seafood, as long as the poor creature's unrecognizable. I mean, shrimps that need beheading and lobsters looking like they've just clawed over the gunwale make me run a mile. To eat, something has to die even if it's only a plate of chips.

'An hour or two.'

God, would I survive? I served Mr Brandau while he talked with the dark Simon Bolivar lookalike who'd exchanged secret glances with Sophie at Nicko's. They talked of percentages, cut-ins and shut-outs. Was this the yacht's secret, a clandestine investment company? Or was there simply no secret, except a bit of body-rodding? La dolce vita was hardly tomorrow's news.

'Who's needs cut-ins, Charlie?' Brandau was saying. 'I can be bored in the Senate!'

The swarthy Charlie laughed, joked his way out of some dilemma. Sophie Brandau's face tightened and she floated over, lovely as a dream.

'Mr Sarpi shouldn't think that politics bores you, Denzie. Think of the effect on the electorate!'

I caught Bill's glance warning me not to listen. I whistled, being busy.

'Hell, Sophie,' her husband joshed. 'I'm gonna *buy* the electorate!'

Moira Hawkins was being introduced to Jim Bethune. The podgy man would have fondled, except Jennie did a neat interception. I noticed Gina Aquilina watching me. I raised my eyebrows in mute appeal, and asked Bill if I could cadge some of the buffet food on account.

'No, Lovejoy.' He had a marvellous delivery, not a decibel misdirected. He should have been a spy.

'Okay, okay.' I carried on serving, smiling, giving out pleasantries.

Charlie Sarpi and Denzie Brandau drifted away, mingling with Nicko's group. Sophie Brandau hesitated by the bar, then did a simulated start of surprise to notice a restless young blonde who was definitely on the toxic twitch. She had the look of a luscious plumpster who'd slid the snake to become skeletal in a matter of months.

'Why, Kelly Palumba! I didn't even see –!'

'Hey, Sophie –!'

The party was so glad the jittery lass and Sophie were glad that even I felt glad, and served Miss Palumba her brandy sour with a beaming heart. Gladness is contagious, I find, even where something murderous is beginning to scratch your spine.

'Beg your pardon, miss.' I was baffled. The blonde had leant close and asked for something. 'Bill?'

He was cool. 'Sorry, Miss Palumba. We're right out.'

'Sheet,' she said distinctly, swigging her drink and replacing the glass with a commanding tap. I poured. And encore. And twice more, to the brim.

She had said 'to lift my drink'. Lift where? To her lips? Or was it Americese for strengthen? But with what? It was already as potent as distillers could make it. I shrugged as Sophie Brandau edged the girl away into the socialite press with the 'How's the family, Kelly . . . ?' kind of prattle. I tried not to look at the blonde, but when you see somebody screaming so silently it's difficult.

Tap on my shoulder. I turned. Prod. 'Hi, Orly.'

'Mrs Aquilina wants you, Lovejoy. Main cabin.'

I heard Bill's warning, nodded, wiped my hands and went.

They were setting out a long table. I would have called it lovely but for its newness. Gina was supervising flowers and suchlike. Blanche was scurrying, two other serfs placing chairs. Somebody was changing a picture, a Philip Steer painted in a milliard divisionistic dots, two girls running on a waterside pier. I smiled, then frowned to show Orly and Mrs Aquilina I was all attention.

'Blanche. A tray of hors d'oeuvres in the anteroom. This way, Lovejoy.'

An archway led through half-drawn curtains to a slender cabin, more of an alcove. She reclined on a chaise longue and gestured me to sit opposite.

'That's all, Orly. Go check the arena.'

He gave me a lethal glance and left me to be dissected by this smiling lady. She said nothing. My feet shuffled as usual under this treatment. I found myself reddening slowly. I cleared my throat, tried to look offhandedly through to see how the other kulaks were managing. Surely not laying for another nosh? But the table was bare, almost. Just small boxes of playing cards. And a couple of computer screens coming to life with that irritating come-hither bleep they make. Like a boardroom. Who cared?

'Thank you, Blanche.'

A silver tray of food. My mouth watered. Blanche returned to her task. I dragged my eyes from her receding form, tried not to ogle the grub, failed on both counts.

'I'm not usually taken in, Lovejoy,' Mrs Aquilina said.

Now what? I was suddenly so homesick. In a new country I find I return home a lot more than I arrive, if you follow.

'I'm sure you're not, missus.'

'Gina, please. Do have something . . .'

I fell on the tiny things. There's not much in one, so I had to take a few at a time. You get famished in sea air. 'Sorry, er, Gina. But it's been hours since breakfast.'

'Of course it has,' she said. She was carefully not laughing, the way they do, but really rolling in the aisles.

'Want some?' I can be charming, too.

She tasted one small biscuit with a fractionated sardine balanced on its rim. It really beats me how women survive half the time. Some biochemistry we haven't got, I suppose. I didn't like that 'taken in' bit, but it's a wise prophet who knows where his next meal will come from.

'Lovejoy. You seem to be troubled. All eyes and ears.' She smiled. 'Then I saw where your attentions really lay.' She indicated the shrinking victuals and shot an appraising look to the preparations in the long cabin.

'Look, Gina. I can't help being hungry. I can't stop women from walking past, either.'

'Of course not.' She gave a sign and Blanche's mob withdrew. 'Tell me about Bill, Lovejoy.'

'Bill?' She was full of surprises, this one. Did she fancy him, or what? 'Nice bloke, good barman. But something's wrong.'

She stilled with a woman's scary tranquillity. 'Explain.'

'Well, I think he's a thick. I tried asking him about antiques. He wasn't interested. Hadn't even heard of your 1760 Goddard-Townsend cabinet makers from Rhode Island – when a single one of their mahogany secretary desks goes for zillions.' She stared back at me. Obviously she was thick too. Annoyed, I gave it her in detail. 'Furniture that exquisite'll never come again, never on this planet. It's all made of mahogany we call *grand*, natural unforced trees, not this spongiform crap – sorry, love – which they force grow nowadays.'

She was still blank. I found myself up, walking about. 'For Christ's sake, love,' I cried, exasperated. 'Can't you see? That's why the values increase faster than the National Debt! It's like a Gainsborough, irreplaceable.'

'You're telling me Bill's odd because he isn't interested in antiques?'

Give me strength. I'd thought all Yanks were fascinated by antiques, but here I was having a hard time telling them about the treasures on their own doorstep.

'Look, love. You know that Manhattan building somebody sold for, what was it, zillions? On the news two days agone. Remember it? Well, the secretary desk I mentioned could buy two such buildings, and leave change. You follow?' She nodded slowly. God, she was beautiful, yet gorgeous women drive me at least as mad as the lesser lights.

'I see.'

'And a *small* Philadelphia pier table –' I held my hand less than a yard above her carpet '– could buy the very next hotel.' I was yelling down at the numbskull. 'You can't criticize Bill for not being interested when you're stupid as him –'

'Sit down, Lovejoy.'

Her tone chilled me. I sat, suddenly less narked. Her brain was clicking, her gaze distant and venomous. I wished I was back at the bar. We sat for a full minute. She stirred.

'Lovejoy. Sophie Brandau. Her jewellery today.'

'Looked genuine, Gina.' Safe ground?

'Was everybody's?'

'What do you think I am?' I said indignantly. 'I was behind the bar. All the tom – er, jewellery – I saw was genuine, far as I could tell. I liked that eighteenth-century Milanese brooch Miss Palumba was wearing, though some nerk had tried to restore it with platinum.' Silence. 'You see –'

'Lovejoy.' She meant shut up. Then why had the stupid cow asked me to speak? I tried not to sulk while she did more of her long-range venom. When she spoke it was muted, sibilant.

'Make up to Sophie, Lovejoy.'

We'd not had a row. 'Beg pardon?'

The curtain glided open, some electronic trick. Nicko was sitting alone at the long board table, reading his endless printouts.

'Become special to her.'

I checked my hearing against memory, decided I wasn't hallucinating. 'Er, exactly what is it you're –'

'*Do it!*' she spat. I shot to my feet, edged away.

'Do you mean . . .?'

'Into Sophie Brandau. And report her pillow talk.'

'Look, Gina.' I retreated, babbling. 'That's something I can't –'

'Nicko?'

Her husband spoke, still flicking along those lists. 'You opened a packet of money, Lovejoy?'

'From Tye Dee?' Maybe they wanted it back.

'Your prints are on it. The money's traceable. It was stolen from a Pittsburgh bank. A guard was killed. The bullet matches the gun in your hotel room.'

My voice went faint. 'Pittsburgh?' I've only just arrived in the US. It's marked on my passport . . .'

'Illegal migrant worker? Criminal history? Now a lethal bank robber?' Nicko brought out my passport. 'No record of any date stamp in this, Lovejoy.'

I'd seen the Immigration man stamp it at the airport. I sat. Gina was suddenly impatient.

'You've your orders, Lovejoy. And keep me informed of the Hawkins project.'

The what? Why didn't she just ask Moira Hawkins? She was only yards away, swanning around the deck arena with Fat Jim Bethune. And why did this megabuck outfit worry about a cheap dream in a cheap bookshop?

'It's just some loony scheme about a missing manuscript.'

'Realistic? A practical proposition?'

'Well . . .' I felt it was time to splash over the side, somehow jump ship and make a run for it. Less than a few hours ago my only worry was being late at Fredo's diner. 'Her sister's the grailer. That's a nickname for crets who waste their lives chasing a rainbow. The Holy Grail, see? The Hawkins daftness is only a Sherlock Holmes novel. It went missing in the Victorian postal system. Every nation has its loonies,' I said apologetically, in case Gina or Nicko took umbrage. 'We have folk who're chasing two of the Virgin Mary's milk teeth, supposedly in a pot in Syria. Fakes are life's real trouble.'

Gina said softly, 'That's so, so right. Go now.'

I decided to play along as ordered but to cut out first chance I got. So whatever I promised now would be superfluous, since I wouldn't be here to be checked on. I'd smile my very best at Sophie Brandau, tell Gina the gossip, then exit pursued by bear.

'How often do I report?'

'Nightly,' she said, making my mouth gape by adding, 'You come to my cabin.'

And Nicko sitting there, deep in his numbers, while his wife tells a stranger to come tiptoeing into her boudoir in the candle hours? 'Er, wouldn't it be best if I —?'

'*Out!*'

I crept away like a night-stealer. Just in time to get pinned against the nearest bulkhead by Orly. He was ten times tougher than he looked.

'Lovejoy. You keep away, capeesh? Gina's not switching, hear? Not to you, not anyone.'

'Okay, okay!'

It was Tye who prised Orly off. I recovered my wind while Tye shook his head and lowered Orly to the deck. He'd lifted him one-handed with barely a grunt of effort. At least I'd one ally. That's what I thought then.

'Leave Lovejoy, Orly,' Tye said. 'He's taking orders, same as the rest of us. You want changes, you ask Jennie, okay?'

Ask Jennie? Not Nicko, Gina? I watched Orly hate me out of sight, and followed Tye towards the sound of the music and glam shambles. I'd be sorry to land Tye in it when I ran for it and shook the dust of New York off my shoes.

Tye paused at the foot of the gangway. 'A tip, Lovejoy. This is big. Nobody gets outa here less'n he's allowed. 'Kay?'

'I'll ask first, Tye. That's a promise.'

He gave me the bent eye for a moment.

'I can't tell if'n you're stoopid or clever. Know that?' He sighed and started to climb to the upper deck. 'Trouble is, it's the same thing.'

With ignorance born of idiocy, I ignored that warning too.

As I rejoined Bill behind the bar the tannoy was announcing that the opening game would commence in one hour. O'Cody, portly grey-hair in the magenta silk waistcoat of a monsignor, chuckled when Jennie joked there was still time for a quick prayer. Others laughed along. Puzzling, because I hadn't seen a cleric come aboard, though somebody very like him had. I shelved the oddity, smiled, located Sophie Brandau in the glittering throng, whispered to Tye to have somebody spill a little *rosso* on the lovely Sophie's dress, caught up a silver tray – gadrooned, my favourite style – and briskly went to start my compulsory courting.

CHAPTER NINE

A spillage on a woman's dress is an indictable offence. Funny, that, when it's supposed to be lucky. The old Queen Mum used to say ta to nervous waiters when they plopped a drop on her lap, for luck given. Sophie Brandau didn't quite go spare, but Blanche hurtled to the rescue when Tye – too clever to commit the crime himself – sent a waiter to accidentally tilt a carafe in passing. Kelly Palumba and a thin straw-haired wastrel called Epsilon were especially concerned. Denzie Brandau gave a bored half-glance, made some remark to Moira Hawkins, causing people to fall about. I diagnosed a husband making capital from his wife's clumsiness. I was beginning to dislike the politician. I took over from Kelly Palumba, who cracked to her pal, 'Better than your TV productions, Epsilon!' I didn't care much for her, either.

'Mind, Mrs Brandau,' I said. 'Don't stretch the material.' People don't think. Her dress was a rich brocade, royal blue with sky sleeves. I commandeered a water decanter from a waiter and drenched a serviette. 'Macon wine leaves a stain otherwise.'

I drew her to one side as the chatter reasserted itself. We were by the rail, landward side. 'A few more linens, Blanche, please,' whittled the gathering down.

That left Sophie Brandau and myself. Fussing like I imagined a meticulous waiter would, I blotted the brocade. It was near the hem, and took a few minutes. During it, I passed comments on the surroundings. Which made me notice the man in the motor opposite the pier. He didn't look much like a photographer, but the motionless Wildlife Internations van nearby with its odd black-sheening windows could be full of them. He was talking into a car phone. So?

On board, however, Mrs Brandau and me were no longer the centre of attention. I placed everything on the tray, and happened to notice her face with a start of astonishment. Overacting, of course.

'Good heavens!' I said. 'I remember you now! That beautiful sautoir, wasn't it?'

The diamond chain was there, worn as it should be from both shoulders (I hate the one-shoulder *sur l'épaule* style so popular in nineteeth-century France, because what the hell's the pendant to do?) The pendant was there, tassel shape, four compound strands. Diamonds genuine as genuine is, and antique old. The central diamond was huge, bigger than the poor lumbering zircon she'd substituted for it. Seventeen carats? Nearer twenty, and brilliant-cut, which was good going for that kind of date.

'You noticed,' she said, quiet and pale.

'Did I stare? I apologize, Mrs Brandau.'

You have to feel sorry for any woman caught out in deception. It's routine for a man. Okay, when some bird rumbles you it's uncomfortable for a few weeks – well, ten minutes – but then you get over it and life's rich pageant rolls on. 'I said nothing, about the pendant.'

'I guessed from the way you looked at it,' she said. 'You're Lovejoy? The one Nicko had the trouble with over the furniture?'

That sounded nasty. 'I'm the one who advised Nicko how not to ruin his antique,' I corrected stiffly.

'You've become quite a joke,' she said, not even near laughing. 'Facing Nicko down over a wine stain.'

I said, narked, 'We don't deserve the antiques we've got. The moron you got to dock your sautoir pendant and substitute with zircons wants locking up.'

'You're good at antiques?' Her eyes were so sad, but still wearing that calculating quality women find hard to forgive themselves for. 'Can you do valuations?'

'Accurately. But . . .' I hesitated. Her eyes were lovely, brown, deep and broad in a slender face. She looked out of place among this lot. 'But sometimes people don't like the truth. Antiques deserve it.' Well, hang veracity. I'd got orders.

'And restorations? Antiques firms give such conflicting opinions.' She said it like lines in a rehearsal. She'd been as glad of the spillage excuse as I. Maybe she had orders, too.

'They would,' I said with feeling. 'Valuation companies are on the fiddle. I do everything free – for genuine antiques, that is.' I don't, of course. Never have. But my life might be at stake.

She thought a second. A gust of laughter rose from the party over something political.

'Tell one of the waitresses to get me a bitter soda, Lovejoy,' she said quickly. 'The Game starts soon. When it's quiet, bring me a drink to my cabin. It's zero two zero.'

American for twenty. 'Right. What drink, exactly?'

She stared at me, shook her head as if having difficulty. 'Anything convincing, Lovejoy.'

What drink was convincing, in Long Island Sound?

'Will there be a stain?' she was asking pointedly as people started drifting from the canopied arena. I recognized feminine obfuscation at work, and loudly played along.

'Certainly not, Mrs Brandau.' I felt like telling her it hadn't been wine, only water, another of my deceits, but I needed all my honesty in reserve. One of the guests was now in a military uniform, I saw as I made my way back to Bill. I hadn't noticed any general arriving. What was it, fancy dress? But ranks above corporal are where the Mysterious Orient begins, as far as I'm concerned.

'Here, Bill. What's three stars mean?'

'They mean you saw nuttin', Lovejoy.' Bill was flipping a last-minute cocktail for Kelly Palumba, who was now sloshed. She giggled.

'Hey, Lovejoy! Tell this hunk I'm gonna get some work outa him real soon ...'

Epsilon was pouting. 'I have to go, Kelly. See you here in an hour.' What card game lasts exactly an hour?

'That's time enough,' Kelly told Bill. A woman leering is not a pretty sight. I was glad when she started to slide.

I caught her as her knees buckled. Blanche and two waitresses flew up, hustling her out of sight with that concealed anger they reserve for a transgressing sister.

The party was thinning. Seeing nuttin', I didn't notice Denzie Brandau smoothing Moira Hawkins's bottom as they strolled off together. Nor did I notice the covert sign the Monsignor made to the General, fingers tapping palms in the universal let's-cut-percentages plot. Nor the unconcerned way Nicko indicated his watch when Jennie started rounding up the strays like an eager sheepdog.

But I did notice the way Bill rearranged my clean glasses which I'd placed on the counter. And the glint of the low sun showing the people on shore. You don't hide a watcher among trees, nor conceal him behind a window sill. You put him in a motor, where shoppers park their cars. Like the man Bill had continually checked on with a casual glance now and then ever since the party had started. Still, all was normal.

Except it all wasn't. We were under surveillance. Bill was in on it, with his signalling glasses and his flashy tricks with cocktail shakers. I was anxious to warn him about Gina's questioning, but got interrupted by a last-minute matron, one who'd had more face-lifts than Tower Bridge. She was a born gusher, had fawned continuously on the Monsignor, and now swigged her sixth martini like medicine, grimacing as it took effect.

'Wish me luck, honey,' she said, pondering whether to go for another. I decided to get shut of her.

'Luck? Here. Take this.' I took out a cent. 'It was my first ever American coin. You know the old saying, your first penny buys an hour's luck.'

'I never heard that one.'

She couldn't have. I'd just made it up. Women who doubt really nark me. 'It's true. Here.' I passed it over with a discreet smile, which mercifully got rid of her.

'Is that proverb straight, Lovejoy?'

'Certainly!' Now even Bill was sceptical. I hate mistrust in other people. We started to clear up.

'Do a deal, Bill?' The deck arena was clear of guests. Gina Aquilina drifted through – changed again, exquisitely sheathed in a risky purple, silver chain accessories – with Orly prattling amusing prattle. He'd changed too, a smoothie's white tuxedo. I waited until they'd strolled inside.

'Could I afford it?'

Witticisms gall me, when they're at my expense. 'Watch your back, that's all.' Zole's words.

'My back?' He laughed, but eyes alert and wary.

'Gina asked about you. I said you were a great barman.' I glanced over his shoulder at the shore, made sure he knew where I was looking. 'I could have dropped you in the clag, Bill. That means you owe me.'

'How much, Lovejoy?'

'The ten dollars Tony owed. I could have said you were hopeless, got you the sack.'

'I didn't figure you for a mercenary, Lovejoy.' He brought out a ten-dollar bill, placed it on the serving basin. He was puzzled now, and even warier.

'I'm working my passage up, up and away. I need every groat I can get. Thanks.' I slid the ten dollars back to him, finished wiping the glasses. The bar might be wired for sound, vision, heaven knows what. Just like the party area, or the rails where I'd attended to Sophie Brandau.

Bill looked at the money. He finally recovered it, said nothing more, except gave a curt nod of recognition. We wound up the bar.

'Reckon Kelly Palumba's recovered?'

'No names, Lovejoy. House rules.'

'Right. Only, it's been about an hour since she went moribund.' I drew breath. Come darkness, I'd be over the side and swimming for it, or being smuggled away in some kind lady's purse. Sophie

Brandau was that lady. 'Bill. What would you call a really convincing drink, for a lady?'

Cabin 020 was midships, port side. That meant its portholes faced the open sound. Light was dwindling now, sailing boats and small craft setting sailing lights shimmering the darkening waters. The *Gina* was starting to sway almost imperceptibly. I knocked, licked my hand to smooth my uncontrollable thatch, and donned a bright waiter's beam.

Mrs Brandau's welcome wasn't much. 'Come in, Lovejoy. Sit.'

Hell, like a dog. Reluctantly I deposited the tray, an old Burmese original lacquer. Criminal to use it. I'd only chosen it to prevent Bill from scouring it to extinction. It was one hundred and fifty years old, living on borrowed time in this company of millionaire scatter-brains.

The cabin was a shipboard compact, folding tables and furniture screwed down and all that. It was highly feminine, three mirrors, of which one was a true Regency that caught my breath. I sat on a low settee, modern crud, and tried to think polite thoughts about the lovely woman opposite.

Worry shreds a woman's confidence, doesn't it. It takes the steam out of the face somehow, shows in the eyes. This lady was never going to bat for America, not the way she'd crumpled inwardly.

'Something I said, love?' I asked.

'You were kind, Lovejoy. I need somebody kind.'

This sort of talk dismays me. We're vulnerable enough without trust raising its fearful head.

'Look, lady. I'm knee-deep in muck and bullets. I've hardly a bean. All I really know, between ourselves, is antiques and nothing but antiques. I'm also...' How to phrase it so I sounded superb? 'Don't trust me, is all I'm saying.'

'Sophie,' she said listlessly. Women take no notice. You might as well talk to the wall. 'It's my husband, Lovejoy.'

Oh, hell. I half rose. She gestured me down.

'How can I stop him?' She noticed my face, which must have debeamed somewhere along the line. 'You're the one doing the Sherlock with Moira Hawkins. Denzie's crazy. It's not the first time he's been stupid. She's dragging him in. We're in over our heads. She's persuaded him it'll bring fame, a fortune. The biggest PR fillip ever. Even push him to the presidency. He's like a man demented. And she's playing on it.'

That was it. Expectancy lifted her eyebrows. 'Well, Lovejoy?'

Clearly this was no seduction scene between randy serf and lusting contessa. Disappointed, I revealed how I'd encountered the Hawkinses. 'All I know is that Moira's sister Rose frequents the bar where I work . . .'

Sophie heard me out. She lit a cigarette, clicking the lighter a few times. 'I'd hoped you would be more cooperative. If it's a deal you want . . .'

I'd nothing to deal with. Yet here was a millionaire's wife offering . . . Suddenly I wanted to know more, more about Moira Hawkins's project, why Sophie was so concerned. I mean, I'd seen the Hawkins place. It was mundane, cheap even. This lady's emerald solitaire could buy Rose, Moira, bookshop and all. I'd been ordered to play along with this delectable bird, so I'd be in the clear with Gina even if I said, 'Okay, love. I'll do what you want.'

Her face lit, losing that waxy cast and hueing into animation. 'You will? Truly, Lovejoy?'

She came to fold herself beside me. 'You know the risks?'

'You're worth it,' I lied, hoping Gina's recorded tapes of this conversation would exonerate me one hundred per cent.

Her eyes fluttered, lowered. 'Don't be under any illusion, Lovejoy. There's a limit to what I can do.'

'That's always the danger.' I felt noble, a knight on a white charger. 'You want me to have a word with Moira?'

She gave a harsh laugh. 'No, Lovejoy. You'll have to end it. The Sherlock enterprise. It's the one thing that'll make him drop that Hawkins bitch.'

End? That all? I cheered up. Moira's plot hinged on a grailer scam, and they're always failures. Dreams are dud, which is why they stay dreams and never become reality.

'Easy, Sophie,' I said. 'Leave it to me.'

'You will? Oh, you darling man! Thank you!'

For one second I knew I could have joined her in communal happiness, so to speak, but I heard someone coming down the corridor. My hand never even reached her breast.

'Invite me to your place,' I said, thinking quickly. 'To, what, restore your antiques.'

She slipped me a card from her handbag.

'I'll okay it with Jennie,' she said. 'I've a convincing collection; Jim Bethune supplied most. You want I should damage one or two, make it look convincing?'

I went cold, nearly throttled her but kept control. Her hand cupped, grasped mine. She kissed my palm, eyes filling. I'd never seen so much gratitude at one go.

'Don't ever damage an antique, Sophie. Promise?'

'I'll do anything in my power for you. I swear.'

I left then, her gratitude flowing out into the corridor after me like a cloying perfume. Mr Sokolowsky was approaching. He said a cheery hello, asked how I was liking life on board ship. I was making some sort of inane reply when he leant close confidentially.

'Help her, Lovejoy,' he whispered, and went on his way, the sentimental old fool. I presumed he meant Sophie. I shrugged it off, only one more bemusement among many.

When I returned, Bill had gone. The deck arena looked uninviting. Nothing so forlorn as drooping bunting. All was left for seagulls and the evening breeze.

Onshore the Wildlife van remained. I looked down at the water. Still enough daylight to make a swim for it. A small white motor launch was purring across the bay, heading parallel to the shore. One crewman, and Bill. The *Gina*'s inshore boat. I yelled, 'Hey, Bill!' but he didn't turn. All right, I thought, narked. Not even the manners to say so-long.

I decided I'd better report to Gina as soon as darkness covered the day, and went to find the galley for some nosh to keep the wolf from the door. It was on the way that I got the key to most, if not all.

The cruiser was almost silent, rocking somnolently with its lines tapping as the breeze flicked them. The companionway led down a deck. You double back towards the stern, for the crew's quarters. I'd been told our scoff was there and nowhere else. Tye Dee must already be there, I'd decided. Like an obedient hound I would report to Gina on the dot, allaying all her suspicions.

'Lovejoy?'

I almost fainted with fright when she grabbed my arm, coming out of nowhere.

'You silly mare! You scared me to death!'

Normally Kelly Palumba would have giggled, having put one over on the universe. She was in no state for levity. She was shaking, teeth chattering and limbs a-twitch. A fleck of vomit touched the corner of her mouth. God, she was a mess.

'Lovejoy. Where the fuck's Bill?'

'How the hell should I know?' She clung and trailed, clawing. She babbled inanely. I pushed her back into her cabin and stepped after. 'Look. Wait here. I'll call Blanche.'

'Wait?' she shrilled. 'What the fuck's with *wait?*' She wept, shivering. Her dress was soiled. I looked away, stuck to my fair-minded task of getting the hell out and leaving her to stew in her own pot. 'Get fo' me, Lovejoy. I'm dyin'.'

Some sort of drugs. 'I'm sorry. I haven't got any.' I pressed the button frantically. This nightmare wasn't the prelude I wanted to my clandestine escape. 'Who's your stewardess?'

'Fuck the stewardess!' She slumped against the door, sobbing, muscles in spasm, retching. 'Where's Bill?' It was a cry from the heart. I tried dragging her away so I could get out. Where the hell was Blanche and her team? 'Bill sees me right every time. You're all against me . . .'

Bill the drug supplier, to this ruin? I almost joined in her wailing from self-pity.

'Let me out. I'll get Bill. He'll bring you your, er, tablets. Honest, love.'

She flailed against the cabin door in some sort of epilepsy. Why had I let her lean against the damned door, trapping me like this? I reached for a towel by the bedside, scattering syringes, silver foil, and rolled it under her head. I vaguely knew there was something about an epileptic's tongue, but what?

Gradually she quietened. I was drenched in sweat, breathing hard.

'They won't even let me play the Game,' she whimpered. 'Just because I've a small habit. Who hasn't, Lovejoy?'

'Mmmh,' I said. 'Rotten sods.'

She sobbed uncontrollably. 'Now I'll be out of the California Game. It happened before.' Her voice crescendoed. 'They'll not let me to LA.'

I tried to step over her towards the door but she clutched my leg. 'They wouldn't do a thing like that. I'll ask them –'

'Fix me, Lovejoy.' She tried a smile. A pathetic eager grin for a horror film. 'I'll be nice for you. Ask Bill. I'll do anything if'n you make me sing.'

I was worn out. The cabin was insufferably hot. There must be something stupendous in drugs to reduce a complete human to this. She'd nearly been exquisite two hours since.

'Right!' I said brightly. 'I'll get the, er, tablets for you. I have nine, maybe a dozen. Just let me pass . . .' All the time I was pushing the bloody button and not one of the idle bitches was coming. I'd belt the lazy cows.

She started her retching, holding on. I got a hand on the door latch, but made it no further, frantically started knocking on the panel calling out Blanche's name, bawling for Tye Dee, anybody for God's sake. She hung on, weeping and stinking, babbling not to leave her like this, promising anything.

'I'll get you a place in the Game, Lovejoy,' she wheedled, her aghast ravaged face staring up at me. 'I'll fund you!'

'Help!' I bawled, sick and shaking almost as bad as she was. 'Blanche, for Christ's *sake* −'

The door handle turned, and Blanche came whizzing in, forcing the girl bodily up from the floor in an amazing display of strength. Tye crowded in after. I reeled out.

'Where the hell have you been?' I yelled. 'I've been pressing that frigging button and knocking the bloody door for six hours, while you idle gets sat on your fat arses and −'

Tye clamped a hand over my mouth and hauled me along to the next cabin. He slammed me in and shut the door.

'You call yourself a friend?' I was yelling. 'Leaving me −'

'Shtum, Lovejoy.' He listened. The faint thumping from the adjacent room quietened, stilled. He relaxed, sat on the bunk.

I went to the bathroom, washed my hands and face, sniffing at my clothes for traces of Kelly . . . and noticed that Tye wore only trousers and a gaping shirt. He was barefoot. My hands in the basin's warm water, I stared at my reflection. Come to think of it, Blanche had hardly been what you might call eminently presentable, either. She'd looked just rising from a good night's, ah, rest.

Tye was pulling on socks, fumbling for shoes beneath the bed. Silk stockings were draped on a chair. The bed linen was disordered. A hard day's night had been had by all. I straightened, found a towel.

'No wonder you were slow coming,' I said evenly.

He cocked an ear, nodded as a buzzer sounded three faint zeds. 'We have to talk.'

Blanche entered. She was pale under her dark skin, almost purple around the eyes. Lovely, but scared and looking at Tye for direction. She carried a small tray holding a syringe, needles, ampoules. They made me feel queasy.

'I've fixed her good, Tye,' she said in a wobbly voice. She looked in a worse state than me. Partners in paradise, while I'd been in hell next door.

'You'd better know something, Lovejoy,' Tye said. 'All that went on in Kelly Palumba's cabin'll be taped, sound and video.'

'Thank God for that!' I said vehemently. 'It'll prove she dragged me in. When Nicko and Gina see the tape they'll see I was bawling my head off for you two . . .'

Aha. I paused, looked from Blanche to Tye.

'You see the problem, Lovejoy.'

Blanche was finishing dressing. I tried not to see her lovely legs sheathing into her silks. Tye stood, buttoning his collar.

'Aye.' And I did. The camera record would show me all innocent, trying to cope with the sick lass – and it would reveal that Tye and Blanche were in dereliction of duty. 'You two'll get your wrists slapped?'

'Sort of, Lovejoy.'

'But this . . .' Like a fool I glanced about the cabin, as if bugging devices would be in view and clearly labelled.

Blanche answered, doing her hair at the mirror. 'I have an arrangement with the recordist, Lovejoy. To default the circuits.'

She evaded my eyes in the mirror. Well, she had powers of persuasion any electrician would accede to.

Tye spoke, fastening his holster. I watched, amazed. It was the first real holster I'd ever seen. I'd no idea they were so bulky. However did undercover agents manage?

'We can erase Kelly Palumba's, Lovejoy.'

Into the ensuing silence Blanche spoke softly. 'If you stay quiet, Lovejoy.'

Now her eyes met mine. It wasn't a simple threat. It was more like, well, a country woman's promise of coming weather, certain it would come but hoping for maximum clemency. A rainstorm, we'd all get soaked.

'What's the risk to me?' I was conscious I was missing some sort of opportunity, but was too feeble-minded to think it through. 'I've promised loyalty to Gina all sorts of ways.'

'Haven't we all, Lovejoy?' Tye donned his jacket. He looked surprisingly neat, if a trifle bulky. So those holsters were tailored! The things you learn.

'There'll be no comeback from Gina,' Blanche said. 'Where's the harm in a little fun?' She did that erotic magic with lipstick that always makes me swallow and think hard unyielding thoughts. She smiled to herself. And Tye smiled too.

'Everybody needs a little fun now and then. Right?'

I swallowed. 'Right, right.'

That was where we left it, we of the good ship *Gina*, me going to change into clean gear then totter along to the galley for a nosh, Tye strolling to resume his patrol, Blanche staring at her reflection slowly sucking her lips in to even her lipstick. And the drugged girl somewhere in that chemical paradise from which few travellers ever really return.

CHAPTER TEN

It was Chanel who came to tell me I was wanted. I liked Chanel. She was personal maid to Mrs Melodie van Cordlant, my one-cent lucky lady. I'd have stayed in the galley to explain that eating was a good means of preventing starvation, but it'd have been no good.

I climbed to the next deck. Think of what that poor Kelly had told me. What was it? They wouldn't even let her to LA, for the California Game. She tried bribing me with her poor ravaged body, just like she'd paid Mr Squeaky Clean Bill for providing her drugs.

Weird words.

The poor lass was just demented – or else she was also addicted to gambling. I knocked at the door Chanel had told me: the long conference cabin. I was glad I'd donned clean and was scented like a rose garden. Maybe this was my reward, Gina wreaking her unsated lust on my poor defenceless frame?

The long boardroom was empty. A few papers were strewn here and there, crumples being fed into a portable shredder by Blanche and two stewardesses. Gina reclined, good enough to eat.

'Yes, Gina?' I said, all confidence and intimacy.

She hardly glanced up.

'Oh, Lovejoy.' I was suddenly new and insignificant. 'To Manfredi's. Soonest.' She looked past me. 'Blanche? Get me that Harvard architect. Two minutes.'

'Yes, Miz Gina.'

'Er . . . ?' I said, still oozing charm.

She noticed me with irritation. 'Manfredi's, Lovejoy. Go.'

I cleared my throat. 'Er, I don't think I quite understand –'

Hands grabbed me, mostly Tye's but with assistance from two other hulks. I was flung into my old gear, mercifully cleaned, hustled into the shore boat, and rushed breathless and bewildered to a waiting motor on shore.

Well, I'd prayed for an end to my servitude, but I was narked now it had come.

I didn't know it, but next dawn was the day I'd start killing people.

Once, I knew this bloke Ted who wrote what he called copy. Ted was a university academic, and like the rest he moonlighted on his

Eng Lit job by scribing for newspapers. A sad bloke, he was simply one of these geezers who'd never done anything except teach – never known an honest day's labour. He was made redundant in the Great Cutbacks. Suddenly he found himself facing the stark truth that he was unemployable. Now he trundles a handcart about Surrey villages scouring for tat, old rubbish which he tries to sell. He does it badly, needless to say. If he'd ever worked, with hands, he'd have been okay. As it is, he's had to invent a conspiracy among his university alumni to justify his bitterness. Tells everybody they were all jealous.

We all do it. I did it, that morning when Fredo arrived and found me disgruntled on the pavement. He said very little, just to get the garbage out in the alleyway because Josephus was having woman trouble.

'I asked Nicko for a few days off,' I lied brightly.

'Sure.' New York's elastic word speaks volumes.

Della was thrilled I was with them again. Jonie came and told me I'd missed a brawl in the bar between two guys berserk over the Superbowl. Lil told me she'd known all along I was crazy over her. Two new waitresses, and a new shabby shuffler to help Fredo in the kitchen, and we were ready to cope with Manhattan. I was angry, dejected in the best Ted manner, fuming to myself as I started smiling, giving out my cheery 'Hi, there!' to all and sundry.

I'm not really posh-minded. No, honestly I'm not. But I really had thought that on the *Gina*, first names with Nicko and all that, I was plugged in to something special. As New Yorkers bowled in for breakfast and my routine banter, I found myself thinking over oddities. Bill – who was he? Nicko owned the world, sure. And Gina ran much of it, sure. But whenever anybody spoke of reporting or checking or approving, it was always Jennie's name that cropped up. And Orly was her oppo.

'I reckon Dallas Cowboys aren't in it this year,' I told a driver I recognized. I didn't understand who the Cowboys were, but remembered he was For. His trigger phrase reflexed him into a soliloquy that gave me time to think.

The California Game? I'd been given orders to report nightly to Gina. Any progress on Moira Hawkins and her loony Sherlock plan. Yet here I was washing and serving at Fredo's joint when Gina and the *Gina* were a-bobbing on the briny of Long Island Sound.

'They're too erratic, for one thing,' I challenged my customer, into his third mound of pancakes. (You won't believe this, but he poured syrup over them, next to four rashers of bacon. Warning: American grub's lovely; its arrangement takes some beating.)

'Tell me who's more consistent!'

'Look at the league tables,' I said, doing that American shrug – a simultaneous grin and nodded headwag which encourages instant denials.

Did Gina *now* expect me to phone every evening with my progress report? There couldn't of course *be* any progress. There never is on a grailer. There can't be, for they're all myths, dreamt up by mystics and purveyors of illicit scams. You can invent some yourself. Do it today: precious diamonds from South Africa bigger than any on earth; limitless gold from the ocean floor; rare antiques in attics the world over. You only have to dream it up, and antique dealers will rush to market it for you. The fact that it doesn't exist won't matter. That's what a grailer is, rainbow gold. I'm not being unromantic. I'm only trying to warn you your friend's scheme of importing rare tapestries from the Punjab, ten cents a time and unlimited profit, is crud.

'Dallas, schmallas.' I replenished my customer's coffee while he went wild and starting calling along the counter for allies to set this jerk straight.

I mean, I know an actor who's umpteenth in line to the Throne. Well, this right royal bloke could reap the world, if you think of it. He's a born grailer. Why? Because he could sell his story, his opinions, even his name for vasto gelto, and live plushly ever after. And does he? Not on your life. He simply ploughs the theatres, does auditions, is downcast when he doesn't get them, rejoices when he does, the whole acting gig.

Why doesn't he? Because he's not thick, that's why. I once met him at an antiques auction. He was bidding for a miniature portrait. I tipped him off that it was on ivory and badly warped. He said ta, slipped me a fiver and we had a bit of a chat. I waxed indignant that the auctioneer – it wasn't a thousand miles from Sotheby's, Bond Street – hadn't sent somebody over to point the defect out.

'Maybe he doesn't know,' he said, smiling.

'You could have told him,' I said. 'Mmmh,' he concurred, '*but then what?*'

And I saw the problem. His life would be an instant media circus. Reporters would rifle his dustbins. Every female he raised his hat to would be hounded to suicide. He would be dissected in public with that well-known frenzy the media reserve for ante-mortems.

'No what?' the Dallas supporter was asking.

God, I must have spoken out loud. 'No way,' I said. 'They ain't got the pitchers.'

'Pitchers is baseball, jerko.'

Hell fire. 'Shows how much them Cowboys know,' I improvised quickly. 'They're advertising for pitchers in the *Herald Tribune*.'

That got a chorus of shouts and laughs. In the middle of it an old and valued customer arrived.

'Hello, Lovejoy.' She was hugging herself.

'Too early for wine, Rose.'

'Coffee, two eggs, toast.'

'Coming right up.' I shot the order through, eyed her. 'I had to go on a visit, love. Sorry.'

'Back just in time, Lovejoy. We've located a precious heap of paper for you.'

I stared. 'You have?' I'd never heard of a grailer actually becoming reality. Fakes do, of course. Trillion to one, I gave mental odds. News indeed for Gina; she was so endearing it'd be a shame to disappoint her.

'Hand it over, then. Let's have a look.'

'I said located, not obtained.'

Surprise, surprise. I tried to look enthralled, but probably failed, being distracted by Bill who blew my theory about then by suddenly not being dead after all. He went straight across to the nooks, sat and read his paper. I made demented small talk with Rose, the Cowboy fan, a state-of-the-city grouse. Bill left after a quick serving, paid Della on the till. No sign from him. Meantime, Rose had been telling me some cock-and-bull tale about letters received, transatlantic phone calls . . .

If Bill wasn't dead, was Tony? I felt a bit let down, decided the entire episode was my spooky imagination. All over. I felt relieved. I smiled at Rose's charming features. A bird in the hand is worth two in the bush, as the wicked old treble-entendre has it.

'. . . to England,' she was saying.

'Really?' How convenient for me, if Moira wanted somebody to cross the Pond and bring it over! 'How interesting, Rose.' I looked into her eyes, sincerely as I could while serving a bloke with a breakfast I could hardly lift.

'Hey, I was in England once!' the customer put in, just when I wanted to tell Rose how deeply I'd missed her.

Conversation struck up from all around. No time for chat with desirable ladies. I resumed my loud comments on the telly newscasts, the plight of City Hall, the nation's finances. And promised Rose when finally she left that yes, I'd be along to the bookshop the minute Fredo's closed, to discuss plans.

Two letters came for me that morning. One was by special messenger, a bicycle dervish with his head clamped into trannie muffs. The other was handed in by a uniformed chauffeur. I saw Della looking, grinned and told her it was the circles I moved in. I stuffed them into my pocket. More marked money from Nicko's Pittsburgh robbery? It could do without my fingerprints.

I worked on, surprised to find myself thinking less now of escape Somewhere Else, USA. Magic California? I didn't realize it then, being thick, but America's favourite risk was already setting in. I was being amused by the good cheer, the bustle, the aggressive glee all around. And the noise, the sheer willing ease of encounter. That American risk called seduction.

My grotty walk to the grotty Benidormo was interrupted. A few seconds after I'd called goodnights to Fredo and Della, envying as I did Della's special friendliness towards Fredo this particular evening, I caught sight of a reflection in a shop window. He was behind me, closing casually but fast. One flash of a passing police car's blue was all it took. I paused to let him catch up, not looking.

'Wotcher, Bill. Not dead, then?' Now I wish I'd not said it.

'Good eyes, Lovejoy.' He was amused, cool, in charge. As a luxury yacht barman, I hadn't been certain. One look on this street and I had him sussed.

'All the better for seeing you, officer.'

He paused to let some theatregoers pass, chasing taxis. 'You have two ways, Lovejoy. Out, or in. Either way, you're recruited.'

Another job? Three, or was it four? Maybe the letters in my pocket were offers from Paramount. I suddenly wanted to be in that museum Rose had taken me to, safe among antiques where life was simple and any other Homo sapiens was a foe.

'Who're we against?'

'Everybody, Lovejoy. Far as we know.'

A three-star general, a Monsignor, antiques magnate, bullion heiress, bankers, drug handlers, property baronesses, television moguls . . . They'd all been there. Plus politicians, and somebody the guests had called Commissioner. As in police?

'I'd come like a shot, Bill. But I'm on my way to a job.'

He was amused. 'That Sherlock gig? We know all about that, Lovejoy. What we don't know is what it's *for*. Suppose you find out from Miss Hawkins and tell us, huh? Your first assignment.'

'Sure,' I promised. One more tyranny's nothing to a serf. 'How'll I contact you?' As if I ever would.

'You agreed too fast, Lovejoy.'

I was so tired. 'Look, Bill, if that's your real name. I'm in a cleft stick. You're in the law. You've given me orders. I'll comply. Now leave me alone. I've a chance of seeing a bird for a few minutes' quiet nooky.'

'Phone number in your pocket, Lovejoy.' He moved off, blending expertly among pedestrians. I thought I saw him fade through a doorway, but couldn't be sure. It was a card with a typed phone number. I walked on, head down and thinking.

Tyrants. It's all very well for them. Even among other tyrants they can make a living. It's us that catch it. I paused, hurried on and found a phone. I caught Fredo at the bar. He sounded a little breathless, relieved it was only me.

'Fredo? I need Gina's phone number.'

'Christ, Lovejoy!' He spoke off phone to somebody. I heard a woman's offended expletive, a door slam. 'I can't, Lovejoy. Even a dickhead like you should know the score by now.'

'Listen. Gina said I was to report in. What must I do, send a carrier pigeon? Tell me Nicko's, then. Or Jennie's. It's urgent.' I hesitated for only a second, opted for betrayal. 'That barman, Bill. He's police. Asked about Moira Hawkins.'

'Wait, wait.' He came on in another second, asked where I was ringing from, and finally gave me a number.

While the traffic rushed past and people tried to hustle me, I got it picked up first ring.

'Hello? This is Lovejoy. I need to speak to Gina, please.'

'Jennie, Lovejoy. Why are you ringing this number?'

I explained I'd got it from Fredo. 'I was ordered to report to Gina.'

'What is it?'

'Bill. The barman on the *Gina*, remember him? He's a bobby. He's just asked me to spy on the Hawkins family.'

'Bobby? You mean police?' She made me repeat his every word. I did, almost with impeccable accuracy.

'Look, Jennie. I don't know what I'm supposed to do any more.'

'You did right, Lovejoy. Just behave normally. Leave things to me.'

'Look,' I started to tell the phone, but it was dead and the queue was threatening my life. I escaped.

Some things go wrong, don't they. Had I caused them to, telling Jennie about Bill? Fredo didn't matter. Anyhow, he was only interested in making smiles with Della.

Zole was in my room. I looked at the key in my hand. I'd had to unlock the door. He was eating a hamburger and watching a small colour television from the bed.

'Hey, Lovejoy ma man. This gasket's gonna blow.'

A cop chase, to gunfire. 'The hotel management upping its image?' I got my soap and towel, still damp from morning.

'You talk sheet, Lovejoy. It's yo' present, y'know?'

He still didn't think much of me. I went the length of the corridor, washed, did a weary shave, and returned as Magda saw a client off the premises.

She came with me. 'You're great with Zole, Lovejoy. He's talked about nothing all day, except how pleased you'd be with the set.'

'Look, Magda.' I hated to say it. 'How did Zole come by it? Might it have been, well, stolen?'

She stared at me so long I thought she was controlling outrage at the scandalous suggestion.

'Of course it's stolen, Lovejoy! Jeech! You know how much they *cost*? Zole works the stores with three other kids.'

She took my arm and walked me. Zole was yelling obscenities, exhorting the gunmen to even greater mayhem. 'Tell him you like it, Lovejoy,' she whispered. 'He'll be thrilled.'

I cleared my throat, put my soap and towel away. 'Zole. That set's the very best I ever saw. It's splendid. Thank you.'

'Ain't nuthin', Rube,' he said, engrossed.

That was it. Zole, aged seven, was also a gang leader. I said so-long, started downstairs with Magda along.

'Look, love,' I said. 'This is a bit awkward to say. But if the police catch me with a stolen television I'll be in real trouble. Can you tell Zole no more presents, please?'

She laughed. We came into the hallway. The desk man was watching a quiz show, impatiently muttering answers to himself.

'Lovejoy. Watch out for yourself, okay? There's people watching you. I just want you should know.'

'Me? You sure, Magda?'

She made to move off. I caught her. 'Look, love. What about Zole? Who's looking after him while you're, er, working?'

All she did was laugh at me. 'Murder, man,' she said.

I must have recoiled because she stopped scanning cruising cars and looked at me directly. She didn't often do that.

'Hey.' Yanks are brilliant at inflexion. She squeezed more compassion into that one syllable than Molière averaged in a Paris rep. 'I mean you're weird, okay?'

'Sorry, Magda. Just spooked, is all.' It was a phrase picked up from a dozing bar bum. 'I just wish I could help. You have a difficult time, the pair of you.'

She smiled. 'Most guys are shovers or pullers, Lovejoy. You're weird because you're neither. You off to see that skinny bitch?'

I said nothing.

'She'll not fly you far, hon. Fly Magda Airlines some time.'

If it hadn't been for the prickly feeling of unease I'd have talked longer. Anyhow, a crumpled motor crawled by and she trotted off to answer the whistled summons. I sighed and walked off. People do what they're good at, I always think.

As I started off, I tried working out this Land of Opportunity's determinants. Like, how come Kelly Palumba was rich beyond the dreams of whatnot, while same-age Magda was a street prostitute? It couldn't simply be silver-spoon-at-birth, could it? Kelly had offered me more money for a pinch of drugs than Magda saw in a month. Maybe our olden-day system was simply continued here in the USA? Except in America the bosses didn't wear emblazoned coats of arms.

Then I heard sirens, denoting carnage somewhere close. It wasn't far, maybe three hundred yards, to where the cars congregated around the man lying near the pavement.

Taxi drivers were yelling and horns blared accompaniment. I didn't bother listening to the explanations and shouts of whose fault it all was, how some car had suddenly accelerated and the man suddenly fell off the kerb . . . I went on past the crowd, sick to my soul. No question of what had happened to Tony, not now I'd seen Bill lying there. The taxi drivers were wrong. It was my fault. I'd assumed the police were invulnerable, that nobody could possibly harm a special agent, or whatever Bill was. Had been. I'd rung the Aquilina number to ingratiate myself. I knew that. Well, I'd made myself secure now. Bill had paid up, for me.

Against all habit I went into a late-night bar up from Times Square. I had some Californian wine, pale and faintly opalescent. I vowed no revenge. How could I? I was just badly shaken, even leaping like a scalded cat when the bar door banged in the night wind. I was frightened. I didn't know what I was into. Stupidly, I'd assumed I was free of obligations to Nicko's crowd once Gina had sent me back to pasture in Manhattan.

In Apple Zee's nutritious joint I pulled out the letters. I memorized Bill's phone number, but kept the card to give to Nicko. It wouldn't matter to Bill, not now. All betrayal is a one-off, complete and entire of itself. The card would add nothing, but be proof of my good faith. The first letter was a note from Sophie Brandau's secretary, on scented notepaper that must have cost a bomb. It said to call on Mrs Brandau at my earliest convenience, Park Avenue. The second was a scrawled note from a Mrs van Cordlant's secretary's assistant, saying to call, on Madison Avenue.

Not much. So? The only way was to feel my way out of New York, along any thread. Rose was my least likely thread. The others? Well, Sophie might reveal most. Except this Mrs van Cordlant coming out of the blue . . . When in doubt, grab for antiques. Therefore Sophie, Park Avenue.

I was about to go when Zole slipped in beside me.

'Two more burgers, ma-main,' Zole sang. He had his star-spangled yo-yo.

'Not for me, ta. And put that yo-yo away.'

'You ain't gettin', Rube.'

I watched him in the bar mirror, grabbing the food. A lad after my own heart. 'Eat well, Zole.'

'Your pal was dead before he got hit,' Zole said conversationally. 'He got *throwed*, man.'

'I guessed.' Bill was no accident-prone stumbler. He was a capable bloke.

'Hey, Lovejoy! You ain't such a rube!'

'He was the one watching the hotel?'

'Him, a bad news pig and two brothers.'

Whatever that meant. 'Brothers? He had brothers?'

Zole guffawed, a gaping mouth filled with a mash of ketchup-soaked hamburger, and mocked, 'Ah mean *black*, Lovejoy. Ya know *coloured*? Jeech!'

Leaving, I made him replace the cutlery and two saucers which had somehow fallen under his tee-shirt. We parted, me to get an armful of newspapers from an all-nighter, him to hustle a mark for Magda, he said. I nearly didn't believe him, but worried in case it was true.

The Benidormo was jumping, forgive the pun. Magda's room thumped to an ancient rhythm. The other side was a pandemonium of a man and bird having a brawl, best of six pinfalls and threats of murder with free abuse.

Before I could settle down to tranquillity, the Bad News Pig shouldered in and stood there apologetically.

'Sorry, Lovejoy. I gotta do this.'

My heart sank. Between the orgiastic moans from Magda's and the howls from screamsville, my own pad had somehow earned a bludgeoning.

'What's up, Tye?'

'Gina says you aren't following orders, okay?'

He said the same okay four times, each time hauling me erect and clouting me in the belly so I whoomfed double. I tried asking what orders for chrissakes but he didn't answer. He was really sorrowful, though, and expressed sincere regret as I crouched and retched onto the bare linoleum.

'It's not me, unnerstand,' he said with compassion. 'It's Gina, okay? You didn't report in.'

I gagged. My sweat dripped onto my hands, into the puddled sick between them. God, I felt like death. 'Okay. Sure.' What else meant concurrence?

An hour after Tye'd left I finished mopping the floor and went down the corridor to wash my towel. Magda came to stand in the doorway behind me. She looked sympathetic. My heart sank further. I definitely needed no more help.

'No compassion, Magda. I've had enough to be going on with, ta.'

'Lovejoy, honey,' she said softly, 'leave N'York. Soon.'

'Am I allowed one phone call first?'

She sighed. 'Dumb,' she said.

For the next hour, until midnight, sprawled on the mattress between two shaking walls, I ogled my gift TV and read the newspapers, under a snowfall of flaking plaster. I'd at last set to, learning New York's news. Then at the witching hour I phoned the number Fredo had given me, and told a recording machine a negative report, but that I was invited to see the lady in question next day when I'd report in full.

And slept, fitfully dreaming of Bill's body being lobbed under an approaching car. I didn't go to see Rose that night.

CHAPTER ELEVEN

America's not perfect, mind. Disillusion's the bus station, West 42nd Street.

Sheer size is agoraphobia's ally. I'd learnt the word panhandler from Zole the day before. The world centre of hustling, panhandling, drug pushing, aggressive dereliction, is surely here. I'd never seen so many buses in my life, commuter roarers and long-distance racers all the colours of the rainbow. It seems they're all private companies. Passengers too are all shades and sizes. Tip: don't go for a pee – bottle it until you reach home.

A whole hour it took me, finding the times and places of the California runs, for my escape. The drifters with their aggressive sales pitches frightened me to death. One shabby bloke wide as a barn stopped me in the open crowd by simply shoving a flat hand on my chest.

'Hey. Whachoo want, man?' he threatened.

'Er . . .' I tried to edge away among some passengers.

'You gotta want somethin', man.' He dragged at me.

'I've no money,' I said feebly.

'Sheet.' He let go so I fell, got up and scarpered to palpitating safety among a horde of people queueing for hamburgers.

The trick is to stay ungrabbable, which means beyond arm's reach of passers-by. This means deep in a queue of ordinary folk, or ensconced in a nosh bar where the proprietor is protection for as long as you're buying. Remember that. Solitude prevails in any loo, except here it's a mangler's mart, with blokes of all ages soliciting, injecting, selling syringes, even fighting over vulnerable travellers with knives. Police are on hand, sometimes. But bloodstained tiles do nothing for confidence.

Japanese tourists are useful, going in clusters like they do. I found them a practical aid, and hopped from group to camera-loaded group like a child crossing a turbulent stream on stepping stones.

And got taken forcefully just when I'd discovered the bus numbers, price, and worked out a policy to avoid the perils of passengerhood. Perhaps midday departure to San Francisco would be the best? Being trapped on a charabanc with a load of streetwise hustlers scared me. Or maybe these weapon-toting clutchers never actually went on the buses at all?

'This way, man.'

Three blokes grabbed me. I tried squawking for help, struggling, shouting for police, anything. I was yanked down some stairs, God knows where. Two prostitutes were having a wrangle on a landing while a bemused city dresser looked on. Four or five blokes were trading money for screws of paper, slick as light. The staircases were concrete. I got bruised against the handrails in the rush downward. A couple were fornicating in a doorway, the woman against the wall, nonchalantly smoking, gazing into space. The tunnels and staircases reverberated to the echoes of shouts, quite casual, distant thunder of traffic, people talking, cars starting up. My mind reeled backwards. Incongruity's supposed to be the essence of humour, not chaos. Down here all rules vanished. We reached some level which stank of urine. My three captors were talking quite offhandedly among themselves, as if they weren't hauling a struggling captive along dank concrete terraces. We seemed to be near an umpteen-tiered car park. The sweet smell of excess mingled aromatically with petrol's thick scent. A man whooped as if in some echo chamber. I glimpsed some geezers around a trestle table under a naked bulb. 'After you wit' heem,' a bird called laconically, squeezing past going the other way and tutting in annoyance when they shoved her aside.

'Hey, Lovejoy ma man!'

We'd stopped in a concrete bunker of some style, the door not hanging off and a score of television monitors on the go round the walls.

I was plonked in front of a desk – desk, if you please, in this warren. Numerous people sat about, several birds. They were talking, watching the consols, professionals of a sort. I tried to get breath, but got giddier the more I inhaled. The fumes were literally intoxicating, sending my mind on a strange unplanned trip. A control room?

'What you doin' here, Lovejoy?' He pronounced it love-jo-a. 'Why 'ncha come ta me, main?'

A little unused air happened into my lungs and I found voice. 'For chrissakes, Busman!' I yelled. 'What the hell you do that for? You scared the hell out of me, you stupid burke!'

The place stunned into silence. Busman rotated his chair, smiling hugely at his people.

'Ain't he somethin'?' he demanded. 'He ain't crazy, jess sorta weird. Squat it, Lovejoy.'

A chair rolled under me. I fell into it, sucking where my knuckles had scraped along the walls.

'Silly sod.' I was really narked, mostly from having been terrified.

He boomed a laugh from forty fathoms. I swear the ground vibrated. 'Lovejoy's the bad who got me shucked, people. Believe it.'

They resumed talking, glancing between their consols and me. The screens showed the concourses, departure points, ticket agencies, the nosh concessions. Even the stairwells were there, hustlers and activities in all their glory.

'Is this where you work, Busman?'

His amusement thundered out. He shook, his desk throbbed, his teams fell about. Typical. I was getting narked and said so. I'd thought I was being polite.

'Love-jo-a,' he said, wiping his eyes on his sleeve. 'You *is* weird, an' thassa fact. I don't work here, man. I *works*.'

More rolling in the aisles from all and sundry. I sat, nodding with a feeble show of interest. Whatever turns this lot on, I thought, then let me get out of here and I'll go by train, canal, hire a yak. Anywhere'd do.

'I *controls*, Lovejoy. You know control?'

Who pays them to watch the concourse so fervently, I wondered idly. I didn't really care. If I asked the question they'd only roar and shake their heads. Even the birds were eyeing me, tittering.

'Lovejoy.' Busman came in to land, leaning forward. God, he was big. He'd make ten of me and have leftovers. 'You sprung me. Why?'

I brightened. A sentence I could recognize, at last. Berto Gordino must have got him out.

'It wasn't me, Busman. I just asked a lawyer to try.'

He closed his eyes, shook his head, roused as if coming round from an anaesthetic.

'You don't work fo' no Bethune, Lovejoy.' It was an accusation. I swallowed, nodded.

'I lied, Busman. I was scared. I'm only a bar help at Manfredi's. I did extra waiting for some society folk. It was Mrs Aquilina in the car. Her lawyer –'

'I got it, Lovejoy.' He beckoned a confrere, sounding mystified. 'See what I mean, Trazz? Anybody else'd claim *serious*. Lovejoy just says it like is.'

'It was my idea, though,' I put in quickly, not wanting to be left out of any free praise.

Trazz was a tiny man of skeletal thinness, warped by some deformity so he stood at an angle from his waist up. He had a cigarette between his lips, eyes crinkled against ascending smoke.

'He's not so dumb,' Trazz said. It was a hoarse whisper so slight you had to strain to listen. 'Not like today's mob. See the screen, Busman? They've hacked the delivery. Makes two times, Busman. We godda *move.*'

'They stupid they have, Trazz.' Busman rolled his chair across the floor, staring intently from screen to screen as buses disgorged passengers and bags. 'Who's the shipper?'

'They's Sarpi's. Got hisself Miamis, Haitians, Jamaican.' Trazz crinkled, went tsss-tsss. I watched a second, scored it as wry laughter. 'He knowed best, Busman, tsss-tsss.'

'Hit his smurfs, Trazz. How many he got?'

'Today? Sixty-eight, not counting Mexican.'

People all about laughed at this sally. I tried to grin along but my face had gone tight. Hit?

'Forty too much?'

Trazz went tsss-tsss some more, said, 'Forty twenny-eight short, Busman.' More hearty laughs. A jocular company.

Trazz swayed away, pivoting on his right hip. Quiet and speed together, for all his deformity.

'See, Lovejoy? N'York's way.' Busman rose from his chair, darkening the known world, nodded me along with him. We walked the screen-studded walls. 'We see the goods come, charge a percennage. Only small, nuthin' spectacular.'

'What's a smurf, Busman?' I had to look upwards almost at right angles.

Folk nearby chuckled. A girl snorted in disbelief, hurriedly composed herself when Busman idly looked round.

'Smurf is a mule, Lovejoy. Carries the bag, see? Drugs, money fo' washing in these clean white streets of ours, guns, anythin' the man wants, see? Six cents on the dollar.'

'Who's this man, then?'

He laughed so much he almost fell down, literally sagging helplessly. I had to try and prop the bloody nerk up. Nobody came to help, even though I cried out when my spine buckled, because they were all rolling in the aisles too. I got him to a chair at a screen showing the panel of long-distance arrivals and lent him my hankie so he could snort and wipe his eyes. What the hell had I said?

'The man's who-evuh, Lovejoy,' he said. 'Poh-lice hack businesses, right? Then they *the man,* see? Canada goods hack mebbe four cents on the dollar by transport's bossman. Broker man's boys spread rumours some bank's foreclosin' so he makes a little zill, *he's* the man, see? Who-evuh.'

'Not just one person?'

'You catchin' own, man!'

He strolled up deeper into the room. It was extensive. At the inner end a row of American pool tables. Trazz was there, allocating jobs to a small crowd of men, all sizes and shapes. We went through a doorway, along a corridor and into a comfortable living room. A woman about Trazz's size came up smiling, got introduced.

'How d'you do, Lorrie?' I greeted. 'Pleased to make your acquaintance.'

Busman loved that. 'We gotta gentleman here, no mistake. He sprunged me last week, that big society mouthpiece. Give him a drink.'

We rested in deep leather armchairs. I was given some hooch that made my eyes water. Lorrie was thrilled, seeing my gasp as evidence of sensitivity.

Busman enjoyed himself telling her how I'd got myself almost dissected by the maelstrom in the concourse. I worked out that we were somewhere deep below West 42nd Street, the bus station heaving and churning away way above our heads. I didn't like the sensation. I looked round. No antiques, which was a disappointment.

'Is this all a part of . . .?'

'Sure is,' Busman said. 'They don't call for the rent, is all.' He laughed. Lorrie laughed.

'Do they know this goes on?'

'Sure do, Lovejoy.' He explained to Lorrie, 'He don't know frum nuthin' Lorrie. Like a chile, so say everythin' two times but start over part way in, see? Tell him it. I gotta check Trazz not too vicious this time.' He went into an inner room which had more screens projecting from its walls.

She was fascinated, started to explain, repeating it slower as if I was gormless.

'You really don't understand,' she marvelled. 'I think it's kinda sweet, y'know? Like . . .' She dug for a word. 'Like innocent, y'know?'

Narked, I said I was following all right. She said hey sure, and went on telling me how Busman's world worked. Cash defaulters had to be punished. Sarpi's drug carriers arriving from the south today would be attacked, their merchandise seized. It was an illegal Customs and Excise.

'Why don't the police stop it?' I said at one point, which called for more repetition, slower still, Lorrie painstakingly mouthing the words as if I'd gone deaf.

'Police got their own hack, see? Smurfers take care of them, like airlines, like property developers, building trades. Like merger capital, see? Like bullion mark-ups that happen of a sudden for no reason. Like movies that bomb, like million-dollar shows go turkey, a politician gets himself elected –'

'Elected?' I'd heard Yanks had universal suffrage.

'Sure. One's elected, the others not paid enough, see?'

'The man?' I guessed shrewdly.

She was delighted. 'You got it, Lovejoy! It's *always* the man, see?'

I said, 'Lorrie, I can't thank you enough for your kindness and patience. I'm grateful.'

'Think nothing of it, Lovejoy,' she said shyly. 'It's our pleasure.'

We talked of homes for a while, me saying about my cottage in England and trying hard to remember the price of groceries and all that so she could be outraged at differences higher or lower. Busman returned, downing a couple of whiskies more and saying that Trazz was putting too savage and that he'd have to go. He was proud that Lorrie had finally explained the way life worked. 'She bright,' he said. I concurred. She was ten times brighter than me.

'Honey, Lovejoy in that shitty Benidormo,' she complained elegantly. 'You not do something?'

'Thank you, love, but I'd rather stay there for a couple more nights, if that's all right. I do appreciate your generosity.'

'You wants, you asks,' Busman rumbled benevolently. We went and I got an usher from Trazz to the upper world of life and pleasant New York skies. It was still a dream, but now tinged with dark-rimmed clouds.

CHAPTER TWELVE

Fredo was mightily soured by the news that I had messages to carry for Nicko and couldn't work today. He complained, whined, appealed to the skies as he opened the bar.

'I'll stay, then. Can I phone Nicko?'

'No!' he screeched, going pasty white. 'Ya wanna get me . . . ?'

Killed? I went my way.

New York's bus system's so orderly it's incomprehensible. You simply buy a ride, and get a permit from the driver entitling you to another ride on any bus whose route crosses yours. Get it? It all stems from this methodical crisscross system of numbering streets. I was baffled by its predictability, finally got a taxi.

'Th'ain't got this in England 'cos they dumb, man,' the driver sang, laughing. 'Like, you live say 500 Fifth Avenue. Eerase that zero, divide by two, okay? Add eighteen gives forty-three. You drops the fare 43rd Street and you's home, man.'

'How marvellous,' I said through a headache.

'Sep you add thirty-five for Park Avenue.'

Fantastically enough he dropped me right at the door. Where the commissionaire only reluctantly put a message through to the Brandau residence. I was told ten o'clock.

That left me walking through lovely New York's morning sunshine. I'd my Manhattan map, which showed these amazing streets. The shops were so varied, the traffic instant mayhem. I stopped just to look. The taller buildings caught sun against the blue. Even the deepest chasms were relieved by a distant sheet of sky, sometimes with an exhilarating stretch of waterway. A couple of times cars nearly ran me down – wrong side of the road, I remembered eventually. Manhattan was so wonderful it was a full hour before I caught myself wandering rather than aiming, called to mind Tye Dee's chastisement and set about finding Mrs van Cordlant's address on Madison Avenue. The names thrilled me, from songs and films. I felt quite proud when I managed to say Madison without adding Avenue. A real New Yorker.

My letter got me into the lift. It flung upwards like a shuttle, casting me out at altitude into a plush ballroom which seemed to function as a corridor. You could have held a concert in it. I was frightened by an instant screech as a lady I half recognized wafted to greet me.

'It's my lucky Libran!' She enveloped me. Perfume cut off my air supply. Something licked my face. I realized there were three of us in there, one a minute dog. 'I'm so glad you could come, my dear. Chanel? Bring this gentleman his favourite drink this instant!'

'Yes, Mrs van Cordlant!'

A maid in full fig – I didn't say hello to Chanel – slicked the doors to and wheeled a tray of drink after us. The flat spread into the distance. Windows showed Central Park, a lake, the scaggy tops of edifices and expanses of lovely sky.

Mrs van Cordlant dragged me to a settee and shoved me down. She'd not been this decisive when I'd given her a cent to get rid of her on board the *Gina*. Then, she'd seemed driven to distraction. Now she was practically on top of me. Enveloping breasts seemed everywhere. I struggled to breathe.

'Just tea, please.'

Chanel almost staggered with shock, but was a game girl and left us to it.

Mrs van Cordlant eyed me eagerly. 'How long have you been clairvoyant, my dear? Was it from birth?'

'Er, well –'

'I *agree*, Lovejoy! My astro-psychic – been with her *years* – had *no notion*! – until she was struck by lightning in South Carolina. Can you imagine?'

'Good heavens,' I said gravely, thinking she was a right nut. The bloody dog, a King Charles the size of a shrew, was trying to hump my foot. I tried to disengage without booting it into the Guggenheim.

She was eyeing me admiringly. I felt odd. Admiration hadn't happened since I'd landed.

'Do you want repaying now, Lovejoy, or shall we take care of the business in hand first?'

'Repaying?' I brightened. Then I remembered I'd only given her a single cent. Repayment on that scale was out.

I rose, frostier than her commissionaire, and toe-flicked her hound aside.

'Mrs van Cordlant,' I intoned. 'If you imply that I would demean myself by accepting repayment for the small service I did you, I'm afraid I must decline.'

'But I –' Her features were quite appalled.

I went all stern. 'No, Mrs van Cordlant. Thank you. But I gave you that coin in all good faith, knowing it would assist. *Any* compensation to me would instantly devalue your luck. I can't accept money. The . . .' What were they? Star signs? 'The forces of fortune are *life*, Mrs van Cordlant. They can't be bartered, like commodities.'

'Oh, I'm so sorry, Lovejoy. I'd no idea!'

'Please may I take my leave, Mrs van Cordlant?'

'Oh, please. I –'

Melodie quickly mollified me enough to have me sitting down. We were frosty friends at opposite ends of the settee, a mere mile apart, while Melodie apologized repeatedly. I was aloof.

'You hear that, Chanel?' she told the maid with brimming eyes while I looked soulful. 'Lovejoy here – a true clairvoyant, though he's Libran – refused twenty thousand, so's not to spoil the luck he *gave* me! Isn't that just beautiful?'

Melodie choked, Chanel looked astonished. I almost fainted, and did a bit of choking on my own. I came to with my ears ringing disbelief.

'Lovejoy,' the silly old bat said, emotion brimming from her eyes. 'You are the most sincere person I have ever met. Do you know what it's like to be rich in New York?'

'No, Melodie,' I said with honesty. Or anywhere else.

Her voice sank to a whisper. Chanel left, looking back in disbelief. 'It's punishment, Lovejoy. Purgatory.'

'It is?' I tried more soulful, this time didn't make it.

'It's people, Lovejoy. Mercenary, grasping.'

Women are odd. I really mean that. A woman doesn't know the effect she has on a man. Any woman affects every man with instant global tonnage every single time. But women all go out teaching each other it isn't true, God knows why. They reach for doubt, where we blokes go for hope. This accounts for much of their behaviour. Here was Melodie, for instance, wanting some excuse to justify our evident valency, and finding approval for her desires in this mystic claptrap. I was glad, wanting desperately to get back to where that fortune had so briefly winked its golden eye.

Chanel safely out of the way, I took her hand forgivingly. 'Don't, Melodie. You're distressing yourself. Distress isn't the way of, er, those psychic influences. We can keep ourselves mindful of truth, and love.'

All that frigging gelt, my baser elements were sobbing. I could have been winging my way out on my own personal frigging jet.

She was filling up again. We were both awash. She raised my hand to her lips, gave it a sucking kiss. 'Oh, Lovejoy. I knew we'd bond. No wonder Gina values you.'

'Please, Melodie.' I moved away, thinking what to say. In the grief of losing all that gelt, I'd forgotten this bird was a pal of the Nicko mob. 'There's something I have to say.'

'Yes, dear?' She came to stand with me, looking over the city. I put my arm round her waist.

'I have a psychic obligation to you, Melodie. It came to me right . . .' How the hell did psychic obligations come? '. . . out of the ether.' I grasped her hands. They were a mass of rings I could hardly get my fingers round. 'I had to guide your actions, transfer my luck to you.'

'You did?' she breathed.

'Had to, love. But there's a psychic condition.'

'What condition, Lovejoy?' She withdrew slightly, eyes narrowing. I recognized suspicion.

I gazed into her eyes, deeply sincere. 'I want a promise, Melodie. Just your word that you'll not breathe a word of our friendship. This psychic, er, thing is solely between us. Is that understood?'

Her expression cleared. 'Oh, yes, Lovejoy!'

'Can Chanel be trusted?'

'Perfectly. Her family's served mine for two generations.'

Two generations? That was only her and her dad. Didn't she mean ten, twelve? I shelved the problem, bussed her, disengaged when she clung.

'Oh, Lovejoy.' She broke down, weeping. 'I have a terrible confession. A moment ago, when you said you wanted something . . .'

'I know, love,' I soothed. 'Don't forget I *am* psychic. Mercenary considerations crossed your mind, didn't they?'

She nodded, sniffing. The miniature hound started whimpering in a corner.

'*Never* think of money between us.' I swallowed, almost blubbering myself at our profound emotional depths. Thoughts of all that money helped my sorrow along.

'Thank you, my dear,' she said.

'Then all's forgiven.' I led her gently to the settee. 'And you can tell me . . .' Brainwave! '. . . about how you carried it off, on the *Gina*.'

We held hands. I stayed her from ringing for Chanel to pour, bravely said I'd manage. It was a modern scrolled silver, rubbish but worth its weight in, well, silver. The porcelain was crappy modern stuff. Unbelievable.

'Oh, Lovejoy. It was marvellous!' Her eyes were shining now. There's nothing voluble as a woman telling a triumph. 'I'd never felt so confident! It was your penny!'

Smiling, I corrected her gently. 'Not the penny, love. The forces act *through* it.'

'That's it!' she cried. 'I felt the forces act *through*! I slipped it under my third ring – you'll know we're all searched. I took quite a risk, Lovejoy.'

Her face was solemn now, serious.

'Risk?' I frowned. 'Not with the force?'

'Oh, no! But I suddenly *knew* I should stake bullion profits. Out of the blue!' She was so thrilled. We were so close. 'You know what I staked?' She tutted at herself. 'Cool as you please! Two per cent! Can you believe it?' She gave a naughty-girl giggle.

I chuckled, shaking my head. 'I'd have loved to've seen you, Melodie. You have such natural grace.'

'Oh, d'you think so?' She fluffed her hair the way they do. 'Their faces! Especially Charlie Sarpi's. After the failure of the Japanese gold commemorative fakes from Europe, he thought his cartel was in the driving seat.'

'I was only sorry Kelly Palumba was unwell.'

'Such a shame, poor dear. Epsilon tried, but I swear that young man's sometimes quite deranged. Really made a hash of poor Kelly's stake. He simply knows nothing of property values. She'll be so mad. He got in, though. Did all right with his silly TV stations.'

'Well, his home ground.' I spoke as if I knew what we were talking about.

'Sarpi didn't even come close, darling,' she told me mistily. 'Only the Commissioner. Jim Bethune's always in at the finish of course these days. Antiques is a crazy world.'

She was telling *me* that? I hesitated. 'You know, love, I feel as if I've known you in at least two previous incarnations.'

'Lovejoy, I feel it too. Deeply. We've known each other a lifetime. Is that silly?' She went shy.

'Of course it is.' You have to deny a woman's suspicions to confirm they're true, but gently. 'If we'd been, well, lovers in a former incarnation, surely we'd probably . . . ?'

Confusion set in, especially when she agreed with me. I wasn't too sure I wanted to associate with her, not without a single antique in the whole rotten dump. Sophie Brandau on the other hand said she'd got several.

'Will it last, Lovejoy?' We'd migrated to the middle of the vast settee. 'For the Game itself, I mean.'

'No, Melodie. I'll have to divine for you, explore the, er, ether. That way I'll reinforce fortune.'

'You will?'

Gold rings clamped on my hands. 'Melodie, Melodie,' I chided softly. 'You think I'd desert you, now we've found each other after all this time?' For a moment I floundered. How long did reincarnation take? Was it like a frog shedding its skin, ten minutes flat? Or was it something to do with the Egyptians?

'I know it! Look what happened last time, darling! That horrible Monsignor O'Cody *cleaned up.* Seven massive Church debts rescinded. You know what that is in dollars, darling?'

'Yes,' I lied with gravity, sighing. 'Amazing.'

She snorted angrily. 'I don't want to seem a sore loser, Lovejoy. It cost me, like it did the others. Costs hurt.' She gave a thrilled moan. I recognized the woe-filled ecstasy of the gambler. You see it every day in auction houses the world over. 'But I think O'Cody's a nerve. His line bid one point nine per cent of total funds last fall, and lost. Know what? He tried all sorts of persuasion. Indulgences, the Faith, every whining excuse you can imagine –'

'I wasn't here then, Melodie.'

'You should have been, Lovejoy! You know what he tried to do? Reschedule diocese loan flotations. Jim Bethune appealed to Nicko, got that stopped. I ask you!'

'Good heavens! Did things go that far?' I was completely lost now.

'They did! How could anybody look the De Beer hackers in the eye after that? Jim'd staked his usual three per cent auction levy. Kelly had some new theme park in the pot. And, I mean, diamonds are *diamonds*, Lovejoy!'

'True, Melodie. Long faces everywhere, I'll bet!'

'And the rest! Of course, this time there'll be none of that. Nicko's had to get quite firm. That's why I think Gina's so worried about this manuscript business. Fell like a damp squib when Denzie staked it. I mean, he talked it up – the Second Coming! Worth quite a bit, I suppose, but nothing compared to, say, the Commissioner's police hack.'

I sighed. 'But you try telling them!'

'One default, that's all it needs, darling. One default, and the whole house of cards falls apart.' She had her arm round me. Her eyes filled my view.

'And antiques, Melodie, er, love.'

'Of course! Jim Bethune could see his whole hack *vanishing.*' She was stroking my face. 'You know, darling, I could easily –'

A distant buzzer sounded. The hound yelped, flew under the

settee. Melodie moved away quickly, smoothing her hair. 'Look at the time!' she said brightly.

I recognized all the signs of a returning husband. Time to go.

I raised Melodie's hand to my lips with maximum sincerity, hoping I was doing it right. 'Until the next time, love.'

She hurried me to the door. 'When, darling? Quickly!'

'Tomorrow? Same time?'

'Yes! I've no visitors tomorrow. Take the stairs until the elevator's gone.'

The lift whirred, on its way. As Melodie's door closed, I ignored the stairs and scooted along the corridor, guessing doors. A faint clatter guided me. I can always sense the servants' entrance, my natural habitat. Chanel was doing the coffee mystique as I ghosted in.

'Lovejoy!' Instantly down to whispers, with her woman's instinct for subterfuge. 'What the –?'

'Shhh!' I made myself more frantic than I felt. 'It's her husband!'

She laughed silently. 'Dumb, Lovejoy. She ain't got a husband, just four exes!'

Four divorces? Melodie wasn't young, but her turnover rate seemed excessive. 'Chanel. I had to see you.'

The kitchen had two closed-circuit monitors mounted above the inner door, and a small wall panel. One showed the downstairs foyer, the other the penthouse corridor.

'Me?' Her surprise melted slowly into a smile. 'You outa your skull, Lovejoy? You passed up a fortune there.'

'When can I see you, love? I wanted to, er, date you on the *Gina*.' A faint buzzer sounded. She reflexively pressed an I'm-coming button. 'She wants me back tomorrow.'

'Horny bitch,' she scolded angrily. 'You watch her, Lovejoy. Come an hour earlier. My room's down the hall.'

The consol showed the lift gate opening. Two men strolled into view, one lighting a cigarette. The doorbell buzzed, its proximity making me jump. Chanel gestured me to stay and quickly left to answer, smoothing her dress. I waited until the screen showed Denzie Brandau and Jim Bethune admitted, then slid out into the corridor. I fled, the one thing I used to be good at.

Outside, New York'd never have known I'd been up to no good with Mrs van Cordlant. Everything seemed so normal. Traffic poured about. People tried to jump the red. Pedestrians survived by the skin of their teeth. Shops traded. A siren wailed the American song.

Hack? What stakes, exactly? Kelly had mentioned a game. What game was played by a Church? Police Commissioner? Silver bullion heiress? Property magnate? And on down the queue of wealth. Right down to the Brandaus with their miserable little stake of a supposed manuscript, supposedly now appearing after a century or so, in a manner as yet unidentified.

Thinking, shallow as ever, I posted off Bill's card to Gina with a note saying it was the phone number I'd reported the night before.

CHAPTER THIRTEEN

America's phones are bliss. Their habit of actually working is very disconcerting: put in a coin, dial and speak to whoever answers. I truly hope it catches on elsewhere. In little over half an hour, I made ten transatlantic calls to East Anglia and London. Cost me an arm and a leg, but I was over the moon. In East Anglia, a public phone is a dangling flex.

'Get through, Lovejoy?'

'Eh?' I wished Zole wouldn't keep doing that, suddenly being there with his bloody yo-yo. Hearing my name in this exotic paradise was queer enough. 'Oh, aye.' I'd told Boyson's pal I'd ring in an hour. If he wasn't home and waiting I'd . . .

'Stay cool, Lovejoy.' Zole was whizzing his damned yo-yo past my ear. It sounded like a mosquito, the sort that wakes you up slapping at air. 'Cool's no fool.'

'Why do you Yanks talk so?' I asked, starting across the traffic with the sudden rush of pedestrians as the green WALK light showed. I didn't particularly need to cross, but in New York you seize any opportunity. 'Gossip's a trash flash, honesty's a sleaze freeze.' I'd noticed this as soon as I arrived. A dim actor of notable physique was a punk hunk, a crosstown journey a side ride. All catch phrases.

'You mad 'cos you cain't talk, Lovejoy.' Whizz, whizz.

'Maybe true, Zole. Coffee?'

We went into a shop I'd never seen closed, perched on stools overlooking the tormented traffic. Zole ordered numerous hamburgers. How had he survived until he'd acquired teeth?

'Lovejoy, you stupid.'

I grabbed him by his tee-shirt. 'Listen, you arrogant little sod. Call me stupid again and I'll —'

'I'm doin' you favours here, man!' He dusted himself down with dignity. 'This is N'York, Lovejoy. You gotta do like N'York, see? Or you don't make it.'

'Make what?'

He sighed, wading into his grub. Seeing him eat made me hungry so I went and bought two of the nearest things they had to a pasty.

'Like, I say you cain't talk, you don't *agree*, man. That's the stupid. I say you cain't talk, you gotta say the same back, but real mean.'

'I have?' I was curious.

'And don't pay the fuckin' phone. You *works* it. Then you gets the call free, understand? You think Magda pays when she calls Tye ever' night?'

Magda, phoning Tye? 'It's illegal,' I said, to keep him going. I was learning.

'Legal's stupid, Lovejoy. Legal's jess N'York puttin' you down. I'll show you.' He looked about for a second, then appalled me by yelling, 'Hey, lady! Where's the ketchup?'

I went red. 'Shhhh, you little —'

'Comin' ride up,' somebody called, quite unconcerned. I smiled apologetically as it arrived. Zole noshed on, mollified.

'See?' he said eventually. 'I hollers no ketchup, you says you're sorry. They thinks you stupid. They *knows* I'm not. Like that book you buying.'

I stilled. How much of my phoning had the little sod overheard? 'Book?'

'Don't send dollars less'n you get it first, see? Stupid.'

I smiled at the obnoxious little nerk. 'Ah. That's just some money I owed him.'

'He don't squeeze, you don't pay, Lovejoy. That's smart.'

'It is?' I wondered if he had any leanings towards being an antique dealer. With his instinct for fraud, he'd do a bundle.

'Get the whole book, Lovejoy. One page is stupid.'

He'd heard everything. 'But what if —'

He glared at me in fury, yelled, 'Who's doin' the buying, man? You or him? You? Then don't pay's smart. Lemme talk to him.'

We discussed this proposition until we'd finished. I said I'd follow his advice, meaning I'd make sure nobody was listening next time, meaning Zole. I just hoped he wouldn't say anything to Magda. With her circle of clients I'd be done for in a day.

Brian Tarnley can't be trusted either, but that's because he's an antiquarian bookseller. The important thing about him is he owns a dingy upstairs room near Floral Street, Covent Garden. There, Easy Boyson works rent free.

It's a strange partnership, founded on two things. First is that Easy Boyson's daughter is Brian's wife. Second is that Boyson's on the run, has been these five years. He was unbelievably a major, as in rank. His august old regiment was understandably vexed when the regimental silver vaporized. The peelers failed to find Boyson, or the tom. Which was lucky for Brian, who'd married Easy's daughter and could provide the scarpering major with a safe nook. Investigations revealed gaping holes where the military's bulging bank accounts should have been.

Neighbours occasionally query the two Tarnley children's tales about a grandfather who lives in their attic and isn't allowed to come out and play. Brian tells everybody that Alice's dad's poorly.

Which is great for Brian, because Easy Boyson's a forger. And the police are still unravelling the handwriting on withdrawal forms in Glyn Mills, bankers of Pall Mall.

Zole followed me to the phone, eager to show me how to defraud the phone company. I declined, and told him I was phoning a lady and my talk was not for little boys. He went off disgusted.

'Easy Boyson? Wotcher. It's Lovejoy.'

'Where the hell are you, Lovejoy? A tank exercise?'

Brisk, military. I warmed to him. He still rises at six, spick and span by seven, ready for action.

'Conan Doyle, Easy. Do me a Sherlock Holmes page. You'll find examples of his handwriting in –'

'Leave recce to me, Lovejoy. Degree of authenticity?'

'Complete,' I said. Another fortune down the nick.

'Excellent!' Forgers love perfection. 'Continuation?' He meant was there a chance the buyers would want the whole thing later on.

'Possibly.'

'Right.' He pondered a moment, named a price that staggered.

'Fair enough.' I told him. 'I'll have it collected.'

'Good luck, Lovejoy. Regards to New York.'

And rang off. I supposed it was the traffic or something gave my location away. But Easy Boyson was an officer and a gentleman. Word his bond. Thank goodness for standards.

Then I used my last dollars to do something truly momentous. I scribbled a note to Mrs Gina Aquilina, saying I didn't quite know where I stood, but had faithfully followed her instructions, and had striven to identify the source of the Hawkins grailer. A sample page would soon be on hand, when I would send it. I signed it, put it in an envelope, and got a cycle courier to come to the coffee shop. He was there in an unbelievable space-age time of two minutes, and hurtled off on payment of my last groat.

Nothing for it. I walked all the way back to Fredo's, signed in for the remainder of the day, and started my cheery greetings to all comers. Until the fire touched the fuse.

Middle of the midday rush it happened, one o'clock and every seat in the place occupied, people arguing sports and politics and prices and traffic in the way I was growing to love, all peace and racket.

'Lovejoy? Take a break.'

'Wotcher, Tye.'

'Hey, what about my order?' a customer called angrily from along the counter as I doffed my apron. I shrugged. Zole had taught me how to yell, but not what to reply. Fredo tore out of his office in a state.

'Glad to catch your visit, Lovejoy,' he groused.

'Not be long, boss.'

Tye gave me a look that sank my spirits, conducting me to his car. It was misparked, but without a parking ticket.

'I don't know what it is about you, Lovejoy,' he sighed, opening his passenger door. 'But you're sure attracting Gina's attention lately.'

When you need a light quip, none comes. Ever notice that?

The road north from New York splits into a frond of motorways. We bent right, and distantly I recognized a stretch of water. 'Hey, Tye!' I went, excited. 'That's where we sailed!'

'Lovejoy. You a wiseass or dumb?'

He'd obviously got out of bed the wrong side. I ogled the scenery. Small towns came and went. Connecticut's pronounced with a load of Ds it hasn't got. The sun lit hills. Trees shone a strange and lovely russet I'd never quite seen before, quite like Chinese amber. We drove less than two hours, to a mansion with porticos and white pillars, lawns which people hate you to call manicured. No gates, but a goon in seeming somnolence that fooled nobody. He bent, peered at Tye, me, the limo's interior, shrugged us through.

'Reckon there's Civil War antiques here, Tye?'

He sighed, made no reply. We alighted and Blanche, lovely as ever but even more distant, ushered me in to a drawing room whose very length tired the ankles. Gina was sitting writing letters at a pathetic rubbishy desk, fetchingly decorating a window alcove against sunlight and olivine curtains.

'Lovejoy.' No sit down either. 'You found *what*?'

'The grailer, Gina. I think.'

She slowly ran her gaze from my scuffy shoes to my unruly thatch. I felt specimened, candidate for a museum jar.

Her slender hands held the card I'd posted, and my scribble. She didn't ask where, how, what. Just examined me. A reaming, draining inspection. Her eyes were bleak as a winter sea.

'What did I order you to do, Lovejoy?'

'Er, well, missus.' My voice quivers when I'm scared and my throat dries so it's hard to get a conversation going.

'*What?*'

I jumped, stammered, 'To, er, make up to Sophie Brandau, report what I learned.'

She beckoned me gently. I went close, stooped when she crooked her finger. Her hand lashed my face. The silly cow nearly ripped my eye from its socket, missing by a whisker. My head spun.

'And did you?'

'I've no money, except the marked stuff that'll get me arrested.'

She considered that.

'Lovejoy. I'm no longer interested in whether you're as innocent as you seem, or double shrewd.'

She could have expressed slightly more enthusiasm. I'd saved her from kidnap, or worse.

'Now I'm changing the rules. I give you orders day to day, understand? You start now.' Why do agitated women clutch their elbows when they march about? I dithered, not knowing if I had to follow her. She returned, halted, gorgeous. 'Tell me about the Hawkins thing.'

I did, speaking with utmost sincerity into her eyes and only occasionally losing my place. Whistling bravely past the graveyard, I said only what I'd rehearsed.

'I spent every cent on phone calls to England. Dealers I know, who owe me, ones I could trust. And I kept it down to no-name stuff.' I fluttered my eyes, the best I could do for shyness. 'A . . . lady I know. She's married. We used to be, well, close friends. I got her to sift her husband's reserve records. He's a big antiquarian.'

'So it's true? This . . .?'

'Manuscript thing? It seems so. She's getting me a single sheet, day after tomorrow. I'll divvy it.' I waited. 'I thought it'd be what you'd want me to do.' I was pleased with myself. She wasn't responding much, but I felt my tide turn. 'See, Moira could tell me anything. In bed or out, I'd have only her account to go on. I know me, see? I'm hopeless with women. I believe them.'

Gina paced, stood looking.

I took her raised brows as an invitation to speak on. 'Moira Hawkins is a lady who wants much more than she has. Deep down, she's ambitious. Look at me, Gina. I'm a scruff. I'm no Fauntleroy. Would she be seen in a restaurant in my company?'

'There's Rose.'

'Or the Brandaus?'

'You mention them together, Lovejoy. Why?'

'They're lovers, Gina. I'm not that thick.'

Suspicions are meat and drink to women, so I kept going.

'Sophie Brandau doesn't want the scam to succeed. She knows it's untrue anyway. Sophie's frightened. It's all got out of hand. She wants him to chuck it.'

'How do you know this?'

'It's plain as a pikestaff. I think Sophie hocked her jewellery so she could maybe buy Denzie out of Moira's scam.'

'What did she use the money for?'

'Buy the grailer?' I suggested, trying the American shrug. I tried it again, gave up.

She stood at the window, fingers tapping her elbows. 'How much is a grailer?'

'Depends on the amps.' Her head shook minutely so I'd explain. 'Amplifying factors. They work to tell you the price of an antique, anywhere.'

I lifted a gilt silhouette sugar bowl from the low cornish. The poor phony thing was trying to be genuine *Hausmaler* work from Augsburg, about 1725. 'This fake's from Berlin – see how they tried to get the proper silhouette of these flying birds? They went mad for Chinese fashion in the eighteenth century. This doesn't . . .' My words run out when I try to explain what happens. My chest should tighten and chime. I turned the lidded bowl over. Zilch.

'It's an 1880s fake. Price? Only two months' wages. If it was genuine, that counts one amp. If you'd got an original bill of sale from Augsburg, that's provenance and counts another amp. And genuine counts a third. Rarity, four. Is it of special material or mint? Five. Signature of the master, Johann Aufenwerth? Six. Then there's the grail factor, last of all. Like, say this was owned by Abraham Lincoln himself! Makes seven. Seven times two is fourteen. Hence the lowest price you can afford to sell it at is fourteen times the average monthly wage. See?' I replaced the chinoiserie carefully. She was listening, saying nothing.

'Some antiques have a base price – that's only the same, but compounded of amps to get the unit. Pearls, say. Get the quality first, expressed as currency units. Our unit is one pound sterling. Say you've a pearl, right? You phone a jeweller: what's this week's unit base average for pearls, ma man?' I was embarrassed, caught out doing my dud accent. 'He tells you it's one. Before you do anything else, you *weigh* the pearl, in grains. It's nine, a whopper.

The cost is exactly nine times nine, equals eighty-one quid *that day*. The price fluctuates. Like, next week's average unit base price might be two. Then your pearl's zoomed to eighty-one times two, see?'

I was suddenly conscious of a stirring behind me. Jennie and Nicko stood there. Malice was in the air.

With one woman I've always the feeling I've a chance. With two, and a criminally-minded lover of one who was also the husband of the first, I was in irons.

'You see what I mean, Nicko?' Gina asked, her job done. She went to her Victorian chaise longue, early repro but none the worse for that. She embellished it by just reclining. I envied it, quickly went back to being humble.

'He's a risk,' Jennie said. I disliked Jennie. She always sounded so bloody cold. I'd reported to her not Gina, about Bill. Then Bill was killed. Then Gina sends Tye to duff me up for not reporting. Aha.

'Maybe worth taking,' Gina suggested.

'For what, though?' Nicko lit a cigarette. 'I can't have any slip, this late stage.'

'For the Game.'

Jennie's sharp intake of breath endeared her to me even less. Nicko stilled her worry with a shrug.

'Where's the gain?' he asked. He stared balefully past me with his black eyes.

'We know Moira Hawkins is fronting something with Denzie Brandau, Nicko. We don't know what. Lovejoy here knows values. You heard him. Okay, so he's stupid −'

'Just a minute, Gina.' They talked on over me.

'− but that doesn't mean he can't be used.'

I tried to look useful, effective, anything to prevent my being taken away pleading like Tony.

'Used how?' Nicko asked.

'Like I tried. A plant.'

Jennie couldn't control herself. 'You tried that, dear.'

Gina's smile was cold. 'I underestimated Lovejoy. He's weird, but oddly effective. He's latched onto the Sherlock thing.'

'He says, dear.'

Women can put malice into that innocent word. It splashed like malevolent oil.

'He said himself it might not be the right one. But it's a superb effort without any resources.'

I liked Gina. She was brainy as well as beautiful.

'He'd have got close to Sophie if we'd funded him from the start.' I wanted to give Nicko a reproachful glance to remind him of his marked money business, but bottled out. 'We take him on staff, tell Denzie openly that Lovejoy rides with them as our inform-ant.'

'Have you thought of risks at all, dear?' from Jennie.

'Wait.'

Nicko sat staring into space. My attention wandered between the exquisite Gina and a piece of original Chelsea porcelain ceiling ornament above me. It was misplaced, of course, stuck there without any other decoration to support it on the walls, but it was exuding a lovely warmth that any genuine antique gives –

People were talking.

'Answer, Lovejoy,' Gina commanded. 'What will you require?'

'A small sum to send for the sample page.' I explained I was getting it on tick. 'And to know enough to stop being scared I'm making mistakes.'

That earned me a blast of black-eyed laser from Nicko's eyes. To my disgust I found myself begging.

'Well, for Christ's sake. I'm on a tightrope every waking hour. I'm given orders I don't understand, not knowing if I'm going to get myself topped or not, beaten up –'

'The number he gave checked out,' Jennie said.

'Right, Gina. Do it. Your can, okay?' Nicko rose and walked from the room. Jennie had to scurry to catch up before the door closed.

Gina was smiling-not-smiling. 'Allies, Lovejoy. Welcome to the team.'

'Do I get the chance of a bath? Paid?'

'Money, yes. But not the reward you're holding out for.' She smiled genuinely now, sipped her drink, feline. 'Plus one very very special benefit.'

'What?'

'You're in the California Game, Lovejoy.'

'Thanks, love.' Like hell I am, I thought. I'm off out.

CHAPTER FOURTEEN

Shopping is hell. God knows what women get out of it, but for me it's Doom City. Today, it was even worse, because I'd been sent out with Orly, who clearly hated me.

'For a start,' I grumbled as we trekked from shop to shop, 'everything's new. Different with antiques.'

'Lovejoy.' He stopped, right there in the middle of Fifth Avenue, arms full of parcels, and tried to stare me down. It didn't work, because I was in the California Game too, whatever it was. 'I don't trust you. You're a loose cannon. You'll roll about the deck and sink our ship. I know it. Okay. But don't try charming me. You're today's Fifth Column.'

'Don't hold back, Orly. Spit it out.'

He didn't smile.

'There'll be a comeuppance, Lovejoy. You'll die the death. After you're buried I'll laugh all I want.'

'Orly,' I said, riling him who was determined to be riled. 'Did you think that silk tie was worth the money? Only –'

He dumped the parcels in our limo – it was following us – and marched imperiously into the next store.

'Orly,' I tried every so often. 'How comes it that you and Gina, well, y'know? While Nicko and Jennie are . . . ?'

'Stupid,' was all he said back.

I noticed Zole ogling us from across the street. He saw me in a brand new off-the-peg suit, trendy shoes, striped shirt. His yo-yo almost froze in mid-air. He didn't come across, though I waved. I wondered what they'd say in Fredo's.

I got into the car after him and tapped our driver on the shoulder. 'Manfredi's Eatery, mate.'

'Orly?' the driver asked.

'Bugger Orly,' I said 'I told you Manfredi's.'

We drove to Manfredi's. I endured a few minutes of leg-pulling from Della and Lil, was congratulated by Josephus in a melodiously outdated rap, envied by Jonie, and caused Fredo moans of outright grief by resigning. No sign of Rose. I made them drop me off at the corner by Hawkins's, and got a satisfactory ping! from the little bell over the bookshop door. Seeing Orly's thunderous face as the limo rolled away was pleasant.

Rose was at the desk, invoicing.

'Lovejoy!' she cried, flushing red as fire. 'I thought you'd left us in the lurch!'

I bussed her cheek, looked round smiling. 'Won a few quid on a, er, betting game.'

'You look splendid! Moira'll be thrilled!'

'How's Moira?'

Her expression clouded. 'Busy. She's at a meeting.'

As ever, I added for her. With Denzie Brandau. I did a stroll. No customers behind the stacks.

'Listen, Rose. This money I've got. It could take you and me to Southsea. We could bring over the Sherlock!'

'Uh-huh.' Another New York enigmatic, meaning anything you cared to read in. 'Well, that's great, Lovejoy!'

Meaning I was to serve, not lead. Okay, but it wouldn't do.

'I'll book our flights, okay?' I coursed over her indecision. 'Tell Moira we'll be there and back within a week.'

'Wait, Lovejoy,' she tried desperately, but I'd already bussed her and was out of the door heading off down the street, calling that I'd be back about four.

For a couple of blissful hours I delved into the public library, Fifth Avenue west side, looking up California and various people, with patchy success. Nice library, though the white marble and the smug lions by the steps cloy, and its marble candelabra are a bit much. I loved it. No sign of Zole at the corner, so I used the public phone. Still amazed by the cheapness of the USA phone system – ours in UK's three times dearer.

'Lovejoy. Locations, please. Moira Hawkins, Sophie Brandau.'

'One moment.' And, less than five seconds I swear, the girl gave me both.

'Ta, love. I'm going to the latter.'

Moira at a hotel restaurant in which, surprise surprise, Denzie Brandau happened to be chairing a campaign fund-raiser. Sophie was at home, so I phoned her, asked her could I see her urgently in strictest confidence. I got a taxi to Park Avenue, where the doorman fawned. Flung to the penthouse by a lift that just managed to judder to a halt before crashing out into orbit, I rang the bell. Sophie herself came to the door.

The Theory of Sexual Understanding is mine. I created it. It works between a man and a woman. It's this: everything's up to her. I coined it years ago over a bird I fell for over some antique she said she owned. God, I slogged, broke my heart, agonized, plotted, just to get near her. Nearly four whole days. I finally gave it up as hopeless on a rainy Thursday at an antiques auction. She came in, offhandedly told me she'd brought along her Roman mosaic glass bowl, about 10 AD. (These small objects, astonishingly difficult to fake, are still pretty common.) I shrugged and went with her to the auctioneer's yard.

In her car, she practically raped me, whimpering and ripping at my clothes. The car windows mercifully steamed up and the auction was under way so nobody saw us. I hope. Her preoccupied husband was at the same auction. See what I mean? I'd set out to win her affections, against all odds, and failed. Then she decides on frontal assault, and it's the halleluiah smile. Of course, the lying cow really hadn't got a Roman mosaic glass anything, so my love didn't stand the test of time and I ditched her for a vicar's widow whose collection of Continental barometers came up for sale about then.

My ToSU worked the second Sophie opened the door. I myself am never quite sure when a woman takes the decision. But I am certain it's always up to her. We blokes just trot along obediently hoping the whim's in the right direction. But I knew I was favoured. Not that she did anything to suggest she was about to. I mean, her reception of me was almost exactly the same as Gina's, by which I mean an erg above glacial. She looked imperial, gowned as if for an evening do.

No maid, I realized, but that incidental's never more than half a clue, and open to misinterpretation.

'No, thanks.' I declined the offer of a drink. 'I didn't come because of your antiques, Sophie.' I didn't need to mimic hesitation. I was worried enough. 'It's that something's really wrong. But I want to help, any way I can.'

'I know.' She didn't mind her hand in mine.

'Look, love. I've been taken on the payroll by Gina, to advise on antiques. I've been told it's to do with the California Game. I'm telling you this, well, because.'

'What are you saying, Lovejoy?'

Why ask me? I wasn't really sure. 'Anything I can do for you, love, I will. I promise.' Aghast, my brain shrieked caution, not to make frigging promises that might get it killed. I wallowed on just because of the way she was looking at me.

'I need help, Lovejoy.' Tears welled in her eyes. She suppressed them, came to.

'I don't mean I'll help Denzie. I mean help you.'

Drive a harder bargain, you pillock! shrieked my brain in a panic. What's she giving in return for lobbing us both in jeopardy?

'Please, Lovejoy. He's not a bad man. Honestly. I promise you. He's just . . . wayward, driven by ambition. He's a consummate politician, capable, kind. Everybody'll tell you. He's in line for the next presidential nomination. People don't know Denzie. I don't know which way to turn, not since Moira inveigled him into taking a half share in the Sherlock stake.'

I let her talk through her exhortations, hopes, fears. I rose and went to stand, as if in deep tortured thought, before a decorative shelf of pewter tankards that pulled me like a magnet. I'd been dying to inspect them ever since I'd stepped into the flat. I was so excited by what I saw I almost shouted the joyous news to Sophie. In the nick of time I remembered I was in spiritual anguish, and just loved that dulled glowing metal. They were stupendous, the only complete set of Channel Isles tankards I'd ever seen. The giveaway is the measure, for obstinate old Jersey people still use the 'pot', which is a cool 69.5 fluid ounces. All six stood there, each with cunning little double acorns on the thumb catches. I stood, warmed with love. How many ancients had drunk from them in their two centuries? You don't get love like that any more –

'Lovejoy?'

Sophie was asking me something. She'd come to stand beside me. I turned away from the pewters, heartbreak coming easy.

'Shhhh.' I put my finger to her lips. 'I promise I'll help Denzie.'

'You will?'

My brain resigned, stormed out of ken shrieking abuse and insults. But what could I do? She was closer, letting her hands touch my jacket and gradually raising her gaze from my chest towards my face and then opening her mouth ever so slightly and keeping her eyes fixed on my mouth as she gave the gentlest of tugs so we were closer than ever and what could I do when it's women decide every single time?

'Darling?'

Sophie moved with a woman's awkwardness from sin into confession. I never have any problem shifting these gears. They do.

'Mmmmmh?'

Women's greatest – maybe only – mistake is to chatter straight after love's made. Beats me why. What's there to say? But they find something, anything. If ever I find a woman willing to stay mum during that transitory death after loving, I'd love her for now. I know I keep on about this.

'Darling. I didn't . . . you know? Just to . . . y'know, Lovejoy?'

'Mmmh?' (See? They don't even know themselves.)

'I don't want you to think, well, just because.'

'Mmmh.'

'You don't, do you?' Apprehension raised the ending, so a denial would suit best.

I gave up, carried the small death along, rolled over to find her propped on one elbow. The bedroom was semi-dark, curtains drawn. We were a million feet off the ground, but she'd had to ensure we were safe from the prying balloonists.

'Look, love.' I couldn't stop looking at her breasts. She covered them by gathering her nightdress with her spare hand. I hadn't remembered her donning a nightie, but orthodoxy rules. 'If you think I'm that cynical, then −'

She shushed me. 'I just want to hear you say you don't think that way.'

'Do I need to, love?' I'm easily confused. Was she asking me to deny an affirmative based on a denial of a suspicion . . . or the opposite?

'Please.'

'Very well.' No chance of escaping with a light laugh. I cupped her lovely face. 'Sophie Brandau, your anxieties are unfounded. I admire you. I fell for you instantly. I'm head over heels in love with you.' I gave her a quiet smile, my sincerity revealed.

She sighed in relief. The answer she'd needed was in there somewhere.

'Thank you.' She lay back, thinking. I waited. After confession, the penance. They go for both together. Sometimes I wonder if it's women whose instincts determine religious liturgy. You could make out quite a case.

'Lovejoy. Were you . . . shocked by, well, by it all?'

What the hell now? 'You want the truth?' I asked with reluctance. 'Yes, quite frankly. It was something . . .' Words are such sods. I never know which ones women want.

'I knew it, darling. I could tell. But you must realize. America's a harsh country. Below the surface we don't make any allowances. It's dog-eat-dog. The California Game's that.'

At last I was in. A moment's thought, so as not to spoil the drift of her talk, then, 'But why need it be quite so . . . ?'

Women are good at jumping to conclusions, even when other people haven't the faintest idea what they're talking about.

'Enormous is America's way. And it isn't necessarily corrupt. The sports percentages would still get slipped to some syndicate no matter who was playing the championship. Political nominations always have been fixed. Drug companies have done secret deals ever since they were quoted on Wall Street. Drugs arrive in tons, not ounces, so payola rolls on over all Federal enforcement agencies. It's the American way to grab a piece of the action. A percentage of major-city real-estate development always gets hived off . . .'

Antiques, business, labour movements, union dues, local politics, imports. I listened, wondering. Game? Stakes?

'I just wish it had stayed at that level for Denzie's sake. But ever since Moira's crazy idea that he'd have a cast-iron presidential ticket, he's been like a mad thing. It was Moira's idea to add it to the stake.'

'Shhh, love,' I said. 'Hold together for a moment. Forget all this. You've an ally at last.'

We lay embracing, langour and warmth stealing over us.

'Darling?' she said at last.

'Yes, love.'

'Are there . . . are there different ways of making love?'

Sometimes, women don't expect uncertainty. They're positive we blokes know everything about sex. You lose credibility by showing hesitancy. It's one of the few times reflexes come to help. Even my brain went along this time. We answered jointly in the affirmative.

Orly delivered me at Bethune's, by 74th Street near Columbus Avenue. I grumbled because I was starving, and Anita's Chili Parlor exuded aromas that made me weak at the knees. Even if it was spelled wrong – America's got rotten spelling – we could give it a try. Orly wouldn't hear of it, hurried me in.

The place itself was another disappointment. The showroom was nearly bare, with a few Edwardian bits of furniture, a silver salver or two, a scatter of paintings that had yet to age into conviction, a couple of scientific instruments – a microscope, sextant, a couple of timepieces – of modern design. Fatty Jim Bethune came to greet us, cigar in pollution phase, waistcoat bristling pens.

'Lovejoy, huh? You're going to revitalize the antiques stake, huh?'

'How do.' I put out a hand. He ignored it, shouted to a matronly assistant to take five, and wheezed into a captain's chair – fake, lacquered brass studs, railings set into coarse six-ply. We sat on a poor 1940s couch fraying in a desperate attempt at authenticity.

Orly gave me a warning glance. Whatever it was, I was in the California Game now. Gina'd said so. Presumably just as much as this gentleman. We were all evidently sharing one stake.

'He doesn't know much about the Game, Jim,' Orly said.

'Then what the hell? Sheet, this ain't no nursery.'

'He's a divvy, a scammer from the old country.'

'Jees.' Bethune wheezed, coughed, spat phlegm into a huge handkerchief. His hair flopped with every breath, side to side with metronomic regularity. I watched it, fascinated. 'What you do, Lovejoy?'

'Do?'

'Jesus H. Christ.' He stared. His eyes were rheumy close to, set small into putty features. 'You think N'York's a pushover? That it?'

'Well, actually –'

'You listen up, dumbo.' He leant forward to prod. 'Jennie passes word, okay we got to. But you're shit here, right?'

The pause seemed long to me, but maybe it was infinitesimal. He took my silence as meekness. He was nearly right.

Ash fell onto his waistcoat. He looked shop soiled. It crossed my mind that maybe Jim Bethune was less than superb at running the antiques side of things for the Aquilinas and their stake in the Game. Maybe I was here as a stopgap? Catalyst?

'We raise our part of the stake, Lovejoy. From antiques. You heard antiques?' His flab oscillated with merriment, settled as the wheezes died. 'We take a cut of selected prices from the auction houses. We're currently adding a national museum to our contributions . . .' More splutters of amusement '. . . They start contributing next week. In time for any little card playing we might wanta do.'

I waited for the jubilation to lessen. 'How do you make them chip in?'

His eyes were beads through a smoke veil.

'This dumbo's going to raise our ante, Orly?'

Orly smiled weakly.

Bethune spoke quite kindly, as if he'd realized at last that I was no threat.

'We make a bomb threat against a museum, right? It's glad to pay a little, stop them bad old bombs. Same with auction houses. It's regular money.'

'You accept payment how?'

His pleasantry evaporated. 'That's no concern of yours, boy, and don't you –'

He stubbed his cigar, lit a fresh one from a humidor younger than himself. In an antiques warehouse? But I was all attention to this mastermind, and clearly listening with nothing less than total admiration.

'Pay? Okay. They see Bethune's gets antiques to the value of the protection money. I sell, and that forms the stake, see? It's simple, easy.'

'That's amazing, Mr Bethune!' I exclaimed. 'Don't they go to the police?'

I felt Orly stir, as if he suspected pretence.

'Police, Lovejoy?' Bethune grinned, charred teeth sausaged in two rolls of pink blubber. 'We got friends there.'

I warned myself not to overdo it. 'But suppose this museum doesn't pay up?'

He was amused at my naivety. 'Why, a little fire in their basement. Nothing serious.'

'Marvellous, Mr Bethune,' I said, clearly thrilled. 'Well, thank you for explaining. Is there anything you want me to do? I'm ready to help.'

He smirked at the very thought. 'Not yet, Lovejoy. I'll be sure and let you know.'

'Orly. Anything else to add?' I asked meekly.

He was puzzled, but a little wary. 'No. Jim's covered it all.'

I rose, smiled, said thanks. 'Then I'd better report in. Can I use your phone, Mr Bethune?'

There was one on the wall nearby. I rang the number, got the girl with the mechanical voice.

'Lovejoy. Urgent for Mrs Aquilina, please.'

Waiting to be connected, I smiled at Bethune, who was telling Orly about some joker who'd wanted to negotiate a reduction in the protection fee. Fatty was very, very relieved I'd proved such a mug.

'Gina? Lovejoy. I've just finished with Mr Bethune. Yes, Orly's here.' I listened, nodding as she asked if everything was satisfactory. 'Yes, definitely. Mr Bethune's done a perfectly neat job. Pleasing himself. He's a dud. Replace him forthwith. Brains of a rocking horse.'

The line was silent a moment. Gina asked, 'Can he hear this?'

'Yes. Bethune's right here.' I looked back. Bethune's complexion had gone muddy, his eyes currants in plaster. I gave attention to the phone. 'Still there, love?'

'That was unwise, Lovejoy. You should have –'

'No orders in antiques, love. Anything else, I'll hear and obey. This cret's ripping you off. He's taking a double cut, first on the levy, then on the antiques' selling price. He's hiving.'

'Hiving?'

'Taking a toll on every transaction. Your income's less than half what it should be. Before you ask, no, he's not told me the figures.'

'What action do you recommend, Lovejoy?'

'Do I get paid this time?'

She got the joke. 'No. You're being well paid – in dollars. Jennie's fixed your account today. You'll be pleasantly surprised.'

'However much, it's second best.' Into her gentle laugh I said, 'Bethune? Save him. Demote to second advisor.'

'But Orly has other duties. So who'll be first?'

'Me.'

'I might have guessed.' She hesitated. 'One thing, Lovejoy. After what you said, you've got to raise the income for our stake in the California Game. You understand? Whatever Bethune raised, you must double.'

My throat was suddenly dry. Maybe Sophie had taken more out of me than I'd realized. 'I understand.'

'I'll send immediate help, in case.' A pretty hesitation, then, 'Good luck, Lovejoy.'

I hung up. 'Right, lads,' I told the pair cheerfully. 'Let's get down to it. Jim, you're sacked. Okay?'

They'd both risen, appalled. The antique dealer was gazing across at the windows, the low-grade antiques, as his world imploded. Orly was motionless. He was an irritation, this one.

'Gina's sending a team along. Here, Orly. Do you reckon that Anita's place does takeaways? Hop across and bring some grub. I'm starving.'

He moved towards the phone. Enemies nark me, especially as I'd done nothing to make him my foe. 'No, Orly. Bring it yourself. Plenty of them bread things. And be quick about it – or I'll tell teacher.'

Orly was white. He swallowed, exhaled long and steadily. The effort to walk out of the door was superhuman, but he did it. Thoughtfully I watched him go. Funny, that. It raised the question of whether Gina was in league with the private scam Orly was running, or whether he was in it only with Fatty Bethune. But I'd peeped from Mrs van Cordlant's kitchen, and seen Bethune and Denzie Brandau paying her a clandestine visit, which raised the question of whether . . . My head ached.

'Jim,' I said quietly to the fat man. 'A quick word.'

A limo slid to a stop outside, illegal parking. Tye Dee and three Suits alighted, came in. I waved. 'Wotcher, Tye. Can you have a quick shufti round, see the doors are locked, and bring the staff? That means everybody, okay?' I was beginning to like this okay at the end of everything. It was sort of inviting, friendly. Tye scattered his people. A neat dapper bloke entered carrying a briefcase. I sighed. Accountants were arriving.

'The office, please. Impound all files, get them in some sort of order, okay?'

'Right.' He beckoned a clone and a secretary to follow.

'Right, Jim,' I said quietly. 'Tell all. Including the private thing you've got going with You-Know-Who, okay?' I nodded to the street, terse and cryptic to show I wasn't bluffing even if I was. 'Orly'll be back in a minute. It's as long as you've got.'

I was in a hurry to find Magda.

CHAPTER FIFTEEN

The Benidormo had slipped into almost total decay. The desk man had crumpled into dust the instant his telly cooled. The phone was layered in rime. I once saw a sea village flooded on the spring tide. This foyer looked like the aftermath without marine life stirring beneath the tatty carpet. Nobody about. For reassurance I went back to peer into the street, shivered, went upstairs to my room wondering if the world had vanished without me. Eerily, a western saga was shooting off to no Zole. For once I was glad to hear a rhythmic pounding from Magda's room.

Ten minutes, then the bloke left. Magda's abuse was crisper than before, more desperate in a way I found hideous. She followed him along the corridor yelling invective. His growled reply was inaudible. I gave her a few moments' grace, tapped on the door. It flung open.

'Who the sheet . . . ? Lovejoy! You're . . .'

'Here,' I said. 'Hello, Magda.'

Her hair was embattled, her face marked. Derelict is as derelict does, where a woman's appearance is concerned. I used to think women were barmy, forever at mirrors with paints. I now admit they're infallibly right about make-up. In fact I'd go so far as to say that cosmetics are essential, the thicker and gaudier the better. You can't have too much, though women of course think the opposite, being wrong again.

She looked ninety, haggard, death on sticks.

'In yours, Lovejoy. Not here.'

She doused the telly, did that swish of hair and sat on the edge of the bed. The lazy hotel swine hadn't made it. How many nights had it been since I'd last slept there?

'He beat you up?'

'A couple since.' She had a sort of defiance, as if she expected me to whale into her too. Odd, because I'm never really narked with people, not often.

'How are you managing, Magda?'

'Not as good as you, Lovejoy. Fancy suiting, handmade shoes. Your lady's a spender.'

'How's Zole?'

'Okay. He brung good two days.'

'Stolen stuff?'

Magda lit a cigarette. She was spoiling for a fight. Her clothes were ragbag, shoes on the welts and soiled. When a woman's lipstick gets ragged at the edges, it's all up.

'Lovejoy, you stupid fucka, listen up. That set's here as a signal, see? Zole brings his loot when it's off, stays away when it's on. I'm getting rubbed off the street out there. Girls team up when hooker bookers move in.' She was trembling, smoking in drags, pluming the blue aside from a twisted mouth. 'You're just too stupid, okay?' She dabbed at her hair, surrendered.

One thing I'm bad at is knowing what to say when a bird weeps. I wish we'd been taught things like this at school, instead of calcium chloride and the Corn Laws.

'When you didn't come back, Lovejoy, I thought they'd . . .'

Done for me? I had money to give her, but not straight off. I'm not as dim as all that.

'I need your help, Magda.'

She looked up at me from the bed, disbelieving. 'Help? Shag's all I do.'

'I may be going somewhere.' I paused too long. 'Okay? I need somebody I can trust.'

'Lovejoy. I got something to tell you −'

I shoved her down when she tried to stand. Give me a battered bone-weary prostitute, I'm as tough as they.

'I know about the phone calls to Tye, how much you were paid.'

She was baffled. 'Whyn't you beat me?'

'I have people for that now, love. They're better at it.' Not much of a joke, but she calmed with a non-smile. I didn't quite know how far to risk the little I knew. There's that Arabian saying, isn't there: doubt your friend, sleep with your enemy.

'If I've guessed right, I'll be travelling out of New York, several places, in a hurry.'

'Somebody after you?'

'No. But I'll need somebody around.' The surprised understanding in her eyes made me speed through a denial. 'Not a bird wanted on voyage. I need somebody close by to do the occasional job, keep contact, be at certain places.'

'You want me? What about −?'

'Take Zole. I'll pay you, and fares.'

She was casting about the space just as Fat Jim Bethune had.

'Outa N'York? I never been . . .'

'You'll need clothes, Magda.' I'm always wary about telling

women things about their gear. 'Though your frock's pretty, er, smart, love, it might, er . . .'

'I'm in fuckin *rags*, Lovejoy.' She ran a finger across her cheek against wetness. 'Is this up real, Lovejoy?'

I pulled out a small wad. Bethune's money, until I'd given harsh orders to the accountant.

'Dress Zole reasonable, nothing way out. And don't take any lip from him. He's coming. I'll need him for couple of specific theft jobs. Okay?'

She looked. 'How d'you know I'll not blow the money?'

'I trust you. Don't show yourselves in your new stuff, or somebody'll guess.

'Be here every even hour from midday tomorrow, twelve o'clock, two o'clock. Understand? Ready to go.'

'Lovejoy, I'm scared.' She still hadn't put the money away, but her pocket was torn and she'd left her handbag in her room. 'I'm not . . . so good at reliable.'

She was scared? I nearly did clout her one when she said that. I drew slow breath. 'Magda. This is your frigging country, not mine. You've got to look after me, okay? You just remember I'm the one who's got to be looked after, not selfish cows like you.'

She appraised me, nodding slowly. Age was slowly fading into youth. A glim of a smile nearly showed.

'You're right about that, Lovejoy. Deedy.'

Different woman, same opinion. 'First job's to collect something from the airport.' I passed her a piece of paper with a flight number. In the safety of Zole's absence I'd dared a phone call to Easy Boyson, who'd been going mad. 'It's a stiff envelope. You'll have to pay out of that money. Bring it with you.'

We said a number of okays, some doubtful. She headed for a mirror. I left then.

The cocktail party I was made to attend could have been better placed. I mean, New York's galleries and museums are famous. Think how superb a splash in some prestigious museum would be, with antiques and paintings all around so you needn't see people swallowing oysters and stabbing each other. Instead, you could respond to the melodious chimes of a Wedgwood jasper, a Blake drawing, see the brilliant leaves tumble on a Sisley canvas.

But it was a posh hotel. We swigged, noshed the groaning buffet and everybody talked. The people were all there from the boat, including Moira, Commissioner Kilmer, Denzie and Sophie – the former paying little attention to Moira except when their looks accidentally lingered. Good old Melodie van Cordlant was there, meaningful with glances and arm squeezes. Jennie was with everyone, curt except with Nicko on whom she fawned. Orly clung to Gina, talking loudly and occupying her every moment. Berto Gordino, lawyer of this parish, came with Kelly Palumba, for whom Epsilon the showbiz magnate competed in shrill tones. Kelly looked a million quid. Long might it last, I thought. Monsignor O'Cody was last to come. Jim Bethune was at the far end of the room, now in his Sunday best, being spoken to by Tye Dee in an undertone. Hey ho, I thought with sympathy.

'Canapes, sir?'

'Ta, Chanel. Home team playing today, eh?'

I was the only one eating. All the rest were swilling at other troughs.

Chanel checked we weren't overheard, said, 'Always is the home team, Lovejoy. You gotta believe it.'

Mr Granger called out that all guests were invited through into the conference salon, where drinks would be available. I complained that I'd only just started, but there was a concerted rush for the double doors. I grabbed a load of rolls, cheese, some slabs of egg-looking thing, while Blanche hurriedly loaded up more for me. No pasties, and biscuits are New York's lack – mind you, they'd only have tons of cinnamon in. I was last into the long room.

Places were marked, as for a wedding reception. Kelly had started giggling, was being shushed by Epsilon and Berto Gordino. I found my name card between those of Orly and Gina.

Nicko appeared, with Jennie, took the position of authority.

'Jim Bethune sends his apologies, friends.' He had one small piece of paper before him, served up by Jennie. 'Lovejoy's taking his place from now on.'

'Is that legit, Nicko?' Denzie Brandau asked easily, smiling round the table. 'First I heard of it.'

'It is, Denzie.' Nicko seemed oblivious of the sudden silence. 'Any questions?'

'Where exactly does Lovejoy take over from Jim?' Charlie Sarpi asked. I wondered how he managed his moustache. Sophie prevented herself from giving him the bent eye just in time. Gina was watching her across the phony mahogany.

'Right away, Charlie. Every level.'

'Look, Nicko.' Denzie did that politician's shift to indicate exasperation. It consists of obliquely arranging his trunk, plonking a hand firmly on the table, arm outstretched, and crossing his legs. 'Who *is* this Lovejoy? I mean, where's the beef?'

'Lovejoy'll double the antiques stake, Denzie. There's the beef.'

A ripple of interest ran round the table. Monsignor O'Cody peered down at me, specs gleaming.

'How'll he do that, Nicko?' Commissioner Kilmer barked. It was honestly that, a sharp yap, grossly out of keeping with his tall bulk. I don't know what he'd been like as a young bobby, but even ageing as he was he put the fear of God in me.

The silence meant me. I was eating my grub, which I'd made into rolls. I can't resist anything in bread. I hurried the mouthful, swallowed.

'Lovejoy?' Nicko said.

'No, thanks.'

The silence now meant???

'What the hell's that mean, Nicko?'

'Stay calm, J. J.' Nicko let me swallow, come up for air. 'Lovejoy. You must bring in double what Jim Bethune did. Do you know how much that is?'

'Yes, Nicko.'

His hands opened expressively. He was so patient, but getting quieter. Any minute those dark lasers he used for eyes might actually swivel onto me and sear the inside of my skull. I didn't want that.

'Are your methods so secret they can't be divulged?'

'Nicko.' I shoved my tray away, showing my sincerity. 'I'm out of my depth here. Oh, I'll get the gelt.'

Nicko's gaze charred nearer, less than a yard from my right shoulder. Even Gina leant away. 'With help?'

'Yes. I'll need two helpers, full time.' Before anybody could cut in, I started my spiel. 'See, I don't know who's on our side, Nicko. I know you are. And Gina. And I think Jennie. But these other ladies and gentlemen I don't even know. I don't know what the stake is to be – everything I cull from antiques? And for what?' I tried to spread my hands like Nicko but it didn't work and I felt a prat so put them away. 'This Game, Nicko. Tell me who's got a right to know, and I'll come clean about my methods, every detail.'

'The Game in Manhattan is finished, Lovejoy.' Nicko looked at Jennie, got an imperceptible assent. 'On the *Gina*. Remember?'

'I was behind the bar, Nicko.'

'He's stupid,' Commissioner J. J. Kilmer barked.

Nicko nearly smiled, leant forward. 'Let's hope you're not this stupid about old furniture, Lovejoy. The Game. We're the players,

Lovejoy. At first, we play against each other here in Manhattan. The stakes are based on personal . . . wealth.' Now he did smile. I wished he hadn't. 'It's up to each player to raise his or her stake. Nobody is allowed to default. The stakes can come from anywhere.'

'Tell him,' Jennie put in. It sounded a question but wasn't. .

'If a player were to bring personal cash, Lovejoy, we'd be limited to however much he or she could withdraw from a bank account, right? So we accept promissory notes. Then the sum waged can be relatively huge.'

Jennie took over. 'Very damaging, Lovejoy, in a city where any major withdrawal is noticed by Manhattan's wallet watchers.' She held the pause, waited for my nod.

'And you can bet next year's takings?'

Jennie smiled. 'You got it, Lovejoy. If the bet's mega dollar, and based on certain illegal practices –'

'Not that word, please,' from Berto Gordino in anguish. 'From selected activities, Lovejoy.'

Once a lawyer, I thought.

'– Why, it's easy to handle. Suppose a Police Commissioner were to bet fifty per cent of the police hack and lost, okay? He'd simply raise his hack. That's the stake.'

I looked round the table. Bullion prices would be lifted fractionally to provide the losing margin if Melodie lost. Hadn't she said something about Monsignor O'Cody fiddling the diocesan funds? Politics was Denzie Brandau's wager – presumably he peddled influence in the time-honoured way, for a price. Charlie Sarpi was a drugs man, Kelly Palumba the real-estate queen, Epsilon the showbiz hacker . . .

'If the game's over, what're we all here for?'

'Because you lost, Lovejoy.'

'I what?'

Nicko smiled. His eyes were miles off now, thank God. 'Everybody here pays their losses into the kitty. That kitty's the stake when we get to LA. For the California Game.'

'Thus getting a share in the New York wager.' Jennie was dying to spiel out a load of figures. I could tell.

'Which I shall bet for us all in –'

'– In the California Game,' I said. 'All New York? One bet?'

'He makes it sound unfair,' J. J. said, inventing the wheel with his first-ever try at irony. People chuckled.

Melodie intervened, dear thing. 'You see, Lovejoy, we gamble to see who wins here. In New York, see? In Florida, why, they're

doing the same thing. Then there's four bets come from the Mid
West, six from California, one from Washington . . .'

'The Game itself's held yearly, Lovejoy. Each bet's the produc
of sectored interests.' Nicko shrugged. 'It's up to each to get the bes
possible finance behind them. The bigger the stake, the bigger the
win.'

'What's the Game? Cards? Roulette?'

Nicko chuckled, hailstones on tin. 'The entire loot of the nation
Lovejoy.'

'For twelve months,' Jennie amended. 'Shared among us, in
proportion as stated. The Game on the *Gina* was to decide who play
in LA and the total stake.'

I drew breath to ask my one remaining question, but Orly was
already sniggering. 'Except you, Lovejoy,' he said. 'You're the one
here with no share. Yet.'

'Methods, Lovejoy?' Nicko could afford to look all cool. He'd
won megamillions. Except now he had to gamble it for higher stakes
still.

'I said double Bethune's stake,' I reminded him calmly. 'I mean
quadruple.'

He tilted his head Jennie's way as if interrogatingly. 'It's in ten
days, Lovejoy. Nobody could possibly hack so many millions from
antiques in so few days.'

'Anybody lend me an aeroplane, please?' I asked, rising. 'And
I'll need a bank account – paying-in purposes only.'

'A moment, Lovejoy,' Gina said, but I twisted my hand free.

'I can hear them clearing away the grub out there. I'm starving.
I gave a bright smile down the lines of faces. 'Can I get anybody
anything . . . ?'

I just caught Blanche and Chanel wheeling the last trayfuls out
thoughtless cows. They only laughed when I ballocked them about
it. You'd think women'd learn, wouldn't you? It's a wonder that I'm
so patient. I warned them that one day I'd lose my temper altogether
but they only laughed all the more. It's no good trying to tell women
off. They're like infants, only laugh and think you're daft.

Somebody inside had come to a decision by the time I returned
with my tray. Nicko promised a private jet, two goons, a secretary
and licence to travel.

Nobody mentioned chains, but they'd be there, they'd be there

CHAPTER SIXTEEN

Jennie was efficiency itself, I'll give her that.

Thirty lasses came, mostly skilled, beautiful, drivingly ambitious. I picked a small timid bird called Prunella, in specs, clumsy, dressed plain. No wonder the US excels. I didn't know a hundred words per minute was humanly possible. They all knew computers and could start instantly. I was worn out, told Prunella to start in twenty minutes.

'You'll never regret this, Lovejoy,' she told me with solemnity. 'This is my greatest opportunity, travelling secretary. I've always been a halfway girl, y'know? Sort of nearly getting there —'

'Prunella,' I said. 'Rule one: not much talk.'

'You got it, Lovejoy.'

We were alone in the foyer of the Pennsylvania. 'There's another thing, Prunella. I'll need certain, er, commercial tasks done in great secrecy. They'll fall to you.'

She was over the moon. 'Economic espionage!' she whispered. 'Lovejoy, rely on Prunella!'

I was to remember that, later.

My team assembled at Pennsylvania Station. Tye was along, of course, monolithically, saying nothing. I'd told him not to come armed, and he'd agreed. I didn't believe him. He needed a secret howitzer. I had a first real look at Prunella in action: today with obvious contact lenses a foot deep and extraordinary flying elbows, as if protecting her files. I'd slimmed my team down to just us, was now having misgivings about my wisdom.

'Prunella,' I said wearily as she scattered her files all over the coffee shop for the umpteenth time.

'Sorry, Lovejoy.' She retrieved them.

Jim Bethune arrived, gave Tye the bent eye.

'I don't believe this,' he said. 'Us? Up the stake in the 'ckin *Game*?'

Travellers were pouring past. Touts were touting. We were scrunged up at a small table, at least those of us not dropping folders. The coffee was dire, first bad quaff in this wonderful land.

'Which museum are you milking, Jim?' If he had any thoughts of undermining my position, now was the time to disillusion him.

'Lovejoy,' he said, confidence swelling, 'this is between you and me, right? I don't discuss business in shitholes.'

'Tye,' I said evenly, 'get rid of him.'

Tye rose, hauled him upright.

'Wait a minute, Lovejoy. I don't mean –'

I gave him my saddest. 'Jim. You've blown your one chance. Goodbye, and good luck.'

He clawed desperately to stay by the table as Tye started leaning towards the exit. A boy with a white forage cap by the popcorn stand edged nervously into the walkway.

'You can't do this, Lovejoy! Metropolitan Gallery of Arts. Bickmore's the boss . . .'

Tye walked him out, returned. Bethune stood outside staring in, kid at a toffee shop window perishing of neglect.

'Right, team. Prunella, you come with me. Tye, you also, but act like a chauffeur or a private assistant, okay? Jim's to be brought in once I've got going.'

'We need him?' Tye asked, surprised.

'Essential. Let's go.'

On the way to the street I told Prunella to phone Bickmore and get an immediate appointment; subject: security.

The Metropolitan Gallery of Arts claims to be the largest in the western hemisphere. It's right, but I'm not too sure about the arts bit. Don't misunderstand me. It's got tons of genuine art. It's also got tons of stuff that is hard to classify. I can't come to grips with a massive cube with a grandiose title. I allow that it's art, but not my sort. I need this big stone block to tell me something about the bloke whose name's on the caption, and it doesn't. That off my chest, I admit that any place with 3.3 million works of art truly is a wonder.

Bethune waited nervously by the information desk while Prunella scurried on ahead, Tye patiently scooping up her dropped papers. I spoke harshly with Jim. It was difficult moving, because of the Madonna and Child. The terracotta was set in a nook by the stairs at the end of the enormous hall. Blue and white glaze is often a giveaway, as here. It bonged like a cathedral bell into me. I believed the Andrea della Robbia label – it was his uncle Luca who enamelled glazes this colour onto terracotta. I'd seen pictures of it, loved it for years. Who hasn't? But to see it in the flesh –

'Lovejoy? Mr Bickmore's waiting.'

Prunella scampered alongside, shoes clacking. 'Are you all right, Lovejoy? You look —'

'Never heard of hay fever?' I told the silly cow, then felt sorry when she fumbled in her handbag for medicaments.

The office was grand. Bickmore was a tall, arid man of the old school. He had a knack of being willowy, so he could peer over his bifocals. I'm used to the worm's eye view. And I've been put down by every trick in the book. I smiled, shook his hand, sat as Prunella's files cascaded around.

'Prunella's been with me a long time, Mr Bickmore,' I said. 'The only polymath in my corporation.'

'You're not American.' He was broad smiles. 'What museum is your favourite back home?'

We chatted a while about the British Museum, a few others, just enough to prove I was on intimate terms with their layout. I supplied him with a card citing me at Nicko's office address, and was in no doubt he'd checked before letting us in.

'It's a matter of security, Mr Bickmore,' I said pleasantly. 'Yours, not mine.'

His split-level specs sloped disapproval. 'You're not selling, Love-joy?'

'I'm not. You are. We bought tickets,' I added, smiling to show no hard feelings.

'Think of it as a suggested donation, Lovejoy.'

'Always makes fees seem easier, Mr Bickmore.'

'Security,' Bickmore said coldly. 'If it's a matter of —'

'Of the protection money you were going to pay.' I let the silence solidify. I'd warned Prunella not to be shocked. She was scribbling it all down, pen flying.

Bickmore gave orders to an intercom, rose and closed an intervening door.

'Protection money?'

'Prunella? Get Mr Dee in, please. And Mr Bethune.'

Bickmore watched Tye and the dealer enter.

'Mr Bethune? Tell Mr Bickmore, please.'

Fatty spoke, face wooden. 'It came to my notice that the Met Gallery was being oppressed by the protection racketeers. I've paid for you, and will continue to do so.'

'For the foreseeable future,' I finished for him irritably. Give me strength. The silly sod had only two lines to learn, and he'd ballsed them up.

'Why would you do that, Mr Bethune?'

'Lovejoy persuaded me by his reputation, Mr Bickmore.'

'Thank you, Bethune,' I said. The pillock's delivery had been putrid. Tye left with him.

'Well, I'm very, very grateful, Lovejoy!' Bickmore said slowly. He waited, Prunella's pen zoomed, I waited.

He was a shrewd old administrator. He cleared his throat.

'This makes a considerable difference to our finances this coming year, Lovejoy. I shall make out a report to the Trustees. The Board of Regulators will be eager to express . . .'

His speech dried. I was shaking my head. 'I, er, influenced Bethune to show my good intentions, Mr Bickmore. I'm eager to see your Gallery of Arts survive. I can't have this lovely . . .' I coughed. There's a limit to falsehood ' . . . this hotchpotch of a building damaged. Millions of customers come every year. Some might get injured.'

He looked from me to Prunella. 'But it is protection? You're after money?'

'No, Mr Bickmore. I'm after painless money.'

There was a plan of the building, floor by floor, occupying one entire wall. I crossed to it, trying to seem sure of myself. I guessed Prunella was coming along from the crash of tumbling clipboards.

'You've got the Rokeman Primitive Museum incorporated here, Mr Bickmore?' I nodded. 'All those Benin heads, Nigerian sculptures, tribal items. Fantastic, eh?'

'Lovejoy. If you're making some sort of threat . . .'

I turned away, knocking into Prunella who was just then rising from having picked up her things. What the hell had she brought all that stuff *for*, for God's sake?

'There are threats and threats, Mr Bickmore.' He was a secret smoker. I recognized his wandering hand, edging under stress towards his waistcoat pocket's rectangular bulge. 'Think of a threat that brings money in.'

His hand halted. Maybe lessening tension.

'A profitable, ah, threat?'

'Plus a percentage of it to someone else.'

He thought for quite a time. I looked at the plans, flicking idly through catalogues and year books.

'Lovejoy,' he said finally, fingers tipping together. 'This scheme, to increase our finances. Is it the sort of scheme that could be announced to the media?'

'Media's a must, Mr Bickmore,' I advised gravely, and his face wrinkled into a guarded smile.

'Can you explain the details, please?' he asked. 'Coffee?'

There are skeletons in every cupboard. The Met Gallery of Arts has them a-plenty.

Just like the British Museum – which has bought fakes, duds, phonys, wasting millions in its time – most museums have spent fortunes on fraud.

I reminded Bickmore of this in detail, until he suggested we send Prunella out for a rest. I declined.

'The Elgin Marbles were purchased in good faith, proper legitimate bills of sale and everything,' I continued earnestly.

'True, true!' He was delighted to find common ground in international law.

'So your Veracruz figures – especially that fifteenth-century Standard Bearer, and the one they call The Smiler – really *should* be here.' Pause. '*I* think, Mr Bickmore. And those Ecuador and Peru vessels too – incidentally, are they really Chavin period? Though I'll bet your Peru gold mask's really a Chimu, right?'

'What are you saying, Lovejoy?' His voice had gone thick. Mine does that.

I leaned forward confidentially. 'Supposing one of those nations' ambassadors started a row at the United Nations . . .'

He bristled. 'Lovejoy. I will not countenance any return of any of our legitimate –'

'Or illegitimate? Like that Maya series of tomb artefacts you bought three years ago?' I wasn't disclosing confidences. Every day brings fresh tales of important scams like the grave-robbers of Italy, the poor old Mayas, the threadbare Aztecs. Civilization spreads at exactly the pace of tomb-raiders.

'I deny every insinuation, Lovejoy!'

'Sit down, mate. Think a minute.' He subsided slowly. I could hear his grey cells starting up with a whirr. 'A series of articles in some Latin American newspaper, raising all hell about the national treasures you've got here. Their national treasures. Or in an Accra daily, with African politicians complaining of neo-colonial exploitation. Get the idea?'

'No.' He spoke only for Prunella's pen.

'Let me explain. World headlines yell: It's those bad old Yanks again, nicking antiques. The world loves shouting this slogan.'

'So?'

'So you issue a denial – the same ones you used over the Tairona Columbia items, the Kwoma New Guinea ethnics. Isn't it a bit odd, incidentally, to have those near the North America exhibits?' He didn't answer. I smiled now, home and dry. 'You raise the admission fee – okay, recommended donation – to that gallery. Cloak it in mystique. You have a special guard, get local volunteers on oh-so terribly vital vigilante duties, maybe even restrict the number of visitors.' I spoke over his shocked gasp. 'You sell a certificate that they've seen it on the Great Dispute Day. Do I have to spell it all out?'

He removed his glasses, possibly for the first time since birth. 'Nothing creates interest like an argument.'

'Wrong – like a *patriotic* argument.' I watched his smile begin, slowly extend, eliminating wrinkles. 'You're the patriot who takes on the might of . . . well, pick a country.'

'There's one thing, Lovejoy. No ambassador has criticized us to the United Nations, not for three years.'

'Not for two years, six months and seventeen days, Mr Bickmore.' I smiled and stood, extending a hand. 'I honestly do think another's about due any day now.'

He came with me to the door. 'We haven't cleared things up, Lovejoy.'

'We have,' I said. 'Six times what Bethune cancelled.'

He spluttered, reeled. 'Six times?'

'It's simple. You up your special ticket. Respond to the news splash, you'll not know what to do with the money.'

His only grief was the thought of a fraction of the income slipping through his sticky administrator's fingers. 'But that's an impossible fee, Lovejoy!'

'Not a fee, Mr Bickmore. Think of it as a suggested donation. Ready, Prunella?'

By the end of the day I was worn out. We'd done over half a dozen museums, all official places with superb antiques, paintings, furniture, stuff I'd have given my life to halt at and adore. But that was the point: my life was the stake.

It's called a 'trilling' in the trade. That is, you introduce a kind of pressure from a third person – nation, ambassador, whatever you can think up – and shove it onto a second person. You yourself are the first person who makes up the prile. The problem is, you're inextricably linked, bonded for life in a trilling. It's not just a once-off, some deal you set up and close tomorrow and it's goodnight dworlink at the door. Oh, no. A trilling's everything but a marriage, though there's even less love, would you believe. The one important factor different from all other con tricks is that big trillings need big organization. And even little ones sometimes do. Our UK trillings occur in London, Newcastle and Brighton. I've only been in two in my time, and was lucky to get out of both.

We did trillings on the Brooklyn Galleries Centre (sorry, Brooklyn Center), the American Numismatists' Society Museum, two Modern Art galleries where I drove a harsh bargain because I was feeling bolshie and Prunella and I'd had a row because by then she'd got the bit between her teeth and was geeing me along like a bloody tired nag. Plus the Museum and Gallery of Broadcasting Arts off Fifth Avenue at East 53rd Street where I drove one harder still on account of I blame them for time wasting. Oh, and the Natural History place. That was a particular difficulty I'll tell you about, in case you ever do a trilling.

You vary the trilling, of course. The threat of an international lawsuit wouldn't work with a Natural History place, at least not much. But I had little compunction, what with the Natural History Museum of the Americas standing on Eighth Avenue, Central Park West, and being the size of London. It chills my spine. I mean, stuffed animals are all very well, but the poor things should have been left alone, and I'm not big on dinosaurs even if 2.8 million New Yorkers see them every single year.

It's a question of tactics. I had to raise the great Disease Scare Tactic on this occasion, telling the gentle Mrs Beekman after an hour's jockeying that she would soon hear a clamour that would close her museum, possibly for good, if she didn't accede to my humble request for a small fraction of the ticket takings. She was a harsh bargainer. I was practically wrung out by repeating my gilded threats under her vociferous cross-examination.

I told her, 'Our London churches are excavating their crypts all over the city. They have devoted doctors to check there's no diseases itching to pop out and grapple with the populace. Understand?'

'London had its problems in the seventeeth century,' she said primly. 'So long ago, wasn't it?'

Okay, so she knew that diseases fade away. 'The public doesn't know that, lady. And what with Aids, series of unknown viruses yet to be announced . . .'

My clincher was promising to have specimen newspapers delivered to her next morning, carrying banner headlines announcing Contagious Disease Risks at Natural History Galleries, adding regretfully that it might be difficult to prevent them falling into the wrong hands. I also promised that she'd be saved the bother of legal claims filed against her museum. She tried the police threat. I asked her to phone Commissioner J. J. Kilmore and talk the matter over with him.

She surrendered eventually, she guaranteeing a payment of fifty cents on the dollar. I guaranteed a bonus: her request for staff increases the following year would be given favourable mention in high places. I wouldn't pass that on to Denzie Brandau, of course, because I was lying. She'd really put me through it. I'd tell Jennie to pay a fraction of each Natural History instalment into a numbered bank account in, say, Philadelphia. In Mrs Beekman's name, of course. Safety does no harm.

Trilling ploys are not necessarily animose. You can have quite friendly gambits. Like the Bickmore one. I mean, that would bring money pouring in over the transom. We'd get a share, but so what? A plus is a plus is a plus. The Numismatists – loony obsessionals the world over – were a pleasure to deal with, because I could faithfully promise a major find of certain hammered silver coins, right here in New York State! The bloke was really delighted, because the carrot (there's always got to be a carrot in a trilling) was that the hoard would be mainly the sort his main foe collected.

'Fall in value of your pal's collection?' I guessed.

'He might be inclined to sell,' he replied evenly.

'Good heavens,' I said just as evenly. 'Whereupon you'd buy them, the day before the coins were revealed as counterfeit?'

He fell about at that, me laughing with him.

'I'll see the publicity's done right,' I promised. 'Fancy some early English hammered silver coins, soon to be discovered at Roanoke? Only, I've got some maniacs back home who'd be really keen to have a regular thing going . . .'

See what I mean? Some antiques people are a pleasure to do business with.

That evening I totted up the sums fleecing in soon, and found I'd bettered Jim's by a clear six-fold. It took me two hours on the phone with Prunella close by reading her notes in the hotel at Pennsylvania Station where Jennie had booked us in. I fixed all the frayed edges, the outstanding threats and promises, settled the transfers, formed up a method of checking on the payments with Gina's accountants, and had the contributors listed at Jennie's.

Prunella was paid. She was flushed, exulting.

'You know, Lovejoy,' she said, transported. 'I'm on a high! I'm flying! The girls back at the agency would never believe me.'

'Will never, Prunella,' I warned. 'Confidentiality. Besides —'

'Yes?' she breathed.

I thought, what the hell. I might never get out of this. 'Would you care to stay for supper, Prunella?'

'Supper? Oh, yes!'

It's the one way to guarantee silence. As guarantees go.

CHAPTER SEVENTEEN

Four o'clock in the morning I sent Prunella home – pedantically reporting the fact on the phone to a somnolent Tye, to show scrupulous observance of the syndicate's rules. He was narked, but it gave me the chance to give Prunella instructions about collecting an envelope from a certain international airline. I gave her the flight number.

'I'm depending on you, darling,' I told her wide eyes. 'It's life or death. Bring it when I send for you.'

'Oh, Lovejoy! Nobody's ever depended on me!'

I tried to look disturbed, exalted. I was knackered. 'I love you darling, okay?' But that didn't sound quite right. There's more to okays than meets the ear.

That was two incoming envelopes, Prunella and Magda. I rang the syndicate number.

'Morning, Gina. Lovejoy. I'm leaving New York this morning on the jet. What guards do I have?'

She made the plumping noises of a woman rudely wakened, tried to unthicken her voice into day.

'Tye'll decide. Where to?'

'I'll be hacking the New York auction houses in a very few days from now. Meantime, I'm flying to six different states.'

'You've already raised the necessary sum, Lovejoy?'

'You might need an edge, love.' I left space for her to explain why now suddenly we needed less money, but she said nothing. Well, suffering women have a right to privacy. 'My list's at reception.'

'No,' she said quickly. 'Courier it to me. Now.'

Christ, I thought. She's in greater difficulties than I'd guessed. I streaked to my room, wrote out a list of addresses culled from the public library, and gave it to the motorcycle maniac. Ten minutes flat.

A word about hotel night staff. They love things to do. I gave them five minutes to settle down, then remembered something very vital, and made them get a second courier. I sent him to the Benidormo with a note to Magda, to hurtle back with her signature as proof. I tipped them, said both couriers should go on the one bill, please, for simplicity's sake. That way, I'd be the only person who knew about Magda and Zole tagging along. Then I roused Tye and told him we were moving.

By nine o'clock we were in the air, heading south in slanting sunshine over the biggest, loveliest land God ever lowered to earth.

The entourage included Tye, two bulky goons called Al and Shelt who sat with knees apart and literally ate non-stop, peanuts, tiny savouries, crisps, popcorn. I'm making them sound friendly, but I'd never seen such menace in all my life. And a brisk stewardess, Ellie, all cold eyes and no repartee. The pilot Joker, his pal Smith, and that was us.

Is America superb, or isn't it? Its hotels can get couriers, any hour. A *pilot*, would you believe, accepts that business considerations are enough! It all seems so normal that you start wondering why the whole world can't be just the same. On the Continent you get the exhausted glance at the watch, vague assurance that maybe sometime . . . In England the pilot − assuming you could speak to such a lordly technocrat − would ask what's so special about your business that it can't be changed to suit his convenience . . .

The coffee was superb, drinks were there, and I could have had a film shown if I'd wanted. A suitcase of clothing was provided, I learned.

So what was wrong?

I concentrated. I'd sent out for two books and nine magazines before breakfast. *And got them!* I wasn't sure how my plan would stand up to stress, but I was beginning to have an idea whose side I was on.

'Tye?' I said about one o'clock. 'Can I get a message sent to the ground?'

'Anywhere, ten seconds.'

'Time the US upped its performance,' I said. 'Joke, joke.'

The lassie swished up, poised for duty. I sighed. There's only a limited amount of efficiency a bloke can take. I put a brave face on it, and asked her to get a print-out of Manhattan's auction dates, and anything she could muster on George F. Mortdex.

'And send word that we're arriving for prospective interview with him or his deputy, from London, please.'

'What name are you going under, Lovejoy?' Tye asked.

'Mine,' I said. 'But we may not become friends.'

He said nothing, but passed his goons a slow glance. They nodded. I swallowed. Maybe I'm unused to allies.

'Is this a ranch, Mr Verbane?'

He beamed, walking ahead in his handmade tweeds, crocodile shoes. We followed his perfume trail.

'We use domicile hereabouts, Lovejoy. Virginia thinks ranch infra dig, y'know?'

He was effete, even bubbly.

The estate – all right, domicile – was not vast, certainly not much bigger than Rutlandshire. Noble trees, vast undulating fields with white fences and pale roads curling into the distance. It was beautiful countryside, which always gets me down. The house was the size of a hamlet. Civilization lurked within.

Swimming pool, tables on lawns, awning against the sunshine thank God, lovely white wood and orange tiles, ornate plasterwork in the porches. George F. Mortdex was worth a dollar or two.

Mr Verbane offered me and Tye seats on a verandah where servants were waiting to fuss. He accepted a tartan shawl round his knees. I avoided Tye's sardonic look, smiled and said I'd rough it without a blanket.

'We don't often get unexpected visitors,' Verbane said. 'We're so remote from civilization.'

A couple of gorgeous figures splashed in a pool nearby. Gardeners were trimming beyond. Grooms led horses along the river which incised the spreading lawn.

'I had hoped to see Mr Mortdex himself.'

Verbane sighed, all apology. 'That's out of the question. He's so old now, always works alone. I have to manage all his personal affairs.' He smiled, waved to the girls. 'Though it's an absolute *slog*. Racing's such a terrible obligation. You've no idea.'

'Responsibility's a killer,' I agreed.

'That's so right!' he cried, his self-pity grabbing any passing sympathy. 'I'm sometimes *drained*. How marvellous that you understand!'

'Like antique prices.'

He smiled roguishly. 'I knew it! You're an antique dealer!'

I smiled back. 'Antique dealers give antiques a bad name. Like boozers give booze.'

He passed glittering compliments to the waitresses over the drinks. He'd insisted on madeleines. I had a few, though cakes that little go nowhere and it was over an hour since we'd left the plane.

'I absolutely *adore* negotiating, Lovejoy!' He yoo-hooed to a sports car arriving at the stables. A lady in a yellow hat waved. I'd never seen such friendliness. I felt in a procession. 'What'll we negotiate *about*?'

'Mr Mortdex's collections,' I said. 'Their falling valuation –'

He sat up, focusing his attention.

'Falling? You're misinformed, Lovejoy. There isn't a collection that has withstood fluctuations better than Mr Mortdex's. I select and buy, on an absolutely personal basis.'

The tea was rotten cinnamon stuff. 'I mean Wednesday.'

He was a moment checking his mind. I knew he was desperate to dash indoors screaming for the computer, but he was perfect so couldn't be found wanting. Finally he swallowed pride, that costly commodity. 'What happens next Wednesday?'

'Your statue gets impounded.'

'Statue?' He tried indolence, then casual when that didn't work either. I'm all for façades, which are valuable things, but only when they're some use.

'Aphrodite. Fifth century BC, that you bought in a secret deal three years ago. Wasn't it twenty million dollars? That English art dealer who lives not far from Bury Street in St James's? Everybody was so pleased – except the Sicilians.'

A lovely bird did her splash, rose laughing from the pool in nice symbolism, yoo-hooed, looked hard at us when Verbane ignored her.

'You're thinking of the J. Paul Getty Museum in Malibu, Lovejoy. They're the ones who bought Aphrodite.'

'I heard,' I said. I waved to the girl for him. She returned the salutation doubtfully. 'Tye? Could you go down to the motor car, please? I think I've left that dictaphone thing.'

'You be okay, Lovejoy?'

'I'll shout if I'm in danger.'

We were alone. During the intermission Verbane summoned bourbon entombed in ice. He quaffed long, had another. I really envy these folk who can drink early in the day without getting a headache.

'I haven't any strong feelings, Mr Verbane,' I said as honestly as I could. 'Hoving's opinions about the Getty purchase aren't my concern. Though I wouldn't like to discount anything Hoving said, especially after he bought the St Edmundsbury Cross.'

'Are you claiming –?'

'Nothing. These rumours about a second Aphrodite being taken from Sicily and sold through London are the sort of rumours that shouldn't be resuscitated.' I saw his brow clear a little. 'Don't you agree?'

'Of course I do.' He coughed, took a small white pill thing while I waited with the silent respect all medicines deserve.

'I deny having Aphrodite, Lovejoy.'

'Course. I'll support you, if anyone asks my opinion.'

This scandal isn't quite a scandal, not as major art and antiques frauds/purchases/scams/sales go these days. It was just before the nineties that the Aphrodite row erupted. She's lovely, an ancient Greek marble and limestone masterpiece spirited – not too strong a word – into the harsh public glare which money provides for any valuable art form. The Getty people made honest inquiries of the Italian Government, and bought. Then nasty old rumours began whispering to vigilant Italian police that Aphrodite was stolen. Aphrodite (her name actually means 'Lovely Arse', incidentally, though the Romans called her Venus) is worth fighting for. The battle continues, though the value's soared in the meantime.

The rumours I'd heard had mentioned a second Aphrodite from the same source. Possibly a fake, my contact had said on the phone two days back. Well, Verbane's delusions were no business of mine. His support was. The antique trade's maxim is: sell support, never give.

'At a price, Lovejoy?'

'No. At a swap, Mr Verbane.'

'I don't trade that way. Mr Mortdex hates it.'

I could see Tye slowly heading back. I'd arranged a series of signals should I want him to take more time, I tried to flatten my hair reflexively. He instantly paused to watch the horses, now mounted and cantering. 'You buy at auctions, Mr Verbane.'

'I heard about you, Lovejoy.' No pansy mannerisms now. He was lighting a cigarette, cold as a frog. 'Doing the rounds, protection racket in museums?'

'You've been misinformed. I made a sale, in antiques. If your informant told you differently, she's lying. Which should set you wondering why, eh?'

He'd stared when I implied his informant was a woman. It wasn't as wild a guess as all that. The second Aphrodite was supposed to have been 'bought' by an American natural history team in search of lepidoptera near Palermo. Natural history, as in Mrs Beekman. I calmed him. 'Mrs Beekman didn't tell me anything. I'm a lucky guesser.'

'What do you offer, Lovejoy?'

'One per cent of your last valuation, paid into an account I shall name. Thereafter, one per cent of all your purchases of sales, same destination.'

'And you'll do what in exchange?'

'I'll tell you of three high-buy fakes, international market.'

He considered that. 'How do you know this?'

'That's for sale. And their location. And who paid what.'

'As *facts?*'

We settled finally. I declined his offer of a meal, though it hurt. By then he'd provided copies of the Mortdex Collection valuation. I promised him I'd have it checked by auditors who'd visit within the day, whereupon the naughty Mr Verbane produced a different sheaf of printouts. Managers of private collections are the same the world over.

He stayed me as I made to leave, reminding me of the promise.

'Oh, yes. Antiques.' I'd already worked out what he deserved. 'The Khmer art sculptures, South-East Asia. Remember the November sales?'

'Yes.' He was a-quiver, almost as if he'd bought a sandstone Buddha. 'I remember.'

I bet you do, you poor sod, I thought. 'Several were fake, Mr Verbane.'

He licked his lips. A girl called an invitation to come and join them. He quietened her with a snarl.

'That sandstone thing's recent, made in Thailand. Mr Sunkinueng who was Phnom Penh Museum curator —'

'But the reputation of Sotheby . . .' He was giddy. I'd have felt almost sorry for him, except I didn't.

'Reputations are made for breaking. That four-armed god sitting on a lion, from Angkor Wat, 1200 AD. bought by a famous American collector.' I looked about at the lovely countryside. 'Who lived hereabouts.'

'Fake?' he whispered. His lips were blue.

'Modern fake,' I said cheerfully.

'You said you'd tell me something I could . . .'

'Make on? Very well.' I thought a bit, as if I hadn't already made up my mind. 'You're rivals to the Getty Museum in California, right? Well, their male Kouros statue from Greece is said to be two thousand years old — by kind friends with a vested interest.'

He brightened, as they all do at the grief of rivals. 'But its attribution is doubtful?'

'Don't ask me. Ask Giuseppe Cellino — he'll tell you exactly how it was peddled round every antiques museum and gallery in the known world by a Swiss dealer for three years. He has all the addresses, times, dates. Don't say I sent you.'

Smiles and grief were still competing on his face when we drove away.

'Lovejoy?' Tye said as our limo paused at the entrance of the imposing estate. 'How much of all that was true?'

'All of it, Tye,' I said sadly. 'All.'

He was driving, taking us carefully out into the two-laner. 'Then how come these big experts don't know from fakes? That Sotheby Gallery place is supposed to be −'

'Tye,' I said, watching the great house recede into the distance. 'There's enough of us already in. Don't *you* start, okay?'

'Capeesh, boss.'

At the airport while Tye and his goons saw to the plane, bags, paid off the saloon car, I phoned news of the hack to Gina. Then phoned Prunella to get moving. I never carry a watch, but checked the time and reckoned Magda and Zole should be about halfway to my next destination. It'd be risky for her, but that's what women are for.

CHAPTER EIGHTEEN

We were airborne in an hour. Joker and his ambling mate Smith cleared us for landing in Chicago by dusk. I felt I'd been travelling for years. Tye's two goons were still uncommunicative, the air hostess Ellie of amphibian responsiveness.

Tye still hadn't mentioned why one of our tame vigilantes hadn't travelled with us to Mr Mortdex's ranch. Or why we'd been followed there and back, by a separate saloon motor that kept vanishing and reappearing. It even changed its colour once. I felt less friendly towards Tye now, because I was doing the business as well as anyone could, right?

'Tye,' I said over a meal of surreal splendour – Ellie ignored compliments – 'I have a secrecy problem.'

He didn't quite stiffen, but he was expecting Lovejoy Deception Hour. 'What things?' he asked. All his food came fried. I'd never met a bloke like him for demanding fried grub.

'It's between ourselves, okay?' I cleared my throat. 'You know Prunella? She's flying to Chicago, should be there now. I told her to book us in, er, together.'

He nodded, methodical with his fried burger slab thing, inch by square inch, regular as a metronome. His dining habits were admirable.

'So? She's secretary, right? Doing her job.'

'No, Tye,' I explained. 'She and I, er . . . in Manhattan last night. I've said she should meet us. I'll need a little time for a special . . . conference.'

'You n'her?' He swigged wine, not breaking his masticating rhythm. 'You got it, Lovejoy.' He paused. Three squares of burger accumulated on his plate. I realized he was laughing, possibly an alltime first. 'S'long as I know you isn't going any place.' Al and Shelt laughed along.

I couldn't get the hang of all that water. There were even ships on the damned thing. I'd thought we were a million miles inland.

'Where are we, love?'

Prunella had a map out in a flash, dropping notes and pencils like a sower going forth to sow.

'The Great Lakes, Lovejoy.'

I looked into the darkness. It was illuminated by a trillion lights, like a city of crystal on a gleaming shore. I shivered. Prunella squeaked I must be cold. I just caught her from upping the thermostat to critical. You've never met anything like the heat of an American hotel.

'You know what's wrong, Prunella? Your country's just too big, too beautiful, too everything.'

'I'm pleased you like it, Lovejoy. But we're a little short on history. I've heard of your lovely old buildings, traditions —'

I wanted to prove to Tye that we were ensconced in snuggery and up to no good. I chose my time carefully to open the envelope she'd collected from the airport. It contained the first of Easy Boyson's Sherlock forgeries, just the one page but pretty good. I was proud of him. I concealed it in my folder, told Prunella not to answer the door until I got back, and wore myself out descending the hotel stairs.

A taxi took me from the harbourside to O'Hare International Airport. I was glad to see the end of all that water in the non-dark dark. I'm only used to lakes you can see across.

Magda and Zole were waiting in a nosh bar. I was delighted to see them. Zole was having some sort of row with the manager over a gaming machine he claimed was rigged. Magda was pale and washed out. She looked smart in her new coat and shoes, matching accessories.

'I'm not used to this, Lovejoy. I done as you said.'

'Well did, love.' She'd never been out of New York before.

Zole came and smouldered, eyeing the one-arm bandits. 'Hey, Lovejoy. All Chicago's fixed.'

'Hey, Zole ma man,' I said. He sneered, joined us. 'You got a broad, Lovejoy? Or you aim t' be stickin' Magda?'

I'd almost forgotten how to have a headache without Zole around.

'Play the machines, Zole.' I gave him all my change. He sauntered away, hands in his pockets, head on the swivel.

Magda passed me her envelope. I took it.

'Ta, love. This address is a theme park, whatever that is. There's a big exhibition of antiques in a barn. Houses, rooms done up like in the nineteenth century. When Zole steals the item I've written down, make sure he walks within a few feet of me, okay? On his way out. Stay with him, and don't steal anything yourself.'

'Will we be all right, Lovejoy?' She hesitated, glanced towards the counter where Zole was having a heated exchange about the food prices. 'Only, you heard about our fire?'

'Fire?' I went cold.

'The Benidormo. An hour after we left like you sent round, your room blew a firestorm. Ours went too. A couple's hurt bad. A man died in the stairwell, burned terrible.'

'The hotel? My room?' No wonder she looked pale.

'I'm sheet scared, Lovejoy. Fires, guns. I had all thet crap, y'know?'

'You won't be, love,' I said, thinking of being followed at Mortdex's.

'I seed it on the news at the airport. Not Zole.'

I passed her some money. 'Love, any time you want to cut out, you can. But I still want your help. Book your flight soon as I leave. Tell Zole nothing except that I want him to steal the antique as a game, to . . .' I'd worked the phrase out '. . . to put the bite on somebody.'

She nodded. She'd had her hair done. I said she looked pretty, which made her go hard and call me stupid.

Zole, tact personified, helped matters along by telling Magda she should lay me quick and we could get back to the Big Apple. I stopped Zole trying to filch a woman's handbag from a table as we left.

'Give my regards to Joe and, er, Gertrude,' I said, bussing Magda a so-long in the main concourse.

'You makin' them up, Lovejoy?' the little nerk demanded.

'Yes, Zole,' I told him, to shut the little bugger up. We exchanged no further information.

The hotel stairs were a hell of a climb. Prunella welcomed me with relief. We made mutual smiles until sleep rewarded us with oblivion.

We flew over Illinois in broad daylight, Iowa, into Omaha with me breathless at the spectacle. I thought: This nation had to invent theme parks? It's one great glorious kaleidoscope. Maybe paradise is already down here, and we're so busy moaning and grumbling that we can't believe our own eyes.

With Prunella primly distancing herself from me – I'd agreed to her stern warning that we should not behave as if there was Something Between Us – the flight map showed names I couldn't honestly believe in. Manchester and Cambridge and Dedham, I'd accept those. And Delhi and Persia and Macedonia I'd take on trust.

'But Hiawatha?' I asked Tye. 'Peoria? Des Moines? Oskaloosa? Sioux City? Come on, mate. Who's making them up?'

Prunella's secretarial training came to the rescue. She had an hour's lecture on name-lore programmed deeply within, and was still explaining why Skunk River was not a myth when we separated at the airport.

The helicopter seemed so small. I'd only ever been in one before, and that under atrocious circumstances. I still get the shakes, and was silent for the whole flight, a little over an hour. I always keep wondering why they don't strap a huge parachute to the bloody things, in case its whirring blades spin off.

We landed beyond a small town that called itself a city, and were driven through woodland and glades, emerging onto a cliffy outlook over a river. You'd call it splendid, if you like countryside. The greeting I got I'd have called splendid too, if I liked phony.

'Preston Gullenbenkian,' the mighty orator intoned, fixing me with an intent beam. 'I'm yours in the service of the Lord of Hosts.'

'I'm Lovejoy, Reverend,' I said, feeling inadequate, like I'd met Wesley. 'You received our –'

Gullenbenkian intoned reverently, as if I was a gospel, 'Your word was heard, Lovejoy. And acted upon.' He paused, hand on his heart. 'It's my way. I want you to know that.'

We were outside a pile – as in vast unbelievable palace. I'd thought Blenheim was still in the UK, but here was its isomer overlooking that panoramic view.

'The mighty Missouri, Lovejoy.' He raised his eyes to Heaven. 'We must give thanks to the Lord for all His generosity.' He dashed off a quick prayer.

I dither in the presence of holiness. He was a tall, suntanned man, the sort who always get lead parts in Westerns. But his gear was perfect, his teeth glittering, his skin oiled and shining.

'And it's simple Prez, Lovejoy,' he resumed, leading me up the great straight drive. 'Sure, I'm in holy orders. But that doesn't entitle a humble, ordinary man to seize on outmoded elitisms.'

'That's good of you, Prez.'

He shot me a glance, casually acknowledged several youngsters loitering about in a not-so-aimless manner. Lads and lasses, they were long-haired, in sun specs. Two of them had rifles. Whatever he wasn't, Gullenbenkian was astute.

'Necessary, Lovejoy. Your people wait here.'

'Tye, please. See your pal gets enough peanuts.'

Tye and Al stood watching as the gospeller and I trod to the verandah. I daresay Tye had planted some sort of recording gadget on me this time, expecting this. Better if he had, so it wouldn't just be my word against anyone else's.

'What hospitality may I offer you, Lovejoy? Not often I audience somebody from your neck of the woods.' He laughed, a practised, all-embracing laugh. I'd always thought only monarchs and popes gave audiences.

'Nothing, thanks, Prez. I just came to talk.'

'Talk how?' The interior echoed. Baronial wasn't the word. It would have done for a duke, a prince. It was brand new, the ceilings vaulted, the stained-glass windows soaring, sweeping staircases curving upwards to a high domed ceiling. It was splendour so garish I almost couldn't speak.

'A money offer, actually.'

We passed through the hall and out into a closed courtyard. Three youngsters faded at our approach. A girl emerged, served a tray of drinks, retired. I wondered why they were all so scruffy.

The gospeller caught me looking after her and smiled.

'Not *my* devotees, you understand. The Lord's servants. They're wonderfully motivated in our service.'

'Who's our?'

'The Lord's. And mine. Instruments of the Lord's intentions here upon earth. Six months only.'

That old one. 'What happens if they stay longer?'

He raised his eyebrows. Every hair on his head seemed mathematically inclined, devoted to giving proper service. Steel-grey hair, bright of eye, gold watch clinking on his wrist.

'They don't. Many try, Lovejoy.'

'No second helpings, then?'

'None. Much better for them to live here a while, restore their flagging energies, the better to leap again into battle.'

He explained how each crusade into the major cities was organized, the thousand proselytizers who preceded him. 'We organize bands, marches, spectacular events.'

'Showbiz?'

'Got to be, Lovejoy. The Lord can't be made to hide.'

We chuckled, such friends. 'Which brings in revenue to build the Own Decree Crystal Dome?'

'Praise God, yes it does, Lovejoy. I'm pleased you've heard of our little enterprise.'

'Cathedral, isn't it?'

'They're already calling it that?' He was delighted.

'I'm afraid I haven't seen your television show, Prez. I haven't been in the US very long.'

He snapped his fingers. A serf darted out, to be sent for a

timetable of his broadcasts. For somebody not quite God, he was an impressive simulant.

'Your money offer, Lovejoy,' he reminded.

His lady – I'd seen photographs – joined us, bulbous and with the face of a doll. Disconcertingly, her voice was a shrill monotone. Her cosmetics were thickly trowelled on, lips protuberant with lipstick, her eyes deep in cream, liner, receder, heightener, lowerers, brighteners. I thought she was lovely.

'Annalou, Lovejoy,' God's sub belled melodiously. 'Come to see our Deus Deistic Theme Park, perhaps worship a little, and make an offer.'

'I'll be right glad to show you round, Lovejoy,' Annalou said. 'You be here for our broadcast?'

'Afraid not, Annalou. I've to be back in Manhattan within the day.' I stuffed the programme details in my pocket and we boarded a small electric car thing, driven by a long-haired kulak called Glad Tidings.

Annalou explained while Prez dispensed papal blessings to bystanders. 'Our devotees abandon all their trappings of the World Without while they sojourn here. Including their names.'

And property, the articles said.

We drove slowly down a gravelled drive through rose gardens, out into lawns and fountain courts where hymns played on chimes. Recordings of unseen orchestras piously serenaded us. People began to appear, wandering and smiling. It was like a film set, the people affluent, blissful, contentedly calling 'Praise the Lord' as we passed. I'm not used to holiness on this – indeed any – scale. I felt unnerved. Annalou fondly took my hand.

'The place gets to you, Lovejoy, don't it? Peace divine.'

'There's the theme centre, Lovejoy.'

Prez's voice was husky with pride. Turrets and towers formed a surround, for all the world resembling a child's wooden fort rimming an enormous glass dome.

We drove up among the thickening crowds of visitors. Prez was telling me it would be finished in two years' time, if investments kept coming.

'Investments?'

'Contributions are investments in holiness, Lovejoy. Joy repays joy!'

To my alarm they began singing a hymn. People all around joined in. I went red, feeling a duckegg, not knowing the words and feeling too stupid to join in even if I did.

We stopped at the main entrance. 'Praise all goodness, friends!' Prez said, shaking hands with anybody he could reach. People slapped backs, cried heavenly slogans. I nodded, tried to smile.

'Good be praised!' Annalou cried in her dreadful monotone, using her heavenly shape to wheedle a way through the crowd. I followed.

We were on a forecourt laid out with biblical scenes in mosaic, with tableaux showing prophetic events in grottoes lining the route. Close to, the glass Deus Whatnot grew to huge dimensions.

'So far, the only entrance we use is the small southern one, cloistered against evil of course by our famous Exhibition of Eternity.'

'It's in connection with that, Prez, that my financial –'

'A second's prayerful thought first, Lovejoy!' Prez intoned, hauling me towards the entrance. I understood: no money chat among devotees.

We paused before a waxwork tableau while he said a lengthy prayer. I paused respectfully, trapped by Annalou's pressing figure and Prez's athletic bulk. Visitors all about paused with us, praying along.

The entrance was done up like a church porch. 'See that it's Jerusalem, Lovejoy? Isn't the symbolism just cute?'

'Great, Annalou.' I wished she wouldn't crush my arm against herself so enthusiastically. Not in a church, even one like this. I was getting hot under the collar.

'Our Exhibition of Eternity reveals the splendour of God's own times, Lovejoy,' Prez said in a blast of halleluiahs as the crowd unglued and we started in.

'The antiques?'

'Evidence of former times when Good walked the earth.'

'I'm so moved,' I said to Annalou. And I really was. I could have eaten her with a spoon. No wonder the contributions – well, investments – came rolling in with a bird like this fluttering her eyelashes on your television set.

'I can tell, Lovejoy,' she whispered. If only it hadn't been in a monotone.

Somebody bumped against me, tripping me. I stumbled and would have fallen if Annalou hadn't been so close. Magda's angry face swam into my ken and vanished in a sea of devotees.

We had entered a kind of gloamy grotto. A waterfall cascaded before lights. Antiques were close. I felt a strong boom in my chest, and turned to see Zole ostentatiously swaggering out.

'Wait, Annalou!'

401

'Yes?' she breathed.

'You're sure all the antiques are in here?'

'Why, yes, Lovejoy!'

'There's one being carried out. By that little lad –'

She caught Glad Tidings, he pressed an alarm. Everybody froze. The hymns stopped. Lights bashed on. Devotees crowded in and marshalled us all along walls, whistles sounding outside. Annalou and Prez dragged me through the crowd out onto the forecourt.

'That way. I felt something really overpowering.'

'Felt?' Prez pondered that, prayerfully I'm sure. I saw Zole with Magda heading for a public long-distance coach, walking with composure.

'I'll tell you who has it.' I closed my eyes, swaying, overdoing things rather, but trying to keep in with the spirit of the place. Pretence is contagious.

'Freeze, everybody!'

Everybody stilled. Glad Tidings muttered that he should shake everybody down, where's the problem. I said to wait.

I stalked towards where Zole stood with Magda, opened my eyes, gave a quick wink at Zole. Magda was furious for some reason, but that's only a woman doing her thing.

'Hand it over, sonny, please.'

I held out my hand to Zole, quickly adding as he drew breath for a spurt of insolence, 'My name's Lovejoy. No harm will come to you, we promise.'

'You sure?' he asked suspiciously, little sod.

'We promise in the name of Good, don't we, friends?' I chanted. 'Forgiveness is all. Suffer little children to, er . . .' What the hell was it? 'And we shall be, er, blessed,' I ended a bit lamely.

'Here. It was just lying about.'

Zole gave me a statuette. I almost dropped it in shock as the red-hot glow spread into me and the bells thundered in my soul. I'd never, ever seen anything like it. God, but it was lovely, lying there in my hand where it belonged.

It didn't look much, just a small hard-porcelain figure of Moses with his tablets inscribed in Hebrew. But it was Chinese, old as the hills, typical feeling and colours. They're not even imitated (yet, yet!) by porcelain fakers on the antiques marts (yet!) so you're almost certainly in possession of a wonderful find if you've got one at home. They're supposed to come in a set of six, various Old Testament characters – Joshua, Noah, that lot.

Weakly I passed it to Annalou, and pulled out a roll of money.

This was props gelt, high-denomination notes drawn through Tye, to be returned in the plane. People gasped at the size of the roll. Ostentatiously I peeled one off, and gave it to Zole with a flourish.

'Here, sonny,' I said loudly. 'Your need is greater than mine, as the Lord sayeth.' Or somebody. 'Now, lady. Go and sin no more!'

'Praise the Lord!' somebody said mercifully.

'Amen!' I chirped. I was so moved I honestly felt tears.

Magda and Zole were ushered away, but I walked after them and beckoned a taxi forward from the car park line. I didn't want vengeful devotees inflicting an impromptu penance on them. I gave them what I hoped looked like a genuine blessing as they pulled out. Show over.

I turned, bumped into Annalou. Prez was talking in low tones to Glad Tidings and three other serfs. I dried my eyes.

'Lovejoy!' Annalou said, dropping her voice three notches and taking my arm. 'You're so sweet!'

It's true. I am. I was thinking what could have happened to me if that Zole hadn't done his stuff.

'God is in each of us, Annalou,' I intoned. 'Though I am the worst of His flock. Can I admit something to you, Annalou? It's this. I'm sore afflicted by lust – yes, even now, even as we were about to enter the temple of the, er, Deus.' I'd forgotten the bloody name. God, it was a mess. 'For you, love. I've never felt this way before, not even since I found the sacred Mildenhall Treasure, or that missing Rembrandt from Dulwich Art Gallery.'

'Not since . . .?' She took my arm. Her breast pressed against my quivering form. 'For little me, Lovejoy? You felt carnal sinful desire . . .?'

'I have to admit it, Annalou. The instant I saw you, I fell. I'm sure Satan sent me –'

'Shhh, Lovejoy.' Prez was approaching. The three devotees were looking hard at me. She whispered, 'Say nothing yet, Lovejoy. Until you and I've had a chance of a prayer together.'

I composed myself and together we went into the Exhibition of Eternity. I paid the admission fee with a large denomination, and managed to look offended when the devotee offered me change.

Two hours later I was breathless and stunned.

Take any – for that read every – art form, cram it into a partly finished glass building arranged as caves, crystal porticos and arches, alleys and terraces, all under one great luminescent ceiling. Add dancing fountains, glass chapels and glowing altars rising musically from the ground. Add moving glass walls with portraits of bad, bad art ('Unfolding in eternal sequence!' gushed Annalou). Add automaton choirs, electrically powered with glutinous hymns pouring out from crannies everywhere, on stages which rose and sank. Add Eternal Damnation with a fire shooting from a bottomless pit where automated gremlins stoked furnaces and electronic groans put the fear of God in you. Searchlights reamed away in dark corners – 'Let there be lights!' Prez crowed ahead of us.

'The greatest scene of all, Lovejoy!' Annalou told me, more friendly than ever. 'Real Genuine People choirs are still the greatest pull!'

The RGP choristers sang, swaying delirious with joy. People clapped in time and rocked to and fro.

They were all dressed in cottas and cassocks, reds and whites and blacks. Microphones, that least sanctified instrument, dangled and amplified.

'A small choir, only a few folks come, see?'

'A big choir means a bigger crowd, more revenue?'

'You better believe it.'

The Sanctum Antiquorum charged a special admission fee. You got a plenary indulgence on a Parchment of Prayer, for an extra fee. It looked like real parchment to me, which raised the unpleasant thought that some sheep somewhere had given one hundred per cent.

'This is a genuine scale copy of the Vatican Museum's forum, Lovejoy!' Annalou claimed. 'We're hoping to buy a church from your Wiltshire, complete with gravestones, and install it as an added attraction in a Cornice of Contemplation.'

The antiques were a mixture of fake, fraud, and the genuine. Paintings, mainly Italian School, mid-eighteenth century, a couple of frescoes, walls from genuine old monasteries, arches and pillars from Germany, a couple of French cloisters. It was a marvellous show, but an impossible mishmash. Yet what's wrong with that?

Silver chalices, gold monstrances, rings claiming kinship with ancient bishops and saints, a chunk of everything vaguely religious was included. There was a hand-shaped left-handed tea-caddy spoon I particularly fell for – once used in Catholic services for shovelling incense into the thurible at High Mass. (Tip: any collector will give his eye teeth for a left-handed one of those, being so much rarer than the right-handed sort.) Madonnas abounded, statues bled and wept with artificial abandon. Crutches dangled from arches, testifying to spontaneous recovery from afflictions.

I'm not knocking all this, incidentally. Whatever your salvation depends on, go to it and good luck. Just don't ask me to subscribe to the magazine.

I spent too long gazing at the small sextet of ancient figures from China, one of which I'd rescued from Zole. Seeing them all together, I honestly wished I'd not bubbled the kid, but sent him back for the other five and waited in the getaway helicopter or something.

'Honey.' Annalou squeezed my hand, having detected but misunderstood my sincerest form of emotion. 'We can maybe work something out, okay? You and me?'

'It's love, you see,' I explained thickly, gazing at the wonderful small porcelains. The Jesuits had these done in seventeenth-century Peking. I reached and touched them one by one, feeling the glow.

'I'll always remember them, Annalou,' I told her truthfully. 'They're what brought us together.'

'Shhhh!'

A few more hymns and we made our melodious way out into the air. I was bog-eyed, and had to sit down beside an Inspiration for Invalids arbour. It faced a Garden of Eden, with a politely clad robot Adam taking perennial bites from a plastic apple while a demure Eve looked on in automated horror at a snake winding its way round and round a tree. I had to look away.

'I can see you're overcome, Lovejoy.' Prez was with us. He'd had a space cleared for us by devotees, the invalids' wheelchairs and stretchers being moved on temporarily while we spoke.

'I hoped it wouldn't show, Prez.'

They exchanged significant glances while I pretended to be superawed by the crystal building. It didn't take much effort.

'Lovejoy. Your financial offer . . .?' He sat beside me, clapping his hand on my shoulder while Annalou pressed close. They were quite a team. 'It's to do with your special gift, right? That was the most fascinating display of perception I've ever witnessed. Why, a gift like that, recognizing antiques by *sense*, why, that's a gift which must be used for Good. I feel we have a rightful claim on your services, Lovejoy.'

I came to, smiled. 'That's right, Prez. I came here to offer my gift in your service.'

'How wonderful!' Annalou pressed my hand. 'That means you'll be able to stay a while, rejoicing in prayer!'

'Afraid not, love. But I will provide a list of items which are fakes. In your exhibits, as they stand.'

Silence. I admired the ghastly Deus building. 'You deserve help, Prez. I was guided here by a higher power.'

'Well, I feel that too.' He was uncertain.

'Those saintly relics from Trier, the pottery on display by the Saints of Europe scenarios. They're fakes, Prez.'

'They're . . .?' He looked hard at Annalou. From the corner of my eye I caught her worried shrug.

'We'll get confirmation from Queen Mary College, London. They do it with physics somehow. Some mumbo-jumbo called inductively coupled plasma emission spectrometry. That'll show it, I'm sure. And that Roman glass from the Holy Land's all rubbish. They use spectrophotometry. I think, but we can give them a call –'

'Fakes?' Prez said faintly. He checked we weren't being overheard. 'Lovejoy. You can't be right. Our Foundation bought those items from the most reputable sources.'

'You have my sympathy, Prez. And so has your lovely wife here.' I dragged my eyes from his lovely wife and gave him my best soulful smile. 'I feel your anguish. Here you are, having built up this great . . . er, thing. And now to realize you've spent a fortune of your income on worthless junk. It's a setback, Prez. I weep for you.'

'Are you sure, Lovejoy, honey? About the fakes?'

'Shut up!' Prez snapped at her in an undertone. I tried to look startled. He smiled at me, abruptly back to holiness. 'Lovejoy. The strain of this revelation's afflicted my soul. Are you sure?'

'Yes. That specimen of Egyptian grain from Joseph of the multicoloured coat fame is duff – er, false, Prez. Like the bowl it's in. I think these science people use something called electron spin resonance for that –'

'Lovejoy, we got to talk.'

He signalled Glad Tidings and the custom golf truck. We drove to his private palace through crowds of adoring devotees, who cried their blessings down upon us. I felt a right prat, and a fraud, but that's par for my course. He gave few blessings on that return journey.

Deals are hard for me. I mean, I'd loved to have called off the whole thing and scarpered, with those precious gleaming Jesuit porcelains as payment. But that would have left Magda and Zole, and Gina, and the Californian Game looming a week away. And dead Bill. And Rose Hawkins. And me on the run from everyone on earth.

So I listened, was offered everything I wanted if only I'd join this heavenly pair and their labours. I was left alone with Annalou for a sordid set of promises while Prez ostentatiously conversed with his special bodyguard of devotees outside in plain view – allowing is time to reach some sort of conclusion, I surmised. I weakened, made promises to return, saying I'd use my services on their behalf all round the religious antiques markets of the world. She sulked, but brightened when I showed fear of my lust being recognized for the sinful thing it was. She slipped me an address in St Louis where she had a private apartment for religious retreats. I pretended to be exalted, thrilled. Which of course I was.

Then it was Prez's turn while Annalou went somewhere. I insisted I simply had to write to all the authorities I knew about this terrible fraud that had been perpetrated on this holy enterprise, giving it maximum publicity for the sake of honesty and . . .

I got two point four per cent of the investments in the theme park. I insisted on refusing the one per cent of the admission fees to the church Exhibition of Eternity, and said it would be my personal contribution to the work. He watched me go, musing hard, as Glad Tidings walked me out to where Tye and his goon waited by the helicopter. I was wringing in sweat as we ascended into the heavens. See what religion does to you? It's catching.

CHAPTER NINETEEN

The risks in antiques fraud are relative. Other criminals risk the absolute. You've never heard of a fraudster involved in a shoot-out of the 'Come in and get me, copper!' sort. Or of some con artist needing helicopter gunships to bring him in. No, we subtle-monger do it with the smile, the promise, the hint. And we have one great ally: greed. And make no mistake. Greed is everywhere, like weather. You get varieties of it, from tempestuous to a benignity so tranquil you kind of forget that it's there. But it's never very far away, thank God. Wasn't there a European king, heavens preserve us, done for fiddling his investments the year before last? See what I mean?

Fraud is the daughter of greed.

Going, that second day in Louisiana, to the house of the famous collector Mr D. Hirschman, it seemed to me that I hadn't needed to be lucky so far. In each case the marks' greed had bolstered my endeavours. Their greed had made them overreach – Mortdex's man Verbane was hiving off a share of the Mortdex millions for himself so couldn't afford a whiff of scandal. Annalou, bless her, had succumbed to that greediest of impulses, the craving for me. She'd believed that her obvious charms would seduce me into helping her and Prez to cull still more ancient religious relics to drag in more susceptibles to the fold. Prez's greed had been more direct – let's shut this bum up, in a manner beneficial to all.

I defy anybody to answer this next question with a resounding negative: Have you ever been a fraud?

Think a moment before answering. That hair tint? That little white lie about being only twenty-four? Your height? Weight? Telling the doctor you honestly stuck to his rotten diet? And saying yes you really stayed home every night your partner was away in Boston . . .? Fraud. The Church is at it, governments, the UN, Inland Revenue, emperors and monarchs. But there's some kind of con that are morally permitted, it seems. Like spying, like in wartime, like when Scotland Yard does a drugs stake-out and captures dope smugglers.

Fraud is a necessary part of our personality. No good complaining. We're all born con artists.

I would have had great hopes for Zole, if it hadn't been for that damned dog.

'Why did you let him buy that mongrel, you silly cow?'

'He's a kid. It didn't cost. Where's the harm?'

'Whose was it?' I grabbed Zole by the throat. The dog growled threateningly so I let him go.

It was early evening. We were in a street filled with sound and ironmongery, scrolled iron balconies and music bands milling away in every doorway. I was having to shout to make myself heard.

'You little sod, you thieved it.'

The dog Sherman was a small white Scotch terrier thing that had seen better days. It kept grinning at me, coming close, wanting an orgy of affection. It forgave easily.

'Lovejoy. That business at the Deus Deistic Theme Park. Did it work out okay?'

'I was worth more'n what you gave, Lovejoy,' Zole claimed, cocky little swine. Just how much he'd been worth for a few seconds while holding the porcelain figure, he'd never know.

'Magda.' I addressed myself to her, forgetting the little psycho with the pooch. 'I have an important visit to make. Did you find out about the Benidormo?'

She told me what she'd learned from the papers – I hadn't wanted to be seen by Tye *et al* feverishly hunting through the dailies for evidence of a bomb outrage in my cooling bed. Unexplained, it seems. Arson, possibly some insurance scam, was being mooted. Ho hum.

'How long will this last, Lovejoy?'

My last phone talk with Gina had been that the California Game would be at Revere Mount, five days hence. I'd wired fascimiles of the two Sherlock pages, posted them express, revealed they were fakes, told her what to look for as proof. She'd seemed pleased. So the Hawkins connection was broken, and Sophie Brandau would be as pleased as I. I still had the rest of the places to hack, then the Manhattan Big Two auctioneers, the hairiest problem of all. After that, I might be able to take it on the lam while they went to play their neffie game.

'Week, give or take, love.'

'Then?' I went uncomfortable. 'Happiness with that Annalou whore?'

'I dunno what. I can't plan.'

Zole's dog peed on a lamp post. Nice that New Orleans still had lamp posts, though. Zole admired its effort.

'And us?'

Meaning her and Zole but excluding me, I hoped.

'I'll think of something, Magda. One thing.' I hesitated, took advantage of Zole's preoccupation with Sherman. 'You don't phone Tye any longer, do you?'

I shifted from foot to foot while she composed herself.

'Once, since we started out, Lovejoy.' She added quickly, 'I didn't tell him about the envelope, though.'

'What's Tye promised you?'

She looked into the distance. Some parade was forming up, bands tuning up, people with banners and flowers. Everybody seemed to carry cornets and trombones. Coloured dresses, floral scarves, a couple of floats surmounted by pretty lasses under arches of blossoms.

'He's said we might, well, get together.' She looked at me, shrugged. 'Some time, y'know how it is.'

Smooth old Tye. I felt my loyalty evaporate, quick as sweat on a stone. I'd practically saved him on board the *Gina*. I'd been helpful all along, really. No more. And he knew I'd a helper trailing along, which meant Magda and Zole were now handicaps, no longer allies.

'You still going to phone him?'

'No. Course not.'

I'd got rid of Tye by being so docile while waiting for Mr Hirschman to fit me into his busy schedule, that Tye'd readily agreed to let me go alone to the collector's home. He was busy making arrangements with Prunella I'd asked for in New York. For a second I thought to question Magda further, but gave in. She could tell me whatever she wanted anyway. I gave her more money, told her we'd possibly be another day here. I wasn't sure. We'd meet at the waterfront. As we parted, something Zole did stuck in my mind. I grabbed him as he slipped something under Sherman's collar.

'What's that, you little tyke?'

'Lemme go, Lovejoy.'

A knife, a shiv about eight inches blade, an etched horn handle. I showed it to Magda, thunderstruck. People in the street took no notice, too occupied watching the loud bands form in procession.

'Magda? This child's got a dagger! For God's sake, woman! What the hell are you thinking of?'

She shook her head wearily. 'Don't sheet me, Lovejoy. We look out for each other best we can, okay?'

'No it's not okay!' I blazed. 'He's still a —'

'Don't say it, Lovejoy!' Zole threatened, all aggression. Sherman growled. I growled back and it gave a canine sort of shrug and settled on its haunches to await the outcome. 'I'm no kid! I already stuck three pimps tried to muscle —'

'You stay a kid until I tell you different, understand?'

I cast the knife into the harbour waters, and marched off in a fury.

'We in a strange town, Lovejoy!' he shouted after me. 'We gotta carry, man! Or you done.'

Ever get that feeling that you're suddenly the centre of a world gone mad? It happens a lot around me.

'Dam, everybody calls me, Lovejoy,' the collector said. 'Would you believe Damski for a first name? Sort of goes with Hirschman, right?'

A humorous man, but laughing without a crack in his face. His dark eyes were humourless. I wondered if every high-fly collector has a façade of mirth, but then remembered Mr Verbane.

The house was one of a terrace, a street actually as I know streets. A curved courtyard with shrubs in pots and trellises supporting climbing plants – wisterias, vines, bougainvilleas at a guess, though usually when I'm showing off with plant names women come and correct me. Wrought-iron gates, pavements and garden patios seemed to be the New Orleans fashion.

We entered through french windows, a comfortable and masculine salon. Hirschman was impassive, rotating his whole body before sitting down, a Bavarian Victorian clockwork automaton. He was pudgy in each limb. Rings shone on his fat fingers. I recognized a pro.

'It's your collection, er, Dam.' I could see no purpose in delay. 'I've come for a proportion of the valuation.'

'Protection, Lovejoy? You don't look the type.'

'Not in the way you mean, Dam. Protection for your unbought, as well as the bought.'

'But I finish up paying you, that it?'

'Yes.'

'Anti-semitic, huh?'

'Some of my best friends, et cetera.'

'Never mind the boughts, Lovejoy. Them I got, a'ready. Tell me the unboughts. I never heard that scam before.'

'The Kroller-Muller Museum in Holland,' I said. He was too cool. I felt the humidity reach into my clothes and sweat start tickling.

'I heard of it.' He lit a cigar like a bratwurst, admired his smoke.

'In that forest, by Arnhem. The robbery took two minutes – smash glass, rush twenty paces into the gallery, grab three Van Goghs, vanish. Remember it?'

He spread his hands, in mock appeasement. 'How'd I remember, Lovejoy? You only just told me. Terrible, terrible.'

'The police were there in a flash. The crooks were gone in half a flash. The museum still has two hundred and seventy-five works by Vincent, but . . .'

'The three have never been found?'

'Not so far, Dam.'

'Why come to me, Lovejoy? I'm one of millions.'

'You've companies in Japan, Dam. You've offices near the Mitsubishi Bank in Tokyo – the one lately held up by the Yakuza street gangs there.'

'And they pulled the Kroller-Muller heist? That what you're saying?'

'No. They're the ones stole the Corots in France. Like the say-so Corot copy you later exhibited, saying you had it painted the same week, copied from photographs.'

'You're alleging my copy's the genuine stolen Corot? I have certificates to prove –'

'I'm a divvy, Damski. Any test you like.'

Which brought silence in on cue, amid smoke and the barking of a dog nearby. I'd been pleased to see the old-fashioned roadstones outside in the street. Tradition dies hard in New Orleans, it seems. I wondered if those marching bands were part of the same tradition. Dixieland? Wasn't that the stuff they played hereabouts? Or was that Nashville? I'm hopeless with music, though I sing in a choir in my home village –

'Eh?' He'd just said something momentous.

'I'm going to have you silenced, Lovejoy.' He sounded friendly, thoughtful. 'But first, I'm going to do you a favour. I'm going to explain why.'

'Silenced?' I said stupidly.

'As in terminal.' He was at pains to seem reasonable. 'Do you know what I'd give for your power to divine, to divvy genuine from fake? Everything. Instead, that power is vouchsafed to an oaf like you. A drifter, on the make for a few miserable dollars.'

'I'm not like that –'

'Instead, I lack totally that extraordinary power which you have in abundance. It isn't that which I find unforgivable. It's you. You, Lovejoy, are a gargoyle not to be tolerated. There's one point more.'

I licked my lips, looked for escape.

'Don't worry. I've more sense than execute you here, in my own home. I'll have it done before you leave the city, parts of which can become very fraught and dangerous.'

'I'll call the police,' I threatened feebly, wondering why I'd told Tye to stay away the only time I needed him.

'The other reason is, I've come from nothing, Lovejoy. I've risen by the exercise of my own brain, astuteness. Triumph of the will.' He smirked at the aptness of the phrase. 'Ironical, no? I'm not going to have you coming in here and talking my – *my* – possessions back into public ownership – ownership of dolts and fools who couldn't look after them as they deserve to be looked after. They forfeited them. They deserved to. I tried the fools in Holland, the idiots in France, before the jury of my own mind. And found them guilty.'

'So you transferred ownership?'

'And shall do more, Lovejoy. Without your assistance.' He smiled beatifically, spent by the effort of revelation.

'You were the barrister for the defence, Lovejoy. You must pay the price for having lost the trial. Goodbye, Lovejoy. Start running.'

Shakily I rose and went towards the patio, through the french windows expecting gunshots any minute. Then the street, through the squeaking wrought-iron gates, into music and flowers and people.

And the lowering dusk.

CHAPTER TWENTY

The bar was a walk-in, more like a shop than anything. The windows were skimpily curtained. Lights were on, shedding gold onto the pavements. And the music was a delight – at least, I'd have thought so if I'd not been scared.

I'd chosen a seat where I could look out. Everybody in the place seemed to smoke. The band was into melodious action. The mugginess meant all doors stood ajar, all sounds mingling. I didn't want to miss Magda and Zole. Almost as if they were a lifeline.

That's the trouble with the confidence trick, especially the extortion kind. It's the Emperor's New Clothes – it only takes some nerk to point out that he's got none, and all barriers are down. I'd tried phoning the hotel, but Tye wasn't available. Prunella was inexplicably out.

First time on my own. Why now?

Anxious, I scanned the gathering dusk. What I'd seen as a harbour front was a river. America's rivers are so vast I can never tell if they're the sea or not.

New Orleans is built in a loop of the Mississippi, between it and a lake, I remembered from Prunella's maps (where *was* she for Christ's sake?). I could see ferries toing and froing to the south side. A few small power boats zipped around. A place on the front advertised boats for hire, but they were shutting up shop. The entire city isn't all that big, not for the US. Say, seven miles by four, with its Lake Pontchartrain only the size of an ocean. Across the Mississippi the land fritters away into swamps and islands. I'd seen it on our approach to Moisant International Airport. Nice for a holiday, not for escape. Except two men had been looking down at me from a balcony as I'd left Hirschman's courtyard, and I was already seeing at least one every few minutes among the people.

A cluster of tourists – so what was I? – went by, calling to each other. I went among them, walking towards the river as they went. A charter boat, Dixieland music stomping from an upper deck, with fairy lights and a spurt of water from the ship's side. The gangway was manned by two pretty lasses who wanted me to sign on for the voyage, or at least have a brochure.

'I'm waiting for my friends,' I said.

They laughed. 'Won't we do?' and all that. Any other time, I thought.

Then I saw him. It was one of the two men, no mistake. He was walking slowly along the front, staring into each café, bar, restaurant. I wasn't wrong. I looked about for his oppo, found him. A steady double act, one strolling into each honky-tonk, the other scanning the crowds. Methodical, gradually advancing, eliminating possibilities. Which meant . . . Oh, Jesus. The other side too, from the ferry concourse. Two more, doing the same, just as anonymous, just as implacable, only they were in jeans and sneakers.

'Here, miss. I'll have one, please.'

'Sure it's not three?' Mischievous with the smile. I could have thumped her.

'Eh?'

'Your friends.'

Magda, Zole and the dog Sherman arrived, all breathless.

'Ah, just in time!' I babbled. 'Cancel the ticket.' I grabbed Magda's arm, pulled her across the road and into an alleyway, Zole expostulating.

'Where the hell've you been, you lazy bitch?' I gave her.

'Hey, stay cool, ma man,' from Zole. I clipped his ear to shut him up.

'There's some people after me,' I stammered, trying for calm and failing. 'They're here, on the riverside. I want you to go and phone Tye now. Not tomorrow, not next week – *now*. Understand?'

Magda was so sad. She stood there, filled with sorrow. Sometimes women are so frigging useless. I almost knocked her down in my terror. It was bubbling up into my brain, blotting all thought.

'He checked everybody out, Lovejoy. You too. Gone. And Al and Shelt.'

'Gone?' I stared at her. Al and Shelt, the peanut eaters? A kitchen hand frightened me to death by suddenly bursting out of a raucous interior and rattling a dustbin into place. He slammed back inside. The alley darkened, the light extinguished. 'Gone where?'

'Just gone, Lovejoy. Everybody.'

'Didn't he say where?' I glanced towards the lights. The gleaming river looked a barrier now, not an escape. But Magda'd promised me she wouldn't phone him, and she had.

'Sheet,' Zole said. He was carrying Sherman. The dog looked knackered. Why do they always gasp when they've done nowt?

'I had to come, Lovejoy, in case you . . .'

Fight or flight? Always the latter, for Lovejoy Antiques.

'Come on. We'll try to hire a boat and go . . .'

'Sheet, man,' Zole was saying over and over. I realized why when I made to drag Magda towards the riverside lights. A man was standing against the glow, in silhouette. He was the one with a snappy hat, rakishly angled, and a suit of many stripes. I'd never seen such huge white cuffs, spats even.

'Mine,' he told his left shoulder, and his mate faded away round the corner. 'I say mine, man,' he told over my head. The two sneakers-and-jeans were deep in the alley.

'Okay,' one called, laughing. 'But he looks real mean, okay?'

They emitted hoarse huh-huhs of laughter. I wanted the loo, a hang-glider, anything. We were left with our killer. I mean my.

'Okay, lady,' the man said. He was about ten feet away when he finally stopped strolling forward. Where the frig was that kitchen hand now, when I wanted him? I could have dashed through the kitchen . . . 'You and the kid take off.'

'Magda,' I pleaded weakly. I was quivering, my voice pathetic. I'm disgusting at the best of times.

'Come on, Sherman,' Zole said, treacherous little traitorous bastard reneger, betrayer of a friend who'd helped the corrupt little sod.

Sherman. The dog. They're supposed to guard us, right?

'Kill,' I said weakly to the stupid hound.

'You got it,' Zole said.

I don't really know what happened next, only that Zole dropped Sherman to the ground as the man reached into his jacket and pulled out a weapon. There was a crack, but near me, not near him. A second shot came from the man into the ground with fragments of stone pavement flying everywhere. Magda yelped, I whimpered, Sherman screeched, any mixture of the three. In that same millisec Zole had gone flying backwards, spinning and hitting the ground. The man was sagging, slowly sinking to the ground, as if trying to pick something up at a party without being noticed much. He seemed preoccupied.

I picked Zole up, tears streaming down my face.

'Zole. I'm sorry. I thought he'd just do me —'

'Let me down, silly fucker,' Zole said, wriggling. 'Where's ma gun? I gotta finish the motha fucka —'

He escaped, searched for something on the ground. Sherman was howling, shivering worse than me. Magda was shouting, holding my arm, pulling, trying to get me to run past the kneeling man who had stilled, slumped ominously against the wall.

416

'Hang on,' Zole was calling. 'I gotta find ma gun an' finish him –'

Sherman howled and Magda screamed for Christ's sake to come on, the others'll be back. Zole was stumbling after, Sherman's lead round his legs, the mongrel howling and whining. And bleeding, I saw as we stumbled up the alley towards the street lights, from a scratch near its nose, presumably a splinter . . . And Zole was fiddling with a gun as he followed, grumbling at the thing. He shook it like a rattle, listened hard to its sound as he tried to work the trigger.

I snatched it off him and flung the thing into the alley. We ran towards the boat, the pretty girls waiting for the last trippers to climb aboard. We joined them. Thank God for New Orleans music. It deafens you to everything else. I paid, and though the girls looked at us a bit oddly, Magda was talking breathlessly to them and I was paying money over, and all was peace and light and safety as the boat pulled away from the mooring and we glided away up the lovely broad flowing Mississippi.

Watching the paddles turn water on a steamer is hypnotic, even a new and utterly phony side-paddler. The trippers seemed to be some sort of convention, fez hats with tassels and secret songs bawled into the universe. Beer flowed. Some other passengers were like us, normal and very, very glad to be there.

Normal? For that read abnormal.

I stood watching the shore line. I had only a few dollars now. Rescued by a homicidal child, supported by a prostitute. And now leant on by a dog that was still trembling with fright. The cut on its face was about a tenth of an inch, the worm.

Tye had gone. Prunella had gone. All right, Magda lied – she'd told me she wouldn't try to contact Tye. But she'd come to warn me.

Zole came, threw Sherman some unspeakable protein, and passed me a glass. I tasted gingerly. Wine.

'Hey, ma man. Whyn't you ball Magda? See, if'n you stick each other, we's team animals, right?'

I turned to inspect him, leaning over the glittering dark river. He was hardly out of nappies, and listen to his language.

'Where'd you get the automatic, Zole?'

'Bought it. Cheaper'n N'York.'

'There could have been another accident. What if the safety catch hadn't been on?'

He snorted scorn. 'Ain't no safeties on revolvers, Lovejoy. On automatics, sure. This wasn't no 'matic magna.'

I scrutinized him. 'You ever shoot anybody before, Zole?'

'Nope. 'Cept a numbers drek near East 43rd one time.' He showed a scar on his shoulder, pulling his shirt down for me to see. 'Got cut bad bad, man. Dee bee recoil, y'know?'

He reached down and embraced Sherman, now wolfing the meat. Drinkers whooped by, yelling something about going fishing.

'Lovejoy? Tye comin' after us?'

That hadn't occurred to me. Leaving me to face Hirschman's hoodlums was one thing. But would Tye hunt me down? Zole saw clearer than I.

'Dunno, Zole.'

'Then what's the plan, ma man?'

'Yes, Lovejoy. What's the plan?'

Magda. Another tour boat creamed out of the darkness with lights and music, paddle wheels splashing. People waved and shouted, and our lot waved and hollered. Zole took a bead on the bridge and went, 'Pow-pow-pow!' I almost clipped his ear as correction but thought better of it.

'I'll tell you the story, love. See if you know.'

Zole went and brought drinks for us both while I told my tale, every detail, including the phony scripts, how I'd tried to bring in a number of fake pages to prove to Gina I'd combed the kingdom for the Sherlock grailer. I explained that would expose Moira Hawkins as a fraud, so allowing Gina the chance to eliminate Moira from the gamesters. I spoke with grievance. I'd done well by Gina. And now Tye makes a mistake like this, almost gets me killed.

'Why, Lovejoy?' Magda asked when I'd done.

'He *dumb*, Magda,' Zole said.

'Well, see, Magda, it's like this . . .' Like what? Nothing came to help. 'It's complicated, see? It's raising millions from antiques and art –'

'So?' She lit a rare cigarette and smiled wrily when I moved to windward. 'So why her people let you get killed when you raisin' so good?'

'Wastin' yo' time, Magda. He but *dumb*.'

'Shut your face. Magda, I think she said something about . . .'

Magda shook her head slowly. 'I'll say for her. She's the hots for Denzie Brandau, right? Along comes Moira Hawkins with the big dig, the dream scheme. Dumb Denzie falls for Moira's play –

that president crap – leaving Gina washing the coffee things. See? So she minds to wreck Moira Hawkins's gran' plan.'

'But ...' But that wouldn't explain Tye's failure to come and protect me from Damski Hirschman's goons, would it?

'Gina Aquilina gets your pages, like you sent. She has them tested. Sure, they're dud. She's all the evidence she needs to confront Denzie Brandau and Moira Hawkins. So out goes Moira. And guess who that leaves to pick up Denzie's daisies?'

'So Gina withdraws Tye Dee ... ?'

And the peanut eaters, and the plane from New Orleans. And the bank credits I was using. And Prunella. And the rest of my little circus. A dead man wouldn't need helpers. Yet I'd been successful. If Gina was sure that she and Nicko would win the California Game, she'd be sure of snaffling Denzie Brandau as well once he ditched the shadowy Moira. Plus his big run at the presidency, with Gina his First Lady, perhaps after Sophie had bought some tragic but convenient accident?

'Lovejoy,' Zole said. 'How you *get* to grow old, ma man? I don't *believe* him, Magda.'

I counted out my few dollars, watched by them both. 'That's it. I'll understand if you cut and run.'

'See how dumb he really is?'

'Stop talking, Zole,' Magda said evenly. And the lad subsided. I didn't believe it. Never listens to a word I say, but heeds her matter-of-fact shush. 'I haven't got much more, Lovejoy.'

Zole rebounded. 'Me too.'

Dog? Gun? Magda's expenses made more sense than any of mine.

'You got your list of places, Lovejoy. Maybe we try shaking them down?'

'No, Magda. I wrote them to Gina, places, dates, names, everything. If she's the one who marked me down ...'

'You aren't thinking of California, Lovejoy?'

'We know where the Game is, love. We know when, who'll be there. Fancy running for the rest of our lives?'

'Running's dumb, man,' from Zole.

'Zole's right, love.'

'Hey, Lovejoy! You'm learnin'!'

We went to join the party, Magda sitting close to me as we spent our last on drinks and food. The old saying is, your last bite lasts longest. It transpired that we were heading upriver on an all-night paddler party, destination Baton Rouge.

CHAPTER TWENTY-ONE

The night was idyllic. What better way to spend a balmy warm night, than sit on the deck of a pleasure steamer on this great river of midnight velvet, watching lights go dreamily by?

At least, it would have been, if I wasn't the quarry of hunters. If the little lad asleep on one of the boat's benches with his dog hadn't shot and possibly killed a man. If the prostitute who was his . . . what? Pal? Mother? I'd not asked . . . if she wasn't probably sick of the sight of me. I mean, before I'd hove into view her life was plain and ordinary, right? Well, not quite those, but certainly ordered. She'd hook a client, charge him the going rate, repeat the process, while Zole stole. Together, a living.

Then me. And Tye Dee, who makes her a spy. Next, they're running like hell because of me.

On the same deck, a sleepy trio of conventioneers were talking about fishing. Music wafted from the big saloon. Women laughed. Occasional shouts. The wheels shooshed and thumped. The warm night felt like heaven. Sweat trickled down my neck, but for once I didn't mind. Even Sherman looked content, having extracted maximum sympathy for his nose scratch from a hundred cooing women, crafty canine. He'd fed like a lord. And he snored.

The shore lights glided past. A couple of late boats strung with fairy lights heading downriver passed close enough for us to hear their music, see the dancers waving. Our drinkers and dancers crowded the rails calling good wishes. You can't help thinking how wrong preconceptions are, can you? I'd thought America was all plastic food, angry motorists, no history. Okay, I thought ruefully, people sometimes hunt you, but that was partly my fault – I should have run the instant Rose Hawkins spotted my lust for antiques.

The boat went junketing musically on under stars through American velvet. No wonder the world and his wife wants to come. That notion finally set me thinking about the plight I was in, the road out. The California Game. Because if I wasn't dead from Hirschman's goons and Gina's betrayal, I was still in.

By the time dawn shimmered into the eastern sky I'd got a plan of sorts. I'd need luck, a little money to start with. Plus a hell of a lot of other people's money to finish with.

Breakfast found me the money to start with, in the form of Magda. She looked surprisingly fresh and level of eye. The main cabin had magically become a dining room – musical still, the Dixieland players pleased as Punch with a capitive audience. Zole stoked his boiler faster than me, almost.

'Lovejoy.' Magda passed me a bulky serviette. 'Don't unwrap it here.'

'How much d'you get, Magda?' Zole demanded through a mouthful. 'These dudes're good for plenty –'

Money. Magda had earned money. During the long exquisite night while I'd thought mystical thoughts, Magda had been . . . I cleared my throat.

'What's this, love?'

'We need money. We got none. I got some.'

'He's but dumb.' Zole fed Sherman a load of ham.

My headaches always try to tell me something. I'm too slow to realize things until afterwards. I'd stopped eating which, in a woman's presence, always bodes ill for me.

Magda picked at her food, the way they do. She was deadly serious. 'They that serious, they'll know we're headed for Baton Rouge. They'll be waiting, see?'

Jesus. I'd not thought of that. I'd assumed it was just a matter of booking a flight.

'We separate, Magda.' At least half of me was thinking. Without Magda, Zole and a Scotch terrier I'd travel faster, maybe stand more of a chance. This was no time to feel guilt.

'Split up, Lovejoy? You on your own?' I don't think she'd ever smiled a wintry smile in her life. Every smile was warm with understanding. I'm not sure I liked it. 'Without us you'd not be here.'

They make you sound helpless, women. I was narked. 'Look, Magda. I'm the one that matters. Let me tell you that a divvy's the rarest frigging creature on earth. Without me . . .' I tried again. 'Without me, the whole . . .'

Hang on. Without me *what?*

Without me, the antiques staker would have still been old stickyfingers, Fat Jim Bethune, the antiques stake maybe a tenth of what I'd made it.

Without me, Moira would have Denzie hooked on her daft Sherlock scam, and Gina and Sophie would both be in the lurch. Which was the opposite of what Gina wanted, if Magda's interpretation was right. Meanwhile, I had Busman as an ally, back in that warren. I'd never needed a library so badly.

'How long've we got, love?'

'The boat docks Baton Rouge at ten.'

Difficult. Zole must have seen my face fall. He snickered. 'He dumb.'

'Call me that once again and I'll –'

'What, Lovejoy?' He noshed on, taunting. 'You can't even –'

'We get off before Baton Rouge,' Magda said. 'Get a car. I've spoken with the man.' She looked out at the gliding scenery. 'There's a smaller place across the other side. He'll set us down in a boat.'

Legit. I'd noticed the lifeboats in the davits, of course, had all sorts of mad plans brewing. She'd simply arranged it. I didn't need to ask how.

An hour later we were on dry land, hired a car and bowled north on US 61. Magda drove while I slept with the dog sprawled over me. When I awoke, we'd passed Natchez, filled up at Vicksburg, and were coasting due east on US 80 with intermissions for Sherman to have a pee.

'Magda,' I said once. 'Shall I drive a bit? I mean, you've not had much sleep . . .' I dried. 'Where'll we stop?'

'Atlanta Georgia.'

I like the way Americans never say a name but what they make a doublet, Memphis Tenesse and that.

'We've missed out a lot of places,' I observed. 'Why?'

'He but *dumb*,' from Zole.

'Stop calling him that,' Magda said before I could draw breath.

Zole looked across at her, and not a word. He gave me a look over his shoulder. Silence. We pulled into Atlanta on the main 20, and found a smallish hotel equidistant between the State Capitol, Cooks, and Emory University. Zole got me every newspaper and magazine under the sun, and I started reading like my life depended on it. Magda vanished, Zole vanished, the world vanished.

Antiques are the norm of my life. For most others, it's time – like how did the Tokyo Exchange perform overnight, how will Wall Street do today. Yet even that isn't constant. I mean, time varies in America – now isn't now in New York if you're in Atlanta, and it's different again in Los Angeles. Fashions are never the same two minutes together. This year's colour's not tomorrow's. Governments roll over and die, and new bums come rioting in.

But antiques *are*. I'm told some mountaineers and astronauts share the same feeling: whatever else happens, there's always Everest or Jupiter. Ambition rules us all, from dreamy starlet to maniac billionaires. But I see life against a backdrop of lovely things – furniture, paintings, jewellery, porcelains, candlesticks to Constables – which older folk made with the love of their hands and left to move us to tears with beauty.

Except everybody isn't the same. Some people would walk past the Mona Lisa without a glance. I used to know a woman like that. Used to sit up all night culling news of investment bonds, yet she had a Turner painting on her wall. Barmy.

My point is that everything valuable has its doppelganger, its fake counterpart. The general rule in antiques is, the pricier the antique, the more serious are the contenders for its throne. This means the fakes are taken more seriously.

And fakes are everywhere.

The list of fakes is enough to stop the average person getting out of bed in the morning. Aircraft parts, cardiac pacemakers, antibiotics for death-dealing infections, even blood transfusion equipment, vie with precious Old Masters, priceless jewels, documents, bonds, share certificates, family records. Everything's up for grabs. Equally so, too. Nothing is sacred to the faker. That children will die from the wrong drug doesn't matter a damn to fraudsters. Nor that helicopters will fall from the sky when some dud bolt shears in flight. Fraud is the achiever's religion.

By four in the morning I'd found the sort of man I was looking for. I put on the television news channel for an update. Quickly I decided I'd move in two stages. I made a transatlantic call to tell a retired Major Lister in Rutland exactly how I wanted him to have his photo taken. I told him exactly what to do and why. I wanted them at the office of a multi-billionaire who was in deep trouble. Then I rested, asking to be roused at six o'clock.

Magda returned our car, and I spent three hours in the splendid public library while she and Zole rested. I'd been on tenterhooks in case either had got caught or didn't show up, or simply vanished having decided they'd had enough of me as a non-paying passenger. They should have done. I'd have ditched them if I'd had half a chance.

She booked us on different flights from Hartsfield Atlanta, she and Zole to Los Angeles, me to New York. It was an awkward leave-taking. She checked me over as if I was a child going to a new school, spotless shirt, briefcase, suit pressed, shoes glittering, tie sober yet crisp.

'Your hair never stay down, Lovejoy?'

'Not really.' I was embarrassed. She'd gone to so much trouble.

'You know to get them to radio ahead?'

'Yes, ta. I've got the list, love.'

'If you need something doing Lovejoy, remember you can hire. You're in Big A.'

'I'm learning, Magda. And thanks. See you in LA.'

'Take care, honey.'

I went red. I'd never been called honey before, not properly.

'And you, love. You too, Zole.'

'Here, Lovejoy.' He gave me what looked like a pencil case. I waved them through the gate, patting Sherman to show I wasn't scared and he was to guard them until we met up.

Heading for my boarding gate, I opened Zole's present. It was a throwing knife. I dropped the bloodcurdling implement into the litter bin. The flight was on time at New York.

CHAPTER TWENTY-TWO

'I've heard of America.' Major Lister had ogled the skyline all the way from the airport. He made the announcement as a concession to fashion. 'Truly amazing.'

We'd rehearsed his part until we were both word perfect. He had the photograph, silver framed, and a parchment citation, sealing wax, everything. I was really proud of the craftsman I'd sent him to.

'Vertigo ask much?' I worried uneasily.

'He says you still owe him. Some lady in Morton.'

'I'll pay.' She'd been keen to have a bonfire of all her possessions, in order to sell them. I'd fixed it for her, with a little bit of help from my friends. We call it a tinder job in the trade. (A tragic house fire loses you all your precious antiques, only it's fakes which get crisped, see? You sell the untraceable genuine antiques at some far-flung auction, and get the insurance as a bonus). I'd taken three months to fake all her stuff. I'd worked like a dog. Vertigo had done three marvellous portraits.

'This gentleman expecting us, Lovejoy?'

'Aye. It may only be his assistants, but it'll be as useful.'

Tramper Tower was the great Donny Tramper's gift to the great city of New York – his phraseology, nobody else's. We gave John Lister's name, and were ushered up to the upper triplex where Tramper's think tank never closed. Its beacons shone ceaselessly to inform the universe of Donny Dynamite's unflagging zeal in quest of the American dream.

A smoothie of each sex welcomed us, with clones. Opulence ruled. I felt positively shoddy, but then I always do. John Lister's bearing carried him through, spick and span.

'This is Major Lister,' I explained. 'Rutland Orphanage. I called you earlier.'

The lead lass shook hands with aggression-filled doubt. The others stood aloof with threat.

'We have no record of the appointment, Major Lister. Nor of a contribution from Mr Tramper to your orphanage. Also, Mr Tramper's real busy right now and –'

'The citation, Wilkins,' John commanded. I leapt to obey. 'Miss, will you let me conduct the ceremony here? We fully comprehend. Mr Tramper's time is of the essence.'

'Ceremony?' The clones swapped glances.

'Of thanks. I have a citation, and a small acknowledgement of Mr Tramper's generosity. It saved our orphanage.'

Lister cleared his throat, conducted the head lady from behind her desk, produced the scroll.

'In the name of the Rutland Orphanage, of Maltan Lees, in testimony of the generosity of –'

'Hold it, please.'

An anxious gent disappeared from the anteroom. We waited. It took two minutes, and we were ushered into an office as broad as the bridge of an ocean liner. The whole of Manhattan was spread out before us. We actually looked down on skyscrapers. My head swam.

The man at the desk rose. Fortyish, smooth and easy, with eyes that had once known humour, but no longer. He shook our hands. I deferred to Major Lister. We explained our purpose, Tramper nodding and listening. Then he lit a cigar, took three rapid puffs, extinguished it with regret into an ashtray piled with enormous remnants of aborted smokes. He waved his aides out, and we were alone.

'Wilkins?' he asked me directly. I was standing near Lister's chair.

'That's me.'

He said no more for quite a few minutes. During them he extracted and read the citation. Then he examined the photograph, carefully perusing the dates on the reverse.

'What do you get out of this, Wilkins?' he asked eventually. His calm was a delight to see. I glowed with admiration of America and all her great businessmen. Hardly a single clue, and he susses out every nuance of the baffling problem instantly. Great.

'A contribution from others, Mr Tramper.'

'You putting me on?'

'No, Mr Tramper.'

He swung his chair, practising, perhaps never having done it before. He wasn't in showbusiness, this genius.

'Nothing would be easier than for me to call in the photographers, pics with you presenting the scroll. The publicity would do me a barrel of favours, I can tell you.' He eyed me. 'You heard about me and Marlene Maloney, huh? It's smeared in the papers, TV.' He laughed mirthlessly, quoted, 'Tramper Tramps into Bimbo Limbo.'

He stayed my comment with a hand, did his non-smoking smoke trick, gazed longingly into the ashtray.

'Bastard doctors,' he said. I agreed, nodding with conviction. 'My latest casino opens in Atlantic City next month, Tramper Xanadu. I'm subjected to the most scurrilous attacks, lawsuits, abuse, since my, uh, friendship with Marlene Maloney came public. It's a feeding frenzy. Every moral vigilante group on the East Coast's after my blood.'

He tapped with a pencil, snapped it, dropped it anywhere. He hadn't looked away from me.

'Major Lister's orphanage is legit, right?'

'Correct, Mr Tramper.'

'How much did I donate?' he asked wrily.

I went red. I'd forgotten what I'd said for Vertigo to put on the scroll. 'I think twenty thousand.'

'The columns'll claim it's a put-up, by my own publicity people.'

'They'd be proved wrong by hard independent evidence, Mr Tramper. Major Lister's certificate acknowledges receipt of your generosity a year ago, before any opprobrium.'

'Before Marlene Maloney,' he mused. 'This out of the goodness of your heart?'

His mind was too slick to flannel. 'Not really. If it doesn't work, I'll try something else, somewhere else. Don't worry. We'll reveal nothing. Nobody knows we're here. Major Lister here'll vouch for me.'

Silence for a moment, while he grew angry with something out of view. 'You know what those bastards are doing right now? Running a'cking *cartoon* about me! I'm suing, but...'

'My mate's come a long way,' I said to soothe him. I didn't want him mad. 'Might as well call in your tame city clickers and get your cent's worth, eh?'

'Twenty thousand's nothing. You can have it anyway. The morality brigades are opposing my casino, threatening to close me even in N'York!'

'Could they?' I was interested.

'They can damn well slow me down. This is America.'

'They'll not close you, Mr Tramper. Not after what happens next.'

I waited while he re-ran the words. 'This is the bite, huh? The bite that costs nothing?'

Honestly, I felt quite sorry for him. Nobody likes to have their genital activities plastered over every tabloid and screen, to the howls of enemies.

'You need to prove anew that you can organize your businesses and casinos in a law-abiding manner.' I felt eloquence effervescing with the glee of fraud. 'Difficult when the moral battalions besiege Tramper Towers. It has to be major evidence.'

'Like what? I've every security agency in the country on my payrolls and it's not enough.'

'Parts of New York are a mess, Mr Tramper. Your Taxi and Limo Commission alone tries four hundred taxi-driver offenders a day for assault and abuse of passengers. The killings, muggings, the crime –'

'Gimme a break. It's not my doing.'

'Supposing you halted all crime in one area for a whole twenty-four hours? Call it a Law Day.'

'That's dumb talk, Wilkins. We got police. They try and fail.' He was the sort of bloke I suppose women fall for, handsome and in the prime of life, but in a cleft stick. His affair had suffered more mudslinging than Richard III. He gave in when I said nothing. 'You know they were tipping me as a presidential nominee?'

'There'll be one fewer of those in a couple of days, Mr Tramper. Work out what you'll say to the cameras. You'll be shyly conceding that you're a secret benefactor, and an anti-crime potentate. You'll contribute this gesture as goodwill to this great city of yours. Clear your path almost immediately.'

He was still sour about other nominees. 'They got that punch-drunk Texan as sellingest contender. And that shifty bastard Brandau. I could lose them any day of the week.'

'I'll lose you Brandau this week, Mr Tramper.'

We talked seriously then, with John Lister's head turning like a Wimbledon regular's between us. It took a little over an hour. Mr Tramper gave the orphanage a donation way above his previous year's mythical donation, following which his minions were summoned to round up the media photographers. I quietly faded. They could do without my picture.

As John left for the airport, dollars winging ahead of him to Rutland, I went to see Busman, to ask a favour and start negotiating a price for Donny Tramper's new invention, a piece of peace in Manhattan. I needed success now.

There's that theory of success, isn't there – confidence makes you win. Lose heart, and you've lost no matter how big your army.

I took a taxi down Eighth Avenue, and walked into the bus terminal. It was getting on for six, the day drawing in. Maybe it was tiredness, maybe from being away from antiques so long, but I was so really down. At the terminal I had a quick coffee while I wondered what I'd do if I failed with Busman. Should I try to see Sophie? But maybe she too thought I was dead. Or Gina? Too risky – I'd have a fatal visit from Tye. Rose? At least she was innocent of all the mayhem. I'd maybe look her up when it was over.

Nothing for it. I was uneasy, spinning out the coffee because it felt safer. I felt unshaven, soiled, tired, almost doomed from dispirit. I went into the maelstrom of travellers to seek Busman.

A small cluster of youths marauding on the outskirts of a passenger group seemed the most promising. I went up to them and said Busman had sent for me. They didn't mug me, just directed me into the concrete warren. I plodded down, feeling the loneliest figure on earth.

The atmosphere had gone, somehow. I walked the tunnels, asking loudly at every molestation for Busman, telling I was sent for, that Busman wanted to see me. Whatever the previous impression I'd had of this subterranean dump, now it was sickly, sordid. The mystique had gone. What had seemed a strange pervading smell had become a fetid stench. The walls were smeared offal slabs. The perverts and prostitutes mauling in corners, the junkies rubbing bloodstained sleeves, the muggers brawling over thieved wallets had once seemed exotic derangements. Now they were a mess of degradation. I ploughed on, saying loudly I was to see Busman and Trazz.

A Flash Harry emerged from nowhere, came along with me the last few airless corridors, telling me stories of problems they'd had with police lately. I said sure and yeah.

The big control place was shoddier than I remembered, strewn with waste paper, more crowded, more smoke and screens but now a dungeon-like tomb. Busman was there, hearty and welcoming. Trazz came creaking up aslant, doing a laugh of surprise, tsss-tssss.

'Lovejoy, ain't it? You made it back to the Apple.'

'Hello, Trazz.' I gave Busman my hand. He took it with more of a practised lean than he had once before. A politician's grip now, but still friendly.

'Wotcher, Busman.'

'You been away, Lovejoy.'

'Bit of a holiday.'

We did some word sparring. He unbent a little more, laughing properly and telling me stories of his activities in the terminal. I eased too, thinking I was just tired, imagining things. Trazz went to check some of the screens' scrutineers.

'Busman. I came with a proposition.'

'I thought, Lovejoy.' The big man beamed. 'I can't agree outright. Gotta warn you.'

'I understand. Could you stifle all the crime here, for twenty-four hours?'

He fanned himself slowly in astonishment. We were at his desk. No phones, I noticed. Everybody else seemed to have several. I gave him time to work it out. Slowly he shook his head, regret uppermost.

'You askin' me to throw a fortune, Lovejoy? Ma money comes in steady, fourteen scams. In N'York scams is business. Halt business, ma people suffer.'

'Suffer how, Busman?'

'No money, that's how. They pay breath, make deals, pay the vig on loans, up cuts, things you never even heard of, Lovejoy. They gotta work, or I displeased.' He chuckled.

'If they didn't work a day, Busman. Got free paid instead?'

He whistled, thinking fast. 'You know how much that'd cost, boah?'

He'd never called me boy before. It had an alien sound.

'The protection for a block of real estate's tenth of the annual rent. A ten-million dollar rental, they pay some syndicate a million?'

'Right.' He swung in his chair, finally put his feet up, like great boats. 'I get five cents on every took dollar, Lovejoy.'

'That, then. Plus what your others'd need?'

'This real?' he asked, figuring as he went.

'Depends on the price, Busman. The man might well be the big P before long.'

He called Trazz. They talked out of earshot, made phone calls, got a girl to work a computer for a while. Then he returned, giving me his new and disturbing beam.

'You got it, Lovejoy. Midnight to midnight, in three hours.'

'From now?' That shook me. I hadn't realized it would happen so fast. I took the paper on which the girl had written the sum, seven figures. I gulped, nodded, said the deal was probably on.

We shook. I was to phone a number in a few minutes. I was given the same Flash Harry guide, and left.

But something then worried me more than it should. As I turned, I saw in a big-screen console angled near Busman's desk a strange reflection move. It was Busman's head, swivelling as he looked at Trazz. He gave a shrug and a nod combined, turning his palm upwards, thumb out. An odd gesture, it seemed out of character, macabre. Yet when I turned to wave goodbye from the door, Busman was beaming in my general direction and gave me a wave. Trazz,

shuffling and angled, grinned after me with the grin of a cadaver. I
didn't shiver. I walked away from my friends, just managing not to
break into a run.

The escort got me safely to the street. I phoned Mr Tramper,
said it was on, how and where the money should be paid, and rang
off.

Then I really did scarper, like a bat from Hell, into the New
York night, not really knowing who was after me but travelling at
speed in case I found out.

CHAPTER TWENTY-THREE

There's a vital difference between being a tourist and being in your own town. That difference is a bed, nothing more, nothing less.

A tourist has nothing, because even the bed, loo, water tap, is rented by the minute. Laying your head down is at somebody else's behest. But if it's your own pad, you can tell everybody else to clear off and shut the door on the blighters. The difference is Tourist Tiredness, that state of utter weariness where you get taken for every penny, when you buy stupid things, when con merchants come out to play on the bones of the gullible. Exhaustion's a grim mutagen. Even the smartest tourist eventually begins trading dollars for dimes, hard currency for zlotniks.

This was me. I was worn out. Not physically, but my instincts were a dud battery.

Friends come in useful about now. But Magda and Zole I'd sent into exile. Bill had died on these very streets. Busman had agreed to a deal, which was likely to start working soon, but somehow I felt under threat. I realized what was bothering me. That gesture I'd seen reflected was the one he'd used before, when telling Trazz to hit Charlie Sarpi's transgressors. I know finality when I see it. It's different from dismissal. That there'd been an element of regret in Busman's manner didn't allay my fear.

I was in theatreland, none yet loosed, so the nosh bars and stalls weren't crowded. I found a darker place to sit and stoke up with grub. I've been hunted before, and know that food and loos lend alacrity. I kept an eye out for enemies, and thought.

Fredo's bar might still be open, but so what? Josephus, Della, Fredo, Lil, Jonie – what was I to them? A fly-by-night, that's what. And I'd flown. That too is the American way, zoom off to a better take. I didn't know where any of them lived, either.

Sophie Brandau, the one I was really drawn to? Her husband wasn't likely to welcome me. Melodie van Cordlant might, but I suspected she was too embroiled among the gamesters for me to fling myself on her mercy. Fatty Jim Bethune? I'd done him a favour, but he wouldn't regard it as such. Orly hated me. Nicko? Jennie? Two unknowables. Was there refuge among the lower orders, like Blanche? Not while she and Tye were shacking up there wasn't. Rose and the Hawkins family? But Moira was Denzie Brandau's busty lusty. Rose ran silent and deep. Maybe she hated me too. Chanel was out.

Which left Prunella, erstwhile lover, Miss Reliability. And I knew her address.

The bus took me some of the way. I walked from Lexington, turning left at the little supermarket into East 36th, and found Prunella's impossible surname on the Apt. 6B voice box. I had the sense to disguise my voice, trying for nasality and a Central Europe accent. The squawk answered with Prunella's inflexion.

'Passel serviss foor, uh . . .'

'Be right down,' she said, careful girl.

I flitted down the slope as far as the Third Avenue corner, and stood hunched. I could see into the well-lit porch. Tye Dee came to the glass vestibule, cautious and slow, looking obliquely, then did a rapid step to stare uphill. The stress was unmistakable. I saw his head rotate, a deliberate scan of the tall terraced houses opposite. I didn't move. A displaced shadow points better than a flashlight. Tye's bulk withdrew. I waited, leaning on the corner, and was right. A full minute later, his head came slowly into view, did its pan, then vanished. And so did I.

Sokolowsky was in the phone book. I had the sense not to bother, instead got a taxi to Perry Street, and walked. The street was more like a street than any I'd yet seen, every house accessible, no transparent double doors manned by vigilantes, local cafés and nosh bars on the go even at this late hour.

The old man was suspicious when I buzzed. I said who I was, but for old time's sake did the lurk-and-lour trick in case he too had a battalion of goons, then trotted forward and up his steps just before he closed the world out.

'Evening, Mr Sokolowsky. Lovejoy.'

The corridor behind him was feebly lit. He nodded, reluctantly admitted me. He arranged complicated chains on the outer door.

'You're hard to remove, Lovejoy. Like my Aunt Esther's lemon tea. Carpets it stained stayed stained.' He shuffled ahead, turning out lights as he went. 'She's staining Heaven's carpets with her tea. You come when the water's off. Can you explain it? Manhattan an island you can spit across, without water twice a week? You give money. For what? For them not to give you water?'

'Mhhh.'

We shuffled inside. An iron expanding gate blocked the stairs.

'You wonder why I've a gate across the stairs? I'll tell you why I've a gate across the stairs.'

'No, honest. I wasn't.'

'I'll tell you anyhow, because you're wondering. I've a gate across the stairs because they break in. People who know nothing break in, like weather. Always there.' He paused, took my arm at the entrance of a small cluttered room, shoved me as though I was inert until I could move no further and had to flop into a chair. 'Technology we got like Africa's got drought. We teach the young miracles my grandfather wouldn't believe. For what? So they can learn nothing. Instead of a job, they break in and steal what they can reach. It's life. Who says life isn't terrible?'

'Thanks for letting me in, Mr Sokolowsky.'

He creaked into a chair. 'Visitors who come through the door I can live with. You'll have some tea. It's Russian style, so the glass burns your fingers. You know anything Russian doesn't? It's life.'

I nodded thanks, unsure whether it was an act. I knew he was an alert jeweller, who saw much and spoke little.

He poured hot water through tea leaves in a sieve, added a slice of lemon, heaped sugar in, stirred, kept the spoon. I felt my eyelids drooping. It was all so peaceful, so innocent. He raised the kettle to remind me of the scandalous water problems, shrugged in his shawl, gently went 'Scheesch!' and painstakingly set about bringing some thick apple cake thing.

The room had a bar fire. Books lined the walls. A globe and worn rugs lent a medieval air. It could have been any century, except for his electric kettle and the water problem.

'You wondering why I have only one table lamp?'

'No, no.'

'You have a question nobody answers, that's suffering. So I'll tell you. I have only one table lamp because electric's had it good too long. I could afford two, three, a dozen. Count the lights in this house. I could have them on every minute every day, but why should I? The electric company's better than the water company? Don't insult my intelligence, Lovejoy. Eat. You've a way to go.'

'Thanks, Mr Sokolowsky.' It was good, a sort of thick apple pie. Was it the famous strudel they mention in pictures?

'You got killed in New Orleans, Lovejoy. I for one don't believe it. I didn't then, I don't now.' He spoke with a grandfather's comforting gravity, everything debatable whatever the evidence of your senses.

'No. I made it.' Somebody had reported I'd got topped. Hirschman wouldn't have, so it must have been the goons themselves. Perhaps they'd have copped it from their bosses if they'd reported a failure? To them I was only a stranger passing through, my killing a job to be paid for and forgotten.

'I thought as much.' He was in a rocking chair. He plucked occasionally at his shawl, the habit of age. 'You see this street, Lovejoy? The notices, what they write?'

'There were lots of posters —'

'And such posters,' he said severely. 'You read them? Karate lessons? Chinese contemplation? Gays, lesbians? Macrobiotic cooking? This is civilization they learn Chinese think, can't think American a'ready?'

'Well, I suppose change is everywhere —'

'Run, Lovejoy,' the old man said sadly. 'Run.'

I'd lost the thread. 'Eh?' He'd just been talking about cooking.

'Run.' He reached and closed the book on his small table. 'Lovejoy. They'll know you're alive sooner or later. My advice is run, run till you've no need. Then you can stop. It's life. I'm telling you because I know.'

'I don't know what I'm running from, Mr Sokolowsky.'

He removed his spectacles, replaced them. 'That's something I don't know, Lovejoy.'

'Run where?' He knew I was honestly asking.

'My advice isn't good, Lovejoy. So tell me what you've done since you didn't die.'

More or less, I told. He poured more tea, holding up his kettle to condemn the water company. I worried it was all some delaying tactic to keep me here while he secretly signalled Tye and Al and Shelt.

'The California Game's a legend, Lovejoy,' he said at last. 'I've lived a lifetime and can tell you legends are nothing but trouble. Like New York's water supply,' he interposed bitterly. 'Legends you've got to handle like bombs. Cover them up, hide from their effects. The rest of the time, ignore them. But their fame spreads. People want to walk with legends. See the problem?'

'Publicity would prevent the California Game.'

He sighed as only old Sokolowskys can sigh.

'You're teaching me, Lovejoy? Oy vey. You know so much, you're running from you don't know with nothing in a strange land?'

'I apologize.'

'No hard feelings. Manners I remember.' I had a sudden image of him elsewhere, fumbling for a fire tiger to poke some nonexistent fire. 'The California Game's the biggest and most illegal. Take a fraction of every business in America, that's the stake. It's always simple faro – you know faro? Your win, my win. Nothing simpler, the one game nobody can cheat, no skill required.'

'Faro?' I'd had visions of some exotic protracted gambling game lasting through nights of smoke and drinks.

'One card's chosen as marker. Everybody sees it. You deal a new deck into two separate piles, one your win pile, one your loser. Whichever pile the marker card falls into, so you've won or lost.'

'Is it worth it?' I'd heard of the great poker championship in Las Vegas, with fans saving a lifetime to enter. 'You might as well do it by phone.'

'It's a secure way of passing power, Lovejoy. Handing over power's where all trouble starts.'

'Whoever wins gets the hacks?'

'And decides who can play next time. Nicko won last year.' His gaze was the saddest gaze I'd ever seen. 'This hurts me to say, Lovejoy. Go from here. I've to phone or they kill me. I'll give you time. But go now.'

I thought I'd misheard, reluctantly decided I hadn't. I finished my tea, thanked him.

'You need a loan, Lovejoy, speak this side of the door.'

'No, thanks.' I paused in the dimly lit corridor. 'If you were me, where would you go until daylight?'

'There's all-nighters. Tell jokes until dawn. Here in America there's so much to laugh at.' His expression was sobriety itself.

'Thanks, Mr Sokolowsky. Maybe there'll be a time . . .'

'Maybe, Lovejoy,' he agreed, and I was out and on my own.

That night I walked, was accosted intermittently by figures and shapes that frightened me. I lurked in all-night diners where I could, ducked out when the going got rough. One seemed to specialize in brawls. Eventually I risked a taxi, got dropped off where comedians talked jokes into a hang of smoke over tables populated by an audience who never laughed. The worst was, those comedians were the best I'd ever heard. It broke what was left of my heart.

Came dawn. I decided I'd risk visiting Mr Sokolowsky to check the details of the Game. I went by Metro, riskily joining the first commuters of the day, lighting at Christopher Street on the Broadway-Seventh Avenue line. I felt death warmed up, as my Gran used to say.

The view from the end of the old jeweller's street kept me moving on. Ambulances and police and fire engines wah-wah about New York every hour God sends, so I'd not sussed the significance of a team tearing past as I'd headed that way. But outside his house a small crowd had gathered, and a covered shape was being gurneyed into an ambulance. I didn't look back.

A suspicious mind like mine might conclude that old Sokolowsky had told his masters that I'd called. They'd possibly hunted, failed to find me, and exacted the ultimate forfeit. My mouth was dry. I was tired, lost.

But antiques beckoned. I went into a huge commercial building that claimed to be the centre of World Trade. I believed it. I submitted to a professional shave which started me imagining gangsters bursting in to do a routine assassination, had a headwash (exhausting), manicure (embarrassing), and shoeshine (most embarrassing of all).

The tonsorialist, he said he was, talked ceaselessly, praising Donny Tramper's brilliant innovation – a midnight to midnight Law Day, which was the talk of the town because it seemed to be working. Grand Central to Tenth, West 34th to 48th, not a single mugging or killing yet, a whole ten hours!

I did my best with the accent. 'Who's this Tramper genius?'

'Here.' He showed me a morning paper a foot thick, Tramper being honoured by one Major J. Lister. 'Tramper maintains this foreign orphanage. He's mad the papers found out.'

Good hearted, and modest with it.

I left, into Manhattan sunshine. I felt prepared. Let me die among antiques.

CHAPTER TWENTY-FOUR

Playing antiques auction houses against each other is the ultimate. It's the dealer's fandango. Sooner or later we all skip the light fantastic, to their tune. The Big Two skip fastest of all.

I'd chosen Mangold, of Geneva, London, Paris, Monaco and everywhere else where money lurks. Nicko's people – I supposed Tye Dee, Al, Shelt – would be watching Sotheby's and Christie's, because the plan I'd formed with Gina included those. Mangold's wasn't big. I'd chosen it from many. The reason was its forthcoming lawsuit against the Big Pigs, as dealers call them.

I simply got a hire car – you can get these in America – and drove there in splendour. Remembering Oscar Wilde's essential for the con trick, I smiled constantly, trying for an aura of wealth. I was Mr Dulane, of Geneva and London. I was also a lawyer. The head man saw me with all the readiness of the smaller company under threat.

We shook hands, some more amiably than others. I apologized to Simon Mangold for my appearance, claimed jet lag and airports. He said it gets everybody.

'You're the son of the founder?'

'Dad died last year.'

His attitude announced that he was going to go down fighting. But that only tells everybody you're going down anyway. It must be something about the antiques that does it, makes bravery ridiculous. We were in a panelled office, nothing old in it except a couple of beautiful Chelsea porcelains that warmed my soul. Here was a man who loved antiques, but whose love was the doom of his firm.

'That's when your troubles started, I hear, Mr Mangold.'

'It's in the papers,' he said bluntly.

'The Bigs are nothing if not acquisitive.' I went all sympathetic. 'I'm here to give you information which may help you.'

He digested this. No fool he. 'Give?'

'Give. As in donate. If you like the gift, I'll suggest a course of action which will benefit us both. If you don't you're free to use the information for nothing.'

That fazed him. He excavated with a toothpick, examined his palms for buried treasure, stroked the surface of his desk. I watched, marvelling. We just ask to be researched by sociologists.

'That clear cut?' When I nodded, he asked to see my business
rd. I shook my head, said I was travelling light.

'Would you hang on a second, Mr Dulane?'

'Not that either,' I said, varying my smile to show no hard
lings. 'Your secretary can check the International Business Direc-
ry, you won't find us. I haven't much time.' I was narked and shut
m up. Hell, it was my prezzie. People want jam on it.

'I've chosen your auction houses, Mr Mangold, because my
formation will damage your competitors, please my principals, and
able you to survive. Ready?'

His mind clicked round. The large auction houses were trying
launch a closed shop, effectively eliminating Mangold's from the
itiques market. They'd both tried to buy him out for years. The
ice for survival was to vanish into either of the Big Two. Mangold's
is suing, despairingly trusting the law courts. Which showed how
sperate he was.

'What if I ignore your information? Or simply use it free?'

With some people doubt's an industry. It was a long way to LA,
id time was running out.

He pressed a buzzer, spoke into an intercom. 'Get Mr Feldstein
id send for Mortimant –'

'Unbuzz your lawyers, Mr Mangold, or I pretend you've mis-
iderstood and you'll look a prat.'

He hesitated, a lifetime's habit, reluctantly concurred.

'And the recorder, please.' I held out my hand for the tape. He
ed telling me it erased automatically, but I didn't continue until
'd lifted the tape from his drawer and placed it on my palm. I
intinued with my true story.

'Everybody knows the story. How the English Lord bought the
urteen ancient Roman silvers, illegally acquired via Lebanon from
igoslavia. All in contravention of UNESCO's embargo on
iuggled antiques. The British Antique Dealers' Association 1984
ode was also broken. No wonder Christie's was furious!' I smiled
easantly, all Edward G. Robinson. 'They hate to be confused with
ch-rivals, right?'

'Sure.' He was weighing me up. 'You have evidence?'

'Who needs evidence?' I asked in all seriousness. 'Mudslinging
ictioneers don't.' I held the delay, then said, 'Do they, Mr Man-
ild?'

'This information, properly used, could seriously damage even a
m as famous as, say, Sotheby's. Or Christie's.'

He meant improperly, but I let it pass.

'True. Like that terrible Louvre Affair, eh?'

'The Louvre Affair?'

'Spelled as in Poussin, Mr Mangold. Can I refresh your memo by quoting, "The Louvre stopped at nothing in its effort to swinc honest people" . . .?'

Once upon a twenty-five years ago, a Nicholas Poussin pai ing of 1628 was auctioned by a French engineer. The auctionec paid him a measly two hundred quid for it, offhandedly telling t owner it was an el cheapo Bologna-school effort. The engineer w sad, of course – but even sadder when the papers blazoned ne of the Louvre's fabulous discovery of (surprise surprise!) his se same Olympos painting! Except it was now rare, authentic, a priceless . . .

As Mangold feverishly tried to keep up, wondering about possit links with his rivals, I listed others for him where the Louvre a other galleries had misbehaved.

'A really malicious person could remember that terrible episo where a certain poor convent sued the Louvre – which had just pa half a million for that famous Lorenzo Lotto masterpiece, the o the Catholic nunnery had just sold for seventy measly dollars, certain auctioneers' advice.' I tutted, doing a lot of head wagging show how I deplored all this. 'Fair profit's fair profit, Mr Mangol But that's too many percents for me. And I'll bet the papers'll thi the same, if you happen to refresh their memories.'

He licked his lips. I'd got him, on his own lifeline.

'There are links between famous auction houses and auctionec who arrange first sales, Mr Mangold. The pattern's there. It's up you to bring them to the public's attention. Viciously, savagely. T public understands ruthless greed, but likes to deplore it in other I heaved a sigh, in memory of poor old Sokolowsky. 'I just ca help feeling sad over that forthcoming announcement of lawsuits th will be brought against Sotheby's of New York.' I stood, smile 'Well, thanks for your time, Mr Mangold –'

He quivered like a greyhound hearing the hare. 'Lawsuits?'

I sat. 'Didn't you hear? Well, I hate to be the bearer of rea bad news, but it's just that the antiques dealers in the UK are f up. So're the ones on the Continent. Tomorrow there'll be a mec salvo about chandelier bidding, from Antique Internationalers, London.'

He thought that one through. 'But any AI member who ma that protest would . . .'

'Be driven into the ground by the biggies? Course it would. B

it'll happen, sure as God sends Sunday. Unless you don't want it
to.'

'You wouldn't link Mangold's with an outrageous —'

'Never. We've got somebody else, who'll do it for a fee. It's all
fixed.'

He subsided, said slowly, 'That will inflict irrevocable damage
on them. Immediate.'

Not so outrageous after all. We both thought over the history
of recent doubts. They centred on what the trade now calls 'Bond
borrowing', and please note the capital.

It came to light when Van Gogh's painting *Irises* went up at a
Sotheby's auction. (Incidentally, why is it always poor old Vincent
who catches the bad glad? It's high time some other poor sod had
a go.) A mere $53.9 million won the hammer, as we say, for brave
Aussie Mr Bond. Everybody was thrilled, especially auctioneers
everywhere. And why? Because prices were through the roof, and
so was their commission. The trouble was, half the gelt was borrowed. Guess who from? Why, the auctioneers themselves!

The world outcry was followed by instant explanations, that the
world's top auction houses hadn't deliberately intended to drive up
the prices of art works by a secret loan, that Sotheby's policies would
change, et yawnsome cetera. Worst of all, the art market went gaga.

'Art dealers began to ask if the Museum of Modern Art would
have paid so high for the next Van Gogh, if Picasso's self-portrait
would have touched forty-eight million dollars, all that jazz.'

'Names?'

I passed him a list of the international dealers who'd complained
to the press.

'You'll combine your diatribe with all sorts of veiled accusations
of complicity, naturally. You'll ask why Thyssen paid over fourteen
million sterling, at Sotheby's, for a painting he already half owned.
You'll scream outrage when the AI hullabaloo is raised tomorrow
about big auctioneers allowing the new relay bid — you know the
old trick, Joe nods to Betty who winks at Fred who scratches his
nose so Jean waves to the auctioneer. You'll holler "Is this fair?"
and all that. You know how to yell, I'm sure.'

'Mangold's has been the subject of abuse from —'

'Sure, sure.' My tone was cold. Asking for sympathy, and him
an auctioneer. 'False high estimates: "anticipatory valuation" to the
trade. That too will be complained about. New legislation will be
demanded from the Europeans, and Parliament. Quote Turner's
Seascape Folkestone — the whole trade knows about that. And cite the

different values given to different museums for the same painting.' I pretended to think a while, though I'd already decided. 'That Cuyp painting simply couldn't be officially worth only three million sterling in Wales, and twice that in Edinburgh, right? Here's a list of suggestions for your press handout, with details and dates. Some you'll already find in your clippings file. Others are my own . . . imaginings.' I smiled. Even he cracked his face a little. 'I'm hoping you'll dish the obvious dirt, Mr Mangold, like telling the world that all those awful hundred-thousand dollar Utrillos are fakes.'

'Three full pages, Mr Dulane?' He read rapidly, looking for his own name, relaxed when it wasn't there.

'I was pushed for time.'

He did smile then. 'Who'll be making the protest to the Antique Internationalers?'

I sighed at the memory of what it would be costing me when young Masterson, Eton and Oxford, suaved to his feet and delivered the speech in Brussels. I'd be paying for the rest of my life, if I lived that long.

'An interested party, Mr Mangold,' I said mournfully. 'Here's your bill: just get me secretly to Los Angeles, at maximum speed. Add pocket money, and we're quits.'

He folded the lists away. 'When your man has raised Cain in Brussels, Parliament, the European Commission −'

'Now, or I cancel.' I stood, the better to run.

He moved even faster, clambering his desk to wring my hands. 'It's a deal,' he said.

'Plus the phone call.' He unwrung, as if hearing me demand that secret four per cent discount on commission which they allow antique dealers, as a bribe. I explained. 'The call I'll make very soon, from LA, asking you to agree that you'll donate to me one hundredth of the joint Sotheby-Christie Impressionist sale prices.'

He gaped. 'That'll be a fortune! Mangold's could never afford −'

'Mangold's will,' I promised. 'Because the Rail Pensions Fund can't risk scandal. Play your cards, and they'll switch the sale to you. Surely you can afford one per cent of their gelt?'

Tears filled his eyes. 'If that comes to pass, Mr Dulane,' he said huskily, 'I'll give you two per cent.'

His mind was orgasming at the thought of failures and suicides among his rivals. I was pleased. I'd hate to see auctioneers mellow. Keep progress at bay, I always say. You know where you are with sin.

CHAPTER TWENTY-FIVE

Mangold did an efficient job. No ostentation, just sent his secretary to conduct me along miles of tortuous corridors. We came out through a shopping mall where a hired saloon waited. A private plane from a small airport beyond Little Ferry, and I had time to think and hope and be relieved the fliers weren't Joker and Smith.

The loveliness whizzing below brought tears to my eyes, seeing it all being wasted because I was zooming to fabulous California and probable demise. I was heartbroken with pity for Lovejoy Antiques Inc's stupidity. So I wallowed and planned, and finally decided I'd better be ready for anything, or else.

Which brings me to a little place called Los Angeles.

One thing you have to admit about East Anglia is that its villages have centres. Each town has a middle. Every city has an area that definitely is bullseye. Like an idiot, I'd assumed Los Angeles would be similar. I'd actually told Magda and Zole to meet at the railway station, six o'clock every night until I showed up. I'd stay at some hotel 'near the town centre'. I remembered using the phrase.

Lovejoy, he dumb. Brains of a Yeti.

For Los Angeles is a tangle of cities, towns, areas, coasts, harbours, suburbs, all by the veritable dozen. I stared down disbelievingly as the massive spread grew beneath us. Strings of motorways wound through cities strewn about the globe's surface, motor cars streaming along umpteen-lane highways that melded, parted, and emptied themselves into the misty distance where still more cities sprawled. I'd seen rivers of traffic before, never floods.

Just as I thought I'd identified LA's town centre, it was supplanted by another. And another.

Shakily I asked the air lass what this place was. She looked brightly out of the window.

'That's old LA,' she said fondly. 'Great, huh? We'll be landing at one of the airports shortly.'

Get it? *One* of the airports? I shrank, didn't want to disembark. I was already lost. I'd thought Los Angeles was a seaside resort. Instead it was a universe.

We landed at a smaller airport near Lawndale. It was as big as most countries, and took six minutes to slot me into a motor car. I laid low, occasionally peering out. The world was rushing, whizzing to God knows where. The driver was a Turk, who talked of baseball for the twenty or so miles.

'You look like I feel, Lovejoy.'

I'd never been so glad to see anyone as Magda and Zole. He'd acquired a skateboard, blew gum between cryptic aphorisms, still swivelled like a periscope poking up from *Nautilus*. Magda looked what my old Gran called Sunday shod, meaning respectable on the surface but don't take too much on trust. Her clothes were bright, her face rested into a youth.

'This place scares me, love.'

We were in a self-service near the station. She had found it, said it was safe.

'I've already seen two people mugged. In broad daylight.' I waited for this to take effect. Magda shrugged, Zole blew a bubble. 'And some of the . . . girls seem as young as, well, Zole here. One solicited me on a tricycle.'

'I'll take you round Hollywood and Vine. Some of them blocks beyond Sunset Boulevard you wouldn't believe, Lovejoy. Two of your friends get themselves happy there.'

'They did?' I asked uneasily.

'Al and Shelt. That Kelly Palumba and her sheet.'

'She dumb. Her man pays dumb dollar.'

'Epsilon,' Magda translated. 'Buys for her. She's stoned.'

'Magda.' It was hard to start, even after a few goes. 'Look, love. I'm really grateful . . .'

I hate saying things like this, especially to a bird, because they're inclined to feel they have a right to you more than they have a right. If you follow. But when Magda and Zole had come into the station I'd almost fainted with relief. And when she told me she'd done as I'd asked I almost filled up.

'I found Revere Mount, Lovejoy. It's Malibu.'

The self-service place was enormous. Two women in studs and black leather were jeering by the till, men round them whooping and cheering at sallies. A weathered, frayed old man was slumped at a table, head on his hands. Outside it was almost dark, traffic glaring and snorting for headway. Nobody seemed to be watching us.

'For the Game?'

'Uh huh. They staying every which way, Pasadena, Long Beach, Santa Monica.'

But Al and Shelt were Tye Dee's two special goons. And Magda'd mentioned them practically with her hello. Which raised the small question of how she'd done so well.

'Where are the Aquilinas?'

'Beverly Hills. They got a house, a battalion of friends.' She told me an address in impossible numbers.

'You've done marvellously, love.'

Zole happened to be listening, picked up a vibe of doubt. He'd been strolling among tables, picking leftovers from plates. Habit of a lifetime, I supposed. There's an old Polish millionaire I know in London does the same. Collects priceless porcelain, but once was a POW.

'Cost us plenny in calls, Lovejoy,' he put in. 'And she done favours for free with a agency man, Boyle Heights.'

'Zole,' Magda said in her special tone. He shrugged, resumed his scavenge. 'It's known, Lovejoy. Society gossip on TV, convention talk.'

'They know to arrange what's said, love. They own everything I've ever heard of. Can you give me names?'

'It was easy at first. That Palumba broad'd been on the movies once, turkeyed out. She was in the papers. Finding the hotel, getting to know waiters, the lounge hustlers, pretending I was looking for a ster.' She half smiled, grimaced slightly to warn there was no way to postpone bad news. 'It's tomorrow, Lovejoy. Big place. Movie people use it, studios, syndicates, you name it. Night, ten o'clock.'

'Where are you staying?' I'm pathetic sometimes. Had I never been in a strange city before? I sounded like a kid trying to join her team, let me play or I'll tell.

She hesitated. 'I got to pay this guy, Lovejoy. Another time?'

'Fine,' I said, my best smile on. 'Look after Zole, eh?'

She shrugged. 'It's what I do, Lovejoy.'

We agreed to part without thinking further, the station to be our meeting place, day after next. After that would be straw guessing. I tried to find something warm and grateful to say. She seemed to wait in expectation, finally collected Zole. We parted. She didn't wish me luck. And with Zole on hand she'd not need any.

I remember her squaring up to walk to the taxi rank. Loveliness sometimes in the eye of the beholder. Sometimes it's just better than beauty, and that's that.

I registered at a downtown hotel which had an armed night guard at the door. I gave complicated instructions about being roused the instant my missing luggage arrived from some mythical but erratic airline, and slept fitfully dreaming of gamblers with knives for fingers.

The sun dawned me on streets gaunt without people. The area seemed oddly vacant, a studio oddly empty. Windows seemed shuttered from perversity rather than need. The few shops which had opened were scored with graffiti, abusive and delirious. LA clocked early didn't look a going concern. It looked raddled, sickening for something yet feverishly determined to conquer. The walls of buildings were pockmarked, as if firing squads had lately been about their business. Vacant ground wore skeletalized cars lying lopsided with one cheek into the ground. I walked enough to be pervaded by the sense of Los Angeles, which is action deflected beyond control, omnipotence revealing its secret neuroses. Then I went and earned the reproaches of the desk clerk for having actually walked instead of travelling by gunship, and booked out, ostensibly for the airport.

Working out my gelt, I had enough left to put me in some sort of social order, and to get me to Revere Mount Mansions. Time was already spinning LA faster than I wanted. Revere Mount was a play on words – wasn't he the patriot who'd ridden to warn of an invasion? More importantly, he was a fabulous silversmith whose work I've always admired. It seemed an omen. Then.

CHAPTER TWENTY-SIX

Revere Mount Mansions deserved the plural. I was glad of two things: that I didn't have to storm it, and that I'd decided to suss it out before night fell.

It stood back from a cliff edge which overlooked a multi-lane highway flooding with headlights. A road nosed the Malibu hillside as if trying to find contour lines among the bushes. Why was the land so dry? Coloured lights arched over the gateway proclaiming that Revere Mount Mansions was Heaven's Gift to California. Close to, it looked as if the paint wasn't yet dry.

Not that I got close to straight away. Nor did I lurk in the undergrowth. I stayed away seeking middle-class mediocrity until the day began to wane, then prepared for action. I'd spent hours being toured around Movie City. I ogled studio sets, saw where the great directors had shot this movie and fought that mogul. On a normal day I'd have been thrilled. Now, I just kept asking the time and judging how long it would take to reach Malibu. People kept giving me brochures, or begging. I've never seen so many people asking to have their clipboard signed in support of some cause or other.

We passed it on a coach trip. In mid-afternoon sunshine it was brilliant, a Samarkand of a place, El Dorado, with golden towers Camelot would have been proud of. Peacocks fanned their tails among the laid gardens. Small pagodas and summerhouses dotted the walks among lakes and waterfalls. The coach guide was in raptures.

'The gardens alone took quarter of a million tons of stone, fifteen thousand plants and bushes . . .'

People photographed, darted from one side of the coach to the other, called for the driver to pause because the sunshine was catching somebody's lens wrong. The guide even said that it was currently a focus of a huge All American convention of charity associations, and LA was especially honoured yet once more folks to be the site of might . . .

I honoured Revere Mount by seeing how far it stood from the road – half a mile. The cliff seemed pretty sheer. When finally the hillside ran out of patience and recovered its slope, the drop was sudden until barricades landscaped some sort of surety for the traffic on the teeming highway below. If I'd been the roadbuilder I'd have gone round, only the opposite side ended in close wooded screes. Distantly, glints of water showed. The hills astonished me by their height and dusty brown dryness.

Men stood by the gateway. They wore livery, but garments do not hinder truth. Smart, vigilant in constant communication. There were seven, taking turns to leap forward to direct drivers along one of the three roads through the ornamental gardens. The main building had more verandahs than a castle, more windows than any Vatican. Outlying smaller places were presumably the kind of separate motel buildings America has perfected. Then the driver called he was behind schedule and we drove on across bridges beneath which no rivers ran, to lose the view among dense cloying trees.

I'd had the shakes ever since reaching America. I couldn't remember a single hour when I'd been quiet, at peace. I'd always had to be running out of the firing line, working out where I was, what the hell I ought to be doing to survive. Maybe that's what folk meant by the American Way? It certainly was Magda's view of her world, and Zole's opinion of his. Things here weren't immutable. What today forbids, tomorrow might make compulsory. Today might hang you, and tomorrow sanctify. But even with dusk rushing the hills into night I couldn't find it in my heart to scold America. Why? Because love is the same, after all. The lady sloshes you with her handbag one day, and the next day pulls you, moaning.

Eight o'clock, I went over my words, trying to spot unexpecteds.

Nine, I phoned the reception at Revere Mount. I tried to sound as if I was delayed by impossible inefficiency somewhere, bullied over the girl's routines, said to get urgent word to the gate supervisor, make sure I wasn't delayed because I'd barely make it before the Game. Then I rang off, sweating. It could have been the sticky heat that drenched my palms, but wasn't.

Sometimes – in love, war, gambling, any sort of risk – time is paramount, no pun intended.

Half past nine I was out on the pavement watching taxis. The third driver looked as if he knew the area and could get a move on. I flopped into the cab and told him Revere Mount Mansions fast.

He drove like a maniac. I would have been frightened to death, but was there already.

I'd worked out my phraseology, tersely gave it the gatemen.

'Point me to the Game. I'm late, a'ready.'

Two barred the way. A third approached, stooped to examine

all occupants. I noticed the lights were clever. However a car was positioned, light entered from every direction.

'Evening, sir. I think we have full complement.'

'You think wrong.'

A list was consulted. 'Have you a number, sir?'

'Alhambra one-four-zero, for Christ's sake. Lovejoy the name. Nicko called it yet? Sheet, I oughta seen Gina and Tye Dee before now —'

'It's here.' The man glanced at the others, flicked open a thick wallet of photographs, checked one against me, nodded, spoke to the cabbie. 'Up the main drag, left, big square annexe on your right. Don't deviate.'

'Got it.'

Two minutes, and I was trying to look casual at the entrance of Revere, having my photograph checked and rechecked, moving into affluent aromas and ascending a staircase out of Elizabeth and Essex with showbiz music accompanying the hubbub of talk.

My scheme included washing hands, smiling at the staff and giving them joke time. Easy to make a show of haste without actually hurrying.

It was one minute to ten when I reached the main gathering. I knew I was going to be the only one not wearing a dinner jacket, and I was right.

I waited, admiring the chandeliers — modern gunge — and the wealthy woe school of dross decor, the sort to impress. There must have been some three hundred people glitzing away, every shade and shape God made. I stood on the landing, ducking and weaving at one side of the entrance as if anxiously looking for my party.

'Lost, sir?' a flunkey asked.

I grinned. 'The Game's my home, man. Alhambra one-four-zero my number.'

'Alhambra? They're all up front, by the dais. You just made it. Here come the announcements now.'

Nicko was tapping the microphone, Gina — not Jennie — gorgeous beside him. I kept still beside the entrance. There were plenty of people, milling, snatching last-minute drinks, plying others. Excitement was in the air. A band was fading with slight rattles, clashes, trying for their enemy silence.

'Ladies and gentlemen — friends all!' Nicko's voice had octaved echoes and an after whine. 'Welcome to the nineteenth California Game!'

People whooped, applauded, crowded closer round the dais. I could see Jennie, Melodie, Epsilon, Monsignor O'Cody, the Commissioner, Denzie and Sophie. No Moira, no Kelly Palumba. Charlie Sarpi was there, but less good-humoured than the rest. And astonishing me by his presence, tanking on booze and twice his natural hue of grue, Fatty Jim Bethune of antiques fame.

'We are gathered here –' Nicko paused for the shrill screams of laughter as Monsignor O'Cody waved to acknowledge the applause '– as guests of the Californians, for which our eternal gratitude.'

Applause, whistles, yells, jokes. Nicko stayed the congratulatory riot. He was a consummate crowd-handler. Should have been a policeman, I thought wrily. My heart was thumping, blood shushing my ears.

'As last year's winners, we poverty-stricken New Yorkers will –'

Pandemonium, ladies stamping the floor and screeching, their men howling affable insults.

'– will lead. All sectors have already nominated their players. Observers in the galleries as usual, please. Ladies and gentlemen – the Game's on! Go go go!'

The elegant throng crushed the far exits. Two, beside the central dais. I hung back, finding my mark. They were an intense, less than jubilant, cluster of half a dozen who didn't scrum forward with quite the same rapture. I strolled up, grabbed a wine from a side counter, but only after checking the half-dozen wall bars were free of Manhattan familiars.

'Don't you Californians praise your traffic to me ever again!' I exclaimed, grinning at a woman shut into a mass of emerald slab silk. Her jewellery was dazzling, but not antique.

'Had difficulty?' She wasn't into the group discussion. I'd seen her eagerness to roam. Women love a party because excitement rules within bounds that they can change any time. 'We're Florida, incidentally. Jane Elsmeer.'

'Raising the ante?' I chuckled, took a swig. 'Tell your friends to throw in the towel. Lovejoy's the name.'

'Hi. You're confident.' Her eyelashes batted. I nearly had to lean into the wind they created.

'You're exquisite, but I fear for your bank balance.' We were all drifting down the room as the crush lessened and the crowd thinned through the exits. 'We got over twenty times our last year's gelt.' I smiled into her astonishment. 'That do you?' I took her arm. 'Jane, honey. I'll see you don't starve, okay? Come to Lovejoy. Nicko's got my number.' I chuckled, squeezed her hand.

'Twenty?' She glanced over to her people, still debating. 'Is that possible?'

I said soulfully, 'With eyes like yours, Jane, I'll let you hear more any time.'

Her hand held me back. 'No stake's more than double, is it? I didn't really listen to the announcement, but —'

'Difference between two and twenty's zero, right?' I laughed. Ushers were begging us tardies to move into the Game arena. 'Twenty, God's truth. See you in there, Jane.'

I strolled down the emptying salon, nodding and saying hi to barmen and generally being a pest. I hoped I'd done enough.

In a mirror I saw Jane Elsmeer talking to her Florida syndicate. They were shooting looks my way. I did my act with another glass, and was almost last in. But not quite last. One of the Floridans hung back even more, and made sure he was standing immediately behind me at the last second, as the doors closed on the gloaming of the Game.

An aquarium. Not really, but like that.

We, the watching crowd, were rimmed round a glass-enclosed balcony. Down below, a boarded arena with one great central table covered in green baize. It was oddly reminiscent of a snooker championship, except with the audience arranged in sloping crystal. We were in semi-darkness. The arena below was brilliantly lit.

Our gallery ran the full circumference. It was difficult to see the faces of the crowd though I searched among them for the Manhattan lot. Glad of the gloom, I edged along, casual pace by casual pace. Happier still to see the avid concentration of everybody staring down into the Game arena.

It was cleverer than I realized at first. The table's wide surface could be seen from every position in the gallery.

Below, Nicko was chatting to three blokes, all as important, all as cool. Power emanated from their stances. One was so fat he should have been a joke. Except for his stillness you'd have passed him over without a thought. But creatures aren't stationary. Nature says move, a sign of life. So we fidget, shuffle, cough in church, look round when the movie hits a dull stretch, try not to yawn when our loved one's going on and on about her damned row with that parking attendant.

Except this bloke stood. You could have drawn round him in a gale, he was so static. Which is another way of saying he was a hunter. Fat, okay. Nobody taking much notice of him, okay too. But he was the frightener. The man.

'Okay everybody!' Nicko's voice on some concealed intercom made me jump a mile. Everybody else started buzzing with expectation. 'Here's Vermilio!'

The crowd applauded, which was a bit daft, seeing the arena people couldn't hear us, though we could hear them. The immense rotund man spoke into a microphone, a surprisingly high voice.

'The successful stakers are the following teams: Alhambra of New York, automatic entrants as last year's winner.'

The crowd fell silent. I saw a couple of birds near me cross their fingers. We'd all gone quiet. Nobody strolling or pairing off now.

'Renaissance from Chicago. The New Miners from Houston, Texas – is that name for real? Will somebody ask Harry? The Strollers, Philadelphia. The Governors, Washington DC . . .'

Ten groups had bought places. The names were greeted with stifled exclamations, cries quickly shushed by others hanging on Vermilio's every syllable. I was enthralled. Somebody nearby was sobbing, whispering about an appeal, third year lock-out and –

' . . . and last the Dawnbusters of Hawaii!'

Hubbub rose. People congratulated people. Some dissolved in relief. Women squealed more ecstasy than the men. Down in the lit arena Vermilio handed over to a bloke in a plum tuxedo, who began to intone lists of figures for each of the teams Vermilio had announced. Nobody took much notice, though I saw the Florida folk, Jane Elsmeer among them, frozen at one of the panes, staring down with a terrible intensity. I eyed the signed exits, hoping I could make it if it came to a dash.

'The grand total staked on this year's Game is the highest ever.' The plum-coated bloke raised his pitch by way of bliss, surely the accountant. 'It is two point oh nine times last year's in absolute dollars, ladies and gentlemen!'

The applause was general and heartfelt. I applauded along, smiling absently. People were muttering with some urgency near Jane Elsmeer. I edged nearer the window, apologizing to a lady whose scarlet sheath dress lacked only a Canterbury Cross in gold – even a Regency copy of the Anglo-Saxon would have done.

'You get in?' she asked.

I tore my eyes from her dress. 'Oh, I'm an Alhambran,' I said. 'I upped our stake twenty-fold. I like your dress, love. Have you thought of combining it with a simpler brooch? I know those Cartiers are fashionable, but a genuine antique –'

She had to amputate herself away from this guff with a low excuse, whispered something to her man. I caught, ' . . . Alhambra's the Aquilinas, right?' before she smiled, returned to collect more admiration.

The talk round the Floridans was causing some attention.

'Are you particularly interested in old jewellery?' she asked, taking hold with a gamekeeper's grip.

'My life's first and only lovelust,' I told her pleasantly. 'Though if I'd met you earlier I'd revise my career moves. Hardly any woman can wear genuine antique gems, love. It's a delight to find one who has the class.'

Not true, of course. Antique jewellery draws any woman's glory. God knows why they buy expensive modern crud, when antique decoratives are cheaper. It always amazes me –

He saw me. Across the arena, in through the sloping tinted glass opposite, Fatty Jim Bethune saw me. The growing noise, now practically arguments, round the Floridans was attracting attention. It had attracted his.

I waved, smiling. No good shouting round the balcony, but the arena lighting struck upwards, picking those faces nearest the glass.

'It's him,' Jane Elsmeer was saying, closing. She had a woman's second dearest wish, total attention. People were following.

'Hello, Jane,' I said. 'Do you get to play?'

'Lovejoy. Upped by twenty. He told me.'

'At least that,' I said modestly. 'Though I can't claim to be in on the totalizations finalizationwise –'

And that was that. My feet hardly touched the ground.

The room felt like a medieval Inquisition chamber. Some houses, even rooms, have an aura as if evil intentions were ingrained by a malevolent hand. In fact, it was to guard against such forces that ancient builders buried holy relics – and sometimes the architect – in the walls. Still done today, except we make polite social occasions of laying the foundation stone.

The man Vermilio watched me come. He was standing by a desk. He was the only bloke I'd ever seen not use a desk for extra authority. The plum-tuxedo accountant was beside him. Nicko was there, staring ominously past me.

Plus a line of goons standing along the panelled walling. Everybody looked at me.

'Lovejoy, huh?'

'Yes.' I advanced, smiling, hand outstretched. 'I don't believe I've had the –'

I was stopped by a gesture. 'No games, Lovejoy. Talk.'

'What about?' I waited, asked Nicko anxiously, 'Nothing wrong, Nicko, is there? I did everything you said.'

'Mr Vermilio wants that you tell him what you tellt the Elsmeer broad.' The plum-tuxedo man said the words with an accountant's terrible pedantry. People come, people go, accounts go on for ever.

'Mrs Elsmeer? We were talking about the Game. She said she hoped they'd get in, their stake was special. I said ours was twenty times up on last year's, so we were sure to play.'

'Twenty.' Vermilio sounded like asking for a gun. 'Coats?'

'Nicko declared a little over twice last year's stake for his Alhambra team, Vermilio.' Coats might well be an exploited nickname, heady stuff for an accountant. Except maybe he wasn't just an accountant.

'I can explain, Vermilio, Coats.' Nicko spread his hands in appeasement. 'This guy's new in. We employed him to see if he could increase the contribution from antiques. He failed.' He smiled, calm personified. 'We got Jim Bethune back instead.'

'But Nicko,' I exclaimed, indignant. 'Mr Bethune's figures were less than a twentieth of —'

'He's a blusterer, Vermilio,' Nicko said. 'We had to give him a try. But he couldn't deliver —'

'I got the concession from Mangold's auctioneers like I promised, Nicko!' Nicko tried to interrupt, but Vermilio silenced him by a look. 'The percentage from Mortdex. God, Nicko. The hack from Louisiana alone is over three times what you had from all the art markets last year! The hacks from Tramper, Gullenbenkian, bring it at least to eighteen times Bethune's figures —'

'He's insane, Vermilio. It can't be done.'

Nicko was green. His eyes did their laser trick directly into me. I didn't care. I was suddenly immune. Once a threat is diluted, it might as well go all the way.

'Let's hear it.'

Vermilio stayed on his feet. Coats called in several tuxedo people from outside. They sat around me in a circle to listen. I was made to talk. The line of goons against the panelling didn't move. Nicko stood beside Vermilio while I spoke quietly to show I wasn't a madman.

'I was working in a bar,' I began. 'I fancied a few antique items worn by a customer. Her sister noticed my interest, guessed I was able to recognize genuine antiques by instinct. It's called being a divvy. Nicko Aquilina came to hear of me, took me on his payroll. I investigated Jim Bethune's antiques firm in Manhattan. It was a front for fraud —'

'Fraud's essential in the California Game, Lovejoy.' Coats, in reprimand. I didn't respond. Let him dig my trench for me. 'All our stakes are hacks.'

'It's not fraud,' I said quietly. 'It's fair, legit legal.'

Coats was irritated, challenged on his own ground.

'You heard the announcement. Washington stakes an extra half billion this year, hacked from the Irish illegal immigrant levy. Houston, Texas, cuts in the same from the environment lobby. Hawaii brings in a new billio from glass pipes – very promising, now ice-crack's on the mainland here. Chicago's brung another half billio from Pentagon hacks –'

'Dull, dull,' somebody muttered. 'What's new? It shoulda been new.'

'Like fuckin' Philly, uh?' somebody in a gaudy polka-dot bow tie shot back. The listeners brightened. I did, with the realization I was relatively small fry among this lot. 'Still workin' the fuckin' Panama Bahama dirty dollar shunt? Jeech!'

'Atlanta's new,' a smooth smiler put in conversationally. 'Except a World Soccer Cup stadium hack only works one time. Once the stadium's been built all over the fuckin's place, that's it, though maybe next time –'

'Lovejoy?' from Vermilio.

They shut up. I was back in the limelight. 'Mine isn't fraud. It's legit.' My attempt at snappy speech was pathetic.

'Your antiques hack is legitimate?' Coats looked for help.

'Ring Mangold. Ask him if he's agreed to chip in a percentage of the shifted auctions. Nothing illegal there, by any country's laws. Check Gullenbenkian. It's legit. Check that Tramper's input's legal. Ask Verbane if the Mortdex contribution's legal or not.' I waxed indignant, almost believing me myself. 'That's what I told Nicko, didn't I, Nicko? And Jennie. Ask Tye Dee. He'll tell you. He was with me all through when I arranged them. He's got witnesses. I've a list of hotels, bedroom reservations.'

I was moving about, pleading for antiques now, not for me.

'The trouble is, people like you come to think of antiques as a commodity. They're not. They're people, the best things on earth. Can't you see that, played right, the antiques world can chip in as much as the rest of an entire stake? Nicko'll tell you. I worked it all out for him weeks ago –'

'A legit hack?' Coats almost reeled. 'There's no such thing.' He looked at the Atlanta man, appealed, 'The World Cup building programme – the hack was twelve per cent of total. Massive!'

'I don't like the word hack,' I protested. 'Or fraud.'

Vermilio pondered massively. 'Check his numbers,' he said. 'Nicko? He's right, you're wrong, okay?'

'Sure.'

'It looks like the Alhambra stakers tried it on,' Coats the accountant said. 'Risking less'n they hacked. Should they lose, they keep mosta the hack. If they win, then nice for them.'

Vermilio smiled, like a mountain parting to show worse mountains in the interior. 'Compensation,' he announced. 'A bet. Nicko's on the line. He wins, he keeps his ass. He loses...'

The meeting dissolved in whoops and an exchange of bets. I looked at Nicko, but received nothing. He knew only what I knew. I was pouring sweat too, and the air conditioning was at maximum chill.

Faro's said to be the oldest card game ever.

You pick a card, and chuck away the rest of that pack. Then you take a new pack, and deal into two piles. If the matching card falls into one pile, you win. If in the other, you lose.

Money, usually. Life, in Nicko's case.

The Alhambra crowd assembled in silence away from the exit signs, when finally the galleries were crowded and rumours had settled into a steady hum of hatred. I'd tried to say hi there to Jane Elsmeer, but she'd managed nothing more than a reflex twitch of the lips. I'd even smiled at the scarlet lady to no avail.

'Play ball!' somebody called. I wish they'd warned us. I came slowly down to the deep russet pile, heart banging enough to shake me.

'The Alhambra syndicate, first. Nicko Aquilina plays.'

A girl was at the green, placing decks of cards. People were examining them, all watched by Vermilio and Coats. The scrutineers nodded, talking as if everything was normal.

'We go first, eh?' I asked a man craning next to me.

'You an Alhambra?' he asked through the artificial dusk, staring. 'Good luck.'

Why did I need luck, for heaven's sake? I'd done the decent thing, revealed the truth about my scams, told Vermilio how everything worked when I was asked. No. It was Nicko, Gina, the rest who were for the high jump if Nicko lost. Tough luck. But I'd soon be out of here... Wouldn't I? Vermilio had said Nicko, not me.

Suddenly I wanted Nicko to win. Not because my throat was slate dry, no. And honestly not because I felt faint at the thought of the terrible crime that would be committed on him if he didn't win. But we'd been, if not quite friends, sort of acquaintances who'd done each other no real harm, and I'd quite enjoyed my stay in America after all, lovely country and everything –

'Ten of diamonds is Alhambra's card.'

Nicko placed the card face up for all us watchers to see. Coats nodded to the girl, who slowly started dealing her pack, one card to her left, another to her right. People murmured. I swallowed, trying tiptoes to see over heads. Word had spread that more hinged on this result than mere money, crime.

'Your win,' she said. Jack of clubs.

'My win.' Three of hearts.

'Your win.' Ace of spades, to a swell of talk swiftly muted. People near me made superstitious gestures.

'My win.' A four, clubs.

Fingers sometimes do their own thing. Mine were trying hard to grasp hold of my palms, hoping for a heavenly ladder.

'Your win. Game over!'

The babble erupted, me whimpering what was it, who'd won, was it – ?

'Lucky,' the man grinned with gold teeth at me. I could have throttled him.

The crowd relaxed, talking, betting, swapping predictions. I pressed through to glimpse Nicko stepping back, taking his place in the line-up as the next player stepped up. God, but he was cool, that Nicko. I saw Gina's expression across the arena fishbowl. Waxen, a million years old. Where was Sophie Brandau? I'd not seen her since I'd arrived. And Kelly Palumba, lucky in her addiction to be out of this. Monsignor O'Cody was grey, talking intently with three grave-suited men, explaining his innocence in everything, the way of all religious leaders.

'Philadelphia to play. Frank Valera the nominee.'

We – Nicko, I mean – were safe for the rest of this round. I didn't listen. All I wanted now was for the rest to lose first round, and Nicko'd be clear. I went to ask for a drink. The door goon wouldn't let me out until the whole first round had been played all through. Then he allowed me into the grand salon, where a good-humoured barkeep poured me lemonade, asking if I'd won much so far. They all wished me luck as I re-entered. The pillocks thought it was routine gambling.

Start of the second round. I asked people in the semi-darkness who was still in, got told to shush. Nicko was just stepping up to pluck the marker card, as the girl's new pack was shuffled in. We – no, *he* – wanted the seven of spades this time.

He made it with only five cards remaining. I collapsed with relief. He had the cool to smile at Vermilio as he withdrew without a wobble. I was almost fainting with fear, my suspicion hardening that maybe Nicko's fate would also be mine. I wanted to ask the man with the gold teeth why he'd called me lucky. It was Nicko who was up for the chop, wasn't it?

People were whispering all round the gallery now. There's something about terror that stimulates. The women were panting, the men steaming with heat. Passion was king. The place felt humid, as tropical outside as in. Hands were moving. Suggestions were being whispered. I heard some woman groan a soft 'Oh *God*', pure desire. A lecher's dream. It happens in cockfights, some sudden lust blamming your mind from nowhere.

By taking hold of people I learned that four had lost in the first round. I stood as if stunned. Gina's face had gone. Instead, Fatty Jim Bethune's stared down beside that of Monsignor O'Cody. His lips were moving. A prayer, even? I was tempted to walk round the glass gallery, stand with them, maybe ask Gina where was Sophie, decided I didn't want to be with a load of losers, and stood shaking while the cards were shuffled. I wanted the dealer girl, now a lovely dark lass who'd removed all her rings, to fall down in a palsy, anything to stop the cards coming.

Six remaining for the second round. Two more lost while I watched and had to forfeit their stakes. People had calculators out, clicking and tapping, in that terrible tide of whispering, the heat impossible.

'Third round,' the caller announced. 'Alhambra, Nicko Aquilina.'

The door was just closing. I made it to the salon, asked for some grub, went to the kitchen, following its noises.

My voice had almost gone. I was drenched, sopping and un-wholesome, wet running down my nape, my thatch of hair plastered down twenties style. A bloke suffering from super-nourishment among the trays and gleaming steel surfaces shouted for assistants, and I was brought a plate of genuine American food, meaning it was bigger than me. I asked could I sit in the air, and they let me through.

It was coolish out on the kitchen step. I sat, noshing. Nicko was up there in the Game, his awful stare now no use. Everything hinged on the turn of a card his way. Or not. I looked out into the night. Sophie, Rose Hawkins, that sister of hers. The ambitions of Sophie's husband Denzie, consummate politician. And the reason they – okay, so Hirschman gave the word – tried to have me killed in New Orleans. And Bill's death. Sokolowsky. And the hotel fire. And upstairs in that enclosed arena of green baize Nicko was even now winning. Or losing. What was the statistical chance, one in four? Racing punters say there's no way to win above two to one.

Behind me the kitchen clattered in its steam. Hideous places, kitchens. The kitchen had gas. Gas from cylinders. I left my plate, stepped out. Two dogs loped by, black and straining. I called a hi to the dog handler.

'Lovely animals,' I called.

'Bastards,' he grunted, jerking and pulling.

God, but dogs can look malevolent. A muted roar wafted out into the night. I almost collapsed. Nicko's win, or loss? The card could fall only one way, no inbetween.

Cylinders. I'd nothing to light anything with, and they were huge great things, shining with dull reflections from the floodlights of the Revere's façade. It was eerie, a waiting film set. Movie memories. I shook. Maybe I was coming down with something. Worse, maybe I wasn't, and reality was knifing my soul.

Another guard walked by, coated in red plaid, a hunter's nebbed cap showing for a second against the lake's distant gleam, his boots scuffing gravel. I called a hi there, got a grunt as he passed. Maybe I'd sounded drunk enough. I'd tried.

Seven cylinders, two already tubed into the wall below the noisy kitchen's half-open windows. Each cylinder had a pale panel, presumably warning of calamities that could ensue if you didn't watch out. I've always been frightened of these damned things. I once saw an accident at school. A cylinder had fallen sideways, being unloaded from a lorry, the valve striking against a kerb and popping off a hundred feet into the air. The oxygen cylinder had shooshed along the ground like a torpedo, smashing through the school wall, miraculously missing us little pests standing frozen to the spot. Nobody had been injured. We'd thought it wonderful, especially as the white-faced science teacher sent us all home for the day.

If Nicko'd lost, they'd come looking for me. I reached, unscrewed each of the two connecting nuts until I could hear an ugly hissing sound from the valve. I wanted a long, slow leak. I went along the row of cylinders and did the same. It's gambling people who are supposed to like fear. I'm not one. My arms were almost uncontrollable by the time I'd done the last. I stood there, legs trembling. Was this liquid gas fuel lighter than air once it vaporized? Did it just float up, to give some future astronaut a fright when he lit his fag in the stratosphere? Or did it sink low and lie on the ground like a marsh miasma? I'd vaguely heard that was what frightened our ancients, when marsh gases lit spontaneously, their sinister blue flames flickering along the roadside swamps and scaring travellers to death. If the latter, I was standing here being gassed, risking being blown to blazes. A stray spark from the kitchen window could set the gas ball off.

I returned the chef's plate, said it was the best nosh I'd had since my wedding, and scarpered back to the salon.

To see a few men and women emerging for a smoke and a drink. They stayed clustered by the doors to the gallery, not to miss the call.

'It's the last play,' a woman told me when I asked. 'Nicko Aquilina's on the line this time! Him and LA are left in.'

She was drooling, kept taking my arm. Everybody was thrilled, breathing fast, loving it.

'It's thrilling, hon,' she told me huskily. 'Know what I mean?'

'Sure do,' I said. I lit her cigarette for her. 'I'm so excited I just can't tell you. You here with somebody? I'm Lovejoy.'

'My husband.' She hid her scorn so only most of it showed. Her head inclined and her lips thinned. 'I'm Elise Shepherd.' A suave man, cuffs glittering with diamond links. Ramon Navarro from some old black-and-whiter. Odd how many here were lookalikes of the famous. Something in the California air?

There was something else in the air.

'Pity,' I said quietly, squeezing her arm. 'Elise, love. I've watched you since I arrived.' I made sure Ramon Navarro was making headway with a slender bird sequined in turquoise.

'You have?' She squeezed my arm, glancing, weighing opportunities. Somebody caught her rapid scan, waved. She hallooed, trilled fingers.

'Is there nowhere we could go for the last round and . . . ?'

'Yes?' Her tongue idled along her upper lip.

'And enjoy each other's company?'

'God, no. I might be able to . . . No, that wouldn't work. Barney'd miss me, the bastard.'

An announcer called the restart. I kept hold of her, desperately needing camouflage. She interpreted my fright as passionate desire, which it was.

'There's a corridor round the gallery,' she said quickly, as we all began to move and talk rose excitedly. Some silly old sod told me this was the most exciting time he'd ever experienced. I could have hit him.

'Where, for Christ's sake?' I could have clouted her too.

A smile flitted across her mouth. 'You're a tiger, hon. Door to the right. We could hear the calls from out there, while . . .'

'See you there. Hurry, darling.'

The goon standing at the gallery entrance had seen me talking with the woman. I winked. He raised his eyebrows, knowing the score. I walked through the corridor door, leaving the gallery entrance.

The corridor was empty. Wide, dark maroon velvet walls, gilded statues with lamps simulating old torches in frosted glass. Pathetic. Twice the price of genuine antique lanterns. Designers are unbelievable. I walked slowly down the corridor, counting steps, hearing the faint hubbub inside. The corridor curved round the gallery. Windows, closed against the thick night's slushy aromatic air, were serried round the curved walls. Ornate, with alcoves every ten yards, plush double seats trying to look Regency.

Except there was a goon, standing against an inner wall. And another beyond him. They'd thought of everything, our Malibu hosts. I walked, nodding as I passed the first. The second was twenty yards further on.

Hurry Elise, you lazy cow. Where the hell was she?

She was coming to meet me at a trot, somehow having escaped from her husband the other way. I grabbed her, nodded to the goon with a feeble smile. He turned away, walked deliberately back towards the door I'd come through. I crushed her close, squeezing the life out of her, pulling her along the corridor.

'Wait! Here —'

'No, er,' I gasped, trying to rush and reveal deep heartfelt passion. What the hell was her name? 'We must have . . . I can't wait, darling.'

'This one!'

She tried slowing into another alcove. Luckily it was occupied, a couple twisting sinuously to synchronized gasps. I hauled her, whisper-babbling. A goon turned aside, arms folded. God knows what they were used to.

'Last round, folks!' The announcer's echo made me whimper.

'Here, darling?'

'Yes, yes!' I flung her down and clawed feverishly at her bodice. Why the hell are their clothes so complicated? You'd think they'd go for simplicity. You can get scarred for life. 'I can't wait, er . . .' Name? Esme, Ellen? 'Darling.'

Directly below us, faint clashes of the kitchen. If I'd had any sense I'd have counted the windows along that side to make absolutely sure, but maybe the dog handlers would have stopped me.

We overtook passion on the outward run, me ripping at her, shoving the dress off her shoulders and scrabbling at her thighs. The more uncontrollable my sheer lust, the more authentic my presence out here in the corridor while the idiot of an announcer called for silence.

'Alhambra's card, the jack of hearts!'

My mouth was everywhere on Esme, only occasionally meeting hers as we mangled and mauled.

'Don't mark me, Lovejoy, for God's sake, honey, no, no –'

'Darling,' I gasped, sprawling over Ella, almost forgetting why I was there in the storm of frenzy. There was no doubt she was gorgeous, a million times more wondrous than any woman I'd ever –

'Alhambra win . . .!'

Thanks, Heaven, I remembered to say as Emma and I sank into that mutual torment, giving hurt and receiving it, wrestling to deny and abuse. She was openly weeping with delight, mouthing crudities, emitting a guttural chugging cough as we –

'Alhambra lose . . . Alhambra win . . .'

Win, Nicko, I thought. At least, I would have thought that if I wasn't sinking below consciousness as Elsa dragged me in and down and out into space and bliss was enveloping –

'Alhambra lose. Jack of hearts, and Alhambra lose . . .'

Eh? I slammed into Esta, listened to that reaching hum which followed me, calling desperately for my mind to realize, and *do* something. I dragged away from Elena with a long wail of deprivation, scrabbled for my jacket which some stupid pillock had cast aside, fumbled, yanked out the cigarette lighter which I'd stuck in the right-hand pocket after lighting the bird's cigarette and hopped with my pants round my ankles across the corridor towards the window, whimpering with fright and seeing Elsa's thunderstruck face gaping after.

You can't open a window with your pants down, nor trying to pull them up. You can't kick, either. I had my jacket. I wrapped it round my arm, averted my face and slammed the window glass, feeling something maybe give in my elbow. I felt the muggy night air wash in.

'What the – ?' somebody along the curved corridor called.

The lighter was a gas thing. I pressed, got light, spun the control for tallest flame, tried to look out and down as a goon hurtled at me, lobbed the thing out onto the cylinders below.

Heat slammed the world, spinning it round. Odd, but all a brain remembers is clatter, clatter, when you find it hard to think what on earth could be clattering, when fire is shooting with a terrible tearing noise and a whole side of a building comes apart with a low screaming sound.

I remember thinking I should have maybe warned Emelda, at least told her what I was planning, but that's typical for me, because by then something prickly was cramming itself into my face and people were screaming about fire, and a great golden shape was mushrooming out of the darkness nearby as a building crumbled and the hillside spread light and flame as a beacon for the world.

CHAPTER TWENTY-SEVEN

Your mind plays tricks. I can see myself running, scrambling up when I fell among vegetation, hauling myself along on all fours when the terrain suddenly let me down. It was some old serial I'd seen when little, funny man at antics to make laughter. Except this one was bleeding, clothes anywhere. And it was me.

Finally laying himself down, spent and stunned, among rocks with a curtain of flames ascending the hillside, something from a biblical epic now, roaring with a terrible grandeur and a massive building's turrets silhouetted against the orange-scarlet. So many colours, so much to see, if only the man's eyes could see. They couldn't quite focus. And people were screaming and shouts coming closer among scrub. And, oddest of all, whole trees suddenly exploding like they'd been fragged by grenades as the heat reached them and their aromatic perfumes caused the night to quiver in a death thrill as they sucked the flames into each burst of spark.

And the wahwahs, flicking their reds and yellows and blues in feeble simile while the mountainside erupted in roars and the fire moved through the vegetation like savage ascending lava.

The helicopters came, and police, and lights shone from the sky throughout the land, and it was all fireworks and spacecraft and people jumping down.

In one last feeble frame, me looking down from some great flying thing onto the forecourt of that great palace, where uniformed people, very like police, were taking orders from a dapper figure standing there in the mayhem and disorder as vehicles and helicopters moved stately all about him, the centre of that swirl. Except it couldn't be him, because he was surely dead, wasn't he? He'd lost the Game. And in any case he was the instigator of the crimes, and the deaths. Hadn't he ordered two people killed, not counting me? And I sank and let the frigging world get on with it. I should have stayed with Irena, and left things alone, let them take their course. Or maybe I ought to have run back in for her after the explosion? Better to have stayed making love, even if it was on that fake antique banquette.

At least I'd have finished something.

'Mr Shamoon? Joe?'

Somebody was tapping my face, like nurses do when you're coming round from the anaesthetic, the swine.

A policeman was sitting by the bedside. Mine. Why mine?

'Statement time, Joe.'

He had a brewer's goitre, the beer belly hauled in by an ineffectual belt hung about with firearms and ominous leatherette cases. All that blubber was presumably paid for. But why is adiposity threatening in uniform? A thin geezer would have seemed friendlier.

'Eh?' Who was Joe? I wasn't up to discussing people yet. I watched the cop. He chewed, more threat. A nurse swept in, swept out. Should be paid by the mile.

'Where were you when the fire started at the Revere, Joe?'

'The fire?' I was Joe?

My mind cranked slowly into gear. A hospital of some kind. Should I recover, or stay slightly delirious? I've been concussed before now. This didn't feel quite the same.

'I remember a fire,' I said slowly. It seemed to take years to get the words out. 'A sort of blast, people running, screaming, helicopter, fire up a hillside . . .'

'You got it, Joe.' He seemed pleased, told a hand recorder the time, place, date. 'What were you doing at Revere Mount?'

Not what you think, officer. 'Waiting for the boss. Some sort of charity . . .'

'Uh huh. You see the fire start?'

'No. I was with a . . . I think there was a broad.'

'Okay, Joe. I'll be back.'

He left. Joe lay wondering why he wasn't Lovejoy.

The jacket? It was surely mine, the one I'd grabbed up. Or was it? The neighbouring alcove had held the moaning couple. They'd been further into reality than Ellen and me. I couldn't quite remember if the bloke had shed his jacket. But I could recollect how I'd had to shuffle obliquely across the corridor to the window, snatching up a jacket as I'd hopped, trying to haul up my pants with one hand while . . .

Good old Joe Shamoon. Hope he made it. Or maybe he was still back there, into bliss?

I slumbered, woke and had a drink. Orange juice.

When I woke it was night. I clambered erect, steadied my dizziness against the wall, checked I wasn't bleeping from any wires into one of their infernal machines or being dripped into.

There was a light switch. I put it on, stared at myself in the mirror. Yes, Lovejoy all right. For a fleeting second I'd had a horrid

465

vision of seeing some other bloke's face, as on corny telly re-runs. I looked almost a picture of health.

My clothes were in a small wall cupboard, but no sign of any wallet. I brooded and dozed until dawn, then got hold of the first nurse I could and asked for my valuables, please. She brought them quickly, openly assuming I wanted to arrange payment for hospitalization. I almost choked on that, but it seems to be their system.

'Sure this is mine?' I checked shrewdly.

'Positive, Joe.'

Still Shamoon. I had Joe's wallet, billfold of money, credit cards with signatures, two sets of keys, driver's licence, spectacles. I didn't need the specs, but took them anyhow, and two chequebooks. Joe did all right for himself. I wondered what Mrs Joe Shamoon was like. Maybe I could finish what naughty old Joe had started so vigorously, when I found the addresses. The two addresses were in LA. Both had phone numbers.

With many a groan and wheeze, I asked the desk girl to hold the completion papers steady while I signed my credit-card gelt over to the hospital. The sum made me gasp, but I disguised it as a sudden twinge. I sent down for new casual clothes, billing it up to good old Joe Shamoon.

Then I left hospital, after a health check with a registrar. They called him a resident intern, as if he was an old-age prisoner. Funny language. He said I'd got off okay, but prescribed a ton of pills for me. I put them in a dustbin as I left.

One thing, I bet Joe Shamoon was having a hell of a time if he was trying to get treatment on Lovejoy's credit in there.

'What's the joke?' the taxi driver asked, surly.

'I just got better in hospital,' I said.

'That's a joke?' He snickered. 'Hell, LA's the joke, man.'

Redondo Beach was the second of the two addresses. It was a low condominium block alongside the seafront road. Joggers were scooping their feet the way they do when finally the taxi dropped me by the sand. Sunshades and the weirdest collection of parasols adorned the coast in numbers I'd never seen before.

I tried dialling both of Joe's homes, in case he should answer and I'd get myself arrested. Also, I was suddenly more worried about turning up, a strange husband for an alarmed wife, maybe a set of babes all wondering who the new geezer was. No answers.

One thing about California, you can wait on a beachside without giving rise to suspicion. It's what the ocean's for. I sat in a line of reminiscing geriatrics from the Bronx and New Jersey and Brooklyn all saying how they'd like to go back but who the hell wanted snow and better get mugged occasionally in sunshine than in an alley filled with ice and falling masonry, huh? Some, especially the old birds, had reflectors shooting hot sunshine up from below under their chins. They wore false white paper noses and a ton of cream. They all agreed retirement was great. I said I could see that, listened until the guard in the condominium block got up from his stool under the awning and went inside. I said so-long to my gang and quickly entered, fiddling with the keys, then climbing to the third floor.

The doorbell brought nobody. I worked the three keys – no flies on Joe Shamoon – and let my breath out slowly as no dogs, pets, families came forward with fast-fade grins.

It was a small place, as America goes. Two bedrooms, a kitchen, a living space with a view of the seafront, and quite a pleasant small balcony with chairs bleaching contentedly in the sunshine.

And Nicko.

Behind me the outer door opened gently, letting the verandah curtains waft out, then closed sibilantly. Tye Dee and his goons, doubtless. I was suddenly so tired. All for nowt, my exertions of last night – or the night before last? I'd lost a day somewhere.

'Wotcher, Nicko.'

He laid aside his book, Moss's *The Pleasures of Deception*, I noticed with curiosity. He nodded, painstakingly lit a pipe. I watched, the old craving coming as always. I once gave a pipe up, still hanker after the ritual. The swine drew in, pocketed his pouch, stubbed the bowl, did the whole, what did they say hereabouts, enchilada?

'Wotcher, Lovejoy.' He managed it, with the vicious shark grin of a born killer. 'We gotta change words.'

'What's the point?' I couldn't help being bitter. I should have taken my chance, let the pig die instead of blowing the damned thing to smithereens. Served him right, the murdering –

'You got work to do for us, Lovejoy. Antiques.'

Well, maybe his killer's grin was friendly.

'Eh?' I might spin the talk out and make a dash for it, hide out somewhere among my geriatric pals on the waterfront.

'We'd no idea about antiques, art, that kinda stuff, being the scale you showed.' He leaned forward, the pipe smoke driving me mad. 'Deal, Lovejoy?'

'Deal, Nicko.'

'You work for us three months, okay? Then you go.'

His features were affable, but knowing. What a pleasant bloke, I thought after quick revision.

'Hang on.' I dredged up a score of suspicion. 'How'd you know where to find me?'

'We planted Joe Shamoon's stuff on you. Easy. Poor Joe's in surgery. He'll make it – until his wife learns the circumstances of his, uh, accident.'

In some helicopter. I remembered being lifted, flying, people cutting my clothes, lights swirling.

'Nicko.' My head was aching. I'd had no rest except for hospital, and their idea of quiet's to clash cymbals all bloody night. 'Who's this we?' He'd just been slain by the Game syndicates for losing. I'd heard it called, while Esmerelda and I'd been making smiles. Optimism's not got staying power like pessimism.

He waited, smiling at the people behind me. 'Got it?' he asked at last.

'Gina?' I said.

She came round, smiling, sat across from me with the sun-filled verandah window playing her advantage. She looked good enough to eat with honey, except you wouldn't need the honey.

'Gina.' I make it a non-question.

'In one, Lovejoy. Well, in a coupla hundred, give or take.'

'You're police? Or crooks who turned coats?'

'You got it. Federal switchers. We got watchdogs, so we play ball.' He was wondering what I'd guessed. I helped him.

'Why'd you pull Tye and the hoods, let me get killed?'

'You did too good, Lovejoy. We want control of money routes, not new shark routes everywhere.'

So I was to be part of their control. At least I'd be alive. Except that wasn't enough.

'It started with drugs pure and simple, Lovejoy.'

'Not pure, not simple.' Gina was gentler but more implacable. 'Ice, heroin for the post-crack sinks, anything to double on, at any cost.'

'The Drug Enforcement Agency started us in, Lovejoy. The Game was dominated by them and the junk bonders and Savings-Loan defrauders. It used to be little old currency swappers.'

'Days of innocence,' Gina said. She could arrest me any day.

'You showed us a new line, Lovejoy.' Nicko went slowly to the window, gestured for somebody to come, but take their time. 'Though we'd learned plenty of other new lines. Property, hacks on harbours, airports, commodities, information tapping, computer miking, showbiz, religious flakes, lotsa old stuff. You showed us the power of antiques.' He turned, curious. 'How come we didn't see it before you came, Lovejoy?'

'You trusted reputations, Nicko. Like famous auction houses – you think the great Fake exhibition at the British Museum could have come about without them? Or that Echt Vals Real Fake Exhibition a decade ago in Amsterdam? Or that terrorists aren't a part of the antiques game, robbing simply to sell or ransom. You should read about Istanbul's go-betweens.' My tone was growing bitter, hating the way antiques get it every time, treated like dirt except when money gets quoted.

'We don't miss much, Lovejoy,' Gina said.

I rounded on her. Somehow I was standing. 'Much you know, you stupid bitch. You miss the nose on your face. Can't you see that in antiques there's *no such thing as theft*? Oh, there's fraud all right, tricks a-plenty. But theft? Antiques laugh at it.'

'Prove you weren't just a lucky bastard, Lovejoy!' Nicko was pointing at me.

'Shall I?' I yelled, in fury now it was all falling into place. 'Shall I, you legalized murdering sods, the pair of you? Shall I? Seeing you let poor old Sokolowsky get crisped just to stay in with the syndicate? Shall I? Seeing you let Bill get run down for the same reason? Seeing you were willing to have me shot down, when they missed burning me in the Benidormo hotel blaze?'

He backed down, with an effort. 'Some things have to be, Lovejoy. It's a war we're in. People get killed in wars.'

'Aye, you murderous pig, but not always the right ones.' I was so mad I couldn't see for a sec, just stood there shaking. Magda and Zole could have died in that alley. Worse, so could I. Just like that Tony off the *Gina,* during my introduction to the whole rotten business. I just didn't know who was right or wrong any more. Both sides played as dirty. I was so frigging tired, worn out.

'I'll tell you,' I said dully. 'Think back. That Gardner Museum theft in Boston – what was it, quarter of a billion, yesterday's giveaway prices? They stole Vermeer, Rembrandt, ultimate antiques. Tot up the thefts of antiques for that and the previous four years, it comes to four billions, yesterday dollars.'

'And there's no such thing as theft?' Nicko scoffed. The curtains wafted out. This time I didn't hear the snick of the latch. I was past caring.

'You think you've proved me wrong? The Japanese Yakuza, the Mafia, all the terrorists and extortionists in the world know different.

Heard of such a thing as the Statute of Limitations? Most countries have one. Time has a habit of passing. In a couple of years Monet's *Impression Sunrise*, stolen from the Marmottan Museum, Paris, will emerge. The thieves can market the damned thing, immune by law. It's legal now anyway – Japan's statute of limitations is only two years.'

Gina asked, 'Hasn't it been recovered?'

I stared. I honestly don't believe these people. 'Aye, love. *Fourteen times!* Each time's the one true genuine one.' I explained to ease their perplexity, 'You see, love, once a special unique porcelain, bronze, ancient vase, piece of one-off furniture, painting, is stolen, there's very little to go on to tell if what's being offered for ransom is the one true original. Or a fake.'

'They do that?'

'The Mona Lisa was stolen in 1911. Half a dozen fakes were sold for underhand fortunes – until the genuine one walked in, years later. It's routine.

'Ninety-five per cent don't even get recaptured. Ransom's a cool ten per cent of value. Your own Foundation of Art Research admits that only one twentieth ever come home anyway.' I smiled, hoping it was as wintry as Nicko's. 'But then the Statute declares the robbers immune, and out they come. If there's any hassle, they simply add some small blemish – slightly change a hue of the sky in one corner, enlarge the canvas perhaps. You law people make me frigging laugh. You think because an antique's catalogued somewhere that nobody'll buy?'

'But they will?'

'Give me the money and a month, mister. I'll buy you any antique or art work stolen in the past two decades.'

'What about the ones heisted before that?'

'Advertise. Orly and Jennie'll tell you. It's quite legal.' I turned, made way for them to enter the conversation. 'Antiques are the one currency that survives inflation, flood, financial panic.'

'Or fund laundering?' Jennie asked.

'Ideal. It's all the better – you don't have to give the artists their cut. They've already starved to death yonks ago.'

'No moral sheet, Lovejoy,' Orly said. He still hated me.

I turned, gave him my bent eye. 'I hated you less when you were only a murderous crook, Orly.' I shook my head at Nicko. 'No thanks, Nicko. No deal. Do your own dirty work.'

'He's the one, all right,' Nicko said. 'Book him.'

CHAPTER TWENTY-EIGHT

'You got that, Lovejoy?'

'Aye, love. Off pat.'

'Your story of what happened after the explosion?'

'I found myself running over the hillside away from the fire. Got a lift, hid out at a filling station in El Segundo. Stole money and clothes from a motorist who stayed over.'

Jennie had worked with me the full twenty-four hours.

'And where are you heading?'

'For Manhattan. I'll stay with Melodie van Cordlant on Madison. If not her, then with Mrs Brandau. Should I check Jim Bethune out?'

'Bethune died in the fire.'

Another. I didn't sigh, just nodded and quoted the contact numbers Jennie'd drilled into me.

'Good, Lovejoy. You've got it. Contact in emergencies.'

So they'd come and save me? Like they did Bill? Like Sokolow-sky? Tony?

'You'll take over the antiques place, tie in with Busman like you did. Peel off the auctioneers, same as you suggested. Then you'll big-buck buy, establish the chain of selling through the international art market . . .'

I went along, listening to her gunge. Loony tunes, for a bloke like me. I'm the one who thrills to a single Chelsea porcelain figurine sold over a nosh bar counter in a Suffolk village. This scale of things was money madness, coin crazy. I only felt right at a village jumble sale, with one woman whose eyes I could safely look at, playing that most ancient of all games.

'Sure, Jennie,' I said most sincerely. 'Exact. I got it exact.' God. I almost sounded right.

'You establish contact first from here. They're still in LA. We got their numbers, okay?' She passed me a typed list. They were all there. Sophie, Melodie, Kelly Palumba, Moira Hawkins. I was into a winner here – as long as I loved what I was to do. 'You arrange to meet them here, play them along. They're in separate hotels.'

'Gimme the phone, hon.'

Jennie frowned. 'Try to keep that Limey talk, okay? It kinda pleases, y'know?'

'Very well, love.'

I spoke to Melodie, Kelly, and Sophie Brandau in that order. Melodie was over the moon, thrilled I should be desperate to check she wasn't injured in the fire.

'I've been worried sick, Melodie doorling,' I said, almost starting tears at my deep sincerity. 'How soon can I see you, sweetheart?'

'Come right away, Lovejoy! We can have dinner, and –'

'I've very little money, honey.'

'What's a dollar?' she screamed softly. I swore I was on my way, and dialled Kelly.

She was more difficult.

'Is that goon Epsilon with you, Palumba?' I demanded. 'If so I hang up.'

'Yes, but don't,' she said, thinking with a woman's natural alacrity when deceiving by phone. 'It's my financial advisor, Eppie. I have to see him tonight. You go to the premier, I'll follow on, okay?'

We fixed for eightish, her place.

Sophie was circumspect, very Grace Kelly, polite and distant.

'You weren't at the Revere, love,' I accused. 'I wouldn't have gone if I'd known you weren't going to come. Though it's marvellous that you didn't. I'd have been frantic you might have been hurt.'

'Denzie?' I heard her call. 'A woman's guild want me to speak on political family life tonight. Will that be . . . ?'

'Nine o'clock, Sophie Brandau,' I told Jennie curtly. 'Pencil her in. Any more?'

'No, Lovejoy.' Her mouth was set into severe disapproval, squared. 'Go whenever you must.'

'Can I get a lift?'

'Cab it, Lovejoy. You've enough. Expenses.'

'So I have!' I said brightly. 'See you back at the precinct house.' We'd arranged weekly reports to begin with.

I got a taxi from the rank six blocks along. I walked in the fading sunlight, which slanted across the boulevard from the lovely western horizon. You don't get horizons like those in California for colours. I strolled, looking out for muggers, sidestepping rogue joggers, watching for falling meteorites. I was learning American vigilance.

'Where to?'

It seemed an age since I'd been elsewhere, in the East, telling a Chinese cabbie to take me to America, fast as he liked. I watched the lovely curved shore line recede as we turned inland and joined the flood of traffic. God knows where everybody was going, but they were all on the hoof.

The central station wasn't quite so crowded.

Twenty minutes to six when I reached there. I'd hung about as distantly as possible − not difficult in such a whopping place. I had coffee for ease of lurking, and stayed off centre until I saw them.

In she came, cool and swinging, being eyeballed and ogled as she entered. Zole was with her, yo-yo zipping to everyone's annoyance, Sherman trotting.

It was a hard choice to make, really, for somebody like me. I'm my own worst enemy, always have been. The choice is always made for you, my old Gran used to say. You think you choose, until you see what there is. Then you find it's all done, choice out of the window and your feet hurrying the way they would have anyway.

The trouble was Magda wasn't going to be easy to bid farewell. She was a typical woman, sticking to your mind like glue just when you wanted to be away out of the starting block like a gazelle. Her and her idiot criminal maniacal treacherous little kid who shot people and thought it right just because it was me going to get gunned down. A cool Bonnie and Clyde couple, except once she'd told me about how she would send Zole to school and he'd be a great doctor, lawyer, a real educated man full growed, able to look anybody in the eye.

Nothing for it. I had to go. This was the moment to accost her, say goodbye, it was fine while it lasted, thanks for everything. She was looking at her watch, pacing. Zole was off somewhere. He'd abandoned his skateboard, was down to walking. Though I noticed he'd been carrying a trannie, to annoy everybody within earshot.

I cleared my throat, rehearsing my time-to-say-so-long speech. I'd the words all off pat, just as I'd decided in the taxi across town. I walked towards her, among the passengers heading for the barrier.

There was no decision to make, not really, not when you thought of it. Luxury, endless love, lusting my paradisical way from penthouse to penthouse, one lovely rich woman to another, panting and groping, ecstatic with delirious lovely wealth flowing my way, and every solid dollar legit as I took a massive percentage for my trouble. That was life. A dream.

'Hello, love.'

She spun, gladness in her eyes.

'Oh, Lovejoy! You came! I was start'n to think maybe −'

'Where the hell's that little pillock?' I said, moving her towards the train. 'Less than ten minutes to go and you let him wander off. Why do you never take any notice of what I say? Silly cow.'

'Don't you start on me, Lovejoy. Not after what I've been through, waiting and worryin' –'

'Hey, man! Time you showed –'

I clipped the little sod's ear. 'Where the hell've you been? I've been waiting this past half hour –'

'Hey, Magda,' the little cret complained. 'Cain't we ditch Lovejoy? Only, I gonna get real mean he does that one more time –'

'Shut it, pillock. And turn that damned thing off.' I gave Magda the three tickets I'd bought. 'Come on.'

'Kansas City?' Magda was clipping along in her red shoes. 'Why Kansas City, Lovejoy? You never tellt we goin' there. I got bags packed back in the hotel –'

'You shut it, Magda. I'm sick of people asking me things.' How the hell did I know why Kansas City? It was just that I recognized the name from the list of places by the ticket office. 'I don't even know where the bloody place is. Does Sherman travel free?'

'Lovejoy, he dumb, Magda.'

We boarded the train, impossibly high off the ground like all American trains. I was telling her how I'd teach her a few essentials about antiques, get her started in a small shop. It's the easiest thing in the world to find one little good antique, then another . . .

Magda was smiling as we took seats. 'Thanks, Lovejoy. Even if it is only sorta temporary. Know what? I thought you'd left without us.'

I settled back as the train began to move. First thing was to make her start apologizing profusely for her terrible wicked doubt of my sterling character. Then we'd have to take it from there.

'I see, love,' I said, hurt and quiet. 'It's always me that's treacherous, is it? When I've risked everything to get here just to make sure you'd be safe, and Zole get somewhere settled –'

'No, honey. Hush. I'm sorry, darlin'. Me and my big mouth. I'd no right to say them things, Lovejoy . . .'

Okay, I thought, and wondered if there was a good dining car on the damned thing. Sherman snored on me, and we rolled eastwards out of LA.

The Lies of
Fair Ladies

For
Charlotte Grace

To
The Chinese god Wei D'to, who
saves books from scoundrels.

Thanks
Susan, as ever.

CHAPTER ONE

Time to get rid of her.

Decisions about women creep up, don't they? They can even reach in, where antiques rightfully rule. I'm an – *the* – antique dealer, and I know.

Joan made love when her husband Del was talking at us. I'm a patient bloke but there are limits. She spat insults at him, jeering until her moans came and oblivion ruled. Can you imagine?

I'd given her the best years – well, two days – of my life. The reason was this antique she hadn't got.

Joan was filthy rich, in a praiseworthy way. That is, she honestly thought everybody else was rich, too. To me, antiques are one of the ten reasons for money; the other nine don't matter.

'What do you think?' she'd asked me brightly at the auction. First time I saw her. She gave me a dog to hold, silly cow. I gave it her back. It yawned, thinking what a hell of a day.

'Dog looks fine, lady.'

I wasn't particularly happy. I'd had a lousy day, St Edmunds-bury. The worst job in antiques is being a tax hiker. You stroll into some auction. Then, obviously suppressing excitement/glee and what-not, you bid for Lot No. X – some duff painting, whatever old dross you've been hired to hike up. Rival dealers see your eagerness, and get drawn in. The more the merrier. The price soars. Guess who eventually buys it? Why, Lot X's owner himself! Then he donates it to some museum, and claims tax relief *on the price he bid*. Good, eh? The painting was one I'd faked, a John Constable *View of Dedham, Late Sun*. Quite good, but wrong canvas. I'd got his greens just right, though mixing Prussian Blue like J. C. is a swine. The owner was Barry Dimmonson. He met me in his Rolls to pay.

'I'll need you again soon, Lovejoy.' He fumed carcinogens from his bulbous cigar. 'This time knock me up somefink else. A pot.'

'What sort? A Ch'ien Lung vase takes –'

'Any frigging sort.' He cruised off snarling into a car phone. Like I say, a tax hiker's a rotten job. I hurried to the viewing day at Wittwoode's Auction Temple, to meet destiny and Joan.

She was exquisite. One waft of her perfume was worth Witt-woode's Auction Temple plus all the crud that lay therein.

479

'I don't mean Jasper!' she cooed. 'I mean *that.*'

The onyx cameo, Lot 66. Passing dealers listened with their directional ears.

Now, there's an obligation among dealers to support each other against the common enemy. And the good old C. E. is you. Punters, buyers. Anybody who wants what dealers want, namely antiques. Auctioneers don't count because everybody hates them. Reason? Because they know nothing, and do nowt. *And* get a rake-off. Makes your blood boil.

The question worried me. Was this bird honestly asking for honesty? Then my mind smiled.

Over in the corner of the draughty old church Wittwoode has the nerve to call *his*, not God's, Temple, Denny was trying to sell this very cameo to a woman called George Danson. A word about terminology here: a 'woman' to the antiques trade is a non-dealer, man or woman. A 'lady' is anyone with money, pure and maybe not so simple. George Danson was a poor old gaffer with a kindly soul. Denny's a shark, that is, an antique dealer. He didn't own the lovely cameo brooch, of course. (Tip: people who try to sell you an item in an auction viewing never, ever own it, so watch out.)

I'd seen Denny come in out of the rain. He tried to con me once, a royal Worcester framed oval porcelain plaque painted by John Stinton. Not really antique – 1928 or thereabouts, but worth a small car. Denny's was a dud. Fake porcelains are stamped out in Germany these days; the colours are wrong. I decided to blame Denny and do this ladylady (sic) a good turn.

'That, lady?' Decibels bring audiences. 'Fake.'

'Fake?' She stared at me. 'I mean the cameo.'

Emphasis was needed. 'Duff. Neff. Fraud. Sexton Blake, fake.'

'But . . .' She had a lovely high colour of a sudden. Jasper growled, bad vibes. 'The catalogue says genuine Etruscan.'

The power of the written lie always astonishes me. And nobody lies like a cataloguer. Except an auctioneer.

'Balderdash,' I boomed. 'Auctioneers cheat. Some pillocks – er, sorry. They hope to deceive.'

'That's positively shameful!' She eyed me. 'You can tell?'

Somebody passing chuckled. Bernese, a luscious dealer in doll's houses and Edwardian domestic furniture. She hates me. We once made smiles.

'Lovejoy's divining rod's famous, dear,' Bernese said with malice, crashing across to up-end a small occasional table, 1906 or there-

abouts. She wants me to go into partnership. I won't because they
don't last. Her husband runs a Civil Service school.

'I'm a divvie, love. I feel it. But get a MacArthur microscope.
Even a handlens'll show the surface scratches from an electric micro.
Modern fakers have no patience. It's supposed to be nicked from
Florence's Archaeological Museum. Cosimo de'Medici's collection of
ancient jewellery.'

The dud cameo was well-nigh perfect. It showed Hercules and
his missus Hebe. 'Beautifully done. See how their profiles are cut,
the brown layer as his hair, beard, cloak?' The bluish underlayer
was left in various thicknesses for the gods' features.

She wasn't taking any notice, just staring. 'You hadn't seen it
before,' she accused. 'Yet you . . .'

People never believe you, first time round. Yet they believe
promised tax cuts, the lies on food labels. Amazing. She looked me
up and down, registered (a) shoddy (b) wet through, so no motor
and (c) resented by all dealers and auctioneers present.

'Right, Lovejoy!' Wittwoode steamed up, frothing. He's a great
frother, walrus moustache and bottle specs. He thinks nobody knows
he fiddles his books. A pillar of the trade. 'You've done enough
damage. Out!'

'I'm going, I'm going.'

Then the lady uttered magic. All froze in reverence.

'I have a valuable original cameo.' She smiled. Jasper whimpered, knowing trouble. 'Would you . . . divvie it, Lovejoy?'

Police or profit? A gorgeous bird, or Wittwoode's goons?

'Well, all right.' I'm good at surrender.

Joan's cameo was a similar fraud. She'd paid a fortune for it. I
explained the sad news.

She heard me out. First time she'd listened to anyone for years.
I talked on, scams I have known. I came to when it was almost dark.
We were served tea by a grovelling serf. I made to go. She restrained
me with skill.

'I have more jewellery, Lovejoy. In my boudoir.' I'd never heard
anyone use that word except on the music hall.

And that was that. Except that, when we were just on the point
of serious smiles, she breathlessly cried to wait, for Christ's sake. Just
another minute . . .

She clicked a radio on at seven o'clock. Everybody's talk-show
favourite, Del Vervain, came on, poisonous with affability.

Joan turned to me, face suddenly haggard. 'See, Lovejoy?' she asked, in tears. 'My husband's famous boyish charm. Isn't it wonderful?'

'Er, very wonderful.' I didn't want any part of this. The bloke was connected with grimsville.

She said, abruptly savage. 'Don't go. It's a live show. He'll not be home for hours . . .'

Sloshed out of his mind, by all accounts. Her dress fell, her breasts appeared. She took hold of me, fingers working. I started a lucid denial, based on pure logic.

I managed, 'Ooooh.'

My second evening with Joan – Del Vervain's show broadcasts between seven and eleven – I escaped by saying I'd go for a present for her. She was thrilled. As her cameo was fake, wouldn't it be luvverly if I wangled her a genuine Etruscan cameo? She wept sincere tears.

'You're wonderful, Lovejoy.' We were still in the after-throes. I was dying to slip into the little death that comes after. Joan, typical bird, talked non-stop.

I filled up. She was right. I am. Emotion's catching, to sensitive blokes like me.

'When do we meet, doowerlink?' My cover.

'Coffee. Joynson's, Sudbury.' She owns Joynson's.

She sent me off in her chauffeur-driven Rolls Royce. I had him drop me at the Antiques Arcade. Closed at that hour, of course. The chauffeur wasn't deceived. His eyes kept giving me sardonic glances in the mirror. I don't like people who are sardonic. What's wrong with trust?

That night at my cottage I slept the sleep of the just.

By eight next morning I was up and whistling, feeding the robin his cheese, the bluetits their nuts, and me fried tomatoes, dry bread, tea with brown sugar. My cottage is Lovejoy Antiques, Inc. – to sound American and affluent, all Americans being rich. Our own humbler description 'Ltd' sounds sternly not-got-much.

An elderly lady was on the doorstep as I launched out to face the world. I sighed. Today, I especially did not want a Yank researching her family tree.

'Morning, Miss Turner.'

She's from Virginia or somewhere. Started haunting me after we met in the grotty town library. Like a fool I'd taken pity on the dingy old crone, corrected a library lass who was telling her wrong about birth certificates.

'Morning, Lovejoy!' She's an eager ninety. She dragged notes from a handbag like a leather trunk. 'I'll only trouble you a moment. Your advice worked! The people at the General Register Office in Saint Catherine's House were charming.'

'Sorry, love, I've no time.' Everybody's always after me for a hand-out. Didn't the shabby old biddy know Americans are millionaires?

She trotted alongside, adjusting specs to peer at some scrap. 'My parents, John Turner and Mary Ann. I have their birth certificates *right here.'*

'Glad you made it. So-long.'

'No, no!' she cried. 'Lovejoy, I'm desperate!'

What now? I cursed myself for a fool. And halted so she could wheeze into the punchline. She looked threadbare as me. I was worn out and I'd only got ten yards. I gave her my last note. Anything to get rid.

'Marriage certificates at the GRO, Kingsway. Alphabetical order. Different coloured form. Guess your Grandpa's marriage date, work back. Only takes half an hour. Ta-ra.'

'Thank you,' she called after, smiling. Daft owd bat.

I yelled over my shoulder, 'Put the right volume number on the form, for God's sake.'

'Thank you, Lovejoy.' Tears of gratitude? Silly old cow.

Our village bus was late – not an all-time first. I was still waiting at the chapel when the Plod stopped and offered me a lift. Not where I wanted to go, but police are poor on direction. I've often found that. We drove in monosyllables to a huge moated house near Manningtree. Set in a vast flat cornfield, a small river snaking indolently past. My heart sank when I saw who the head ploddite was.

'Morning,' I offered heartily, going to stand beside him at the drawbridge. 'Black Knight challenged yet?'

He snorted non-amusement, stood there examing the edifice. Lovely, turreted, windows in serried ranks.

'Ever heard of pace, Lovejoy?'

Drinkwater's some sort of inspector. Though the Bill come heavy with titles these days. Ever noticed? The more titles, the worse they behave. Odd. I'll have to think about that. It may be a universal law or something.

'Pace?' Be helpful. 'Speed? Alacrity?' His cadaverous features didn't improve. 'That poison gas?'

Drinkwater's a Midland's reject. He has four spoonfuls of sugar in each half-pint mug of tea at the nick. His false teeth clack when he talks. His left ear twitches.

'That's Mace, you prat.' He never sits either, even during interrogations, just walks about, hands in his trouser pockets. I've never seen him without a mac. His adam's apple yoyos hypnotically. He focuses attention. A one-man carnival. 'P.A.C.E., Lovejoy, Police and Criminal Evidence Act.'

'No. Have . . . ?' Maybe he had? I coughed nervously.

His bleary eyes took me in. 'This interview will be deemed to have satisfied that Act's requirements, Lovejoy. Follow?'

'Yes.' I wasn't to complain.

'Did you pull the robbery herein?'

Herein? Trust the Plod. Archaisms deceive the innocent. 'What's been nicked? Looks empty to me.'

He chuckled, gave me the benefit of his features face on. You know he's chuckling because his skeletal chest jerks.

'Not empty, Lovejoy. Gutted. Fireplaces. Balustrades. Tiles. Wall-paper, even. Pelmets. Kitchen ranges. Chandeliers.'

This is called a turkey job in the antiques trade. Whether Turkey specialised in them, or cleaning out as in your Christmas fowl, I don't know. Drinkwater waited. A uniformed bobby lit a fag discreetly.

'Must have been strong lads,' I offered. Silence. Another bobby lit up, coughing in the morning stillness.

'You see my problem, Lovejoy?'

Quite honestly I didn't, but you daren't disagree. Then I began to wonder.

'Left empty some time, eh?'

'Six months. Council conversion, planning offices.'

Late Georgian, it was imposingly set, moated amid this flat field. No trees lined the little river's banks. I began to smile, trying hard not to. The only road ran straight as a die across the field to the mansion. No cover. No way to creep close.

'How'd they get pantechnicons and robbers in?'

'*And* the antiques out, Lovejoy. A wheelbarrow would be spotted a mile off, let alone a van. The river's out.' He indicated a cottage where the road joined a narrow wooded lane. 'The security specialist house. Three men, on shifts.'

Then I did smile. It was the old locked room mystery, for the most unlockable site in the known world.

A smile's dangerous to Drinkwater's kind. 'You know something, Lovejoy, you frigging dross.'

'Me?' I said indignantly. 'I've never even seen the blinking place before, Drinkwater! I didn't even know . . .' . . . *I didn't even know Prammie Joe was out of gaol.*

The change in his eyes warned me.

'. . . this building was here,' I finished lamely.

He stared me down. 'Know what, Lovejoy? I wish you was one of them crets as boils shredded soap and diesel, for homemade bombs. But you're a chiselling shagnasty, living off any woman with enough in her purse.'

'Here, Drinkwater. I don't have to put up with —'

'Sooner or later, lad, some item from Cornish Place will turn up in your hovel. And I'll fit you for life. Follow?'

'My cottage isn't a hovel,' I tried indignantly. He simply walked across the drawbridge, left me to make my own way home. Ten miles, through the dullest countryside you ever did see. I got a lift from a sales rep disappointed I wasn't going to Norwich.

Prammie Joe out of nick, though. Well, well. He must have worked like a dog, doing a turkey on that huge place all on his own. Good old Joe. Class tells. I decided oh-so-casually to meet up with Prammie Joe. Maybe his brilliant theft was a commission job for some big roller (= rich antiques buyer who doesn't really care what stuff he buys, for swift resale). Then I'd best keep out of it. But if it was a loner, I'd cut in for a share. And why not? The only loser would be the taxpayer. And local politicians, of course. That made me smile wider still.

CHAPTER TWO

Things surge up or down in antiques. Never two days alike. Antique dealers live on their wits – they possess none, hence their vaunted penury. In fact, most dealers couldn't make a living at all, were it not for the honest old public, which lives for greed while pretending the opposite. This is why I like women. They *know* they're greedy, that everybody else is too. But it's okay as long as you keep up appearances, like offering your last macaroon to a visitor, hoping she won't take it.

So that fateful day I strolled hopeful into the Antiques Arcade (think a dingy covered walk of counters offering dross) because, remember what I said? Antiques are either on a down spiral, or soaring. Even in Ancient Rome, with barbarians howling at the gates, antique dealers made a killing, street stalls getting priceless valuables for a song, burying the loot in the yard. My advice: Don't waste pity. Save it for the starving. Antique dealers are born with a whimper, like those terrible Christmas dolls that wet the bed. And the whimper goes: 'Times are 'orrible bad, guv'nor, so please don't quibble about the price; this is a genuine Van Dyke I'm practically giving away . . .'

They also hate talent, as the chorus of abuse I received testified.

'How do, Lovejoy.' Gunge was waiting. 'This big ring any good?'

'No.' No, because the answer's always no. At first. If you don't believe me, take that precious heirloom your Great Aunt left you – let's say a genuine Hepplewhite shield-backed upright chair. You *know* it's genuine because you have a portrait of your own great-grandad posing beside that selfsame brilliant piece of crafted wonder. Take it to any – *any* – antique dealer. Pretend you want to sell. You ask, 'Valuable, eh?'

What does he reply? '*No. Sorry.*'

He gives reasons to knock down your reasons. He has a trillion put-downers – sneers, scorn, sighs, reproach. You have documents? He sneers, Lady, everybody tries *that* on. Your chair's in Gloag's *Dictionary*, and its vase splat (the middle bit where your spine rests) is identical? Faked, he sighs, and offers you a pittance. Lovejoy's Antiques Rule One is: *It's always no.* Tell you about exceptions later.

'The ring is Jeff Dalgleish's. I'm on ten perk.'

That made me hesitate. All about, dealers were making crude

comments on my dishevelled state. A happy band of siblings, all cut-throat.

'Watch your language,' I shouted down the Arcade. 'I'm the only customer today with any money.'

That shut them up. Their ribaldry faded. It might be true, antiques being the ultimate switchback ride.

Perk is per cent. I took the ring. It was genuine but fake, if you follow. Some antiques truly are both. 'Papal' rings would fit no finger except some panto giant's. They are so huge, they rattle around even on your thumb. Mostly gilt bronze, with a prominent bezel and a stone of rock crystal or plain-coloured glass. They're pretty common, and not much sought. For all the world like a child's idea of an impressive dress ring. We aren't really sure, but suppose them to be worn on a cord round some ancient legate's neck, symbol of authority. They never have a seal die, for impressing wax on documents. I weighed Gunge up.

Gunge Herod, like me, suffers from his name. His first means unmentionable, his second slaughter. His nickname comes from his usual response: 'No; it's gunge.' He's disliked because his barrow blocks the Arcade entrance. A barrow exempts him weekly dues, so you can imagine. He does jewellery and household antiques.

'Jeff's got a weird one here, Gunge.'

Usually papal rings aren't valuable. But unless I was mistaken this monster was solid gold, and the stone was brown topaz. Don't knock topaz; its pink, honey-yellows and blue varieties are some of the loveliest of gems. I saw most of the other dealers were carefully not watching, and took out my polaroid sunglasses. Every jeweller carries them. Mine are simply lenses from an old pair somebody chucked away. The trick is, put the gem on one polaroid lens, and look at it through the other. Rotate the top one. If the stone stay dark for a complete rotation, then it's one lot of stones, including diamond and simple glass; if it alternates light and dark, then it's a group including topazes, sapphires, rubies and a million others. Mind you, the polaroid trick only tells you what a gem is *not*. Like, if a gemstone shows darklight every quarter turn, and a jeweller is trying to sell you this amazingly cheap genuine diamond, you know he's lying. And if an auctioneer invites bids for a spectacular 'antique sapphire pendant', and the gem stayed dark to your sunglasses ploy, then that auctioneer – perish the thought! – is a crook, and the 'precious sapphire' is probably just a chunk of polished bottle.

The stone changed, light to dark, light to dark. I was honestly surprised.

'May be honey topaz. Done the gold test?'

'No.' He shuffled in embarrassment. I moved aside so he could shuffle without crushing me. He's a huge bearded bloke, six feet eight, wide with it. Has to go in pubs sideways. Size always amazes me. I mean, Gunge comes from my country, and we're average everything.

This annoyed me – not Gunge's hugeness, but that the miserable sods in the Arcade wouldn't do him a gold test. It only takes a second. There wasn't one who didn't have a gold-testing kit. I looked along. Connie was in.

'Connie? A favour, love.'

'No, Lovejoy. You owe me for those boots.'

'Boots?' I did a theatrical start. 'Ah, yes, I remember. I got a fair price. Settle up in the Bricklayers Arms tonight?' She'd got me a pair of Victorian ladies' boots. A Dulwich collector pays me on the nail. I'd forgotten to pay Connie. Well, who can remember every damned thing?

She dithered, a delightful sight. She's about twenty-two, comely, dresses classy instead of this current shop-soiled fashion. High heels, swinging skirt, spends two hours every morning in front of her bedroom mirror ... I mean, I'll bet she possibly does. Has rich parents who fondly think their daughter's beavering at Manchester University doing astrophysics. To me, women and lies are unknowable. I mean, why did't she pretend she was doing sociology, a phoney subject nobody cares about? Then she could carry the lie with total conviction. Real sociologists do it all the time.

'Gunge's shy his dues, Lovejoy,' she lectured severely, drumming her fingers prettily. 'It's cheating.'

Which was rich, from an astrophysicist running a crummy antiques stall among a load of deadlegs. But pointing out a lie to a female's considered impolite.

'Just a bad patch, doowerlink. One dropper. Please.'

'You'll divvie some stuff for me?'

Sigh. I took the papal ring to her stall – three feet of plank, a homemade glass case, a strip of black velvet. 'Deal. Where is it?'

'They're not here, Lovejoy.' I brightened. They is plural.

'Bring them along to the Bricklayers.'

She shook her head, a lovely sheen. 'They're not handies.'

A quick look. The dealers had lost interest. 'A lot?'

'Several. I'll take you. It has to be tomorrow.'

No longer mere plural, but multo. I swallowed. I wasn't sure if my throat was dry from her astrophysical nearness or the thought of a dream warehouse crammed with antiques.

'Here.' I passed her the papal ring. She didn't examine it immediately, another surprise. I go by feel, some inner bong that homes me on to genuine antiques. But other dealers have to look, scrutinize, weigh. And she wasn't doing any of that. Preoccupied with her cache of antiques. Must be worth a mint. I warmed to her. No, honestly. I quite like astrophysics. For all I knew, so did she.

'Deal, Lovejoy?' She gazed straight at me. Not exactly Drink-water's look, but with a hint of the same quality. Judging, goading even. For the first time I felt something wasn't right. As if Connie'd only come to the Arcade that day waiting for me. But Lovejoy Antiques, Inc. was a supersurvivor.

'Deal, love.' I was starving hungry. I'd have touched her for a pasty or two, except I owed. Mistrust is catching.

I left the Arcade, blithely irritating the dealers by yelling for them to stick at it, customers. They bawled outrage back. Lovejoy's Rule Two: Always look on your way to a terrific bargain. It depresses rivals no end.

Prammie Joe isn't on the phone. Some say he isn't even on Planet Earth. He's a true loner, living on this promontory on the banks of the Orwell. Waterman born and bred, he makes a meagre living among the waterways. Canals, rivers, estuaries are his world. He isn't quite the scruff I suppose I'm making him sound. He's impeccably clean, always shaved. He was a sailor once, and they're precise of habit. He's a worry to any antique dealer, is Prammie Joe. Has a disturbing habit of coming up trumps from nowhere. Bound to dismay the Arcaders, when you think.

Like, once, Prammie showed up with two serpents – musical, not fire-breathers. The serpent is six feet of carved walnut, or even sycamore, with a brass mouth-piece shaped like a, well, guess. You hold it crossways, a phenomenal boa constrictor on your lap, and play it with breath and finger-holes. First showed up in France about 1590. A lovely sound. They are unbelievably rare. Prammie Joe's two antique serpents – just one would have left the Arcade thunder-struck – were both true as a bell, about 1635. I actually played one, to round off my feeling. Everybody was asking where the hell an old swamp tromper like Joe found them, for heaven's sake. None of us found out. You never do, with blokes like Prammie. One-offs.

No hope of the taxi fare from the railway station, so I set off along the by-pass thumbing a lift. I got one after trudging three miles, a schoolteacher rabbiting about educational precepts. I went 'Mmmmh' and similar until we reached the river. He was pleased to meet an antique dealer, and gave me his address to call and see a genuine ancient coffee pot with a perforated spout. 'Maybe it's an early teapot,' he said brightly. 'Know what I mean?' I did, and thanked him most sincerely.

'Look,' I told him as I alighted. 'I'm no reconnaissance. Christie's of London. Keep it under your hat.'

'Right!' he exclaimed. 'That why you're dressed shoddy?'

'Er, yes.' You can go off people pretty quick. 'I'll send one of my deputies along.'

'Splendid!' He drove off beaming.

A carter's wagon gave me a lift at 2 mph down towards Prammie's marshy abode. It was getting on for four o'clock when I plodded through the hedgerows. Prammie was at the water's edge with his pram. Not pram as in perambulator, that vehicle you shove babies about in. Pram as in short, blunt-prowed dinghy, propelled by a single stern oar. Shallow of draught, it floats joyously on any piddling stream, unseen and silent. Hence my reason for thinking of him and Cornish Place.

'Wotcher, Prammie. I covered my tracks at the hedge.'

He crouches like an Aussie, one leg thrust out before. You wonder how his arms reach. He was mending his lever. Lying supine, he can scull the pram forward. He sighed. I was narked. I'd suffered a lot of sighs.

'Thought you'd be along, Lovejoy.'

'Don't you sigh at me, Prammie. I could've shopped you.'

'Drinkwater have you, did he?' He has one of those moustaches that fluff in and out with each snuffle. It looks borrowed off a dog. What with him and Drinkwater, I'd had enough chuckles, too. 'Burk, he is.'

Confidence makes me uneasy. It never lasts. Like good health, it's on a loser.

'Take care, Prammie. He's a nutter.' A nutter is a bobby of singularly malevolent disposition. No rarity, but functions unimpeded by law, justice, similar myths.

'Bad as those security blokes.' He almost tumbled into the river with merriment. 'Know what? They *wired* that cornfield!'

Well, some things do make you laugh. I'm no countryman, but you've only to glance at a field of standing grain to see the tracks of every newt that wended through.

'Searchlights for hang-gliders, eh?' We fell about. Sobering, I reverently asked how long the robbery had taken. You have to admire class.

'Every night bar Sundays, eleven weeks, Lovejoy.' He doesn't work on the Sabbath. He's churchwarden at St Michael's. His old eyes misted over. 'Know what, son? I'm really proud. My swansong.' He rolled and lit a cigarette. Strikes the match on his thumbnail. I wish I could do that. I once tried but burnt my thumb.

'Anybody would be, Prammie.' Praise where it's due.

'Had two rafts. Towed them. There are spin-offs. I saved a little lad in the —' He paused, chuckled, having nearly given a location away. He pointed down to the shallow creek. 'Lucky I went at Cornish Place from downstream, eh?'

Well, that really set us rolling. We finished up in his hut with a drink, wiping our eyes. You need only watch a great mansion in a river moat in the middle of a plain from upstream. One watcher there, the place is impregnable.

'Marry that lassie yet, Lovejoy?'

That set me thinking. I remembered. 'Well, no, Prammie. I would have, but . . .' I couldn't even recall her name. Blonde? Or not? Harriet Something was it, strong opinions on celery juice and pollution? 'Er, Harriet moved away.'

'Pity.' He sobered, eyeing me. 'A nice girl, Lovejoy. I don't think you played fair.'

The reason I'm the only dealer in the Eastern Hundreds who'd know that Prammie Joe did Cornish Place was that I'm the only one ever seen him in action. And that was pure accident.

Harriet — if I've got her name right — was a carnivore from Wapping. On a sweep for some Antiques Road Show. (A sweep is scavenging ahead of the main shoal of predatory televisioneers.) She fell on me, lit. and met. Knew nothing about antiques. I had to stop the lads selling her collections of pre-1842 trademarks and French Revolution photographs. She and I were making heavy-duty smiles on the banks of the Deben, when a gentle rhythmic shushing disturbed the rural peace. I thought it was Harriet, until somebody ahemed in my earhole. And there was Prammie Joe, in his modified boat. His bare foot worked steadily at his stern-mounted oar. He lay on his back, holding the gun'ls.

That would have been a quick embarrassed adjustment of clothing, and the usual sheepish conversation until he'd gone by. But in the prow of his pram stood a Martinware jug. I'd seen the same one sold seven days before at Southwold. Martinware is grotesque — salt-glazed stoneware, mottled as hell, so grey and muted you wonder why the Martin brothers bothered. Anyway, they're no earlier than 1873. The Martins packed up in 1914. The jugs often feature hideously contorted faces, or supposedly comical fishes and ducks. Horrible.

'Mister Martin, I presume,' I managed, as Harriet squealed and we rolled apart. I thought that pretty witty in the circumstances, on the Deben, in flagrante delicto.

Prammie had paused, peering sideways at us. He nodded, sussed fair and square. Simply mentioned a tavern near Woodbridge, saying he'd be there about eight. We all three then resumed our activities, some more carefree than others. I christened him my secret nickname Prammie that very evening.

'You could have been anybody, Lovejoy,' he told me inside his hut. 'A godsend it was only you.'

That 'only you' stung. He could have met a blackmailer, is what he meant. He's got a sense of fair play – which should tell you straight off he's no antique dealer.

'I feel it too, Prammie,' I said most sincerely. Harriet had mauled me bog-eyed. I was almost at death's dark door when she had to move on. She wrote to me hourly for five months, made sudden unnerving visits. My guardian angel made sure I saw her Ferrari coming. 'I was heartbroken, Prammie. Truly. Her mother's an MP. Well, my face didn't fit.' I sniffed, quite overcome by cruel fate and Harriet's snooty bitch of a mother who came between us. In the nick of time I remembered I was making this up for Prammie's benefit.

Prammie murmured, 'Never mind, son. Time the great healer.'

Sometimes you have to stare. I mean, this old goat'd just pulled off a robbery anybody would be proud of, and deep down he's a sentimental softie.

'Er, ta, Prammie.' Kind, though. 'Got any tom handy?' I was dying to see the stolen stuff.

'Nar, Lovejoy.' His rheumy eyes were shining. He's a teetotaller, non-wencher. 'Know why I risked it, son? My plan. You know I breed?'

Breed? I didn't even know he had children. I was just about to say, when I looked out through the window.

His cabin is an old reed-cutter's hut. Low down among reeds and bullrushes. You haven't a hope of seeing it unless you know it's there. He has a way through the hedgerows. He uses the waterways for getting anywhere. For proper journeys, he uses a proper dinghy. His night-stealing's all done on his pram. He keeps it buried in the reeds. Even anglers don't come down this marshy stretch, and they're daft enough to go anywhere there's a tiddler. Breed. He had mentioned waterbirds a few times with passion.

492

'Ducks and them?'

He smiled. 'That's Lovejoy,' he said. 'Yes, ducks and them. Migratories, transients, indigens. I foster and propagate them all.'

'Well, Prammie,' I said, rising quickly. 'Nice seeing you –' Passion for antiques and women, inevitable. But passion for pigeons? 'Time I was off.'

'Stay, son. Tea's ready.' He poured out of an old tin teapot. He explained, 'Notice how I brewed up?'

Almost worth another sigh. 'Kettle,' I observed shrewdly. Living on your own sends you bats.

'How?' He was amused. 'Coal fire? Logs? Primus stove? Paraffin? Gas?'

'You plugged it in, Prammie.' Humour a loony, I always say.

'Electricity, Lovejoy. Pinched from the mains.' He chuckled with flaps of his doggie moustache. 'No smoke, see? No National Insurance card. No tax. No post. No family, save my birds. I'm not even here!'

'I know you're here, Prammie.'

'Ah, but you're as barmy as me, Lovejoy. If you hadn't been . . . admiring Harriet that day, you'd not know either.'

'You got gaoled, Prammie.'

'Bad luck, Lovejoy.' He was tranquil. He makes good tea, for all his rustic isolation. 'Taken for wrongful possession, a Daniel Quare clock. Caught in football traffic. Two bobbies helped me across the road. Saw the lable, next day's auction at Gimbert's. I'd no fixed abode . . .'

'Rotten luck.' My heart bled for him. Remove the label, you lower an item's value to any decent fairminded receiver of stolen goods. 'Still, if it was Daniel Quare, it might well have been a fake, eh? Look on the bright side.' The other favourite clockmaker for fakers is Breguet of Paris. It's joked that clockies – fakers of anything that tells time – can sign Quare's and Breguet's names better than they can their own.

'No, Lovejoy.' He was serious. 'The Lord's work. He moves in mysterious ways. It was in gaol I met the scammer.'

I saw light. He'd met a blackguard. 'On commission?'

'Flat fee, son.' He spoke with eyes glowing, doubtless seeing a million migratories, or whatever, laying eggs and nuzzling mud. A really great vision. 'I'll have enough to buy this stretch. Can't you see it? A sanctuary!'

'Lovely, Prammie.' I ahemed. 'Can I, er, help?'

He shook his head, still friendly. 'Lovejoy. I took every fireplace, every speer and pelmet, with my own hands. I *know* every item is genuine. I hand the last over Monday.'

'Sure? Be careful, eh?'

His smile was beatific. '*You* are telling *me*, Lovejoy? It was me caught you in the very act of –'

'Yes, well.' I stood with finality. 'No harm asking.'

He saw me away from his hut. At the hedge I turned to look back. Only eighty feet away, you couldn't see a damned thing. A few cows grazed, providing yet more cover. It was true. He was the careful one all right.

And that, said Alice, was that. Goodnight, Prammie.

CHAPTER THREE

That afternoon was murderous. Not death. Money. Some people spend, spend, spend and gain nowt. Like Big Frank's joke: 'If I won a trillion on the sweepstake, I'd just carry on being an antique dealer until it was all gone.'

Think of the price of stamps and melons. I was having a blazing row about a melon. Savvy Savvy's a supermarket. Their only superlatives are their blinking prices.

I'd reached the till girl after only ten years of battling through hordes. 'Four quid? For one measly melon? You're off your frigging nut!'

'That's the price, Lovejoy.' The girl was heated. People behind were murmuring angry agreement. 'It's marked.'

'It's still not fair, you silly cow!'

'Our melons are not measly!' The manageress, steaming up with more falsehoods. 'Lovejoy. You're barred from shopping here,' this boss hood thundered. 'Savvy Savvy's for respectable shoppers. Get security, Nelly!'

'Barefaced robbery!' I'd only come in for some cheese and tomatoes. They don't do pasties. I get those from Barm In The Barn near the railway, Tuesdays. 'Don't come to me when you go broke. Thieving cow.'

The town was crowded, mostly with people delightedly grinning through Savvy Savvy's windows at the chiselling within. I dumped their grotty cheese and tomatoes, yelled, 'They used to be four shillings, proper money.' Pre-decimal prices always get to them.

'He's right!' an old crone cheeped. 'I can remember . . .'

The babble of reminiscence rose to a hubbub, which let me out unscathed. No, though. It makes my blood boil. These posh shops'll have us in our graves. Cost-efficiency tactics never work, do they? Prices'd go down if they did. I headed down East Hill to Sandy's Dutch Treaty, fuming. Same with antiques. Look at stamps. I pick stamps because they're utterly boring. Yet they're the classic example of antiques holocaust. A lesson to all antique grabbers, like you and me.

Lately, there'd come a mighty flood of philately. It was worrying me sick. In fact, this was the reason I'd gone to the arcade, to suss it out. Somebody said Sandy – more about him in a minute – was offering a whole stamp collection portfolio. In this day and age! Can you believe it? A caution: avoid stamps.

Back in the fabled Good Old Days, when singers sang the words and gold was simply colour at Christmas, bureaux used to bring out catalogues listing prices of British Colonials and Persian Commemoratives and whatnot. That set the scene for ever and a day – or at least until the next catalogue. Then things changed. Inflation (remember that old thing?) happened. Currencies wobbled. Oil did, or didn't, do something vital. Stock markets seethed. One fateful dark day in 1980, London awoke jubilantly to the Stamp World Exhibition. To find the floor had vanished. Nobody wanted stamps.

Prices fell like a stone. Stamp empires were engulfed. Down through the widening cracks plummeted dealers, traders, speculators' portfolios. Amsterdam to Tel Aviv, Geneva to New York, the philately world went crunch. This is my point: if you want to speculate, fine. Anything you like – gold, stocks, shares, land – and good luck. But speculate in antiques? Stick, please, to those *where collectors provide a permanent floor to market prices*. Better still, don't speculate at all. Be a pure collector, you can have the top brick off the chimney.

The Great Stamp Catastophe of 1980 was odd. All portents were favourable. Times were mindbendingly boomy. Wasn't the 6 May the 140th anniversary of the first Penny Black? Wasn't the Cold War dissolving? Everybody was over the moon, joyous with profits.

You see, nobody bought.

Dealers wept, gnashed, pleaded. But the only sound was the popping of speculators' bubbles, the splashing of tears.

Since that date, there are two markets in old stamps. One's the top market, where unique stamps still bring buyers for the yawnsome little things. Here sells the 1849 vermilion tête bêche for a fortune, and the American 1918 24-cent airmail with an upside-down middle. The other market is down here, you and me. Forget dealers, portfolio managers, that lot. Think only of Joe Soap next door. How often does he come home rich and rejoicing? He's your market.

See? Not boring at all. I wish it were. It's something far worse. It's really rather scary. Because there's a terrible hidden question here: What *exactly* turned the floor into Scotch mist in sunny old 1980? Answer: *Nobody knows.* Which is when fright creeps night-stealing into the soul. It crouches, chewing its nails and blubbering every time the door goes. Antique dealers want straight upward graphs, not ones that nuzzle the lino.

If I knew all this, what was my problem as I fumed down East Hill? The sudden influx of old stamps. Like swallows at midwinter, they just don't, aren't, can't. But they'd come to town, via Sandy. And he truly is your rare bird.

Sandy was alone. This was the other meganews of the century. He was determinedly showing he Didn't Care by setting up shop near the Ship tavern. He'd rowed with Mel – cerulean taffeta for a wall hanging – and ended the only permanent partnership our local antiques scene has. Had.

The door blared *YMCA*. I blocked my ears.

'Wait, too lay mond!' a voice trilled. 'Coming!'

East Hill's a trailing string of small dumps. Never been any different since the Emperor Claudius slithered cursing down it on his decorated war elephant, the Roman legions grinning him a safe journey home. For a king's ransom in rent you get a square room, and a curtained back the size of a confessional.

The curtain slowly opened. A recording blared *The Entrance of the Queen of Sheba*. Sandy emerged. I watched, irritated. It's gormless. He wore a sequinned bolero, a caftan, scarlet Cossack trousers. His T-strap ribbon-trimmed high heels were French, 1920s. His turban was beige velvet decorated with Mameluke points and pearls. He spun, eyelids fluttering. His cosmetics could have filled a pint pot. Ridiculous.

'The music, Sandy,' I bellowed, suddenly embarrassed because it silenced in the middle of my yell.

'You adore, Lovejoy? Worship, positively drool?'

My tongue almost spoke the truth. Then I remembered. I wanted his help. I managed a feeble smile.

'Magenta?' I said. Doubting colours works with women. By extension . . .

He leapt to the half-cheval mirror, advertised as a genuine Sheraton and priced for any passing tycoons.

'Scarlet! You dare *doubt*, Lovejoy?'

'No. Honest. Maybe it's the light.'

These vague things are what you've to say when you've not a clue. It saves you knowing what they're on about. Sandy's inspection satisfied him. He perched on a high stool, eyes twinkling maliciously.

'Face it, Lovejoy. You're not Beau Brummel, are you, dear?'

You have to hand it to Sandy. His sense of décor is superb. The grotty shop was tasteful. Style comes with wit and elegance. Him and Mel could make an alcove in a garret into a cathedral, just by panels, mirrors, lights, textures. Sandy had a small bar counter, spirits, wines.

'In spite of all, you may deliver your message, Lovejoy.' He gushed coyly, fingers glittering striped plum and madder nail varnish.

'Don't *tease*, Lovejoy!' He actually blushed. I thought, Oh, Christ. 'Mel's sent you, hasn't he? To apologise?'

He lit a cigarette in a rotating ivory fag-holder. It chimed *What Shall We Do with a Drunken Sailor?*

'Don't make excuses for him, Lovejoy. I *know* he's headstrong. He *begged* you to make the peace. Poor lamb.' His lip quivered as he struggled not to cry. 'Give him this letter. Tell him it *won't* be easy. Not after what he said about my carpet.' He glared, spitting spite. 'I mean, you've only to *see* what he *did!* Chandeliers like Woolworth earrings . . .'

'Sandy.' I felt stricken. This was serious stuff. I'd never known them part before, though they're always swearing lifelong malice. 'I've not seen Mel.'

He paled. He gathered himself and swept grandly into the back room. The curtain closed. Then he wept, sobs so total they almost shook the walls.

'Sorry,' I called after a bit. I honestly was sorry for him. I mean, where love flourishes and all that. But I hadn't got time for all this. Gunge Herod's speciality is household pre-Victoriana. Was he in with Prammie Joe? Today wasn't one of Connie's usual days at the Arcade. That papal ring business felt a put-up job. By Connie? She alone offered to do a dropper. And she'd seemed unnaturally tense. Or was it my imagination?

'Er, I'll come another time, Sandy.' I was leaving gingerly, when the curtain swished aside and Sandy stood there dramatically attired in a black sheath dress, beret with a diamond clasp.

He swished out, sat smouldering on a cockfighting chair.

'Ay shell neffer foor geef'eem, Loofjoy.' He snapped out of it instantly, doing his eye-shadow with stuff from his handbag, and said, 'Right. Who was I?'

'Ginger Rogers? Betty Grable?'

'Marlene Dietrich, buffoon! Don't you know *any*-thing?'

'Mind your fag ash. That reading chair's Sheraton.'

'It is?' He was suddenly all dealer. I never know when he's being Sandy or not himself, if you follow.

'It's a reading chair, Sandy. See how narrow the back is? You sit astride it, facing backwards.' The rear ledge sticks out for a book. 'The mistaken name, cockfighting chair, comes from engravings of blokes watching cockfight mains seated in them.'

'Anything else, Lovejoy?'

'Your half-cheval's dud.'

'*Bitch!*' He examined it. 'It's eighteenth century!'

'It's last month, Sandy.' Giving bad news always wears me out. 'Free with some crummy magazine, I shouldn't wonder.'

A cheval ('horse') glass is so-called because of its 'horse' pulley for swivelling the mirror to different angles. The plate-glass revolution brought in the 'full' cheval, instead of the mirror in halves. This faker had used chunks of genuine old mirrors, a common trick.

'Spiteful beast! You're saying that to buy it cheap!'

Enough. I opened the door. 'See you, Sandy.'

'Please, Lovejoy.' He looked stricken. I didn't go back. It might be another mercurial mood switch. 'I'll behave. What?'

'Those stamps. You tried touting them ten days ago.'

'Flat fee, Lovejoy.' He simpered. 'My friend had a dreadful terrible time in gaol, poor dear.'

Flat fee? My slow neurones clunked into gear. Another ex-gaolbird? Nobody likes selling antiques for a flat fee. Like, fifty quid if you sell this antique turk's head hour-glass. You lose money, if it goes for a thousand.

'Did they sell?' They couldn't have.

'No. Parcelled them into job lots, Wittwoode's next auction. Best I could do, dear.' He tittered. 'He'll be furioso!'

So would anybody. Sending antiques to auction is an admission of failure. So why do it? Because somebody was desperate, that's why. Somebody who'd come out of nick after a number of years.

'Didn't you warn him?'

'It was all he had.' Sandy shrugged, admiring his reflection. 'Got this horrid dollop broker to store his stamp cache until he was released. Lovejoy, do you think I should go platinum blond? Mel would *rage!*'

That adjective meant the dollop broker was a woman. Sandy's vernacular. Also Sandy's ex-convict pal was desperate for money.

Time to scarper. I risked one last dig. 'Wish Mel's friend good luck with his Penny Blacks.'

'Mel's friend?' Sandy cooed after me. 'With *his* colouring?'

So Mel also knew who it was. My mind was working out: this old lag emerged from a stretch of long porridge. He wanted money. So he unearthed his portfolio of stamps – they must have seemed a cast-iron investment, way back when. He gives them to Sandy to sell. Sandy can't, because the floor's vanished. Sandy sends them to Wittwoode's, for costly auction. Flat fee, too. The cheap way. Any dealer on earth would hang on, for the market to recover.

And, surprise surprise! Monday the massive haul of household goods from Prammie Joe's turkey job *had* to be handed over. Joe said so. And Connie wanted me to divvie a load of heavy antiques without delay. A pattern? With the conviction of the unlearned, I went to meet The Great Marvella and her talking snake. I like her. Not sure about the snake.

CHAPTER FOUR

There's a joke: antiques is the hobby God would have, if only He had the money. Like all cracks, there's a grain of truth. Antiques is a bottomless well. This parable proves it:

A bird bought a small hotel hereabouts. She made a go of it, started discos, bingo, resident band. Then bought a garage, import concessions for foreign motors, flashy dress shops. A ball of fire. The town hadn't seen anything like Gervetta. Then she got antiques, like people get beri-beri. A deficiency disease.

In her case, she wanted paintings. I mean hungered, craved, would do anything for. Now, paintings are the one antique everybody *knows*. We look and go 'Yuck!' or 'Yes!' We may not react the same, but we do it. Gervetta looked, waved her bulging chequebook. Paintings flowed in. The trouble is that liking is light years away from being able to *recognise* that Rembrandt, that priceless Turner or Monet. Paintings are the frightening game of Spot the Dud.

Gervetta knew she *knew* she knew paintings. She didn't.

She started on scenic English watercolours, pre-1851. This expansive market is one where, dealers sadly remark, a collector can't go wrong. Oh, fakes abound: David Cox, Samuel Palmer, Turner, John Constable even, the Rowbothams. But usually a competent friend can more or less guarantee good odds of authenticity. So, dearly beloved, Gervetta drained the countryside. Dealers scavenged for watercolours like maniacs. Then on a whim she changed – old Irish and English drinking glasses. She'd have been wiser to choose American blown-three-mould glassware, which is classy, identifiable, and plentiful. And not much faked – yet.

Our fakers had a riot. They sold her recycled glasses barely cool from the furnace. In sets of six, would you believe. They sold her Jacobite drinking glasses so rare nobody had ever seen their like – meaning, the faker had got it wrong but was reluctant to chuck the damned thing away. Then by mistake Gervetta came to me. I'd heard of her. Who hadn't? She wanted to sell her precious antiques.

'You understand, Lovejoy,' she explained after introducing herself in my workshop, a tumbledown ex-garage in the overgrown garden. 'It's tax write-offs.' She smiled winningly. 'The Inland Revenue's caught up, and wants a cut.'

'Why me, lady?'

'You're the only dealer in the Eastern Hundreds who hasn't sold to me,' she said frankly.

Aye, well. I'd been away overseas. Still had the scars. Anyhow, crooks don't trespass. We – I mean, *they* – daren't.

She watched me work. I was repairing a worm-eaten Charles II cane-bottomed day bed. For all the world a low chair with the seat inordinately stretched. They're unbelievably rare. This lovely piece was 'relic', too far gone to be anything but firewood. All six worm-holed scroll legs were shredding sponge.

I use that thin plasticky stuff shops use for packing porcelain. Here's how wormy furniture's restored: make a cup of this, and fix it beneath the moth-eaten wooden leg with elastic bands. Pour in a thick cream of rabbit-skin size, chalk, and plasterer's whiting, with a drop of formaldehyde to kill the woodworm. Let it set a couple of days. Harden it off three or four days.

The leg I was working on was the fourth. I test the stuff with a pin. Hard as stone. Then you can file it, like real wood. I include a few artificial cracks, of course, filling them with stained beeswax. This trick is unnecessary, but legally allows you to advertise the furniture as 'restored'. The buyer then has no legal claim on you.

'You're good, Lovejoy.'

'You're beautiful, love. But your antique glass isn't.'

She stared. 'How do you know it's glass?'

'You lifted the box out of your motor like, well, glass. And I'm the only real antique dealer on earth.'

It was all beyond her. 'But you haven't seen it unpacked.'

'Don't bother. It's fake.'

Naturally, being a bird, Gervetta was all doubt. I had to show her the simple glass trick. Put a fake antique glass down. Stand a brand-new glass, bought today, next to it. Shine an intense light at both, equal illumination. Look at the rims. The new glass rim seems whitish. So will a fake. The antique glass shows lovely greyish crescents.

'Yours, love, are white. See?' She also had some Stuart crystal, ho ho ho, engraving white as snow, edges sharp. 'Born yesterday.'

'Me? Like the glass?'

She took it well, give her that. But women are fifty times more practical. She wouldn't believe that all her 'antiques' were duff. She asked me to come and check. I said no.

'Why not?' She was outraged. 'I have to know, stupid!'

'Can't you see, you silly bitch?'

We were in the cottage. Her Rolls Royce besmirched the garden. Inside, bare flagged floor, no furniture, no fire, no light, bare windows. She looked, the bewilderment of wealth.

'You said your Carolean bed was highly valuable, Lovejoy.'

'It's somebody else's, missus. Now clear off. I've done you an expensive favour. Free. Now let me earn my next three meals.'

That was when she hired me, and learned the ghastly truth about her collections. Her real heartbreak was an antique David Wolff glass. He was a Dutch bloke, whose stipple-engraved glasses are famous. He worked on English drinking glasses shipped to Holland, his tiny dots so fine you need a lens. This fake (*white* dots is a give-away) even had an English shilling of 1782 in the glass as 'proof'. It's the oldest trick in the book.

Me hired meant we moved on to other kinds of linkage. The dealers wouldn't speak to me for ending their spree. Women dealers were doubly scathing. Females don't like other birds. Dunno why.

Gervetta and me were friends for almost a fortnight. She suddenly sold up and went to live in Charlottesville, USA, among the ineffably rich. She left me a fake Ch'ien Lung tea-dust glaze bowl, having paid a fortune for it. The five phoney certificates – British Museum, Sotheby's – were still stuck on. You didn't need to check the absence of that curious green hint to the dark brown glaze, or peer through a surface microscope to see the unnatural smoothness. It *felt* dud. Poor – poorer – Gervetta.

The lesson? Bottomless wells take any amount of gelt and echo for more. Parable ends.

So I went to see Jeff. They call him a different nickname, but he's Dalgleish. Geordie, from the Tyne. He lives with Eleanor, blind and bonny since birth.

The bus got me down the estuary in time for dark. Jeff teaches tense people relaxation. Antique dealers always do a spare-time catchpenny. Jeff's was the easiest I've ever heard of. 'Sit down, lady. Nod off. Next.'

'Wotcher, Jeff. I warn you I want a lift to the Bricklayers Arms in a few minutes.'

'Come in, Lovejoy.' He called my arrival ahead. They live in a cottage. He's levelled off every floor so there are no ledges, no sudden steps. The lights are always apologetically dimmed, in self-rebuke for Eleanor's misfortune. 'Glad to see you.'

Jeff has the lowered gaze of the blind minder, forever checking protrusions. They never lose it. Eleanor on the other hand has the strange merriment of the afflicted, her laugh straight poetry. She's lovely, vivacious. Makes me wonder what the rest of us have done. She immediately was up to buss me, hurrying to make tea. I always dawdle at Jeff's, never move anything. I'm clumsy enough.

'Jeff. You sent a ring through Gunge Herod?'

'Yes.' He looked too hopeful. I sighed inside.

'Take a hint?' He hesitated. I'd been right to come. He had it bad, lured by some big scam. 'Yes or no, Jeff?'

'Anything wrong, Lovejoy?' He glanced to the kitchen door.

'I think so. Suspect.' I corrected.

'I own the ring, Lovejoy.' A guarded little speech.

'Jeff. Before Eleanor comes back.' We both spoke softly. 'My guess is, you've been asked to put some money in a scam. Big. Cast iron. The money's needed fast, tomorrow. Am I right?' Silence. 'Cut out, Jeff.'

He licked his lips. He doesn't have much savvy. I should talk. He's the one with the gorgeous bird.

'You don't understand, Lovejoy.' He indicated Eleanor's trilling. 'I'm her mainstay. I'll need help as we grow older. A nest-egg's vital.'

'What if the nest-egg's a myth, Jeff? You in clink?'

He searched my face. I've seen that look a million times, the ineffable hope of the wistful buyer.

'You two conspirators done?' Eleanor came swishing in, carrying a tray. I think she hears everything, and pretends not to.

'Yes, Ellie.' Jeff smiled, as if she could see him. Did she feel smiles? 'Lovejoy's come to warn us. No unwise investments.'

I felt rather than saw her hesitation, speaking of feelings. She said evenly, 'Thank you, Lovejoy.'

And the chat turned from antiques to innocence, which is never worth reporting. Over and out.

The Great Marvella and her talking snake is (you'll see why the singular in a sec) an institution. We've had our wizards, sure. But TGM and HTS hit us like a typhoon. Nobody quite believed her until they actually clapped eyes on. Then, worryingly, some people did. And she was made.

Jeff dropped me at the door, by St Botolph's Priory, one of the ruins that Cromwell knocked about a bit. I could see torchlights among the gravestones – a local amateur drama rehearsing towards catastrophe. I bumped into Acker Kirwin. He's an affluent buyer from Nine Arches, village of specialists in tax evasion. He carried something that pulled my bellrope. My chest went boiiing.

'Acker!' I cried, shoving him into the lamplight to see. 'Great to see you! Musical box? Nicole Frères?'

'Shhh, Lovejoy, you burk!' Acker's the only dealer who always sounds furtive. He wore an alpaca overcoat, lined by camel velvet. Done up like a dog's dinner. Women say he's a handsome devil, with his Errol Flynn tash. To add insult to injury, he deals money in your hand. I don't like him. He has connections among the grim, same as others.

'Is it mint?' A musical box in mint condition's worth four times the amount you'd get if it has a tooth missing from its comb – the metal bit that plucks the tune from prongs on the revolving drum.

This box was just over two feet long, the right size. Get one with a fat cylinder, with the names of classical pieces on the lid's escutcheon, and you've found a genuine long-playing 'overture' box. Top value. They are wound by a simple key.

'Yours for a year's wages, Lovejoy.'

'Eh?' I gasped at the price. We talk in fractions of the nation's average annual wage – monetary values being the shifting sands they are. I mean, King William III – of William and Mary fame – bought all Kensington Palace for 14,000 quid. See what I mean? 'That's robbery!'

Acker sniggered. 'You know it's a steal, Lovejoy.' Acker means a.k.a. – 'also known as'. He uses aliases.

If he wasn't going to sell me the Nicole Freères box for a song I'd annoy him back.

'Marvella in? Had a chat with her snake?'

'Not seen her, Lovejoy,' Acker said, and strolled off.

Odd. The only doorway with a light on was The Great Marvella's. I'd seen him emerge from it. I'd never heard so many lies in one day before. A record even for the antiques game.

A buzz on the door's voice box got an aloof, 'Who?'

'Never mind who's out here, Vell,' I rasped back. 'Who've you got in there?'

The grille laughed fit to burst. 'Geronimo's caged, Lovejoy. Promise.'

'Okay,' I said, peeved. All very well for the silly cow to laugh, but a snake's a snake. 'Good evening, Marvella,' I began again, politely. 'It's Lovejoy. May I come in?'

CHAPTER FIVE

Stairs are the most boring structures on earth. You can't do a thing except go up or down. Sometimes what's at the top is less than pleasant. I mean Geronimo, not The Great Marvella.

Her upstairs flat is over a florist's, facing the chip shop (Fantle's chippie. Not bad, but it's gone curry-with-pasta and other uncon trollables. Plastic spoons are the end of civilization). It was still open I'd no money. The aroma wafted in after me and clung. A pause i always wise at a top step.

'Hello?' I knocked. I'm pathetic, but snakes are definitely no my scene. Although I remember an auction duel over a stuffed cobra that brought the house down.

'Come in. Coward.'

Her voice is unnaturally whispery, a come-on, maybe pas trauma. You don't ask.

Slo-o-owly I entered. There she was, sixty inches of female flowing dark hair, dressed only in a man's buttonless jacket. That's only. Not even shoes. She was reading elegantly on a sofa. Sh pointed to the table.

Geronimo's cage, Geronimo coiled inside. I sweated relief.

'Look, Vell. Can't you put him away?'

She raised her eyebrows. 'What *are* you suggesting?'

Cages look secure. But snakes can wriggle, can't they? And climb Ugh.

'Don't muck about. Lock him away, Vell.'

She asked, 'What d'you think, Geronimo?'

The snake replied, 'If he'll come in with me, Marvella.'

'Geronimo agrees, Lovejoy. On one condition –'

'I heard, I heard.' It's only Vell's voice-throwing act. She say she was on the professional stage, really quite famous. We don' believe her. Ventriloquists aren't, are they? I mean, you can alway see their lips move. They're embarrassing. The audience all wan the act to end.

'Going to stand there all evening, Lovejoy?'

There's nowhere to sit. A straight chair, opposite her couch Perching on the table was definitely out. She has a bedroom and kitchen, sumptuous by comparison. But this was her intro room fo clients. She tells paranormal fortunes in her inner sanctum, the

506

Marvella Revivification Clinic. She revivifies by massage and asking Geronimo what next, and other symbolically penetrating questions. Unbelievably, people actually pay money. They bring real problems – about Auntie's cancer, should the daughter get the cottage, is he sincere, the wide world's moans. The snake diagnoses. Vell interprets, to satisfying massage.

Many antique dealers, Connie among them, have regular appointments. My reason for risking Geronimo.

'No, Vell. I'm just going.' I shuffled uncomfortably. She was all but naked, the big jacket hopelessly inadequate. 'Heard of any big antique scam, love?'

'My clients' disclosures are confidential, Lovejoy.'

That old one. Everybody – insurance companies, charities, governments – claims your secrets are 'confidential'. They mean they stick your precious secrets into files clerks read for a laugh when the office is slack.

'Did Acker Kirwin say owt?'

Puzzlement on her brow. Quite good acting. Maybe she had been on the stage after all.

'Come to bed and I'll tell you, Lovejoy.'

'Er, ta, Vell. But I'm . . .'

'Running for a train?' Getting mad. Not my fault. I'm the one should be narked, not her.

It was from a time she and I nearly made smiles. We'd met at an auction. I'd actually sold her a lovely circular supper Canterbury, 1810, beautiful mahogany though not Sheraton. I'd mended the railing round the top myself. Four legs, and very rare, with two drawers in the railed drum layer between the legs. Castors original. She'd got in my way when I carried it into Wittwoode's. I got narked. She made slighting remarks back. She and I swiftly became polarised as well as passionate – until I knocked over a cage on her bed table, reached down to pick it up. And found myself staring into the stony eyes of Geronimo while his tongue flicked in and out. I was off like a cork from a bottle. I'd babbled, hurtling out of the bedroom door, that I was running for a train. Vell's hated me ever since.

'Sorry, Vell.' I backed out, eyes on Geronimo.

'Don't be stupid, Lovejoy.' She rose, her bottom dragging my eyes. She strolled indolently to a wall hutch – modern crud, veneered chipboard – and poured some wine. 'I thought it was only me scared you.'

'I'm not scared.' I declined the wine. 'Got anything to eat? Snake and onions?'

'Cut that out, Lovejoy,' the snake said. Vell's throat moved, her lips stiff. I wish she wouldn't do it.

'The chippie's open,' Vell said. 'Nip out and get some. We can chat.'

'No, I won't bother.'

Her eyes shrewded up. 'Broke, Lovejoy?'

Women nark me. Nothing but criticism. Like when you're ill. It's a real excuse for them to go to town bullying you back to health.

'No, I'm not.' Her accusation stung.

'No,' she agreed quickly. 'I *know* you're not *broke*. I meant you'd forgotten your wallet. Look.' She brightened. 'I've not had anything yet. I'm peckish. Would you slip over to Fantle's? Fish and chips twice.'

I shot out with her gelt. This was lucky. If she hadn't been starving . . . I ran across the rain-glistening black road, and wolfed two lots of chips, brown sauce, before returning sedately with a scalding hot newspaper parcel for us both. Geronimo watched as I dined regally from the fat-soaked paper. Vell luckily had lost her appetite, so I had hers as well. Anyway, women never eat much.

Vell watched me nosh with that patient detachment women bring to observe appetites. She was kneeling revealingly.

'Geronimo has to go away, Lovejoy. For a day or two.'

I paused. This was worth thought. 'Got relatives?'

'His medical's due.' She was smiling. God, but women are cruel. I mean, it's basically unfair for a gorgeous bird undressed only in a jacket to sit near when you're full.

'I thought he looked peaky.'

'Nerve,' Geronimo said, through Vell's tight lips.

Even tight lips aren't fair in these circumstances. I mean, tight lips make you think of loosening them, and what with.

'That rich bitch Mrs Vervain left your scene, Lovejoy?'

'Who?' I never blab. It's the road to dusty death.

Vell nodded slowly, her smile returning. I screwed up the empty newspapers. Actually, this was another fluke. Because if Vell wouldn't disclose what Acker Kirwin was up to, maybe she would if I stayed a while? But I could only come, so to speak, when Geronimo wasn't here.

'When do you go?' Like a fool, I asked the snake.

It flicked its reptilian tongue, dead eyes swivelling my way. Said, 'Soon. What's on your mind?'

'Nothing,' I told it quickly, and smiled weakly at Vell, who smiled back and handed me the wine, which I took.

The rest of the evening was uneventful. I got nothing out of Vell about Acker or Connie, though I tried. I left, backing round the wall as if pinned in a searchlight, to keep clear of Geronimo. Vell waved bye bye, her breasts making me groan with lust as I hopped it. I'd promised to come next evening for supper. We'd be alone.

Outside in the cool drizzle, the shoe-black night sheened on the town like polish. I drew breath. A motor swished past, spraying my legs. Fantle's was shut. The florist's was lit by a single fluorescent strip. Farther down, the night was lit by an orange sky glow from the town's ring road.

The bus station's a couple of hundred yards, through a narrow gateway in the Roman wall. I went along the alley that passes the Priory ruins.

'Is that you, Lovejoy?'

'Martha?' I couldn't see a damned thing. They've cut street lights for efficiency, so we can all break our legs after dusk. 'How's the show?'

She's a pleasant lass. Acts with the St Hilda Players. A pleasant lot on the whole, though each'd kill to get the lead part. Summer performances in the ruins with floodlights. She has a boutique out in the villages, and a husband.

'Fine, thanks. We're doing *Titus Andronicus.*'

'Comedy? I'll come.'

She put her arm through mine. We walked along. 'Why do you, Lovejoy? Pretend you're thick. I've seen you, creeping in.'

'I can't afford a ticket. Who can?'

'Our prices are cheap!' The actress's dictum: it's proper, charging people to admire me.

'You're rolling, love. I've heard about your new benefactress. Cassandra Clark, isn't it? You should make the plays free.'

And suddenly it fell into place. Acker hadn't been coming out of The Great Marvella's doorway. He'd been ducking *in*, hoping not to be seen, when Jeff's car had dropped me off. He hadn't come from the shuttered pawnshop, Fantle's chippie, the florist's. The only other place was the Priory ruins. And the rehearsal.

'Just because we've found somebody public-spirited in this God-forsaken town, Lovejoy! People are unwilling to pay to see a wonderful show. Yet they watch endless grot on telly –' Et yawnsome cetera.

'I agree, love,' I said.

Astonishment stopped her tirade. 'You do? I *knew* you approved of us, really.'

'Cassandra Clark there tonight, was she? Only, I saw Acker Kirwin take an antique . . .'

'Came briefly.' Martha's tones had the reverence actresses reserve for people who put up money. 'Cassandra's wonderful. She never interferes with the artistic side. A *true* philanthropist.'

We entered the bus station to the sound of heavenly violins, Martha waxing eloquent about philanthrophy and me thinking there's no such thing. Waiting for the last bus out to our respective villages, I got a rundown of those present at rehearsal, and the loan of the fare home. Martha didn't explain why a lovely rich lady would pour money into shamateur drama in an ancient ruined priory.

Bits were adding up. I wished Prammie Joe was on the phone, or that message bottles flowed from my river directly into his. But it was late. Countryside frightens me at the best of times, let alone when bats do fly and trees start watching you. So I didn't go to Prammie's marsh. Wrong again.

CHAPTER SIX

The day dawned with brilliance. One of those that makes you understand why some folk actually like countryside. I've even heard some take country holidays. A white frost, hard as iron, the grass stiff with the spittle of a full moon, sky blue as childhood, air still. The birds were nodding the ground as usual. A squirrel fooling about, dashing along branches. I yawned at the window, perished with cold.

Telephones are counter-productive. Their absence is the same. I considered this philosophy while cooking my breakfast. The swine had cut me off, non-payment of debts to robbers. The gas and electricity were temporarily off – a disagreement about fiscal policy with energy barons. I used my home-made stove. A tin bowl half-filled with sand. Put in a little oil or petrol, drop in a match. It woomphs into flame. Perch on it your pan containing margarine, sliced tomatoes. Bread, and dine like a king.

The trick's dangerous, so I do it between two bricks in the garden – a wilderness of fecund greenery engulfing my cottage. The birds stay away.

I washed – standing at the sink, on a towel to protect the valuable Wilton carpet (joke), towelled myself dry, gasping at the cold. Cold permeates like nothing else. Odd, that. Warmth doesn't, so why should cold? The bare flags set me shivering. My underpants were dry, thank God. Socks were barely damp, though frigid with that cunning old cold. I was down to my last tea bag. An apple – plenty of those – and I was off to my daily slog singing that Tallis *Sanctus* everybody else gets wrong.

My garage is deep in the foliage near my back door. It functions without any modern aid – the only way to fake antiques. The greatest workshop of the western world, sez I.

It was a relief, getting back to real life. Joan Vervain had taken it out of me. Drinkwater was worrying, though the Cornish Place robbery was more recycling than theft. I mean, our local councillors don't *own* the buildings, do they? They only look after them for us people. If they can't be bothered, they must take the consequences.

This train of thought narked me, as I set up the lathe. I'd make an issue out of it next local election, and vote against everybody.

My lathe's dentist's old treadle drill. I use a Singer strap, gears from a machine spindle. I've given up sitting on a stool when turning wood. You have to move about. I was repairing/restoring/faking a small tripod table. Not the most profitable antique, because small genuine antique tables are still cheap. It's a question of the things that can be done *in the way they were done* that matters. A decent fake has dignity. It's trying to be as superb as Hepplewhite.

This tripod table had been shattered during its theft from a Lowestoft antique dealer's. Not by me, I hasten to add. There was only the top and tripod feet left. The single pillar was broken to smithereens as the lads hoofed it. A tripod table's so simple it sounds cheap, but don't be fooled. No antique is easy.

A woman was watching me. I didn't look, kept going.

Tripod tables – actually split three ways between me, Desdemona Sands from Rowhedge, and her cousin Luke Brennon the thief – are simple. Flat circular top, stem, three small feet radiating out. It sounds easy, doesn't it? Dealers still speak of a 'claw foot' table, as in the eighteenth century. Nowadays you don't hear that term. The public gets confused. (The feet are usually plain, turned in, smooth, or merely bulbous. It just resembles a bird's claw.) Mahogany's the wood. My job was to make a new pillar, to be its single leg. It would look 1780, give or take a yard. I'd got a piece of mahogany, brand new, uncured. Which needn't stop you nowadays. The woman still didn't speak.

There's this stuff called PEG. Means polyethyleneglycol. Fakers call it peg. You put granules into water. Drop in your new wood, and forget about it – two days to six weeks; depends on thickness. Mop it with a dishcloth and start work. Simple. The new wood becomes easy to work, hardly ever flakes, and planes like a dream. Normally you need eight years of careful curing in the open air. Monks used to pee on new timber in lined pits, but they didn't have PEG to speed things along. I'd pegged this mahogany piece, and it was ready.

Odd feeling, to be lathe-turning new wood when it feels old. Slippery, too smooth, yet the chuck bites as if the wood . . .

'No tongue, missus?' I hate creeping people.

'Lovejoy, isn't it?'

Cassandra Clark, as ever was. I sighed to a stop, elbows on the work. I approve of lovely women. They bring a glow to, well, a drossy workshop. Hair lustrous, skin blooming, eyes to dazzle. Clothes that make other women swivel with that up-down rake of instant envy. Which raised an all-important question.

'To whom might I have the pleasure of addressing of?'

She smiled. 'Where are they, Lovejoy?'

Stumped, first go. I thought hard. The place was bare except for tools. Maybe she wanted a fake, I thought hopefully.

'They're here, love.' It was true. Whatever I had was here.

'Your antiques, Lovejoy. The ones you make. Fake?' She smiled, not hard to watch. 'Create?'

That was more like it. 'It's this tripod table.'

She inspected my crude lathe. 'Ordinary mahogany, Lovejoy?'

This ignorance is typical. Untrained, unlearned, unread. Hoodlums have more sense.

'There's no such thing. Mahogany's more than sixty different kinds. Matching them up is a pig. Three genera are mahogany proper. Others say only *Swietenia* is the true stuff – Cuba, Honduras, Guatemala. It's unbelievably rare.'

'I know. Rose mahogany.' She was narked, tapped her foot. I really love ignorance. No, honestly. To be that thick needs genius.

'Rosewood's not mahogany, love. It pretends to be . . .' I beamed, hoping to annoy her into some relevation '. . . something it isn't.'

That set her wondering whether to march out, forget this little encounter ever took place. Or stay . . . and what?

Time to needle. 'Duckeggs – meaning you – don't know a thing, love.' I got fed up, resumed my treadling. 'Auctioneers at least dig out a few glib phrases.' I knew I was getting to her. Any woman who hangs around the town's antique dealers and buys not a bauble is up to something. And this one didn't hang around by accident. She'd had to clump through the undergrowth in high heels, for a start.

'For somebody who's broke, Lovejoy, your arrogance is –'

'Don't buy this table, love. It'll look like a Chippendale. Everything matching. Dealers call anything that vaguely looks right "genuine mahogany". But you know what?' I lowered my voice, all furtive.

'What?' she was caught in the pull of a secret.

'They're lying.'

She tutted, decided I wasn't worth a candle. 'And to think that I was actually con –'

'Good morning,' Joan Vervain said sweetly. 'Considering what? I do hope I'm not interrupting.'

She was. The silly cow had cut through the only vital word.

'Not at all, Mrs Vervain.' Cassandra Clark glared at me. 'He has absolutely nothing to offer.'

They passed like cruisers from different navies, at distance but

513

measuring threat. Dear Mrs Vervain started on me, where was I, who the hell did I think she is, et howling cetera.

'It's no good, darling.' I looked broken-hearted. Which wasn't difficult, seeing I was screaming to do the furniture. Desdemona would be screaming for the same thing. Not to mention Luke the thief, only he doesn't scream. He stabs people. 'I can't go on.' I rose, stared soulfully into the garden. 'We have to stop seeing each other.'

'We . . . ?' She swung me round, blazing. 'Is it Del? The drunken bastard send his thugs round? I'll poison the pig –'

'Not that, dwoorlink. It's . . .' I scuffed the flag floor. It's what, exactly? If you let it, your brain finds lies, any shape and just right. Try to work one out, you come a croper. 'Look about, love. Everything I own. Even that's mortgaged, borrowed, nicked.'

That should do it. The idea is to give them a start. They'll provide the rest of the lie for themselves.

Joan leapt in on cue. 'Oh, darling. You're hopeless!'

For one moment I thought she'd rumbled me. 'I know,' I said. More soul, to hurry her. I'd never finish the work at this rate.

'Listen, darling.' She'd reached some conclusion, thank heaven. 'I've got lawyers working on a settlement. I'm not going to be palmed off with pennies . . .'

Her conclusion was appalling. She actually thought that I . . . ? I changed my inward scream to an inward groan.

'Lovejoy?' More bloody arrivals.

'Eh?' I realised I'd sounded joyous, so went sombre. 'Yes. I'm Lovejoy.'

A man and a woman stood blocking the light. The man said, 'I'm Mr Carstairs. My wife. An interview.' He looked doubtful. 'Is this the right place? Lovejoy Antiques, Inc.? The Employment Training . . .'

God. I'd forgotten. I'd applied to the Employment, saying I was an employer willing to train somebody. I didn't actually want the stupid sods to send me a real live person. I'd only registered for the money. What did the Government want, blood?

'Oh, yes. Could you wait a moment, please?' I let them retreat, said softly to Joan, 'Dwoorlink. You bowled me over. You just don't understand.'

'Yes, Lovejoy. I do.' Belief that she alone understands is a woman's credo. And nobody credoed more than Joan. She dragged me down to her mouth. We parted with a plop. 'How soon will you be finished?'

'An hour. They're . . . er, Sotheby's Educational Section.'

'I'll send the car. Love you, lover.'

We parted. I'd bought time.

Mr Carstairs wasn't the Employment Learning Opportunist. It was his missus, Luna if you please. There was an ugly little scene. I heard them arguing hotly.

'It's a dump!' Carstairs said. 'He looks off the road.'

'It's my chance, Oliver. I've made my mind up.'

A shocked gasp. 'Luna. This is a mistake –'

'Oliver. If I don't do it now, I'll never do it.'

A bird after my own heart. She knew I was the opportunity of a lifetime. A discerning bird if ever I saw one.

The lathe treadled into action, so I didn't hear the rest of the heated exchange. Later I was interrupted by a timid shout that made me jump out of my skin. I'd forgotten the silly cow.

'Lovejoy.' She was there when I came down. She looked scared, defiantly twisting her handbag strap into gangrene. Oliver was severely blocking the light. 'I'm Luna Carstairs. EOTSC.'

The what? Forty-odd, plumpish, fair, dressed by some 1950s B feature. I liked her. 'Did you bring the paper?'

'Yes.' She rummaged eagerly, gave me a letter. I tossed it aside.

'Right. Sleeves rolled up, Luna. We've work to do.'

'Now?' She unbuttoned her coat. Give me strength.

'Metaphorically, love.' I shouldn't call her a silly cow, not right off. 'You'll freeze to death out here.' I didn't want an apprentice who moaned about draughts.

'You mean I've got the job?' She was thrilled.

'Insight, Mrs Carstairs,' I said. 'I can tell worth.'

Oliver the Indignant left, in some deep-throated engined monster tethered by the gate. To Luna I explained the most important tasks in her life for the next four weeks. The first was to brew up, in my special manner.

She had enough money for us to get the town bus. She'd enough for me to buy us pasties, mushy peas and chips. Woody's is grot city, home of saturated fats and antique dealers. Noshing to repletion, I realised that a lady of Luna's restricted lifestyle brought a new dimension. She solved the local scam problem in half a sentence.

'Mahogany's beautiful material,' I was saying. She had an annoying habit of looking about. Getting on my nerves. I had to keep jerking her attention back. 'Oak was king until about 1660. Walnut came anciently from Persia. Extensively planted, Elizabethan times on. Hence, walnut furniture – *for Christ's sake pay heed!*'

'I'm sorry, Lovejoy,' she said, startled to vigilance. She was flying, blue eyes shining with excitement. I was mollified. Enthusiasm isn't far from passion. With this smart bird the lads'd see I was up-market.

'Then mahogany ruled, say 1725 on. Sauce, please.' She passed the sauce. I lashed out a pool of it. True to female tradition, Luna ate little. She actually picked up a chip on her fork and inspected the damned thing. The Employment had slipped me some extra-terrestrial. 'The main problem for the faker – er, antiques expert restorer – is that mahogany has what we call thunder shakes. An upset. Fracture across the wood, that you can't see until you've cut into it. Every time you cut mahogany your heart's in your mouth, wondering if it has one of these concealed cross-fractures – *what the frigging hell's the matter?*'

She was all thrilled-to-be-here. The lads were smiling back, taking the mickey. Was she on the run, or what?

'I'm sorry, Lovejoy. I've never been in one before.'

Woody's is a shambles of filthed tables, peeling chrome, reject lino shredded to catch the settling grease. A dozen bloated dealers were in, convincing each other they were having a hard life.

'One what?' I was baffled.

'A *dive*,' she whispered conspiratorially, head almost in my plate. I hugged my grub closer. She had her own, largely untouched. I eyed it. It would hot up pretty well.

'Dive?' I'd drawn Priscilla of the Lower Third. 'This is Woody's, love.' It is the least exotic place on Planet Earth. Woody's barrel gut, fungating triangle of pubic hairs visible in the fumes of frying crud, adds to the authenticity.

'The *food*, Lovejoy! Hairs in the bacon!'

'Don't you like it?' I asked, hopeful.

Pause. 'It's a little wholesome, Lovejoy.'

'Don't give offence, love. I'll try to finish yours.'

'Oh, would you, Lovejoy? I really would appreciate . . .'

Where was I? 'Our problem is that tripod table, Luna. They practically never have a carved top *and* carved tripod feet. Carved table top means the feet have *got* to be plain. Tell me what I've just said.'

She repeated it faithfully, solemn eyes watching my reaction. I mopped my plate with bread, swapped it for hers.

'The second clue. If a tripod table's top is *exactly* circular, it's probably a fake. You measure its diameter. It'll have shrunk since the eighteenth century. Ours is almost five-eighths of an inch out. Repeat.'

'Oh, Lovejoy!' she cried, excited. 'To think I was actually concerned about you!' Her hand flew to her mouth. 'What's the matter? What have I said?'

I managed, 'Nothing, love. Just remembered something.'

'You've gone quite pale.' She foraged in her handbag. 'Have you got a headache? I usually find these tablets –'

'Repeat what I've told you.'

'About the table? If you're all right . . .'

To think that I was actually concerned about you . . . Was what Cassandra Clark said, almost. Joan had finished the word for her – but wrongly. Not 'considering'. *Concerned.* Which equals worried. Cassandra had come because she was worried I would chuck a spanner in her works. My transparent poverty reassured her: I clearly presented no threat. But to what? She was rich. I'd seen her at the Arcade, not long ago. When I'd sussed out Gunge Herod's/Jeff's papal ring. She'd ignored me, of course. But now? For a brief spell, I'd had her worried.

Whatever I'd been up to – and I wasn't sure what – presented some threat. Luna had finished her recital.

'Lesson Two begins now, love.' I almost added an apology, for chucking her in the deep end.

'Here's a list of local museums, love. I'll expect you to look at the furniture in them all. Quickly.' I finished the grub, rose amid merry grins from the lads and a blessing from Psycho, our religious nut.

'Who will teach me about them, Lovejoy?'

I pinged the door open, called so-long to Woody. 'Teaching antiques? No such thing. Come on, love. We've a lady to see.'

I needed to check on Tits Alors (rhymes with doors). She'd be lurking – well, not exactly lurking; more like flaunting brazenly – on her beat about now. If Luna was going to play the antiques game she had to learn it wasn't played in a nunnery.

CHAPTER SEVEN

Luna Carstairs had 'occasional use of my Oliver's motor', she told me. You get the feeling spouses communicate by memorandum. We were still on Shanks's pony when we cut past the Welcome Sailor pub. Tits Alors was at her post. Willowy, short-skirted, booted, black fishnets, enough make-up to export. Beautiful.

'See Tits Alors? Ask how near she is to a load.'

'A load?' Luna abruptly de-thrilled. I went to the Arcade, pausing to watch two Brighton blokes unload a long case clock ('grandfather', as goons like antique dealers insist on missaying). Plain case, in bur-walnut veneer on oak, done well. Fakers nark me. I mean, whoever'd faked got it perfect – then forgot these early clocks are never above six-and-a-half feet tall. And the chapter ring (its hours circle) was twelve inches, two inches too big. I hate carelessness.

Luna was blocking my path, her face flaming. 'Lovejoy! That . . . that *lady* is a . . . a . . .' She flapped her hands.

'Prostitute? So?' If you want something doing, do it yourself. I crossed over. 'Hello, Tits.'

Tits smiled through rouge, mascara, a plaster of cosmetics. 'Lovejoy! Nice to . . .' She saw Luna. 'She with you? I thought . . .'

'Sorry. Luna Carstairs, apprentice. May I present Tits Alors, antique dealeress.'

Tits smiled. 'Not dealer. Collector, Lovejoy.'

I had to laugh. 'How near are you to a load, Tits?'

'Ten days, give or take. But it's spoken for.'

'It's what?' This was unprecedented. 'Who's buying?'

She wouldn't say. I said so-long, walked Luna off for a think. Except Luna was dazedly bent on interrogation.

'Lovejoy. I've actually *spoken* to a *real* one!'

Wearily I spurred my tardy cortex, to calm her.

'Look. Tits solicits. Blokes take her to some hotel. Home even, if the wife's away. She performs, takes her fee. Nicks some tom – er, steals jewellery, a small antique, anything.'

Luna gasped. 'Doesn't she get reported?'

'Never.' I quickly forestalled the obvious. 'The client would have to explain about Tits. Get it?'

She trotted alongside, baffled. 'Lovejoy. When Ti – ah, Miss Alors sells the antiques, don't the police –?'

'She sells them to *me*. Now shut up. Just listen, watch.'

That silenced her until I reached the Arcade, thank God. Gunge Herod was there like a parked troll. In his russet sheepskin he looked off the Himalayas. Luna gaped when he shuffled to meet us.

'Lovejoy. It's Connie.'

'Connie?' My innards squeezed in alarm from the way he said it. He shook his raggedy mane to allay panic.

'No. She's fine, but mad you didn't show.'

'Show?' Everybody wants me. What about me?

'You owe her a divvie. And bunce.'

I weighed possibilities. He was bigger than ever. Me and Luna together couldn't make a single sumo. 'Got wheels?'

'No. She's at the station.'

Luna paid for a taxi. We tried to balance Gunge's weight, but the taxi was practically on two wheels. Luna was thrilled. I was getting sick of her being thrilled. She said, eyes aglow, 'This is so exciting, Lovejoy!' She couldn't keep her eyes off Gunge. Never seen a Yeti before.

'Who's this, Lovejoy?'

Connie looked pretty as a picture. We made the station forecourt just as it started raining. I want one of those folding umbrellas. I had one but it got lost. My shoes reminded me they still leaked. I'd cardboarded them again only this morning. You can't depend on shoes.

'Luna Carstairs, apprentice,' I introduced. 'Miss Connie Hopkins, antique dealer of this parish.'

Luna was ecstatic again, I saw tiredly. 'Am I really your apprentice, Lovejoy?'

'No strangers, Lovejoy,' Connie said. 'Today's confidential.'

See what I mean about confidential? A lady with a ton of antiques for public sale and they're confidential. Is it just me?

'Luna's okay. She's got my firman.'

Connie eyed Luna mistrustfully. Gunge dwarfed the area. Passengers, hoping one remaining train would amble in, queued aiming vaguely for the ticket offices where clerks read newspapers.

'Lovejoy! How fortunate!'

This was one of those days. 'Hello, Miss Turner,' I said miserably. 'Er, I'm just off —'

My scruffy old genealogy-daft Yank twittered up, delved for certificates into her cavernous leather.

'I have Scots ancestors! But I didn't find —'

'– records in London?' I gave Luna the bent eye, rubbing finger and thumb. She reached for her handbag. Connie was impatient. 'English ancestors from July, 1837, General Register Offices, London. Edinburgh for Scotland, starting 1855. The General Register Office.' I said it slowly. 'Don't go to the wrong one, okay?'

'You have the address, Lovejoy?'

'It's in Edinburgh's bloody phone book.'

Luna sidled up, slipped me a note. I stuffed it into the old bat's bag. 'Only take pencil. They strip-search you for ink up there. Remember "Mac" and "Mc" are separate, or omitted, or just "M". And Peter and Patrick were interchangeable names the further north you go –'

'*Lovejoy!*' from Connie. I told Miss Turner so-long.

Connie's impatience had decided her about letting Luna come. Much more odderer. She was frantic. I mean, what was the big deal? Miss Turner warbled a distant goodbye. I waved absently.

Connie drove us out through Polstead, towards the old airfield at Boxtenholt. The *three* of us, note. When everything was – what's the vital word, begins with C?

'Are you cold, Lovejoy?' I'd shivered, an angel on my grave. 'You should have stopped for your overcoat.'

Thank you, Luna. 'It's countryside. Nothing but scenery.'

'He's not got one,' Gunge boomed after some miles. He's not quick. Who is?

'I'm sorry. I didn't ... Wouldn't for the world ...' Luna apologised for the remainder of the journey.

Connie took me aside as we alighted at the disused airfield. 'Lovejoy. You're sure she's all right?' I said give over.

Boxtenholt village is in a hollow, a tributary vale. The common pasture stands higher, a windy exposed stretch of scrub with a couple of ancient trackways. During the war it was an aerodrome, American bombers. There's a derelict breeze-block building, a tumbled control tower, sheep. A wooden sign clumped mournfully against the gaping window space – had the damned thing been doing that since 1945, for God's sake? Enough to give you the creeps. Kiddies fly kites and lovers snog on Boxtenholt Heath. There's an ancient tumulus in the centre, now rudely marked by an Ordnance Survey stone.

'This way.'

Connie's idea of deception was to park at one end of the heath, and march us to a grey guardhouse on what was the aerodrome's perimeter, down a flight of concrete steps. She had a flashlight. Me and Gunge shifted some fallen slabs blocking a metal door. Connie had a key.

'Wait, please.' I drew Luna to one side as Connie entered, Gunge close behind. We were alone. I spoke in the gloaming. 'Luna. If you say "Isn't this wonderful" once more, I'll give you a pasting. Capeesh?'

'Oh, Lovejoy! *Gangsters* say capeesh!' She scanned my face for signs that I was sharing in all this excitement.

I gathered her garments in a fist about her throat and lifted her. I can do it, with the weak. 'Do you understand? Silence. Your last chance.'

'Yes, Lovejoy.'

We followed gunge and Connie. They had lit candles.

'Something to sit on, Gungie?' I asked. 'Pile a few blocks.'

Evidently cells, below the guardroom. Dank, now, with seepage from rain. It felt lovely, glowing with the beauty that only antiques can give. They were covered with dust-sheets. Somebody had had the wit to roll an old carpet for the mound of vibrating brilliance. Concrete beams above, concrete walls around. These cells would be there in a million years. I felt queasy, told Luna, then Gunge, then Connie, to see the cellar door was propped ajar.

Divvieing is a dour, rather sickening business. Idyllic, of course. It's to do with antiques. The poor old divvie suffers every time. I've known, over the years, eight or nine of us with this gift. Some have it just for furniture, paintings, jewellery. Whatever, it's hard on the soul. Sin's easier – you get something for that. Though aphorisms are always wrong.

For a couple of minutes before starting I have to pace, hum, walk, not look at anyone. Luna couldn't take it. In fact, Luna was an outright nuisance, especially when she gazed blankly at each of us in turn while I ambled. She finally erupted, 'Well? Shouldn't we start –?'

'Shhhh!' Gunge and Connie rounded on her.

She was startled into silence. Which interrupted my feelings, so I had to start again, strolling, jingling non-existent coins, staring at the wall, whistling. This is the trouble: antiques are human. They have feelings, doubts, hesitations just like us. I mean, you don't rush straight up to perfect strangers and grab hold, tip them up, prod, dig your fingers into them, scrape their skin, all to 'take a look'. You'd soon get your eye blacked. But nobody thinks twice about doing that to antiques. Think how the poor things must feel. And *feel* they do. Believe it. 'Taking a look' is being presented at court. A cat can look at a king. But with grace, please.

'Right,' I said. Ready.

I sat on some breeze blocks. Gunge's stack was a yard away. On it burned two candles, in a pair of dazzling silver candlesticks. Not much to look at – cast baluster, less than seven inches small, only twenty ounces put together. Simplicity ruled, when refugee silversmiths came scrambling across the Channel after the Edict of Nantes was revoked in 1685 and persecutions became the norm. Pierre Harache was a shrewd nut. He got a head start. This first immigrant silversmithing genius was already making silverware in London in 1683, his simple fashions instantly all the rage. I grinned all over my face.

'Wotcher, Pierre,' I heard my voice say. 'Can I, loves?'

They didn't mind. I touched them, simultaneous so as not to give offence. You've only to see one, and that milky sheen streaks naked into your soul. That's the trouble with people who collect antiques: they'll go any distance to see dross, but won't 'waste time' visiting a free museum to see these breathtaking exquisite wonders.

'Thank you,' I told the lovely pair. 'Next.'

A small bowl, Egyptian Black, meaning that Wedgwood simply fired it once. Iron oxide type, mere earthenware stained with the stuff and fired at a low temperature. Made over fifty years, from 1720 on. This bowl was true unglazed basalt; it could be cut, even polished on a lathe with care. Josiah Wedgwood's supposed to have introduced the term 'black basaltes' about 1768. People suppose there were no black wares made before that. But there were. Two brothers called Elers had made them early in the century. This was Wedgwood. *Plain* bowls are very, very rare. You can touch the great man himself by touching one of these.

'Next.'

Quartetto tables, Battersea enamels – half a dozen snuffboxes if you please – one tiny wooden masterpiece shaped like a lady's high-heeled slipper with a sliding wooden lid. There was a carpet burned (actually no more than singed) to alter the colour and to age the back (rogues do it with a spirit blow-lamp). This is the only sensible fakery you get in carpets, because if you order, say, a dozen modern copies of a lovely Turkish Ghiordes prayer rug, about 1785, well, they're still all clearly handmade, though dirt cheap.

Connie had several classy items of furniture, all small. I like Victorian furniture, though I'm daunted by the immense grandeur of some sideboards. Three straight chairs had top rails which stuck out wider than the back; sure sign of 1840 or later. I explained this didn't mean they weren't class; they were. But it put paid to their having to fly under false colours. The chairs were pleased, I think.

Pewter tankards, small metal boxes for miners (they carried their chewing tobacco in these – they're dated, nineteenth century, often with colliery names on). A handful of *inro*, enough to make your mouth water: small cases on cords when wearing traditional Japanese dress; you stuck your favourite medicines in. The *netsuke*, a sort of toggle, on one end of the cord, is some of the most superb creative carving ever executed. Witty, amusing, hilarious, scarey, everything you could wish. My favourite was a grazing horse, carved from a bit of stag antler, barely three inches tall. Connie had a mass of antiques, with a leavening of fakes. Good as you'd ever see.

My headaches are famous. I was some time coming to after they'd put the candles out. I went reluctantly, stumbling up the dusty steps and into the Suffolk wet. I inhaled the drizzle for size. It didn't feel too bad, so I breathed more. The pity is that rain wets your head. I went and stood under a tree, listening to the solid taps of the rain. Drizzle gets steam up by soaking leaves. Then the leaf gets fed up and sags its drop like a bird plop.

Connie and Gunge were trying to talk. Luna stayed with them, occasionally glancing across. Wearily I beckoned. She trotted across the grass, heels sinking. I walked the crumbling runway to Connie's motor, leant against the bonnet.

'Lovejoy,' she said hesitantly at last. She tried the car doors, tutting like they do as if discovering a malicious plot. 'Was that little cardboard tube really worth two of these cars?'

'Mmmmh. Don't call that masterpiece a cardboard tube. It was a genuine Campani. He made "perspective glasses", telescopes. Samuel Pepys used one for ogling pretty ladies in church, naughty old devil. That colouring and decoration is tooled leather.'

She went quiet for a bit. 'You knocked over that beautiful square knife-box, Lovejoy. Unforgivable. I have a lovely one exactly like it, Queen Anne.'

'Oh, aye. Is its herring-bone inlay veneer sunk? Or dead level, too? If so, it's a fake, like that one.' I could see she was aghast at horrifying possibilities. 'You see, love, that veneer rises in a couple of centuries. It has to, see? Changes in temperature, humidity. Only new fakes are neat and level.'

Her eyes filled with alarm. She drew breath to ask. I saved her the trouble. 'I know, I know. Why didn't I have to examine it. It felt wrong. The real antiques recognise you, and say hello. They warm me. Fakes don't. It's like . . . well, like love.'

She was still trying to remember, seeing her favourite piece in her mind's eye, when Gunge and Connie came up. We embarked without a word. I settled soggily into the back seat.

'Good, Lovejoy.' Gunge, activating a neurone.

I said nothing. Connie was driving. We came to Polstead, and she went left at the crossroads.

'Lovejoy. Do you want in?' she asked along the old Roman road. They're our only straight bits in East Anglia.

'How big, compared?' I meant how big a sample had I divvied, of the whole. My mind was going: *Connie's scam isn't Prammie Joe Godbolt's scam.* Seriously bad news. In fact highly dangerous.

'Quarter, Lovejoy.'

I hadn't a bean, let alone enough to cut in on a scam this size. I said I'd think about it. She said she'd give me until tomorrow. Lots of tomorrows lately, too.

She dropped me and Luna at the cottage. My apprentice made the yuckiest brew I'd ever had. It was horrible. I didn't know if I'd last the full month on this, and told her so. She was proud of herself, said stop complaining. We sat drinking it, Luna saying the cottage was so cold. Daylight faded.

'Lovejoy?' Here it came, sum total of misgiving. 'Why is that Mrs Hopkins', er, scam in that disused airfield, and not in her showroom?'

'Some are stolen, love. A scam is a robber's scheme.'

'*Stolen?* Shouldn't we tell the police?'

My turn to stare. 'No, love. The less we have to do with the police, the better. We're not on the same side.'

'Not on the same side as the Law?' More mind-boggling.

'Do you know anybody who is?'

It was then that the police came clumping in. Drinkwater wanted me at the police station to see if I knew anyone called Godbolt. I told Luna to lock up, please, and count the silver after the constables had departed.

But *why* wasn't Connie's scam the same as Prammie Joe's? Dozy old East Anglia doesn't run to two major scams in one week. Tits Alors had already pre-sold her own load. To somebody forming up a third? Jesus. Luna, full of unasked questions, hopped from one foot to the other at the cottage door as the ploddites drove me away.

CHAPTER EIGHT

Imagine a flattish area of land, pretty big and wide, with only fields, woods, rivers, farms, villages, and cities here and there (actually two). East Anglia in a nutshell. The rivers wander into estuaries that are basically sea marshes. It's truly rural. I mean, the whole Kingdom jokes about it. Like, in showbusiness they say, 'He's the best comedian in East Anglia – how *is* the other feller?' All that.

But if you know this creaking old country of ours, you'll have sussed our trick. Nothing is what it seems. Peaceful? – take care, something's going on. Tranquil? – mayhem lurks. Sleepy? Watch out, that's all. Hereward the Wake is one of our heroes. Not as well known as Robin Hood, perhaps, but at least the Normans never caught *him*. He never slept, drifted unseen through the fens, vanishing during the day to emerge more powerful than ever when the sun sank. They say he did sleep, but with one eye open. Maybe two.

'Know anybody called Godbolt, Lovejoy?' Drinkwater's clacking pot teeth asked. Twitch. Ear flick.

'No. Live around here, does he?'

'Note that, Cradhead.'

The other ploddite said right, almost as if he'd been taught to write. Really lifelike. His name is variously pronounced.

We drove out to the River Deben. The police motor was full of misgivings, mostly mine. There's a bridge not far from Shottisham, and a small uninhabited island. We alighted and peered at the soggy countryside. I'd had enough of the wretched stuff today. I blame the Government. What's wrong with concreting it? Mother Nature's had her chance for a quadrillion years, and failed spectacularly. Look at the damned stuff.

'Into the dinghy, Lovejoy.'

Cradhead couldn't row to save his life. Lacked coordination. Prerequisite for his job, I suppose. Fearing the goon would drown us all, I took the oars myself. I'm not much good, but can get by.

'Upstream, Lovejoy.' Drinkwater of the Rolling Main.

Not easy old downstream, oh no. We went about a hundred yards, Drinkwater saying 'Left a bit' and all that. I was puffed out.

'Stop here,' the nerk actually commanded.

'Reach the brakes, Drinkie, there's a pal.'

He glared. I glared back. We drifted a moment, clumping

gently into the islet. That is, we would have, except we banged into something solid. I looked over into the water. Cradhead reached past, almost upsetting the boat, to grab on – to a 1713 brass chandelier, beautiful and genuine. Strapped on a semi-sunken raft.

'Comments are invited, Lovejoy.'

Here's a definite antiques tip: a brass chandelier is English or Dutch. It'll have an ugly-looking globe with waggly brass radii curving out for the candles. Travel half a day hereabouts, you can see half-a-dozen churches where they still dangle. I think they're horrible, but antique they are. Oh, and some public buildings have them, too. Minus one, Cornish Place, I guessed.

'Brass chandelier, Drinkwater. Very collectable. London decorators are always after them from redundant churches.' I rested on my oars. 'That it?'

We waited. I scanned the river. Something splashed with evil intent, like all countryside splashes. A little black duck with a yellow beak chugged by. I yawned. It was all happening.

'I want more comment, Lovejoy.'

'Well, these chandeliers often have a little brass dove for a finial, if it's from a church. I've never seen one with a coat-of-arms, but hear in the Midlands –'

'You dross. Why is it bobbing in the river?'

'Why ask me, you prat?' I yelled back, just as if I was really annoyed instead of frightened to death for Prammie Joe. 'There's a thousand antique dealers in East Anglia. What the hell's got into you, Drinkwater?'

'Robbery's got into me, Lovejoy.' He sat staring with his eyes just like Geronimo's. His pot teeth clacked, his ear twitched. 'This brass thing's from Cornish Place. The raft is described as one possibly belonging to Joseph Godbolt. Who finds and sells antiques.'

'Can I go home?' Biased police records, mostly false.

'The Mayor's wife'll wait, Lovejoy. I don't suppose she'll behave any different from your other tarts. Godbolt was known to be of this locality, no fixed abode.'

'Why not make the bloke who found this thing take you to this Godbolt, if he can recognise his flotsam?'

'Angler, Lovejoy. Works in a sawyer's yard near Woolverstone. He sold Godbolt this wood. It's marked.'

I drew breath, but said nothing. Woolverstone isn't even on this river. It's south, opposite bank of the Orwell, above Harwich. Where the ferries leave for the Continent.

'Clues?' I suggested idly. 'Fingerprints? You must have ... Godbolt's down at the nick.' I nearly said Prammie.

Cradhead spoke. A cultured bloke, fair of hair and plum of voice. You just know he's got friends in Whitehall.

'Can you, ah, contribute any personal knowledge, Lovejoy? Of any, ah, scam of such, ah, quantity as Cornish Place?'

Ah, no. Which troubled me too. I found myself being looked at directly by Cradhead, first time. It wasn't pleasing. Maybe he wasn't a nerk at all. I mean, a handful of idiots like him, with exactly this casual offhand manner, had run empires.

'No. Not heard a thing.'

'Shut it, Cradhead.' Drinkwater gestured for me to row us away. 'Tell the lads to bring this brass thing in.' He caught himself. I grinned. He'd almost said for questioning. 'Lovejoy. We know you talk to that poofter on East Hill. And other dealers in that thieves' Arcade. You tell me anything you learn, hear, get hinted. Right?'

'And if you find Mr Godbolt, ask him ...' Suddenly I wished to make no merry quips about Prammie, went quiet.

'Yes, ah, Lovejoy?' from Cradhead.

'How come you aren't doing this, Cradhead?' I said nastily, getting the oars. 'Didn't you row at Oxford?' I was narked. They'd let something terrible happen to Prammie Joe. 'That Oxford-Cambridge Boat Race is a fix, anyway. It's always –'

'– the same two teams reach the final?' he capped, smiling.

The problem was, careful watermen like Prammie Joe don't let rafts of ill-gotten plunder go drifting downriver towards the cold dark sea. Not unless ... I backed oars, put our prow into the bank.

Cradhead knew I knew something. Nasty bloke. He was new to the district. Maybe he'd not stay long, with any luck.

They gave me a lift home, a driver who lectured the world on the problems he was having with his bird, a pub dancer in Manningtree.

That evening, Joan Vervain cornered me, and we had a supper filled with Chinese nourishment brought in by the chauffeur. She was disappointed I had no television, electricity, gas, running water.

'You see, doowerlink,' I said with heartfelt sorrow but unyielding take-it-on-the-chin pride. 'I won't come to you as a pauper.'

'But darling,' she cooed, hands cupped beneath her chin. God, but women's tactics are unfair. And candlelight's treacherous. Everybody knows that. 'I already pay for – no. I didn't mean I *pay*. But I can't see you ...' She licked her lips. Her eyes were huge. '... go *hungry*, can I?'

We managed to make smiles, though, in spite of her husband's unavoidable radio absence. I found to my horror, as I woke from that terrible moribundity of after-love, that I'd promised to leave with her the following week. We were going to Monte Carlo, to live for ever in a state of sexual ecstasy and wealthy wassailing. Our address was to be the Caribbean in midwinter, Geneva in summer, San Francisco and Florida for inbetweens. I roused blearily into panic.

'What are London and Hong Kong for?' She has ten homes.

'Shopping, you silly darling!'

She had brought blankets and some heavy coverlet that heated up when you pulled a strip thing. Breakfast was delivered by a lass in a small white van. No hairs in the bacon.

It was seeing Joan off that Luna arrived. I won't say caught us, because she didn't. Why *is* it that women always make you feel as if they've caught you red-handed?

'Your jobs are two-fold, Luna,' I was giving out as she drove us to the auction. Oliver had let her have the car.

'Isn't she well known?' Once a woman leeches on to another woman, you can't prise her off. 'I've seen her in the paper.'

I scotched this right at the outset. 'A lot of people think that. I was asked only yesterday if she was the Mayor's wife!' I chuckled merrily at the idiocy of some people.

'Impossible, Lovejoy. *I'm* the Mayor's wife.'

Headaches, like age and lawyers, never come alone. 'Go to this address.' I passed her the teacher's card. 'Tell him the Sotheby's agent he gave a lift to says there's no market for his coffee pot, but buy it.'

She was thrilled. 'We represent Sotheby's? Oliver will –'

'No, love. We lie. Otherwise they won't trust us.'

Adjustment took ten minutes of analysis. 'I *know* I said to tell him there's no market, but . . .'

Makes me wonder how folk do it. Where I come from, she'd starve.

'Second, go to the auction. I'll be there. I'll bid for a beautiful tôle tray, I forget the lot number. Make sure you come in late, all casual. When you see me shake my head, there'll be only one bid left. You bid then. Okay? Make sure you get it, but look worried.'

'How will I know how much to bid, Lovejoy?'

Honestly, women amaze me. I mean, they love spending money, by all accounts. Yet send them along to spend some, and it's Prime Minister's Question Time.

'I told you. When I drop out, there'll only be one bid to go.'

'Whose, Lovejoy?' Her eyes were shining with excitement. 'Shall I make arrangements with him to. –?'

'*For Christ's sake!*' I yelled. 'Just do it! Stupid cow!'

'It's no good getting cross, Lovejoy. What if I pay too much? And what *is* a tôle tray? How much –?'

'Pull in. The auction's by the market. Park near the lights.'

'It's no trouble, Lovejoy. I'll take you to the door –'

'No thank you, Luna.' I struggled down to her pace. 'We pretend we don't know each other.'

Her brow unfurrowed. 'I see! Ignore each other's presence!' She blocked all the traffic. Lucky we were in dozy old East Anglia, where motor horns never parp.

'That's it. Buy the tôle. Leg it to that teacher's.'

'Leg?'

'Proceed in an orderly manner. Good luck.'

She was still firing worried, but terribly thrilled, questions after me as I walked down to the auction. I don't understand some people.

The auction went like a dream. I bid for Lot 18, the lovely tôle tray. One bloke made the running, your friend and mine Acker Kirwin. Just when he thought the lot was going to be knocked down to him, I did my bid. The auctioneer today was Irving, a dour Fifer with a dehydrated sepulchral voice. A tip: don't bid early. Enter late, keep your nerve. Think for a sec, and you'll guess why. It daunts the opposition. They realise that you've judged it just that wee bit better than they have.

On cue, Luna's mellifluous but shaky voice quavered, 'Yes, please.' Good girl, I thought, and left smiling to myself, but frowning in apparent distress to show others I was upset. Now all it needed was for her to get to that schoolteacher and buy his 'coffee pot' and we'd be in business. I'd owe her the money, of course, and pay her out of the profits.

CHAPTER NINE

Something was nagging. I alighted from the lorry and called so-long to the driver – pleasant Ipswich chap, kept ferrets – and set out to walk the last two miles to Prammie Joe's hideout. I mean, those surnames. Hopkins is common, right? Clark's common. Godbolt? A bit uncommon. Maybe I'd heard them together in some pantomime, a play. Old poets, the sort you have to learn incomprehensible snatches of at school? What are the chances of any three names coming together? I was imagining things. With a moniker like Lovejoy, I have a thing about names.

The day was waning smartish. I found myself walking quietly. The path narrowed, then split off the lane proper and became an old track down to Prammie Joe's creek. You get these sudden deflections in East Anglia, usually where the Romans built a temple, like at places called Mile End, so marching legionaries could chuck votive offerings to some god for the success of their campaign. Or where Middle Ages improvers built a footbridge near an old water-splash, so making the old crossing redundant.

I walked quieter still. I've had practice, one way and another. The path – it was hard to find, nearing the undergrowth where the muddiness began – narrowed further. Occasional cows must come this way, judging from the state of the ground underfoot. The hedge was tattered, losing the battle not to become a thicket. I supposed vaguely that gravel was anciently cast into the river here, to make the bed firm enough for waggons. Our roads have always been abysmal. Forget the engravings of rollicking coaches bristling with ruddy-countenanced passengers waving bottles. When Emperor Charles VI visited Petworth, the fifty miles from London were a nightmare – Sussex stalwarts were hired to walk alongside, propping the coach upright. The Emperor was only up-ended twelve times.

There was a faint hum. Hum? Up and down, like a pub singer trying for his key before launching into his gala melody. Rasping, sort of. I cracked a twig, hissing and sucking my finger when stabbed by a hawthorn. The humming ignored me. I know little about countryside, but I do know its sounds go silent when interrupted. Except some.

I stepped through the hedge gap. Prammie had made it oblique, from cunning. Stand alongside the tangle, you've to face the way

530

you've come even to see it. You step through, take three paces or
so, and you are in this overgrown field with blackthorn and reeds.
Your only way is down, towards the creek. And that constant, terrible
humming sound.

From Prammie Joe's shack. I saw the shack when my feet felt
suddenly cold. My shoes were water-sogged. I could see the hut door.
Open? I'd never seen it open without Prammie Joe here.

'Prammie?' Nothing. The hum continued. 'It's Lovejoy.'

The humming rose and fell. Zzzzz. A sleeping giant. Always
inhaling? A faint blur hung about the doorway. Dark, shifting, a
feeble shadow trying to become something definite.

And an aroma. No, a smell. Not smell, even. A stench. A stench
of something having . . .

'Joe? It's me. Lovejoy.'

Something came at my face. I brushed it away. It came again,
troubling me. I brushed it off. A bluebottle. Flies. The hanging
shadow was a cloud of buzzing blow-flies. Which breed –

'Joe!' I screamed. 'For Christ's sake, Prammie!'

Maggots breed in soldiers' shot legs, in cattle wounds. I drew
breath, moaning, took my jacket off, covered my head with it, ran
at the hut, paused a second and stepped in, gagged, saw Joe's face
one heaving mass of maggots and bluebottles that actually dripped,
dripped on to the wood floor beside him, things squirming in his eyes
sockets. I turned and ran, retching, swiping madly at the bluebottles
that followed. Some were even in my jacket. I waved it round my
head fifty yards up the field. My hands were shaking. I felt my eyes
streaming. I was going, 'Argh, argh . . .' I tried not to, but spewed
and retched and wept. I was pathetic, disgusting. I found two
blow-flies buzzing in my sleeve, stamped one to death like a madman,
and chased the other round the universe until I collapsed, sobbing,
on the marshy ground. When I'm a prat, I go for gold.

As penance, I made myself walk home, nearly getting myself
killed by every night joyrider. After the pubs closed it was a
nightmare. Hardly any pavements in East Anglia.

Two o'clock in the morning I reached my cottage. All night long
I heard buzzing, buzzing. I didn't sleep. Fault is everybody's for
everything, people say nowadays. It didn't feel like it. It felt like
mine.

Came dawn, bluetits were tapping for their bloody nuts, the
robin was flirting for his cheese, the hedgehog wondering what had
gone into me. I shut them all out. Let them get on with it. I'd had
enough Nature.

'Morning, Lovejoy.'

Luna was an atrocious call on my resources this early after a non-night night.

'Notice anything?' she asked, shy with hidden glee.

'Rain coming?' The tide turns our weather to the opposite of its dawn doings. I wondered for a ghastly moment what bluebottles do in bad weather.

'No, silly. Electricity! Water! Phone! They're coming!'

There was a van in the garden. Boiler-suited blokes were milling, unloading ladders.

'Your television licence is paid, Lovejoy.' She was especially thrilled at this, hugging herself. 'A TV set will be here soon. And radio.' Radio? Joan Vervain really would be pleased. We could shag during Hubby Del's radio show.

'Who paid?'

'Why, we did!' She drew me aside as boiler suits marched in.

A horrible feeling was growing within me.

'Where did we get the gelt, love? Money,' I explained, to smooth her forehead.

'I had the most extraordinary stroke of luck, Lovejoy!' She drew me to the divan and sat us down, breathless with delight. 'No sooner had I bought the troll tray, than a gentleman offered me a good profit. I sold it there and then!'

Carefully I didn't strangle her. 'Don't tell me. You only made one bid, and Acker – the rival bidder – folded?'

'Yes! Wasn't I clever?'

'You silly bitch.'

She gasped thunderstruck. 'But that's what we *do!* Buy and sell!'

It's called the lop. Only happens at antiques auctions. When somebody does the shuff – that is, what me and Luna had planned, one partner displacing another to confuse bidders – a cunning opponent does the lop. This means he stops bidding, allowing the shuffer to win the item. No sooner is it knocked down to her, than the lopper's colleague pants up and says, 'Missus, did you get Lot 18? Parking is such hell in Penny Lane. Will you sell? I'll give you a good . . .' Et predictable cetera. Duckeggs get lopped. I don't.

She listened, stricken. Well she might. She'd lost us a beautiful tôle tray. Tôle's manufacturing process is beautiful, combining art and science. The French did it wonderfully in the eighteenth century.

'Tôle, not troll. You take sheet iron.' I described it from the pit of a terrible memory. 'They discovered a heat-resist varnish and paint. You put many coats of paint on your iron. Then black it by holding it in smoke from a torch dipped in pine resin. Any resin for that matter. Fakers use teak oil on pine twigs.'

'Lovejoy?' Luna said, ten miles off.

'Smooth it with brickdust. Many layers of varnish. Then you *paint* in coloured varnishes. The earlier the date, to 1740, the more beautiful. They copied Sèvres. You get pots, food-warmers, a million household wares in tôle.'

She blotted my face with a hankie. 'Please don't cry, Lovejoy. We'll find another one. I'll go to Sotheby's.'

'I'm not. Silly mare.' I struck her hand away. She took no notice. They never do.

'Where do these two TVs go, lady?' A bloke was standing on the porch between two large cases.

She bridled. 'I only ordered one television.'

'Two, lady. Paid outright. Is there an aerial?'

'I only ordered one . . .' And so forth.

Prammie Joe had been killed, head bashed in. Had a cord been round his throat? Some sort of wire? Country folk have wire like city folk have rubber bands, plenty and all lengths. Snares, traps, hay, fencing, those rural things.

Luna's car. In silence I went out, was unsurprised to see her keys in the ignition. She'd wisely left her motor by my hedge, where waggons used to rest when clambering uphill from the river crossing below. I got in and headed for town.

Hereabouts in Ruritania, so to speak, you can't help knowing people who live up to their umbilicus in fens, marshes, rivers. But knowing isn't quite the same as a mere nodding acquaintance. I mean, everybody on earth 'knows' antiques. But not everybody *knows* antiques. See the difference? Or we'd all own Christie's and have a British Museum in the yard.

There were quite a few possibilities for help. One was Brad, boat repairer down on the estuary, early flintlocks. Except nothing had moved much in Brad's direction since the Tower of London clearing sale. There was Fesk Dynson, on the canals. Lock-keeper. Painting is his life. He worships oils, any Victorian. Not changed much there, either. Antique furnishings I'd already learned about the hard way – or Prammie Joe had. No mega moves in silver, local furniture, collectibles, or I'd have heard from our silver man, Big Frank from Suffolk. No major scam recently, except the great clandestine smuggle to the Continent after that massive crisp job in Norfolk. In a crisp job, you fake copies of all the antiques in your decaying mansion house. You replace the genuine antiques with the fakes. You then burn the manor house to a crisp. You get insurance money for (a) the manor (b) the burnt antiques. Naturally, you also (c) sell the antiques abroad where the prying eyes of the constabulary never go. Plus, you are relieved of that massive expense, namely your poor old Queen Anne building. You buy a villa in the sun, a pool and a blonde, and live stinkingly richly happy ever after. That was six months since.

No. I'd have to explore Prammie Joe's death through the waterways of this fair kingdom, and trust to luck. There's only one true waterways man in antiques. Rye Benedict, at ye olde mill by ye stream.

He was in, working the machinery for a group of school-children, telling the three who listened how the millstones worked. The other thirty were smoking behind the river wall or groping each other on the embankments. Education, hard at the learning curve.

'Wotcher, Miss Brewer.' Therla once taught in our village school, but the kids had run her a merry dance and she'd retired in hysterics. She was fetching, desirable. Why did I never have teachers like her? I'd been taught by amorphous cylinders of black cloth called Sister Hyacinth for my first six years. They had no legs. Miss Brewer had legs, and morphology.

'Hello, Lovejoy.' Some kids paused, looked across, sniggered. My name elicits this response. 'Interested in water machinery?'

Therla Brewer is ever hopeful that somebody keen will take her next lesson.

'No, love. You?'

'The school's Outdoor Activity Interaction Expression. Two OAIE sessions a week.' She gazed about, dispiritedly trying to convince herself they were all enthused. 'Design of waterways last week. The Stour. One boy tumbled in. Saved by an ocean barge, thank heavens.'

'Amen,' I said piously, bored. 'Rye be long, will he?'

We stood listening. Rye's really quite good, giving out water heights, great sailing barges from the Thames, the current mania for petrol engines. The antiques dealer in me smiled approval. Like I keep saying, passion rules where antiques hold sway.

Therla eventually herded her brood out, after begging Rye to come to give her children an hour's lecture on sailing vessels. The duckegg agreed. Therla has means of persuasion.

'Hello, Lovejoy.' Rye looked tired as he came back from seeing

Therla's mob off. He's one of these men people call clean-shaven, as if he somehow deserves a knighthood for using a razor of a morning.

'Tell me, Rye.' I paused. Hang on. Tell what *about?*

I gaped because he'd recoiled in sudden alarm, stepped back so swiftly I had to reach, pull him away from the great millstones. You can lock the colossal discs by means of a lever. I gave him what for. You stupid burke, Rye!' I yelled, mad as hell. 'You nearly went into the damned things! You're always on about safety, you pillock!'

He'd gone white as a sheet. 'I thought you meant –'

'What?' The barmy conversation was concluded when he shook his head in mute denial. We walked to his office for a brew.

The walls were covered with maps, levels of water tables, canal widths, cross-sections of every river in East Anglia. This old water-mill's a hobby. The Council give him a pittance to maintain the great quiet engine. Why him? Because he owns the garden centre and plant nursery on the river. His family's from Wenham, big landowners. To them that hath shall be given. Some deserving pauper like me should have Rye's job. Makes you sick, but I'm not jealous.

'I'm after advice, Rye.' I saw his guarded look disappear when I asked if he knew about some big shed, warehouse, anything new on the rivers.

'Nothing that isn't filled with container loads from the Hook of Holland, Lovejoy. It's rivalry time since the Channel Tunnel thing.'

'Any new stream? A dam? Canal being drained? Workings reopened like they did at Dedham's Stour? You know, the ones Constable painted by that teashop?'

That gleam of caution came and went. I put it down to my fatigue over Prammie Joe. I was seeing things. And I'd selected Rye practically at random, hadn't I? Well, hadn't I? Near enough, yes. Except Rye was the only waterman as learned about tides and rivers as Prammie Joe.

We talked a while. He praised our three consecutive bad winters. Nothing improved the Eastern Hundreds' water table like snow and hard frosts. He waxed enthusiasm. I concurred, wondering what the hell I was doing there.

'Ta, Rye,' I said, bored sick. 'Think of anything, eh?'

He was too casual. 'What's the interest?'

'Oh, some old, er, canal tokens are on sale at Wittwoode's Auction. Sometimes a batch comes ahead of a rush.'

The relief on his face was a pleasure to see. He came to the car.

'Special edition motor, Lovejoy! Business booming?'

'Not bad,' I said modestly. 'Want to make an offer?'

'I'll soon have enough for something *really* special.'

I drove away, thinking there was something I'd missed. Like a fool I'd forgotten what Prammie had told me, when we were laughing about his loading up the stuff at Cornish Place.

He'd rescued a schoolboy. From a place . . . Therla said something about nearly losing a boy. From drowning? In the Stour? But her lad had been rescued by an ocean-going barge, not a small pram propelled by an old ex-convict laid horizontal in the thwarts. His last journey, had Prammie Joe told me? A week ago, had Therla said?

Luna was at the cottage, fuming with the electricity, gas, water, TV men. I beckoned, pulled her in.

'Luna, love.' I drove away immediately. Movement distracts women; any sort will do. 'I want you to −'

'What on earth?' She gaped round. 'Leaving all those men in the cottage? They could steal −'

'We've nothing to steal,' I shot cruelly. 'You gave it away.'

'There's the schoolteacher's coffee pot,' she said, stung. 'I've made the men some coffee in it.'

My headache started skull-splitting. 'You did *what*?'

'I had to pay a fortune, unfortunately, but you said −'

She was insane. I gave up. 'Ipswich, Luna. *East Anglian Daily Times*. You're a reporter from London asking about a schoolboy rescued from the River Stour last week. Okay? You're thinking of a national feature, local bravery, hazards of the eastern rivers. Tell them anything. But find out.'

'Won't they be busy with their next issue? Only, reporters are always in such a rush.'

'They won't be today, love,' I said bitterly. 'They will be tomorrow.'

Fraud rules. It rules because everybody loves deception. Who has never felt that sneaky twinge of admiration, hearing of some nerk who tricked a gullible bank out of millions? Don't let's fool ourselves. We love it. The most secret twinge of all we reserve for ourselves − regret that *we* didn't dare do it. Imagine the ecstasy when, shacked up with the birds in Bahia's sunlight, you dream of old Fanshawe opening the vaults on Monday morning to find your cocky little note saying ta-ta. It's your dream, my dream, everybody's dream. No good being offended by my accusation. We all admire Robin Hood

In moral terms, he's a common thief. Legally, a rascally felon. But to us? He's superb, a riot, applauded down the centuries. *Because he got away with it!*

Come what may, fraud rules. Who leads in the Great Fraud Handicap Stakes? Well, bankers are front runners (sorry about the pun). Lawyers are contenders. Clerics closing on the bend, charity workers. Civil servants are also-rans, left standing by local government councillors. The fraud field is a cavalry charge. Politicians as fraudsters are the rule rather than the exception. Antique dealers are total. Consider them auctioneers minus respectability. For me, auctioneers are the pits. They defraud under false colours, priests who poison the chalice.

I went for the walk round the village, not to think so much as to not think. That's the way. Let learning in by osmosis. Suddenly you'll realise that you knew all the time, but didn't want to let on to yourself. Perhaps the truth reveals the treachery of a friend. Perhaps that flash of understanding proves that the ultimate nerk is none other than your very own self. I found myself watching Leone's nags.

They like me. All pets do. If I nod off in the garden hedgehogs come and kip nearby. Cats doze on my belly. Birds poof on my shoulder while I kip. I'm like Francis of Assisi. Leone's nag is Harry, a giant beast that slobbers like a baker's drain. I quite like animals. I'd like them better if they'd keep their distance. Leone's a blonde thirty. She rides up our lane from Seven Arches where her beasts fool about on the grass. She rides without a crash helmet the better to be seen. She's gorgeous.

'Hello, Lovejoy.'

'Wotcher, Leone. What's he running round in a ring for?'

'Exercise. He loves it, don't you, Harry?'

Harry looked fed up. Three littles came to hang on the fencing. Candice is their leader, aged six. I babysit for these three when their mums are desperate.

'Ooooh. Look, Lovejoy! Harry's got new feet on!'

'And skin,' added Jondie, a tiny four-year-old who steals my flowers for his rapacious guinea-pigs.

'Can't have,' I informed them loftily.

'Lovejoy's wrong,' Violet announced. She's three, can whistle through her fingers.

Then I noticed Leone had gone pink. I looked at Candice. 'New feet? What colour are his other?'

'Fluffy white. Or brown.'

'Grey sometimes,' said Jondie. 'My Dad does it.'

'Boils grass in a pan. It stinks. My Dad only plays cards.'

'Tough luck, Violet,' I commiserated. 'Hear that, Leone? Your horse Harry is fashion mad. He'll miss the point-to-point at Webberswick now, eh?'

She slowed her nag, let him crop the grass. I watched her stroll over.

'It's the usual thing, Lovejoy. That's all.' Harry was a big animal. Reputedly fast. I worked it out. Here a stain, there a stain, might help in shifting the odds. 'Does no harm, Lovejoy.' She pressed my arm, the way wheedling begins. 'It's only foreigners get bled. Not locals.'

She waxed about her fraudulent arrangements while I listened. Every so often, little Candice and her pair weighed in with small technical details. Violet's card-playing dad did a good line in false tails, it seemed. Not all poker, then.

Leone wheedled, 'Who minds if a few rich strangers lose a penny here, a penny there, Lovejoy?'

'What if I turned up and bet?'

'You never do, Lovejoy. Anyway, we'd put you right.'

Local approval justifies bleeding dry the nerks from elsewhere. Antiques in a nutshell. I'd forgotten the obvious.

Candice said disarmingly, 'Daddy gets lots of pennies.'

Leone pinked nearer red. 'Time you three got home,' she said quickly.

They left, calling so-long. Candice told the others, with the gravity of her six summers, 'Leone wants to suck mouths with Lovejoy, like she does with the vicar.'

And . . . silence. Leone blood scarlet now. The whole village was in on it. Except me. Mind you, I'm the last person to watch nags trot, phoney feet or no phoney feet.

'It's not fraud, Lovejoy. It's usual. Good heavens, it's a saying: horse of a different colour.'

'Come here, you,' I said roughly. She came closer. I leant over and we sucked mouths. She broke away breathless.

'You won't let on, Lovejoy?'

By then I was walking quickly away, calling over my shoulder, 'Why should I? It's usual.'

And it is, truly. I'd missed it. Candice made me carry Violet piggy-back the half-mile uphill into the village. She promised not to tell the vicar that me and Leone sucked mouths. I didn't believe her. She'd blab. Females start fibs early. They made me sing *Curlylocks*, my one pathetic tactic for getting infants to kip. They listened gravely, little Vi silently mouthing the words. I felt a prat. My showstopper done, I waved the trio of wide-awakes off at my gate.

Which left me sitting on my wall. It isn't every day you discover a new universal law. But how important it was. *Small* local deceits have their own inbuilt honour. Everybody local has a right to know about them. On demand, you might say. But major ones are different. They're alien. They are the biggies, the grandies.

How many massive antique scams could I think of? A score, offhand. Leaving aside the atrocious Hammer monolith of Los Angeles, grand scams come clamouring for attention. But beware. The legitimate collection of Mona Lisa fakes covering Cartier's wall, for example, doesn't count.

Some things do. The uproar over the Dead Sea Scrolls – who should have access to study them – gave rise in 1989 to shoals of scholarly fraudsters who flitted through the groves of academe offering complete copies for 165,000 pounds sterling, in advance. Collectors fell for it. Strapped universities desperately struggled to fall for it, but couldn't raise the advance – and thereby saved their reputations. For the Scrolls are the most jealously guarded hoard in the world. Gelt in the vault. The paranoid secrecy of minders – i.e. greed – plays, as ever, into the hands of grand scammers.

If obsessional neuroses can do it, so can fame. I've seen thirty, maybe forty, valuable pieces of the Marcos silver sold in auctions never noticed by the press, when everybody knows that Christie's in New York handled the real Old Masters and silver in 1991, of course, raising a cool 10.6 million pounds. A Paul Storr silver dinner service, George III, made a fortune. Bidders wept because fame forced prices over the top. Poor them. Still, if they will go for the genuine stuff...

And everybody knows about war booty. If you don't, you ought. It's the commonest grand scam around. After the German Government bought some war treasure in 1991 – Quedlinburg, World War II – for, word is, a million, it became open season. You hire front men ('mouthies' in the trade) of the right educational background. You invent some treasure. Your mouthies tour museums, collectors. They whisper the terrible fact that, alas, the jewel-encrusted illuminated Gospel of 1558 is, with its ancient silver chalice, actually war loot. Good heavens! the eager buyers cry, sending the mouthies packing – only as far as the corner pub, where the secret deal is struck. Discount applies, for there's the risk that Gold Coast countries will play hell over the priceless Benin metalwork heads, or Italy over that Leonardo drawing. Inevitably, lawyers help, for where lawyers roam illegitimacy rules. Grand scammers recently offered that cache of Chesterton letters in at least three countries, though the real cache of two hundred poems, plays, prose works, now slumbers ignored in London's British Library. And law courts everywhere rejoice over the Sevso silver treasure that the whole world will be suing over until Doomsday. The repayments newly offered to Czarist bondholders (Czar Alexander III himself pulled this majestic scam in the 1880s) has started a giddy spiral of phoney printed bonds. (Take care: the ones I've seen so far are simply Russian laundry lists, printed in Fulham.) See? Greed again.

And the world spins in its happy course. China's gigantic Orange Ape-Man. Saints' replicas (the all-time favourite grand scam). Bronze Age ferry boats discovered in river beds, the whereabouts known only to my friend here who will offer *to you alone!* this priceless genuine ancient map revealing its location for the cheap sum of . . . And the gems smuggled out from Afghanistan during the Mujahedin war, which my friend has a sack of and will offer *to you alone!* for the cheap sum of . . . Et incredible cetera.

They work. Every time. Always. Read here, they seem daft. But if somebody actually *did* come up to you – Oxford, titled family, dressed to the nines, a bishop in tow – and sadly told you he was having to broker the sale of a valuable church treasure, on account of fiscal difficulties the diocese didn't want revealed, and that His Lordship the bishop here would take you round St Winston's to meet the church synod's secretary. And that the price *to you alone!* was the unbelievably low sum of . . .

Temptation? A little, maybe. And a little temptation always wins hands down. There's no recorded instance of a big temptation. Superfluous.

Now, I'm a titch in the antiques trade. We don't have grand scams hereabouts. They're for the Continent, London, Birmingham, the high levels.

My thoughts ended there. Some foods are too rich.

CHAPTER TEN

The worst of other people's admiration is that it's deceit. I mean, even a statue of God wears a pigeon on its head, right? Feet of clay. I pulled myself together and got going.

Luna was dispatched to Ipswich – maybe she'd get the right city, of East Anglia's two. She had to get something right, for God's sake or mine. I went to the Arcade. Sandy's Dutch Treaty shop on East Hill was shut ('Catch Me If You Can,' the CLOSED notice was subtitled). No answer either at Connie's small one-room shop which stood one door uphill. I wanted to know what Drinkwater had asked him about.

Big Frank from Suffolk was in, buying silver like the maniac he is. He was especially mournful today.

'Not another, Frank?' I asked. It was my way of checking if the news of Prammie Joe was out. Big Frank has no one place, just scoots round the small coastal villages after silver.

'You wouldn't chuckle, Lovejoy.'

Indeed. Big Frank has marriage like the rest of us have black-heads. I forget how many wives he's had. He pays maintenance to a monstrous regiment. I've been to six of his weddings, plus four engagements.

'What happened? Your latest wife was bonny.'

'She accused me of having it away with the woman in the farm opposite.'

'Look, Frank.' I was disappointed, because I'd been their best man. 'These new wives. Once or twice, but isn't Dodie your eighth? Why don't I explain? After all, the woman in the farm opposite . . .'

'Her sister, mmmh. What about this, Lovejoy?'

He showed me a lovely rectangular standish, silver, with its inkwell and pounce pot absolutely unblemished. Connie Hopkins was hovering nearby: it was her inordinately extortionate price ticket. Connie uses the SUTHERLAND code I once told you about, reversing the letters every quarter day. S = 1, U = 2, and so on. Other dealers use their kiddies' names. Really truly mind- boggling clever, no? Stroll through any antique shop, you can crack their code in the time it takes to ask the price of two single antiques. Remember that they mark the price *they paid*, not the price they'll sell at. For that, nowadays, add two hundred per cent. Modern retail jewellers mark up new bangles, rings, pendants, earrings, exactly that. Test it out. Buy a new gold-and-sapphire ring, take it to a different reputable jeweller, and try to sell it. If he offers *half* the price you've paid, you've done well.

'Got the original gum?' I asked. The pounce pot was not filled with sand, as commonly believed, but with powered gum sandarac, to re-buff the paper if the old writers had to erase a mistake.

It looked right. It felt right. But sadly it made me feel as if I was sort of leaning over. Right but wrong.

'What metal?' It felt really queer, almost rippling in my hands. I stared hard at the hallmarks. 'Better Nine?'

A certain horribleness began in December, 1478. Every St Dunstan's Day, 19 May, a twenty-year cycle of letters was stamped on silver, A the first year, B the second, so on. Once King Charlie II came in 1660, the change-day became his birthday, Oak-Apple Day, 29 April. But still the letter cycle went relentlessly on. Except 1696-7, when the Britannia standard upped to 11 ounces and 10 pennyweights (95.8%, if you're a decimal crank). This means 8 pennyweights more to the Troy pound than sterling! Astonishment! New silver was worth more! (This was necessary because the naughty old public were clipping coins). And, gasp-shock-horror, the twenty-year letter cycle was interrupted! A seated woman, Britannia, showed up on the mark. There's been one other interruption to the letter cycle – in 1975, but that doesn't matter, being modern.

'It's old standard, Lovejoy, looks like to me.'

'Mmmmh.' Meaning, oh, sure, but no thank you. Its matt quality disturbed me.

Lately, we'd been seeing a lot of these pieces. All desirable, all beautifully made. And all having that lovely matt look to the truly ancient (genuine) silver. I'd bet all I had – well, all I owed – that, if this piece was tested in London's Queen Mary College by flame photometry or whatever, it would be pristine medieval silver. The hallmark was a letter T on a little barrel (T on tun, for Taunton, get it? They loved puns), and Britannia. And a maker's mark, initials, four times. The old silversmiths were past masters at dodging tax duty, and repeated their marks a few times – four's usual – hoping customers would assume that one mark was the official Government-decreed one.

Well. Beautiful. But that terrible matt look. I polished the edge of the box on my sleeve. It felt ancient, bonging gently, but it felt wriggly. 'How many'd it take, Frank?' *I had him.*

'What're you talking about, Lovejoy?'

'Frank. Take a crucible filled with silver Saxon pennies. Clean them. Melt them down. Get Heppie to make you a lovely new standish like this. Stamp it with a few marks, and take it all unsuspecting to Lovejoy. He divvies it. After all, it's genuine ancient silver, right?'

These tricks make people shrink in my eyes. Big Frank looked heartbroken, but that was only the spectre of no bunce, no profit. He'd chosen the place, his audience. Now they all knew he was on the fiddle. Just to get more wealth for a new wife. Marriage has a lot to answer for. I'd thought better of him.

'You that desperate, Frank? That you'd try to con me?' On the same level as that Vienna bloke who worked the *Lucona* sinking. He claimed 18.5 million dollars insurance, after having the 11,000-ton ship blown to blazes. Fine, eh? Except for the half-dozen who went to watery graves. Horror makes you bitter, sad for us all. We only pretend civilization.

'Sorry, Lovejoy.' He sounded really down.

Everybody in the Arcade had stopped talking. Connie was studiously scanning some Christie's Impressionist catalogues. Even Acker Kirwin, apparently in to hump some old Sir Johns – chamber pots in wooden boxes, sometimes (but rarely) built up like square-topped stools – stood observing the drama.

Unpleasantness makes you feel in the springtime of senility, the dawn of decay. And Prammie Joe was no nearer seeing tomorrow's sunshine.

I drifted off. Connie didn't meet my eye. Big Frank came after me as I walked down to Woody's caff. He tried buttering me up, 'It's these payments, Lovejoy. I'm going under.' I walked on, head down, seeing only that terrible cloud buzzing in that low doorway among the reeds. Then I stopped all of sudden, by the Bugler pub near the war memorial.

'What was that, Frank?'

'Well, Lovejoy. There *is*.' He shrugged. 'It's a oncer, see? Things have been rough. I've tried a million other lines, but silver . . .' His eyes glowed with the fervour of the lunatic. 'She said I could come in, if I'd chip a tenth. Endless profits. I could buy into Continental silver, even English Huguenot . . .'

He rambled on in delirium. In the town centre, traffic swishing past and people hurrying with prams. I hadn't a clue what he was on about. But I'd never seen him like this before. I eyed him. Another huge-scale scam, for Christ's sake?

His eyes were afire. 'I'd need a year's wage, Lovejoy.'

So the scam meant at least ten times that. Bridge loans in antiques cost a tenth.

'Frank. I'll try to lend you, if I can. Can you trust her, though?' With Frank, it's always a bird, sometimes even one he's married to. I was fishing.

He looked about, for ex-wives skulking among the shoppers. 'Janny's straight as a die.' He smiled shyly. 'We're engaged.'

Par for his course. 'I'll see. Chop straight, eh?'

'Lovejoy, you're a pal. Yes, even share-out. I really appreciate you not being narked.'

'About the standish? Nar, Frank. Some punter'll happen by.'

We parted amicably. But I was now frantic, as well as baffled. Something was turning all the dealers into maniacs. I alone was sane and fair-minded, as usual.

I called in six antique shops more, and emerged triumphant. Jenny Calamy lived out near Woodbridge, and had been in Big Frank's company closer than somewhat. Calamy sounds like calamity, and Calamity Jenny's the name of her shop. J. Calamy had met Big Frank over antiques, yes, but they both attended The Great Marvella and her talking snake. For massage and conversation, the latter being three-way, four-tongued psychoanalysis. And I had an appointment with her. Had had? Some tense or other. I invented excuses as I hurried that way, in case I'd got the date wrong.

The buzzer changed to the snake's fluty voice instantly, clicked the door open. I went in slowly. One day, maybe there'd only be the snake there, fat about the middle, and no Marvella. There were two voices.

'Watch this, Cassandra,' Vell's voice said, choking laughing. 'Come in, Lovejoy. He'll dither for hours. Geronimo's gone to bed.'

Inchwise I peered round. There on the couch was Vell. And Cassandra Clark. Even lovelier. Never mind them, the snake was in its cage. It looked without hostility. I'd rather it hated me. Or loathed. That anonymity was the killer.

'Cassandra's just finished, Lovejoy.'

They smiled at each other with merriment. I didn't get the joke. Finished?

'Told a good fortune?' I said, trying jocularity. Geronimo watched. Its head moved slightly.

'Quite fair,' Cassandra said. More hidden smiles were exchanged, but women do that all the time around me. I didn't attach too much importance to it. 'Geronimo was particularly optimistic.'

'Good old Geronimo.' I didn't really want to be on speaking terms with him. I felt awkward with Cassandra here.

She's a hard lass. Looks as if butter really truly wouldn't. Cassandra Clark had quality, but her hand-bag was sure to be loaded. I thought about her visit to my workshop. She had a Past, the Arcade hinted. Touched antiques, examined them. Never, ever bought. Word was she used a whole shoal of buncers – dealers who buy solely on commission – sworn to secrecy, exporting to the USA. I could eat her with a spoon. Or without, though chance'd be a fine thing. She was dressed to kill, everything matching, with that casual oh-what-a-mess hairstyle that costs the earth. It needs lustrous youth, plus what Chinese dealers call Vitamin M. Money.

A man between two women doesn't have much of a chance. And knowing what they say isn't exactly the same as knowing what they mean. A man between two birds feels about four years old, and that's a fact.

'What is it, Lovejoy? Brought your problems to Geronimo?' From Cassandra, laid back, smart.

Cutting my losses, I smiled apology to Marvella. 'Look, love. About money. I wonder if you're flush. Only, I've had a few expenses and . . .'

'What do you think I am, Lovejoy?' Vell bridled. Geronimo hissed a snakely chuckle. 'Made of money?'

That sounded authentic. My begging patter sounded right, so maybe I'd convinced Cassandra I was simply here on the cadge.

'I know, love. But it's for something special.'

That seemed to stop the conversational flow. I swear there was a kind of tension in the room that hadn't been there before.

'What special?' Vell asked.

'I'm trying to escape from under,' I said apologetically, wanting out.

'A woman? You mean a woman, Lovejoy?'

'Yes.' I added lamely, 'It's a bit difficult. She wants to divorce her bloke, and marry me. I've got too much on –'

Cassandra nodded. Vell said smoothly, 'How much?'

'Grub. Today, tomorrow. A taxi to the auctions, maybe enough to deposit on something.'

Cassandra nodded again. And immediately The Great Marvella said, 'Honestly, Lovejoy! You'll be the death of me. I thought you'd come for an ephemeris analysis.'

With that snake in the room? People are daft. Vell gave me a few notes. I said thank you so very sincerely and Cassandra smiled and Geronimo watched and Vell and Cassandra smiled and I retreated down the stairs calling thanks until I was safe among pedestrians and sweating heavily, not knowing why. Sweat trickled from my chin.

Luna picked me up from the war memorial, and I borrowed this beekeeper's gear.

Torrance is a fat geezer you wouldn't ever imagine keeps bees. He lives down on the Colne, where you wouldn't think there are many bees anyhow. He sells the honey, and brews mead and sells that. He talks to them, which all beekeepers do, as if the hives were filled with real people.

He charged me a fortune, the swine. He was desperate to know if the bees I was going after were wild bumble bees, or a cultivated stock. I told him my girlfriend's dad was mad about bees, to shut him up. The goon followed me out to the car wanting recruits for his manky bee-keeping society. What a nerk. I loaded up and told Luna to drive to the cottage.

There we inspected the depredations done by the skilled artificers of the Eastern Hundreds. Mercifully, the pot was still intact. It was the first thing I looked at, but the phone shrilled. Phones are a mistake.

'He's just here. It's urgent, Lovejoy.'

'Ever known a phone call that wasn't?' I said sourly.

'Hello, Lovejoy, I'm in Edinburgh.' Miss Turner. I glared, threatened Luna with a fist. She smiled serenely back. 'It's so different! Can you tell me where I am, please?'

One day I'll escape. Then what will the world do? 'Where are you? *Exactly?* Read the name.'

Pause, clatter, a breathless hello. 'General Register House, Lovejoy. Opposite the North British Hotel. It's really quite nice.'

'You stupid old mare!' I yelled in fury while Luna tried to calm me down. I clouted her away and bawled, 'I distinctly told you not to go to the wrong place. Didn't I? *Didn't I?*'

'Please don't be angry, Lovejoy,' the old lady quavered. 'But I'm on my own and —'

Bloody fine. Loses herself, then rings me to sort her out. Typical. 'Listen, you daft old bat. Is there a big statue outside? Duke of Wellington?'

'Why, yes!' She was delighted. 'Very imposing, with —'

'You stupid mare! You're in the Scottish Record Office's place. You want the General Register Office for Scotland, silly cow. Births, marriages, deaths and census records.' I made her write it down, read it back. 'Got it, you silly old fool?'

'Got it, Lovejoy,' she cooed happily. 'Now, where exactly . . . ?'

'New Register House,' I said, broken. 'It's next door to where you're standing. Go there immediately. And never ring me again.' I slammed the receiver down on the crazy old loon. Honest to God. Where was I? Luna's pot.

Luna was quite put out. 'You haven't noticed, Lovejoy!' She indicated the cottage. Electric light, bulbs and everything. Gas, on. Water, on. Phone, on.

'The cost was too great, love. That tôle tray was something we'll possibly never see ever again in a lifetime.' I smiled at her, held up the lovely stoneware nipple-spout Castleford feeding-pot. 'This makes up for it, partly. About 1795. Like it?'

What a stupid question. She smiled tentatively. 'Well, yes. But those holes in the spout. Why isn't it proper?'

Headache time. I sighed. Baby feeders are called 'bubby pots' in the trade, because Dr Hugh Smith in 1777 invented one sort and called it that. Transfer-printed ones were made by Wedgwood, or plain cream-ware. They are lovely. Specialist items, of course, but so far hardly ever faked or even copied.

'You did well,' I said. She was pleased, and we rested a bit. I asked if she'd ever heard of The Great Marvella. She said yes, several acquaintances went to her. Did I know she actually had a talking snake? I said I'd heard.

Then I had the wit to ask if she'd ever heard of Cassandra Clark. Luna said yes, she did improving social causes. In fact, Miss Clark was on the Mayor's fund-raising charity committee. Oliver knew her. She Had Money.

Dusk falls slowly at first in East Anglia, then suddenly tumbles over the edge into the pitch black. I didn't want to be on my own, not knowing what I'd have to face, so I told Luna we were going to work late and would she drive me. She was doubtful until I said it was a secret. Then she was all thrilled and shrieked of course and we went out towards the estuaries, down where the marshes meet the tides and the rivers end in low mudflats.

CHAPTER ELEVEN

'Lovejoy.' Luna dropped me off at the lane head. 'Why the outfit?' She meant I was getting out of hand.

I gathered it in my arms. 'You'd be surprised how much clobber you need to look at a bee.'

She looked worried. 'Lovejoy. Oliver always asks what I've done each day. What shall I say?'

'It's confidential.' Others can use the lie word, so can I.

'But this —' She gestured at the darkening country-side, the loneliness of it. 'It's nothing to *do* with antiques.'

I leaned into the car. 'Everything I do is to do with antiques, love. Remember that.'

The buzzing was fitful. I heard it from quite a distance. But I went through the hedge and donned the protective gear. I had a smoke gun to doze them, but wasn't sure how to use it. Did it make me sleepy as well? Or, worse, did it act on me but not the bees? For bees read another kind of flying object.

There was just enough daylight when I reached the little hut. Except I could hardly see a damned thing. Torrance hadn't warned me about this net mask. It blacks out your sight. No wonder beekeepers always get stung. But I made it into the hut and gagged a few times, avoiding Prammie Joe's buzzing horrible thick black teeming mess of a face . . . I won't describe it. There was a squirming mound on the floor beneath his chair. It stank, the whole place. I tried not to stand in anything, leave footprints, but who could see? Ugh. I retched inside the mask, searched his cupboards, drawing my hands away sharply in disgust when blowflies came between my fingers. Nothing. You never do. But on the planking floor, near where he Aussie-crouched to watch the birds of an eve, was a fold of paper. I grabbed it and shot out. I'd had enough.

Gagging, I escaped, blundered, crashing, down to the water, still retching. It was some time before I had the sense to peer up and down the small tributary. I got a stick, prodded the water. A few inches. How much did a boat need?

There was an ugly moment when I found three bluebottles were trapped inside my hood with me. I shouted, ripping off the mask and batting it on my thigh, struggled to get it back on before the rest of that hideous swarm came buzzing on my face, my eyes. I found I'd held my breath like a fool. I was almost fainting.

Which, I resumed weakly, raised the question of where the pram was. I knew about one of Prammie's rafts – safe in the hands of that Cradhead. But the other? And the pram? If hereabouts, it would be well hidden. Prammie Joe hadn't been detected by the vigilant watchers of Cornish Place. So he wouldn't be spotted by home-goers from the village pub, would he?

Twenty minutes later I'd changed, and met Luna.

'Did anybody see you?' I asked, all nonchalant, Lovejoy the countryman, pally with ornithology or whatever bees are.

'No, Lovejoy.' She stared hard in the dashboard lights. It was now quite dark, our sudden fall to blackness. 'You've been sick, Lovejoy. And that clothing smells.'

Trust her, silly cow. 'Remember Ipswich?'

Half an hour's lecture on the state of Ipswich's traffic, then she told me. Zilch. Nothing. No reports in the papers, no boy falling in the water and being rescued. I'd have to suss out Therla Brewer myself.

'Luna. Ever heard of anybody called Calamy?' No. She hadn't. 'Or Godbolt?' Not that either.

But the names were worrying. Godbolt. Calamy. Hopkins. Clark? Funny, but I knew somehow there was yet another. A quite ordinary English name. I couldn't for the life of me think. I put my head back on the seat as she drove. So far, I'd heard of a scam that had vanished, lost an old pal by foul means, searched for knew-not-what, and found nowt. Now I was trying to remember something I'd maybe never heard of. God Almighty. What a pillock.

To please Luna, I told her to sell the feeding pot in Wittwoode's Auction. She'd done quite well. I had to teach her some antiquery, besides murder, or Oliver Carstairs, Mayor, might get narked.

Joan Vervain came to the cottage that night. She did her screams of abuse at her husband on his radio show while we made smiles. Wondrous, of course. That rush to paradise can't ever be anything else. But I was fed up. Her rabbiting on about Monte Carlo or Mustique narked me. I felt bought, for development. I mean, I'd ditched the bloody woman days ago, yet here she still was, more here than ever.

A pile of agents' brochures, showing Mediterranean places, was provided for me to approve. The lawyers would meet Del Vervain next Monday, and the news of the divorce would hit the world.

Together, she said coyly along the pillow, with the announcement of our impending marriage. Which saw the night through, to the pale feet of morn.

Two things: I'd somehow see Jenny Calamy, and discover if she fitted in to Prammie Joe's scam. I had only met her once, and even then we'd had a row about a piece of Meissen. She swore the decoration was 'genuine factory'. But crossed swords marks which have a nick in them show the piece was sold 'in the white' and decorated elsewhere. It would have been better if the crossed swords had had an 'S', signifying Samson of Paris, a notable copier/faker whose work is highly sought. You can't tell some folk.

Especially you can't tell Big Frank that your visit to his next wife is entirely platonic – i.e. sexless. He's dynamite on fiancées. I'd have to think up some legitimate reason. I fed the birds – the lot of them were sulking, because I'd had a bad morning last time – then had my breakfast. Fried tomatoes pall sometimes, but there aren't many alternatives when they're what you've got. I went to do my washing. I've got one spare sheet, change it every week. The blanket rarely needs washing, but I hang it on the washing line sometimes. I forget to bring it in, and have to wear all my things to get to sleep. Night dew falls early on the coast.

There's a launderette in the village, up by the Bungalow Stores. It sells you a cup of powder, and you watch the washing going round, trying not to listen to the daft taped music. Some children came in, larking about. I watched them playing ghosts, springing out and frightening each other. One took the broom from the corner and rode it round. It wasn't All Hallows Eve yet, nowhere near. Some American horror film in town, I supposed. The dump felt empty when they were shooed out by Old Bessie.

The second thing was La Brewer. The discovery of Prammie Joe's body by the Old Bill might take a day, a week. All hell would be let loose. Why had Drinkwater been to see Sandy? Plenty of other dealers were interested in antique furnishings. In fact, you could even say that every dealer was. Maybe because Sandy and Mel were the wealthiest of our local dealers? The Cornish Place turkey job was a matter of millions, biggest scam we'd had in years. No wonder somebody killed Joe.

Had Joe wanted a share? Was that the reason?

Surely it had to be. Why else? Prammie knew what he was doing. Theft is theft, however skilled. I was the only one who knew how he'd done it, because . . . Hang on a sec. I thought about that as I counted my socks – they get eaten by Old Bessie's machines. I *couldn't* be the only one who knew, could I? I mean, whoever had commissioned Prammie Joe to turkey Cornish Place also knew, right?

Prammie had mentioned some bloke he'd met in clink. Somebody he was in gaol with. That same killer had known that Prammie Joe, elusive waterman, was the only bloke in the Eastern Hundreds who could pull it off.

Who else had been in nick lately? Answer: Acker Kirwin. Easy peasy. Acker had done Prammie in. QED? It seemed logical. Those names came into my mind, and I dozed.

'Lovejoy?' Bessie was shaking me. 'Lovejoy? You've done your washing three times. Did you mean to?'

'Mmmmh?' God, it was ten o'clock. 'Mmmh? Oh, aye, Bessie. It was, er, messy. I've been gardening.'

Bessie's an old crone who knows I don't garden. She got my stuff in silence, bagged it up for me. Wet washing's horrible stuff. Ever noticed that?

'Big Frank's his name,' I told Luna. She was waiting in the porch. She looked really attractive, pastel twin set and smart suit, the skirt well cut. Her rings were too classy for an antique dealer's apprentice. At first I'd said to dress down rather than up.

'Whose name, Lovejoy? And good morning, Luna.'

'Good morning, Luna. The dealer. Ask him if you can go and see Jenny Calamy. Her address,' I added grandly, 'will be in my new phone book. You misappropriated my money to have us connected, so use it.'

'Here, Lovejoy.' She took the washing. I followed her on to the grass while she pegged out the wet things.

She'd given me an envelope. Cheques from the gas, electricity, phone, television people. Rebates? Now, our local services don't make rebates except on the rack, not even if they owe you.

'It's money I didn't spend. The tôle tray.' She had pegs in her mouth and spoke past them, the way they do. I try this, but I choke. Women's mouths are fantastic, a life of their own . . . 'Somebody else had already paid, Lovejoy. They'll repossess the spare TV set. We can leave it in our porch.'

Our? Well, she was an apprentice. 'Good girl.'

'I read until very late last night, Lovejoy.' She paused, faced me. She looked lovely against the green grass, the hedgerow russets. 'I apologise. I realise now what a wonder that antique was. To me, it was simply an old tray. Seeing you do that dividing –'

'Divvying.'

'– in the old aerodrome cellar explained a great deal.'

A But was on the way. Women have conditions; we have deceit.

'But why are you so, forgive me, poor?'

'I'm not poor,' I gave her, stung. 'It's just I have a lot of friends. And I . . .' I shrugged, looked for escape.

'You're hopeless, Lovejoy. A scatterbrain. Money, clothes. Your cottage is upside down. And . . .'

More praise? I always get this. She'd start staying late, tidying me up so I couldn't find a flaming thing.

'You are taken advantage of, get into scrapes. Incur obligations and escape them by your love of these old things.'

'These old things, love,' I cut in, narked, 'are all that matters. I keep telling you. Frigging well listen.' I envy Americans. They have this commanding phrase, *listen up*. It means harken intently or you're for it. 'Up,' I added defiantly.

'Lovejoy. I'm worried by all these journeys you make me do.'

She hadn't enough pegs to hang the remaining wet things out. I said not to worry. They always blow about the garden anyway. I once found a pillow case with a nest in, low down among the hawthorns. I didn't know I'd lost it.

One day, I'm going to stop explaining. 'They're vital. Jenny's engaged to Big Frank. Go carefully, because of his wife. His mistress, her sister, lives in the farm opposite.'

'Lovejoy,' Luna said. 'Are we in difficulties?'

'Us?' This time I rather liked the plural. We walked back up to the cottage, my arm through hers. 'Never in a million years, love. Remember the feeding pot. Wittwoode's. Don't accept an auction number below ten, nor in the last eight.'

'Why not?'

'It's where gunge goes.'

She plugged the kettle in, cast about for cups. 'I couldn't help noticing those bee clothes. They're still sort of slimy. I'll have my maid see to them. That veil thing . . . Lovejoy?'

Quickly she stood close, taking my arm. I sat on the divan. 'We'll have some tea before we go anywhere. You look quite pale.'

'Fine,' I piped heartily. 'Take it to Torrance. Tell him ta.'

'And what do I buy from Miss Calamy?'

'You do something really sly, Luna,' I said. 'Nothing. You're just my apprentice, seeing how an average antiques shop is run. Don't go without Big Frank's permission.'

When I felt better I dialled Sandy, to get him to explain some of the nastier antique dealer tricks to my new apprentice, a lady called Luna. He was in, and garrulous.

'So you *flew* to me, fountain head of deceit, Lovejoy!' he shrilled. 'How perceptive!'

'You be nice to her, Sandy. Y'hear?'

'Could I fail, dear? What colours is this perfectly grotesque obese cow trying to wear?'

'Er . . .' I avoided looking. 'I'm not sure. I haven't seen her yet this morning. She's putting a piece in Wittwoode's. Guide her, will you?'

'Very well, Lovejoy. It will be a change from that *oaf* Drinkwater, though his friend Cradhead –'

Quickly sussing, I put in. 'Troubling you?'

'I mean, I don't even *know* Spoolie. He's *far* too plain!' Oscar Wilde's line. 'I shall pretend your tart's a customer.' He tittered. 'Lovejoy, I want to thank you for sending her. A perfectly *marvellous* opportunity to *shine.*'

Click, burr. 'Sandy's, er, mannered, Luna,' I said. 'Sort of eccentric. Tell me everything he says. Especially names.'

We went to the motor. I dropped her off at East Hill, then drove to The Ghool Spool.

Antiques are funny, meaning you never know where they begin and end. Some antiques are rightly seen as national treasures – like the famous Badminton Cabinet. Made in Florence in 1726, it was recently up for sale to an American heiress. Then political outrage set in, and people started bawling the usual old lines, selling our antiques is unpatriotic, all that old rubbish. It's what you mean by 'treasures' and 'antiques' that matters.

Antiques once meant only things from the Ancient world – Greece or Rome (but especially the latter, because the Romans never had any consumer protection laws. The Greeks had). Then, modern times, antiques meant pre-1837. Gradually it crept nearer and nearer. 'Collectibles' arrived then, and 'Groupables'. Finally, 'To-morrow's Antiques', the ultimate in fraudulence.

And the word began to spread its meaning, as well as its precisions. Anciently it meant only statuary. It then became jewellery, paintings, any artefact, and finally (fanfare, please) any marketable rubbish.

Which brings us to films, theatre ephemera. The Ghool Spool.

Of course, everybody's fascinated by the knick-knacks of the famous. Bits off an emperor's gown, letters from Dickens to Harrison

Ainsworth, pages of a Beethoven manuscript, anything that lends a name. They're only valuable, these googaws, because we the public make them so. Whether it's a bass guitar from the Beatles, or a Leonard Bernstein baton, age doesn't matter so much as the fame on the tag. But remember that in the shifting sands of ephemera, authenticity rules. You've got to be able to *prove* that doodle of crochets on an old omnibus ticket really was done by Delius.

Spoolie's not really called that. It's his nickname.

'Lovejoy, I've got nothing,' he said sadly as I entered under his clanging doorbell. 'Everything's less than a hundred years.'

'Just passing, Spoolie. Suppose I had a customer?'

As Spoolie launched into his spiel, I wandered round his little shop. It stands on the outskirts of Mistley, on an uphill road between two leaning pubs. I honestly can't understand the fascination of emphemera. Yet it powers mighty collectors. I know a bloke who mortgaged his house just to bid for old Ealing Studios furniture.

'That's honestly probably almost virtually nearly positively genuine, that shoe.' Spoolie waxed eloquently. 'Carmen Miranda – remember her? She used to keep drugs in the huge heels of her dancing shoes. Did you know she danced without any knickers on?'

'Mmmmh, great, Spoolie.'

The shop was hung about with bike wheels, once ridden on by some movie cyclist. Clothes dangled from the ceiling. A rocking horse, once used on the stage. A dress, reputedly worn by Ava Gardner. (Spoolie: 'Ava said she got sold like a prize hog in that.')

'I'd love a pack of Bogart's cigarettes,' Spoolie wound on. He never sells videos, scorning secondary sources. 'I've written to the Mayor of Hollywood. I'm opening negotiations for that capital H in the Hollywood sign. You know the one? Just think, Lovejoy. Peg Entwistle chucked herself off it to her death in 1929. RKO wouldn't renew her contract. Can't you just see it? This place would become a Mecca for ephemerists.'

'Mmmmh, great, Spoolie.'

'Signatures are rare,' he told me mournfully. 'I'm down to autographs of cameramen, soundists' diaries, hankies with Orson Welles' initials. Vivien Leigh, though. I've two autographs of hers, but post-Olivier. A Marilyn Monroe cost me half a wage. Ronald Reagan's frigging *mother* signed all his postcards.'

'Mmmmh, great.'

'It's my ambition to do the Grave Rave Tour, Lovejoy. Hollywood. They finish, *Life is no rehearsal*. Pure magic!'

He had postcards, signed books, placemats and coasters, a guitar once played by youthful hopefuls long since insignificant. His shop was a hang-up trying to enter dreamscape.

'I'll kill for a photo of Mary Martin's ghost. Did you know she keeps appearing in Weatherford, Texas? Here, Lovejoy. You're always broke. D'you think I'm doing the right thing? When I came out of nick —'

'You been inside, Spoolie?' This was why I'd come.

'Oh, a few months. I was fitted up. You know the Plod. A drainer, not even in my manor.'

A cat-burgling, outside his area. 'What got stolen?'

He shrugged. 'Money. And some letters. I thought . . . I mean,' he corrected quickly, while I affected not to notice, 'I'll bet the burglar thought they were from somebody famous. They were a professor's, to some political tart.'

I gauged him. 'Know anything about stamps, Spoolie?'

He smiled, shifty. 'So you know. Bought big into antique stamps before I went in. Left them with a dolloper.'

Valuable news. 'You jugged with anybody local?'

Spoolie's face closed. 'No. Drinkwater asked me. Some bloke called Godbolt. Never heard of him.'

'Lovely shop you got, Spoolie.' I said so-long and left, the door playing that scratchy introduction from Flash Gordon serials. Blank. Which only left me Therla the schoolteacher and her non-story of the non-drowning, and Luna's escapade with Jenny. Calamy's not a local name, but it was bothering me. I decided to look names up.

On the way I noticed that Rye Benedict's plant showrooms were up for sale. A decent crowd queued at his mill. Maybe he was going full-time into history, and leaving Nature alone. I was all for it. A shop opposite Therla Brewer's school had a headline about a savage local murder. It made me stop until I could go on, but I didn't buy a paper.

CHAPTER TWELVE

Schools dismay me. It's their air of assumption. Ever since learning that Dickens had to tone *down* the ghastly events at the real Dotheboys Hall, to achieve realism, they've given me the willies. I sense chains, cross the road even yet. I parked the car in the school, though, to avoid prying ploddite eyes. It was in this vehicle that Luna had taken me to suss out Prammie's hut. The countryside might have whispered.

Therla was in the common room being merry with a dozen somnolents. Children, all taller than children used to be, milled about the corridors, looking bored. I wish it had been boredom in my day. I can only remember worry. She came and we walked to her classroom, empty except for two snogging youngsters who marched out, the lad glaring, the girl giving Therla an impudent challenging stare. Therla sighed apology.

'I do my best, Lovejoy. You can see they're horrors.'

The girl was pretty. I could easily dislike the boy.

'That accident, love. The boy in the river.'

'Andrew? He climbed once too often. It was in the Stour. I think I said? An old man on a strange little boat fished him out. He had the oddest way of propulsion, some sort of –'

It's odd how a few words can send you really strange. 'You said he was rescued by an ocean-going barge.'

'Yes. Beside a great barge . . . What's the matter?'

'You stupid cow. You meant *nearby?*'

'Of course. I told you.' She was exasperated. Teachers are trained in it. 'It was fastened to it. For heaven's sake, Lovejoy. I don't understand how ships tie themselves to each other, do I?'

'Ta, Therl.'

'Lovejoy. Don't you think you owe me some explanation? You come here as if your life depended . . .'

It had been Prammie Joe himself. In the Stour? But Prammie's hut lies deep in the tributary marshes of the next river north, the Deben. I'd assumed wrong. I'd been mesmerised by Cornish Place.

'His dinghy was tied to the barge?'

'Yes.' Her forehead wrinkled prettily. 'Under the back, so to speak. Most odd. There were ropes, loading things on to two punts he had. Andrew was very lucky. I honestly do try, Lovejoy,' she sighed. 'Field trips are a nightmare. Next year I take forty-eight teenagers to the Urals. Can you imagine?'

No, I couldn't. 'Did the old man say anything?'

'No. In fact, he was most offensive. He hadn't the slightest intention of making Andrew feel forgiven. Just bundled him ashore – only a few yards, really.'

I said, 'Honestly, some people. What barge, Therl?'

'Therla, please. One of those slow sailing ones. They race them. It was all ready. Here.' She pointed.

A watercolour on a wall. Three Thames barges. 'Big? Like that?'

'Yes. They're quite pretty moving. Ugly just lying still.'

'D'you still teach history? Or has it died of education? There's something on my mind.'

She was pleased at my interest. 'Josh Moss.'

I kept getting these dim flashes in my mind's eye, those names. Oddly, written in an old court hand. I was sure I'd seen at least two, maybe three, on parchment somewhere.

Josh Moss was fetched from the gaiety of the common room. He seemed relieved to escape. I parted amicably from Therla. She does evening classes in poetry, keeps wanting me to enrol. I promised. I remember hardly anything of school poetry, just dim drums throbbing, and only that because we made rude rhymes of *Lepanto*. But Therla's really pleasant. You could get to like even poetry.

'It's a silly thing, Josh,' I said. Instinctively I adopted my old tactic before the teacher, looking downcast and sorry-I'm-such-trouble. 'Some names keep going through my head. I've a, er, a bet on. A mate at the pub. He says they're footballers. I think something historical.'

'Names?' He was a fresh-faced bloke, looking about fourteen. He didn't like my joining Therla's poetry class.

'Godbolt. Calamy. Clark. Hopkins. And one blurred.'

'Easy, Lovejoy,' he said, grinning. 'You're missing Fairclough.'

'That's it!' I cried. Fairclough? 'Who are they?'

'Were, Lovejoy. John Godbolt. Edmund Calamy. And last but certainly not the least, Elizabeth Clark.'

Still I waited, thick as a post. 'Yes?'

Josh sighed. 'See, Lovejoy? You too. Local history's ignored these days. It provides such useful insights. Matthew Hopkins not ring a bell? The Witch-Finder General. He was born hereabouts. Wenham, I think.'

'Wenham?' I stared. Who was from Wenham?

'A bad time. Elizabeth Clark was a witch.' He shrugged, smiling. 'So they said, the day they hanged her. It's not far. Take the main A12 from the roundabout. Be careful of the signs from –'

'Thanks, Josh. Great.'

'Lovejoy,' he called after me. 'D'you win? Your bet.'

'Er, no. But ta.'

From a street phone – one of the six was accidentally unvandalised – I reached Wittwoode's, and Luna. She seemed thrilled. I said come to the school, stat. She said she'd no motor because I had it. I told her to do as she was told. I'd had enough of being buggered about. What are apprentices for, for God's sake? I honestly think women give me lip just to annoy. I can't come because you've got my motor. Gormless.

Coincidences are coincidences, right? But four flukes in a row? Names don't mean much these days, do they? It was all possibly imagination or something.

The point was, it wasn't. Sourly I watched Luna's taxi draw up. 'What's your name?' I signalled her taxi to wait.

'Lovejoy. Whatever's the matter? You look white as –'

'Don't keep saying that. Stop frigging about.'

She stared at me, a sheaf of papers in her hand, ready for a whole Wittwoode saga. 'You *know* who I am, Lovejoy. Mrs Luna Florence Carstairs. Is it a game?'

'Before you were married, stupid.' I'd actually recoiled.

'MacIntosh.' She followed along the pavement. A valeta.

My griping belly muscles relaxed. 'Prove it.'

'Prove . . .?' She delved into her handbag, hauled out a photograph of a beautiful girl. 'That's me.'

Words on the reverse eased me more. *Everybody says Lola's 'a ringer for Luna MacIntosh' when you were nineteen! Love, Dad.*

'Lola?'

'My daughter, Lovejoy. Are you ill?'

Drawing breath, I demanded her mother's name. Her mother's mother's name. Her great-granddad's . . . The family came from Fort William. I should have detected her accent. Fright had done my cortex in. I put my arms round her, bussed her in relief. She backed away, murmuring she was the Mayoress, for heaven's sake, and in public. I gave her her car keys.

'Right, pal. Ditch that motor, for good. Okay?'

'Is it making that clattering noise again? I thought they'd mended it.' She unlocked her car door. 'That garage is becoming so unreliable.'

'Meet me at the town library. Don't be late.'

I borrowed the taxi fare, and left. Talk to some birds, you might as well talk to the wall.

CHAPTER THIRTEEN

Our town library's a non-library. A theory of a library, it's run by Scotchman, a skeletal prat whose sole function is thwarting. To him it's a good day when he's successfully obstacled the whole public from borrowing books.

'I need a book, please, Scotchy.'

'Sorry, Lovejoy, but –'

'Allow me.' I captured a young loafer. 'Look, pal. I don't know how to work the computer here . . .'

The pimply youth's eyes ignited. He shot round the desk, shoved Scotchman up and away, activated the computer. 'Wotcher want, mate?'

'Anything on Matthew Hopkins. Old timer, three hundred and fifty years since.'

Tap tap tap. I'm computer illiterate. These infants aren't. They live for them. But writing by any other name.

'Witch-Finder General?' The youth gazed admiringly at me. 'A pop group? This library's no books. There's one at Grays, Thurrock. Plenty in London.' The security guard was being fetched.

'What is it?' Miss Campbell was beside us, assistant librarian, intent on social justice for the disadvantaged.

'This lad is showing me your technologistics, communication-wise, Miss Campbell.' I said it in one breath.

She dithered, righteous anger foiled by jargon. 'Well, if –'

'Here, mate.' The computer wizard handed me a print-out. I said ta. He slouched off to be bored again.

The nearest tome on Hopkins was in St Edmundsbury. I'd no motor, so it would be bus. I made do with various dictionaries, got the names, deeds, trial details. Reference libraries have been turned into Local Studies Resource Centres. The baffled serving the baffled. Children on school projects take a folder, copy it out for teacher, and move on to their next feat of intellect. I made the bus home, but had to walk from the village outskirts because some nerk insisted on the correct fare.

Luna's origin wasn't local. Bless her. I warmed to the woman, my one trusty ally. I had a few scribbled notes on the ghoulish doings of yore. I brewed up, sat out in a cold rising wind, chucked the birds some cheese, and reflected on what I now knew.

Once upon a time, our fair land was going about its humdrum business. Good Queen Bess had faded from memory. Came James, a spectacular anti-witch nut. Thanks to him, anti-witch mania was burgeoned.

Piecemeal bits garnered in the non-library worried me worse as I began to read my scrawl. There's a lot of balderdash talked about witches nowadays. People think of them, if at all, as cranks having a bit of spare nooky in the woods at summer solstices, or encouraging Mother Earth to produce leaves.

Except there's more.

Like, seventeen people were burnt at St Osyths, near here, in 1676. As late as 1863, a poor elderly French bloke was dragged from his home in Castle Hedingham, ducked to see if he was a wizard, and died from the experience. King George II had some sense, thank God, and repealed our ancient witchcraft laws in 1736. Isolated incidents occurred, though. Like the burning of poor Bridget Cleary at Baltyvadhen in Tipperary in 1895 by her husband and his five mates. Fine, okay, it's history. But read it, suddenly it edges close. Suddenly it's not so long ago. And suddenly the evenings draw in.

The terrible feeling comes, that the people who did those horrible frightening things were *here*, on this ground. They *lived* here. This village, that seaport. They walked our streets, maybe drank from the very bowl you see in the antique shop. Get the point? They laughed and joked *here*. Then they burnt, hanged, imprisoned, gaoled, drowned the innocent. In the name of holiness.

And nobody did this dreadfulness like the ghastly Witch-Finder General.

His dad was a Puritan minister of Wenham. Matthew Hopkins became an Ipswich lawyer, chiselling contentedly at whatever could be chiselled. It was back around the Great Civil War (Cromwell versus Charlie I, on whether Divine Right of Kingship should rule instead of Parliament. People won, making us the modern world's first ever Republic).

Lawyer Hopkins suddenly went ape. Off his own bat he decided he was gifted. His gifts lay in a particular direction.

Abruptly, he began to 'find' witches. He started with a mere handful, at Manningtree, where he lived. Soon, witches were here, there, everywhere. Politicians use the same trick. You know the ploy: there's a witch/treason/a conspiracy/plot/whatever. The cry goes up. Good heavens! All will be lost if everybody doesn't support the prosecutors! And all that jazz. Don't mock the Puritans of Salem,

New England, of 1692. Or the people in Scotland who burnt thousands. James I, a loon of sorts, even prosecuted a whole assize for acquitting some poor soul. Or the witch-persecutors of Pennsylvania. Or Kalisk in Poland. You don't need to look far even today. Especially today.

Lawyer Hopkins appointed himself the Witch-Finder General. And rode out on his anti-witch crusade. He demanded twenty silver shillings a time, a whole pound. (Get it? The more witches he spotted, the richer he got.) This odious reptile rampaged through East Anglia, intoxicated with the power of life or death – and, terribly, it was always death. Exulting, the maniac invented a modification of an ancient 'test' for 'finding' witches. It went:

First identify your witch (that is, pick anybody). Bind her/him. Lob her into a pond. If she floats, why, she's guilty – for the Lord's pure water has rejected her. So she must be hanged. If she sinks, why, she's innocent. You see the problem. Either way, you're dead.

The evil spread through East Anglia like wildfire. Norfolk, Suffolk, and Essex. The horror scourged hamlets, villages, towns, cities, and finally whole counties. Bedfordshire, Huntingdon, Cambridgeshire, all suffered. Folk lived in fright. Some women, knowing their innocence, actually volunteered to come to trial to get it over with. And, Hopkins blithely reported, were hanged for their pains. The witch-hunts went on. And on. Anything was a sign of being a witch – a neighbour's roses wilting, a friend catching a cold, some skin blemish. It was wholesale utter madness. One elderly one-legged Manningtree woman was brought to trial for having a cat she called pet names. She was 'swum' – that is, tied up and ducked, Hopkins' famous test. She failed to drown. So she was hanged.

Her name was Elizabeth Clark, God rest her.

Sick and crazy, the witch-hunts stormed on, in the name of God. Even reeling from the carnage of civil war the nation was appalled by the murderous progress of the Witch-Finder. But everybody did nothing. Just like you and me would have done. Like we do today. Everybody kept quiet – and watched their innocent friends and relatives tortured, drowned, hanged. One poor old octogenarian, Reverend Lowes of Brandeston, Suffolk, was kept awake for over a week by running him about. His parishioners did nothing. The witch-seekers bound him, threw him in Framlingham Castle moat. He floated, so was condemned to be hanged. The poor old cleric begged for a burial service. The laughing Witch-Finder forbade it. The parishioners – you, me – did nothing. The old priest shakily read his own funeral service. And was hanged. His friends, neighbours, parishioners watched. And d.n. He'd been their vicar for fifty years. Of course, the Witch-Finder was a holy Puritan who would make money from the judicial murder. Sound familiar? Piety is lucrative, properly applied.

The reason I was so distressed was something I knew, in my heart of hearts. Had I been there in 1646, I too would have stayed silent.

And d.n. Like now. Like you.

But even crazed bloodlust ends, thank God. It came to pass that one man in the Kingdom suddenly thought, What the hell is going *on?* To John Gaule, of Great Staughton village, it seemed absurd for a so-say civilised nation to be torturing itself on the whim of a madman. *And, unbelievably, he stood up and said so!* One frightening, ghastly day, this brave cleric actually strode to the pulpit – it's still there – and preached against the Witch-Finder General himself. He even had the nerve to publish his conviction that the real witches were the witch-hunters themselves. And then walked home from his appalled congregation and waited, trembling but firm in spirit, for the heavens to cave in.

Great Staughton held its breath, stunned. All Huntingdonshire – home of Oliver Cromwell the arch-Puritan himself, remember, whose Roundheads clanked on every skyline – waited for the Witch-Finder's vengeful team to ride into town.

And waited.

They didn't come. They bottled out. Chicken.

So let's hear it for brave John Gaule of Great Staughton. Drink to his eternal memory. What makes a wimp suddenly heroic? God alone knows. I don't. Because all his life John Gaule had been wet, a drip. He'd fawned and grovelled, bowed and scraped. Until that fateful day when he became a lion. Light a candle to his courage. He deserves it.

The Witch-Finder General complained – but he never came.

And suddenly everybody halted, looked at each other. The witch-finding stuttered. It was the Emperor's New Clothes. People read the vicar's rebuke, and were ashamed. Then they smarted, felt cheated. Then furious. With whom? Why, with the Witch-Finder General! They invented a legend. It goes that, on an angry day, they rushed to where he was staying, dragged him out and lobbed him into a pond in savage mimicry of his own witch-finding test. He floated, so they hanged him from the gibbet.

History is more mundane. After John Gaule's denunciation, East Anglia simply calmed down. The Witch-Finder died in his bed in 1647, of tuberculosis.

He was a local bloke. Wenham's but a stone's throw from here. On the bench alongside him sat two sombre figures, Edmund Calamy and Sergeant John Godbolt. Famous names, when you bother to remember. They had a grim sergeant, one Fairclough, to play the heavy. I'm sorry it's such a horrible tale. It's the worse for being true. Mistley-cum-Manningtree knows that. Theirs is the unenviable distinction of having the Witch-Finder General sleeping soundly – or maybe not so soundly – in their churchyard.

No names I'd managed to find in the non-library matched any of Luna's family names. I was still sitting on my half-finished wall when Luna arrived in a snarly two-tone Ford. She approached across the grass in trepidation. I watched her.

I must have been something of a tribulation. She must be at the end of her tether. She stood in front of me. A worried woman. My one ally, whose patience nearly equalled mine.

'Hiyer, pal,' I said at last. 'Friends?'

She gave a radiant smile. 'Oh, Lovejoy! You're better!'

'I haven't been poorly,' I said, narked. 'Come inside.'

She put her arm through mine. 'Antiques at last?'

'Lots, love. Lots and lots.' I meant enough to make a huge scam, the sort East Anglia doesn't have.

The answerphone, a real nuisance, had a message.

'This is Mayor Carstairs, Lovejoy. I want to know what's going on. This degree of interaction –'

There's an off switch, works a treat. 'He got nothing better to do, love?'

'It's only the motor,' she said, quite cheerfully. 'Oliver wanted me to use the one you don't like any more. I borrowed this from Oliver's cousin Emily.'

'Tell Emily ta, love. She pretty?'

'No,' she said evenly. 'Hideous, nasty.'

'Pity. We're going to need help with the forgery.'

Luna turned, kettle in her hand. 'Did you say forgery?'

'Eh? No. I said copying. An antique, for a friend.'

In silence we sat and listened to the news. One Joseph Godbolt had been found dead, possibly some days, in a reed-cutter's hut in a marshy area off the River Deben. His death was being investigated. The police suspected foul play, had set up an Incident Room in a local tavern.

I held up a warning finger as Luna, instantly thrilled, drew breath to exclaim at the extraordinary coincidence that Godbolt was the very name . . .

'Don't,' I said. She didn't. And I started convincing her that forgery was nearly, but not quite, the same as faking or copying or simulating. Words are great, aren't they? Prove anything, used right.

CHAPTER FOURTEEN

'Strip off, Lovejoy, or I'll bring Geronimo.'

The threat did it. I felt a right duckegg. It must be great to take your clothes off and not feel daft. We look misshapen, a clown's joke. Women look exquisite, tailored by an expert. I didn't look at the mirror.

'Not underpants and socks, Vell?' No, maybe socks. Men's socks look the last laugh.

She tutted. 'Lovejoy, get *on*. You've paid for an hour. Prospective fortune, para-psycho analysis, massage. So far you've wasted ten minutes. I can't oil you with your clothes on.'

'Oil?' I cried, alarmed. 'What oil?'

You use oil for motor cars and painting, not for Lovejoys. Though there's one antique called an oil clock, where time is marked by the fall in an oil reservoir as a flame burns –

'Stop *talking!*' She was getting really narked. 'Oil's for the massage, Lovejoy! For heaven's *sake*.'

I'd made Vell's inner sanctum by making an appointment for The Great Marvella's services. There didn't seem any other way. A casual call meant possibly running into her clients. For once, I wanted to avoid a big seduction scene. Wondrous exalting, yes, but with death now dealt into the antiques game I needed mileage. Fortune-telling meant looking into Geronimo's terrible flat-headed gaze while he decided what the next month held for me. I also passed on the para-psychologic analysis, because Geronimo did the analysing with Vell's demented ventriloquism. That left Reconstruct-ile Autosynthetic Massage. It sounded like a set of girders.

She started undoing my clothes. I tried to deflect her.

'This is ridiculous!' she cried, determined. 'You're like a child. Stand *still!*'

Hell of a way to get an interview.

'Listen, Vell.' I struggled to keep my shirt. I'd conceded shoes in token gesture of seriously wanting her bloody massage. 'I haven't really got any aches. Maybe if I do some gardening –'

She brushed a wisp of hair away from her forehead as we grappled politely. 'I think I must be mad, Lovejoy. I've given you open invitations before now. And you've run a mile. Now you are here you're wriggling like a –'

'I'm stripping! I'm stripping!'

I looked about for somewhere to put my shirt. She snatched it, exasperated, and flung it on a couch. The inner sanctum had plenty of furniture. It was a vaulted place, really surprising. Old roof beams quite chapel-like. I mean, the little street hardly seemed to have anywhere to keep a space this size. It must have been an old meeting hall, from the seventeenth century when new sects came in grace abounding.

The massage table stood grandly in the middle, ready for a Lying in State. She had heating, I suppose for her female clients. Women are always on the search for draughts, real or imagined. They'd choose a different masseuse with a different snake if it wasn't warm. She had a large expanding divan, embroidered damascus cushions and everything, and some good Edwardian upright furniture.

'Have I to get up on that?'

That left my trousers, no socks, and underpants. Clean on, as if I was going to the doctor. I'd even done my teeth a second time, just as if I was going snogging.

'Up, please. Remove *all* outer clothing before ascending the Autosynthetic Rostrum.'

These catchphrases are meaningless, aren't they. Delivered in an even, bored tone, they sound full of weighty authority. Sheepishly I lowered my trousers, folded them with defiant slowness, and dropped them on the floor. I wasn't walking the thirty or so feet to put them on the clothes mane provided, not with her looking. A bloke in underpants looks as daft as he does naked. No. Delete that. He doesn't. Couldn't.

The raised table was like in Doc Lancaster's surgery. Pillow the wrong thickness. A blanket, cream-coloured, with a red stripe. No compound light glaring down at me, thank God. If there had been, I'd have been off. I could almost hear the sound of clinking instruments and the hiss of sterilisers.

'You lie, prone. I can't do a massage with you propped up on your elbow like that.'

Prone, face down. Supine face up. Right.

'Lovejoy. The blanket over your *feet*. Let *go!*'

'In a minute –'

She ripped the blanket away. 'Lie still. Relax, please.'

Some trolley trundled near. Bottles chinked. Her hands slapped.

'Only oil.' Warm, her hands in the middle of my spine. 'It's unscented. Is this your first massage?'

'Mmmmh.' A lie, because I've been out East. I wanted to get information out of her, not put information in.

'You'll be pleasantly surprised. People have wrong ideas. They think sordid goings-on, instead of psycho-physical restorative contactile stimulus.'

'Quite honestly, I think we do,' I agreed. 'Er, forget the psycho-restoration, er, thing.' I wanted to butter her up, get her to talk. 'Do you have plenty of sufferers?'

Her hand smacked me smartly. 'Clients, Lovejoy. I don't inflict suffering.'

'I meant clients. Honest.' I thought only lawyers and prostitutes had clients.

'Business picked up about a year ago.' She was working. 'Even among your cynical profession.' Profession was a laugh. Antique dealers call rich antique-buying smoothies professionoils (oily professionals, get it?). Sotheby's and Christie's are full of them. And TV nowadays, those road-show people with antique shops syndicated on the side.

'Vell, I came on condition you don't tell.'

She laughed. 'Men all want confidentiality. Not the women. And Sandy, of course. But he doesn't count. As if it mattered! Massage is therapy, not something to be embarrassed about.'

'I know, I know.' Smooth, smooth. I think I meant that I was being smooth, not that her hands were moving so pleasingly. I began to feel sleepy. I could see how folk got to like this sort of thing. 'It was Connie suggested I came. I've been very, er . . .' Why did people come, anyway? 'Er, fed up, lately.'

'I heard Tinker's away. And your little fat cow. Doing quite well for yourself. Selling wood, isn't she?'

'My apprentice? Mmmmh.' Vell hated Lydia. My erstwhile apprentice had given her the sailor's elbow once in the Arcade. Lydia's very beautiful, but if Vell wanted to bitch Lydia up, fine by me. Lydia was seconded to an august antique furniture showroom off Bond Street for a year. 'Selling wood', as Vell sweetly described it.

'Arms extended. Over the end of the reclination.'

Reclination? I noticed there was a blemish in the door, like for a cat flap. The infilling wood was wrong. The door itself was lovely ancient English oak.

'Had a flood?' We were on an upper floor.

She looked, laughed. 'Oh, you know. Clients like to hear tales. Geronimo –'

I shot up, shoving her away. 'He comes in here?'

Vell shoved me down. 'No, silly. He stays in his cage.'

Calmed, I felt myself slipping into a quiet bliss. Vell was really good at rubbing. I made myself come to.

'How do you advertise, Vell? I don't see your postcards.'

They're still called sixpenny cards, from thirty years ago. You write out your advert on a postcard and a shopkeeper sticks it in his window.

'Honestly! What do you think I'm running, Lovejoy? I advertise, when need be, in expensive magazines. Not in alleys.'

'Course not. Big stuff, eh?' I was there at last. 'I know. Cassandra Almighty Clark.'

Vell gave one of those half-embarrassed laughs that make you wonder. 'Cassandra and I are friends. Sort of. Except she went to a different school.'

A little bitterness there? I could imagine, though. Cassandra Clark filthy rich, Vell peddling ventriloquism.

'Nice you've met up.' Time for a shot in the dark. 'I'm hoping to sell Cassandra some good stuff soon. But she's not bought much since she arrived in the area.' Meaning never. Not a piceworth. Yet I couldn't remember an auction Cassandra Clark hadn't been at. How odd. A dealer groupie?

'You are?' Very guarded, all of a sudden. Had the hands stilled a fraction before smoothing onward?

'I can lay my hands on a mountain of superb stuff.'

She trilled an unconvincing laugh. 'Cassandra might not like them, Lovejoy. She's very discriminating.'

'She will. I'm looking for a really wealthy, er, client.'

'Over, please.' I could have sworn she was so sad. I'd thought she was jolly. 'Lovejoy. Stay in your own league. I know it's none of my business, but –'

'Antiques are my league, love.' I smiled up at her. 'The others aren't on the scale I want. Hey, Vell. You're making me nod off. Is there a surcharge if I do? I'll have to owe.'

She was smiling in a queer way. 'Thought as much, Lovejoy. Wait.' She went to the outer room. I heard her bleep some message service. 'No calls until further notice.'

She returned, and got on with her work. Refreshing.

It was three o'clock before I rose from her divan, bathed, found all my clothes. She lay on the damascus cushion watching me go. It felt odd, like farewell. Yet in one sense we'd only just met. But with women you can't ever quite work out exactly what you should be exactly working out, if you follow. I've often found that.

Time I went down the estuaries. But not with Luna in her snarly two-tone. I didn't want Drinkwater wondering what sorts of motors Mayor Carstairs and his wife possessed, in case he lucked on to some report of her near Prammie Joe's place. I should have thought of that beforehand, but you're sometimes too scared to go to some places on your own. I've often found that, as well.

'Lovejoy, dear. Old scrubber Luna is positively *charming!* I told her *everything* about your dreadful past!'

'Hello, Sandy.'

He came gushing to welcome us. 'Oh, here she very *is*, Lovejoy! Woolworth's, dear, your wig? A bargain seconds?'

'Sandy,' I warned, uncomfortable. Luna didn't seem to mind.

'We got on very well, Lovejoy. Didn't we, Sandy?'

'Like my outfit?' He drew Luna inside. He looked loony. A long eastern caftan, a decorated print blouse, pearls, and mirrors on each fingernail. 'Wait!'

He snapped his fingers. The fireplace rotated. A bar, complete with stools, pivoted out. 'You worship? Admire?'

'I'd rather have the fireplace.' It wasn't anything special, but Carrara marble and nineteenth century is something you don't see every day of the week. It made me think of pricey house furnishings. Cornish Place would make some dealer a prince.

Sandy fluttered his eyelashes at Luna. 'Isn't he the one? *Nothing* but antiques. He must adore *you*, Luna! Are those still your own teeth?'

'Now behave.' Luna was smiling. Women always seem so well adjusted to, well, Sandys.

We hadn't had time to do much. I'd been preoccupied. Luna was relieved we were moving into antiques. I'd given her a session on jewellery. Costume next. Riches to rags.

'Sandy told me that antique dealers use delaying tactics for payment, Lovejoy.'

'He did?' I said, while Sandy did his eyes in another ton of mascara. The lashes were like bat's wings, stuck out a mile. 'Let's hope he pays The Great Marvella on the nail. She has a snake for a debt-collector.'

'Isn't Geronimo perfectly *sweet?*' Sandy crooned, pouring a vodka and vermouth in a glass with a five-foot stem. It stood on the floor alongside him. 'So erotic! Visual! Drinkie-poos?'

Luna asked for orange juice. I had nothing.

'Question One!' he announced. 'Who used a wine glass exactly like this in a film?' He tapped Luna playfully. 'You ought to guess this, dear. He too wore a blonde wig!'

'Dirk Bogarde. I loved the Mediterranean terrace!'

Sandy's smile vanished. *'Aren't* we a clever cow, then?'

'Sandy has a pal,' I explained to Luna. 'Spoolie. He's showbiz ephemera. The Ghool Spool. He's not long out of gaol.'

Sandy eyed me. 'That doesn't make him a bad person.'

Luna frowned. 'Rod Steiger? Played a multiple murderer?'

I yelled, 'Shut up, Luna!' She thought Sandy was playing his famous film quotes game. 'Which gaol, Sandy? Parkhurst?'

'Not the same,' Sandy said quickly. Which meant he'd already been on the phone to Spoolie, discussing Prammie Joe's demise. The rotated fireplace was one I'd seen auctioned some time since, so nothing suggestive there.

'That's good,' I said. 'See, I want a place burgled.'

Quietness supervened. Sandy's face set to mutiny. I looked at a breakfront bookcase. It was a really pleasant fake. I'd done it myself out of an elderly wardrobe.

'Luna. Come and look. Remember I was telling you about fakes?'

'Fake?' Sandy shrieked so loud I reeled, but kept doggedly on. Time to stop mucking 'about. I wanted help, not tantrums.

'There was an old furniture man in antiques called Crawley. He published a number of maxims. He had records of fifty-three thousand pieces of furniture he'd worked on over twenty years. Either altered, or complete fakes. That shows the size of the market.'

'I think it's lovely.'

'Thank you, love. I made it. Of course it's lovely.'

'You?' Sandy shrieked. *'You?'* He burst into tears, to Luna's consternation. She rummaged for a hankie. I wearily made her desist and listen.

'A million pointers give it away, love. Look on the inside of the doors. Usually there are graze marks, because the tray-shelves slid. Some housemaids didn't push the shelves all the way back in, see?' I opened the doors and showed her the marks. 'Proves it was an old wardrobe. I cut these glass windows from old framed prints – dealers are always chucking the glass away. You can find marks – the glass can never quite be cleaned free of them.'

'But it looks original, Lovejoy.'

'Don't talk. Listen. The smaller a break-front book-case, the more expensive. The easiest test is this: lower the writing flap, and sit as if you're going to write a letter. Measure its height from the carpet. It should be two feet seven inches, give or take. If it's not, then some faker has miscalculated.' I shrugged modestly. 'This is two foot seven, dead on.'

Sandy was bleating, but still holding out.

I looked about the shop. 'See this little Pembroke table? Oval's more costly than serpentine or rectanglar. Here, you see, the faker –'

'Delia,' Sandy said murderously, giving in. 'Delia's the burglar you want. I'll ring for you. But don't think I'm your friend any more, Lovejoy. This is *war*. You made me *cry*.'

'Oh, now, Sandy,' from Luna, all worried.

Sandy squared off, narrowing his eyes, trying to jut his chin. 'This – is – no – easy – assignment – men!' He smiled, confident. 'Right, trolls! Who? Have to hurry you, gargoyles!'

'John Wayne?' Luna spoke before I could tip her the wink to guess wrong. 'I never like those war films, do you?'

Sandy glared malevolently. It was hopeless. I started to leave. '*What* a clever little whore our *dear* mare-ess is turning out to be, Lovejoy! Isn't it time you went back to Jessica? Or Lydia? Connie, perhaps? Or that Berlin bombshell who positively *begged* to be thrashed, and collected Georgian silver stirrup cups? Or Dolly? Why *didn't* you marry Dolly? The poor bitch was on *heat* every single *hour*, I mean practically *wet* trailing you round the market with her hubby, I mean *sobbing* –'

'Sorry about that, love.' I spoke over the door's farewell tone *Marching Through Georgia*. We emerged into East Hill's cool wet air. 'Sandy likes to be clever. Forgot to tell you.'

'But I love the cinema, Lovejoy.' We walked towards the museum. 'What was the joke about the burglar?'

'Shhh,' I said. I waved cheerily to a friend across the road. 'Hiyer, Jeff. Eleanor okay, is she?'

'Fine.' he called across cars. 'Get my message? Gungie wants you. It's important.'

'Ta, Jeff. Love to Eleanor.'

We went to see if any of the graves at St Mary-at-the-Walls was dry enough to sit on. When we were perched in comfort, I began. 'Luna, love. We want a robbery carried out. I need to know which antique dealers go to a particular fortune-telling masseuse. I can't ask Marvella directly. So we want somebody to do a drainer – er, burgle her establishment, by climbing down her drain-pipe – and delve in her records.'

'We do?' She was wide-eyed.

'Exactly. I'd go myself,' I lied candidly. 'But I have scruples.'

'Oh, scruples are *right*, Lovejoy!'

Sometimes I'm lucky. Luna might become an ideal partner.

'Let's get to Woody's and have a bite.' I'd never used a female burglar before, but Sandy knew his business. If he said Delia, Delia it had to be. 'Tell me about Jenny Calamy.'

The rain came down in torrents as we left for Woody's caff. Luna had forgotten her umbrella, the stupid cow. I sometimes think I draw the short straw. Apprentices get my goat. Why are they never efficient? I'd have got wet through if I hadn't sent her off for a taxi from outside Marks and Sparks while I sheltered in the church porch. Women basically have no organisation.

CHAPTER FIFTEEN

We tore back to the cottage with some shopping, at Luna's insistence, the motor full of plastic bags. I deplore shopping. You can't just pop in, can you? You take ten hours instead of three minutes. Its gets me wild.

The answerphone wanted attention. That winking eye riles me. Worse than a bird asking where you've been, and who with.

'Lovejoy,' Joan's voice said, all tense. 'We have to talk. Del's not going to take this lying down. I'll call.'

Why? She'd already been, left two vases of flowers and three envelopes, one containing money, the other two various instructions about lawyers and where we were to meet every hour from now to Doomsday. And a couple of air tickets to Monte Carlo. Luna, distributing the shopping, paused at the sight of the airline logos.

She gauged me candidly. 'You have no intention of going, Lovejoy. Have you?'

'Eh?' I'd not given elopement much thought.

There was a nervy message from Connie. 'Urgent. Please find me, Lovejoy. Arcade, Woody's, Dennison's Auction till five. White Hart thereafter. Gunge's looking out for you.'

I smiled weakly at Luna. 'Everything's always urgent. Ever noticed?' We were leaving, but Luna had to delay us by answering the phone.

'I'm out,' I hissed frantically, but she passed me Miss Turner, smiling. 'What now?'

'Hello, Lovejoy. Have I had *success!*' Might as well talk to the wall. 'But I'm at a dead end. Though I did find –'

Take the shortest way. 'What religion were your Scotch ancestors? Nonconformist? Protestant?'

'Of course, Lovejoy! Though . . . ' The old bat's voice lowered to guilt. 'Some English ancestry was . . . Catholic.'

I did a pretend gasp, bored out of my skull. 'Have a go at the Census Records. They might get you to 1841. Then go to the Scottish Record Office. Look there for your Protestant people. For God's sake don't miss out the congregation number. They get ratty.'

'Oh! I simply didn't *think!* How very clever, Lovejoy –'

'Chiseller.' I hung up, rounded on Luna. 'There's books galore

on finding your ancestors. Tell the old boot I've emigrated next
time.'

She was smiling. 'You're so sweet, Lovejoy.'

We drove down the estuary then, and finished up standing on
the banks of the River Deben. Along its course it has a small islet
or two, but essentially is a straight, uninteresting river. For me its
importance lay in its end, in the North Sea. A mile south along the
coast lies the port of Felixstowe. Sail down a couple more miles for
the Orwell Basin. It doesn't sound much, but it's the conflux of two
others rivers, the Orwell, and the Stour − John Constable's river.
You can take your pick of any number of estuaries, tributaries,
moorings, marinas, small islands, lowly sea marshes, and come
gliding in of a dark night −

'Lovejoy?' Luna was shaking me.

'I'm just thinking of the water.'

The river looked innocuous, really ordinary. From Ramsholt to
Hemley where we were standing was barely more than a mile, the
river between. There's a promontory on the south side where we
were, with a couple of creeks joining the main river from the marshes.

Luna was thrilled by the onshore wind and the sea birds.
'Lovejoy. Isn't this near where . . . ?

Fine like now, with the air dry, no more rain this afternoon so
far, the wind whistling across the sedge and a wherry or two gliding
serenely down to the sea. Fine, too, in sun, with children playing
and a few small boats enjoying themselves. But bleed the sky's light,
and it becomes very, very different. The pitch night has a solidity
that chills your soul. Then, the wind's brisk whistle loses it flute
quality. It becomes a sombre moan. The breeze drains warmth, tugs
fretfully. Your feet slide in the mud. Rain slashes at your eyes,
vicious. The very night air can shove you over, send you down
slithering into the water, where the river has gone mad −

Luna said brightly. 'Time to go! We're going mental!'

'Right, right.'

We drove off, me telling Luna to go via Rye Benedict's.

It could be done. A waterman born and bred could easily scull
a shallow pram from those creeks. He'd have to choose his nights,
of course, and know the tides. Then it'd be easy to reach the sea.
All right, so I couldn't decide how Prammie Joe had got along the
coast from the Deben to the Orwell Basin. But once there he could
paddle upriver to Cornish Place.

Yes, that was how he'd done it all right. But where had he taken
the stuff? Stripping a mansion of its furnishings is a major task,

cubed. The fireplaces alone would weigh tons, taken together. Consider doors – not the least valuable items. They'd have to be wrapped up against getting wet, or they'd spoil. So Prammie didn't carry the blinking things once he'd got them on to his rafts, but it was still a mighty feat. I mean, there you are in your cosy little hut, with the wind howling, rain slashing, onshore gales, you'd naturally want to read, listen to some music. But no. Up gets old Prammie, and night after night sculls off down the river . . . Down the *same* river? Wait a minute. Or somewhere else?

'Is she the friend?' Luna was asking as we reached Rye's mill. I saw the garden centre's notice had a red *Sold* poster diagonally across it.

'Who?'

Luna pointed. 'Connie. You said, helping a friend. Faking. I mean, copying,' she amended neatly as I drew breath.

Connie was speaking with Rye. I didn't realise they were friends, not 'calling friends', as country folk say. But here was Connie, fetchingly attired in beige, speaking intently with Rye on the forecourt. The mill was motionless, the millrace burbling into white froth below. We'd had enough rain lately. No school mobs, thank goodness. The mill shop was closed. I realised with a faint smile I'd never seen it open. Some businessman. But he'd seemed hooked on some massive investment last time I came by. At least, that was how I remembered it. And here he was, chatting – no, conversing intently – with the lovely Connie.

Luna drew in, parked. I waited. Their deep talk went on. Not at all animose, but certainly profound.

'Do I interrupt, love?'

'I should. Or they might think . . .' She pinked. Women are strong on not prying, because they can do it sly.

I alighted, making din enough to wake the dead. Connie and Rye moved apart. I was unobservant. Luna came with diffidence.

'I see you've sold your garden centre across the river, Rye. Into history full-time, then?'

It honestly was an innocent remark. Hang it all, there was the notice for all to see, nine feet tall. But he looked positively shifty, which is definitely not Rye Benedict.

'Not really, Lovejoy.' And he put a big envelope under his arm, shoving photographs back inside it. I pretended disinterest.

'With all that profit, you can buy your own mill,' I chuckled, until I noticed I was chuckling on my own. Connie looked strained, Rye nervous as a kitten.

'What a lovely old place!' Luna enthused, womanlike, wanting to blot up the silence. 'And how beautifully kept!'

Rye unbent slightly, but licking his lips nervously. 'Yes. Thank you. I run it for the Council.' He looked at it wistfully. 'I wish it were.' He waved across at the nursery garden. 'That seemed more profitable to my family. Everything was steam, electricity, coal. Now, we're beginning to realise. Old-fashioned mills were clean.'

He spoke almost bitterly, as if he resented the mill some way. Weird. I saw Connie looking at me.

'Don't knock the great inventors, Rye,' I said. 'I love the Victorians.'

He unbent with an enthusiast's instant fervour. 'Oh, you can say that again, Lovejoy! They really were the greats. Think of them – James Watt. Telford. Brunel.'

'Rye –'

He wouldn't let Connie interrupt. I didn't want him to, either. 'Lovejoy. I really believe there should be an order, sort of sainthood, for people like Brunel. They are the true immortals! More than any popes or politicians.'

His eyes were shining, hot, almost afire. Another acquaintance gone ape.

'Brunel your hero, Rye? Pity he never worked locally –'

'Oh, but –'

Then Connie really did interrupt, with a firmness that made Luna take a step back. 'Look. This is all very well. But Lovejoy, I wanted to –'

'Connie,' Rye said. It came out vehement. He caught himself and smiled. It wore him out, but he managed. A lot of past argument went into that negative.

'I have a proposition, Lovejoy. About my antiques.' Connie said it with some kind of sadness I couldn't fathom, looking at Rye as she spoke. Luna was pinker than normal, I saw with surprise. I thought, God, more eyebrow play than a melodrama.

'All right, love. Meet at the Treble Tile?'

'Give me a lift?'

I asked Rye for a table of tides. He said he's send me one, because his shop was shut – as if the door had just slammed accidentally and him with with no key. I had to laugh: a non-shop.

Connie sat in the back. Luna drove us. Connie sussed Luna out first, though she already knew Luna was my apprentice. A typical woman, judging how far things had gone between me and the Lady Mayoress of the Hundred.

'My antiques, Lovejoy. Can you fuff them?'

'To what?'

'Double what you divvied?'

That made me swallow hard. The fuff is a con trick. You pad
out a number of genuine antiques to make a larger number by adding
some more. Except there's one small detail: the additional 'antiques'
are fakes, look-alikes, sham. Now, don't get all indignant. Prestigious
auction houses the world over do this. Of course, they catalogue the
fakes, replicas, the false, in eloquent vagueness that makes the bidders
think they too are genuine. The auctioneers, who can't ever be
trusted, may even point out that there's been 'controversy' over this
'interesting' item . . . Read the words carefully, and you'll realise the
auctioneers are being their own glib selves, pulling a con.

Luna listened to my explanation, trying hard not to be so
appalled she could hardly keep the motor on the road.

Connie kindly added her pennyworth. 'It means buying or
creating fakes, Luna. Or multiplying them somehow. Lovejoy's the
expert.'

'But you already have so many, Connie . . .'

'Why us?' I put in. 'Because buyers, on this sort of scale, will
believe the lot if I authenticate a few.'

Luna coloured even more when I'd said 'us', pleased. 'And you'd
do that, Lovejoy?'

'No. I'll fuff, all right. But passing them all off as genuine
antiques is the buyer's responsibility. Correct, Connie?'

'Yes.' She wanted me to say I'd do it all, but I wouldn't. Too
many things were going on in this drab old countryside for me to
start carrying the pots and pans. I'd already decided before she asked.
That didn't mean I'd carry out the whole sale. Fair's fair.

Another thing. Until I knew exactly what was going on, I was
a swinging compass, no direction.

'Any particular antiques you want?' I asked casually.

'Anything, Lovejoy. Furniture, silver, jewellery, clocks, weapons,
furnishings, treen, instruments, microscopes, household, dolls,
ephemera . . .' Onward, ever onward.

The list pleased me. It included household furnishings. So she
wasn't in on Prammie Joe's scam after all. Her voice hadn't even
wavered. So she was going it alone. I could tell she was a very
worried bird. As worried as Rye Benedict. Had she been trying to
borrow money off Rye, knowing he had the profits from the sale of
his market-garden estate? That didn't quite ring true, somehow.
She'd asked my help – 'urgently' by phone, sending Gunge looking.

'How soon?' That's the only problem with a fuff job. Dealers want it done yesterday.

'As possible, Lovejoy. On the drip feed.'

When they become available. 'Local, or abroad?'

'Oh, overseas.' Easier still. Local fakes sell afar, as far fakes sell near. It's a saying. The point being that real antiques sell anywhere.

We dropped her in the old station yard, where nobody waits for buses any more. 'To seem unassociated,' I explained to Luna.

We went among heavy traffic – two buses and a brewer's dray – towards the village. Coming off the station round about a tall, precisely dressed gentleman – you couldn't simply call him a bloke – stepped out into the road, bowler hat raised politely. Luna felt obliged to stop.

'Good afternoon,' he said in the window, smiling. Military tash, Old Etonian tie. Pin stripes, patent leather, a symphony of upper-crust wealth. 'Have I the honour of addressing one Lovejoy?'

'And one Luna,' I said, smiling in spite of myself. His sort usually narks me. I was surprised. 'Whom does one have the honour of addressing one?' That old Etonian tie was no sham, I bet myself. 'Osbert Sitwell said he'd been educated entirely in his holidays from Eton.'

He chuckled. 'Sandy said you would be odd, Lovejoy. How d'you do?' Odd from Sandy was rich. He got in with swift grace. Which was really strange, because I distinctly remembered locking the rear door. He'd slid in as if it was wide open.

I looked at him in the rearview mirror. 'Delia?'

'Pleased to make your acquaintance.'

Luna opened her mouth to say something, but I gave her the bent eye, and all was well.

CHAPTER SIXTEEN

'Thanks, Delia. Sure you can get a lift?'

'No,' he chortled, straight from those children's comics where everybody always chortled. 'Better to walk. Opportunities.'

'Well, do my drainers first, eh?'

'Willco, old bean.'

And off he strode. I shut the door, and we sat and looked at each other. Luna was sitting on the divan, her head on one side.

'You told him to burgle The Great Marvella. And to watch out for the snake?' It'd take too long to explain, my sigh told her. '*And* Mr Benedict's watermill shop, Lovejoy?'

'Look. If you're going to pick on every little thing –'

She became heated. 'Every little *thing*? For heaven's sake, Lovejoy! I'd no idea it would be criminal! I mean, I've even started lying to Oliver! I'm never deceitful!'

'No? What about when . . .?' I saw her eyes widen in apprehension, then calm down as she got the joke. She smiled a bit.

'Be serious, Lovejoy. Oliver's not only the Mayor. He's a lawyer. Secretary of the local Bar Association and everything.' She flapped her hands helplessly. 'And now I'm an accessory. I'm *embroiled*. Burglary. On commission. I don't mind the money.'

I'd had to borrow a bit from her, to pay Delia his earnest penny. Uncomfortably I totted up what Luna had paid for lately, and gulped. I always cut corners adding up what I owe.

'I'm sorry, Luna.' I was so sincere. If I'd not had to flog my phono I'd have put on hearts-and-flowers. 'I honestly am. I'm not usually like this.'

'That's not *it*, Lovejoy.' Then why mention money? To lead into obligations, that's why. 'I just don't know where I stand.'

And miraculously the door thumped. I leapt, joyously reprieved, to welcome Big Frank. He entered, darkening the world for miles. Luna gaped, never having seen his like before in her august circles. First Gunge, our gungey giant. Now a clean one. Thank God he was smiling. I introduced them.

'Oh, you're the gentleman on the phone!' Luna was so pleased. 'Miss Jenny was lovely. We had such a lovely chat. I'm so glad you and she . . .' She halted, stricken. She wasn't supposed to be glad about Big Frank's impending marriage, because he was still wed to Mrs Big Frank.

'Thanks, missus. Silver, Lovejoy?'

'None, Frank.' He sat on the divan, so he could adjust his head to the vertical. Normally he stoops anywhere within twenty feet of any doorway.

'Lovejoy. I want you to help Jenny.'

'What with, Frank?' More help? From me again?

Abruptly I too wanted to sit on the divan of a sudden, but there was no room. Already Luna was tilted high in the air from Big Frank's weight compressing the universe.

'She's got something really big on. I mean, really ginormous. Bigger than anything in the Eastern Hundreds, Lovejoy.'

Another? My cottage was headache city. I've already explained that East Anglia isn't given to mega blitzes, nor scams of international proportions. We're more your actual one-offs. I cast about for the kettle, finally gestured for Luna to brew up. She smiled happily, as Big Frank gave it out.

'Lovejoy, she won't even tell me.'

'She won't tell *you*? But you're going to be . . .'

'Husband and wife.' The great goon's face melted into soppy fondness. If I hadn't been his best man so often, my own face would have melted too. 'But she's right, Lovejoy. The sums are fantastic.'

'Fantastic?' Now I really did slide down the wall and sit on the bare flagged floor. 'Look, Frank . . .'

The best dance of all, the exit shuffle. If it had been one silver chalice, fine. Big Frank could at least recognise some makers' marks, and knew to assay silver content. But that had taken him thirty years to learn, from birth. The silly loon was so infatuated with his Jenny that he was willing to step outside silver to serve her whim.

'No, Lovejoy. Straight up. She only needs a few more days, and it'll be England.' He beamed at the image. 'Then we can spend for ever on antique Georgian silver.'

His eyes glazed at the very thought of unimagined paradise. 'England' is antique dealers' slang for perfection, the triumph of profit. Comes from the sailors' cry when leaving foreign ports on the journey homeward: 'England, home, and beauty!' Meanwhile, my mind had gone dreamy too, wondering what on earth was possessing us all. Scams so huge, with money so vast, that the National Debt would shrink if the Chancellor could get his hands on the wadge? Barmy.

Luna brewed up while Big Frank and I thought our mutually

excluding thoughts. I was helping Connie, from past love. I was also helping Prammie Joe, if you can call it that, from sorrow. I had the feeling somehow that I should be helping Rye Benedict – correction, please. Delete that. I ought to be helping myself. It was me that was broke, not this load of deadlegs.

'Help how, exactly, Frank?' As if I didn't know.

'Lovejoy. How many divvies are there?'

'Me,' I said miserably. 'I did hear there's an old dear near Saxmundham for porcelain –'

'One, Lovejoy.' Frank's voice is so deep you sometimes have to actively listen out for it, like the deepest bell. 'You. I want you to be there when Jenny accepts the antiques.'

Plural. Plenty, again? 'Frank. I'm pushed at the minute. How about a dollop broker? I've heard there's a really superb one around these days.'

'Yes, she's great. Jenny'll be using her.'

She again. Same one. Sooner or later I was going to have to think about this mysterious person, and tell Luna what a dollop broker actually is.

'If your Jenny's working up a dollop, and you know a dollop broker, then where's your problem, Frank?'

He stared at me sadly. 'Tracing the seller, once the money's been handed over. That's the problem, Lovejoy.'

So the vendor was foreign? Crikey. Jenny, soon to be his wife, wouldn't even tell him who was going to sell her all these valuable antiques? For a brief instant, as Luna dished out tea and biscuits, something occurred to me. Something wrong, but notably right, if you follow. I tried to hang on to it, but it was gone.

'It's sensible, Lovejoy.' I stood, to look out of the window and think a bit. Frank rumbled on. 'I mean, who tells anybody?'

Except a fiancée wasn't just anybody, if she was going to be his eighth – ninth? – wife. Maybe that feeling I'd nearly had was the dawning realisation that I was in greater demand than I'd ever been.

'About the old soldi,' Lovejoy. I'll see you get a fee.'

'You will?' Big Frank is quite a good payer. But never up front.

'Up front,' he promised. Queererer and queererer.

'Right, Frank. I'll go and see her. If it's okay?'

'Any time, Lovejoy.' He looked down into his tea and didn't grimace. 'Your bird here will show you the way.'

He left, politely thanking Luna for the hospitality. Which would have left me food for thought, if I hadn't been thinking what it was I'd almost been thinking about.

'A dollop broker?'

We were going to nosh in a restaurant, to celebrate Luna's first ever sale of an antique at auction. She'd got word from Wittwoode's that she'd made a week's wage on the bubby pot. Of course I threatened fire and slaughter if the lads dared to ring it. They'd thoughtfully stayed out of the bidding. I didn't tell Luna that I'd asked Jeff to bid it up. I didn't want Luna disappointed, first time out.

'Is it an antique dealer, Lovejoy?'

That was a laugh. 'No, love. All they do is hide stuff for you.'

'Hide? Not sell?'

'It works like this, love. If you're going to gaol, or having to do a runner – that is, leave the country for any reason – you use a dollop broker.'

It was dark. We were under the station bridge, queueing at the traffic lights so commuters could come staggering off the train in droves.

'There is none in the phone book.' So she'd looked.

'They aren't legal, love. They store stolen antiques, any quantity, for you to recover when it's safe for you to come home. Or out of clink. Or when the Statute of Limitations has expended – in Japan it's only a short time. Give you an example: you pinch paintings, say, from France, anywhere. You give your dollop of stolen paintings to a dollop broker. He guards them until you come for them, maybe years hence, and gives you them back, against a fee. You take your stolen paintings, whatever, to Japan. And sell them.'

'Why don't you hoard them yourself, where it's safe?'

I stared. Why can't people see the obvious?

'Well,' I explained as we started to move on the green. 'Just think. You're inside gaol, ten years for robbery, right? You have dolloped up – that is, given into the hands of a dollop broker – your loot, your valuable sculptures nicked from the British Museum. If you'd hidden them in Friday Wood, you'd have to wait until you got out. You'd be old, right? But with the loot in the hands of a dollop broker, why, you can sell the loot. To any other crook you wish to name. Bill of sale and everything. The loot is described somewhat differently than if they were coming up, say, at Christie's – in some code you've previously agreed with the dollop broker.'

She drew breath as we started up North Hill. 'Don't,' I said quickly to forestall her saying but that was illegal. 'It's done everywhere. All you need is to identify yourself to the dollop broker, and he'll surrender your goods –'

'Your *stolen* goods, Lovejoy,' she reprimanded primly.

'Until they get to Japan, or some other country where the Statute of Limitations is short. Then it's all legit. Out come your stolen Monets, Rembrandts, and you invest in Switzerland's holier-than-thou banking system, with the other mafiosi.'

'I've never heard the like.'

'You did it yourself, love,' I pointed out quietly. 'Today. You bought a bubby pot, a very valuable item, from an unsuspecting teacher, for a fifth of the value it realised at auction.'

'But that was legal, and *fair*, Lovejoy.' She gave the woman's too-patient smile.

She was proud of that, but somebody had to tell her. 'Will you send him the balance?'

'Of course not!' she cried indignantly, swerving in the traffic at the fork. 'You're talking of hiding, well, *stolen* goods! Crime's ill-gotten gains!'

'If you say so.'

Truce time. We arrived at the restaurant in the friendly silence armistice brings. But to me there's not all that much difference. I mean, on the one hand a bloke thieves some precious work of art and stashes it away in a dollop broker's shed or wherever, maybe gets caught, does his time. He then comes out and shifts it overseas and sells on the open market, possibly even at a famous multinational auctioneer's. And retires to blondes and a casino. On the other, you give a person a pittance, hoof it with his antique and keep the profit. The only difference is that one defrauds you of *all* the antique's value, and the other denies *most* of it. It's the sort of scandal everybody dreams of, you and me, kings and presidents. Oh, and antique dealers.

We dined, had a lovely candle-lit supper, becoming friendly and apologetic as the hours turned quiet and the town edged into slumber. She dropped me off at the cottage, and I went in to find my own brand of hell waiting.

At first I thought there was only one man waiting for me.

He was sitting on my chair. Bulky shadows behind the door told me he was well gooned.

Del Vervain's show is a scatty prattle-and-tune radio thing. Really boring, but so popular for so long that everybody knows his voice. It's interviews with the flighty and mighty. He does a written-

out patter of mind-bendingly dull boyish wit. Every so often he ushers
a new guest on, who grovels to set up Del's next punchline. He
occasionally slips into the vernacular, you-and-me friendly, changes
accents admirably. The standing joke is that Del's jokes are utter
dross, lines deliberately wrong. Del tops them with infantile slickness.
The audience is milked of every handclap. You've probably heard
it. It's really crud.

'Lovejoy. Sit down.' That magic accent.

I didn't, hoping a run was on the cards. In the corner of my
eye a shadow stepped a yard. I stayed where I was.

'You recognise me, I'm sure.' Del Vervain seemed about to make
a quirky remark, then remembered I was the only audience. Odd
to see him real, so familiar from the tabloid supplements. But
threatening.

'Yes.' I cleared my throat, tried it without falsetto. 'Yes. You're
on the wireless. Heaven With Vervain.'

'Bright, bright.' Somebody snickered behind me. 'You know my
wife Joan.'

Flat statement, denial out of the question. 'Yes.'

'You've been fucking her ragged, Lovejoy.'

Put that bluntly, my breath went away. 'Well, I, er –'

'She's going to take you away from . . . all this.' A casual look
brought a roomful of snickers, snuff-snuff-snuff.

'Nothing definite's been arranged. Honest.'

'No air tickets? No grand Rolls booked in Monaco? No marriage
ceremony? No media notified? The banks?'

'She's *talked* of a, er, flight. But the rest is news to me.'

'Honest?' He leant forward, smiling eyes questing over my face
as if in wonderment. 'Do you mean honest, Lovejoy?' Snuff-snuff-
snuff. Two goons? Three?

'Well, yes.' My squeaky throat had gone again.

'Honest is a word you seem to use rather a lot, Lovejoy.' He
clicked on a hand recorder. It whittered and a snatch of my
conversation came on, scratchy, but definitely me. I seemed to say
honest every second word. It was me in Woody's, fixing up a chop
on an item in Wittwoode's Auction.

'I'm an honest bloke.'

He smiled then, with relish. Sickeningly I knew what was going
to happen. He reached some letters off the table. They'd been
opened.

'Here,' I said indignantly. 'Those are my . . .'

'Air tickets, Lovejoy. New lease, apartment in Monte Carlo. Bank

accounts in your name. One account in joint names, you and . . .
guess who?'

I groaned. The stupid, stupid cow had jumped the gun. Monte
Carlo? I live here, for God's sake.

'I was going to talk her out of it,' I whimpered. 'Honest.'

'There you go again, Lovejoy. All honesty, no reality. I gather
you're famous for it.'

'It's a mistake. I wasn't ever going away with her. Honest – er,
truly.'

He stuffed the letters into a pocket, dropped an embossed
envelope on the table. Two nerks came into the light where I could
see how very big they were. Their noses were crushed, their foreheads
corrugated iron. Vervain went out as they started on me. First time
he's left anywhere without an exit line, I bet.

They belted me silly.

Some time later the phone rang. I dragged myself to it. Joan's voice
came on, breathless with secrecy and urgency and, I daresay, confidentiality.

'Lovejoy? Darling? I want to warn you. Del is absolutely *furious*.
We must go tonight. Be at Stansted Airport in three hours . . .'

I went to soak my face. Little bruising on the features, though
my ribs creaked and my skin was sore as hell. They must have
punched me unconscious, because somebody had stolen four hours
from the clock. I could hardly move my right thigh, swollen to a
tree trunk. It stung every time I moved. The fancy envelope contained an invitation from Mr and Mrs T. E. Vervain to nosh, days
hence. My mind was in its ? mode. It required no reasons.

Another hour later, the answerphone bleeped to tell the county
it was recording. A man's voice, old and querulous. 'Is there a
Lovejoy there, please? I have need to dispose of my son's antiques
business. I wish to obtain guidance – for a fee, of course. Please ring
Mr Fairclough, South Corn Mart, Norwich, any time between –'

Fairclough?

I reached for my one glowing neurone, and flicked it to snore.

CHAPTER SEVENTEEN

There's something wrily humorous about being beaten up – when you see it on that inert cinema screen. When it's real, well, no. It hurts like hell. Quite as bad, the shame makes you vomit and shiver even when you're over the worst. In fact, you're never sure which is the worst. Bruises mend, after all. Skin heals over. But the degradation lingers, festers, a core of hatred that never ever leaves. Like foxhunting must seem like poetry in motion – to the hunters. To the fox it's less than a giggle. I'll bet foxes never forget.

That morning I didn't answer the phone. I ignored sustained knocking. My curtains stayed drawn. Ignored the post girl's shower of catchpenny missives. Hermit Lovejoy. It was all of noon before I surfaced. I must say, superficially I looked pretty good. Not a mark, just a faint graze or two on the knuckles. I left the cottage – at a careful strolling pace, definitely not wincing at each step – as some bloody airport phoned, frantic about flight reservations. The messages could have a nice uninterrupted chat amongst themselves.

Delia welcomed me at St Peter's Church at the top of North Hill. That is, he was waiting to cross at the traffic lights near the linen shop and ignored me. People like Delia have this strange skill of directional non-greeting, to call attention to one specific person even in a crowd. Before I'd realised, I was strolling slo-o-o-wly, thigh hurting like hell, up the alley to the theatre coffee shop. The military figure in smart Savile Row clobber marched briskly ahead. Nobody goes there for midday nosh so there are crannies for people to meet.

'Bad, old bean?'

Delia hadn't glanced at me, but he knew all right. There must be something in Eton that tunes pupils in to the plights of others. Maybe so they can mostly ignore them, I shouldn't wonder.

'Wish I'd gone to Eton. Like Captain Hook.' I rummaged in my useless labyrinthine memory. 'Were you a contemporary of James Bond? Tarzan?'

Delia smiled. A waiter brought him coffee, none for me. He unfolded his *Financial Times* and absently started to read.

'Is it true you bounders literally used Shelley as a football?' Eton has this peculiar Wall Game. Nobody's scored since 1912.

The counter was vacated before he spoke. He hadn't risen to my jibes about Eton. 'Rum friends you have, Lovejoy. You might have warned me about the snake.'

Burglars have to take their chances, but I was ashamed.

'I did hint, Delia.'

'Put the fear of God in me, old boy.' He looked unruffled. I wondered if he wore his bowler hat on a job. 'When I depart, Lovejoy, you'll find a folder under the table by the door. Only imitation leather, I'm afraid, these days.'

'Oh, aye.' His faint headshake made me refrain from looking. Had he accomplices, then? 'What impressions?'

He read on a minute, tutting at some Share Index perfidy. 'Rum thing, all those tiresome underwater photographs, Lovejoy. Some old boat. Amazing hobbies, people, what? He's taking too low a price on his market garden. By a mile.' Tut tut tut.

He must mean Rye. 'And TGM?'

'You've got the lot, old fruit. Scan your folder.'

Photocopies of all Vell's clients' records? I gulped at the price Delia'd charge. Class tells, on an invoice.

'Money, Delia.'

He told the bill. I would have gulped again, but I couldn't. Delia's sort are deceptively casual. Default would leave me permanently damaged, with plenty of reproach that I lacked principles. No anger, though. A sigh or two, then on to the next job. Delia knew I knew this.

'Right,' I said heartily. 'Ta, Delia. I'll leave the money with Sandy in two hours. That okay?'

'Fine. If he's closed, drop it through his letter box.'

'But what...?' If you can't get in, I was going to say, like an idiot. I rose with a whimper, having to push myself up with fists on the table.

'Er, Delia. I'm sorry I was narked about Eton. Jealousy.'

'Don't give it another thought, old boy.' He smiled in reminiscence. 'We play a Wall Game, sort of rugby. I scored a hat-trick. I was pretty famous.'

'Great. Wish I'd been there. Cheers.'

'Chin chin, Lovejoy. I advertise in the Personals, if you need anything.'

Honour indeed. 'Ta, Delia.'

The folder was under the table. I collected it and left, feeling ashamed. Delia was class. So what, he pretended he'd been to Eton. I'll bet Eton wished he had.

'Mayor Carstairs?' I phoned from the bus station among throngs. Everybody seemed to be noshing enormous flat hamburgers. The place stank of fried onions. What did you call a Mayor, for God's sake? 'Lovejoy. Er, I need to contact Mrs Carstairs urgently –'

'You need to contact *me* urgently, Lovejoy.' In the permafrost, another angry bloke. I sighed. What is everybody always so narked about? I mean, have they nothing else to do? 'We have to discuss the degree of interaction which you and Mrs Carstairs have established –'

Well, once an administrator. 'I'll call, sir,' I intoned gravely, trying to disentangle my legs from some corgi yapping in pursuit of its minder, a little girl of six laughing her head off. 'I too see the necessity for analytical interim negotiation –'

'Are you being frivolous, Lovejoy?'

The frigging hound was back, barking deliriously. 'Her next antiques lesson is vital. Starts in half an hour.'

'Very well. I'll motor phone her. Where is this lecture?'

'I've arranged transport, sir. So if Mrs Carstairs could be at the post office in twenty minutes . . .' Et phoney cetera.

She came in a tearing hurry, eagerly hoping she wasn't late. I warmed, then quelled the feeling. I'd been as good as warned off Luna, and we hadn't yet made a single smile.

'I had to stop off for a notebook, Lovejoy! You should have *said!* I tried to catch you at the cottage, but you'd gone!' That explained all that knocking. 'I'm so looking forward to the lecture, Lovejoy. Should I have brought a lens thing? Only, the chemist's shuts for lunch and –'

A bus came. I drew her out of earshot.

'Luna. Take this folder. I had it stolen. Don't lose it, or we're sunk. I need a load of money. Now, to pay him.'

'You . . .?' She gaped, except her sort doesn't really gape. They raise eyebrows, look round vaguely then back to stare some more. But it does pretty well, as gapes go.

'There's no lecture, love. We're going to produce a load of antiques. Very speedily.'

'We are?' She did the gape. 'No lecture? We *are?*'

'Once you get the money to pay Delia, yes. To save somebody from being murdered.'

'Like that poor old –?'

'Very similar, love. Ouch.' She'd put her hand on my arm. 'Watch it, Lune. I, er, fell.'

She stepped back to appraise me, slowly nodded. 'Are you being blackmailed, Lovejoy?'

'No,' I said impatiently. 'Silly cow. You need a reputation to be blackmailed.' I would have glanced at the post office clock but there's only this red-glow digital kidding that the world is permanently fixed at 09–37 am and 68 celsius. 'The bank, love.'

'Have you had anything to eat, Lovejoy?'

'We had such a big supper last night.'

She went and got the gelt. She drove us down East Hill and I shoved it through Sandy's letter box in good time, so relieved I almost stopped groaning. Sitting in a motor when you've been kicked silly's even more painful than a bus ride.

'Are you all right, Lovejoy?'

'Fine, ta. Take us somewhere we can read Delia's loot, eh? Then the swimming baths. Then Calamity Jenny's.'

'Should you be going swimming if you're so stiff? Only –'

'Lune,' I said wearily. 'Just drive.'

She was frightened, or she'd have told me off. She hated being called Lune, but that was her fault, not mine.

We'd almost started to pull away from the kerb when a police car slowed, blocking us in. Cradhead got out, and approached at funereal pace.

I smiled and waved. He leant down, quite affable.

'Sorry I can't stop, Chief Superintendent. But I've a valuation for our Lady Mayoress. Perhaps some other time, eh?'

'Now, Lovejoy. You know I'm only a corporal.' He opened the door. 'Forgive me, Mrs Carstairs.'

He stayed there, holding the door wide. Cars crawled past, faces peering, the swine. I could be being kidnapped for all the action they took. They wear the same expression when having a nice drive out to ogle some shambles of a motorway accident.

'Very well, Commissioner.' I got out, unable to suppress a groan. 'Please don't think this happens every day, Mrs Carstairs. I do assure you. I am the most respected antiques expert in the Eastern Hundreds, for valuations, estimates, repairs –'

He coaxed me away, which is being dragged with your heels trailing. I saw Luna's stricken face, mutely urging her to get the hell out of it, seeing we'd just paid off Delia for stolen materials now on her back seat.

She called, 'Shall I follow, Lovejoy? Your folder –'

God Almighty. *Wave it around, you silly bitch* I tried to radar, but she dithered on the pavement.

'We'll go over your list later, Mrs Carstairs.'

'My list?' she asked, baffled.

My grin felt it weighed a ton. 'Of your antiques. And thank Oliver. I'll call him, soon as I've done with Superintendent Cradhead.'

That did it. Her expression wiped clean. 'Oh. I *see*, Lovejoy!' she said brightly. 'I'm to take the folder until you come for it!'

Put it in neon lights, love, I raged. I'd throttle her. We went to the police car and I got in, grunting.

'Gardening aches,' I said quickly. My ribs must be busted.

'Sitting comfortably, Lovejoy? Then read on.'

'A telephone number?' I looked on the reverse. Blank.

'It's yours.'

The other bloke in the motor chuckled, shaking his head. 'He's a one-off, right enough.'

'Mine? Fancy that.' I gave it back, waited. My heart was sneaking down nervously to my boots.

'Written in the shaky old hand of one Godfrey S. Fairclough. He'd not long phoned you, Lovejoy. Left you a message.'

The other nerk snickered. All ears and nicotine teeth.

'Here,' I said, narked. 'You had no right to break in and listen to my messages. It's against the law.'

Cradhead said, 'Lovejoy. One Godfrey S. Fairclough was injured by intruders. Fortunately, the assailants were disturbed by a door-to-door charity collector.'

'Why didn't you catch them?'

'How do you know we didn't?'

'You wouldn't be working up to your daft question.' He opened a palm, inviting it. 'Where was I on the night of the fifty-first? And did I do him.'

'And?'

'Daft, like I said.' I stared back at the other ploddite, who was trying to give me the bent eye. A laugh, really. Witnesses all around. A couple of kids were staring in, noses pressed to the windows. Drinkwater might be a nerk, but this Cradhead seemed to possess a rudimentary cortex.

'The collector almost caught a glimpse, but the foliage . . .' He hesitated. 'You know this Fairclough?'

He must be seriously injured, poor old bloke, or they'd be asking him instead of having to take my word for it. I shrugged.

'Parker. Go for a walk, will you?'

'You what?' Parker said, amazed. But he went.

'One of your brightest?' I said.

Cradhead sighed. 'It's these frigging courses, Lovejoy. They're never on the job. Sociology.'

I warmed to him. Somebody who hates sociologists can't be all bad.

'I don't know much, Craddie.' I thought I'd better get in first. 'Except that old bloke Godbolt who got topped was involved in some antiques thing. I've not heard for sure, but word is some shipment out to the US is on, through the Midlands. It seems a bigger shipment of antiques than we're used to.'

'Is it out, Lovejoy? Or in?'

In? This startled me, because it hadn't occurred to me. I decided I was wrong to warm to Cradhead. In fact, I wanted him on the next sociology course, preferably in Aberdeen.

'In?' I would have shrugged, if I could have done it without a screech. 'We don't *im*port antiques much, Craddie. don't you know the local scene? We *ex*port them, for coin of the realm.'

'Just a thought.' He patted my shoulder, harder than he needed. 'That was some gardening you did, Lovejoy. No hard climbing, no clobbering old gentlemen?'

'Del Vervain.' I had to admit it, or he'd turn as nasty as his gaffer. 'He got some thugs to do me over last night.'

He took the news calmly. 'Not going to Monte Carlo then?' He let me go, smiling and shaking his head. 'Time you settled down, Lovejoy. Oh, Drinkwater wants to see you. About a whole series of burglaries.'

'Series?' I said like a fool, startled.

'Sorry. Only two, weren't there? Ta-ta, Lovejoy.'

Delia's break-ins had been sussed, which was fine by me. Good old Delia, in the clear. I wished I was.

By the time I found Luna again, I'd almost worked out how much I owed her. It made me pale around the gills. No wonder hubby Oliver was having doubts about his wife's behaviour. But could I help it if she liked antiques? One thing: if Drinkwater wanted to see me, why did Cradhead let me go?

Poor old Fairclough.

CHAPTER EIGHTEEN

The swimming bath was heaving like a tin of maggots. Children of all ages screamed, plunged, had water fights. The echoing racket was deafening. Plasher was vigilant, never taking his eyes off the turmoil. He's the lifeguard, always in swimming trunks, never looks at you. He has a voice like thunder.

'Wotcher, Plasher.'

'Wotcher, Lovejoy.'

A score of children ran past, leapt howling on to the seething mass in the water.

Plasher bellowed, 'Less of that!' And unbelievably for a second the pandemonium faltered slightly before redoubling. I wish I could do that.

Luna was all admiring, thrilled at the spectacle of a zillion infants wriggling in water.

'Plasher, I want your brother to suss out some shipments. Big. Anywhere. Recent, within say a month. Back or front.'

'Okay.' And in his foghorn voice, a yell, 'Smithson – *out!*'

'Ta, Plasher.' I gave him the note with my phone number on and we left, almost deaf.

'What a marvellous man!' Luna said through a cotton-wool tunnel, thrilled. 'Controlling all those children! What did Mr Cradhead want?'

We drove out of town to Calamity Jenny's antique shop. I explained the way antiques were distributed by night lorrymen. 'They accept illicit loads, from laybys. You pay on mileage, plus extra for each switch, one lorry to another.'

'And that back or front business?'

'We want to know what big shipments were made last month, or are booked by night lorries next month.'

'Aren't they ever caught, Lovejoy?'

'The drivers? Their bosses know. If they stopped it, the drivers would walk out. So they condone.'

She drove without speaking until we were parked outside Jenny's. Here it comes, I thought. The big morality blip.

'Lovejoy.' She switched off. 'Why should I continue? Your apprentice, everything.'

'Eh?' It wasn't at all what I'd expected. But then nothing ever is. Even retrospect usually lets me down.

'It costs me a fortune. You don't pay me the money the National Employment pays for me. You don't tell me what we're doing. You are bad-tempered. Then you do *that*.'

'Do what?' Women can't be stopped when they're gabbing like this. It's like verbal sweat, has to come out. Then you can get on.

'You tell that hulk Plasher to do something, he agrees without question. You look so murderous sometimes. Then you picked up that little girl when she'd grazed her knee and was crying.'

See what I mean? There'd been this titchie girl with a leg that needed blotting. She'd shaken my trouser leg, so I'd sucked her knee pale to stop it blooding. Because I was nearest, you silly cow, I thought in exasperation. So?

A girl – no more than nineteen – was peering out of the shop and beckoning. Jenny? Big Frank's wives were getting younger every single marriage.

'There's Jenny!' I exclaimed, and escaped out.

The welcomes over, I had a quick look about Calamity Jenny's place. Very affluent, very splendid buying. Not all true stuff, of course, but it surpassed Luna's feeble description of 'Really quite nice, Lovejoy'. And Jenny herself? 'R.q.n, Lovejoy'. That had been the sum of Luna's earlier exploration.

She was beautiful. Pretty with that wicked winsomeness any man'd go for. I could see why Big Frank had placed her top of his next electoral roll, so to speak. Luna overdid the merry prattle, until I told her to nark it and come and look. She tried telling me she'd already seen most of Jenny's antiques. A laugh. She might have been in their presence, but hadn't *seen* one.

Big Frank had succumbed to Jenny's beauty, yes. Another reason was that she had a ton of silver, some fake, some Belgian and north French and not hall-marked. And (watch out for this) plenty of the new silver they've been turning out like Ford cars in Lebanon and Egypt. The trick is to take a genuine piece of antique silver abroad on your holidays, complete with Customs and Excise stamps, all that 'snow', as necessary documentation is called. Then in Alexandria, Cairo, Calcutta, you have the piece copied by their silversmiths of prodigious skills. Reimport them into Great Britain's frantic antiques silver markets, and sell them as genuine antiques. If you're going to try this, go only for 'clean-line' styles. That means the earlier the better. In fact, I'd even say fake all silver before 1730.

'Any of these Indian, love?'

Luna smiled, clapped her hands. 'I've *checked* the hallmarks of those sugar tongs, Lovejoy! They're Paul de Lamerie's marks, 1728.'

She was being all thrilled again. 'You see, Lovejoy? I did what you said. *I looked them up!*'

'The marks are fake, love,' I explained as Jenny blushed fetchingly. 'They're not sharp. If a silver mark looks sort of soft, blurred a bit, it's probably fake.'

'Fake?' Luna rummaged for a little paperback which listed silversmith marks. I'd come across her reading it. 'But –'

'Fakers are greedy, love. They think in shillings, pennies. And they're slovens, usually. They know they're duff workers. They make fake dies out of soft metal, see? Brass, copper, even tin. Not the hard metal required.'

'You mean . . .?' Luna coloured up, looked at Jenny, who was still being winsome. 'Shouldn't we tell the . . .?'

God Almighty. Still thinking like a member of the public, and her an apprentice antique dealer.

'Jenny had them made, Luna,' I laboured. Luna was proving heavy load. 'She wasn't tricked into buying them. And they aren't sugar tongs. That's a tongue scraper.'

'For . . .?' Luna felt at the sprung silver's spatulate ends.

'A tongue scraper. For – forget it.' I flapped my hands. I was talking a private language, no means of contact.

'It's no good getting ratty, Lovejoy.' Luna was now unthrilled. Deo gratias. 'I'm doing my best. You never tell me what we're *doing*. You were cross yesterday because I couldn't remember how to tell a real chastity belt from a modern –'

Et reproachful cetera. I'd told the silly cow ten times. Let her get on with it. I ignored her. 'They Indian, Jenny?'

'The silvers?' She reached into a small decorative inglenook taken from an old cast-iron industrial fireplace range. 'These were done in the Isle of Man. What d'you think?'

The punches weren't too bad, but soft metal again. Possession is illegal. I interrupted Luna's deplorings to tell her this small fact. She silenced, stared in amaze at Jenny.

'The silver-mounted meerschaum pipe bowls are Cairo,' Jenny said proudly.

She had a collection of pipes, all eroticas – mouths doing wonderful things, frank anatomical organs, and figures of couples busy, er, coupling. Very valuable now, if genuine mid-Victorian.

Luna said, 'I thought those looked almost . . .' She paled. They looked almost because they were.

'Erotica's in, love. Especially tobacciana, which is a dying thing. Forgive the pun.'

Luna gave up, settled for wonder. As soon as we were driving away she'd tell me sternly that Jenny wanted a good smacking for being so, well, absolutely *bold* . . .

'Meerschaum means sea foam, Lune,' I relented. 'It's a sort of natural porous mineral, silicate of magnesium. You can carve it, work it even with a small file. Chosen because it keeps the tobacco smoke cool, see? Insmoked and new, it isn't that meerschaum amber colour. That's only the nicotine. But fakes −' I smiled fondly at Jenny. 'Fakes come ready stained.'

'They're *horrible*, Lovejoy. They're people *doing*, well, *things*.' Luna was so distressed, poor lass.

'Any one'd buy a car, love. If really Viennese.' Austria made them a national art in the nineteenth century.

Yes, silver was one of Jenny's things. Her collection was incoherent, in spite of this. She must have vaccuumed all that Big Frank had missed. And she'd imported fakes enough to sink a ship. Ship? Time I looked at the photographs and papers Delia had burgled for me. He'd mentioned some sunken vessel. But erotica was distracting, making me think of Jenny. Big Frank's Jenny. Not mine.

'Jenny. Big Frank wanted me to call.'

'Yes, Lovejoy.' She glanced at Luna, still being mesmerised by the meerschaums, and raised her eyebrows faintly. She was making the oldest offer. I brightened, then sombred. Big Frank was going to wed this lissom lass. Minimally I shook my head. Jenny gave a rueful smile, shrugged.

'I want some things divvied. Imported. High class. Soon.'

'Where?'

'Hawkshead.'

'Okay.' I smiled, but with an effort. 'Fix time with Luna.' I bussed her. She moved her mouth more than is customary. I was still gulping when I waved at her shop window. Big Frank was in for multo hallelujah choruses, once he'd got rid of his wife and got wed.

And in the motor it happened. Luna suddenly proved her worth. We were hardly on to the Lavenham road.

'That young lady's up to no good,' she said reprovingly. 'She should still be at school. I mean, all those holidays to Cyprus! If she were my daughter I'd censure her.'

We'd gone miles before the penny dropped. *What* was that?

'Pull in, love.'

'I can't just yet. That little tractor has right of way −'

I yelled, 'Pull in for Christ's sake can't you do a frigging single thing I tell you just for once instead of giving me frigging lip back everything I say?' Hardly the English of Milton. She pulled in, to a merry cacophony of motor horns and one bawled obscenity. Ignition off, and furious reproach.

'Lovejoy! I will not be spoken to −'

'Cyprus? What about Cyprus?'

'Cyprus?' Her brow unwrinkled. 'Miss Calamy goes a lot to Cyprus. I told you, Lovejoy.'

I leaned away to look at her. 'What did you tell me?'

'Of all the . . .' She saw my raised finger, drew a calming breath. 'If you *must*, Lovejoy. She said she only went once, to Paphos. But she was fibbing. She goes to the eastern side. And far too often. She's a child. My daughter Lola's age!'

'More than once?' Jenny saying she holidayed once when she went plenty was a very, very significant lie. Not without serious implications for life and death.

'Several times. I only discovered it accidentally.' Her mouth set sternly. 'This is confidential, Lovejoy. You promise?'

'Hand on my heart.' Some folk never leave Planet Mongo.

'I was in her shop, first visit. She was on the phone. Some stupid airline clerk. Though I know how she felt, Lovejoy. Sometimes they are hopeless. Once, Oliver took me to −'

'Cyprus?' I cued desperately.

'Yes.' Luna was Mrs Surprise. 'You don't even have to go via Geneva at all. Jenny said she *always* went that way. There's an excellent direct service from Heathrow, though the arrival time −'

I swear I'm the most patient bloke on earth. I can prove it. I didn't even thump her. She tutted at being restrained from criticising a pretty younger bird, but clinched it.

'Jenny told the stupid booking agent she'd been seven times lately and *always* caught the same flight. To meet her friend.' Luna shook her lovely hair in admonition. I suddenly saw how very gorgeous she looked. 'I should have gone straight to the managing director −'

My mind pretended to hear her out. 'Turkish Cyprus, then?'

'Yes. I'm not exactly sure where she goes, but −'

But I did. Clear as day, sure as taxes.

'Come here, Lune.' I dragged her head close, sucked her luscious mouth longer than mere approval allowed. She came up gasping, pink-faced, looking round in embarrassment in case gawpers lurked nearby. A passing lorry driver bipped in cheery salutation, earning a serious tut.

'No more of *that*, Lovejoy! What on earth would Oliver think? No wonder he −'

'You're beautiful, Lune,' I said. She was radiant. All women have allure. But some really reach in. 'I could eat you.' She was doing her stare. 'Drive us home, love. Sharp.' I honestly don't know how I managed to keep my hands off her.

She drove, looking at me from time to time.

In the end, she compromised. Which to a bird is doing exactly what she wants. She dropped me at the cottage and drove away in a racing start.

A pity. In the end it didn't matter much. Using my new water-cooled phone I got Hilda – receptionist in Knowles Travel – to come by on her way home.

Hilda's a constant and smiley long-time-no-see but what're-we-doing sort. A friend, I suppose I'm saying. I chucked her brochures away as soon as she'd gone. Then I caught the bus into town, hired a car from Ogden's on Luna's credit. Then lit out north. I reached Hawkshead at eleven o'clock.

Hawkshead. Roar up the motorway through Lincolnshire, after a couple of hundred miles you come to a service station. Loos, nosh bar, restaurant, slot machines, and inevitably one of those widespread yellow-lit shops filled with things you'll never need in a million years – London policemen dolls, toffee moulded into gruesome creatures, plastic bugles. Outside, roaring traffic, and acres of vehicles pausing to buy chocolate dwarfs.

Until night, when suddenly you notice how lonely the place actually is. An oasis of light in a dark and louring hilly landscape. It's then that it happens.

The place becomes an antiques market. Vans arrive, and park far from the lights. While the motorway below roars with night traffic, dealing begins. A score of pantechnicons drop their tailboards and reveal interiors crammed with antique furniture, porcelain, flintlocks, paintings. It's joked that you can buy back your precious bow-front corner cupboard, stolen in the morning, at ten o'clock the same night in Hawkshead.

Some very heavy goons lurk there. Like a nerk I'd left my pencil torch behind. I depended on the dealers' rigged battery lights. I wandered, had sweet tea and a pasty – good pasties at Hawkshead – and sussed out the place. It felt like home.

The people to avoid are the bloggers. Tonight they were here aplenty. These hoodlums follow you home, and burgle/rob/mug, stealing the antiques you've just bought. They're in collusion with the antique dealers themselves, who get their – read *your* – lovely antique back an hour after they've sold it. They sell it again tomorrow and tomorrow and tomorrow. Recycling at its best. I was tempted, but desisted. There were a couple of baluster pewters – waists, a handle, a lid with a knob. Tip: go for hammerhead knobs, ball knobs, or bud-shaped ones. Of course, they'll be expensive. Pewter is definitely in. Find a King James vessel taller than seventeen and three-quarter inches, you can spit in your boss's eye and retire for life.

This far north I didn't know too many faces. I was glad. It gave me the chance to talk to Nuala (you've to say Noola) from Belfast. She's a pretty lass with Celtic colouring – blue eyes, hair jet. She runs a ferry line with her dad. This doesn't mean they steer ships, only that they operate two businesses – Belfast and Liverpool – as one, using the ferry. Nuala is heap big business, and she's only twenty.

'Hello, love. How's Sean?'

'Lovejoy! Nice to see you. Dad's fine, thanks.'

You don't buss Ulster folk as greeting, only in serious snogging. Meekly I kept my distance. 'He doing anything?'

'He'll be down East Anglia, soon. He'll call.'

'And be welcome.' News indeed. Four blokes suddenly were standing close. Nuala travels mob-handed. I prattled inanities until they drifted off, disappointed at not having to club me insensible. 'Here, Nool. Sean interested in a Snettisham?'

Nuala raised a beckoning finger. A couple of wiry Liverpudlians stepped from a pantechnicon and took over her pitch. We climbed into the driver's cab. She lit up the longest cigarette I'd ever seen. 'You serious, Lovejoy?'

'Not for me, Nool.' I shrugged, looking down. These cabins are high off the blinking ground. Like flying. 'Too rich. You'd need a dollop broker in your pocket. And who's got one of those?'

'Dad, Lovejoy.' She's a cool girl, is Nool. I wish I had one like her. In fact, she herself'd do at a pinch. Except she's married to a Manchester racecourse grifter. You leave those alone. Sean, her dad, had done time for a series of church robberies. He'd made a fortune selling the antiques when he got released. Which meant he'd used a dollop broker.

'That your stained glass on the blanket, love?

Antiques placed casually on a blanket at these fly-by-night gatherings claim to be genuine. Fakes stand on the tarmac.

'Interested? Genuine, Lovejoy. I had Donk lift a piece of calme to show the glass's edge –'

'Tch. Silly cow, Nool.'

She laughed. 'Sorry, Lovejoy. I forgot you'd know.' Medieval glaziers had no steel-wheels or diamond knives, so they nibbled the glass's edges with a notched thing called a grozing iron. Moth-eaten margins under the lead calmes mean genuine ancient stained glass. I've never known this test lie.

'Scotch, is it?'

She laughed again, getting the joke. There is no surviving medieval Scotch stained glass.

'A dollop broker's too big for me, Nool. You have to deposit, what, ten per cent? Jesus!'

'That'd be my problem, Lovejoy. Whose Snettisham?'

'Promise you'll use an East Anglian?' I glanced about, all suspicion, worrying I was overdoing it. 'Reason is, we've a local lady dolloper. Once did me a favour. Okay?'

Nuala's frown vanished. She grinned. 'Miss R is the one Da used! She's marvellous. Deal?'

'Deal, Nool.' I chuckled. 'Miss R's great.'

'Da was annoyed she wasn't willing at first. He had to take *me* along! I was only fourteen! The year she started broking.' Oh, how we laughed.

I chanced an arrow. 'Same with me. My sister.'

'Once a teacher, always.'

My mind went: Miss R. Teacher. East Anglian antiques dollop broker six years. *Deals only with females!* I haven't got a sister.

I quickly invented, 'The finder's one of three Beccles treasure-seekers. They've shown me a torc. Genuine. There's the usual gamekeeper trouble. The gold is being sussed by a tame museum scientist. Okay?'

We mused possibilities, then shook hands on it. I lowered myself to resume my earthly wanderings.

A Snettisham is a major treasure-trove find. Called after the mega one at Ken Hill in Snettisham, Norfolk. There, over thirty-eight precious torcs – neckbands of Ancient British tribal kings – were found, with two dozen bronze torcs, coins, bangles, ingots. The decent old gent whose gadget bleeped them into King's Lynn Coroner's Court was a sterling character. He was unbelievably honest. Actually had asked the land-owner's permission to treasure-hunt. And reported his stupendous discovery to archaeologists and the British Museum. Knowing he might not get a penny (our daft Law of Treasure Trove dates from 1195 AD, believe it or not), still this gentleman behaved with absolute propriety. It's true.

Other treasure-hunters are not so loyal or honest. Our loony law states that treasure originally *hidden* goes to the Crown – i.e. national museums. Treasure originally *lost* is the finder's. (Get it? It's the very opposite of finders keepers. Finders = losers). Since we're talking 70 BC, outguessing some pre-Roman warrior chieftain means you'll probably get zilch from your mind-boggling discovery of, what, 30 million pounds sterling.

Is it any wonder treasure-seekers, 'moonspenders', 'moonies', as they're called, mostly sell their loot secretly and say nothing? Rotten laws make rotters.

A couple of hours more I strolled, noshed. Saw antiques come and go. There was only one fake I'd made myself, a lovely 1852 painting by C. J. Lewis of two ladies with dogs on punts. Chocolate-box sort, of course, but now all the rage. I was pleased to see it go in exchange for a trio of 'traveller's pieces'. People think these tiny pieces of furniture were salesmen's or apprentices' samples. They're not. They were simply for doll's houses, children's toys. Highly sought these days. They show us the authentic furniture of the time.

Smug, I drove homeward at two in the morning. Miss R was the dollop broker for Jenny Calamy's importing trips to Cyprus.

That lovely island is split into two chunks. Turkish, Greek. I'm not knocking any one political system, honest I'm not. And people conquer people, don't they, bend them to their will. We of these islands know this. I merely report that, with Cyprus split, a mighty change came about in Ancient World antiques. All of a sudden, great shipments happened. Geneva's the centre, Munich the residence, of the modern loot bootleggers. The fact that the antiques are plundered from the churches, houses, schools of Cyprus is ignored. Buyers have plenty of money for the genuine thing. The Greek Government has been forced into being a serious buyer, to recover Greek art from the looters' middlemen. It's not new, in this terrible world. In 1258, when Baghdad was sacked by Hulegu the Mongol, the Tigris ran black – with the ink of the city's priceless manuscripts dumped in the river. We're the predators.

It would be somewhere not far from Lythrankomi, where Jenny went so often, via Geneva. Had to be. The buyer would probably be from Munich. The loot would be priceless mosaics, ikons, paintings, church furnishings, religious jewellery. The shipment would be large – and for large read *large*. Everything would be unbelievably genuine. Jenny'd gone to a deal of trouble and expense to acquire Big Frank's marriage proposal. Birds do this sort of thing. I once knew a Southminster girl who pretended she loved cricket – went to matches all through one long wet summer, finally married the opening bowler. Never seen another match since. Fiancée fans, you might call them. Love-stricken as Jenny purported to be, she'd all but offered me the family vault when I'd hesitated. So she was more than a little desperate to have me divvieing. She'd needed Big Frank, so she'd acquired some silver, as a lure. It's the one thing he could never resist. She'd persuaded Big Frank to ask my help, to divvie her imported loot. Big Frank for protection, Lovejoy for authenticity. She was going to import a huge Cypriot shipment, via Hawkshead, direct to the mysterious Miss R, dollop broker.

Good old Luna. I'd catch it tomorrow – today – from her, of course. I retired smiling at the thought of her eyes, staring wide and astonished into mine.

CHAPTER NINETEEN

It was the day of the nosh party at Del Vervain's. No chance of ducking it, of course.

I was tying my tie the new American way. There used to be two ways: the old over-over knot, and the Windsor. Both slip. It took umpteen centuries until a 92-year-old Yank invented Method Three. Start seam out, wide end under wrap wide end over and again under the short bit. Tighten. Cross wide bit to your right then under, shove it through down. Voila! Right way out, and non-slip! Good old Yanks. Mind you, a cravat'd be the thing. James II's coronation cravat, lace of course, cost thirty-six pounds ten shillings. You can buy genuine ancient lace cravats for less than that even today. If only I knew which lace cravat was King James' . . .

'Think what we've done, so far, love,' I told Luna the instant she arrived. Different motor, I saw with admiration. A low sleek job, shape of a sucked toffee, electric blue. I set her cooking my fried bread and tomatoes while I thought. 'We've got facts, but no solutions. And antiques.'

'You ought to explain, Lovejoy.' She looked good enough to chew. Style, high heels and smart, better than a New Year sale. No mention of my earlier gratitude. 'I'm confused.'

Explain what? I didn't know myself. But the Lunas of this world expect omniscience from adjacent males.

'I'm almost sure what's going on, love,' I lied easily. 'I'll sum it up tomorrow.' For me too. 'Say what you *think* we've done. I'll say if you're close.'

'Well,' she began doubtfully, slicing tomatoes. 'Poor Mr Godbolt died. The police still think foul play.'

'Right!' I praised. Actually, the Plod would be at the boozer, until Prammie Joe faded from memory. 'Anything else?'

'Connie asked you –' I raised a finger. She smiled shyly. 'Connie asked *us* to divvie her antiques at the disused aerodrome. And to fuff them out for a major sale.'

'Excellent!' I started on the bread and tea. My technique is mop-and-nosh, unaided by cutlery.

She coloured up slightly, attended to the stove. 'Miss Alors, the, ah, street lady has diverted a load of handies, small stolen antiques, to another buyer instead of yourself. Jenny Calamy wants you to assist the sale of her antiques.' She deftly stepped back as the next load of sliced tomatoes slid into the hot margarine. 'I don't care for that young lady, Lovejoy.'

'Mmmh. Very forward.'

'She's had everything. Splendid school background . . .'

Hang on. I paused, slice of sopping bread halfway across the plate. What had Vell said? Some marvellous school? She was from one not so posh, something like that? Of Cassandra Clark.

'. . . especially Big Frank, all those wives. Of course, I blame the woman. I mean, a man's obviously swayed by anything flighty . . .' Woman blame woman. But interesting. Schoolmates?

'We've burgled Rye Benedict's mill shop that's never open. And Marvella's flat at the old Meeting House. We went to the River Deben. You asked Miss Brewer about the little boy falling into the water. We've asked Plasher at the swimming baths for a great many fake antiques . . .'

'What's up?' She was slow with the next plate, silly cow, staring into space with rapture. 'I'm starving.'

She turned, thrilled times ten. 'Did you *hear* me, Lovejoy? I've talked with prostitutes, fakers, thieves, rogues!' She spoke the word with relish. '*Gaolbirds!* Can you believe it?'

'I will, if I survive.'

'Oh, sorry.' She hurried with the grub.

'Which leaves us with quite an interesting day. You'll meet Tinny today. Object: to come gathering nuts in May, Lune.'

'Luna, please, Lovejoy. And you gather –'

I held up a soaked slice. 'It's a saying, Lune. You *can't* gather nuts in May, see? Soon as you've fried the next lot, get out the stuff Delia stole for me.'

'Us, Lovejoy. Us.'

That gave me pause for a second. I agreed, 'Us, love.'

The folder held two sections. One was Vell's records of her clients. I was surprised at the diversity of people who went. Luna raised her eyebrows at my name there, but I explained I'd been trying to get the list, legit means first.

A score of antique dealers were in. Connie, Tits Alors. And, making Luna go quiet, one Oliver J. Carstairs, Mayor. Regularly, once a fortnight. More women than men. Now, some things are really certain. It's that women go to dentists, health classes, all those sort of things, more than men. They're more practical. We hide; they don't. But I'd seen Cassandra Clark chatting in Vell's after a massage-and-horoscope session. And Cassandra Clark wasn't in the records at all.

'Odd,' I mused. Delia was the ultimate pro. He'd not have missed a card. How the heck had he photocopied this lot?

Which left Rye Benedict's dull stuff. I told Luna to get on with sussing those while I finished dressing and saw to the birds' nuts. She was sitting staring at them – just a series of rather blotchy photographs and a few maps – when I said I was ready.

'Lovejoy. Why do people go to The Great Marvella?'

'Eh? Why . . .' Then I thought, yes. Why? To do what? Massage? Then horoscope? Talk with Geronimo about the future? I suddenly realised I honestly didn't know.

Luna clearly suspected Hubby Oliver went there to make smiles, thinly disguised. Maybe Vell was a posh kind of . . . well, a Tits Alors with a meeting house of a special kind.

'Dunno, love. Honest.' I'd told her about the snake, the fortune-telling act, the ventriloquism,˙how daft it all was. I didn't tell Lune that Vell feeds Geronimo on live mice. I looked over her shoulder at Rye's secret photographs.

An underwater boat? That shape, anyway. I found myself tracing its outlines with a finger while I explained to Lune about how a man with work stress would need a massage.

'Oliver maybe has to go, for Council reasons.' I expounded a new theory of commercial development of Priory Street and the old ruins. She looked disbelieving.

'He's never mentioned it, Lovejoy.'

'No, of course he couldn't!' I cried, mechanically shuffling Rye's photocopies while I tried to invent an alibi for her bloody husband. More than Oliver'd do for me. 'It's confidential! All Council work is. Look, love. If people knew there was some development going on, why, the Council would lose a fortune! Everybody would snap up those small shops . . .'

Boat. Sunk, but definitely a boat. With a huge arc project-ing from the mud. A paddle-wheel? The photograph looked murky. A fish faced the camera, thunder-struck at light where there should be none. The maps were charts. Sandbanks. Submerged wrecks, marked with symbols. Photos of a wreck? Maps of submerged sands? Surely Rye wasn't falling for the old I've-got-a-sunken-galleon con? Then I thought. I actually recognised one particular map. The coast between the Colne and Deben estuaries. Weakly, I faced what I knew I'd been shunning, and drew out of a drawer the folded paper from Prammie's. One was a tracing of the other, done by a slow patient hand. A pencilled note: *Only place X, if less than 40'.*

I leafed through the photos as Luna explained her deep trust in her Oliver. And found it. One picture was jubilantly overwritten, massive initials in ballpoint: *IKB!!!* with half-inch marks along it. Somebody's scale, of a sunken paddle-boat? Isambard Kingdom Brunel, IKB. Who never worked on the east coast. His was the *Great Eastern*, the mightiest iron ship of all. Rye Benedict's hero.

'Eh?' Lune was still on about her frigging Oliver.

'Do you suppose Oliver has had a premonition? He has a bad back –'

'Sod Oliver. Get your knickers on, Lune. We're off.'

That quietened her down, otherwise we'd be there yet. Some people simply ask for it.

'Tinny, Luna. My apprentice.'

Tinny's a container bloke from Felixstowe. He's always ready to do a deal, any antiques, any size of order. He was admiring a painting, *The Falls on the Caravogue* by Jack B. Yeats, the Irish painter. In fact, so was I. I'd painted it about a year since. I love it. Sold it to Suki Sharland for love, one terrible lonely night. She happens to be the most beautiful bird in this land. Tell you about her some time.

'Tinny? How d'you do?' from Luna. She'd worried all the way about Oliver's possible need for Marvella's massage. Her powerful prowly motor turned out to be a Jaguar, one of the sort you have to call by letters, XKX and that. My face felt three miles back.

The yard of Tinny's small firm looks like a builder's supply merchant. Bricks, pipes, paving flags, sheds, timber. It's a front. He gets really narked if genuine customers come, wanting nails and suchlike. It's a staging post for containers shipped to and from Belgium, which are filled with renegade antiques.

'Tinny,' I corrected. 'When was it, Tinny?'

He smiled modestly. 'Three years gone, Lovejoy.'

'Tinny had himself shipped inside a container. Room size. Filled with antiques. Takes his job seriously, does Tinny.'

'Ever since, they've called me Tinny. Tin Can, see?' He smiled with pride, a wizened little bloke with an oddly protruberant belly, waistcoat, watch-chain and all. He looks a dehydrated bookie, but is all there.

'It was that fire in Norfolk. The great house at –'

'Pentlesham Major?' Luna cried. 'I remember it! Seventeen

paintings, all burned!' Her thrilled mode again. She was getting the hang of the antiques game. Not before time.

'And?' I prompted, with mute apology to Tinny.

'And . . .' She worked it out, after apologising to Tinny. 'And Mr Tinny took the paintings to the Continent to sell, because . . . *they hadn't been burned at all?*'

'Bravo, lady!' Tinny patted her hand while Luna blushed. I liked that. She fluffled out like a preening bird.

'We want at least a can, Tinny.'

'Christ, Lovejoy. You don't ask much, do you?'

A customer drove in, parked, got out and looked around at the fence-posts.

'How much, mate? There's no prices marked.'

'Get stuffed,' Tinny called over.

'You *what?* You'll never make any sales with that attitude!' The customer drove off in high dudgeon, shouting that he'd go to Blakeson's at Nine Ash Green, serve everybody right.

'Get on my nerves,' Tinny grumbled.

Luna stayed silent. Like I said, learning. A couple of days back she'd have given him a lecture on business charm.

'Right, Lovejoy. Two weeks?' It was very reluctant.

'Sooner, Tinny. Four days?'

'I'll do what I can.'

Luna asked what had we asked for. I told her Tinny would get us a container shipment of antiques four days from now. Tinny never lets me down. Except I'd caught his worried frown. It was old time's sake doing me the favour, not Tinny.

So others, probably instant payers, wanted the same. And just as fast. I told Lune. She was indignant, said the very idea and what cheek it was for others to want what we wanted.

'Now,' I said. 'Station, please. Got enough for the train?'

'Can't we go by car?'

'No. It's their London flat, not their local shed.' Also, I didn't know if I was going to get beaten up again. Del Vervain's mobsters might abstain if they knew I had Luna along. She wouldn't go over big with Joan. True love never does run smooth.

The Vervains occupied one of those flats that seem divorced from reality. In darkest crammed London, they stand aloof, away from it all behind tall iron railings. The gate was surmounted by lions. Paving, mostly, with a few jardinières but no Sèvres porcelain. That would be a real find. I told Luna I live in hopes.

'What are we here for, Lovejoy?'

'Eh? Oh, this invitation.'

She looked with horror. 'You mean you –?' She would have clawed my eyes except the door opened.

'I thought you'd be pleased,' I grumbled. There's no pleasing women. Here I was, taking her to the lovely London home of a famous radio personality, and she flies off the handle.

'I'll kill you, Lovejoy,' she said through a fixed grin as Joan and Del Vervain advanced to welcome her. Luna started apologising, for not having known, that she hadn't had time to go and change, the whole grovel.

'So you're Lovejoy!'

Vervain announced this. He meant, pretend we haven't met before, Lovejoy, or else. It felt like being given gracious permission to hereafter call myself my own name. He was definitely tubby. He was living up to his reputation, already well-soaked. Irish whiskey, by all accounts.

I shook his hand, a flabby dough-filled glove of a thing, made the feeblest stab at bussing Joan. I'd have been clouted as a little lad for such a half-hearted calling kiss. Her eyes startled me. She looked lovely, cocktail frock in a rich royal blue. Real pearls, a double choker, and a pearl bangle. Mid-Victorian, and suffering, but that's what pearls go through. I could have throttled the stupid bitch for the slow murder she was inflicting on such lovely jewellery. Pearls must *never* be worn against a skin sprayed with perfume. Yet the silly cow had –

'Eh? Oh, may I present Mrs Lune Caterer, Mayoress of –'

'Luna Carstairs. I've met Mrs Vervain. At your workshop, Lovejoy.' Luna raised her game, smiling, admiring the lovely hallway, but I could tell by the red dots on her cheeks that she really would murder me when she got me somewhere safe.

'Come in. What's your poison?'

'Orange juice, please.' Luna bravely faced the flak of Joan's interrogative gaze. I said and me. We were taken by the hail-fellow-well-met sweaty Vervain into the company.

Three other guests, all seemingly stamped out by some machine round the corner. Girls, lank of hair and drab of garb, skeletally thin and smoking with edginess bordering on the frantic. All were well into their poteen. One quite stoned.

'This is Lovejoy. Count all available rings!' Vervain held the shot for some imaginary applause. Pause, two three, then a quick capper, 'I mean jewellery, nothing anatomical!' Chuck-chuck-chuck and move on. The girls tittered, looked at me with hard appraisal.

Christ, I thought. The bloke's a cipher, a print-out.

'Catch my show, Lovejoy?' asked His Heartiness.

'A few times.' I was going to say only the start, but caught Joan's sharp reminding glance and went, 'It was quite good.'

He'd actually started to preen when the words hit him.

'*Quite . . .*' He managed the word. It hung alone in the vast room. I waited, looking out into the lovely walled garden. I bet myself those bricks were truly William IV. It was about then that red brick became imperative for gardens.'. . *Good?*'

He sounded choking, ready for a duel. What had I said? I thought I'd given him a compliment. Amiably I looked about.

'Hey, Lovejoy,' one slightly staggering lass said. 'You in the presence of thee repeat twice thee Mister Personality of ever-ee radio band in the wide countree, y'know it?'

'Yes, we have met.'

Once before, I met some broadcasters. They frightened me to death. Like now. But none of them scared me like the look in Joan's eyes. My view kept finding her bright, brilliant eyes somehow even if I wasn't looking. They looked wrong. And women don't as a rule have wrong eyes, do they? I'm hooked on faces. I can't help it. Sometimes I'm caught staring at a face just for nothing, and create the wrong impression. But faces are great, aren't they? Except when they're wrong. The eyes are something people forget. Babies and little children know the truth about faces and eyes. They can spot a dud miles off. I think that's why they always grin at me straight away, knowing an easy touch.

'He for ree-yull, team?' The staggery one flopped, beckoning for more sustaining fluid.

'Exactly my question!' Del Vervain cried. He affected a suit that looked cut by some trainee tailor with the wrong scissors. Image again.

I hadn't a clue what they were on about. Luckily Luna took up the gauntlet.

'Oh, Mr Vervain! My husband and I think your show is absolutely marvellous! Why don't you do it on Sundays too? It's lovely. The way you say that . . .' The three lankies from Alpha Centauri nodded, flicking ash, sipping, murmuring.

Del grinned modestly. 'All er-rightee too-nightee!' he intoned. The girls beamed, 'Great-great-*great!*'

And Luna, to my embarrassment, almost fainted with delight, exclaiming, '*Yes!* Oh, Mr Vervain! We think it's the best thing!'

That was what I'd done wrong. I'd forgotten to worship his ego.

He was addicted to worshippers, fawners, acolytes. Without them he would vanish. In fact, as I turned to That Look in Joan's eyes, I actually saw him become a different person. Genuinely twinkly, humorous, jokey and welcoming. To Lune, that is. Me, I was written out of his script of existence. It gave me a chance to talk quietly to Joan.

'I'm sorry, love,' I told her. 'I couldn't escape the invitation. His blokes beat me up. Is there somewhere we could meet?'

The best I could do to stay in her good books. It gave me the chance of a look at her eyes.

They were a-glitter, expectant, almost as thrilled as Luna's. I'd expected anger, calm shielding her inner distress. But she looked like some bird about to go to a boxing match. You know, that deep intensity which women show at savagery. Mystically charmed, by the prospect of violence. She smiled a confined smile, wetting her lips, and drifted me aside.

'Shhh, Lovejoy. Careful.' A roar of laughter from Del's admirers gave cover. 'Go along with what Del suggests. It's the best thing ever. For us, darling. I'll come soon.'

'Come?' I said in dismay. Tried again, brighter. 'Come?'

'Your cottage. He's starting a new contract. I've missed you, darling.'

'I've missed you, Joan.' Not with those eyes I hadn't. I'd rather have her old eyes, brittle with anger, delirious with –

'Hey, Lovejoy. Do your divvie trick, hey?'

Sod it. Party time. 'If you want, Mr Vervain.'

'Del, if you pull-lease.'

Another riot. Admiration's great in a way, but in excess becomes worrying. Like the chanting mania you see on television sometimes, with a uniformed general sitting in some council chamber acknowledging his voteless subjects' plaudits. You think, Christ, isn't somebody in that crowd simply bored witless?

'They're here. Props!'

The three girls fell about, stroked Del Vervain, did the subtle-monger's near-accidental touch. Open day here at Betelguese House. I wondered which he'd had, if not all.

A maid brought six plates. Four fakes, two authentic.

'These, Del?' First-name terms with the great.

'Don't break –' he caught himself theatrically, twinkled, '– the ones that *cost*. Break the BBC canteen crockery!'

Oh, the merriment. I nodded gravely. Luna was being super-thrilled, laughing at every non-witticism. Marvellous what fame does for sham. Like in the antiques game, really.

'Take your time, Lovejoy. What special effects, sounds . . . ?'

The rioting stopped. I'd taken four of the plates and dropped them on to the carpet. Two crashed and broke.

'Bristol delft,' I said over Luna's faint scream. 'Don't worry, Lune. They're modern fakes. Junk.'

Her face looked imploring. 'What if they're not, Lovejoy?'

The question didn't arise. But I politely stepped aside to give her room. She lifted the two unbroken plates and put them reverently on the table.

'I'm so sorry,' she was telling everybody.

'Gunge is best broken, love.' One of my maxims. I never do it, except for effect.

They were looking at me in silence. Luna was trying to say we'd get replacements, but Del shut her up with a slowly-growing smile, his first sincere response.

'Oh, yes,' he said softly. 'He's the one. Definitely.'

'I knew it,' Joan Bright-Eyes said.

'You didn't even look, Lovejoy.' Del was still smiling. And his eyes looked the same as Joan's.

'There'll be a faint bluish tint to the white glaze,' I said, 'if you held them up in daylight. There'll be three little uneven marks beneath where the plates were put on stands for the kiln firing. That indigo decoration isn't quite the proof of Bristol delftware it's cracked up to be, but –'

'But nothing, Lovejoy. You're the one.'

I'm still not sure if it was Del's forceful personality that moved us across to the buffet, or whether he actually shoved us. Power is as power does. Joan's eyes glittered as brittle as her husband's. I realised I didn't know her at all.

The buffet was some of the best grub I'd ever had. Luna ate sparingly. The Martians only picked, but drank with the solemnity of purpose. Joan also picked. Del noshed with vigour, raising his plate for minions to leap and replenish. Twice he sent the maid back. She'd guessed wrong. The usual display of moronic power.

Fifteen minutes after we'd started – I'd hardly got going – two people arrived. One was a rotund misery, the other a febrile nervy woman chained to a briefcase. Both denied hunger, both smoked, both cried for vodka. They were producers, I learned. They accepted Del Vervain's pronouncement that I was The One, and got down to business. One of the girls tried to chat me up, but I was starving. I mean, it had been a hell of a journey.

Joan watched. Her eyes said I was being fattened.

'Glad you're on the show, Lovejoy,' she said. 'It'll be the all-time winner.'

It wouldn't, because I wasn't on any show. I'd once done an *Antiques TV Showtime*. It was pathetic, a real fraud.

'Glad to hear it,' I said. 'Any more flan, please?'

'I'm afraid it's finished, ma'am,' the maid told Joan, but smiling properly at me. 'We have several quiches, sir. And salmon. The fish pie is –'

'Ta very much, love.' I accepted with elegance, in spite of Lune signalling me to refuse. It's all right for women. They can go for days on the smell of a grape. But the maid was pleased, and we settled down to a supply and demand.

The three thin birds gawped, Lune smouldered, knees together but smiling tightly. Joan circulated. Del and the producers guffawed mirthlessly. And me? I noshed and agreed with everything. I was to go on Del Vervain's show. He was to milk laughs by pretending to drop a priceless Ming vase. I would 'react'. The script would make the best impression – as if broadcasters could do such a thing.

The grub was great. We left about four o'clock. I'd quite taken to the maid. The *Del Vervain Show* script would be ready the following Tuesday. He waved us off with, 'All er-rightee too-nightee!' Lune reeled in ecstasy.

Quite honestly, I was glad to get on the train. Lune wasn't speaking. I wasn't sorry. I thought about telling her why Bristol delfware's properly before 1800, that the name applies now to seven or so factories as far apart as Wincanton and Bristol itself. Of the master painters' different designs – who'd slyly nicked their styles from China and Japan. But one look at her face and I sat thinking about Rye Benedict's underwater photographs of the great Brunel's non-existent paddle-steamer. And Joan's eyes.

Then things started to look down, because Lune's gorgeous Jaguar XKX whatnot motor had been stolen. I sighed. I'd had a lot of days lately. We got into the car, Lune fuming. She turned the ignition key, and started to pull out of the station car park.

'Turn right, love,' I said. 'Head for Drackenford.'

'I'm sorry, Lovejoy, but no.' She said it coldly. 'I for one need to know where you and I actually *stand*. Your conduct –'

Enough. I reached across, switched off the ignition, and took the key. She screeched and struggled with the locked wheel. The motor glided to a stop, nudging the kerb.

'Lovejoy! If that isn't the most irresponsible thing –'

I'm sorry to say that I clocked her. I let her come to. She started to get out. I restrained her. She might be madder than me, but I was tireder.

'For fuck's sake listen. You've had a robbery.'

She gaped. 'I've . . . ?' She tried to speak, looked at a housewife who was pushing a pram on the pavement. *I've . . . ?*

'You've,' I confirmed gravely. 'Your home has been entered, broken into by thieves five hours ago. Your very own antiques have been stolen. By a master thief. Taken away. To Drackenford.'

'My home?' Tears welled up in her eyes. I honestly felt sorry for her. Well, I would have, if she hadn't made me so mad. 'My *home*, Lovejoy? How do you know?'

I put my fingers against her cheek. 'Drackenford. Then we'll make up, eh?'

CHAPTER TWENTY

Drackenford's one of those wood-and-plaster hamlets. Nothing much to its name except plenty of black-and-white architecture, leaning cottages, leaded windows, and pavements so narrow you always have to look behind in case some cart's going to run you down. Four shops, a school the size of a kennel. A river, one bridge, a church filled with ancient alabaster saints, tombstones frittering away into yews and copses. And a war memorial, five names. That's your average East Anglian hamlet. You could guess about six hundred souls on a lusty night.

'Left.'

'There's no road, Lovejoy. It definitely says.'

'Ignore the signs. Right, at the end.'

She braked, turned, at a rocketing two miles an hour. 'It's a farm, Lovejoy.'

'Straight on.'

One mile an hour. We crawled past the farmhouse, down past ornamental gardens and an oxbow river bend. Two small pools large enough to swing a cat. I smiled, squeezed Luna's hand.

'That gravel drive, love.'

'What are you smiling at, Lovejoy? This is private property. I shall get a summons for trespass —'

'And Oliver will be narked,' I finished for her. 'Stop saying that. Pull in by the taller of the two barns.'

I was out before she'd got the brake on. I cupped my mouth and yelled to the sky, 'Same-Same! It's me! Lovejoy!'

Rooks rose, cawing and creating at having their idleness disturbed. Well, I was hard at it. Time they did a bit. 'Lovejoy.' Good old Lune with yet more reproach, buttoning her coat against the rising wind. I was heartily sick of her. 'Couldn't we go over to the small barn and simply knock? This place is . . .' She shuddered, pulling her lapels tight.

And indeed this place was . . . I scanned it. Big, dark, no life. No tyre marks. Broken windows stuffed with old rags. Sacks trailing from fractured glass. Sealed and shuttered and barred.

'Plug your ears, dwoorlink.' I cupped my hands and bellowed, 'Half a minute, Same-Same. Then I'll damage your shed.'

Luna was pacing, distraught. 'This is *positively* absurd, Lovejoy.

Shouting at a disused barn is ridiculous. There's a farmhouse back there to make enquiries –'

'Fifteen seconds, Same-Same,' I howled. The birds did their annoyance thing.

Then a faint noise came from inside the great barn.

'Step aside, Lune.' I drew her back a few paces. A part of the old barn's side began to swing in, making a humming sound. Lights, the clink of metal on metal. Somebody whistling. A voice called casually for turpentine. And out stepped Same-Same.

'Wotcher, Samie.' I'd forgotten how tall Same-Same was. Gangly, with that deceptive ease lanky folk possess. 'Notice anything?'

He waited until the panel whirred back into position. He walked round Luna's motor. 'Nice job. How much?'

'Not for sale, Samie. It's Luna's here. My apprentice.'

He'd been kicking the wheels until then, the way buyers do. Now he stopped, looked at Lune, at me, and groaned.

' 'Cking hell, Lovejoy.' He was disgusted.

'Sorry, Samie,' I said.

'Sorry?' he yelled, apoplectic. I'd been trying to let him down lightly, but he gave me stick. 'It's all very well saying sorry, mate. But I've worked all 'cking afternoon on bits of 'cking rubbish.' He glared at Luna. 'If you'd pay for one of those touch-locks, missus, you'd have saved me a 'cking deal of time.'

'Well, I'm sorry, Mr Same,' from Luna. 'But they're far too expensive. My friend Betty put one on her motor and it went off in the night, and she lives near the hospital and the police –'

'Lovejoy?' Same-Same gestured to me, and walked off shaking his head. 'Do I honestly believe this?'

Luna came to stand beside me. 'I don't understand, Lovejoy.'

'Samie's just gone for your antiques. Unlock your boot.'

'Mr Same's *got* them? *My* antiques?'

'Aye. He used your car to nick them from your house while we were away at Del Vervain's.'

It was all too much for her. I explained the 'samer' con. You go to the railway station car park. You ignore commuters, who're likely to leave wife, children, grandads at home. You wait for the mid-morning crowd. The man-and-wife off to London for a jaunt, who take luggage out of the boot. That means they're off for the day, at least.

'Pinch the car. Nobody's surprised to see the car in its own drive. The more expensive the motor, the more likely is the house to be posh, with tall hedges. The milkman and post girls have all done by noon.'

'Same-Same does that?'

'He's famous for it, among dealers. He never pinches big antiques. Always small, that can fit in . . .' I shrugged apologetically. 'Open your car doors, love. Wide.'

Same-Same came carrying her antiques. I nodded approval as she gasped, recognising each one.

An Austrian bronze, only Edwardian, that made her glance guiltily in my direction. A desk object, really. A bronze rock on a bronze pool. Luna knew, but did not say, that the rock would open at a touch to reveal a naked nymph in a singularly naughty pose. These items are highly collectible, especially if the nymph looks as brilliantly golden as the first day she performed her erotic perversion hidden in her bronze rock. A painting or two, Victorian sentimental – the sort you couldn't give away twenty years ago but now can't buy for love nor money. Then the two things that made me gasp.

Globes. One terrestrial, the other celestial. Mounted, so as to stand on the carpet of some master's study. The surfaces are printed, if they're right, done about the end of the Napoleonic Wars. Printed amendations were issued, to be stuck on the surface as more lands were discovered and new seas charted. I glimpsed one patch with 1828 on it, quite like an ordinary printed addendum label in a book. The surround is usually boxwood, like a girdle. Three beech legs stained to pretend they're rosewood. It doesn't mean fake; it means fashion of the times. They would stand about three feet tall. Lovely, Lovely. I heard myself moaning. They can be dry-stripped of their old yellow varnish and made like new. New, in their instance, being 1816 or so.

'That it, Samie?'

'Mmmmh.' He was disgruntled. Everything my fault.

'Going to the Kensington Antiques Fayre this year?'

'No.' He smiled a cold smile. 'Sending stuff, though.'

'I'll look out for it,' I joked, though I was really far from merriment.

'See you, Lovejoy.'

We left. I looked at the garden ornaments in the farmhouse's lovely ornate garden. Tudor design. The river was charming, only shallow but with a pair of swans gliding serenely along.

'D'you know swans mate for life, Lune?'

'Don't call me . . .' She bit back the rebuke. 'Oh, really?' she said, all casual. 'That's lovely.'

A mile further on I told her to draw in by the Drum Major, a pub. I told her to wait, in the scree of a low hedge.

'Parking light off, love.'

We waited for almost thirty minutes, but nothing came past except a tired tractor and few cows urged on by a cowherd.

'Home, love.'

Some days I'm really thick. I got Luna to phone from a roadside phone box, to tell Oliver not to call the Plod in when he arrived home and found his belongings thinned.

'He rather disbelieved me, Lovejoy.' She sounded miffed. 'He thinks I borrowed the antiques for your purposes.'

Well, that's what the Olivers of this world tend to believe, thinking themselves treble shrewd. Once a prat, and all that.

We drew up at their substantial house. No palace, but certainly the inhabitants weren't going hungry just yet. It's times like this I wish I had a watch. You can look at it, go tut-tut, and scarper.

'Look, love,' I said uneasily. 'Could you give me a lift to the Volunteer? Only, Sandy might have some news –'

'Us, Lovejoy.'

'Er, us, Lune.'

She was already out. Oliver emerged instantly. He marched down, shot glances into the car, turned on me.

'What's all this, Lovejoy? Not content with purloining my wife, embroiling her in goings-on, you have the effrontery –'

'Sorry, but –'

'Oliver. Please.' It was a humble request.

Oliver gave way, but only because I was a potential vote. He didn't know it, but I was now of an opposing political persuasion. They withdrew. I waited for the verdict.

Luna came back, Oliver in self-righteous attendance. 'Lovejoy. Could you please tell Oliver how . . . ?'

'I notice the place you'd parked, love. There was a crack in the tarmac. My side of the car, just below the door. When we left for London, that is. When we came back the motor was a good foot to one side of the same crack.' I waited. It was now quite dark. I should be in the White Hart trying to chat Connie up. 'While we were on the train, your car had been used, then returned to the station car park.' I looked from her to Oliver. 'That your question?'

'Yes.' She turned to her husband. 'See, Oliver?'

I'd threatened her not to disclose Same-Same's scam. I'd drilled her to say it was some lunatic chancer, and we'd managed to catch sight of him off-loading the antiques from the bridge over the by-pass. Best I could invent at such short notice.

'Well, thanks,' I said into silence. 'Is there a bus?'

The police came just then, and I was borrowed from the Mayor's parlour to receive the intentions of one Drinkwater.

Police stations have a curious pong of dried sweat. I suppose they import it wholesale. Drinkwater didn't let me sit. He paced, ear twitching, pot teeth clacking.

'Fairclough, Lovejoy.'

'How is the poor chap?'

'Convalescing. Remembers nil. His son's a fitter on a North Sea oil rig.' Clack clack. 'Had an antiques business. Went bust in a bad patch. The old man decided to sell. Somebody gave him your name.'

'Who?'

'A tart on the by-pass. Tits Alors.'

'Her recommendation was, ignore Sotheby's, and ring me?' Well, an old geezer's entitled to his perks n'jerks, as they say. 'Good stuff, is it?'

'Stolen. All of it. Neighbours saw a van loading up. Very usual at the Faircloughs'.'

Not too convincing, but as it was Drinkwater's tale it'd have to do.

I looked at a map on the wall, seeing we were both strolling about each other like sparring partners wondering whether to have a go. Same-Same's river was a tributary of the Orwell. And 'room to swing' a cat's supposed to be from swinging the cat o'nine tails, naval punishment in confined deck spaces. Except river people hereabouts say it of shallow rivers. Because a cat's a sort of boat. Several different sorts, in fact, from sailing colliers of the mid-nineteenth century to fifty-oared galleys. I'd noticed that Same-Same's little oxbow river had two pools with room enough to swing a cat boat round and start it back down the Orwell for another load.

And Same-Same now had several workers, all busy in his massive sound-proofed barn. People who whistled while they worked and called for the frigging turpentine and look sharp about it. I hadn't seen a thing, but I'd heard enough. Samie used to work alone.

'. . . be inadvisable, Lovejoy.'

'What would?' I came back.

'Going it alone. This thing's worth more than the country.'

'I don't understand.' This the first recorded case of Plod benevolence?

He leant close to me. God, his breath stank. 'You understand all right, Lovejoy. Give me a share. I'll see you right.'

A bribe? 'I wish I could, Drinkwater. But I've heard nothing. Honest.'

He let me go then. It was as clumsy a bribery act as any I've yet come across. He was as bent as a ruler, just trying me out. You can tell a bent ploddite on a foggy Alp. Drinkwater hated me too much to forgo the pleasure of clanging me up. I sighed, taking my leave. And ran into Sandy, yoo-hooing away outside. I tried to duck into the night, but he drove alongside, parping his horn and waving. He had Mel with him. As if I hadn't enough trouble, I'd now got allies and, worse, they'd obviously come to help. Friends plus allies plus help meant utter total immediate disaster.

Resigned, I went towards their motor, hoping the populace was early abed tonight.

CHAPTER TWENTY-ONE

The White Hart was thronged, thick with smoke. Dealers were crammed in, all pretending (a) they'd just pulled off the biggest sale on earth, and (b) a group of Americans were coming tomorrow to buy even more. For human grandeur there's nothing so moving as the sight of antique dealers on the make.

I wanted to creep in last, after Mel and Sandy had Entered (note that capital). But Sandy insisted I go first.

'Swell the audience, Lovejoy,' he trilled, roguish with eyelashes.

Mel said nothing. He doesn't talk much, just glowers. Sandy's the verb, Mel the pronoun, so to speak. He told me to admire the various aspects of their main motor, an old Rover the size of a tram. It's never the same twice.

'Admire the silk curtains, Lovejoy.'

'Great, er, great.' If you like bamboo, strings of rock crystal and strips of purple sacking twined with orange shot silk. I was worried for non-artistic reasons. Didn't Highway Code rules like car windows you could see through?

'Admire the fringes, Lovejoy.'

'Er, yes, Sandy. Great.'

He went through a litany, once sharply pulling to the kerb to admonish my lack of enthusiasm.

The Rover was probably a good motor underneath the crud. I'm sure it was decoratively brilliant. But it always reminds me of those fashion shows where clothes look straight off a tat-monger's street barrow. Talk about rags and bone.

The thing was ribbed on the outside with small windmills, perhaps a hundred or more, flashing the whole colour spectrum. The windows were back-lit, Sandy at the wheel. Fluorescent strips ran round the car's outlines, reds, orange, opalescent plum and a creamy green that almost made me puke. Each headlight wore enormous eyelashes, the rear lights golden. A large red kid-leather tongue trailed panting from the boot. The bonnet's grid was shaped into an enormous chrome pout. The steering wheel wore projecting digits like spokes of a nautical wheel.

You have to accept a lift from this pair, partly because they never let up and partly because they're clever rich antique dealers. I needed to know who was being cleverest.

'Great, great,' the umpteenth time.

I went in, to a welcoming chorus of abuse. Sheepishly I gave Ted the shrug that told him to get ready for Sandy's Entrance. This entailed banging a gong, and balancing a tall glass of crème de menthe on a kneeling plaster cherub on the bar. The outside lights came on over the pub forecourt. Everybody crowded to the windows for a look. Sandy's Entrances are famous.

'It's Sandy! How this time, d'you think?'

'I hope it's the steps,' from Liz Sandwell. She's admired Sandy ever since he poisoned a Birmingham bloke who was giving her a hard time. 'I *love* the steps.'

'It'll be the trolley,' from Flavour John, a rugbyplaying gorilla dealing in porcelain and musical instruments.

Somebody wouldn't have that. 'They did the trolley Entrance last Monday. Bet, four to one against, Flavour?'

Wagers were struck. Some dealers crowded out to see. I hung back, tried to get served. I think the whole thing's stupid. I can't honestly see the point.

A military band struck up from the Rover in noisy intro, blaring. God knows what the country ducks thought. *The Entry of the Gladiators* stunned us from the radiator grille's chrome mouth. You can't help watching.

The roof slowly opened as the music reached its crescendo. Mel was standing beside the car swinging a thurible, the cloying incense wafted on the evening air. To murmurs of appreciation, Sandy slowly rose through the unfolding car roof, as the Statue of Liberty without the torch. He was swathed in her robe. A corona of stars circled his head.

'It's like them pictures!' somebody cried. 'United Artists? I know it's somebody –'

'Two to one against the steps from now –'

I wondered vaguely where the motor got the energy.

'It's the waterfall! The waterfall!'

Amid a shimmering spray of golden fireworks, Sandy was carried down on a small escalator that protruded from the motor. The music pounded. He held his pose, smiling nobly into the distance. Mel's thurible chinked, incense drifting into the taproom. God, but it was a sight. Flavour John came to join me.

'Lost my week's takings. Bloody poofter.'

'So why bet, Flavour?' He'd bet on the trolley Entrance.

'I thought I'd win,' he said. The inveterate gambler's logic. Sometimes the dark thought comes that maybe they hope they'll actually lose.

Sandy was gliding forward to applause from the pub crowd. Flavour John gave a hopeful glance, but no trolley. So far I'd wasted almost an hour, including Drinkwater's hamfisted bribery act. Which only went to show that Drinkwater was worried as me. Cradhead was an unknown. I started asking Flavour if he'd done much at Wittwoode's Auction Temple lately.

Meanwhile, back in showbusiness, Sandy was being showered with rose petals from a gilded bucket.

'Take that fire risk out of here, Mel.'

Ted had lately been prosecuted for letting Mel carry in six candelabras, one an exploding variant. The thurible was bundled out. Sandy smiled and waved. I saw his gaze rake the assembled company, and wisely applauded the nerk with the rest.

Flavour was complaining. 'Been shunted off some flavour porcelain this week. Frigging criminal.'

'Tough luck, Flavour.' Everything he admires is flavoursome. But I've no sympathy. Rugby four days a week and antiques three – when it could be seven days of antiques? No wonder dealers like Flavour John are never satisfied.

'Tough luck?' he said scathingly. Sandy opened his mouth. Mel stood on a stool to pour the crème de menthe in his gob. 'Where's the frigging *luck*, Lovejoy? Acker warned me off, the swine.'

My ears tingled. 'Look, Flavour,' I said, steaming him to further revelations. 'There's not a dealer here won't chop a deal.'

'Go shares?' He laughed hollowly. 'Think I didn't try? I'd have bought the bugger off if I'd had the gelt.'

Flavour owed me. Recently I'd warned him off a mathematical treatise dated 1491 AD. The faker, a real pillock, had filled it with the = equal sign. And that was invented by Robert Recorde, much later.

I said, still steaming, 'Maybe the stuff wasn't good –'

'Good?' He said it so loud people turned round. 'Good, Lovejoy? Nantgarw porcelain four plates. No, straight up. So translucent you could almost read through it. That's *flavour*.'

This sounded the real business. When Bill Billingsley set up the Nantgarw (rhymes with shoe, sort of) porcelain factory in 1813, his factory crashed – his plates were warped, full of firing cracks. So clever old Bill and his son-in-law Sam Walker worked in Swansea for three years. And learned superior technology. Their new super porcelain became craved by wallet-wielding tycoons everywhere, because Bill Billingsley in his second go managed to make porcelain whiter than white, yet somehow so translucent that we say, 'Is it

Nantgarw clear?' meaning so translucent when you hold it up to the light that you can imagine it's oil-soaked paper. The trade nickname is sodden-snow translucency, believe it or not. I moaned inwardly. My life was becoming a saga of antiques missed. The stuff was everywhere, but just gone.

Then I remembered that Nicole Frères musical box. I mentioned it. Flavour snorted a sardonic snort.

'That should have been mine too, Lovejoy. And them old cameras – you know Acker Kirwin's a photography nut. Very flavour, them. They've gone too.' He'd have won my sympathy vote, except he was an antique dealer. 'I'm leaving the Eastern Hundreds, Lovejoy, going up Smoke. No flavour left here.'

'London? Where, though?'

'The Belly. You know Wheatstone? Invented the concertina, made thirty-five thousand of them. They're always around, right? Not now, Lovejoy. I saw six last month. None, this.' He was a broken man. 'Even Salvation Army are scarce.'

'The old black bellows issue?' I was frightened.

'Can you credit it, Lovejoy? No, it's the Smoke for me.'

Well, rather him. Portobello Road has broken stauncher hearts than mine. 'Well, Sandy'll be giving up his shop now him and Mel are back.'

'Haven't you heard, Lovejoy?' Flavour tried to beckon for another pint. 'He's already sold up. This is the celebration.'

'I don't believe it, Flavour.' And I didn't, yet I did.

'True. Don't know who to. Mel's sold up too.'

What the frig was going *on?* It was getting beyond me. Just when I thought I'd sussed out the main buyer of Prammie Joe's turkey stripping of Cornish Place – Acker – and so learned who'd done for him – ditto – the pattern crumpled again. I was sick of the whole thing. I'd never known antiques move about like this before. Antiques go in dribs and drabs. I mean, when the Countess in Long Melford does a tin can for the States, it's corkpopping time in the local taverns. Yet now we were drained of antiques. And in dollop numbers. Beyond belief.

As Sandy did his parade – Mel goes before, strewing rose petals while people clap and have a laugh, Sandy waving with queenly magnanimity – and Flavour John groused in my ear, I started to watch faces. I've told you how much they matter. And there was something not quite right. People were laughing, oh, sure. As usual, blokes were mock-whistling and the women admiring. But there was the occasional glimpse of tautness. Nobody, but nobody was doing a deal. Margaret Dainty was talking to the exotic Jessica who lives down the estuaries in sordid circumstances. They should have been talking antiques, but instead seemed to be commiserating. Margaret raised her glass, inviting me to come and join them. I smilingly declined. She's an older woman, friend for years, with class in spite of her limp.

There was Dyllis Washburne, sitting alone. She has a friend who isn't in the trade but helps her out. They go on holidays together, but he's loyal to his wife who's got hard religion and wants to bomb Non-Conformists. Now, Dyllis is very gregarious, mostly dressing furniture and pen-work japanned furniture. Dyllis alone and palely loitering? Impossible.

And Big Frank, talking to Mel, saying right, right, with many nods. He caught my eye, waved, mouthed 'Ta', presumably for my having visited his red-hot mini-mamma Jenny Calamy. I must do something about that promise, if I could remember what the hell I'd worked out to do about whatever promise it was.

'Cooo-eeee!' Sandy, pausing to do his Queen Empress wave. He wore elbow-length white lace gloves with jewelled glove-bands, very seventeenth century. One thing, Sandy gets it right. 'Admiration?'

'Sandy. You didn't say you'd sold up to Big Frank.'

'Don't spoil my moment, Lovejoy. There's a dear. Sell to Big Frank? Have you seen his *nails*?'

Connie came in, with Rye Benedict. I waved, but she moved on Mel with smiley determination. Big Frank shrugged the shrug of the loser. Mel allowed Connie to buy him a drink without quite looking at her. She began talking animatedly. He sniffed and kept his distance, but they were dealing.

'Reckon Connie bought Sandy-Mel out?' I asked Flavour.

'It's some bird right enough.' He didn't look round. 'Frothy Lane was saying that yob who runs that poxy old mill's sending the vans. Word is the dollop broker's flitting around. Who knows?'

Some days everything goes wrong. I realised now why Sandy and Mel had insisted on giving me a lift. Sandy knew I was worried about the big antiques shifts round the area. He wanted to tell me he and Mel were contributing to it. Maybe he lost courage on the way over. Or maybe he didn't want anything to spoil his Entrance, the night of the big reunion between him and Mel. Whatever. I'd come for solutions, and everything was more tangled than ever. The dollop broker was coming nearer. I said so-long to Flavour John and left.

Some days everything only *seems* to go wrong because deep down something is chancing its arm and going right for once.

As I walked down the lane to my cottage between the hedgerows I saw a light in my window. I thought, oh, hell fire. Another duffing up from Del Vervain's mob? Or Drinkwater brewing up looking for the sugar, waiting to arrest me?

'Hello, Lovejoy.'

It was only Luna. Supper was ready, a delectably sinful meal of all the things you've got to leave alone or Doc Lancaster'll get you. The place was depressingly tidy, honed to brilliance.

'Don't worry,' she said, a little breathlessly. 'I had Elsie and Madge here. They do for me at home.'

'Er, look, Lune.' I didn't go in. Just stood there looking round. 'I'm in enough trouble without Oliver —'

'He's had to go to Manchester. Finance meeting.'

Manchester? Quite a way. It was late. No means of getting home for some time, I should suppose. I didn't say this.

'Manchester's quite a way,' Luna said, checking the stove was still doing its stuff, the quick suspicious way they do. 'He probably won't be home tonight, I shouldn't suppose.'

'Really?' I cleared my throat. She looked up, tutting.

'Well?' Are you going to stand at the door all night?'

Obeying women is in a man's nature, really, in spite of the party line preaching the opposite. I thought of Oliver's powerful position as Mayor. But a man never really leaves a woman. We can't. We haven't the power. We can only go if we're shoved. A woman can leave a bloke, though, and often does. I decided I'd better find out which version was in operation, and stepped inside.

By the time I'd reached this conclusion, Luna had shelled me from my jacket, close and warm. She wore a lovely woollen dress, pale green. I like those. They fall round shapes.

'Coming,' I said. There isn't much you can do when a woman extends an invitation. Choice is a luxury for others. Not me.

CHAPTER TWENTY-TWO

'I didn't intend this, Lovejoy.'

'I'm glad, love.' We spoke along the pillow.

'I want you to know I don't . . . I *don't*.' She looked away. 'This is the first time I've ever . . . apart from Oliver.'

'Shhh.' I think God got emotions wrong. We've too many. Remorse heads my list of redundancies.

'What do I do about Oliver?'

Why ask me? I sighed inwardly. These questions are irrelevant. Who's got answers? We'd had a short session during the night, after we had made our first smile. I'd been desperate to fast fade, but she'd clung on, interrogating until I thought I'd never slide out of the minor death. It makes me wonder sometimes if women ever understand. I mean, all they need do is stay quiet a minute, give your soul time to climb back in. But no. Rabbit, rabbit, rabbit. One day, maybe some bird'll have the sense. She'll be my goddess. I'll follow her for nowt.

It was early morning. We'd made our morning smile. Luna was a willing rider, too anxious to rush us to orgasm, thinking that right. It's basically too much rote in love-making that creates this misunderstanding. It's better slower. She found time to rejoice, to her utter astonishment. She questioned her being flabbergasted, daring to rollick in lust.

'Is he back early?'

'About noon.'

'We've time to go to Rye Benedict's. I must see him.'

'The pictures you were looking at? Delia's?'

'Mmmh. The charts, but they're beyond me.' A submerged I.K. Brunel miniature paddle-steamer would be priceless. If available. But I didn't believe in its existence, let alone the other factors. I think Rye Benedict was being had, his market garden's sale profits the reason. I mean, is anything easier to fake than a photograph? Flavour'd said Acker Kirwin was a photographer. Oho, I thought. But found I'd baffled myself again. Oho *what*?

Daybreak comes too early when a woman is around. I've found that. Bluetits woke us about five-thirty, greedy little sods. Never leave you alone.

'Lovejoy?' Pause. 'I had no intention of . . . of sleeping here. I just thought you deserved a good supper. Getting my things back off Same-Same.'

'Least I could do. Still mad about the Vervains?'

'No. Though you could have warned me.'

'You might not have come, with a scruff like me.'

She leant over me, propped on one elbow, smiling as her breast touched my face and produced the inevitable.

'You're always wrong, Lovejoy.' She frowned. 'Was there ever anything between Mrs Vervain and you?'

I never betray confidences, so I hummed and ha'd, finally told her to mind her own business when she pressed. That led to a struggle, then a protracted smile that made us late, with a rushed breakfast and her nearly burning the blinking tomatoes and too little margarine on the fry-up. I can't drink hot tea, so I had to do that business of pouring it into a bowl and blowing. We made the town road by about half-ten. I grumbled as we left the cottage. Rye's mill would be heaving with infants. I wanted a quiet conversation with the bloke. Luna tried mentioning Oliver, but I wasn't having any. I'd just escaped being married to Joan Vervain. I didn't want another divorce impending, just yet. Though in fact Del and Joan now seemed accomplices. Maybe my influence worked equally well both ways, for reconciliation as well as division? I'd have been a great marriage counsellor.

'What was that, Lovejoy?'

'Eh? Nothing.' I'd been talking to myself.

'There's that Connie you wanted to speak to. Quick!'

I held on while the car slowed and juddered to a halt. Other motors parped. She tutted at their impatience. Connie was coming from the station forecourt. At this hour? I told Luna to wait and nipped through the traffic, calling out. She paused, more of a hesitation, before hurrying on. I raced, caught up.

'Hey, Connie! It's me, for heaven's sake.'

'Hello, Lovejoy.' She smiled, with effort, didn't stop to chat. 'I'm in rather a hurry. Sorry about last night.'

I remembered. I'd beckoned, she'd declined. 'Okay, love. You did the deal everybody's talking about, eh?'

That stopped her. 'Everybody's *what?* But it's . . .'

So there was a deal. 'Sandy and Mel. You bought them out.'

'Oh, Lovejoy. Yes!' It was wrung from her. She seemed distraught, beside herself. Where the heck had she been so soon?' And why hadn't she gone in her car? Or was it somewhere overnight? 'Yes! On commission. You'd only find out.'

That terrible word's enough to cause most dealers I know to keel over into the custard. To sell on commission's only one step from going on the knocker, which is virtually begging from door to door. Sell on commission means you starve until you sell – then the dealer for whom you're selling takes the whole price except a measly ten per cent.

'What favours did you do Sandy and Mel, love? I thought I was the one fuffing your stuff out.'

She twisted, right there in the weak morning sunshine. As if I had her entangled in a net.

'You are, Lovejoy! Don't think I don't still need your load.'

'Thank heavens for that.'

'I must go, Lovejoy. I –'

'Where'll I leave it, Connie?' I had to ask the question, exactly as if I believed her. And explained, when she looked blank, 'Your load I'm assembling.'

'Oh.' She thought quickly of this problem, possibly for the very first time. 'At Boxtenholt aerodrome. See Gunge. Okay?'

'Right, love.'

We bussed, she sprinted. No night ticket on her windscreen, so it had been this morning that she'd hurtled off down the bright silver road. She made a Le Mans start, her face tense and staring.

I walked back to Luna's motor. Luna also did a racing start, but talking, asking, informing.

'Shut up a sec, love.' Thinking's bad for you, some say. Let her do some. 'Luna. Who of all the people you've met is untrustworthy?'

'Among the dealers?' She thought. 'Calamity Jenny. I didn't like her one bit.' Which wasn't quite my question. 'She's too saucy for her own good, that one.'

'And who is trustworthy?'

'Sandy,' she said immediately. I pressed her for more names. 'Big Frank, though he's hopeless. Quite different from that Mr Kirwin.'

Hang on. How come she knew Acker Kirwin? 'You've met?'

'Yes. He bought ever such a lot at Wittwoode's auction. You remember? You sent me.'

'So I did.' I made her describe the scene in detail.

It was the collar job. He'd worked it on unsuspecting punters as the crowds had dwindled. It's not done much nowadays. It's quite simple, puts the average public bidder, the 'women', off bidding. Thus:

You wait to bid, at an auction, say, for a small carriage clock

for your mantelpiece. Say Lot 200, about teatime. Happily you wait.
You stand quite near it. You don't want to be startled into bidding
for the wrong thing, so you've pencilled a ring in your catalogue
round the number, Lot 200. All clear. Then something very worrying
happens.

A suited gentleman, smart, dour, unsmiling, shoves his way
towards you. He looks at the carriage clock, Lot 200, and compares
it with a photograph he pulls from his pocket. He murmurs a curse,
checks a list of items on a clipboard. It bears the police insignia. He
quietly asks, 'This item yours, madam?' in sepulchral tones. 'No, no!'
you gasp, by now convinced something sinister is going on. He peers
at the marks in your catalogue. 'It's just that I was thinking of bidding
for it,' you bleat in terror. 'For my Auntie. A present . . .'

He whispers gruffly that he's police. Would you please bid for
it? And bring it to court, present it as evidence? It would only mean
a few days at the Old Bailey, appearing as witness, you see, ma'am.
The clock was stolen, you see . . .

'No, no!' you exclaim. And depart.

Leaving Acker – for that's who the 'inspector' will be, or some
pal – to buy the carriage clock cheap, having got rid of the one
serious bidder.

'I knew he wasn't a police inspector,' Luna told me.

'How?' She was shrewder than I'd thought.

'I know the inspectors,' she said blithely. 'We were guests of
honour at their annual dinner.' Silly me. 'I told the gentlemen
attendants. They only laughed.' She bridled in annoyance. 'No sense
of vocation. It's not good enough.'

Whizzers, the scene shifters at auctioneers, are always on the
take. Asking them for morality is whistling wind.

'Terrible, isn't it,' I sympathised. And it's then that I think I
looked at Luna for the very first time.

Oh, I'd had a gander, shufti'd her in passing, so to speak. But
actually looking . . . ? No. I'd missed the sureness, her quiet cleverness. She couldn't exactly be the humdrum duckegg I'd assumed.
Maybe because she'd gone along with most of what I'd decreed, I'd
assumed she was a mundane housewife tremulously peering at the
great world beyond her front door. And maybe I despised such,
thinking why the hell hadn't they already got on with life instead of
whinging about being oppressed, that 'jargoneering', as Florence
Nightingale called it.

There were other attributes. She drove sedately, but better than
me. She was composed, attentive when I spoke about antiques. She

didn't believe me on anything else. Rightly, I suppose. She did things off her own bat, sometimes got them right. She was smart enough to notice people, suss out their character. Gulp. Might she actually be more astute than I am? I'd already awarded her a secret medal, for she had made love hesitantly at first but eventually very, very well. Luna Carstairs had pleased me more than any woman I could remember. I looked away. She'd caught my glance, coloured up.

'What, Lovejoy? Did you say something?'

'No.' I was gruff, dismissive.

'And Rye,' she added. 'We can trust him. Not like Mr Vervain.'

'Not at all . . . ? But you were all over Del.'

'I was nothing of the kind, Lovejoy! I was merely . . . attentive. He's a famous broadcaster. But shifty. And so scared of the producer people –'

'Wrong, Lune. *They* were scared of *him*. He's the star.'

'Lovejoy. You have it the wrong way about. He *is* frightened. He was frantic lest you didn't show.'

'Really?' I remembered that strange glint in their eyes, the hot expectation. And Joan's rather sinister glitter. What were they planning? I remembered the rumours, Del's links with the rough toughs of Whitechapel. I felt suddenly cold and told her to put the heating on. She did so, looked at me, said nothing.

'Gawd Almighty, love.' The mill grounds were heaving with school-children. 'You made us late –'

'I?' she blazed, pulling in at the far end of the car park. 'Lovejoy?'

Therla Brewer was somewhere in the maelstrom. Josh Whatnot was trying to make four lads come off the waterwheel. It was locked static, thank goodness, but two of them were wet through. Why didn't they take this mob to the pictures instead? The thought of a hundred screaming ikes in the tumult of a dark cinema made me delete the question unanswered.

'I want five minutes of Rye's time, that's all.'

'He's lecturing. Look.'

And there he was, the trustworthy Rye Benedict, leaning out of a hoist window, hanging on to the dangling rope of the hoist's pulley with one hand, speaking through a megaphone with the other. His feet were on the window ledge.

'Good heavens. I hope he's safe, Lovejoy.'

'Course he is, love. As houses.'

'Knee, Lovejoy.' Red-cheeked, she angrily pulled her skirt over her knees. 'Not here. This is a *public place!* With school-children everywhere.'

'Sorry.' My hand had accidentally fallen on her knee, but the space in front car seats is always cramped.

'He's winching the rope thing. What's it for?'

We watched. 'They unloaded the grain from waggons on the ground. Winched the sacks to the top of that pulley. Then swing it in.'

A horseless waggon stood beneath the hoist. We watched desultorily. The children gathered below watched desultorily. The teachers expounded, pleased at Rye's activity. Three or four sacks were arranged on the waggon. Rye was leaning out, speaking down to the children, indicating something up above the hoist, probably some control rope to stay the pulley's speed.

'That way,' I said on, cursing my luck for being late. I could have been at a viewing day in Norwich. 'That way, all the grain's on the mill's top floor, see? Fewer rats, as well as being able to chute the grain down into the millwheels when required.'

Rye was calling for somebody to hook the pulley rope into a sack on the waggon. Josh sprang on the waggon to do it, amid jeering applause. He took it in good part, leaping spectacularly off when he'd done and bowing to the mob of children. Rye reached inside. The pulley started moving. The sack rose.

'See? Simple. The old folk knew a thing or two. Used the waterwheel power to lift the grain.'

'The waterwheel's stopped.'

'Probably got an electric motor inside, make it easier to demonstrate to children. Principle's the same, though.'

We watched idly, Luna saying how marvellous that people like Rye took interest in these old things like watermills. He'd tried to buy it from Oliver's Town Council, offered substantial money, she was saying quite casually, but the Council weren't allowed to sell. It was a trust.

The pulley slowed, stopped. Rye disappeared inside to check something. Emerged, smiling, feet on the space ledge, looking down at the children some eighty feet below, the waggon with its sacks. And at the sack being winched higher and higher to the hoist window. Him stretched out, steadying himself. I couldn't hear what he was saying, with the car windows almost closed and the children making a din.

'Benedict offered for the mill again quite recently. He has the river rights, on account of the market garden . . .'

Rye reached, failed to find the rope for some reason. He turned as if to look behind into the dark interior of the mill. And started to move outwards.

I thought, what is he doing? Quite idly, my thoughts went. He's going to fall, isn't he? Looks quite like it.

Luna shrieked. The children screamed. Rye was in the air, reaching, still with one hand outstretched. Still with that smile on his face as if to say, This is what shouldn't happen, children, so you will be careful, won't you? and suchlike.

The screams rose as he tumbled over. Once. Twice. And a half. And smashed into the edge of the waggon beneath. Blood spurted upwards, oddly, moving outwards in a graceful arc.

Luna was clutching my arm, weeping madly, crying out my name. I only sat staring. The children began to run in every direction.

Somebody knocked on the window, opened the door. Josh looked in, shouting had we a car phone for Christ's sake couldn't somebody call the ambulance or something because a man had fallen from the mill hoist.

I got out then, walked to the office, and smashed the window, got to the phone and asked for ambulance, and police. I said to send Cradhead. I got Luna's car blanket from her boot, went and covered the body while children and people shrieked and wept.

CHAPTER TWENTY-THREE

Rye Benedict's fall drew the short straw. Drinkwater established a Star Chamber in the mill, ground floor, to waste everybody's time. Police surged. Ambulance people tore up, had a fag, ogled the schoolgirls while the police photographer flashed and ogled the schoolgirls. We were questioned.

'It wasn't me, Drinkwater,' I told him in case he got ideas. 'Four million witnesses'll tell you.'

'That's enough from you, Lovejoy.'

'Here.' I gave him a list of registration numbers on a card.

Luna had started keeping ruled cards in the glove compartment. As soon as we'd come down to earth (sorry) I made her list all the car registrations. There were maybe a dozen parked motors.

Drinkwater read. 'What's this, Lovejoy?'

'Car numbers, Drinkwater. Shall we check?'

He flung the card back. 'Pathetic. Get gone, Lovejoy.'

'I'm a valuable witness, you burke. I was actually here –'

'You were actually groping the Mayoress, Lovejoy.' He gestured me away. 'I know you. About your level.'

Luna was with the children. Astonishingly, she had been out helping the teachers to round up the screaming children and line them up by the river, looking across to the market garden. She had the bloodstained ones go down to the little landing stage and rinse the ghastly splashes off. It was a brisk, businesslike act, and I admired her for thinking of it. In fact, the teachers started coming to her for orders. I was proud of her.

'He's chucking us out,' I told her. 'Come on.'

A reluctant ploddite tried delaying us at the gate, hurt that we were being allowed to go about our lawful business. I enjoyed myself, walking over to tell Drinkwater his orders had been countermanded by beat feet. We drove away in silence. I made to chuck her card out of the window, and paused.

'Hang on, Lune. What's this line?'

'The other car park, Lovejoy. You said list *all* the cars. Twelve at the mill. Three more across the river, Lovejoy, in the market garden.'

'Pull in.' Near somebody's gateway, I counted. The river, though small, was too wide to leap. There was some sort of footbridge round the river bend, beyond hedges, trees.

'How could you see into the other car park?'

She tutted. 'The footbridge, Lovejoy. I knew you'd get cross if I forgot some cars.'

Me? I'm hardly ever cross. In any case, it was only an incidental, right? But the world's made up of atoms.

'I'll walk on, love. You drive round to the market garden. Ask whose cars they are.'

She caught me up ten minutes later. I was walking along the approach road to the dual carriageway by then. I was narked as she drew up.

'Where the hell have you been?'

'Talking with the old lady who does the bedding plants. They were all down in the potting sheds, on the far side. They'd only just been told. She was most upset about Mr Benedict. Of course it's bound to've been a shock –'

'Was one motor his?'

'Yes. The estate car's the sales lady's. She's done the job since the father's time. There are five locals, four girls and a gardener for the outdoor work.'

'Whose is the third motor? Customer?'

'No. When they move the potting plants for public parks, like today, they admit no one. It had gone.' She almost smirked when I grabbed the card. 'Yes, I *did*, Lovejoy.'

And she had. Two numbers below the line were ticked. She'd drawn a ring carefully round the third.

'Did you say anything about the third motor? Ask them or anything?'

'No.' She drove meticulously as yet another police car tore past, shrieking its important way to the next pub. 'I wasn't sure if I should.'

And another, following an ambulance. No lights and sirens this time, more sedate, without haste. Luna pulled in to let the cortège pass, then drove after towards town. It was starting to rain. To wash Rye Benedict's blood off the waggon.

'The garden has a second entrance. It stands ajar on potting days. A notice on it says so.'

I found myself looking at the car number, said casually, 'Anybody could have just dropped in. Fuschia for their Dad's birthday, eh? Sort of thing anybody'd do. Easter cactus.'

'Benedict's is terribly expensive,' Luna said. 'Cheaper at Bellows and Calder's nursery. Except for bulbs. Their shrubs are better value, because Oliver –'

The sky falling, Tinkerbell dying, the ticking crocodile rising from the swamp, and Luna goes ape on the price of daffodils. I slumped in my seat, and said to drive to Cambridge. She complained she hadn't left a note for Oliver. I said he'd be too busy planting cheap shrubs to notice. She flared up at that, and played merry hell. Lulled me to sleep in seconds.

It had to be Cambridge University. Not Oxford – I can't forgive Balliol College for rubbling its lovely medieval chapel and replacing it with a pre-Walt Disney clone. And for mangling the exquisite medieval stained-glass windows when they reset them. Incompetent sods. Dr Dymond was the bloke they dredged up for me. He arrived in his office, swirling his cloak and dropping things. Some student followed him in, languidly arguing for exemption from something. The little bald-headed don was equal to the challenge. He shoved the student out, patting him like a ball player.

'*Omnium rerum principia parva sunt*. Cicero, Tomlinson.' He entered, rubbing his hands.

Half of what these dons do is an act, I'm sure. Music halls did the damage, making all professors absent-minded and all clowns heartbroken. If I hadn't been there, Dr Dymond would have let Tomlinson off his next essay or whatever.

He sat in a swivel chair – modern crud – and placed his feet on his piled desk. He was untidy. If I'd not sent Luna out snooping antiques, she'd have had the vacuum out.

'*All things begin small*. Sort of.' He twinkled at some declension. 'Local history, eh?'

'Only societies, if you could, please.' I told him of my colleague's growing interest in the events of the 1640 decade. 'Not proper research, Dr Dymond. Just a hobby.' I smiled. I didn't want to be banished with a Latin tag like Tomlinson. 'He's quite elderly, so I had to come for him.'

'Local history societies are often least help, Lovejoy.' Dr Dymond opened his palms, started one of his diatribes. 'But I'll list the most active ones for you.' He did, but I knew them all. I'd looked them up. 'I suppose your friend has tried those? Particularly . . . ?'

'It's some trial thing, I think.' I chuckled in embarrassment. 'The mid-1640s. St Edmundsbury. We're waste metal dealers. Our own lorries and everything,' I said proudly. 'Course, old Fred doesn't do as much as he used to. Getting on.'

Hell fire. I was getting carried away, waxing lyrical about my imaginary old pal. It was me wanted to know, not old Fred, interfering swine.

'One trial was held in the house old Fred lives in. It used to belong to . . .' I wrinkled my forehead in perplexity, let it clear '. . . Calamy Somebody. I'm almost sure –'

'Doubtful, Lovejoy. Edmund Calamy – did you know there were several of that name? – didn't actually *own* a house there. In fact, I'm practically sure he lived in Holborn, London. Very famous family.' He sighed, genuine regret. 'You can't trust the *Dictionary of National Biography*. Most history societies are frivolous. Like the Sealed Knot, who enact Great Civil War Battles. Plenty of interest, little academic focus.'

'Have you a section dealing with it?'

'That period, Lovejoy? Heaven help us, no! It's as much as we can do to keep the colleges solvent these days.'

Blank. He took my name and address, in case he dug something up. He told me a great deal about the hideous Witch-Finders, recommended a million texts, wrote them all out. I said thanks, and went down through the college grounds to meet Luna.

Cambridge's antiques were disappointing. Too dear and too new. That didn't mean they weren't desirable. I needed tons of antiques, even if some were fakes, but I didn't want a third fraudulent mortgage on my cottage. She'd tried hard, though. In fact, her eyes were thrilled. Just like she'd always been before poor Rye Benedict was topped. I mean, just before poor Rye Benedict fell accidentally.

'I think we've had enough, Luna, love.'

'Home now, darling?'

'Home, er, right.'

I didn't maul her knee once. I made her phone home as we left Cambridgeshire, to check Oliver would be there. I asked her could I come and say hello. She was pleased, but became quiet as we turned into her lane.

'I don't know if I have a cake for tea, Lovejoy.'

'I don't mind, love.'

'One thing. Please.' She pulled to a stop in the drive, made a prolonging fuss with her seatbelt. 'Perhaps you should stop calling me that. In Oliver's presence, I mean.'

'You mean "love"?' I was amazed. Where I come from you get a thick ear for rudeness to a lady. 'Is it feminism?'

'It's . . . it's relatively unusual in these parts, Lovejoy. Oliver might see it as . . .'

'Oh, well,' I said, cheerily alighting. '*Omnium rerum principia parva sunt.* Seneca.'

'*Operae pretium est!*' she riposted merrily. Then halted, stricken. I thought she'd suddenly remembered something terrible about Rye's fall at the mill.

'What is it?' I whispered, frantic, my heart pounding.

'Seneca? Wasn't it Cicero?'

I could have throttled her. 'You stupid *bitch*! I thought –'

'Hello, darling!' she cooed, quickly edging me aside. Oliver was standing there, glowering. Well, bitch isn't love, is it? 'Oliver, Lovejoy wants to . . .' She paused, her smile frozen. I hadn't told her what I wanted to.

'To ask you something, Oliver. A proposition.'

'Oh? I regret I haven't all that much time.'

As near a no as I'd ever get before asking.

'No, Lovejoy. It's out of the question.'

Oliver was one of those who pose before fireplaces, staring solemnly ahead as if at infantry.

'I haven't explained yet.' I did my ingratiating smile, trying to copy Dr Dymond's open-palm gesture. It had really added to the don's eloquence.

'Your explanations, Lovejoy?' He breathed a stoic breath. Ready. Take aim. 'It smells of one of your antiques machination situations.'

I forgave him his language. A Mayor is a politician. Probably called sleeping with his wife an intercourse opportunity situation. I cancelled the thought instantly. Him and Luna.

'Good heavens, no!' I exclaimed. 'It's honest, quite legal. And profitable. I don't mean for me! I mean Mrs Carstairs here!' My joviality was just this side of hysteria.

You can always see a politician's mind whirring because the cogs are on the outside. His went: profit = money; and money = votes!!

'But I understand, Oliver,' I said, all kindly. 'You wouldn't *want* profit. In case your opponents accused you of amassing money.'

'You said it's confidential, Lovejoy.' From Luna, bless her little heart. On cue. I'd not even told her to say it.

'Of course it is!' I said stoutly. 'Well, was. I'd best be wending –'

'A moment.' Oliver paced, even steps. 'Do no harm to hear you out, eh?'

'If you promise not to divulge a single word.' I drew up a chair. 'It goes like this. You embark on a fund-raising, for some deserving charity.'

His disappointed frown washed itself away when I continued, 'You purchase a load of antiques. And sell them at a considerable profit. Everybody gains – you, the charity. Your wife gains the commission.'

'How do I gain?' asked this philanthropic politician. Not how does the poor children's charity gain, note. Nor even how much commission Luna'd get.

'Oh, you gain the sum equal to your investment, Oliver.'

'Spend fifty to make fifty? That's nothing, Lovejoy.'

'No, Oliver. You *gain* one hundred per cent.'

'Gain?' He glanced sharply at Luna, rocked on his heels, came to rest. 'You mean profit?'

'Gain.' I smiled, knowing he was hooked. 'Antique dealers call it profit, alas. Anybody can do it, Oliver. Luna. You. I'll be the front man. But there's one thing. You'll be open to accusations.'

'What accusations?' He paled at the thought.

'The worst of all, Oliver.' I parted my hands to show honesty. Nothing concealed here. 'Your opponents will accuse you of electioneering. Making political capital out of charity.' As if a politician ever lost votes by giving to an orphanage. He'd be Prime Minister within a week, play his cards right.

'Oh.' He nearly said, Is that all? He smiled, bravely. 'Facing false accusation's my bread and butter, Lovejoy.'

Indeed. A thought crossed his brow, possibly an innovation. 'If anybody can do it, Lovejoy, why don't you? You're poor as a church mouse.'

'Oliver!' cried Luna, scandalised.

'Me?' I was so beatific. 'I do it all the time, Oliver! How do you know I haven't got millions stashed away?'

'Then why do you need me?'

Shrewdness is a pest. Bloody politico. 'Because I'm known. Not that I'm a real antique dealer. I have a brain and everything.'

'He is good, Oliver. Honestly. I know,' Luna caught the double meaning and rose suddenly to hide her confusion. 'I'll make some tea while you talk, shall I?'

'Please.' We both said it together.

CHAPTER TWENTY-FOUR

Sleeping the sleep of the just that night, I imagined all sorts, dozing in snatches. I kept seeing Rye Benedict's accident. Over and over he did his fall, taking me with him so I shot upright crying aloud as I tumbled. I sweat like a pig – always do. But this night was worse. I slumbered in damp sheets, my hair drenched and glued to my face, tormented, dripping wet.

He fell again. But that smile, as if . . . Always he turned in before starting his fall. One hand outstretched to the pulley rope. One hand outstretched behind, into the interior of the hoist space, as if expecting to take hold of something. Feet on the hoist's sill, rope dangling in front, free hand outstretched. And his other hand holding on to something. Then suddenly it wasn't, and he began his stately descent, smiling the smile that became tinged with horror as . . . I woke, whining and breathless, soaked. Had Rye's mouth moved? Was he saying something just before he started to fall? *To someone standing there behind him?*

By five o'clock I was up, checking for dawn, hearing the first birds hesitant about cheeping. I have a pint of skimmed each day. Koala delivers it about half-past five in good time for the bluetits. The little sods drill a hole through the foil cap and somehow suck the milk out. Like a fool I pay through the nose for peanuts. They have a wooden holder I fill each day, Michaelmas to Candlemas. Koala's an Aussie artist who paints triangles. He swaps jobs with his cousin, our local milkman, six months in Sydney. Koala pulls my leg about the birds. I'm sure he whistles them down.

'I'm going to have to do some night milking, Koala, prices you charge.'

'Send your cat, like the witches did.' He reached up and pulled the pear tree branch down to take the nut-holder. He's lanky, and I'm not.

'Ta.'

Koala hooked the string over a twig and let the branch go. It sprang up into place. He left, laughing. Like witches did? Anciently, villagers stole out to milk other folks' cows on the sly. A punishable theft in country areas. Herds whose milk failed were called bewitched. And culprits had to be sought, of course. Witches sent cats to do their thieving for them. All stupidity, folk fable nonsense.

For a minute I stood in the cold morning air, watching dawn. I looked at the pear tree. Koala had reached up, held the branch with one hand, took the nut-box with the other ... Had Rye's hand slipped? I was going barmy. I went inside for my breakfast. Fried tomatoes in margarine again, fried bread, tea with one sugar. I'd have eggs and bacon except you have to handle them raw. Anyway, nowadays you've to starve yourself to live healthy.

Odd, but even sillier thoughts kept coming back. I should have been thinking about money. Oliver had guardedly agreed to give half the wadge I needed. Once an accountant, always blinkered. He heard me out, said it seemed cast iron, then offered half. In vain I'd pointed out that his profit would be reduced. He'd smiled the glacial grin of accountants everywhere, and said, 'Circumstances preclude totality.' Beyond belief. It's a question of the scam being a biggie – 'grandy' in the trade – or a titch.

Tip: In antiques, major scams, the grandies, begin about ten times the average wage. Now, some scams have no *material* theft. Lincoln Cathedral's goings-on over its Magna Carta Exhibition would be an example – what was it, quarter of a million? Others depend on stolen reality. Say for the sake of instance you live in a country where 20,000 dollars is your national annual income. Then ten times that is where grand antiques scams begin. Nor need they not be stolen stuff, like a fifth of all antiques sold these days. It could be one single precious painting stolen from the Prado in Madrid. On the other hand you can amass a hundred legit pieces of crummy old near-derelicts, and the whole lot might not qualify as a grand scam. Anything less, therefore, than $20,000 \times 10$ would be regarded as ordinary. Of course, among the lower orders of antique dealers – and there are plenty down there, here – even a few quid profit is cause for rejoicing.

Then again, there's the sword of Simon Bolivar – or Simòn Bolìvar if you insist on accents. This hero of 1824 had a sword. In February of 1991, Colombian rebels returned it to a Bogota museum. This kind of fanfare gift is a godsend to the world's fakers, who instantly turn out a trillion fakes, sell them, whispering the fatal words, '*This* is the original, mate. You don't *really* believe anyone in his right mind'd *give away* the real one, do you ...?'

Why am I telling you all this? Because I needed, vitally important-antly urgently desperately needed, to move out of the titch class and into the grand, at speed. Sod Oliver. I found myself out looking at the pear tree for the millionth time. Koala had reached out with one hand –

'*Aaaargh!*'

'Good morning, Lovejoy. Did I startle you?'

'You silly old bitch!' I'd have clocked the stupid hag if I hadn't been in a state of collapse. 'Why can't you knock first, frightening me out of my skin? First thing in the frigging morning. I'm hardly out of my pit, you ignorant old . . .'

'Do forgive me, Lovejoy. But I can't knock if you're out in the garden, can I?' She smiled up at me. 'We've rather reached a dilemma.'

'We have, have we?' Beware birds using plurals. It means they've elected you to do their next job. Plurals and confidentiality, my bane.

She looked more dilapidated than ever. Reluctantly I reheated my tomatoes, and shared them with the old biddie. I gave her my other chipped mug.

'We've reached the end of our resources.'

Oh, aye. 'Datewise? Geltwise? Genealogicalwise?'

She examined the tomatoes doubtfully, cheeky old sod. Had the nerve to prod the fried bread. It was a beautiful breakfast. One day I'll cure myself of charity. Then scroungers had better watch out.

'Eat it,' I ordered. 'I'm not going to have you fainting on me.' Tomatoes are a Yank invention anyway.

'Thank you, Lovejoy.' She looked around, steeled herself, and noshed along. 'The information you gave me was most helpful.'

'Giving you the address of the building you were in?' I was narked. I'd hoped she wouldn't eat, but she trenchered away like a guardsman.

She reached over, eyes misty, touched my hand. 'I've written to my friend in New York commending you.'

Jesus, she was importing more spongers. Time to get rid. 'What now?'

She smiled. I looked away. These crones get to you by having lovely old eyes. Well, I'm up to their game. I'd cut and run as soon as I was dressed. The social security could have a riot with this poverty-stricken New Yorker.

'It's 1837, Lovejoy.' She accepted more tea, the mare. I had to brew up again. 'And 1855, in Wales.'

She rambled on while I got my jam. It's local, the usual half-pound jars you get at bring-and-buys in any village in the kingdom. Oddly, she was enraptured, asking how I'd made it. I said I'd write out the recipe. She said blueberry must be some sort of relative of our whinberry, because –

'In Scotland,' I told her firmly. I'd never get shut. She was whittling through a loaf, and reaching for my last bit of quince jelly, I saw with rage. I snatched it away with a second to spare, thieving old bitch. I ought to put a lock on my kitchen alcove. I will, when I get a minute from genealogy. 'In Scotland, they've the Register of Sasines. Land's feudal, held ultimately of the Crown. A good system. Only one channel for ownership, see? Their Register of Sasines is from 1617. If your Scotch ancestors had land. Some's in Latin.'

She cried through a mouthful of my bramble jelly, 'My great-great-great grandfather had a croft in Fife!'

I caught her reaching for my fried bread, got it back with a polite wrestle. 'Deeds start about 1554 – contracts, selling something important. If your ancestor died without heirs, search the Ultimus Haeres records, Scottish Record Office. The Crown, the final heir, took charge.' I looked for the fortune-hunter's gleam but saw only unbridled enthusiasm. So she was simply what she seemed, a loony coot hoping Grampa was Henry V.

Wearily I sided up while she rabbited on and I rabbited back. Yes, for Wales go to Chancery Lane – hatchings, matchings and dispatchings in nonconformist registers from 1700 to 1858. 'Court of Great Sessions in Cardiff,' I told her, snatching her plate in case she wolfed crockery too. Christ, she'd scoffed more than me. I was astonished she could still move. 'And St Cat's House, of course.'

'*Wales*, Lovejoy,' she said patiently. Like I'd never heard of it.

'Best combined records of all, has Wales. The one thing Wales lacks is surnames.' I paused, suddenly hopeful. 'Philips? Morgan? Evans?'

'All those!' she cried, clapping her gnarled old hands. 'How *did* you guess! And Jones!'

I brightened. Once she started excavating that lot, she'd vanish into some dusty file and never be found. Genealogy searchers make a surcharge for Welsh ancestors. Not quite fair, because combine PRO and GRO files and you're back to 1837 in an afternoon. I was so happy that I handed her a note as we finally left. I marched her up the lane.

'Sorry, love. I'd have liked a longer chat. Don't forget about Regimental Registers of Births, for ancestors born into regiments from 1761 – abroad from 1790. Okay? Your US-born Britons are harder – the PRO's earliest are Texas, I think. They're only 1838.'

I made the top of the lane by the chapel, and heard the bus coming. Farewells are quite pleasant, sometimes. She was trying to scribble everything down.

'I think the bloody Government should let you see family wills free. I mean, whose wills were they, for God's sake? Your own Grampa's. The Record Office charges, stingy swine.'

I would have gone on – it's one of my grouses – but the bus hove up and I had to run. Which meant cunning old Lovejoy escaped, old biddies being a mite slow.

'No, Percy,' I said. 'She's only out for a walk.'

'Thought she was waving, Lovejoy,' the driver said.

An odd thing. As I'd paid, a bonny girl was alighting. She changed her mind, came round and got on again. Percy charged her another fare, mean sod. Maybe he'd worked for the PRO in some earlier incarnation. He pulled us away. We left Miss Turner wheezing.

'Lovejoy?' The girl came and sat by me. She was brilliant with youth, loveliness. 'Laura. My only name. All surnames are remnants of feudalistic paternalisms.'

Dilemma time. Should I have exchanged Miss Turner for this? 'Lovejoy,' I admitted. But it only takes ten minutes to town, then I'd be shut of her, 'It's all I have.'

She toyed with the idea, found it gratifying. 'You're against pseudo-religious degeneracies.'

Time to change my seat. I couldn't stand one minute of this, let alone ten. Is there any ism worth a thought? We were the only passengers on the lower deck. Plenty of space.

'Excuse me, love, but I –'

'Money, Lovejoy. To invest. No strings.'

She smiled. I froze. I'd admired her comeliness, her pure adorable style, of course. But now I looked deeper, I saw the mystic loveliness in her, the brilliantly dazzling glory of her nature. I'd been a fool.

My voice wouldn't get going for a second. 'How wise, er, Laura. And I agree about, er, names. They really are degeneracy things.'

She told me the sum she had in mind. It was enough to lift a small country firm called Lovejoy Antiques, Inc. from a titch to a biggie. I listened admiringly to her lecture on totalitarianisms all the way into town. I agreed totally, every word.

We went to a bank. I wrote out a receipt, specifying how the spoils would be divided. Laura fell about at this. I grinned amiably along. I quite like mirth at these moments – not that I've had many such. Signed, sealed, and, most important, delivered. The manager wrung my hand. He gave me a chequebook, pen, briefcase and a set of stationery. He'd have blessed me, if he'd known how.

'One point, Lovejoy.' She waited by the bank door, looking into the busy thoroughfare.

My heart sank. 'Yes?' Too good to be true?'

'I insist on absolute confidentiality. Understand?'

Only ethics. Phew. 'Confidentiality's my other name!' I was so jolly with this delectable angel. 'What if I run short, Laura?'

Then she really took my breath away. 'I'll give you more, Lovejoy.'

She swung off into Head Street, leaving me standing. I wondered if she was unmarried, and would take a bloke like me. I'd get my hair cut, maybe even buy a new jacket. Yet I'd done all right with Lovely Laura as I was. Never change a winning team. A faint superstition nudged my mind: maybe my heartfelt charity to old Miss Turner brought me luck. You know, the leprechaun gambit? I was rich. Bulging. Loaded. Word would get around. And I would fly into a heaven of antiques, antiques.

For the first time I felt I was winning. I tore round by the post office in search of Luna. I was exhilarated. The chequebook felt the size of a ledger.

I was going to spend, spend, as in splurge. My heart was filled almost to bursting, with true happiness, that only money can buy.

CHAPTER TWENTY-FIVE

We drifted into Woody's caff like thistledown, me and Luna. Tip: if you've money – I mean serious gelt, not your piggy bank raped by a nail file – don't advertise. Not in antiques. Because antiques are different. Luna didn't understand.

'It stands to reason, Lovejoy.' She grimaced delicately, swiftly controlled, and put aside her chipped mug. Woody's tea was in fine fettle, a slimy sea of liquid grot. 'With money –'

'Shhhhh!'

She bent to whisper. The dealers leaned in, ears on the wag. 'Why not simply tell everybody? Then they will come to *us*. Think of the petrol we'll save!'

I managed not to groan. Women are better money managers than us. Where they fall down's on little things. I once knew a lovely middle-aged bird, Doris, who missed buying that Rembrandt nicked from Dulwich because she paused to have a row with a shop girl about the price of envelopes. Honest to God.

'They'll up their prices, love.'

Her expression changed. 'They would do *that*, Lovejoy?' She glared round Woody's caff through the blue fog of fat fumes. The lads looked away. 'But they're your friends! It's scandalous!' There was more of this. I pinched her tea, sucking through the film of scummy leaves, waited for her storm to blow over.

'Lovejoy.' Eyes downcast now. Still, a little guilt does a woman good. 'I tried with Oliver. He's had second thoughts. I'm so sorry.'

My heart dived. 'He's backing out?' It really had been too good to be true.

'No. But he's cut his offer.'

'It was already inadequate.' I thought I'd explained all that. 'A scam's titch or grand, love. To go upmarket –'

'I'll make up the difference, Lovejoy.' She misinterpreted my gape, and said quickly, 'His quarter, I mean. So we only need the other half.'

Oliver a quarter, Luna a quarter. *And Laura half!* I didn't tell Luna about Laura. She'd get the wrong idea. I just had enough money. The point being, that only one great dollop of antiques would leap to the dollop broker. Logic.

'Here, Woody. A couple of pasties.'

Woody's rotund belly shook with mirth. The cholesterol king is the only spherical bloke I know. His clothes gave up years ago, and now split majestically. Modesty was satisfied by an apron stiff with decades of solid grease.

'Come into money, Lovejoy?'

The world stilled in reverence at the mention of the great god M, the way congregations stop coughing at the Consecration.

'Aye. I've found Mark Twain's *Huckleberry Finn* manuscript.' There was a general laugh of relief-regret. Another version of this find had lately hit the antiquarian scene. It happens in America once a year, give or take. 'On the slate, Woody. Hang the expense.'

The world relaxed, Lovejoy still the indigent quirk.

'Can you afford it, Luna?'

Worried, I gazed at the lovely woman opposite. Luna had been more on my mind this past couple of days than she had a right. I mean, what did my old Gran say about women? 'A rag, a bone, and a hank of hair.' Affection doesn't come alone. It brings obligations. And who has time for those? But a bonny bird bringing money is a goddess of unsurprising beauty. I ought really to tell her the risks. I mean, if you own a favourite Royal Doulton piece, then you're at risk from roaming dolts, burglars, dealers on the knock, plumbers coming to mend your bathtaps, visiting priests, Aunt Jessie. But that's simply opportunistic theft, done on the spur. Titch antique, titchy risk.

But there's something else. Something far more serious. Big league. It's the ominous death-dealing malevolence that lurks in the world of the grand scam. It's dollop broker country. There's only a dozen genuine dollop brokers in the entire kingdom – I mean those operating well outside the law. All honest, God-fearing hoods and crooks in the known universe keep shtum about them. For the dollop broker is sacrosanct, the Machiavellian figure behind the biggest of the grand scams. Local, national, and international.

There are a million stories, mostly true. Of the English noble who did a humble Italian to doom for failing to deliver his promised tomb-robbings in Tuscany. And to whom is attributed the appalling statement, 'A promise paid for, is marriage; infidelity justifies fatality.' Needless to say, the antiques trade thinks this the height of logic, and praises the nobleman's propriety. And of the Yorkshire blokes, dealers all, who sank their three friends' boat in the North Sea by simply cutting it in half with a larger vessel one dark and stormy night, having transferred the smuggled antiques. (It saved having to pay, a tiresome chore.) Word is that a Dutchman survived, and broods vengeance. He's expected in Newcastle later this year. I'll let you know what happens, if I hear. And of the Turkish lady whose very special girlfriend took this Egyptian antique dealer under her wing. She caught them in flagrante, but was very good about it, and said never mind these things happen don't they. And then framed them for the attempted robbery of a French museum and murder of a Levantine security bloke doing a job for that Munich-Swiss combine –

'Lovejoy.' Luna took my hand. I withdrew it sharply. The dealers were sniggering, nudging. 'Please accept.'

'Eh?' Who'd refuse an offer like this? The pasties were gone. I hoped I'd had hers as well. 'If you insist, Lune.'

She went misty, smiled. 'Thank you, Lovejoy.'

The favours I was doing! Laura's thanks, Luna's gratitude. I felt peeved about Oliver. I was trying to do the selfish pillock a favour, and not a bleep of gratitude.

'Think nothing of it, Lune,' I said magnanimously.

We left then, after a sordid verbal skirmish with Woody over when I'd settle his wretched slate. Luna had a fit of conscience on the pavement, wanting to discuss the problem of world debt. I simply walked on, round to the auction rooms by the Beehive tavern. I mean, Woody had a thriving business, right? So why continually try to exploit travellers like me? It's just not fair.

'That's the wrong way of looking at it, Lovejoy,' Luna countered, trotting alongside. 'We *should* pay. It was the same with that registration. The girl proved most impertinent. I had to speak very firmly to the manager, I can tell you.'

'Love,' I said wearily, halting. She bumped into me. 'I'm crazy about you. Making love was the peak of ecstasy. But for Christ's sake button your frigging mouth. We're bidding this afternoon. Sod ethics.'

'You're . . .?' She searched my eyes. A woman's gaze is never still, is it. Switches side to side, thousand times a minute. Even baby girls do it. Boy babes simply look, steady and level. Sometimes I wonder why.

But not for long. Priorities established, we zoomed to Wittwoode's Auction Temple. Viewing ten to one o'clock, auction at two precisely.

A viewing is such a wonderful experience it's no good trying to describe the sensation. You must see for yourself. And I promise. You'll fall in love with antiques. Oh, I know every viewing day's disappointing when you glimpse the load of tat, crud, dross. But your job is to go in *knowing* that bliss awaits. The bliss is antiques. And every antique is worth any amount of money. Why? Because money's machine-spun paper. And antiques are legacies from the hand of Man, the gifts of angels. Never mind that money is the modern religion. Only idiots preach that money counts. Business barons know that they're duckeggs. Sooner or later, they come to their senses. They frantically start buying like maniacs – and they buy antiques. They are trying to capture Time, encapsulate it as if Time is theirs to re-use. Is there a mighty dictator who fails to stuff his presidential palace with antiques? Trade tycoons raise unedifying edifices – museum, art gallery, foundation – to their self-glory, and thereby prove themselves prats. The megalomaniacs who carry on this way expect knighthoods for caressing their own egos. Quite barmy. When you're that far gone, remorse should be silent grief. Building bizarre cathedrals simply embarrasses the rest of us. (Of course, we're green with envy, which is why we scorn their 'achievements'. Like I'm doing, I suppose. It must be great to be well-adjusted.)

Wittwoode's Auction Temple.

'Drift. Don't look. Don't seek or search.'

Luna was puzzled. 'But you said –'

'I've told you before, Lune.' I pulled her roughly behind the stack of chairs and occasional tables the whizzers chuck together near the long wall. Nobody was close. 'The antiques will pull you. They're here – somewhere. They'll shout, call, maybe just touch your mind as you walk by. But they're here.'

'They'll . . .' She looked at the chair legs sticking out at all angles from the mound. 'Are they here now?'

'Yes. And when you find one,' I begged, pleading, 'don't shriek and wave your handbag. Just tell it hello, then tip me the wink.' I shook my head. Give me strength. 'Not *really* a wink, Lune. Metaphorically. Direct my attention.'

'How?'

'Lune. You directed my attention the other night –'

'Shh!' She pulled away, prim. 'Twice you've mentioned that episode. Lovejoy. Don't think I don't deplore my . . .'

'Shhhh,' I said. 'Please, Lune. We're in public.'

'Yes, well.'

'Here.' I stopped as we emerged. Something she'd said. 'What registration? The impertinent lass?'

'Registration? Oh. The motor car.' She lowered her voice. I
bent, anxious. 'Do you think I ought to complain? Officially, I mean?
The girl's rudeness –'

'No, love.' I was broken. She'd worn me down. 'Don't complain.
She might have trouble at home. But what car?'

'At the garden centre. Poor Mr Benedict's. Don't you remember?
It belonged to a Mr G. F. Cooley, Waylance Street, Weston Hammer. It's quite a nice village, in Staffordshire I think . . .'

Hopefully, sanity lived. Somewhere. I left her, and drifted.

It happened in the first pass. I called Luna over. She came eyeing
the dealers, mistrustful. I held up the bottle-shaped carafe to the
light, smiling.

'See the medallion on the side? Enamel. Trying to be German
eighteenth century.'

'I think it's rather nice.'

Loud with merriment, I chuckled and wagged my head. 'Sorry,
love. Fake. Look through the other side. The glass is quite clear.
Somebody's ground out depressions, enamel pastes in and fired it
anew. It seems true enamelling. Authentic enamelled glass has *no*
sign of grinding. The grinding wheel's marks show up as a slight
prismatic effect. See them?'

'Well, no.'

There weren't any to see, so I was glad she said no. I replace the lovely antique carafe among the job lot of pressed glass
jugs and butter dishes, mentally apologising to it. It stood there,
regal.

'That's inexperience, love,' I said airily. 'It'll come.'

There was a small collection of decoy ducks in a wicker basket.
They're collectors' items, but take care. Most aren't genuine, because
wandering fairgrounds have started selling new ones, suitably aged,
on the now-fashionable 'country antiques' stalls among their side-
shows. I make some myself when I'm desperate. As ever, antiques
bring surprises. Some collectors'll pay a year's average wage for some
rarities. I think they're horrible, but A. Elmer Crowell's Black Duck
Preening – East Harwich in the USA – or Black-Bellied Plover are
current favourites. I mean, who wants a wood duck? Once you've
seen one, and all that.

I called loudly to Betty O'Connors – lives down on the wharf
postal-selling thimbles and stitchery by subscriber catalogue – to bid
for a porcelain firemark for me.

'Bid yourself,' Betty called back.

'Misery,' I grumbled. 'I can't stand this heap of dross. Just bid, eh? I'll owe.'

Dealers snorted, but sidled across to inspect the firemark.

'All right, Lovejoy,' Betty relented.

'Ta, love.' I waved a piece of paper between my fingers, and left it with Alf, a whizzer famous for having lost a leg in the service of antiques corruption. He fell through a wardrobe one night. He'd been bribed to swap the decorated surrounds of two pieces of furniture before the following day's auction. It's a common practice (swapping, not falling through wardrobes). Alf was trapped. His leg went bad, and he was discovered by a charlady who had hysterics. He's a blabbermouth. We call him Radio Alf. I'd chosen carefully. The price I'd pay – a month's wage – was about right, for an Atheneum Fire Office porcelain firemark. They're rare, especially mint.

'People had them on their houses,' I explained to Luna. 'The fire insurance firm would reward the firefighters.' I didn't explain the fertile grounds for corruption and extortion that fire insurance provided in early days, as now. Luna would find some reason not to believe me.

'Now, love,' I said, having sussed the entire place. We were outside, strolling down a riverside walk by some cottages. I quite like trees now and again, even in towns, as long as they don't gang up and threaten to start their own countryside among our harmless streets. 'Your first job.'

'I've *done* several, Lovejoy.' Her lip was quivering. What the hell now?

'This one's your own. Pick seven or eight pieces of furniture. Any. Buy them, changing your mind, hesitating. Now and then start bidding, then drop out. Look . . .' I searched for a word that described her to a tee. 'Incoherent.'

'What if I guess wrong?'

I smiled. I was going to turn them into antiques anyway. 'You can't. You won't. Believe me, love. I know.'

Her eyes filled. 'Oh, Lovejoy. You *do* trust me!'

'Eh?'

She sniffed, did the hankie bit. 'You wanted Betty O'Connors to bid for you, when I'm perfectly –'

Well, I rolled in the aisles. 'Betty? She won't.'

'But she said she would, Lovejoy.'

'Of course she did – so I'd say how much I'd pay. I wrote it down. She'll buy it for herself.'

Luna instantly went nuclear. 'But that's . . . *dishonest*, Lovejoy! Actually to *resort* to such –'

I heard her out, shaking my head sadly at the perfidy of an unkind world. 'Go in this afternoon. Bid for the German carafe, the one shaped like a retail sherry bottle. And that job lot of decoy ducks.'

'But you said they were fakes, Lovejoy.' Wide eyes and all.

'Er, did I?' I'd just deplored Betty O'Connors' lies. 'Er, yes. But the vendor's been in hospital, and wants to move near his daughter's. To, er, Bognor.'

She looked about for lurking observers, decided and gave my arm a surreptitious squeeze. 'You're sweet, Lovejoy.'

'Lune. A little kindness to an old soldier . . .' I welled up at my fictitious old git, controlled myself manfully.

'Should I bid higher than necessary, Lovejoy?' She was thrilled again. 'I mean, the old gentleman would appreciate a little extra. Is his daughter married? Just think how happy he'll –'

Luna got out of hand fast. 'No, love,' I said firmly. 'He's very proud. He would hate charity. Some of these old folk . . .'

'You're so *wise*, Lovejoy! I had a great-aunt once –'

'Look. I'd better go. Remember what I've told you.'

'Yes,' she said solemnly. We walked to the road by the bridge. 'That horrid Mr Cooley was looking at the carafe after we looked at it. Did you notice?'

'Cooley?' I didn't know any Cooley.

'Who owns the motor you wanted to know about.'

Cooley? I halted. Who had been in, milling around among the women non-dealers? Acker Kirwin, Betty, Marjorie, Olive Bremner from Stirling, a few of the Brighton circus, Big Frank, Jeff for ten seconds, Chris who collects hammered silver, Mannie the maniac clock-faker in his caftan and cowbells, Connie Hopkins, Deg the parchment forger, Lonnie Marklin who makes model coaches. Who else? Stan Tell who's furniture. Liz Sandwell, today unfortunately guarded by her jealous rugby-playing monster lover. A scattering of lesser dealers. One I like particularly is Rhea Cousins. She's Georgian furniture – pays in very personal services administered in the privacy of her own home. Her husband Willis is her accomplice. They're very, very rich. I ran down this list, checked myself. I was speaking aloud. Luna's eyes were like saucers, the list making her weak at the knees.

'Cooley?'

'The one I told you about at the other auction, Lovejoy.'

'Acker Kirwin?' I described him.

'Yes. He's not very nice, Lovejoy. Shifty. He's the same one who
. . . conned us before. I *told* you.'

'Give us a lift to the mill, love?' It wouldn't take long. A breath
of country air would do us no harm.

CHAPTER TWENTY-SIX

The watermill was on a flow from the river. Artificial, of course, meaning manmade. A small fishing lake lay above, fed from a little tributary that came from a valley a mile or so off. The influx passed through the mill. Undershot, they call it, the water flowing beneath. You don't get as much power as from an overshot wheel, but that's just hard luck. If you have hills, like in Lancashire, you get significant power from big overshots.

Luna went in the car for the key from the garden centre office. It's quite tall as watermills go. Red brick, with a warehouse for sacks, and a loading bay where Suffolk horses clomped in with their waggons. Gingerly I looked, but the rain had washed the flint cobbles clean of crime, except for moss. Did I think *crime*? Wrong. Everybody saw it was an accident. Witnesses can't be wrong. The victim – sorry, the poor unfortunate – was in full view. Well, nearly full view. One hand was reaching in, out of sight. Taking hold of something, keeping him safe. Dead safe.

The surrounding countryside was quiet. Somebody was whistling across the river, in the market garden I shouldn't wonder. A motor started up. A dog barked, was ballocked crossly for not coming when he was told, the whole family was late now, bad dog. Slam. Rev, and off. Two anglers walked the riverside path, turning in to seek the lake. More gear than spacemen, camouflage jackets, rods, wicker baskets. Bet they only lived a hundred yards away. A laugh.

Somebody had shut the hoist door. A notice said *Council Property Keep Out*. The mill was closed until further notice; trespassers would be prosecuted. I felt indignant. We common folk owned the frigging place – but once a robber baron, always a robber baron. Calling it politics fools only the perpetrators.

The mill doors were locked, and the windows on the second floor wore wire mesh. You'd have to be Delia, at least, to get inside. That set me thinking. Had Delia himself found something in the offices, and come back later to kill Rye? But why? Delia came highly recommended. And asked for more jobs, any time. That's not the chat of a secret murderer, not round here. Also, he seemed as ignorant of antiques as any antique dealer, which is ignorance of a pretty stupendous degree. Here came Luna with the keys.

'I want to see the hoist, Lune.'

Oliver's Council hadn't the sense to use the original ancient locks, still functional. They'd spoiled the great doors by adding enormous metal bars, with modern padlocks. Typical.

The mill inside felt lovely, cool and spacious. The millstones were not turning, which was fine by me. Stairs you could ride a horse up led to open floors, substantial beams across each ceiling to carry almost any weight. 'Jolly' millers were hated down the centuries – think of the extortion they could perpetrate, controlling the only means of processing grain. And their ancient technology is beautiful to behold. Normally I would have been smiling but today I wasn't. We climbed higher.

'This is it, Lovejoy. The hoist.'

It was closed, that great wide window through which the sacks were pulled in. I'd expected a gap, like a fool.

'Why are we here? Do you think Mr Benedict left a clue?'

'How the hell should I know?' And why were we whispering?

I cleared my throat noisily and clumped with giant footfalls down the length of the room. Skylights, walls red brick, patches rimed to white. Only a single sack. One, by the hoist. I'd seen Rye reach out, swing it in. The selfsame sack? Or had Drinkwater taken it away in his extensive investigations of the tragedy? They'd lasted all of ten minutes. Really thorough.

'Luna,' I asked her. 'What happened? You were watching.'

'You saw, Lovejoy.' She gestured helplessly at the hoist window. 'Poor Mr Benedict leaned out. And fell. It was awful.'

'We saw him do it before. Why didn't he fall then?'

She thought, trying. 'Because he was hold of something?'

'What?' I nodded, go and show.

'That line of sticks, perhaps. There's nothing else. This hand.' She spun, aligning her hands. A pretty sight. I'd have reached for her, except this was where Rye was murdered.

Into a long oaken beam, fixed to the wall, was a line of wooden rods. Belaying-pin fashion, the sort you get on old sailing ships. Basically a simple wooden rod, tapered, thick at the top so it won't fall through. Purpose? To tie a rope on. Several pins. Simple.

Except?

Except, take hold of a pin at the top, and move about vigorously, as when pulling in a heavy sack through a hoist window, you might just waggle the stick enough to pull the damn thing out. And down you go. But Rye had no belaying pin in his hand when he fell. Even Drinkwater might have seen one.

'Hold the bottom of the belaying pin, love. And lean away from the wall.'

She took it carefully. 'Like this?'

'Keep your feet together, close to the wall. Now lean away.'

Suddenly I pulled the pin up and out, and she fell away, just regaining her balance.

'Lovejoy! That was a perfectly silly thing to do! I could have got splinters in my hand!'

'No, love. You couldn't.' The pin was worn smooth as silk.

Rye always used that first pin to hold on to. By its projecting *base*. Waggle it as you may, it couldn't come out. Unless somebody unseen in the mill, exactly where we were standing, perhaps chatting amiably as Rye had conducted his demonstration for the children below, had quickly lifted the belaying pin from its hole, leaving Rye's hand grasping nothing.

Acker Kirwin, alias Cooley, whose motor was waiting in the market garden across the river footbridge for him to escape. In the confusion, we'd all been too busy being shocked, running about phoning ambulances, controlling children. A good time to slip away. And it was clearly an accident, no? We'd all seen him miss his footing.

A man starting to fall to his death might well scrabble with his feet when the world is taken away from under for the first time. And last.

'Lovejoy?' Her voice seemed miles away. I was sitting on the floor. 'Lovejoy?' Her arms were round me. She was scented peach, some blossomy thing. 'Don't take on, darling. He went quickly, I'm so sorry. Please don't.'

Roughly I got up and shoved her away. 'Don't what, you silly cow?' I rounded on her, narked, pointing a finger into her face. 'You stop giving me orders. I won't have it, y'hear?'

'Yes, darling.'

'Just get that straight, all right?'

'Certainly, darling.'

Which having been decided, we descended and locked up, and she drove back to the Wittwoode Auction Temple to do her – read my – bidding. And I went to prepare my workshop for the labour that lay ahead. Serious, from now on. I was working for Prammie and Rye Benedict. And, who knows, some old bloke called Fairclough.

On the way, I caught a bus. More on a whim than with anything

serious in mind. An advert had caught my eye. The sailing barges
were gathering. Fifteen minutes later, in the estuary, I stood among
a scatter of old salts, children, and the odd housewife, to watch the
boats.

'They loaded up, all ready for the race?' I asked one elderly
nautical. A spherical whiskered gnome, smoking a foul pipe. I stood
to windward.

He snorted. 'Loaded? You'm thick, booy. Don't load for a race.
She'm travellin' loight.'

These Thames barges, few left now, are massive great things.
Two-masted, with a heavy spritsail. They stain the sails with red
ochre and oil. A real mess.

'Why're they so low in the water then?'

He spat past his pipe stem, the grottle donging a well-spattered
bollard quite ten yards away. I admired that. I knew I'd be trying
it myself, soon as I got home. I'd fail.

'Thames barge is flat-bottomed, son.' He scathed me with a look.
'These coasts, see? Leeboards instead of keels. Let her move to
leeward in shoal water, stay upright if a-grounded. Her mast's
lutchet-stepped, so she can go under bridges.'

He told me a lot, the way of coastal folk yapping about boats.
I stared at the three great sailing barges. So they sail up even shallow
rivers, these things? And race the Blackwater Race cargo empty? So
the use of one as a depot for tons of stolen antiques would be purely
temporary, while it was moored. Decoys are temporary. So Prammie's
heavy stuff from Cornish Place was still ashore.

'Ta, Dad,' I said to the old seaman. And went to work.

It isn't much of a place. A converted garage with a home-made
furnace and bellows. Toolracks. A window for north light, when
painting fakes. A folding bench hinged to the brickwork. Saws,
planes, nails in screwtop marmalade jars – they keep moisture out.
Paints in a cyclist's plastic expanding box (buy Italian-made boxes;
they're cheapest and best). Brushes in earthenware pots (cover them
with plastic freezer bags, with a rubber band). Containers of turpentine,
various painting oils. Linseed oil I try hardening in sunshine,
like the old sixteenth-century painters did. But rushing out
with the jar the instant our watery sunshine creeps over the garden
has seriously weakened me over the years. Canvas, woodstretchers,
glues, ancient nails nicked from various things. It's a mess.
Perfect.

It took me a good two hours to get going. I carried out some
precious pieces I'd been harbouring.

Clearing up is one of those postponable jobs that, when they're done, makes you feel surprisingly holy. I'd been saying I'd get the workshop ready for two months, but I hadn't. Now there it all was, pristine. Ready for action. Pleased, I went inside and brewed up.

Plan: with a massive number of antiques, fuffed out by fakes, I would be in a good position to demand from Connie Hopkins, my partner, access to the dollop broker. Maybe even meet her. Ex-teacher, Miss R. Find out from her who owned the Cornish Place dollop she was guarding, and goodnight, nurse. Proof for all my suspicions.

'Two lumps, Lovejoy.' Joan Vervain, in the porch, smiling.

'Still not reached Monte Carlo?' Gorgeous as ever.

She strolled in, spread herself on the divan. 'You're quite tidy.' She gave me a firm stare I didn't like. The new sort. 'Had any assistance in that line?'

'Women find it difficult here, love.'

'The Lady Mayoress been busying her little self in your service, Lovejoy?'

I wish I could do that, give words twice their meaning. I made tea, gave her some. She tasted it, grimaced.

'She hasn't taught you any domestic skills, Lovejoy.'

'Don't drink it then.'

She smiled, lay back, kicked off her shoes. 'Discontent, darling? You always were impatient.' She was doing the woman's laugh that isn't a laugh at all. I was the butt.

Something amiss in that smile. Still lovey-dovey, but with a secret joy. Del Vervain had shared it, when last seen.

'I'm delighted, love.' I came and embraced her, to get her over with. She embraced me back. We were so pally.

'Did you hear him last night?' She traced my features with a finger. 'Del announced your coming . . . appearance.'

'Soon at this theatre?' I quipped, but unhappy. I've no illusions about broadcasters. They march to a distant drum, out of sync. Del and she were planning something. To my detriment, if not destruction. Were the other producers, who came and read sheafs of documents at the Vervain's party, in on the giggle? 'One of those producers asked me to give her a call —'

'No, darling. Don't do that.' Too quick. '*I've* been asked to take care of you. Those stinking girls bother one so.'

Answer: the producers weren't in on the giggle. And in Joan's phrases lurked a concealed joke. I felt it.

'I'm a bit unhappy, love, I mean, me and microphones . . .'

'Darling.' Her gentle hands were everywhere, urgent and moving. I felt my shirt come undone. When Luna might come thrilling in with waggonloads of antiques? 'Darling. Trust me. This setback with Del is only temporary. We'll be away soon. I promise.'

'If you say so.' There isn't anything a man can do when a woman comes on like this. Her breasts, her shape, physiology, take command and it's yippee and waves on the seashore and passion blinding you to the entire galaxy.

So it happened. Mercifully, Luna was elsewhere, and occupied.

As I came round and Joan's cigarette smoke curled to the ceiling, her satisfied smile revealed she'd ditched me. No Monte Carlo. No escape to happiness to violins. No stealth to wealth for Lovejoy. I was to be sacrificed in some noble cause, namely and to wit, Joan and Del Vervain. Lovejoy would be down in their lion-infested arena with a chocolate sword. I used to watch the faces of women at cockfights when a tiny lad. As the poor feathered creatures slaughtered each other, the woman's faces wore identical uglinesses that I could not then name.

Now I know it well. It's passion. There are other words. Rut. Ecstasy. Orgasm. But none does half as well as that word from the darkness of Man's uncharted past. Joan had been bought back by Del, by the promise of a passion she had never yet experienced. What woman could resist? I was glad. I'd started all this when deciding to ditch her.

She went after an hour. We promised to meet tomorrow somewhere I forgot instantly. I spent a few troubled minutes on the telephone, and got through to an agency, pretending I was the *Bolton Journal & Guardian*. I was the Arts and Entertainment Correspondent: I wanted the ratings for Del Vervain's talk show.

'You've heard, eh?' the chap said, laughing. 'Jesus! The north got pigeons listening to the wire services? It's down the chute, mate. Word is they're going to pull the plug. I mean, four million's goodbye country. Two months'll see it off.'

'Ta,' I said gutturally, and Luna arrived.

Babbling, she hurried in, showing me notes, chits from Wittwoode's, catalogue photographs, ticks on lists. Her face was almost delirious with delight.

But not ugly. I put my arm round her. She stopped talking, possibly an all-time first, and asked what was the matter.

'Nothing,' I said. I bussed her. She pulled away, breathless.

'Lovejoy. This is no time for that. The vans are coming. The . . . whiffler said so.'

She noticed the divan. I hadn't straightened it.

'Did you have a doze?' She rounded on me. 'Lovejoy. You distinctly promised you'd tidy the workshop. Now we'll be hours behind. Get started *this instant!*'

'I love you, Lune.' I'd said it before, differently.

She drew back. The words seemed outside her experience. 'You. . . ?'

No good asking me. I was as astonished as she. Hesitatingly she made to come towards me. But three whizzers from Wittwoode's were suddenly bawling and clattering in the garden, and the waves on the seashore would have to wait. Luna must have power beyond Man's knowing. They'd never been on time before.

CHAPTER TWENTY-SEVEN

'You didn't do so badly, Lune.' I scanned the stuff.

She blushed with pleasure. 'I had to pay highly for the carafe, but it helps your old soldier friend.'

'My who?'

'The elderly gentleman, moving to his daughter's in Bognor. The German enamelled bottle –'

'Ah. *That* old friend.' I'd forgotten. 'Bidding rough?'

'No. That Acker Kirwin tried, but I outwitted him. I pretended to give up, then re-entered. He became discouraged.'

Well, well. I warmed to her. 'Acted like a veteran.'

She was primly disapproving. 'Some of the dealers' practices I find reprehensible.' She swung on me because I wasn't taking notice. 'Especially your friends, Lovejoy.'

'No!' I said, aghast. 'Acting dishonestly?'

'It's true, Lovejoy.' She shook her lovely hair, deploring all crime. Here was me eager to turn this junk into priceless antiques, and she was giving me bleeding-heart morality. 'I saw Sandy swop lot numbers' tickets.'

'Are you sure?' I asked weakly. I don't know anybody who doesn't do this elementary trick. I should have asked Luna if she was real, never mind sure.

'And I saw that . . . that lady. She *propositioned* a Brighton gentleman.' Her face was flaming. 'Her husband made the arrangements! Exchanging sexual favours, for a small oaken Canterbury.'

'Rhea Cousins?' Payment in kind's routine in the antiques trade. Like in every other, I might add, except not quite so obvious. Rhea's husband Willis keeps records on a home computer. Rhea's pretty, but worn out in the service of antiques. Luna must mean Lot 146, mid-Victorian but nice. Good old Rhea. 'I told you.'

'Yes, Lovejoy. Arranged *out loud!* I *mean*.' She was stunned, thrilled. Sweet Mary among trolls.

'Listen, love. It's normal. It's life. It's antiques.'

'But the first auction wasn't like that, Lovejoy.'

'It's just that you were new. Now, you're learning.'

'But . . .' She flapped her hand, sat on the divan beside me. 'But even Mrs Dainty, who's so . . . well, *proper*. I saw her move a battered

old painted chair from one job lot to another. She was most put out
when I explained her mistake.'

Margaret Dainty would be. I suppressed a grin. The trade calls
it 'waltzing'. You examine some item, forgetfully put it back in the
wrong lot. That way, you steal the item from whoever buys the first
job lot, and give it free to whoever buys the second job lot (and
that'll be you, of course). Waltzes are so prevalent that auctioneers
started taking photographs, but gave up. The law says sale happens
on the fall of the hammer – is it your fault if whifflers have misplaced
the stuff, for heaven's sake . . .?

Luna was staggered. 'Surely Mr Wittwoode supplies lists –'

'Come on, love. No chatter in work-time.' There's no telling the
Lunas of this world. I pulled her up and we went to haul the
furniture. 'Mrs Dainty pays the whifflers to turn Nelson's eye.' Like
the rest of us, I could have added, but didn't.

'She actually *paid?*' Etc, etc.

Luna had got twenty-one pieces. I got my trolley – pramwheels
and a plank – to lug them round to the workshop. She had done
very, very well. I told her so because women like approval. I don't
know why. They're strange. I couldn't care less whether people
approve or not.

'One. This dumb-waiter.' Small pieces first. 'It's a small single-
pillar table, right? It should have three circular mahogany trays with
raised margins – dishtops, we call them. It's only got two, right?'

'Yes.' She was looking about, downcast.

'Pay heed. That tips you off that the tripod feet and the top tray
have been taken away, married up, and sold as a tripod table.
Remember the one I was working on?'

'Is it no good? I shall take it straight back –'

'No, love.' Luna was serious effort, for all that she looked lovely
in her smart suit and high heels. Dressy. I like that. 'We'll make it
look antique and original, see? All we'll need is some flat-matched
mahogany to replace its third tray. The previous faker couldn't be
bothered. Well, we can.'

'Is that honest, Lovejoy?'

Untruth called. I looked her straight in the eye. 'Of course. We'll
describe it accurately.' I did my injured expression. I wasn't going
to stomach her woebegone dolour every blinking time I faked a
veneer. Best fight the battle now, and have done. 'Lune,' I said
quietly. 'If you doubt my moral standards –'

'No, Lovejoy! Of course I don't!'

'Please let me finish, Lune.' I closed my eyes, opened them, clearly seeking strength to go on. 'You harbour suspicions. It's too . . . too distressing to even think of.'

'I *know*, Lovejoy. I'm sorry I even *spoke* –'

God, the emotional turmoil. 'I won't conceal the truth, Lune. I've developed an . . . an attachment for you that's deeper than, well, I . . .' I'd almost reached the shaky lip. 'I want you to feel sure.'

'I do, Lovejoy! I was wrong to even *think* –'

I looked into her eyes. 'We stay within the law. Every item.'

Her eyes were brimming. 'I'm for you every inch of the way.'

'Very well,' I said quietly, smiling nobly through anguish. 'Then I forgive you. Load that dumb-waiter. Shove it round to the workshop.'

She was looking down at her lovely stylish clothes. 'I can't. I mean, are we actually going to . . . well, *work*?'

'Of course, you silly bitch,' I yelled. 'Get frigging started!'

'My suit will be ruined.'

She was worried about her high heels. Can you believe women?

'In the cottage you'll find trousers, wellingtons. There's an old shirt.' I bawled after her, 'And wear your own knickers. Them underpants are my even-dates pair, d'you hear?'

She trotted in. I started on the furniture. My spirits rose.

Three Victorian work-tables she'd bought were pedestal sup-ported. I up-ended them. Easiest and commonest job in the world, to remove the pedestal (carefully keeping it to make another fake) and plug the four (sometimes six) screwholes underneath. Add four lovely tapered legs. That would add a good seventy-eighty years to each table.

'Beg pardon, Lovejoy?' from Luna. I'd been muttering.

'Remind me to order three sets of legs from Channie in Long Melford. I've got some veneer to cover the traces of the screw holes.' I straightened, beamed. 'We'll have created three new fake antiques – er, restorations, I mean – by six this evening. Channie fakes – that is,' I corrected carefully, 'he's a master woodworker specialising in supplies to the antiques restoration trade . . . Hellfire, Lune!'

Luna was blushing, shifting from foot to foot. Where was the elegant, edible woman? She was shapeless. She rattled about in enormous wellington boots that seemed to reach into her. My old trousers hung on her like twin sacks. A tee shirt – surely mine could never be that gross? I'm dead average – was draped over her. A marquee after a storm.

'Am I all right?' she asked anxiously. 'For helping?'

'Yes, love,' I said gravely. 'You look really, er. Wheel the tables in. We've a lot to do.'

We found a table with four round legs. Only a crude Victorian wash-table, and battered almost to dereliction.

'We'll make this eighteenth century,' I explained. 'You simply take off each leg, and lathe it down to about three-fifths of its diameter. I'll show you how. Thick veneer from Herman the Gerbil at Eccles, and taper each leg on its inner face. Hey presto! It'll look eighteenth-century London!' And be as phoney as St Peter's bones in the Vatican.

'Me? The lathe?' Luna was really into it. 'Properly?'

'Of course, Lune. I trust you.'

'Oh, you.' But she was pleased, and set to willingly.

'The problem is that the legs will finish different, as they say. From a distance they'll seem a strange colour. So we'll dress the top to match. Then distress it a little, knock it about a bit.' I smiled at her sudden consternation. 'Customers expect it.'

'If you're sure, Lovejoy.' Her brow swept itself free of doubt, as always when a bird has a man in her pocket. Women are a great invention. No wonder sex caught on.

We set to.

It was bliss. Don't knock what we were doing, incidentally. I mean, if you knew how to change your old (or even new) chair into something antique and highly valuable, wouldn't you give it a go? And emulating the great masters of Georgian London, unexcelled for artistry before or since, gives a thrill of utter delight.

We had a tallboy – a stack of drawers, the bottom three wider than the top set. Hepplewhite was the tallboy king; though this was a feeble Edwardian copy, nicely aged. You separate the two sets. The top set consists of three single drawers plus the top level of two matching smaller drawers. We had a table top spare – the Wittwoode vannies had used it to offload the smaller items Luna had bought. We would cut it, then use it as a top for the lower stack of drawers, making a luscious early Victorian chest-of-drawers. The surface finish would be a problem, but that's always so with a faker. We'd get round that somehow.

Showing her how to use the spindle lathe, I was astonished at her proficiency. In half an hour she'd learned to keep the foot-treadle going while balancing herself to keep the pressure even on the chuck.

'Do you know prices have gone up two hundred per cent this year?' I groused, measuring a derelict piece to see if it could be turned into a bachelor chest. It was nice walnut, the right wood, but the bachelor is usually shallow – not more than ten inches, back to front, and only two feet nine inches wide. So a crumbling old bureau has to be savagely reduced. There's a giveaway: when you pull out a bachelor-chest drawer, it's 'tit-heavy', meaning tending to fall forwards –

'Luna!' The voice made me jump. 'What on earth?'

Oliver, marching in and nearly falling over the peg bath I'd set up yonks ago.

'Hello, Oliver.' Luna was being thrilled on the lathe. Not bad, either, turning her wood slowly, tongue out (Luna, not the spindle). Tousled but accurate. I liked her. 'Lovejoy's taught me! I'm thinning it, so –'

'Look at you!' Mayoress, he almost said.

'I hadn't time to come home. Lovejoy said I'm doing superbly.'

'Lovejoy!' Oliver's whiplash command was one I'd have instinctively disobeyed, but Luna was there so I followed him out. 'Lovejoy. I will not have my wife consorting with the district roguery! And where did she change? Dressed as a scruff!'

'Oliver.' I'm noted for my patience, but this was too much.

'No, Lovejoy. I've had a call from Del Vervain urging me to attend a rehearsal, with the Council, in our Moot Hall, of his radio show. How do you think this will make me look? I demand –'

'In, Oliver.' I pushed him into the workshop. This was an Oliver *vs* Luna conflict, nowt to do with me. 'Sort it out.'

Which made me think. I searched for pieces of cock-beading round drawers among the pile. This is moulding, semi-circular in section, that sticks out round the edges of drawers. Classically pre-1800, mahogany or walnut. Too much to hope for original post-1720 cock-beading, but plenty of Early Victorian lookalikes would do. The mistake fakers make nowadays is to fix them with minute pin-nails. The originals were glued. So to a criminal faker (I mean an honest restorer, like me) an authentic length of cock-beading is worth its weight in gold. I kid not.

'Look at you, Lovejoy.' Oliver was out, lip curled in scorn. 'Junk. To think I sent my wife to work with you.'

Oliver was a wart, but I heard him out. I've been slagged off by champs. I needed Luna. I'd no other loyalty. And, I thought indignantly, I was paying her, wasn't I? Well, nearly. I had that girl Laura's gelt, and Luna's. And possibly still Oliver's. Maybe I should pay her? A cheque had come this morning from the Employment Office. To me, not her. Transferring it seemed an unnecessary labour. I needed to cut down my administrative costs. Also, Luna was rich.

'I'm withdrawing my finance, Lovejoy. Completely.'

'Maybe I'll withdraw from Vervain's show in the Moot Hall.'

'You can't.' He was smiling. What else did he know?

'I can do anything I want, Ollie.'

'Don't call me Ollie,' he fumed. 'Attend. Or you'll suffer harassment every hour, on the hour.'

'Threats, eh?'

'Yes.' He said it simply enough for me to believe. 'See that Mrs Carstairs is home never later than five.'

'Yes, b'wana.'

But I'd found two small lengths of glued cock-beading, not a nail-mark on them. I went inside happily, but wondering what deal Oliver had struck with Del Vervain.

'All right, Lovejoy?' Luna asked, worriedly watching me.

'Don't stop,' I told her. 'It's difficult enough to get you women started.' She tutted, smiling, returning to her task. I added laconically, 'The circus is coming to town.'

665

CHAPTER TWENTY-EIGHT

Those working days made Luna realise that antiques are, if not everything, so nearly everything as to make no difference. News spread that Lovejoy Antiques, Inc. had money. We became a mecca. Dealers beat a path to our door. They came singly, of course, which is always a problem, because you don't know who's done a deal with whom. That matters, because you can force prices up or down with that knowledge. Without, it's free fall.

Luna showed amazing aptitude, especially for somebody with no experience. She learned to lathe table legs, to plane even. She could use a routing plane almost better than me within three days. And she was neat, so neat I had to ballock her and say for God's sake stop putting the chisels in order of size, and to leave the solvents alone instead of arranging them with the darkest shades near the window. Can drive you mad.

She liked seeing who would come next. Of course, she had likes and dislikes. She hated that evil swine Acker.

That week spent itself in buying from dealers, and making stuff. We didn't allow dealers into the workshop, of course. And every day as the light faded Gunge arrived in borrowed vans. We stopped for tea about then, and he'd load up while we discussed the evening plans. Luna had contrived an arrangement with Oliver so that she went home to change afterwards, while I made myself some grub. Then we'd meet in the White Hart and buy, buy, buy handies from dealers in the saloon bar. Mostly jewellery, miniatures, portable antiques like porcelain, small statues, glass, silverware, châtelaines, a few books – though I hate booksellers too much to buy on the hoof. Some stuff was memorable – a velocipede, early nineteenth century. And a collection of mustard pots brought in by Bullrush, a tramp with an eye for a window catch. Don't laugh at mustard pots, incidentally. Odd but large mid-Victorian silver gilt ones are even more valuable than small genuine sterling silver ones. Supposedly on account of their usefulness as marmalade pots, but I doubt that. Look for one with a monkey approaching a barrel. Chances are it's a John Bridge, 1825-ish, and costly as a small car. Mostly they're only a week's wages.

Luna had something of an eye for jewellery, I discovered to my delight. I'd taught her to fake amber, of course, using various resins (copal's the faker's standby) and incorporating dead insects or chips of dried bark or pine cones shredded in a food-mixer. The usual. (Don't overdo it, if you try this. I had to admonish her for stuffing the fake ambers with everything but the kitchen sink. One insect wing's fine, a zoo's a giveaway.) By Friday, I wore strings of her fake ambers under my shirt to get the right shine. I'd carved a few into small religious scenes from an invented saint's life. Future archaeologists will write theses on them in years to come.

Another curious thing: Luna was red-hot on modern stuff – 'tomorrow's antiques', the oldest of frauds. I mean, she bought a watercolour sketch by Leon Bakst (never heard of him). Costume, like nothing on earth. She was ecstatic, hugged me afterwards in the car park. It was from *La Boutique Fantasque,* 1918, apparently, worth a new motor. Can you believe it? I shrugged. Not antique at all. I liked the hug. I'd taught her erotic tobacciana at Jenny Calamy's. She snapped up, on description alone, a score of cigarette cases – some cheapish Birmingham Edwardian enamels, others French Art Deco 1920s, others German Edwardian in debased silver. They all had sexy scenes: 'risqué' if you're posh, naughty if you're not. Ladies up to no good, in various postures. The rule is, the more erotic the more pricey. She bought from a wandering shuffler, the sort of bloke no respectable dealer will look at twice. Luna paid him on the nail. He vanished for an hour. Just when I was getting uneasy, in he shuffled, stinking and bleary, carting this old sack of tobacciana. I was proud of her.

Yet she missed others. I can't understand it. There's a pretty famous bronze called *Tiger Devouring a Gavial.* It's gruesomely explicit. In 1831, Bayle the Frenchman exhibited this bronze – they're faked a-plenty by now, of course – and created a sensation. Within milliseconds, all Paris was churning out little animal bronzes. Tigers devouring elephants, lions chewing serpents, even innocents like rabbits and kipping cows. Bronzes vary from Viennese cold-painted cheapos to stallions being boring (a month's wage). Bronze-workers are called animaliers, in the antiques trade, but the posh pronounce it through the nose, prefixing it with 'les'. This enables you to charge double, if the buyer's a nerk. Luna missed a 1585 bronze she-wolf, probably Padua, when it was worth all the rest put together. I told her to stick to modern.

There's a limit to what you can buy in a night pub. You have to travel for the bigger-priced antiques, furniture, paintings, collections of porcelains.

I developed a strategy.

'See, Luna,' I told her after we'd unloaded that night. 'We're vulnerable.'

'But Mr Gunge takes it away safely, Lovejoy.' She instantly checked the latch. 'Don't we trust him? We should.'

Luna's sound instincts: trust Gunge. 'Look about, love.'

She did. The place was crammed with antiques, fake antiques, going-to-be antiques. I'd given IOUs like confetti. Later tonight, when she'd gone home to Grolly Ollie, I'd do my late-night ritual reckoning, how close I was to the thin red line. I must be skating on the very edge. Money really gets me down, the way it spends itself.

'I've taken options on some paintings. And church woods – old pews, lecterns, vestry wall panels. No. It's all right, Lune. The Church Commissioners have approved their sale.' I smiled disarmingly. The Church Commissioners would have hysterics, if ever they heard about the transactions.

'So we have to travel?'

Divvieing antiques is prodigious emotional effort. It's not like the January sales. It's draining. And recovering's like a shattering re-entry from space. It was a long time since I'd done something straightforward and pleasant, like making a fifteenth-century manorial table out of redundant chapel pews. The profit on these is fabulous. Cost: about five or six quid, going to press as they say. London selling price, two months' wages. On the Continent, about six months' wages. All for enjoying yourself, a day's light handiwork.

'We can't, until after next week's meeting, Lovejoy.'

'Can't? Meeting?' I'd promised myself this reenergising therapy. I wasn't going to be baulked. We'd set up about thirty meetings, pubs, auctions, an oyster fishery even. 'You do the meetings, love. You're a natural dealer.'

She coloured, smiling. 'Silly. Mr Vervain. It's tomorrow.'

'What?' I didn't remember any meeting.

'The answerphone. You agreed to attend. The Moot Hall.'

I would have collapsed on the divan, but it was covered with mounds of Dux porcelains wrapped in tissue paper. Scantily-clad nymphets draped about mirrors and marine shells are the vogue. There are plenty about, from 1860 on. Think of unglazed surfaces in pastel colours, and you'll make a fortune.

'I can't,' I said, narked. Just when I'd got my own scam going. God, I was nearly within reach of Miss R, the mighty dollop broker, where all would be revealed. And now this media mouthie was –

'Oliver has gone to inordinate lengths for Mr Vervain, Lovejoy.'

Reproach time. Luna looked soulful, but the divan was inaccessible. 'Think of the benefit for our town! Such an important personality . . .' She wasn't a Mayoress for nothing. Oliver must have worked on her. Why did he want *me* there?

'Can't I postpone it?' It was more than worrying.

Sod his ratings. Vervain's tactics were as transparent as Oliver's. Politicians and broadcasters are in the same game: grabbing acclaim. The slightest wilt means lying awake night after night as the fear burns into the brain that you aren't loved out there. They'll stop at nothing. And Oliver had as good as admitted that he and Vervain were fellows in a common cause.

'No, Lovejoy. You've given an undertaking.' I couldn't remember this conversation. But she was honest and true, right? She said firmly, 'You can't shirk it.'

One word I'd ban if I were king for a day is shirk. It's always used *at* me. As if the word itself aims blame. People missile the bloody word at whatever I want to do. I hate it, my cross since Day One.

'What have I to do?' my traitorous reflex asked dejectedly.

'Come to the Moot Hall to examine the Borough Regalia. A crowd of dignitaries, headed by Oliver, will be present. Del Vervain will make a speech about the community in local broadcasting, and declare it open.'

'Declare . . .?' My headaches wait until I run out of aspirin. You'd think doctors would get off their fat bums for once and find a cure. And chemists these days only sell batteries.

'The fund. To launch the Borough Broadcasting Station.' She smiled fondly. 'It's my idea. I mentioned it to the Vervains. Oliver won Council approval.'

'What's this got to do with me?'

She spoke at length on community bondings, whatever they are, Oliver's need of revenue enhancement . . . Once a Mayoress, always political.

After she'd gone, with much hesitation tonight, I did my sums, reaching a sorry conclusion. Money spends fast, earns slow. I tend to re-learn old truths every day, with surprise.

I came into this through Drinkwater's mistake. Him thinking I'd done the Cornish Place robbery. Then Prammie Joe's death drew me deeper – police now guessed some wandering psychopath. Then came the inexplicable clustering of antiques into grand-scam patterns. So unlike East Anglia, home of the titch scam. And they multiplied:

Tits Alors the prostitute, Connie, anybody with money, plus dealers without, Big Frank's next fiancée Calamity Jenny . . . Mostly clients of Marvella. Then Rye's fall to death.

Which was frightening. Unprecedented, as politicians say when they've ballsed up the economy yet again.

Money. Luna's wadge and Laura's formed quite a sum, but I needed more, thanks to Oliver's defection. I had Laura's number, to ring at ten-thirty each evening. She'd made me swear in blood never to ring at any other time.

'Hello? Lovejoy. Laura?'

'Wait.' Clatter, mutter. To another phone? 'Yes, Lovejoy?'

'I'm running out of groats, love.'

'Hasn't a certain politico's spouse funnelled you enough?'

Birds have this knack of inferring you're sleeping with another woman even when they're only asking you to pass the toast. Narked, I said, 'Look. There's nothing between Mrs Carstairs and me –'

'No? Why is *she* supplying your wants, Lovejoy?'

See what I mean? Ten meanings, one set of words. 'Investment,' I snapped. 'And if you can't talk about money without bringing –'

She purred, 'Don't take on, Lovejoy. I'm on my way.'

On her way? I hadn't asked her to come. It took four goes to replace the receiver.

She arrived in less than half an hour. We sat and talked. I got a cheque for another quarter. With that, I'd be well in. We talked for a short while. Not long enough. I tried sussing what she was playing at, her funding a shoddy like me.

'You're an investment, Lovejoy,' she told me several times. 'Don't look a gift horse in the mouth.'

'Investments aren't a gift.'

'No. They have strings attached, called profit.' I found some sherry. She was amused. 'The last time I was offered leftover Christmas Tio Pepe I was fourteen, Lovejoy. Is this how you seduce Mrs Carstairs?'

'Mind your own business. It's all I've got.'

She did that slow-waggle stroll, touching the antiques, feeling the divan. I'd cleared part of it, for sleep.

'Is this where you . . . what's the term you people use, Lovejoy? Shag?' She smiled, cocky, watching my face. 'Lay? Bonk? Hump? . . . our esteemed Mayoress, Lovejoy?'

'Listen, you.' I was getting hot under the collar. She was gorgeous, agreed. But she had no right to come hard. 'I don't disclose confidences about birds. It's my way. If you think your gelt buys you confidences, you can take it and shove off.'

No good. It only fuelled her interest. Her eyes were shining. 'You love antiques so much, yet you'd abandon them? Just to preserve . . . ?' She came close. I was having hell of a time getting the sherry cork out. Rusted in, probably. 'She must bed really fantab.'

'That does it. Out.'

I slammed the bottle down and pushed her. She fell back, on to the divan. I just managed to rescue two Royal Dux pieces before she hit.

'You silly cow!' I blazed, gathering them safe from this marauder. 'These damage easy! Don't you know the effort that went into making –?'

'Best you've ever had, Lovejoy, was she?'

'Any one of these is worth two of you, you dozy bitch.'

'Better than you think I could be, Lovejoy?' She was swinging her foot, her shoe almost off the upturned toes. Her legs were slender, beautiful. Might as well talk to the wall. I surrendered.

'What is it, Laura?' Wearily I put the Dux pieces on a harmonium keyboard out of her way. 'After a bit of rough scruff? Between college romeos? Mrs Carstairs beat you at tennis? Doing down Daddy's hand-picked fiancé? What?'

'All nine, Lovejoy.' She moved the rest of the porcelains to the harmonium. 'I hope these are new sheets, Lovejoy.' She stood, shivered elegantly. She was beautiful. 'Turn the heating on. I'll catch my death.'

'Heat spoils polishes.' My voice had thickened.

She laughed, dropped her clothes, slipped into bed. 'My teeth are *chattering*. In, for Christ's sake. Get me warm.'

'Look,' I tried weakly. What's the use? Women can do what they like. We pretend for our self-respect that we're making decisions. We're not. It's a woman's world. The proverbs lie.

Next morning she was gone by seven o'clock. She stared astonished while I made us both breakfast, followed me about saying how on earth, all that kind of woman's incomprehension. She dressed after I'd had both our breakfasts. She wasn't hungry. She smiled, paused in the porch to ask who said thank you and to whom.

'Etiquette doesn't cover this, does it, Lovejoy?'

'What's etiquette?' I said, making her laugh. She seemed so familiar, her face filled with life. Almost as if I'd known her in a previous incarnation. Lovely.

'Verdict, Lovejoy?' I had to work that one out. Was she better sex than arch enemy Mrs Carstairs.

'That's confidential.' I was narked. 'I have no relationship with that lady.' Who keeps score, making love? Love is yippee, hundred per cent of itself. Believing there are grades of totality is a woman's myth. I didn't tell Laura this. They never believe me.

She left in her colossal motor without a wave. It howled off up the lane, round at the chapel, then silence.

Reliable old Gunge, the dealer who could be trusted, came about thirty minutes later, to make his usual daily collection. He was in distress. Connie Hopkins had gone missing. Gunge asked did I know where she'd gone. He'd searched high and low. No sign of her in her shop. He seemed to have a key. Interesting, this. I didn't know he and Connie had got that far. I went through the daft rigmarole that telly series have taught us: where did you see her last, have you phoned her parents. Quite lunatic. Lost is lost. The only person who'd know about Connie was sitting on the divan, head in his hands, stuttering, in a state of collapse.

Luna arrived, bright of eye and bushy-tailed. Within seconds she was contributing stupidity.

'You should have put an advert in the newspaper, Mr Gunge!' she said cheerfully. Then wrinkled her nose. 'Is that perfume?'

Another of those days. I took her outside by the elbow. 'Luna, love. Just for today, stay mum unless I say. Understand?'

'It's a perfectly sensible suggestion, Lovejoy. Newspapers are a sound medium –'

'Gunge can't frigging well read, you silly cow.' I waited until it sank in, saw her face discard thrill for horror. 'Haven't you noticed that I mutter the catalogue descriptions out loud when he's close by?'

Her eyes filled. 'Oh, Lovejoy. I never dreamt –'

'It's all right. He's used to stupidity.' I tried to look thrilled, Luna-style. 'I'm quite looking forward to the, eh, Moot Hall.'

CHAPTER TWENTY-NINE

'The antiques, Lovejoy. Do we keep adding?'

'You've our lists, Gunge?' He keeps me a handwritten tally somewhere in his massive bearish presence. Doesn't need any, of course. Illiterates have a fantastically accurate visual memory. I've seen him spot a dud Wellington chest from a reflection in a window across the road, because its veneer had changed since it was auctioned a year before. Hawkeyes.

'Aye, Lovejoy.' To my dismay great tears began to roll down into his beard. I looked at the floor. 'I don't want anything to happen to Connie, Lovejoy. She's scared. Even before Rye died.'

I'm really useless at times like this. 'Look, Gunge. Who else did Connie confide in?'

'Nobody. Not even you. She wondered, but said you're unreliable about women.'

Bloody nerve. Typical womentalk. What do they know?

'What was she frightened of, Gunge?' Luna, ears wafting in the breeze. I glared at her coldly. This was supposed to be a private conversation.

'Of being killed. She talked a lot about spells.'

Spells? Was Connie going off her trolly? I'd met her that day off the train. She'd been edgy, definitely spooked about something.

'By whom? Why didn't she go to the police?' Was it an antique dealer? I think we should –'

My bent eye made Luna peter out, sulking.

'Right, Gunge.' Leaving the antiques in the old Boxtenholt aerodrome would be asking for trouble. 'What help've you got?'

'Just me. Connie didn't want it any other way.'

'Then we're in business,' I said. I felt as near to a smile as I'd been for many a day. Or night. 'Find Sandy, Luna. Tell him and Mel I want to contact the dollop broker. Today.'

She inhaled a gale, only said, 'Will he know how?'

'Not himself, no.' But telling Radio Sandy is our equivalent of BBC One. 'Gunge. You and me will gather everything I've got, ordered, can find, before nightfall. Okay?'

'Will it help us to find Connie?'

'I don't know, Gunge. But we'll try, eh?'

'Thanks, Lovejoy.' He heaved his enormous mass upright and

shambled off to start the loading. This morning he had a pale-blue three-tonner. You never see him twice in the same vehicle. I wondered if he simply nicked them.

He'd been gone an hour, with me and Luna finishing frantically in the workshop, when Drinkwater visited to say that one Miss Connie Hopkins had gone missing, and did I know anything about her, I said no, how terrible, and had he checked her parents. He issued warnings, and left with his teeth clacking and ear all atwitch.

Cradhead appeared in the workshop doorway about eleven, stood watching a while, wandered in, careful not to waft off slices of walnut veneer, and pausing to observe Luna putting the finishing touches to a prunt. These are small glass medallions, very rare alone. They were incorporated into antique roemers, actually only stuck on to the wide hollow stem. I honestly don't know why the German Rhineland liked these great spherical-bowled drinking glasses with the trailing-decorated foot (think of a thread of glass wound round and round), but they did. You have to admire style. These prunts, especially knobby-surface ones dealers call 'raspberries', are highly sought after in their own right now. God knows why.

'Only ordinary soda glass, Craddy,' I admitted before he asked. 'I borrowed glass tubing from Therla Brewer's school. Lower temperature, see?'

'The Lady Mayoress is very adept, Lovejoy.'

Cradhead shouldn't have such a quiet posh voice. Makes you think he's thinking. Only disguise, him being a peeler.

'Thank you, Inspector!' from Luna, so pleased at yet more praise that she paused to discuss her prowess. 'I'm –'

'Get on with it!' I yelled. Then smiled weakly at Cradhead's raised eyebrows. 'Er, Luna my dear. Please don't let it get cold.'

'Deadline to meet, Lovejoy?' He wandered. My back prickled. I wished he'd sod off so I could get on.

'No. Only, the Employment want a report on Mrs Carstairs' progress.'

'Connie Hopkins, Lovejoy.' Cradhead bent to sniff at the surface of a medieval apothecary's measure. Nice, simply two pewter cones joined at the apex. One cone was a half-ounce measure, the other one-ounce. Very pricey. I'd made it myself today. I didn't like Cradhead sniffing it – you can tell a new fake; the lead smells for quite five days after it has been made. Was this fascist swine cleverer than he seemed? 'Absent,' he went on. 'She was collecting antiques fast as . . . well, as Big Frank's new wife. And her studying astrophysics at university!' So he'd checked there too.

'Maybe she's gone off with a boyfriend.'

'Gunge Herod's her boyfriend, Lovejoy. You see him about. Six feet eight, giant, runs a dealer's barrow without a street licence. Can't read —'

'At least he admits it, Craphead! Unlike you frigging peelers . . .' I petered out, swallowed, resumed my varnishing.

Cradhead's eyes lit up at my response. The nerk had goaded me and I'd fallen for it.

'You're worried too, eh? Like us frigging peelers. Apologies, Mrs Carstairs.' He drifted to the door. 'What's on tonight, Lovejoy? Council meeting in the Moot Hall. Schoolchildren. Women's Institutes. Local history societies. Del Vervain. And . . .' He smiled a sleet-shaped smile. 'And you, Lovejoy.'

'Some promotion thing. Charity.' I was off-hand.

'Seven o'clock, Mr Cradhead.' Luna interrupted her glass-making. I'd throttle her. 'Would you like a ticket? I could speak to Mayor Carstairs.'

'Unnecessary, Mrs Carstairs.' Cradhead found his trilby. 'I'll be there. Duty calls, you see.'

'Goodbye,' my silly bitch trilled. 'Good luck finding Miss Hopkins!'

Chintzy chintzy cheeriness. I snarled at her. She bent quickly to her labours. A woman's job is never done, because they can't be bothered. From then on we really moved.

We did seven places, bought some paintings of the oil-and-slush Victorian sentimental schools. Tip: dealers are consters, the lot of them. They still preach there's no demand for sentimental paintings of the Pax Britannica heyday. So they offer you about one-fiftieth of the going price for that lovely stag painting on your parlour wall. And I mean one-fiftieth. Not even a twentieth. Two per cent. Well, thirty years ago that was true. But now? The pendulum's swung. Heartrending paintings of little girls waving doggies goodbye from nursery windows, children building sandcastles while Fond Father Dotes, are pure gold. Tear-jerking's in. Just learn your fifty-times table, that's all.

Speed was the essence. I'd bought wisely and fast with Laura's extra gelt. Luna was hard put to keep track, thank God. Payment on the nail for instant delivery. I'd had five bike couriers tearing up the tarmac for days. Every five hours we returned to the cottage, Gunge loaded up like a stoker raising steam. I rejected some fake furniture and a few porcelains, but mostly the dealers, braying after instant coin, played fair – as always, when all else fails. Luna wanted a serious chat about where the extra money had come from, simply quelled.

The answerphone went odd. Its number promised several messages, but only gave bleeps, to Luna's annoyance.

We discovered the reason about three o'clock. The phone rang. I answered, from the strangest of premonitions. I knew it was the dollop broker before the gruff voice spoke.

'Lovejoy? Who d'you know?'

'Sandy. Mel, Nuala. A load of locals collecting antiques.'

'Who for?'

'Some dollop broker.' I waited. 'Who do you know, then?'

'Everybody. Except your sister, Lovejoy.' The voice waited for me to fill in. I said nothing. She'd heard about Hawkshead. 'Your problem's not lessening with time, is it?'

'No.' This was the one all right. 'What's the arrangement? I've never dealt this big before.'

'Be outside your cottage in ten minutes.'

I was going to protest, but old gravel-throat had gone. I felt scared. Who climbs highest does so by a winding stair. Gulp. I told Luna I had to go out.

'Get Gunge to collect what we've got. Now.'

She was worried, referring to lists, ticking things off. 'I've run out of wrapping paper, Lovejoy. And those Royal Doultons are . . . What's the matter?'

'No more, love. It's all done. Anything you can box, parcel, shove into Gunge's next vanload, do so.'

'Done, Lovejoy! But some are still to be faked up.'

Faked up, if you please. I had to smile. Two weeks ago she'd have fainted at the thought. I embraced her. She tried to pull away, looking through the window in case some arriving vanny jumped to conclusions.

'It's come, love.'

'What's come?'

'Gawd knows. But it's here.'

CHAPTER THIRTY

Luna went up the lane to wait for Gunge. I was nervous as a kitten, now I'd actually made it to the big league. I'd never dreamt I'd actually do it – me, meet a dollop broker! Mega trade.

The car sent for me was a common station taxi. It dropped me at the local hospital. I was collected again by a hire car. The driver knew nothing, took me to Toll Gate shopping mall. Among scores of people loading their wheelies I was collected by a third car, driven miles to a countryside crossroads. By a lonely bus stop, I was met by a saloon car with heavily tinted windows.

The last two drivers were women. Neither spoke. I was in the rear seat. The penultimate motor was replaced after a couple of miles by another. My head was spinning. Why not a chat in Woody's instead of all this motor mix? I thought I saw a blonde driving a car following, but couldn't be sure. In a pub yard I was swapped one last time. One with black windows, no vision at all. Coward to the last, I tried the handles. Locked. The driver was a thin lank-haired girl wearing reflector sun specs, the sort that puts mirrors where eyes should be. I'd only seen her when embarking. For thirty minutes I sat looking at the car's interior.

Ten miles, twenty? I was dropped in some estate. The motor cruised away. I was alone.

From where I stood, at a mansion house door, I could see ornamental gardens. Tallish chimneys, Tudor in style. But fake. A smallish red-brick dwelling stood visible through the trees. An old tennis court, now overgrown. A hockey-size field was newly planted into rosebeds. Trees everywhere. No rivers. It wore an institutional air. A phoney coat-of-arms, modernish stained glass, adorned the main door. I was left to knock.

Silence. I turned slowly on the top step. Balustrade, lawns neatly cut. Tidy flowerbeds. No wheelbarrows, rakes or mowers left lying about. I could see a green-house roof. It felt weird, almost quite alien. Home for retired gentlewomen? Too many steps, no wheel-chairs. No car park. Ancient family seat, Lord Lieutenant of the County? No serfs.

And the door opened.

Thin women I can take. Medium to plump, fine. Old, young, superb. But voluminous? So obese you can't see the edges? Every

677

step a waddle, a susurrus of rasping clothes? Each breath was an orchestra of squeaks. Chin to knees formed one long convexity. Contours were definitely not this lady's thing. I found her eyes, fixed on them like a pointer dog in case I lost them.

'Lovejoy,' I told her.

'I suppose you'll have to come in.'

Spoken with disgust. I followed. Her incredible jeans moved ahead like heaving strato-cumulus. The corridor passed between rooms stacked high with food, crates of tuna fish, sacks of beans, cereal packs, bottles of sauce. Other rooms we passed were rimmed with hanging dresses. Folded jumpers and woollens filled shelves to the ceilings.

'Expecting war, missus?'

'Exploiters don't dun me, Lovejoy. I stock up.'

'Antiques too?'

'Be funny and I'll bin you.'

Funny? Antiques? 'Love isn't funny, missus.'

'Phoney philosophy's what I don't stock, Lovejoy.'

She reached the end room and sat, back to me, on an old garden bench before a television set, some game show with constant applause. She overflowed the seat, lapping in pendulous sags nearly to the floor. A plastic bucket half-filled with salted peanuts was handy, to suppress lurking anorexia. She slumped into the viewer's sprawl, feeding her face handfuls. A crate of cola tins gave fluid support. I was left standing. Was this the famous Miss R, Super Planner herself? Scam Superba? Or merely another intermediary lackey?

The screech frightened me out of my skin.

'It's beheaded, you stupid fucking mare!' she howled at the television screen. 'Anne Boleyn and Catherine Howard were beheaded!'

Roars of dismay from the TV as the contestant was banished back to Hartlepool. 'Just bad luck,' the idiot presenter bawled.

The dolloper was a rage-filled blimp. 'It's fucking ignorance for fuck's fucking sake!' she screamed.

I covered my ears until the din subsided. 'Missus, I'm a delicate flower.'

'Where was she educated, the unlettered bitch?'

There was more. Invective's dull, so I won't summarise the next hour. The fat lady blasted the game show, the news, a fashion parade, a scene with dog-handlers.

'Just watch!' she thundered, immense mass quivering. 'Parading like stuffed cattle! Cruft must be spinning in his grave, the way they're handling those dogs!'

'Cruft wouldn't care, love.' I was fed up. 'Charles Cruft of Cruft's International Dog Show fame kept cats. Never owned a dog.'

The world swivelled, looked at me. The screen clicked off. 'You're in difficulties, Lovejoy. You've taken over Connie Hopkins' stuff, brought it to the right level.'

I drew breath, but it didn't have anything to say.

'My preference is to broker for females. As you now have female partners and backers, you'll do. These are my terms —'

'Here. Just a minute —'

'Silence! I don't accept people wanting hideouts. Nor immigrants. Drugs are acceptable, but only those not requiring special storage conditions. I store any type of criminal deposits, as long as the dollop's owners are clearly identified. I specialise in caches left for the duration of a prison sentence, and for Statutes of Limitations of specified countries. Understand?'

Uttered with the feeling of a copper's caution.

'Fine.'

'Terms: build-up from three perc, one perc weekly to max of ten to a fifth one year and over, inflation adjusted. Take or leave.'

Queen of précis. She'd summed up the usual dolloper's arrangement. Three per cent of our antique's total, rising to ten per cent. She'd conceal the antiques for ever, but charge us a tenth when they were finally sold, even if we were imprisoned.

'Final charge?'

'Two perc after the second year. Flat removal fee, plus mileage.'

I didn't smile. Flat-fee mileage meant you couldn't guess how far your stuff had travelled. That implied her storage space was here. Except I didn't know where here was.

'Okay.'

She picked up a control slab. A woman's voice came on.

'Yes for Lovejoy,' said Miss R. 'Go now.'

'Herod's van is south of Lavenham,' a loudspeaker said. 'I'll let it do its drop in the cran before evacuating. Willco.'

The broker huffed to her feet. 'Settle any arguments between you and Connie before final audit.'

'Right, right.' I felt like in school. You wouldn't want to cross this formidable lady and her slick team of women.

A bleep sounded. She listened to earphones, barked, 'South American bonds, after *that* escapade? The answer is no.'

'They offer to bank through Georgia, USA,' the control panel persuaded.

'Still no. Unless they bank via Washington, DC.'

I felt slim and willowy following her bulk out to the front door. No visible telephones with giveaway numbers. No local scenes. The place was stacked for a siege. Crates of apples rose in a serene curve, upstairs to the landing. Sacks of lentils and dried peas filled the hallway. Yet the place was spick and span.

'Pay one per cent today, Lovejoy.'

'Who to?'

'Whom, cretin. A courier.'

'How do I know I'll work one per cent out right?'

'Correctly,' she corrected, in reflex. 'I shall judge.'

Aye, I thought sardonically as the door shut firmly on me. I'd better get the money right. She would have my antiques. I stared about a moment or two, looking for clues. I'd found the right dollop broker all right, but learned nothing. No chance to bring up Cornish Place. I was dying to know which dealers had been here. I couldn't quite see Sandy or Big Frank making much of a mark with this formidable lady. Calamity Jenny, now, seemed somehow to be right for the place. Or Cassandra Clark? Not Vell, though. Connie? Maybe. Plum-in-the-mouth country.

The black-glass motor came. I got in. It drove away. I tried the door and windows. No views, for the likes of me.

We did the car switches in reverse, and I learned nothing.

Gunge told me he'd called at the old aerodrome in Boxtenholt to drop off three Victorian desks and a case of Edwardian jewellery, final afterthoughts Luna couldn't resist, but the place was cleaned out. He'd had to bring the afterthoughts back.

'Fine, Gunge. Just leave them here.'

I sent Luna to unload them, and sat on my unfinished wall to feed the birds and think. Miss R had spoken in tones so precise it made me think of school. And a massive mansion like that. Big rooms – never mind the clothes and grub stacked everywhere. Obviously she was a nutter. Well, a dollop broker had to be, harbouring stolen antiques until such time as the robbers served their prison sentences and came back to spend their ill-gotten gains. She was class, despite her appearance. Worked out foreign bond percentages without conscious thought. Able to hold together a band of women. (*All* women?) Forceful, authority unquestioned. Shrewd as all dollop brokers. The word trick again, though. A dollop broker doesn't broker anything. Just stores stuff, safe from police, law, other gangsters, insurance companies.

What did I know about her? Only the scams she'd catered for. I guessed she was the dollop broker who'd handled the German medieval treasures until Greck got sprung from gaol. Who'd handled the marijuana from Holland after that Spalding bulb fiasco (the lorries got caught on the bypass from Felixstowe). Who'd handled the French paintings, and brokered their return when the museums and galleries bought them back on the sly. So, a genius. Who could organise a cool lift of three hundred and eighty antiques from a disused aerodrome, while watching TV and eating a bucket of nuts. Not bad, seeing I'd not said where the antiques were.

But that place. The tennis court, traces still visible but now given over to bushes and lawn. A pitch, now flowerbeds. Grass always grows thickest by corner flags. I remember my cousin Glenice playing hockey when she was a little girl, the pitch smaller than the football pitches I'm used to.

School? A girls' school. The big house, gatehouse of red brick. The scrupulous neatness. Her private cursing, public propriety. Her exasperation at the clueless woman contestant who'd not known some elementary history about Henry VIII's wives. Calamity Jenny, she of the august social background, belonged there, and Cassandra Clark. Connie. But not me, not Big Frank. An ex-girls' school, now engaged in a different sort of activity.

What was it somebody had said? I called across for Luna to brew up. It was Vell. She'd said something about Cassandra Clark, being from a different school. With bitterness.

Connie Hopkins? Cassandra Clark? This was the first time I felt something true. Had they been together at school? Yet I'd never seen them as much as swap a greeting. Avoiding each other? Or was I jumping to conclusions, as usual?

Luna emerged. Gunge sat with us on the wall. He could dwarf Miss R, just about.

'Lune,' I said eventually. 'Where did you go to school?'

'Me? Stirling. Quite nice, really, though games was the thing they . . .'

I didn't listen after that. Libraries list schools. They were open tonight until eight o'clock, plenty of time before the Moot Hall gathering. I had Luna try to reach Cassandra Clark, but she could get no answer. Still ruminating, I told her to check the phonebook. It said E. C. Clark.

'E for what?' I asked.

'It doesn't say.' Luna sat primly beside me, finally hunting. 'Why are you interested in Cassandra Clark?'

'Dunno.' I asked Gunge where Connie went to school, but he didn't know. 'We'll find Connie soon, Gunge,' I said, wondering how.

We sat glumly, three monkeys, each with our thoughts. I honestly did feel I might be edging close. Honestly. Gunge sat in silent misery. He saw me as his one last hope. Pathetic. She could be anywhere. I felt she was somewhere not far. Miss R's school? That was the most likely. All I lacked was reason, logic, and a load of troops to storm the place. *If* I could find it again. With caches of criminal loot littering the grounds, there'd be aggressive security. Not just a fat lady with sacks of beans.

An hour later I came to, and told Gunge to ask around after Connie. 'Miss out nowhere, Gunge,' I ordered. 'Everywhere. Strangers, even. But especially the Arcade. Antique dealers. And call in at the cop shop.'

'Peelers, Lovejoy?' He stopped, already halfway to his van.

'No time to be proud, Gunge. Find me at six. I'll look round Connie's place.'

'Me, Lovejoy,' Luna asked. 'What have I to do?'

It was late afternoon. The day waning, birds having a last scour about the garden. She usually went home about this time, after Oliver's tantrum.

'I want you inside, love.'

She took my arm. 'Don't sound so sad, Lovejoy. What is it? You're so soft-hearted. I mean, so upset because poor Gunge's ladyfriend has gone away for a few days. She's having a day or two away. That's all.'

'Yes.' We started inside. 'Draw the curtains, love.'

She already had. And the window fastenings were locked. She was slipping off her shoes even as I reached the divan. Like I say, women are miles ahead of us. Still, I don't like women who are mean. Surely everything's not too much to ask? The cottage felt coldish without so many antiques around. It warmed.

CHAPTER THIRTY-ONE

Gunge showed me Connie's miniature shop. Tiny, sparse. Modern chair, trestle table, kettle and enough to brew tea. Nothing else. I wrestled the town library for facts, scoring best of three pinfalls. The immortal I. K. Brunel's *Great Eastern* paddle-steamer, wonder of the nineteenth century, 18,915 gross tons, launched in 1858 at Millwall. She was marked by disaster.

Not her fault. She was just eerie. During her building, accidents multiplied. Workmen died, were maimed. Brunel himself had a stroke as she readied for sea trials. An explosion in September, 1859, killed six seamen. Brunel relapsed, died. It was a grim paddle-steamer that finally hit the long wet road.

Long before, even her launch was doomladen. She simply stuck for years, the 1 in 12 hopeless. Legend says Isambard built a secret model with his own superb hands, tried it out somewhere. Five funnels, six masts, side-paddles. Like the pictures Delia nicked from Rye. Those features were on the murky photographs. Was it here that Brunel came? Was his model brooding the river serving Rye's watermill? The part of the river Rye'd sold his birthright to try to buy from Oliver's Council, as Luna said? Or was it a con? A photo of a cloudy underwater model would be easy to fake. Any photographer, blindfold.

The unhappy question came. Connie seemed keen on Rye – as long as he funded her drive into the big antiques league. When he'd offered for the mill and its river instead, she'd turned to me. I was a replacement. Frigging cheek.

Nothing for it. We had to find her. She'd gone missing some hours. No bird on earth assembles a wealth of antiques, then strolls away leaving them for others, does she? I made the Moot Hall in good time.

Every town has an ancient meeting place. The Moot Hall is typical – meaning the Borough Council has let it crumble, and now whines for handouts to restore it. You can see it's been patched by cowboy builders hired for a pittance.

'Oliver's so proud, Lovejoy,' Luna whispered as I walked into the hallway. 'This is the biggest event of his mayoral year!'

Some year. Luna had to go. She looked smashing – dress

midnight-blue velvet, genuine pearls, four-carat diamond ring. A brooch would have been too much, but her Edwardian pearl-drop earrings were just right. She was thrilled to bits, of course. I wished her luck.

The Hall was once splendid. Now, it's virtually derelict, faded walls hung about with a few oil paintings in a sickeningly bad state. They depict our ancient councillors avariciously welcoming Huguenot refugees – yet more immigrants to exploit – and two unarmed Royalist knights being gunned down (another form of East Anglian greeting) and the like. The place of honour's reserved for Queen Boadicea, who razed the town in Roman days and rewarded local developers by crucifying everybody. Dealers keep wondering whether to nick these paintings (Big Frank's offered them to a Swiss dealer in Rotterdam. I'll keep you posted).

The place was filling. It smelled musty. The stage was hollow, every footfall rolling thunder. Dust, the Council's hallmark, lay everywhere. Housewives drifted in, excited about the great radio hero Del Vervain. Commercial fawners were filing in to the front rows, so they could be seen to be worshipping those in high places. A few old winos drifted in.

'Wotch, Lovejoy.' An old soak hawked up phlegm and swallowed with relish. 'Reckon they'll have nosh?'

'Wotcher, Forage.' He used to run errands for me once, but finally couldn't leave the pub long enough. 'Doubt it, for the likes of us.' The ante-room, the only one properly restored, had busy waitresses laying an enormous buffet.

'Bastards,' he croaked, settling in one of the rear seats. 'Junketing on our taxes.'

His mates muttered agreement. Marmalade Emma's the second of Forage's trio. She's mostly in black, with a black lacquered wicker hat and two bobbing cherries. The *My Fair Lady* prototype. Grimes is her bloke. Stays stout on booze, God knows how. I've never yet seen him awake. Moving about, yes, but that's not the same thing.

'Forage? Sit at the front,' I suggested. 'It's warmer.'

'They can chuck us out easier from here, Lovejoy,' Forage said. 'The door guard is Grimes' cousin's lad Andy.'

'Oh. Right.' They'd embarrass him all right.

I sat down with them. Marmalade Emma was reminiscing. She makes me wistful. I don't know why. She sings outside pubs – inside, wherever she's allowed – and does a shuffling clownish dance that makes people laugh. They throw pennies to make the drunken old lady show her tattered soiled knickers. You can imagine what an admirable and merry scene it is, in this rural corner of Merrie England. Our village social club hires her to do her dance. They pay her in booze. And critics say wit is a dying art.

'There used to be big chandeliers up there, Lovejoy. See?'

'I don't remember them, Emma.' I looked.

'Ooooh, yes. Very grand. People say they wuz real gold. You're too young.' She quavered a few bars of a waltz. I lalled along. My Auntie Alice was a great laller. She could turn any melody, Handel's *Messiah* down, into lal-lal-lal.

'Did you dance here, Emma?'

She demanded indignantly, cherries bobbing, 'Did I dance here? Lod, Lovejoy!' She nudged Grimes, who chuckled in his sleep and said Lord too. 'Lod above! I danced to dawn, in this very hall! With the Mayor! Old Alderman Adamson. Very grand.' Slyly she checked that Grimes was kipping. You could have heard her whisper in Harwich. 'He kissed me. After a polka. Under the painting of the two girls with lanterns. My favourite.' Her rheumy old eyes searched the walls to point it out. There was no painting there. I thought, odd.

'Lovejoy.' Forage nudged me. 'They're calling you. What you done, son?'

A red-coated Master of Ceremonies was bawling for attention. People were still filing in. 'Nothing. Yet.'

'Lovejoy.' A custodian tried to prise me up but I wouldn't go. 'On the stage. The Mayor said.'

'Tell him no thanks.' Andy, embarrassed after all.

A number of dignitaries were slowly filling the chairs on the podium. Oliver and Luna weren't yet in, nor Del, Joan. Arriving audiences always create a hubbub.

'He won't like it, Lovejoy.'

Emma cackled. 'Lovejoy'll worry chronic, Andy.'

It was quarter of an hour before the proceedings showed signs of starting. Emma talked nonstop, tales of ancient goings-on amongst the nobs of yesteryear. She must have been quite prominent in her day. Grimes hadn't been prominent at all.

'Here, son,' Emma asked as folk hushed and had a last cough. 'It true you're shafting the Lady Mayoress, is it?'

'Mind your own business.'

She fell about at that, Grimes laughing along in his slumber. Forage looked frosty. He disapproves of immoral talk.

'Lovejoy, we loikes you, booy. Even not local. But shafting carriage trade makes for bad blood.'

Other people didn't like me, I noticed wrily. The four of us were in an island of space. A school of children was in the body of the seating. Shoppers gossiped in the back row. The hall was about two-thirds full. Blokes adjusted microphones. I was disappointed. You'd think radio would need spectacular wiring, tons of transmitters. There'd been just one radio van outside. That was it. Television's better value. No wonder Del Vervain was worried sick about ratings if this was radio's only technology.

People quietened, the children enjoying making shushing noises, making such a racket they had to be silenced separately. I was glad Therla Brewer was in. She and Josh were sitting closer than teachers ought. I sighed. That's life.

'Ladies and gentlemen. The Mayor and Mayoress of the Borough!'

Recorded fanfare, barely making it. People stood, some applauding. The line of dignitaries beamed. Oliver and Luna entered. He wore his chain of office; she was merely beautiful. Lights held them as they took their places. People sat, scraping the floor. Why do people *do* that? There's no need. You just sit down, for God's sake. But have you ever heard an audience sit quietly? I never have. It's a queer world.

'Pray silence for His Worship Mayor Carstairs!'

Oliver rose, to feeble clapping. Councillors and front-row fawners were ecstatic. Luna's eyes were shining as she clapped longest of all. I wondered if remembering how differently those hands had behaved at my cottage was jealousy or something, but gave over and listened to Oliver, resplendent in his regalia.

'Councillors! Members of the Social Promotions Committee! Broadcasting fraternity! Last but not least – ladies and gentlemen of the Borough!'

This drew a roar of laughter from ingrates. Housewives tittered, with that anxiety women always show on posh occasions, hoping all will go right and nobody will be ashamed.

'He always was a smarmy bleeder,' Emma whispered shrilly.

People looked around. Oliver pressed on, delighted with the sound of his own voice and a multitude.

'A famous local radio personality and his lady are gracing our ancient town tonight. Even as I speak, this event is being broadcast *live* on Radio Camelod!'

Thinner applause. Oliver raised his hands, quelling a riot of adoration.

'His dad was a ram,' Emma confided. 'All fingers, he was. His wife left him. No bleedin' wonder.' She plucked my sleeve. I bent close, though I'd have heard her if I'd been out sailing. 'His father shagged half his wife's pupils.' She cackled. She had about three teeth left. I wondered vaguely why she didn't have a good false set. 'Headmistress, at Colney Varr.' She gathered herself for a joke. 'Wish I'd gone there, Lovejoy!' Colney Varr was a posh girl's academy somewhere, once famous.

'Silence, please!' Some uniformed guardian on tiptoe.

'Sorry, mate,' I said. God, but Emma ponged. I began to wish I'd sat further forward after all. Grimes snored and twitched. He always does. In solemnity Forage now wore his spectacles, one lens a cracked bifocal, the other missing. I wondered vaguely why *he* didn't have proper glasses.

Our Mayor was waxing lyrical. 'This evening is a Council initiative, to raise funds for the restoration of Council buildings such as this noble edifice in which we currently speak. We are displaying Council regalia and . . .' he twinkled, signifying impending wit '. . . baubles, ha ha ha!'

A few grovellers tried to get applause going, failed.

'All the Borough wealth – portable variety only! – is out for inspection. Under guard, of course!'

He was sweating heavily. Forage nudged Grimes, for snoring. Emma was on about some soldier she'd known. I felt myself nod from the warmth, came to when the celebrity of the evening was announced.

'. . . Del *Vervain!*'

In he strode, laughing, shaking hands all the way down the hall. Bouncing on to the stage and grabbing a hand microphone. He was made up. Astonishing: He looked about twenty years younger.

'Here we are! Radio Camelod, in the oldest Moot Hall in the known world!' He roared with laughter. Everybody roared with laughter. The Mayor and the councillors roared with laughter. I looked about. What gets into people?

'Here, Emma,' I asked. It was narking me. 'Why have you no proper teeth? Or Forage specs?'

'Shhhh, son. I like old Del. Used to be a pub singer.'

Del Vervain was babbling, striding. 'Folks, this is your opportunity! You'll hear the dulcet tones of my gorgeous wife Joan! Come own a-here, honey!'

Applause. Oliver went forward gallantly, escorted Joan. Del was being poisonously jocular. God, having to do that for a living? Broadcasters think imitation New York accents entitle them to instant fame. Lunatic. You'd spend your life wondering why people do what they do, if there was hope of an answer. I was getting narkeder and narkeder.

Joan said hello and how marvellous and everything. Excited, brilliantly dressed in lime green, flouncy skirts a little youngish but delectable. Del displaced her in two sentences.

'We're here, listeners, by popular request. Our first outside broadcast! No phone-ins this time. So save your pennies, ha ha ha ha!'

A bloke seated at the rear of the stage signalled. Del grabbed Oliver and grinned at us with aggressive confidentiality. The show was on. One measly microphone.

'My first guest is His Worship Mayor Carstairs. Oliver, how does it feel, Mayor of this ancient Borough?'

Snoozetime. Oliver intoned his feelings. Del quipped hearty quips. Excruciating. Emma occasionally whispered bits of slander, Oliver's randy Dad and fading family fortunes after Oliver's Mum slipped the traces.

Between gossip and guests, I really did nod off. They were electric. An octogenarian who'd once known the Prime Minister. A historian with theories about Normans. Somebody else – the coast was eroding, we'd all get wet. Yawn city. Del Vervain made me wonder how boring blokes like him get to be broadcasters in the first place. He was hopeless. He'd need a miracle to revive his fortunes, not a pathetic outside broadcast in a dingy old hall. People had come because anybody on the air is still a wonder to behold. But radio doesn't have the appeal of television. Not half so degrading.

People started to drift out, fed up. I was almost on the point of joining them, when Del Vervain struck.

'Now a special treat, listeners! A famous antique dealer. Lovejoy by name. And, by nature, ha ha ha!'

To my alarm here he came, actually walking down the aisle at me, grinning, his microphone a staff of office before him, our modern totem. The prick. I wondered what to say.

'Er,' I managed. My mouth was dry.

He posed, winking at the audience. He was drenched in sweat. No wonder, if this was the best he could do. He ought to leave this sort of thing to the BBC. They've been doing it for years. Better. 'Isn't it true that you have the gift of . . . divvieing antiques?'

'Er, well. Sort of.'

'No?' More winks. He was leaning confidentially on the seat in front of me, grinning round. Smarmy sod. Just how deep my dislike went I only just then discovered. Maybe I disliked Joan too. Why didn't he *look* at me, for God's sake? Maybe broadcasters are trained not to. 'This divvieing. What is it, actually?' Twinkle twinkle midget star. Somebody sniggered. He spun towards the sound grinning hopefully. 'Do I have to slip you a fiver to find out? Ha ha ha!'

'Well,' I said, looking nervously round. 'Well, you touch an antique. And it lets you know if it's genuine.'

'Is that it?' He strode about the aisle. 'Hey, folks! Challenge time! Trial by antique! What say, hey?'

He paced threateningly, chatted up elderly shoppers, got an indistinct ripple of applause.

'Bring out those baubles!' Del commanded. He addressed the microphone. 'By kind permission of Mayor Carstairs – my good friend Oliver! Hi, Mayor! Okay up there? Ha ha ha ha! – we can test the regalia of this great and ancient town!'

His voice had sunk to a sepulchral hollowness, clearly deeply-felt reverence. He grabbed my arm. I shook him off. He tried to pull me up. I wouldn't go.

'Bring the Great Mace, please!'

Sweating heavier. I thought, what's the big deal? Okay, I admire it – huge, gold and silver, a John Flaxman design. Paul Storr, one of the greatest precious-metalsmiths, made it about 1838. Not long, as antiques go, but weighing heavy, adorned with gems. Too ornate, but that only makes it more praiseworthy. How can you fail to admire . . . ? I watched the mace-bearer come. A stout old military bloke, decorated from a million battles.

He stood at attention in his grand livery, the Great Mace on his shoulder. There's a proper way of holding them.

'Here it is, Lovejoy.' Del Vervain, his awed grave-digger's voice. 'Listeners. Honestly most sincerely! You should see the majesty of this great emblem of authority, nay local civic pride!' His voice caught. 'Most sincerely. The atmosphere is electric. Lovejoy, the, ah, divvie man will prove that the stupendous array of silver plate, jewellery and golden, ah, emblems, which we so admire, nay, applaud, are truly genuine repositories of this ancient Borough!'

'Er, Del,' I said. He was talking codswallop.

'One moment, Lovejoy.' He was milking this. As on edge as any bloke I'd ever seen. Too sweaty, in fact. 'This, listeners, is a moment to savour. Lovejoy is one of those special people – I mean that most sincerely – will enter a mystic trance –'

'Er, no, Del,' I tried. He raised a restraining hand.

'Lovejoy. Take your *time*! Listeners. You should see Lovejoy's intense gaze as he enters that zone of ineffable mystery, where the spirits roam in search of the splendours of antiquity . . .'

Emma was chuckling. Grimes was snoring. Forage was nodding behind his spectacle with episcopalian gravity. Del Vervain was going on and on, however I tried to interrupt. Pillock.

He posed, frowning. 'I'm sure some might think Lovejoy is pretending. After all, they say antique dealers try confidence tricks, even robbery. But here in this ancient building we are privileged to see a trial of the truth . . .'

The bearer was holding the Great Mace. I looked at it again, but only for show.

These things are usually precious, often silver gilt, emblems made to signify authority, whether royal, parliamentary, whatever. Essentially a posh stick. Each town has one. No use, of course. Symbols. Which really raises the question of what a genuine symbol is trying to be.

'. . . Lovejoy seems ready, folks! Finally willing his mind into that great abyss where the answers to life and death lie hidden. He will now, at this moment in time, touch the Great Mace, live! And will know whether this vital, nay holy, emblem of this great town's historic past, is genuine.'

'Well, yes, Del. Except the . . .'

'Ladies and gentlemen, listeners! The atmosphere is breath-taking.'

It wasn't. Grimes was snoring so loudly Marmalade Emma had to nudge him quiet. Forage looked grave. I saw a flea leap from his clothes on to Emma. I edged away another inch, touched the Great Mace. I nodded.

'What?' Del Vervain asked. He looked aghast. A couple of security people from the back were standing beside the mace-bearer, blocking the aisle. Everybody was looking. A security bloke in every aisle. By every doorway.

'Yes, Del. Lovely.'

'What?' he asked again. He looked round. Oliver was looking down, tense. Joan was on her feet, stepping forward. I could see Luna glancing in wonderment at Joan, at me. 'Fine?' He was thunderstruck. 'Fine?' he asked as if the word was new.

'Sure.' I paused, helpful. 'Want me to tell you a bit about the silversmith? Actually, I think he sometimes went over the top in design. You see, silver has this terrific high refectivity . . .'

He went to pieces, tried to start an interview with the town crier, but it was no good. The show disintegrated. It was pathetic to see him trying to speak the sort of coherent gibberish he'd made famous, but failing worse with every bleat.

People began to drift. While the proceedings were still limping on, I nudged Marmalade Emma. The four of us made the ante-room, after a decoying exit through the main doors, and waded in to the grand nosh provided for the councillors. The buffet waitresses didn't say a word, just backed away from us at their clean and aseptic tables.

Well, I thought indignantly as Grimes woke and swigged the first bottle he could grab. Serves them right for rigging their crummy broadcast with a dummy Great Mace. They'd assumed I'd blurt out the astonishing truth, that it was a fake. Skilfully made, but still dud. Then presumably there'd have been consternation. Maybe an arrest? And a swift rise for Del's ratings. Pathetic.

'Here, Grimes. That wine properly chilled?'

'Not bad.' He dropped the empty, got another.

Emma cackled. 'Here, son. We in trouble for nicking their victuals?'

'No, Emma,' I said, offering Forage a florentine. I can't resist them, though they're too small. 'They'll let us leave untrammelled.'

'Why?' Forage was stuffing his face, going down the line of filled glasses like a conjuror.

'I just feel it, Forage.' I could have asked why they'd brought me along to recognise the Great Mace for the fake it undoubtedly was. I'd seen it on display not less than eight months since. It had been genuine then. So what had happened in the meantime? Oliver had been Mayor almost a year. I said nothing.

Lovejoy's friends had grown too big, that's what. And I'd fallen among thieves. And listened too often to the lies of fair ladies.

We finished our repast, and departed with dignity.

CHAPTER THIRTY-TWO

'Lovejoy!' the old lady across the road trilled. 'I've been waiting for you!'

Miss Turner. Just when I thought it was safe to go back into civilisation. She trotted over among the traffic, said good evening.

'They wouldn't let me in, dear.' She giggled. 'Three policemen stopped me. Aren't your policemen wonderful?'

That old one. Drinkwater hovered in the brightly-lit doorway of the Moot Hall. Cradhead stood with him, observing life's rich pageant. All roads led here tonight. Which raised the question why. Three and two make five. Eleven Borough security guards. Sixteen? For a radio broadcast? Whose arrest did they have in mind?

'Miss Turner, may I present Marmalade Emma . . .' I did the honours. Miss Turner said she was charmed. My lot said how do.

'Lovejoy has been most helpful,' she told them. 'My lineage goes back three centuries. In East Anglia! Delightful!' She fluttered her lovely old eyes. 'We might be related.'

Great. 'Not me, love. I'm not from –'

'I need more help, Lovejoy. Some of my English ancestors were soldiers, but –'

'Ah, well. If your regiment's after 1660, you're quids in – lucky. After the Restoration, we began a standing army. The PRO has some War Office soldier's records. And the Imperial War Museum, the National Army Museum, regimental museums dotted about. Regiments often started up in taverns and inns, so . . .'

Suddenly I thought, what am I *doing?* I was lecturing to three derelict alkies and a nut, on the rainy pavement, splashed by passing motors, glared at by a cluster of peelers. I must be out of my skull.

'Interesting point, Lovejoy,' Forage interposed, removing his spectacle. 'St Cat's House *does* have Army births and weddings from 1761, but I'm a critic of their records. Madam, you must devise a plan . . .'

With sinking heart I recognised Forage's papal grandeur. It can go on for days. 'Look, folks,' I said quickly. 'Here's a couple of notes. Go to Woody's caff. Nosh up.' I threatened Emma with a fist. '*Before* you swill yourselves stupid in the four-ale bar. Okay?'

Emma fell about laughing. This is typical. Whenever I try to assert myself, women and babes roll in the aisles. They can always spot a dud.

'Lovejoy.' Luna was suddenly there, blazing. 'I want words with you.'

'Hello, Lune. Marmalade Emma and Miss Turner, may I present the Lady Mayoress –'

'*Lovejoy!*' Lune stepped away a pace. '*If* you please.'

And suddenly I'd had enough. Her and Oliver up to their political tricks. Del Vervain up to his, Joan to hers. Connie Hopkins vanished. Rye Benedict dead, murdered by somebody who'd stood chatting all pally. Prammie Joe battered, left for maggots in a marsh. And me summoned like a dog. I'd been introducing her to my friends, for Christ's sake.

'Forage,' I said. 'Your specs. Why're they duff?'

'Ah, Lovejoy. Thereby hangs a tale. I'm *persona non grata* at the eye clinic. No fixed abode, you see.'

'Same as Emma's teeth?' I glared at Luna. 'No health provision for folk without an address?'

'Lovejoy.' Lune was out of her depth, but still apoplectic.

'I'll see you right,' I told them. 'Miss Turner, Grimes. Tell Emma if you've secret bunions. Meet you later.'

Dispiritedly I watched them go. From one sponger I'd worked my way up to four. At least I'm consistent. Pathetic.

'Lovejoy!' Lune exploded. 'You deliberately wrecked –'

'Meaning I didn't do as I was told?' I'd have clouted her, except ploddites skulked in the Moot Hall doorway. 'Lune, I'm done with doing what everybody else expects.'

'You never do what anyone expects, Lovejoy.'

'Never?' I said bitterly. 'Or just hardly ever?'

'You realise what this means, Lovejoy,' Luna rasped, keeping her voice down. 'I withdraw, forthwith. Return every penny by nine o'clock tomorrow morning. Or I'll have every stitch off your back, every antique in that load impounded. And you arrested for fraud.'

Her hand was trembling as I reached out and shook it. 'A deal, lady. Now sod off. Leave me alone.'

She stormed away, her heels clicking on my eardrums. I called up the steps of the Moot Hall, 'Cheers, Drinkwater.' Don't know if he heard.

Hurrying now and uneasy, I went to the Ship Inn to see if there was any word of Connie. Nothing. I phoned Margaret Dainty, then seven other dealers. Nil. I tried Sandy's number, then remembered where he'd be. Music was coming from Sir Isaac's Walk. I took a short cut, so I'd guessed right.

Sandy and Mel were doing their dance in the precinct square. It has a covered way, glass roof and ball lights. I don't think Mel likes these lunatic events, but Sandy claims his public demands. Tonight they'd hired a harpsichord girl from the music school. She wasn't bad, but her instrument was made from a kit. I can't think of anything more ridiculous than a prefabricated harpsichord – except maybe two blokes dancing a gavotte watched by two tramps and a dog. I waited for the end.

'Didn't you *exult* at my minuet, Lovejoy?' He wore a glittering lametta sheath dress, a cavalier hat with genuine ostrich feathers. Mel was dressed as a Spaniard, all black and high-heel boots. I just can't understand two people spending a fortune to look barmy. It's beyond me.

'Great, Sandy.' You've got to go along or he weeps himself into a tantrum. 'Where's Connie?'

'The trouble is, Lovejoy,' he said, adjusting his hat in a mirror. 'This mall's lighting is absolutely *criminal*. Don't you agree?'

'Absolutely, Sandy. Bad lighting. Seen Connie?'

He smiled with malice. 'You've been positively *rummaging* in the Lady Mayoress' for *weeks*, Lovejoy –'

Mel groaned in horror. '*Don't.* I've not had my tablet.'

'Perhaps you could . . .' Sandy tittered wickedly '. . . persuade her to wheedle better illumination.'

'Maybe, Sandy. Seen anything of Connie Hopkins?' The bad feeling about her had started out a mere foreboding. Now, I was scared, my hands wet.

'Promise you'll *stir* Lusty Luna into *passionate* action?'

Mel shrieked, hid behind the harpsichord. Good veneer, correct for 1750. Repro people take a lot of trouble.

'Promise,' I said. 'More lights. Incidentally, heard anything about Connie Hopkins, Sandy?'

He came closer, fluttered his eyelashes roguishly. The musician girl turned a page, oblivious. She was nodding slightly to some inner rhythm as she read the notes, warming up for the next gavotte. She had a small torch for better light.

'You're third in the queue, Lovejoy. *Naughty* Connie! Dear Gunge, Acker Kirwin. Now you! *Do* ask the bitch where she gets her perfume. She had a terrible row with her ladyfriend. Yesterday.' He whispered, 'Was it jealousy? Connie's ladyfriend's been seeing a lot of Big Frank's Jenny.'

'*Sandy!*' Mel screamed in a temper. And that was it. Sandy rushed back. The harpsichord started up again as I headed for the Priory ruins. The whole town centre is only a mile square, for Roman reasons. Not far to go.

I was startled to find Cradhead jogging alongside me. On his own.

'Thought Keystone Kops went in groups,' I said.

'Any idea, Lovejoy?' He wasn't breathless. 'Connie Hopkins.'

That slowed me to a quick walk. I looked at him sideways in the occasional street lamps.

'Not much. You?'

The old aerodrome was out. Not after sussing Oliver's scam at the Moot Hall. I had enough trouble, without getting help from the Plod. The Priory was too frequented, what with the amateur drama people being Othello in every nook and cranny most nights. The dollop broker's school? That was the likeliest place. The Mayor's grounds? Too dangerous, seeing that Luna knew nil. But it was Oliver. Takes a thief to know one.

Too long replying. 'I'm not sure, Craddy.'

'You're off to find Gunge?'

'Yes,' I lied. 'At the Priory ruins.' No lag then. I was proud of my swiftness in deception.

'Don't lie, Lovejoy. I believe Connie Hopkins is being confined against her will. By whom, I don't know. For why, I don't know. But hereabouts, in the Eastern Hundreds.'

The old mill? No – Luna and I earned our squeaky clean alibis there, hadn't we?

'Go your own way, Lovejoy, eh?' These peelers kill me. I'm never anything, except alone. 'Which ladyfriend did Sandy mean?'

'Ask him, Big Ears.' Cassandra Clark, Marvella?

My final shot. I offed through the narrow town lanes like a rabbit. I'd wasted too much time on negatives. I shot down Eld Lane, past the corner pub – still heaving behind its smoke-frosted windows – and by the old almshouses, the steep lantern-lit steps through the Roman wall. And to the Priory.

Visitors are astonished to find spectacular remains of a great priory, somehow secluded in the very heart of a town. There's a new priory – gruesome mustard-coloured Victorian replica – in the grounds. I suppose it sounds like a scenic garden, all laid out really posh. It isn't. It's as close to waste as land can get. The ruins are behind a low wall, set among scrubby trees and gravestones. Occasional winos swill and murmur, desperate lovers gasp deep among weeds and bits of old bicycles. The perimeter consists of small shops that face out on to the street, a semi-derelict railway siding, and that little thoroughfare I mentioned, where The Great Marvella and Geronimo live. It's an ancient part of town. Not spooky, not really.

Except tonight the Priory was empty. No rehearsals. Just a clink of a bottle somewhere among the gravestones. Smoke from clean wood. Jake must be in. He's a hitchhiker, Norwich to Bradwell eleven times a year. Got to do this barmy pilgrimage four hundred times before he dies. He's thirty-one, done over a hundred so far. Work it out.

'Jake?' I blundered forward. The ruins are set low. The ancient monks had fish there.

'That you, Lovejoy?'

He's too cunning to let firelight show, in case a bobby comes a-strolling. He might be near the old ruin's looming gateway. How come ruins always have gateways standing, when their roofs and walls are tumbled? Odd, that.

'You scared me, Lovejoy.' Filth conveys status. Nothing so convincing as a tramp's dignity. 'Thought you was the Plod.'

'Oh, aye.' There's never anywhere to sit. 'How many, Jake?'

'Eight. Three to go this year. I'm on schedule.'

He had a fire, packing cases. I warmed my hands.

'I'm searching for Connie Hopkins, Jake.' I described her, antique dealer who worked the Arcade, empty shop on East Hill. 'Just wondered if you'd clapped eyes, Jake, you working the Ship tavern a few doors up.'

'Blonde tart? Didn't you have your feet under her table?'

'That's private.'

He chuckled. 'Saw her when I woke yesterday.' He nodded towards the top road, over the little wall. 'With that snake tart.'

'Vell?' There was no light from Vell's sparsely furnished parlour. I could see. 'She went in?'

'Went off in a motor. Some tits on that Vell tart, eh?'

'Mmmmh.' Jake wakes at teatime, then retires sloshed out of his mind at two in the morning. So, five o'clock, give or take. 'Hear anything, Jake?'

'No. Just them two birds rowing. Couldn't hear what.'

Sandy said, having words with her ladyfriend. Connie, a special friend of Vell's? I'd assumed somebody else.

'Ta, Jake. If you hear, eh?' I went off through the trees and regained the narrow side street, pausing under the lamps.

Behind, Jake's overgrown grounds of the ancient Priory. Here, the shops and town proper began. Through there, the busy town bus station through the Roman wall. To the right a Congregational church hall of antique red brick. Facing, the pawnbroker's, florist's, the stairs up to Vell's barn. As unmysterious as you can get. This was once consecrated ground in old times.

'Hello?' I buzzed Vell's door, shouted like a pillock when nobody answered. 'Hello? Vell?'

Nothing visible through the letterbox. Just the oblique shaft of light from the streetlamps showing the stairs, the door ajar at the top. Nothing. Except Vell had no real friends that I knew in the district. And where was Vell? My head throbbed. There was an aroma, oddly offensive, as I looked through the post-flap. Couldn't place it, put it out of my mind.

One of the nine public phones in the precinct was still working when I got there. Sandy and Mel had gone. Only the dog remained, forlorn under the glass canopy. I rang everybody I could think of, including Vell's number. Answerphones, nothing. Then I had a stroke of genius, and rang my own number. They give you one of those bleep things, comes with the set. There were three messages. A dealer from Bedfordshire offering an Act of Parliament timekeeper. (A five-shilling tax was slapped on clocks in 1797; taverners hung these wall clocks in taprooms. They're highly sought-after with their big wood face and thin body. They don't strike or chime, so count as 'timepieces' proper.) He'd missed my boat, but had timed and dated his message. A pal.

Second was The Great Marvella, saying she was going away and would I miss her. She'd call in a couple of weeks. She gave an address in Stourbridge, Worcester. Some snake farm, I shouldn't wonder. I'd almost hung up, having got the important negative I wanted, when I heard another voice. Luna, whispering. She shouldn't have said those horrid things. She would come to the cottage as soon as, etc, etc. Nothing from Connie. I set off through the rain to find Gunge, and ran him to earth in the Welcome Sailor about an hour before closing time.

The Welcome Sailor is a traditional East Anglian pub. That is, it's been on its last legs for nine centuries. You couldn't insure it to save your life. The joke being it'll outlive Lloyd's of London. Creaking doors hang longest.

The regulars were relieved I'd arrived. As well they might. Gunge's idea of tactful interrogation is to lift you up into his bearded face and stutter, 'S-S-Seen Connie?' We leant on the taproom bar, safe from ears. He'd had no success, I could tell from the slow tear that rolled down into his vast beard. I'm quick at clues.

'Listen, Gunge. We're going to take a risk.' I waited respectfully while he wiped his eyes with an arm like a hairy log. 'I have an idea where – Gunge. Put me down.' He lowered me and undid his fist so I could move. 'Where we might *look*.'

'Let's go now, Lovejoy.'

'We need a mob, Gunge. Not just you and me.'

He stared, the astonishment of the giant. People his size simply can't understand. They've never been pushed around.

'I have an idea she's in an old school. Eastern Hundreds. Trouble is, it's a dollop broker's.'

'Where? How many we need?'

More giant think. Notice he didn't doubt his ability to storm Dollop Towers? I was shaking in my shoes.

'Within thirty miles. Famous, now closed. Luna knows. But we'll have to be mob-handed. Twenty, thirty. An army.' I felt weary.

'We ring the fire brigade, Lovejoy,' he rumbled. 'That gets us past the door, see?'

I nearly fell into my ale. 'Fire brigade?' I went all casual. Gunge having an idea was a shock. 'Right. I know a torcher –'

'No, Lovejoy,' his bass vibrated. 'A fire might hurt Connie. We only *say* there's a fire.'

Typical giant idiocy. 'Gunge,' I reasoned. 'We need the hoses, the shambles of it. Otherwise the gatemen will –'

'No, Lovejoy.' I was tired of No, Lovejoy. 'We're firemen, see?'

Narked, I drew breath to correct this hulk's tardy thought processes, then exhaled without a word. I felt redundant.

CHAPTER THIRTY-THREE

'Sure it's the right place, Lune?'

'Don't keep *on*, Lovejoy.' Luna was getting snappier by the minute. 'The eighth *time*.'

The van was stiflingly hot. I was soaked inside the fireman's suit. The helmet alone weighed a ton. Mine was yellow, Gunge's white. Was one of us a pleb, the other a boss? I'd begun to lose heart as I recognised the faint outline of the red-brick gatehouse in the head-lights. The tiny van had no space for anyone except Gunge in the front. Me and Luna rattled around like peas in a tin all the way. Now, we were concealed in a layby about a mile off. Apart from a couple of disappointed snoggers who'd left when we disturbed their tryste-spot, we went unnoticed.

One in the morning. Sandy had kitted us out. He always knew somebody, this time a theatrical widow who catered for local thespians at mind-boggling prices. He'd enjoyed himself, asking could he be the first to light Gunge's fire, or be the damosel on the burning balcony, all that. He wears you out just listening.

'I mean,' I pleaded, 'what if it's a real school. See what I mean?' It had been such a great idea in the Welcome Sailor.

'It's the right place.' Luna had her woman's voice on. 'The school Jenny Calamy went to, Cassandra Clark, Connie Hopkins. Credit me with sense, Lovejoy. It's quite bad enough to be a *vandal*. The excuses I had to make! A trace of scandal is enough to −'

'Silent, please,' Gunge rumbled.

Quiet descended. Not even Luna would argue with Gunge. I fidgeted, played I Spy with myself − only you can't cheat when you're your opponent. I tried to remember *The Green Eye of the Little Yellow God*, but couldn't do the first stanza. I hummed 'She went and married a lawyer,' until Gunge swivelled to look back, whereon I shut it. It seemed hours before he spoke.

'Ten past. Phone.'

'You, Lovejoy.' Luna passed me a handphone. Women are skilled shirkers. Nine nine nine, and the nasal twang saying emergency fire ambulance or police.

The fire office sounded itching to go. I made myself breathless.

'The school − you know the old Sampney Young Ladies Academy? It's all afire. Come quick. There's . . .' I gasped, cried out, made a crackling noise, getting really worked up until Luna furiously snatched the phone, tapped it to mute.

'You're simply ridiculous!' she cried. 'I've never *known* . . . Overdoing every single thing.'

'Shush.' Gunge wound the van window down.

We listened. The countryside was silent as only East Anglia's rural quiet can be. You could hear worms crawl. I heard a crinkly leaf skitter along the road. Grass gave faint groans. It would have made me sweat, except I was already pouring with the stuff.

Then in the distance a thin wahwah, instantly deafened out as Gunge turned the ignition and we roared off. I'd have had a pee from nervousness but for Luna. We careered between the tall hedgerows. Gunge took from his vast paunch a light, reached a hand out. I heard it clunk on to our roof as we zoomed along. An intermittent cobalt-coloured glow revealed that he'd nicked a Plod light. We were now a copmobile.

'There!'

Luna saw them cross the flyover, lights a-flash and sirens wailing. Gunge slowed to let the fire engines go, then accelerated so swiftly my face shifted on its bones. We tore along the lanes after them.

The school gates were already ajar. Gunge rolled us inside. Two security uniforms were there. The fire vehicles were already at the front door. Lights switched on. Somebody was looking out from a second-floor window, immensely blocking the light, shouting instructions, demands. A security uniform trotted alongside us. Gunge did an expert curve into the foliage.

'What the hell?' A bloke, young, cool enough to be armed.

'Keep clear, sir,' Gunge said, braking. 'Where's the fire?'

'What frigging fire?'

'Fifth-degree blaze, major casualties.'

I alighted, listening with admiration. God, Gunge was a better liar than me. I heard a scrabbling inside the van, saw the security man turn, and yelled, 'Do I signal for more help, sir?'

'Ascertain status first, Schuller,' Gunge rumbled.

'Very good, sir.' Schuller? 'This the way?' I demanded.

The security man was distracted by uproar from the house.

'Inspect residential perimeter, Schuller.' Gunge, curt.

Schuller. 'Yes, sir. How many resident?'

'Fourteen,' the man said. Reply by reflex.

The real firemen were calling, hoses unwinding. Christ, a searchlight. I swore. Who'd think? Like Bonfire Night. I'd no idea. Did every blaze get this? Fantastic.

'All residents mobile?' I barked. 'Lame? Wheelchairs?'

'No.' Instant again, therefore true.

'Schuller,' Gunge boomed. 'Keep that drive clear. More vehicles coming. How many entrances?'

Schuller, I muttered darkly, hurrying off. I'd give him Schuller. Made me sound like a Transylvanian cobbler from a Disney cartoon. I fiddled with my pathetic little Woolworth hand torch, stumbled off among rose bushes while the guard followed Gunge to the action.

A couple of minutes among the bushes watching the consternation develop, and I returned, knocked on the van's side, three long, one short.

'I'm ready, Lovejoy.' Luna slid into the driver's seat. She was in a policewoman's uniform, so fetching it made me wonder for a second about fetishes, uniforms, leather buckles.

'You look terrific, Lune. I'm off, then. Got my bag?'

She passed it. My ordinary clothes. 'Lovejoy. Be careful.'

But I was already eeling through the black night, falling over. Why didn't roots grow down, for God's sake? Roots are supposed to.

The side of the mansion seemed a mile long. A security bloke came round the far end as I reached there. I talked into a bleeper, like I imagined firemen do, and barked a question about how many entrances. He hesitated, told me five. I told him to open the kitchen door, not let anyone else in.

'Understand?' I shouted, professional in a hurry.

'Right.' He unlocked the door. 'What the hell's going on?'

'Any signs of the oil fire?' I rasped, wishing I could go octaves down like Gunge. 'Straight ahead to the main hallway?'

'Oil? Er, I think so. Fire? There's no –'

'No lights. Fire risks, lights. Close it after me.'

I snapped an order, meet the senior officer at the front, and was inside and free. So he'd never even been inside, this security man. I trotted after my torch-beam.

Kitchens revolt me. I mean, they say even a cabbage screams. This one shone, chrome and steel on black. Marble floor. I stepped round the inner door, switched my lamp off, listened. The suspicious sod was hesitating out there. I could hear him, shuffling on the gravel. A torchlight shone in, roamed about a bit. Then he moved off. His sort gets on your nerves. I could feel the blighter thinking he should have demanded my pass.

Boots are problems. Socks are almost as difficult. Slippy on wood floors, fine on carpets. Outside came the distant hullabaloo of order, counter-order, disorder. Inside, somebody came downstairs, a woman's light tread.

'What is it?' a woman's voice called. Nobody I knew.

'The fire station.' Another, distant. 'Is there a fire?'

By the kitchen door was a wall cupboard, the sort you keep brooms in. I pulled the door, lifting it for possible squeaks, and stepped inside. But what excuse can a hidden fireman offer? I was soaked, enough sweat to put the bloody fire out without hose pipes.

Then the stentorian voice I knew. My favourite dollop broker. She must be a vision in curlers. 'Who heard a fire alarm?'

Five or six female voices denied hearing a thing. A man's boots clumped. A fire officer shouting, who was in authority?

A general search, I was done for. A walk-in freezer at the far end of the kitchen? No, ta. I'd seen too many mafia films to hide there. I could always nip out into the garden. What if the suspicious security man was lurking among the hydrangeas, the swine? I'd have to brazen it out, join the real firemen – except had Sandy's widow got the garb right? One wrong epaulette and I'd be exposed as a fraudster.

'You check, lady.' The fire officer was disappointed the entire place wasn't going up in flames. 'I'll run smoke tests.'

'Is that necessary? You can see quite clearly –'

'Regulations.' He wanted tea with a dash of Glenfiddich.

'I run the test, chief?' some hopeful bloke asked, concealed lust in his voice. I imagined a bevy of beauties on the staircase in fetching disarray, and swallowed. At least he could see them. I was stuck in a cupboard.

'I'll do it, Polkinghorn. Outside. Check the roof.'

Mutters of reluctant obedience, the low thunder of boots.

The voices receded. I risked opening the door slightly. Light fell obliquely in from the corridor. Silence. I wavered, put my boots on. I should have asked Gunge where they did smoke tests. Upstairs? Stairwells? I realised with a shock that I was silhouetted in the doorway, tiptoed out of the kitchen. Three steps up, I was in the hall, where I'd first met the dollop broker, among the stacked lentils and jerseys.

Dejection set in. Sweating, cursing, quivering, I stood like a lemon. The plan seemed so simple: get in, wait until quiet night sanded everybody's eyes, then find Connie. But with fourteen birds wafting about could they possibly keep a fifteenth imprisoned?

The question I hated: Was Connie still alive? Voices returned. I ducked under the stairs, a small cupboard with meters, gas, electricity. Wires everywhere. A couple of metal boxes hummed steadily. I kept well away, scrunged into a ball, switched my torch off, prayed.

'. . . country vandals ought to be tackled by the Government.' The grumbling fire officer.

'I agree,' gravelled Miss R. 'Flogging too good for them. None of my girls ever . . .'

'We'll check again in the morning . . .'

'I blame the parents . . .'

Talk, farewells, doors slamming, men distantly calling, engines starting. I prayed Gunge and Luna had got away, that Luna had done her rehearsed little act with the gateman. I was just congratulating myself when shock struck.

The women's voices approached. Lights in the hallway clicked on. More voices. Sets of feet slapped by – slippers. The kitchen lights. Somebody filled a kettle, women talking. If I hadn't moved to under the stairs I'd have been caught. I almost fainted. Killed by a dozen birds in their private mansion.

'Right. Post mortem.'

The dollop broker clapped hands. Somebody said Mary and Eliza weren't here yet. They were shouted for, somebody finally going to fetch them. Cups clinked, saucers rattled. Midnight feast in the dorm.

'Versions, everybody.'

'I think I heard the sirens first, Miss Reynolds,' a voice offered. 'I called Maria.'

'I answered the security gateman's phone, Miss Reynolds. Fire engines had already entered the drive, and a police van. They ignored his signals to halt.'

'Norma. You're D site supervisor tonight. Any action?'

'None.' Norma was crisp. I imagined her in jodhpurs, riding crop and waisted tan jacket. Mustn't get the wrong side of old Norma.

'Carol.' Saying Carol's name was the nearest Miss Reynolds would ever come to cooing. 'You checked the electronics?'

'Nil for person activity, Miss Reynolds.'

The signal for relief all round. Except the mention of electronics was worrying. I didn't want anybody probing my nook. Talk began, a few mild quips about the firemen's expressions, vandals who thought it funny to phone the fire brigade.

'We'll double Norma's watch. Patricia's next on call.'

Patricia groaned, but accepted her duty. They moved out, Miss

Reynolds calling for two to come back this instant and clear away. She scolded them all upstairs – just because they were a business partnership didn't mean the Sampney Ladies Academy encouraged slatternly behaviour . . . Sounds diminished, leaving me solitude.

D sites. D for dollop sites? Where constant nocturnal supervision was required? Very likely. Electronic surveillance, rotas of vigilants from within the mansion, not mere security hirelings. The gatehouse could be left to men, never part of the dollop broker syndicate.

It was simple. Headmistress, her school going into liquidation, has a ready-made team. Maybe their adoring daddies brought in the first dollops. Educated, socially elegant. And eminently trainable. Who would suspect a schoolhouse of being involved in international roguery? Playing host to the revenue of great robberies, storage of antiques filched from museums and country houses. Poor old Prammie Joe had died because he realised the Cornish Place stuff wasn't going abroad on the Thames barges, but somewhere inland. Here, in fact. But whose dollop was it? The killer's, that's who.

Which left the problem of Connie. She'd presumably been to this school. Wasn't that what Luna'd said, back in the van? And so had some other birds who were now into antiques. But some must be nurses, teachers, politicians. So?

Barefoot time. I got my socks off, edged out of the cubby hole, bumping my head with a blasphemy as I stood erect too quickly. Gloaming coming from the distant front door's side panels, but not enough to move by. A door slammed upstairs, some bird calling sorry. Silence.

Houses are queer places. Not only that. This was female, a nest of those unattainables. One on her lone's pretty formidable. But fourteen? Benign, the house seemed to be smiling, we ladies are caring, sweet. You have nothing to fear, Lovejoy. Oh, aye, I thought sardonically. That chestnut. Then why was I trembling, sweat maddening me down every sloping surface I possessed? I stood a second, moved across the spacious cold floor. Stairs curving up, me giving the bottom step a wide berth. I'm clumsy at the best of times. A door at the far side, shown by a single click of my torch. The damned thing blinded me. I got there, turned the handle. My boots were hung round my neck, instinct bringing them the safest way. I halted – what the hell had I done with the bag, my mufti clothes? Christ. I'd left it outside in the bushes somewhere. Or inside the broom closet? I heard a faint sound that scared me witless. It was me moaning in alarm.

Then I sussed myself. Typical. Four whole minutes I'd been

standing in the semi-dark, hand on the door knob of this mystery room, about to go in and discover . . . what? Connie hanging, dead? Thoughts are only deceits, ways of avoiding doing. I stepped inside quickly. Not a sound. Closed the door after me. Darkness, wholesale. No windows, no light. Not even a wash of nightglow from a curtain edge. I fumbled the torch in my hand, and felt a faint reverberation. The place was vast, panelled. Only spacious cathedrals and banqueting halls do that. I switched it on.

Vast was right. For a country mansion, that is. Width, distance, length, a roof of lovely rafters. The panelled walls receded. It could have been an assembly hall, a decorated gymnasium. I guessed it once doubled as the dining room as well, in the way of private schools.

But it felt cold. Parquet flooring, polished. Round the dark oak-panelled walls were photographs. I moved forward, careful not to crash on my bum to bring the bevy down on me. The wall photographs showed schoolgirls by the dozen, the score, the hundred. Coloured, then black and white, then sepias. I inspected one – a daguerreotype, I could swear. The place was a mausoleum, the record of the Sampney Young Ladies Academy over the years. I shivered, cold. Nothing to cause a draught in the silent place. But it felt . . . tomblike. A shrine. Nothing living, except a vase of flowers on a central table – by Ince, I felt, smiling. It deserved better. A luscious mahogany dining table like that should have been living with people, not stuck here in this sepulture.

Now, you can't trust pictures – whether paintings, photos, or engravings. I mean, in 1644 our first-ever illustrated newspaper, the *Mercurius Civicus*, publishing engravings of Prince Rupert and his sworn enemy Sir Thomas Fairfax – different issues, same portrait. It turned up later as Prince Maurice, et al. No, pictures aren't trustworthy.

How old would Connie be? From her deception about that barmy astrophysics, I worked out a possible date, started along the lines of photographs. Maharajah's daughters were among the fresh faces, African nobility. It was weird, seeing the dress styles evolve through the decades, right from 1840–something. Hockey matches, cumbersome skirts for tennis, punting in impossible but lovely high-neck, long-sleeved blouses properly covering every inch of forearm. Straw hats. One sad Indian girl wearing a black armband on Speech Day, bravely trying to smile, learning the Stiff Upper Lip first go, God help the poor little lass. Except she was long passed on.

The faces came closer. Now war-time, a group of girls laughing fit to burst in Women's Land Army uniforms. One rolling up her sleeves, about to blow up a barrage balloon. Girls falling about as a mistress tried to stay sternly in control as shy soldiers manned their anti-aircraft gun, crocodiles of Sampney Young Ladies filing past. VE Day, clownish celebrations. Long trestled tables on lawns, this mansion in the background, strolling dignitaries taking tea and cake.

Years moved nearer. I inched down the panels, flashing and peering. Brighter photographs, hints of variation in dress. A scarf here, a watch there. School plays, tableaux of improbable history. Scenes from Empire eased into Commonwealth. Faster changes as educational theories tumbled, to balls learning up into the current shambles. Lines of girls depressed at computers. Nervy teachers trying to look jocular at Last Day celebrations. Diploma lists.

My breathing felt funny. I was getting close. I knew it. The girls were modern now, dates recent. Bicycles, a motor cycle even. Sleeker motors parked by this mansion, now captioned Big School House. Foundation ceremonies, blokes in chains of office, improbable gleaming spades and sham trowels, breaking the sod, laying foundation stones.

Plays, even dances, standards tumbling as the years rattled numbers. One long school photograph, Miss Reynolds the headmistress looking moronic in a mortar-board and gown. Democracy wasn't going to raise its head at *her* Young Ladies Academy. Then the shortening. The school dwindled, few from overseas. The school uniform looked archaic. Biology laboratory's closure, Miss Reynolds smiling defiance at the camera. The last sixth-form physics class. Chemistry no more, as costly subjects bit the dust. One bright spot as the Academy launched a Grand Joint Venture with somewhere else – a stiffy segregated arrangement of imitation smiles as two groups of school governors learnt the cruelties of double-entry accounting. Then the end game, desperate Sampney Goes It Alone photographs. One sad spurt of hope as a new boat-house was donated by a new up-and-coming local politician. Good old Oliver Carstairs! Luna not with him – before they were married? Hardly. She'd mentioned some troublesome daughter, wouldn't work or go to college.

The This Year's Intake pictures ended. The Academy dwindled, down to the last pained photograph. Jennifer Calamy, happy to be the smallest. It hurt – not that I loved my school; I hated the damned place. But these lasses and their teachers didn't seem to. Are all school photographs frauds? Dated some six years previous: Miss Reynolds, chin raised, among her charges. I could tell she'd deter-

mined to punish society for the degradation suffered by her beloved
Academy. Her expression was no longer defiance. It was cold, aimed.
Aimed out there, at the horrid world that had shredded her dream-
time. At us. And us was anyone.

That final year was something. Parties, merriment, a veritable
Waterloo Ball of devil-may-careness. And the ending, motors arriving, girls tearful on steps, parents shaking hands. A final cheque-
donation ceremony but this time amid piles of packing cases, stacks
of books, desks balanced. The hallway. A vigorous local politician,
electioneering even as the crew ejected. Ubiquitous old Oliver.

The photographs ended in Favourite Memories. The last of the
girls. Girls looking up from desks in bright sunlight, so lovelily young
they pulled at your heart. The last team match, hockey, lacrosse. A
dash of craziness at tiddleywinks, an illicit dorm party with – gasp
at madcap naughtiness! – two bottles of beer and a bra on show,
girls rolling in the aisles with laughter. Then one photograph I stared
at closer.

A fancy dress party, with faces I knew. Connie Hopkins, close
to tears, in a witch's cloak, pointed hat, astride a broomstick.
Cassandra Clark, more mature, in a tricorn hat and gentleman's
frockcoat, white flat cravat on black. Cromwellian, a Puritan? And
a tiny girl, an executioner with an axe. In that get-up, was it Jenny
Calamy? I peered at the names below the picture. Difficult with a
torch, small lettering. E. C. Clark must be Cassandra. C. A. Hopkins
the witch. Yes, J. E. F. Calamy.

How long I stood there I don't know. But now there wasn't any
point in staying. Nor even, I realised, in keeping quiet. I only needed
to know one thing now. And I could go. Time Cradhead and
Drinkwater earned their cost-of-living adjusted monies. I walked
away, switched the lights on. The place shrank, became sadder,
unthreatening in the harsh glim.

Across the hallway, me putting the lights on as I went. God, but
the lunacy of storing all those dated school-books, desks, struck me
more than ever as I made the kitchen and found more switches.
What did Miss R hope to do, reopen the Academy with her ill-gotten
gains? My bag wasn't in the broom cupboard. Sod it. I must have
left it outside. You can't depend on things.

And, I noted bitterly, the bloody tea they'd brewed was cleared
away. The biscuit barrels were sealed inside a glass-fronted press. I
was really narked. Typical selfish women. No thought of an intruder
happening by during the owl hours and feeling hungry. Oh no. I
clattered the kettle, got it going, but the bloody tea was locked, and

I can't make coffee to save my life. But there was a radio, and a smoke alarm. A smouldering hankie takes only seconds to do. Wake up, idlers.

They came at me mob-handed. By then I was sitting on one of their crummy stools, whistling along with the golden oldies. The fire alarm was shrilling its intermittent bat-squeaks. It set off others through the building.

'Anybody got the key to the grub?' I asked them while they stared. Miss Reynolds shoved through.

I was right. She *was* a fantastic sight. A nightgown big enough for four. No curlers, but perfection shouldn't be ruined. The girls were gorgeous, but threatening. Being a barefooted fireman saved me.

'Wait, please.' I counted them.

One or two had rounders bats, I saw uncomfortably. Twelve, thirteen, fourteen. I'd reached the total. Still no Cassandra Clark. No Connie, because she was being tortured, chained to a chair elsewhere. No Jenny Calamy. And of course no Vell – too poor to have shared in their exalted upbringing.

No more theories.

'Thank you, ladies,' I said. 'Could you call the police, Maria?' I didn't know which one she was, but I sounded as if I did. 'And waken those idlers at the gatehouse, will you, love?'

The kettle shrilled piercingly, adding to the din from the wireless and the smoke alarms. I'd be glad to get home.

CHAPTER THIRTY-FOUR

They gave me more than tea and a wad, as it happened.

It was like being in a beautiful assembly – it *was* being. The police still hadn't been called. Maria quelled the vigilantees outside by a terse call. No fire brigade. No blue lamps blinked on the lawns. It was three in the morning. Four sorts of cake on a silver gadrooned tray. I felt a hobo gone royal.

Miss Reynolds was holding forth in her private drawing room. She looked wrapped in a linen shroud. 'You see, Lovejoy, we give an essential service.'

The girls murmured, nodding. I liked Maria. She could nod to me any time she liked.

'Yes, I see that,' I said, to general relief.

'We're looking after a dollop of yours, for heaven's sake!'

'And I'm glad, Miss Reynolds. After seeing your organisation. Cast iron. I'm very pleased.'

More satisfied smiles. Only one lass yawned, and she'd tried not to. Infected, I yawned as well.

'The point is, Lovejoy, we manage well. On our own.' The silence hung. Heads moved, paused in mid-nod. 'We don't need partners.'

No dollop broker ever starves. They take virtually no risks. Company fronts, banks in Jersey or the Isle of Man, and they live the life of Riley. People with stolen goods have simply nowhere else to go. If a thief wants to be safe from arrest, he has to use a dolloper. Or take the staggering chance of burying the loot under his pal's shed. And we all know what happens to loot stashed with friends, right? It vanishes, along with the friends.

Something in my expression must have showed, because there was a faint stir. Any other time I would have sat mesmerised to watch so many birds stir, but I hadn't long. Forty hours since Connie went missing. I – no, Connie – had few hours left.

'We know how you antique dealers see us, Lovejoy.' Miss Reynolds was all prim. 'But somebody has to maintain standards. Morality is preserved here at Sampney Academy. We're proud to –'

'I need a phone,' I interrupted, to show whose side I was on.

Miss Reynolds nodded. I was given one from a wall compartment.

709

'Gunge? You there?' I went even redder, because he'd just answered. I'm hopeless on phones. Only Italians and Yanks have telephone skills. Genetics, I daresay.

'Found Connie?' the receiver rumbled. My hand vibrated.

'I think I know where she is, Gunge. The place near the Priory ruins. Upstairs. In the massage –'

'Marvella's? Where are you?' I heard Luna demanding, let me speak to him this instant and all that.

'Where you left me.' I fixed Miss Reynolds. 'Connie Hopkins isn't here. I've not searched, but –'

'What if she is?' Deep voices have more threat, haven't they.

'Then I'm wrong.' Blood drained from my face. All very well for me to be wrong. Connie would die. 'Am I, Miss Reynolds?'

Her face looked genuine. The girls' responses seemed so. One or two were asking each other questions, tilting their heads like they do when confidential.

'Connie Hopkins? No, Lovejoy. Is she why you're here?' She interrogated her lasses with sharp glances. They all looked back, shaking heads, wanting to ask what was going on.

'Everybody says no, Gunge.' Just me, trying to spread the responsibility. 'Go now.'

The phone burred. I looked about. I was sick of my fireman's uniform. I'd taken my helmet off. I didn't know whether to wait for Gunge to rescue Connie, or to get going myself. If this lot was having me on –

The doorbell went, one long peal. Again. Miss Reynolds gave an imperious flick of a finger. A lass scampered off, nightdress billowing about her form, making me swallow.

'Listen,' I told her. 'I need a lift. Can I have a motor?'

'To what purpose?' Miss Reynolds was a bargainer.

To the purpose of stopping one of your illustrious young ladies horribly murdering another of your IYL. I thought it, but could not say.

'Evening all.' Cradhead entered briskly, doing the thick copper joke. 'Bit much even for you, Lovejoy.'

He meant so many birds. I was up, beaming. 'Can you drive fast, Craddie? We've a way to go.'

'Fast as I like. Evening, ladies.'

Miss Reynolds came after, her bulk darkening the hallway. 'Lovejoy. You will keep us informed, won't you? This establishment always had prided itself on the welfare of its young ladies. We shouldn't want anything untoward –'

My hate suddenly broke. I turned, thrust my face at hers. She recoiled, actually lifted her arm to ward off a blow. I never swung it.

'I just don't believe you never saw the plight of little Connie Hopkins in your rotten school,' I heard myself say. 'Or realised the horror Cassandra Clark was planning. Keep your fucking standards, Headmistress. Find out what happens any way you can.'

Cradhead was alone, I saw. An unmarked motor car. He set a siren going somehow, me saying left, head for town.

'Anything to tell me, Lovejoy?' he asked conversationally as he roared and braked, battling the narrow lanes with swift gear changes. 'Seeing you've told the whole school.'

We were on the trunk road before I recovered enough to think. 'Do us a favour. Tell them not to nick Gunge's van for speeding.'

He called on a squawk box. 'Description?'

Whoops. I cleared my throat, looked at the speeding night. 'Sort of Bill box, actually. Blue light.'

He inhaled, gathered himself. 'It's a phoney police van, lads. Let it through. Follow —' He glanced at me for confirmation. 'Do not detain.'

I asked if this frigging wheelbarrow couldn't go any faster. He set his mouth in a thin line, and drove on, grimmer than before.

The town seemed derelict, empty. But that was only night's hand, cold over everything. The traffic lights, changing for no traffic to obey, always gives me the spooks. And that part of town, one of the oldest, never was Piccadilly. Like I said, it's got old buildings antedating the Tudors.

No light in the upper storey where Marvella held her rejuvenation clinics, or what, while her pal's snake eyes stared.

'She has a snake,' I told Cradhead. 'Watch out.'

'Snake snake, old chap?' he asked.

'Real. It's enormous. In a cage.'

Gunge had barely arrived. He was trying the door. Two Old Bill cars were winking blue fractiousness, five or six uniformed bobbies milling uncertainly. They hadn't been told what brain cells to use — always assuming, of course. They're taught to surge to no effect in basic training. They stared at me, a barefooted fireman in part of a uniform.

'Break it, lads,' Craddie said.

Neurones chugged into life on command: break it.

They leapt and crushed the door in, stood back with pride as me and Cradhead bounded up the stairs after Gunge's massive bulk ripped on and through. He was so worked up he didn't put the lights on. I did, knowing where the switches were. Cradhead noticed that, said nothing. The constabulary came thundering after.

'Phew. Christ.'

The stench was appalling. Nothing in the sparse outer room. Nothing really in the massage room, the long upper storey with its beams and plain ancient walls. I was struck by the curious resemblance to the chapel-like form of the place.

'That's where she held her.'

One chair, plain wood, still with its auction number on it. Ordure, excrement, urine stained the poor old thing. Quite good, just mid-seventeenth century, when chair-making became a craft separate from village joinery. Basically a chair in medieval joinery style, panel back with a carved crest, flat seat, plain front legs neatly turned. Its arm supports were missing. I saw those, crudely sawn off and chucked against the wall. Chain links trailed to new iron rings set in the wall. Sampney taught its young ladies all manner of skills. Maybe she'd practised, I thought queasily. On what? On whom?

'Lovejoy?' Cradhead asked, wondering.

'She kept Connie here, chained. Forty-eight hours was her goal. I knocked some time since, no answer.'

'Search the place, lads,' Cradhead called. The uniforms plodded downstairs, meeting another load coming up. He exclaimed in exasperation. 'Well, Lovejoy?'

Consecrated. This place was not a church exactly, but a Meeting House. I was looking at it. A prerequisite. The Witch-Finder General used holiness like a net. Was this the selfsame holy place where the witch trials were held? I didn't know enough to be certain. But the door to this upstairs hall was original. And that horrible chunk anciently cut out of it, like a cat flap, clumsily repaired with wrong beechwood by some nerk. For the familiar, the gremlin spirit that accompanies a witch. That's why Vell had gone, maybe knowing something evil was about to happen. Maybe her message to me was a kind of warning.

'The Priory, Craddie.' The one place left. 'She's there.'

'Why?'

Because Connie would be too ill, after over forty hours chained to a chair in her own filth, maybe maimed or battered, to walk anywhere. Had her kidnapper helpers? Like, say, Acker Kirwin, who'd killed Connie's business partner Rye at the mill? I wasn't sure.

I was already clattering downstairs, thrashing my way through the useless Plod in Gunge's wake. I said nothing. Forty-four hours. Four left. It would be dawn when Connie died.

'Jake!' I yelled, tearing across the narrow street into the ruins. 'Jake! It's me, Lovejoy!'

Like an idiot I'd forgotten my torch. I realised I was still barefoot when the churchyard path started hacking my feet. I've a brain like lightning. Gunge crashed ahead. Somebody running with me among the old overgrown gravestones shone a lamp. Others took up the cue. Somebody with sense rushed along the street to the main Priory gate, and now shone torches into the steep ruins from there. Cromwell's men, Fairfax and his lot, had crunched this religious foundation in the Great Civil War. It had stayed crunched.

'Go right, Gunge,' I called, still yelling for Jake.

But the fire was out, cold some time. No Jake, presumably wanting a quiet night, or starting off early to notch another trudge to Norwich.

'Lovejoy?' Gunge, tears a-trickle, looking at me. 'What've they done with her?'

'Wait.'

A plodmobile, its driver brighter than the rest, drove in from the street below. Its beam heads shone through the elder and birch. Surreal. Browns, creams, russets, of the gaunt ruins stretched into the night sky. Scrubby little shrubs clung to the mortar, hung over the toothy remains of arches. Pillars always stay last, don't they. Eighteenth-century gravestones, several dozen. Connie could be in any one. Or not. Could we search them all, underground vaults, in, what, three hours? It had been an enormous Priory, supporting scores of religions. They'd had fishpools for Fridays, two wells . . .

Wells. I looked up, astonished to discover rain teeming on my upturned face, oblique light catching the drops as they came at me out of the night sky. Wells. I wish I'd asked Therla's friend Josh more, fought the library harder for a book about the Witch-Finder. I'd had time, once. No time now.

In the old days, they'd caught the poor old crones, the so-say witches. Strapped them to a chair. Tortured, as a matter of course. Kept them awake. Extracted confessions. Then, forty-eight hours later, they'd 'swum' them. Float equalled guilt. Drown, innocence. Water. You needed water.

'She's here, Gunge. In a well. Or in the fishpools.'

'Fishpools are dry here, sir. The wells aren't.'

I stared at the tall constable. Cradhead asking him details.

'I come painting here, sir,' the constable said, embarrassed. 'The fishpools dry four or five times a year. Like now.'

'Lovejoy. What wells?'

'The abbots had wells. The Colne's half a mile off, downhill.'

Cradhead started calling orders. Uniforms rushed off. More cars came, more lights. Somebody rigged up spotlights – in the wrong places, of course. Gunge was like a mad thing, tearing aside the great gravestones, anything that possibly might be a well-covering, blubbering in panic that infected us all. The tall constable came with me.

We wasted an hour. They'd put out a call for Elizabeth Cassandra Clark, but that only warns miscreants to get the hell out. Some hopes. Wet through, worn out, I found myself at Jake's cold fire.

And finally began to think. Jake usually seemed to camp hereabouts. Never up slope. Never down slope, below the last level of wall. Yet he'd be just as well hidden there as here – and he could use the old crumbled Priory as a windbreak for his sack tent. Yet he camped here. I borrowed the copper's flashlamp.

The ashes of a good dozen fires, Jake-style, were within twenty feet. Why?

Because he forever brewed up. Find a tramp, find a brew. For which you need water. If fishpools dried often, you'd need a well. Shopkeepers on the street wouldn't give a tramp like Jake the time of day, let alone fill his billycan.

'Here, Craddie,' I yelled. Within yards of where I was.

You go in rings, make circles to search. It was a patch cleared of vegetation that gave it away. A gravestone about six feet long by three wide in the undergrowth, covered loosely by brambles. I hauled them aside. They came easily, which is something brambles never, ever do. They cling and rip your hands. I once rescued a blackbird in my own bramble-riddled hedge from a cat. The blackbird flew off without a word of thanks. I got cut to blazes.

A patch of earth, a crescent, scoured clean of vegetation. Pure dark earth. I tried shoving it, calling. 'Connie? Connie?' Then pulling. I tried knocking on it. Tramps must be tough, if they do this all the time. I was having another go when I got lifted, literally lifted and lobbed aside. Gunge bent, grabbed the stone and flipped it over, nearly driving the constable into the ground like a tent peg.

'Lights! Lights!' Cradhead was shouting.

Big size twelves crushed the earth about my face. I peered over the edge of the well, down. Down into the face of Connie, alive, looking up.

'Lovejoy?'

Inaudible. She was trying to croak out my name, but only managed to move her lips. She was tied to something in a sitting position, maybe on a stool, hands behind her back. Her hair was matted about her face. She was breast-deep in water. A dead rat floated by her shoulder.

There were ominous marks on the well's walling. The stones were shiny to a point some two feet above her head. Even as I gaped down into the fetid chasm, it seemed to me the water rose a fraction.

'We're here, love. Have you out in a trice, eh?'

Then people were bawling for ropes, stand aside, get ladders, and fire engines were wahwahing about the ruins. I only hoped they didn't think it was me this time, or I'd be for it. Suddenly I felt so tired, got up and stepped away. It's times like this I wished I still smoked.

'They found her, then,' a woman's voice said, casual. 'Thanks to you, Lovejoy, I hear.'

A shrug. 'I'm thick. Should have been hell of a sight faster.' Then I looked round, keeping my footing as the Plod milled uselessly about.

'Elizabeth Cassandra Clark, I presume.' I thought a moment, managed dully. 'Descendant of Elizabeth Clark, witch?'

'That's right, Lovejoy.' She looked so pretty and assured. Women never lack confidence, do they? It's us blokes lose heart at the ways of the wicked world. Women are in the thick of things, enjoying it all, good and bad. 'Of course, one hopes Connie Hopkins may not survive even yet. I rather put her through it.'

'Aye. Along the same time-honoured lines.'

'Why not?' Cassandra looked almost winsome. 'Her ancestor murdered mine. He was the most repellent specimen of the human race. Connie deserved at least this.'

She watched as some stalwart fireman was lowered into the well on an impossible array of ropes, pulleys screeching. She chuckled prettily. So very lovely.

'I had to send poor Rye flying – took his little belaying pin out when he least expected it. Very appropriate, don't you think? Death by flying, for Connie's friend?'

'No, love. You can't go about killing folk.'

'But one can, darling, when necessary.' I felt Cradheard come and stand listening. 'Joseph Godbolt's time had come. It was so easy, to become his prison visitor. I was actually fond of him.' She laughed.

'You see how deluded you can become? Fond! Of the spawn of a hanging judge?'

'Connie, though. Your schoolfriend.'

'Don't worry, Lovejoy. I shall get her. You can't imagine the temptation! The times I almost ended her life at the Academy! Only tradition held me back.'

'You still have no right, Cassie,' I said doggedly.

Her eyes filled. She leant and kissed me gently.

'Poor Lovejoy. Always wrong. Knows all, knows nothing.'

Then she drew a knife out of her sleeve, and stabbed me. I looked about, puzzled, thought hey, hang on, then started to die.

CHAPTER THIRTY-FIVE

The fact that there was a woman in the bed opposite amazed me. As soon as was I able I asked the nurse, why I was in a woman's ward.

'There's no such thing nowadays,' she scathed. 'How long since you were in hospital?'

'Two years.'

'Things change.' She was gone.

You never see a nurse coming towards you, do you? Only receding at a rate of knots. Where the hell are they all going? Off-duty, I suppose. Sister spent all her waking hours at her desk doing the nurses' Off-Duty Rota, as they cheerfully call their on-duty rotas. You never see the same nurse twice, either. But the noise in hospital's the same. Clash, bang, wallop. All night long the din of nurses playing cymbals. Sirens concentrate on the forecourt below your window. They have lifts that sound like the Brigade of Guards. The trolleys and gurneys whine shrilly, gnats in your earhole the livelong night. Wheels squeak, patients snore and groan.

By the fifth day I was on quite good terms with the woman opposite, in for something excruciating. She was delighted to learn I was the one the papers were on about. She was less excited when the police started taking statements. Several times she asked me what I'd done. Then she went home, made well by some doctoral mismanagement.

Cradhead came to stare about and make oblique references to criminal charges, forgery. Drinkwater never came once, not even to gloat. Miserable sod wouldn't know sympathy if he fell over it.

Early on I'd told a hurtling nurse to clear a table for the flowers all my mates would be sending. She said, 'Clear one yourself!' and sprinted on to rendezvous with her next percussion section. I did, my side hurting from physiotherapy. And waited for the stream of visitors who'd come and give thanks for my deliverance, praise my astuteness, rejoice that I'd tottered from the brink of death.

And waited.

Wai........ted.

It was only in the second week, refused phone access by your friendly surgeons in collusion with your friendly police, the penny, dropped. I began to smile. I knew what my friends were doing. They were ringing in to check on my progress, but warning the nurses not to give It away. And I knew what It was.

Surprise party. They'd all jump out of the woodwork the instant I got sprung. Then it would be the inevitable tussle for my body, the women giving me the hard time that I loved deep down. The deeper and downer the better.

'What are you smiling at?' a nurse cried, charging past.

'Nothing, Nurse,' I called, beaming.

'Why've you no flowers, Lovejoy?' I got next morning.

'Get on with you,' I rebuked fondly.

And the great moment dawned, two weeks to the day. The surgeon came round with his entourage, peered short-sightedly at my belly, said hmph, asked Sister did Lovejoy do his physiotherapy.

'Yes, sir. On the hour,' she lied slickly.

'Rum name.' The surgeon strolled affably on. 'He can go.'

Sprung! I dressed, got taken down to Reception. There I waited, smiling knowingly. They would come for me in some daft decorated motor, balloons all over, streamers and banners. I bet Big Frank'd arrange it. He's always keen on barmy jollification at his weddings.

Two o'clock came. No motor. Nobody asking for me. The Reception staff started glancing at me and whispering. I smiled, sure of the loyalty of friends. I'd rescued everybody from everything.

But you can't expect the traffic to ease up just because friends plan a surprise welcome, can you? Maybe some football team was playing, or an accident on the town by-pass interfered. That was it. I got a taxi, and rolled out to the village. I was wearing borrowed stuff. My fireman's uniform trousers cleaned by the hospital laundry. They lent me hospital slippers. I'd had to sign I'd bring them back. I was cold in the taxi.

In the lane I had a row. The driver wanted paying. I had to go in, breaking in because I'd lost my keys, presumably still with the bag of my own clothes in the grounds of the Academy. I found just enough to pay him.

The cottage was empty. No hullooing friends pouring from the wainscoting, no sudden cork-popping. I knew why. They were all waiting at the Ship, or the Welcome Sailor. I knew them. A rough bunch, but they'd all be there: Margaret Dainty, limping in with her gentle humour; Connie Hopkins, shyly suggesting she should come and stay the night; Luna, eager to resume where we'd left off; Jessica, wearing enough perfume to fell an ox at forty yards, every

come-hither sign blazing; and the rest, cheering me to the echo –
Gunge, Chris Mallon, Sandy and Mel, Liz Sandwell from Dragons-
dale, the whole tribe of good friends. Rivals, yes. But friends deep
down.

All except Joan. There was a card from her:

> *Lovejoy darling,*
> *I've just heard. Do get better, sweetie.*
> *If you don't, well, this message won't*
> *matter, will it? Del has given me a*
> *permanent bodyguard. Geraldo is sworn to*
> *obey – if you know what I mean! I'm taking*
> *him to Monte Carlo, where we'll marry and*
> *live happ. ev. aft. If you see Del, give the*
> *poor dear a hand-out. Thanks for the ride,*
> *darling.*
> *Joan.*

Which set me wondering. Had Joan Vervain known our noble
Mayor, and Luna, before I'd 'introduced' them here? Was the
Vervain's party a put-up? And good old Del in cahoots with Oliver
Carstairs long before? About Luna: honest, or not? I had a yoghurt
aged past its eat-by date.

The bluetits recognised me, though. They started tapping on the
windows. I filled their nut-hangers. Indoors, the diet sheet the ward
sister had given me made my mouth water. I had no cereals,
skimmed milk, oats, bread, bran flakes. I wondered if the birds'
peanuts were for human consumption, thought, well, it's those or
nothing, and ate handfuls. My belly would have to learn to cope. I
have to. There's a limit to the allowances you can make.

Getting on for five o'clock. The pubs would be opening soon.
Pleased, I worked it out. They'd have booked the George carvery.
My peanut-laden stomach rumbled enthusiastically. I dialled Jacko
to come round with his coal lorry and give me a lift. He's been
raised on my IOU scheme. Waiting, I composed my speech of thanks
and acknowledgement.

'Dear Friends,' it began. 'I never expected . . .'

The Ship was heaving, but nobody seemed to be in, if you know
what I mean. I tapped Gerda for news. Absently she asked if I'd
been away. I bit back a rebuke just in time. Of course! All my friends
must've warned everybody to act as if nothing was up, my return

was an everyday occurrence! I cadged a pint on the slate, then judged the time right to leave.

Naturally, I was getting more excited than I should. But it's unusual, isn't it? To be fêted by your friends, a hero, veritable champion of the underdog. I noticed the clock. Getting on for seven. Foolish to turn up too early. A surprise party spoils if the surprise arrives before it's ready.

I timed my exit from the Ship to perfection. Seven o'clock, and the day waning. Walking up East Hill into the town centre was tiring, but I made it.

The Welcome Sailor was practically empty too. No, people hadn't been in – wasn't it Birmingham's Antiques Fair? No Mrs Dainty, no Rebecca from the wharf, no others. The barman supposed there was something on. Maybe the George – he'd heard there was a gathering there.

That was it! The George after all! I was just leaving when a car pulled up, three women inside screaming joyously. The motor was covered in streamers, balloons. At last! I recognised Jenny Calamy. Dressed to kill.

'Lovejoy! You darling!' She raced across the road and bussed me enthusiastically.

'What about Big Frank?' I asked anxiously.

'Wish me luck tomorrow!' she cried.

'Tomorrow?' What was tomorrow?

'My wedding!' she screamed. Her friends in the car screamed along. 'In France! Can you *believe* it? See you when we come back! You really *must* come round! Bye-eeee!'

'Bye-eee!' everybody cried but me. The motor sped away.

Well, you can't postpone a blinking wedding, just because the would-be best man's in hospital. Stands to reason.

I made the George, just in time to see Luna descend from the Mayor's grand motorcade. She was positively shimmering. It was coming on to rain.

She seemed to falter as the flash blulbs of our town's three feeble reporters dazzled. Her smile faded. She sized me up. Then she swept inside, mouth tight, hatred in her eyes. I waited until the little crowd dispersed, talking over the Mayoress' lovely dress, then went inside. I'd rather be going to my party than hers any day of the week.

'Party? No.' The receptionist was a tubby girl. She hides a tot of gin under the counter. 'Try the boozer next door.'

The Robin Hood's not my scene exactly, but the Arcade was closed – an hour early. I perked up. A good sign, especially after the way business must have picked up once news of my rescue of Connie broke.

I drew a blank there, except for a sighting of Harry Bateman, who shot off with a scared look in his eyes at the sight of me. Out of the back door. I smirked. Tatty old Harry nearly gave the game away! My surprise party must be in the one remaining waterhole, the Marquis of Granby on North Hill.

Cunning of my friends, to hold the gathering down there, eh? Behind St Peter's Church, where I'd least expect it. It was coming on to rain harder, and black night a-fallen, when I finally entered the thick fug.

Gunge came to meet me. Connie, pale but happy, was on a stool at the bar. Gunge took me across. I can't say I was relieved, because I'd never doubted. I mean, what are friends for? Goodness can't exist alone. It needs people.

'Hello, Connie.' I felt quite shy. Silly, really, after what Connie and me had been to each other. God, but I wanted a woman. I needed one like . . . No good trying to explain. Blokes don't need telling, and women can't understand.

'Hello, Lovejoy.' Her eyes were misty. I wondered how to get rid of Gunge when she said, 'We want you to be the first to know, Lovejoy.'

She did? I thought I already was. 'That's nice, love.'

'Gunge and I are going to live in the Isle of Man.'

'Fine. I'm . . .' I always forget. Do you congratulate the man, and wish the bride-to-be well? Or vice versa? I bussed her anyway, and Gunge gripped my hand to a mince.

'You judge our dollop, Lovejoy,' Connie said, adoring eyes on her man. 'We'll send our address once we're married.'

God knows how long I stayed. They spoke of a little antique shop near the Douglas ferry, shipping stuff Belfast to Liverpool. The Customs Paper re-imports trick, New York via Glasgow. Something in Guernsey with Southampton shippers. Gunge said hardly a thing.

He followed me to the door when I managed to break away.

'Ta, Lovejoy. Pike on, lad, eh?'

'Ta, Gunge. I mean it. Good luck to you both.'

Into the rain, steady now with a stiff breeze. I went slowly uphill into town.

There was no surprise party. I hadn't asked after the mob. Just as, I told myself finally, they hadn't asked after me.

The town centre was almost deserted. Just the George, with its lights. A couple of small restaurants. The Red Lion's upper floor's curtains showing where some vast nosh was taking place. I think hospitals make you tired out just lying abed. Maybe they want it that way, so you can't start injuring yourself again and come back in for more.

'Lovejoy!'

Glad to hear my name, I swivelled so fast I almost dinged myself unconscious on a lamp-post. Miss Turner. And Forage. And Marmalade Emma, with the sleepy Grimes reeling dozily along.

'Hello,' I said. For once I was willing to tell her all sorts of genealogy. As usual she got in first.

'Such excellent news, Lovejoy! We're related! Mr Forage and I! In the sixteen-eighties! First cousins in common. Can you believe it? You were exactly right!'

I looked at Forage, at Marmalade Emma. I would have looked at Grimes, but he can never look back so it's a waste of a look. This was more than a rejoicing of ancient cousins.

'Who's getting wed?' I asked, smiling.

'Mr Forage and I,' Miss Turner said. 'In New Hampshire. We've discovered a branch of our family there.' She plucked me close, whispered, 'I do believe they're very wealthy, Lovejoy!'

'Wonderful!' I said directly to Forage, who had the decency to look away. 'Almost too good to be true, eh?'

'Fantastic!' Miss Turner cried. 'We go tomorrow, Lovejoy.'

Et heartwarming cetera. I heard them out. Wherever love flourishes, let it. Even if Forage was working the old Cousin Horace scam. Maybe in her heart of hearts Miss Turner knew it too. I had the grace to refuse when she offered me some notes she said she owed.

'They were a gift. You can't repay gifts. It's their nature.'

We said goodbye. Off they trogged to the Ship to celebrate. It was all happening tonight. I wondered how I'd get home.

'Evening, Lovejoy.'

'Craddie.' I walked along, stiff, whatever direction he was going. A police car, unmarked – hence as obvious as a horse in a pub – pulled to the kerb. Acker Kirwin looked out. Two black eyes, lip swollen. 'How's Acker, Craddie?'

'Resisted arrest, old chap. Said he's innocent.'

'Lovejoy,' Acker croaked. 'Tell them, mate. I never helped Cassie. Only mocked up photos for her to sell to Rye. Honest.'

I halted. God, my belly was stiff. 'Would you have let Connie drown, Acker?'

His face answered me. I limped on, despising him, me, the police for doing him over, every last one of us.

'You not arrested Mayor Carstairs yet?'

'On my way there now.' Cradhead chuckled. 'Drinkwater's at the Mayor's Oyster Feast, guest of honour, I'm wondering what sort of entrance I should make.'

He laughed, wagging his head. I was beginning to quite like Cradhead. Dangerous sentiment. There couldn't be any good in him, because he was the Plod. Logic.

'Sorry, Lovejoy. I'll have to question the Lady Mayoress. Did she *really* not know her husband offed the town silver, Council property from Cornish Place? Cassandra Clark testified Mayor Carstairs put up the money. Hard to believe, eh?'

'Indeed.' I wondered how he'd spotted Oliver's scam.

'I spotted the Mayor's scam by watching your face, Lovejoy,' Cradhead said mildly. 'At Del Vervain's radio show. Good old Del was in it too, of course. Hence the outside broadcast.' He laughed, a surprising sharp baritone. 'We were there to arrest you the instant you cried fake. You being the only true crook in the audience. You had the sense to keep mum.'

'Instinct, Craddie. It lights paths already sure, though some lead daftwards.' Which made me wonder if he'd had the wit to raid Sampney Young Ladies Academy yet.

'I expect you're wondering if I had the savvy to raid Sampney Young Ladies Academy yet.'

'Mmmmh?' This creep was an odious nerk, and no mistake.

'Answer's yes. Found nothing. That Miss Reynolds shifts fast, what? Pity you can't come and watch me arrest the Mayor.'

He started across the road, towards the George. Two police cars, lights dimmed and sirens mute, crept to meet him.

Good old Miss Reynolds and her all-girl team! Marvellous what women can do when they finally stir themselves.

'Mind you conform to the Police and Criminal Evidence Act, Craddie,' I called. 'Got to be a first time.'

Which left me alone and palely loitering. I imagined I saw Rhea Cousins' grand motor drive by, husband Willis driving, some Continental dealer already mauling Rhea in the rear seat. Willis was some spouse. You don't get many of him to the shilling, not even round here.

There was a bus home in half an hour. The shelters by the post office had all been vandalised, so I decided to wait under the shopping mall arch. As I trudged wearily down Eld Lane I heard the plaintive tones of a cornet. The *Emperor Waltz*? I'd forgotten: Sandy's dance night.

The square was empty, except for them. It's open to the sky, but for colonnades leading off under the glasscovered ways I've mentioned. The Old Library's a bookshop now. Glossy shops with spread windows look out. A young musician from St Leonard's was playing solo cornet, the waltz too slow but right for the mood. He was standing on top of the fountain, water splashing over his feet, over the side of the ornamental basin. I had to squint to see properly.

Sandy was waltzing in stately fashion with Mel. The latter was attired as a soldier, original shako from Waterloo time, all except his spurs authentic. Sandy looked even loonier. He wore a fantastic silver wig, Carolean tall, with a wide crinoline, an Isabeau corsage dating from about 1846, quite wrong but, since it was white satin covered with pearls and glittering cubic zirconias, accuracy was hardly tonight's theme.

The slowness of the forlorn cornet's melody irritated me. Then I thought, oh well, heaven pardons love's perjuries.

What was I doing here? Wanting to cadge a lift. The pair waltzed gracefully on. I smiled, finally laughed, shaking my head. Who knows why this weird pair did this? Or why any of us ever do anything? Money, love, greed, all motives come nowhere near the truth. Everybody knows nothing.

'Sandy,' I tried for the hell of it. 'Lend us the fare.'

'Loser!' he spat without pausing. 'You almost *ruined* the dolloper. Idiot!'

'To save Connie,' I explained.

'With *her* dress sense?'

They danced on. Well, I had to laugh. I was still falling about twenty minutes later at the bus stop. I don't carry a watch, so have to rely on the town's wayward clocks. I was just beginning to wonder if the last bus had been cancelled when a car drew up.

'Lovejoy?' A girl's voice.

'I'm busy.' Add exhausted. Had enough.

'Get in, you proud fool you.' Sarcasm's the one thing I can take on the chin. I stepped inside, sat with my eyes closed. 'I was going to take you to supper, as a reward.'

'You don't understand.' The car moved off down North Hill. Homeward, thank God. I wondered if I'd any margarine. I could find an apple in the garden, fry some slices. They fill you for about an hour. 'The dolloper you invested in's safe, but a dollop stays inactive for a year after police give chase. It's the rule. No chance of cashing the antiques in for a twelvemonth, love.'

This was where she'd ditch me, fling me out by the old horse trough by the bridge. She just laughed.

'We women are right. Men *are* stupid.'

This was a different car. I opened my eyes. Laura was truly beautiful. Why wasn't she angry? Women are very particular about gelt. They go berserk when bread goes up a penny a loaf. I've actually seen it happen. Yet she was delighted. Seemingly with me.

'Lend us a note, love. I'm a bit short at the moment. I've some money coming tomorrow . . .'

She stopped to buy hot food from a Chinese place at the Middleborough, three great paper sacks of the stuff. I almost fainted from the fragrance. I could remember food, but only just.

We drove to my cottage. I let her carry the nosh inside. There I fell on it, elbows flying. She did nothing, simply observed me like a cat smiling at cream. Except the cream wasn't me. It was something that had happened in town, and very very recently. In normal times I'd have wondered what. Now, in my state of dereliction, I was past caring.

During nosh, the answerphone did its stuff. A familiar husky voice went, 'Lovejoy, darling. It's Vell. Geronimo's on holiday. I'm back. Come soon. Glad it's all over, with those terrible females —'

Laura blocked my reach for the phone, tutting rebuke. I fed on. Who pays the piper.

Two hours later, I managed to stir myself. I noticed she'd locked the door. The curtains were drawn. I saw her erase the answer-phone's messages, saw her curl her legs on the divan. They do that when they're settling in.

'Thank you,' I said hesitantly. Fine time to remember I couldn't brew up.

'Thank you, Lovejoy.'

Well, you couldn't blame me for asking. 'What for?'

'For having my parents arrested.'

She moved, placed her mouth on mine. Parents? I'd had nobody arrested. Except Mayor Carstairs. And maybe his lovely Lady Mayoress, at the ceremony in town.

'Luna? Oliver?'

Laura's alacrity in replacing Oliver when he withdrew came to mind. And her instant payments for Luna's share . . .

'This means that I'm your boss, Lovejoy. Right?'

'Look, Laura. I didn't know you were, er, her daughter Lola when, er, when we . . .'

'Get them off, Lovejoy.' She reached for me. 'Lola's their pet name. They try to keep me a baby. And I'm not.'

'Laura.' I tried to back away. 'My side's all strapped up. This bird knifed me. I stink of ether and them yellow chemicals –'

She laughed. 'You mean, be gentle?' She was falling about.

The door pounded, almost falling in.

'Lovejoy? Come right out this minute!'

'Christ! It's Luna!' I'd rather be back in the rain waiting for the bus. 'Your mother!'

'Marvellous!' Laura cooed, pinning me down. I was so weak I just lay there. 'Never underestimate the hatred within families, Lovejoy. Or the ecstasy that comes from assuaging it.'

'Laura. Look, love.' I tried. 'She'll bring the police –'

'There!' She was laughing breathlessly as the hammering continued and I started to be breathless too. 'Not *so* fatigued, are we, darling?' I knew how George IV felt, sprawling helpless in his new Queen's bridal chamber. At least he was drunk. 'Laura . . .'

'Lovejoy!' Luna frantically tried the windows, the door. I could hear her knocking on the glass. 'I know you're in there!'

'See, Lovejoy?' Laura was moving over me. I was enveloped, entering paradise, bliss-blind. 'Mummy knows you can get her off all charges by refusing to give evidence. But you *will* give it, darling, won't you? Condemn her, Lovejoy. Just a little. Say yes!'

'Ooooh.' I hardly knew what she was on about. Or cared. I was in that helpless phase. All a bloke wants from a bird is everything. Surely everything isn't too much to ask?

'Say yes. Promise me, Lovejoy.' She started to move off me as threat. 'You'll give evidence against her?'

I clasped her close, yelled, 'Yes!' surrendering in a gush of true honest perfect romantic love or something. It's a woman's world, and that's not my fault. 'Oh, yes, love. Anything you say.'

Ecstasy blotted out the entire world to a sound of distant thunder outside on my door.